LOST LIGHT

A Novel

J. M. Halis

"Two hearts separated by the sea will never be,
For loving thee is my destiny..."

North Royalton, Ohio
United States of America

This book is a work of fiction. Any resemblances to persons living or deceased are purely coincidental.

ISBN 978-0-9968903-1-1

This book is dedicated to my father, Kenneth H. Aldridge, Sr., because in my eyes he will always be the "Master Storyteller."

Chapter 1

The island was now in sight through the early morning mist, and to the extreme southwestern shore, she could see it surfacing out of the ash-colored sky like a reluctant sea serpent. The South Bass Island lighthouse—her new home for the next six weeks.

She watched a gull glide on the lake breeze before swooping down to fetch a cracker thrown by a passenger. Elyse Montgomery smiled to herself as Perry's Monument came into view to her right, and the sun turned the lake into a huge crystal geode, creating thousands of sparkling sequins on its surface.

She knew the small island, also known as Put-in-Bay, like a favorite pair of faded jeans. It was roughly three nautical miles from the mainland in the Bass Island region in the western basin of Lake Erie, and every summer she had stayed at the old lighthouse with both her parents and grandparents. Elyse's mother, Rose Dugan Montgomery, had given her daughter the same first name as her own mother, and Elyse was considered an islander. Everyone was proud of the Montgomery's only child when she eventually landed a job as an editor for the popular magazine *Personality* in New York City.

It was her great-grandfather, Joseph O'Reilly, who had first brought the family name to the island in 1897 as the original lighthouse keeper. His tenure lasted forty-two years, during which time he married fellow islander Margaret Neal and had two children, Elyse O'Reilly and Joseph O'Reilly, Jr., who was quite a bit younger than his sister.

Both children were forever connected to the island and Lake Erie. Joseph Jr. became a merchant marine, and

Elyse became the wife of the last lighthouse keeper, Patrick Dugan.

Elyse hadn't been to the island for seventeen years since the summer before she left her hometown of Cleveland, Ohio for college in Columbus at The Ohio State University to pursue her degree in journalism. It was also the same year her mother and grandmother had their falling out—the year things changed forever.

The lighthouse eventually became more automated as did the world in general. A separate steel tower was erected in 1962, which was used in lieu of the lighthouse's lens tower. Elyse's grandparents decided to stay on as caretakers of the property until they purchased the land from the government's Division of Surplus Property.

The property had recently been bequeathed to Elyse in her grandmother's will, so she had no choice but to pack her bags and head to the shores of Lake Erie.

The ferry's air horn blew a welcoming sigh of relief as it docked at Lime Kiln dock, just like it had countless times before. Elyse disembarked from the ferry and stopped to close her eyes and breathe in the lake air, slightly fishy, yet refreshing. She had been so lost in thought that she didn't notice someone standing directly behind her.

"Hi, stranger," a familiar voice said as Elyse came back to reality.

"Uncle Joe!" she replied as she turned around and gave the rotund, gray-haired man with the handlebar mustache a big hug. "It's so good to see you again!"

"And you too, Little Bit. Even though you've outgrown the nickname, you'll need one to be like the rest of us islanders. You know, I can't remember the last time I called anyone by their real name."

"Didn't you always used to say, 'You can call me anything, just don't call me late for dinner'?" she teased.

"Right you are, my dear! Now let me take some of that luggage for you. I'm just glad it's on wheels. Just wish *I* were. Will you be staying in the village?"

"No, I'll be staying at the lighthouse," she said as she looked forebodingly in its direction. "I took a family leave from work to settle Grandmother's estate. It's going to be a bear. The only good thing about this whole mess is seeing you again."

"Flattery will get you everywhere, my dear. Give me a call, and we can go fishing one afternoon. That is, if you're not too busy."

"I'll never be too busy for you, Uncle Joe. After all, you're the one who taught me how to catch and fillet my first walleye. That's one remarkable feat."

"Hey, Big Joe, we're going to be pulling out soon!" a voice beckoned from the Miller ferry.

"I've got to be going, Elyse, but if you need me for anything at all, just give me a call. If you get lonely up at that old lighthouse or hear anything strange, I'm just down the street. Hell, I reckon everybody is just down the street on this four-mile stretch of beach."

"Don't worry, Uncle Joe, I'm a big girl now. If I can live in New York City, I can manage here."

"And if you can make it there, you can make it anywhere. Isn't that how the song goes? Here's one last hug for the road. I'll be seeing you soon," Uncle Joe said as he gave her a big bear hug and kissed her on the forehead before heading back down to the dock to load another round of vehicles, bicycles, and passengers going back to the mainland.

Elyse took her big suitcase and wheeled it behind her as she walked up the steep incline to the top of the hill. Her backpack was strapped securely, and since she was tired, she decided to take a taxi to her final destination.

As the taxi drove up the gravel driveway through the overhanging tree branches, the sky unfolded its generous arms to embrace the lighthouse with the morning sun's rays. It was almost as if the gates of heaven had swung open to let her in.

At first glance, the lighthouse didn't appear to need many repairs. Perhaps the company that wanted to buy it from her would be willing to negotiate the repairs into the contract. She really hated dealing with businessmen. She was a creative person, after all, and they didn't seem to understand her. Everything was so methodical to them—no emotion, strictly business.

"Here we are, lady," the taxi driver said as he stopped before the looming structure. "Need a hand?"

"No, I'll manage," she replied. "What's that come to?"

"Five bucks will do it." Elyse paid the driver and threw in a generous tip. "Hey, thanks! You're not from around here, are you?" he asked.

"Not for a long time," she said under her breath. "Thanks for the ride."

As the taxi pulled away, Elyse stood before the lighthouse and the red brick, two-and-a-half story, Queen Anne-style home as if for the first time. She thought she could sense her grandmother's presence, but shook it off as a light breeze floated in off the lake.

She reached in her wind jacket and took out a skeleton key, the big brass key her grandmother had always kept on a thin leather cord wrapped around her waist. It opened the door to the sunporch immediately. Once inside, she took off her backpack and placed it on the floor with her luggage as she looked around in amazement. The place was frozen in time and hadn't changed one bit.

To her left was the lighthouse tower, which was enclosed within the actual living quarters. The painted brick walls of the tower surrounding the steel spiral staircase were peeling slightly, but when Elyse looked up to the top of the staircase, she saw no structural problems with the staircase itself.

She peered around the corner, and her attention then focused on the walnut-brown bureau and mirror in the main hallway. The framed photographs of her grandparents and family were exactly where they had been seventeen years ago. She picked up a favorite photo taken with her grandfather before they ventured out on their first fishing expedition together, then smiled and put the photo back down on the bureau before walking into the living room behind her.

The furniture was covered with sheets, but was arranged the same as during her last visit. She lovingly touched her grandfather's favorite chair and continued her walk down memory lane through the adjacent dining room toward the kitchen at the end of the hallway.

There it stood: the old cast-iron stove her grandmother had used day after day to bake fresh breads, muffins, and cookies when Elyse stayed there with her parents during their summer vacations. The long narrow pantry at the back of the kitchen had many cupboards for storing canned goods, flour, cereal, and whatever else was needed to sustain someone during the bleak and barren winter months when the island became more of a remote retreat than a vacation getaway.

But those were the good memories, the ones she liked to remember. The bad ones, like the night her mother ran from the house in tears, remained too. She never did find out what her grandmother had said to her mother on that fateful night because her mother died before revealing the secret.

When her grandmother died recently, Elyse had conflicted feelings about her love for her. In her eyes, she had contributed to her mother's death. But now she was thirty-four years old and knew better. Life is a complicated web of secrets that we weave during our lifetimes, and sometimes the silence is what gives us away.

The sound of a slamming door broke Elyse's concentration, and she immediately dashed up the stairs to investigate the matter. She envisioned finding a cracked windowpane with the wind whistling through it. When she opened the master bedroom door, though, she saw that her grandparents' double-wedding-ring quilt still enveloped their iron bed. The window was open about an inch, and white lace curtains blowing in the breeze made the room feel ethereal.

She closed the window as she looked around the room at its contents. It, too, was exactly as she had remembered, even down to her grandmother's comb, brush, and mirror set on the antique dresser. She looked at her reflection in the dresser mirror. Her strawberry-blond hair was in her light-blue eyes, and she looked exhausted. A shot of caffeine was in order. She could take stock of the rest of the house after unpacking.

Elyse went downstairs and threw some wood in the stove to make tea. She removed the covers from the living room furniture, then opened her luggage and began to unpack her minimal belongings. The rest of her clothes and equipment would arrive via Put-in-Bay Airlines the next day.

She turned on her grandmother's antiquated AM/FM radio. It was still tuned to a station that played the old standards. Elyse didn't mind one bit; she liked all types of music, and somehow, this music fit the room. In fact, it fit her too. She instantly became engaged in Frank Sinatra singing Jerome Kern's *The Way You Look Tonight* and began dancing around the room while unpacking.

Fortunately, Elyse did not see the large, luminous figure quietly observing her from the staircase. It watched her dance for a few minutes, with expressionless eyes that had long since forgotten how to laugh, and then disappeared into the dusk before Elyse could sense its unearthly presence.

Chapter 2

The next morning, Elyse came down the stairs, yawning and stretching all the way. The lake air really did a number on her, but then it always did. No matter how much energy you had in the beginning of the day, the lake air just zapped it out of you by evening. The water lapping on the jagged rocks below the house always rocked her to sleep like a mother's lullaby, and now she was well rested and ready to tackle the day.

Since she had time to kill before the plane carrying her belongings arrived, Elyse decided to take a look at the lighthouse tower. Even though the tower was no longer in working order, it still seemed to send a message of security to the passing boaters as it silently stood watch on the edge of the cliff.

Elyse remembered her grandfather had once told her that its intricate Fresnel lens was manufactured in Paris, and it held a rainbow of hope and faith within its beautifully carved prisms—like the rainbow Noah and his family had seen after the Great Flood.

When the light had operated from March to December, the rainbow of hope stretched out over the lake like a huge fishing net, bringing in its "catch" to safety. Now the lens was showcased at the Lake Erie Islands Historical Society on the island.

As a small child, Elyse had always enjoyed exploring the lighthouse tower with her grandfather. He loved to take her up to the top of it to stand outside on the surrounding balustrade platform and look out over the lake.

His face would beam as he proclaimed, "This is as close to heaven as we humans can get, Elyse. We're like birds up here. We can almost touch the clouds and soar into the sky. We can feel the wind on our faces and taste the lake air. This is heaven on earth, my dear, heaven on earth."

Her grandmother was another story. She never talked about the lighthouse or even showed any interest in it.

Elyse proceeded to walk up the forty-two stairs to the top of the sixty-foot tower. She passed five windows and three landings before opening the trap door above her head, which led into the lamp room's circular tower where the lens was once kept, and through another door to the outside.

Elyse looked out at Lake Erie from this familiar summit. She could almost hear her grandfather's voice again.

"You were right on the money," she said aloud. "This *is* heavenly!"

Her grandmother would usually break the spell by calling them to come down to go into town for supplies. Which wasn't all that bad because going into town meant going to Ken and Greta's souvenir shop to look at the latest trinkets, toys, and odds and ends. Back then she would press a metal coin at the stamping machine with her name and date, plus a special word or two to help her remember that particular summer.

The last coin had "Elyse, 1982, Disaster" stamped on it. She ended up throwing that one into the lake by the lighthouse before leaving that summer.

She looked down at her old sandals and sighed. Ken and Greta's had closed years ago, but maybe she could find a pair of moccasins at The Country House store this summer.

On the way down the circular staircase, Elyse noticed a brick out of place in the wall. She immediately reached over to push it back in place when something behind the brick caught her attention. It was some sort of paper.

She gingerly removed the paper and then repositioned the brick. She carefully opened the tattered stationery but could barely make out its contents. It was a poem:

"The night awakens my senses to the memory of what was before and can never be. The lighthouse beckons like your open arms, tenderly reaching out for only me. Your sapphire eyes sear my soul to its very core, as my forsaken ship slides past your *forbidden shore. But I know now that you will always be a refuge from the storm called fate that summoned me out to sea. Love Forever, J"*

A chill ran up Elyse's back as she gently folded the poem back into its original shape. There was no date, but given its appearance, it was at least as ancient as her grandmother's wood-burning stove. *Who could have written it? Did my grandmother hide the poem?* she wondered. She decided to tuck it into the pocket of her wind jacket and show it to Uncle Joe later. Maybe he knew who "J" was.

Elyse looked at her watch and then sprinted down the stairs to call the cab company. Her bicycle would be on that flight, and she was looking forward to some early morning exercise.

The ride to the airport took less than ten minutes. She told the taxi driver to wait because she would have many boxes and suitcases to load into his cab for the ride back. She walked up to the office of the Tri-Motor Plane Company and learned that her shipment would arrive in a few minutes.

As she stood there, looking out at the crystalline blue sky, she felt as if someone were watching her. She casually looked over to her right and saw a striking man with dark-brown hair and blue eyes smiling at her. She looked away and then looked back at him again. He was still doing it, smiling, actually grinning as if he were keeping a secret from her. Now she was becoming annoyed and decided to approach him.

"Excuse me, sir," she began, "but are you going to let me in on your private joke?"

"Please don't take any offense, but there is something stuck to your behind," he replied.

Elyse reached around and pulled a sticker off her back pocket. It was from Burger King and read, "Home of the Whopper."

"And I suppose you were just going to let me wear it all day then?" she asked.

"Sure, if it gave me a good excuse to keep staring at you!" he replied.

Elyse finally laughed at the ludicrousness of the whole episode, and so did the stranger. *He even has a nice laugh*, she told herself.

"Let me start over by apologizing and offering my assistance when your luggage arrives," he said. "My name is Jack."

"And mine is Elyse. I'm sorry, but I haven't been out of the city for ages, and I guess I'm still on the defensive. That sticker must have gotten stuck to my pants on the ferry yesterday. I can't believe I didn't notice it!"

"No harm done. Here's our gear," Jack added when he removed her luggage and boxes from the shipment as she pointed them out. He even helped take them to her cab. She couldn't help but catch a faint drift of his cologne, which was unusual and very sexy.

"I hope to see you again soon, Elyse—minus any form of advertisement. If you have a taste for something besides fast food, stop by LeClare's. Rumor is they've recently hired some hot new chef from an upscale restaurant in Philly."

"I'll keep that in mind. Thanks again, Jack. At least I won't be the 'butt' of anyone's jokes the rest of the day."

"But you'll still be a pleasant memory the rest of mine," he teased.

She waved good-bye to him as the cab drove away. Maybe that line about the restaurant was a hint to meet up with him later. She would definitely follow up on his invitation.

After dropping off her belongings at the lighthouse, Elyse attached a sports bottle filled with spring water to her mountain bike, put on her helmet, and was on her way. The crisp wind blowing in from the lake made the ride to Uncle Joe's pleasant.

She always enjoyed visiting Joe; he lived in one of the most intriguing places on the island called the "Ship House." It was actually the bow of an ore freighter named the *Benson Ford.* Once owned by Henry Ford, Uncle Joe and Aunt Martha had transformed it from a 124-ton chunk of iron and steel into a three-and-a-half-story house. Uncle Joe often threatened to sell it, since all 4,000 square feet of it was becoming a lonely place for one person to live. His beloved Martha's death ten years earlier had made it that way. Still, he hosted weekly poker parties for his cronies in town.

When Elyse rode up to the landlocked ship, Uncle Joe waved to her.

"I never did put an elevator in this old tub," he said. "You'll have to use the ladder."

"Okay. Just have a pitcher of ice tea ready when I get to the top."

"Sure thing, my dear," he replied.

The climb to the top was more challenging than Elyse had remembered. "Wow, what a haul…it was easier when I was seventeen!"

"Tell me about it," Joe began. "I'm just waiting for someone to fall off the ladder after one of my poker games. I have to cut off the drinks early or just let the guys sleep it off here."

"Some things will never change, Uncle Joe. How did Aunt Martha put up with you all of those years?"

"As I've said many times before, the woman was a saint. I remember how much you used to like Aunt Martha's chicken salad, so I tried my hand at it. Hope it's edible."

"I'm sure it will be delightful," Elyse responded. Then she turned her head west. "Just look at the view from here!"

Elyse admired the view of Rattlesnake and Green Islands off the bow and remembered watching quite a few sunsets from this vantage point. Then she sighed and said, "You know, it's a saving grace that some things never change. Like you and this gorgeous view."

"Little Bit, let's go inside and catch up on your life. Mine is pretty much the same week after week," Uncle Joe said.

He motioned with his hand for her to go inside the cabin, and she followed his lead. Once inside, she poured two glasses of ice tea, and they reminisced about old times. Elyse reminded her uncle about the time he and her father had decided to rough it and didn't shave or bathe for a week. Aunt Martha and her mother had decided that enough was enough, and gave them each a bar of soap and literally told them to "jump in the lake." They ended up taking baths in Lake Erie with their clothes on while smoking cigars.

Every morning, her dad and Uncle Joe would head to their favorite watering hole in town, The Round House, to start the day with a boilermaker. As they drank their shot and beer, it wouldn't be too long before Elyse rode into town on her bike to retrieve the two rascals for her mom and aunt. They never returned home quickly, though, since the men bought her beef smokies, barbecue potato chips, and pop in exchange for her silence. Ah, those were the days: no responsibilities or deadlines to meet. How she wished she could revisit those days again.

After a while, Elyse reached into her wind jacket and brought out the letter. She wanted to see Uncle Joe's reaction to it without warning him about its contents in advance.

"Where did you get that, Elyse?" he asked with the utmost concern. "It looks pretty old."

"I thought you wrote it. I found it behind one of the bricks on the stairwell leading to the top of the lighthouse tower. Do you know who "J" could be?"

Joe's face darkened, and his demeanor immediately changed to a somber one. "I know who wrote this, Elyse. It had to be Jacob Flannery, the sea captain your grandmother was seeing before she married your grandfather. I don't remember much about him, though, because I was so little when your grandmother met him. I do remember hearing that he had a stormy temper, and that our parents were upset when they found out she was seeing him."

Elyse leaned forward with anticipation and asked, "Do you think they were lovers?"

"Anything was possible with your grandmother, Elyse. She was always the wild one, the free spirit. Besides resembling her, you two are kindred spirits. Maybe that's why your mother named you after her."

Elyse didn't know whether or not to take that as a compliment, but she knew her uncle was right. After all, she had just ended an affair with her mentor Roger Strong. They had both worked for the same magazine, and he was legally separated from his wife when they first met. He was ten years her senior, but possessed the energy and stamina of a man half his age. However, Roger had returned to his wife, and they moved to Paris.

"Joe, is there anyone still alive who can tell me more about this Jacob fellow? Since I'm staying on the island most of the summer I may as well get a story out of this."

"The only person I can think of is Sam Smith, a former Ted's Tackle employee," Uncle Joe began. "His father and Jacob played poker now and then. Ted's was sold years ago, but you can reach him at the Lake Erie Islands Historical Society; he still works there part-time. I don't know how much Sam can really tell you, though."

"Ah, but you've forgotten who you're dealing with here. I'm relentless when it comes to sniffing out a good story," Elyse said.

"So I've heard," Uncle Joe chuckled.

After lunch they did the dishes while singing the theme songs to the old television shows *Gilligan's Island*, *Petticoat Junction*, and *Green Acres*.

She kissed Uncle Joe good-bye, and promised to invite him over to the lighthouse soon. After climbing down the ladder, she jumped on her bike and sped off toward town. She touched her pocket with the letter in it. Uncle Joe had seemed so eager to give the letter back—almost as if it were cursed.

Chapter 3

Elyse's ride into town seemed shorter than usual. Since she was thinking about her conversation with Uncle Joe, the surrounding buses and golf carts didn't faze her. She parked her bike in the rack close to the grocery store and walked inside to pick up a copy of the *Put-in-Bay Gazette*. The pint-sized store had now grown bigger to accommodate the many tourists who visited the island.

Elyse went out the door and looked down the street. She was surprised to see the old Parker gas station was now the home to Parker's Inn. Across the street she saw a new microbrewery, the police station, gift shops, and Tony's. *It's still there!* She raced up to the windows of the combination bar/malt shop and pressed her nose up to the glass. It looked just like an old movie set. The billiard tables were in the same location, and so were the foosball table and bowling machine.

Tony's looked like it was still in business, even though no hours of operation were posted on the screen door. She would have to visit it later. She had spent many evenings shooting pool here with the islanders, and it was where Uncle Joe had taught her to put an "English," or spin, on her ball.

A smile spread across her face, and she whistled a tune as she walked around the corner of the buildings and down the alleyway leading to the Lake Erie Islands Historical Society.

She noticed three separate red buildings at the end of the road. One was labeled "Boats"; a second one read

"Wildlife"; and the largest one looked to be the main building.

Elyse walked inside and immediately began looking for the Fresnel lens. Once she located it, she noted that its revolving light reminded her of a dutiful soldier guarding the entire museum and its contents.

She spotted an elderly woman behind an information desk and started her investigation by questioning her. "Can you please tell me if Sam Smith is working here today?" she began. "I'm Joe O'Reilly's niece, and I would like to speak to him."

"I'll give him a call upstairs," the old woman said as she picked up the telephone receiver. "He's presently sorting through some odds and ends recently donated by a deceased islander."

Elyse gave her a friendly smile, and pretended not to listen in on her conversation, as the woman dialed an extension number on an old phone on top of her desk.

"Hey, Sam, some lady is here to see you. She claims to be the niece of Big Joe." Pause. "Okay, I'll let her know." The woman turned to Elyse before hanging up the phone and said, "He'll be right down," before sitting back down on her wooden stool.

A wiry man poked his head from around the corner to take a look at Elyse. "You don't look anything like Joe," he remarked.

"Good thing," said Elyse. "That handlebar mustache wouldn't get me many dates!"

The man chuckled. "You're his niece all right, same sense of humor. What can I do for you?"

"Let's take this somewhere private," Elyse began as she noticed that the old woman at the counter was now eavesdropping on their conversation. "I need to ask you a few questions."

Sam led the way to the second floor. It was a narrow space with bookshelves lined with information about the Lake Erie Islands, an oversized wooden desk, and a computer. Sam sat down behind the desk, and Elyse took the remaining seat across from him.

"I think I remember you coming into Ted's for your fishing license when you were just a young girl," Sam began. "Sadly, Ted's been closed for years now. It seems the tourists aren't interested in fish unless it's precooked on their plates. What can I do for you today, Elyse?"

"My uncle believes that you may recall a man by the name of Jacob Flannery. Apparently your father knew him," she said.

"Yes, my father told me that he was a solidly built man with gray eyes, auburn hair, and a close-cropped beard. Apparently, he could be the nicest man on earth if he was your friend, but if he didn't like you, look out. His temper was legendary. He owned his own shipping company, and his ship capsized and sank on the lake one night in October during a horrific thunderstorm. His body was never found."

"Does he have any family on the island?" Elyse mused.

"No, can't say that he does," Sam continued. "He mostly kept to himself, but there were rumors that he kept a mistress hidden away. He probably had one in every port. The women would always give him a second look, if you know what I mean."

"Yes, I do. I've been known to linger like that myself." They both laughed.

"Well, that's all I know about the man," Sam confessed. "I do recall that my father kept some photos from his younger days in an old trunk in the attic. Some he gave to this museum. How long will you be staying on the island? I might be able to take some time to go through the trunk after I get my inventory done."

"No hurry," Elyse said as she got up to leave. "I'll be around here all summer, so I'll be stopping in from time to time anyway."

"I'll contact you if I come across something of interest. Until then, welcome home," he said.

"Thanks for your help, Sam," Elyse said as she shook his hand good-bye. She thought about that last comment as she walked back down the steps. Was this her home? It certainly had felt like it ever since she'd stepped on shore. She really had missed it here; even though it had changed tremendously, it was still her summer island.

Before walking out the door, she stopped by the information desk one more time. "Do you happen to know where a restaurant called LeClare's is located?" she asked the old woman.

"Since you're familiar with the islands, all I need to tell you is that it's where Lonz Winery used to be," the woman replied.

"Oh, really," Elyse mused.

That piqued her interest. Being an avid historian, Elyse's grandfather had told her that Paramount Distillers once owned Lonz and its 123 acres of property. It had originally been known as the Golden Eagle Winery when it opened during the Civil War, and the roughly 4,500 square feet structure resembled a Gothic castle. It was also comprised of sublevel hand-hewn limestone wine cellars, three residences, a 158-slip marina, and additional outer buildings and property.

By 1875 the winery was the largest wine producer in the United States, and Peter Lonz took ownership in 1884. His son, George, was the owner from 1922 until his death in 1968.

Although no wine had been made at the winery for years, it remained a popular gathering spot for tourists traveling the short distance of a little over two miles to Middle Bass Island. Private boats or the Sonny S ferry brought guests there from the mainland and Put-in-Bay, respectively, and by the looks of things now, someone named LeClare apparently owned it.

Elyse thanked the clerk, got back on her bike, and crossed the street to DeRivera Park, where she could see the winery from the shore. She eagerly retrieved her mini binoculars from her backpack, and looked across the bay to Middle Bass Island. Sure enough, the large letters spelling out "LONZ WINERY" on the outside of the building had been replaced with "LECLARE'S."

That chef must be pretty hot, Elyse thought, *if his name was emblazoned across the building like that.* Maybe she would take Jack up on that offer after all.

Elyse headed back to the grocery store to order some supplies of her own. The clerk told her that a delivery van would stop at the lighthouse with the supplies later that day. Elyse thanked the clerk, and was on her way out the door when she literally ran into the handsome stranger.

"I see we frequent the same places," Jack said.

"That wouldn't be too difficult to do on an island this size," she replied.

"Now where did you say you were staying?"

"Actually, I didn't."

"A woman of mystery; I like that! Well, maybe we can have a planned rendezvous sometime soon."

Elyse took the bait. He was much too gorgeous to let off the hook. "Well, how does dinner tonight at LeClare's sound to you?" she asked. "I'll expense it on my account."

"That's generous of you, but I think I can work something out with the chef. We're old friends. Does nine o'clock sound good to you?"

"Fine, I'll meet up with you then. Would casual dress be appropriate?"

"As long as it doesn't have anything stuck to it."

"I left myself open to that one didn't I?"

"You did, but I promise I won't bring it up again. I just like to see you smile," Jack replied.

Damn him! He sure can pour on the charm. He's not even from around here. Where did he say he was from? Elyse couldn't remember. She would ask the questions tonight. That is, if she didn't get lost in those blue eyes of his.

Elyse spent the rest of the day unloading her food and supplies and hooking up her computer. Before she knew it, it was time to dress for dinner. She slipped on a little black dress and put a delicate rhinestone comb in her hair.

When the taxi came to escort her, the driver drew out a long whistle.

"Didn't I see you working at a construction site at Rockefeller Center last week?" Elyse teased the driver while they both shared a laugh. After the taxi dropped her off at the dock, she boarded the Sonny S ferry to Middle Bass Island.

The boardwalk to her left overflowed with tourists collectively laughing, eating, and relaxing. Weekends were always like this on the island. People would sail in from Detroit, Cleveland, Toledo, and Sandusky for a few days of rest and relaxation. When the regattas were in full swing, things could get a bit crazy. But that was a good month away.

The Sonny S glided up to the dock by the restaurant, and everyone got off. Elyse was looking forward to spending more than a few minutes with Jack. He was the first man she had been remotely interested in since her ill-fated affair with Roger.

Elyse walked up to the maître d', a short, impeccably dressed older gentleman with salt-and-pepper hair and a thin mustache. "I have reservations at 9:00 p.m. for two, but I'm sorry to admit that I only know that the other party's first name is Jack," she said.

"That's all I need to know, Mademoiselle," the man answered in a heavy French accent.

She was impressed. *Maybe Jack did have some clout at this place.* Elyse was whisked through the dining room and into the kitchen, where she was seated at the (usually reserved) chef's table. *This is getting better all the time*, she thought.

A bottle of chilled pinot grigio was brought to the table along with an appetizer of petite crab cakes. Elyse wasn't going to eat anything, but the sous chef smiled at her and said, "You'll want to eat them now while they're still warm, Mademoiselle, to appreciate their full flavor."

Oh, what the hell, she thought and proceeded to pour a glass of wine and indulge. She was in heaven but still wondered when Jack would arrive. Her stomach growled. She was just putting another crab cake in her mouth when she heard a familiar voice. She looked up to see Jack wearing a white chef's jacket with "LeClare's" embroidered on it and almost choked on her crab cake.

"I had no idea you worked here," she said.

"I told you I had connections," Jack replied. "I'll be off work in two hours. Until then, I've told my friend Jean-Louis here to give you a sampling of what's on the new summer menu. I hope you're not in any hurry to get home."

"Well, I was going to catch a special on Egyptian mummies on the History Channel, but I guess they're not going anywhere," Elyse said with a smile.

Just then, the maître d' headed straight for Jack. "Jacques, I do not know how this has happened. Mrs. Wingate was to be seated at table number ten to view her yacht from her seat. Now someone else is sitting there, and she is *livid*! The situation is impossible!"

"Pierre, I'll take it from here," he began. "I will speak to her in person; perhaps a bottle of our best champagne is in order."

Pierre immediately looked relieved and dashed away, muttering something in French before attending to the other customers. Jack looked at Elyse and saw a big smile pasted on her face. He just shrugged his shoulders and smiled before heading back through the double kitchen doors.

I might have known he was the head honcho, she thought.

Jean-Louis continued to send epicurean delights to Elyse's table for the next several hours. The escargot with wild mushrooms and a bacon-and-cream sauce under a phyllo canopy was as good as anything Elyse had eaten in any five-star restaurant in New York City.

The food was truly spectacular, but Elyse really enjoyed watching Jack handle his employees even more. Nothing fazed him; he was in total control. He would come by her table now and then to ask if she needed anything, and one time he brought her a single, long-stemmed red rose.

She picked it up and let its scent waft up her nose and into her dreams. The wine was starting to get to her now, so she decided to wait until later when Jack was free to finish the bottle.

At the end of the evening, Jack took off his chef's jacket to reveal a tight-fitting European T-shirt that complemented his trim physique and walked over to Elyse. "Would you like to join me upstairs for a nightcap?" he asked. "My apartment's above the restaurant."

"Lead the way." Elyse motioned to Jack before stopping abruptly to turn around and add, "Jean-Louis, thank you for the hospitality."

"I think he's actually blushing," Jack whispered to her.

"Will they be okay without you?" she inquired while following Jack up to his suite.

"Oh, they'll do fine. Sometimes I attend charity events across the country, and they always survive," he began. "The secret is to make them believe they can't do it without you. I wouldn't want to lose my staff to the competition."

"Why didn't you tell me you own this place?" Elyse asked.

"Wasn't it more fun finding it out this way? After all, you seemed to enjoy yourself immensely."

"Don't get me wrong, the food was divine, but watching you in action was worth the price of admission."

"I do love my job, so coming to work is more like play for me."

Elyse tripped on the last step before they reached the room. "I didn't even finish that bottle of wine, honest!" she protested.

Jack laughed. "That's okay; it must have been a long evening for you. Let's sit by the fire and relax."

"Sounds wonderful." She noticed a cabinet containing CDs and walked over to it. "I see your taste in music is as eclectic as your cooking."

"I'm partial to jazz, rhythm and blues, and old standards sung by the legends," he said. "Feel free to put on whatever you like while I open a bottle of wine."

Elyse smiled as she noted CDs by various contemporary artists in addition to Frank Sinatra, Dean Martin, and Bobby Darin. She decided to play one by Brian McKnight. Jack came out of the kitchen with a bottle of wine and two wine glasses.

Elyse immediately became lost in the moment as Brian McKnight's beautiful song *Could* played in the background.

Jack put the wine bottle and wine glasses down on the small table near the fireplace, and took her hand in his. "*M'accordez-vous cette danse*?" he asked.

"*Oui, Monsieur*," she answered as he took her in his arms.

Elyse noted that they danced well together, and she was a bit nervous about being so close to him. She could feel the heat of his body next to hers and his breath on her neck. She didn't want to appear too forward, yet she was so drawn to him that it was difficult to keep her emotions in check.

Once in a while, she looked up at him. It was if they were the only two people in the world. The song's lyrics seemed to fit their situation perfectly. He turned her to the beat of the music and pulled her closer. She thought, *Am I actually falling in love so fast? Could he possibly be feeling the same way?*

When the song ended, his searing eyes penetrated hers, and he seemed to be contemplating his next course of action. Elyse stood breathless, waiting for him to make the first move. But instead of kissing her, he pulled back, almost as if he were afraid of his feelings. Or maybe he was too aware of them and couldn't be responsible for his actions if he started to kiss her.

A small table was situated in front of the fireplace with a vase of roses in the middle. Jack pulled a chair away from the table and Elyse sat down.

"So, do you prefer to be called Jack or Jacques?" she began.

Jack poured them each a glass of wine. "Well, my name is legally Jacques, but I started using Jack when I arrived in the States," he began. "Jacques seemed a little pretentious then, but it's part of my whole persona here as far as the restaurant is concerned."

"Jack it is then. I've never been known to be pretentious either. Were you born in France?" she asked before she took a sip of wine.

"Actually, I hail from Quebec; my grandparents were from Provence. I inherited my love of cooking from my mother, who died when I was eighteen years old. We used to spend hours in the kitchen making sauces and meals from scratch, and she passed down her secret family recipes to me so they would not be forgotten. My mother used to joke that everyone in her family was given aprons at birth instead of bibs. Since my father and I never really got along that well, I hopped a freight train to Pennsylvania after my mother died, and the rest is history as they say." He sized her up as he took a sip of wine.

"Interesting." Elyse continued, "Do you ever go back to Quebec?"

"As little as possible," he answered as his eyes turned as dark as the depths of the ocean. "My father died five years ago. I didn't even find out until years later since we hadn't kept in touch. The 'father of my heart' is a little Italian man named Roberto Rossi who still lives in Philly. He owned a restaurant and took me under his wing when I arrived in town. He taught me how to make the best chili dogs on the East Coast, but, more importantly, he gave me the love and support that my father never could. He and his wife couldn't have children, so I was like a son to them. They even paid for my classes at the Culinary Institute of America."

"I'm sorry if I seem too nosy. I guess it's just the journalist in me," she said.

"I guess *Personality* magazine is lost without its star editor, Ms. Montgomery," he said with a smile.

"I don't remember telling you that," Elyse interjected.

"Like you said at the grocery store, it's a small island," Jack replied.

She didn't believe that one. *Why was he checking up on me?* They soon finished their wine and Elyse yawned.

"I'm so sorry," she apologized. "It's not the company, believe me. I guess I'm still a bit tired from unpacking and all. Thanks for one unforgettable evening." Elyse got up from the table and walked to the top of the stairs.

"That's okay. Why don't we plan a picnic brunch for Sunday morning when we'll both be more rested," he said as he moved dangerously closer to her.

"That sounds wonderful. Do you know where Oak Point is?" Elyse asked as her heart began beating faster.

"You mean that small park before Peach Point?" Jack's eyes focused on her intensely, leaving no question as to his desire.

"Yes, that's it."

"It's a date then. Just show up at 11:00 a.m." He was devouring her with his eyes. "Did I tell you how stunning you look tonight?"

She blushed. "I guess you have now."

"*Puis-je vous*?" he asked as he leaned over to kiss her.

Elyse melted in his arms. His lips were moist and warm, and his touch was tender and loving.

"Sunday, then?" he inquired.

"Sunday," she affirmed.

She carefully walked down the steps and put a little extra wiggle in it for good measure. Halfway down she turned around to see if he was still watching her, and saw him smiling from ear to ear. She smiled back, and continued down the stairs. *Now, that should keep him coming back for more,* she thought.

When she got to the bottom of the steps, she ran into Pierre. He was closing up the restaurant, and a small white poodle was following him around as he finished his duties.

"What a cute dog," Elyse said as she bent down to pet the creature. "What's the pup's name?"

"His name is Fifi," Pierre replied. "Don't ask me why! My late wife always wanted a girl. It's no matter, though. He is like a son to me. Don't worry, Mademoiselle, a boat is waiting to take you ashore."

"*Merci*, Pierre," Elyse said as she walked out the front entrance.

"You know, Fifi, I think *that* one is going to give the boss heartburn," Pierre said to his little companion. "Of course, I mean that in a good way. Come *mon petit ami*, let's shut off the lights."

Jack's private boat and driver took Elyse back across the bay. Elyse couldn't stop thinking about their kiss and the raw emotion she'd felt coming from him while they danced. She hummed the song *Could* all the way back to South Bass Island's shore. Jack already had a taxicab waiting for her on the other side.

Back at the lighthouse, Elyse took off her shoes and rubbed the bottoms of her feet before ascending the stairs to the bedroom. Then she threw on an oversized OSU T-shirt before opening the window to enjoy the natural harmonies of the wind and water at night.

It didn't take long for her to fall asleep. She never felt the ghostly hand brush her hair away from her face, nor did she hear her name uttered softly before the shapeless form vanished into the night.

Chapter 4

The next day was Saturday. Elyse opened her eyes to a torrent of sunshine streaming into her grandparents' bedroom, or rather *her* bedroom. At least that would be the case for most of the summer.

Elyse casually strolled into the bathroom, smiling as she recalled Jack's kiss from the night before. He was something else. She was still stinging from her love affair with Roger and wasn't quite sure where this relationship with Jack might lead. She decided just to enjoy it for what it would probably turn out to be: a summer romance. She hadn't had one of those since she was a teenager. After all the pain she'd recently endured, a summer romance would be fun. No strings attached.

There was one thing about the night before that still puzzled her though: *Why is Jack checking up on me*? Her instincts told her to get on this right away, so she called her friend, Rachel, at the magazine. Rachel was usually at the office for several hours on Saturdays after her jog through Central Park. She handled the celebrity gossip beat and was quick-witted and funny.

"Hey, it's me," Elyse said. "Please pick up the phone."

"Is this really you, Elyse?" Rachel teased. "I thought you drowned."

Elyse laughed. "Not yet, but I do have an assignment for you."

"Was there a celeb sighting on the island?" Rachel quipped.

"Nothing that good, but it does have an air of mystery to it."

"Ooh, I like it already! Give me all the details and I'll get on it right away."

"I need you to find out everything you can about a chef named Jacques LeClare," Elyse began. "Check your sources in Quebec and Philly. He claims to be a native son of the former and a transplant to the latter. He seems to know quite a bit about me already, even though I just met him a few days ago. I need to know what his angle is."

"He's probably angling to get up your skirt, girl. That's usually the case," Rachel said. "How are you handling things?"

"I'm managing. Let's face it everything sort of hit me at once. Have you heard anything about *him*?" Elyse asked, meaning her former lover.

"Nada, the new boss is a straight shooter. You'd really like him. Anyway, I bet Mr. Roger Strong is sulking in his latte and crying over his croissant. He's so well done, honey, just kick him to the curb."

Elyse smiled at the thought of it. "Let's hope that lying creep *chokes* on his croissant!"

"That's more like it," Rachel said. "You're back to your old self again. When are we going to do lunch? I've got some hot gossip about a Hollywood hottie's double life that will curl your toes, and maybe even that baby-fine hair of yours."

"Now, Rae, I did officially take a family leave to handle my grandmother's estate. And I wish you could see this place; it should be on the National Register of Historic Places. I'm going to go through her things today. That should take me a while. Then I need to schedule an inspection of the lighthouse before I meet with the people at

3R Corporation. Hey, while you're at it, could you please do some checking up on them?"

"No problem. If I can get exclusive interviews, I can move mountains. Is there anything else I can do for you?" Rachel asked.

"That's more than enough for now," Elyse replied. "I'll be in touch periodically. I'll email you my home phone number after we hang up. I purposely left my cell phone home in my loft. Have fun with the upcoming 'Sexiest Guy of the Year' issue."

"Darling, it's more work than you know," Rachel joked. "Don't forget, I'm just a fiber-optic cable away. Bye."

"Thanks for everything, Rae. Love ya!" Elyse sighed as she put the receiver down. The difficult task of sorting through her grandmother's belongings was ahead of her. It would probably be a boring ritual, but after finding that secret love poem the other day she was beginning to wonder what else she might find.

Elyse decided to start with the drawers in the living room. One of the end tables contained a bible, playing cards, dice, and an old church bulletin. *Interesting paradox*, she thought.

The other end table contained a box of beautiful stationery, an address book, ink well, and an exotic-looking pen. There was also a narrow purple ribbon with two keys on it; one fit the lock on the address book with no problem, but the other did not.

For some reason, Elyse instinctively ran her hand inside the back of the drawer and felt a rough edge. She then removed all of the other contents from the drawer before physically separating it from the end table. She cocked the drawer on its side and saw a compartment with a keyhole at the other end; the other key fit it perfectly. Elyse put her hand in the drawer and pulled out a lavender journal with a silk moiré cover. She was stunned. *Why did my grandmother feel the need to lock the journal in a secret place?*

She opened it to the first page:

"Today is my nineteenth birthday. My parents gave me this journal as a present since they know that I love to write. While I was outside painting a picture of the lake, I noticed a strange boat heading toward the shore. By strange, I mean unfamiliar. After all, I am familiar with all of the supply boats that frequent the island.

"When I saw it, I put down my brush and just stared. I can't say why I did that, only that it was as if a feeling of doom encircled my heart like a black cloud. The feeling passed after a short while, but I wasn't quite myself for the rest of the day. So much so, that mother took my temperature and made me some tea. She attributed it to too much time spent in the sun, and had me lie down for a while."

The next entry was a day later:

"When I went into town with father today I caught sight of a stranger out of the corner of my eye who kept staring at me. When I turned to get a better look at him, father abruptly grabbed my arm and hurried me off to our wagon. I turned my head slightly as the horse pulled our wagon onto the road and caught a glimpse of a very handsome young man standing outside of the general store. He was observing me with such fierce intensity that the thought of it is still unsettling. Perhaps we will see him again in passing."

Elyse knew that this wasn't the account of the first day her grandparents had met because both of them were islanders. *Could this stranger have been the mysterious Jacob Flannery?* Sam had told her that Jacob cut a very striking figure. Why had her great-grandfather been so eager to rush her grandmother off like that? Was it just the reaction of a protective father looking out for his only daughter, or was it something else?

Elyse read on:

"Today it has been a week since I saw the stranger at the general store. I have been very busy helping mother with the upcoming church bake sale. Father is performing his usual lighthouse duties, and Joseph is forever getting into mischief. He is only a child, but is already fascinated by the numbers on father's deck of playing cards. Father thinks this is a funny occurrence, but mother scolded him for letting his child be influenced by the 'devil's playthings.' I, on the other hand, do not believe any of this will have a lasting effect on him."

Elyse had to giggle to herself at that last sentence. Oh, if her grandmother had only known at the time how wrong she would be on that one.

The next entry was on the day of the church picnic:

"I don't know exactly when it happened, but after mother left me to go tend to Nora Findley's aching back (she is with child and needed to sit a spell), I was visited by the handsome stranger. He bought a piece of strawberry rhubarb pie from me and said that I was the prettiest girl he'd ever seen! Being quite embarrassed by his remark, I actually felt flushed in his presence. He made me laugh by proclaiming that the color of my checks had turned the same color as the berries in the pie. He told me that his ship was scheduled to come to the island once a week for the rest of the summer.

"He asked me my name and then told me his. It is Jacob. I have never known anyone to be so charming! He is from Ireland and will be going back there in the fall. He asked if he could see me again soon, but mother returned

before I could answer him. He thanked me for the pie and then tipped his hat before walking off into the park while whistling a tune. Mother looked at me in a curious way and then asked me what he had wanted. I told her that he had only wanted a piece of pie. I don't think she quite believed me."

Elyse looked at her watch and thought, *Where did the time go?* She had slept in late, and now it was almost four o'clock in the afternoon. As usual, she had been sidetracked by something more interesting than her real objective and hadn't done much sorting at all. She decided to mark the place where she had left off in the journal with the thin purple ribbon and grab an apple as a snack. She was heading back into the living room when the phone rang.

"Miss Montgomery?" an older gentleman's voice inquired. "This is Sam Smith. I finally had the time to go through my father's chest in the attic, and I found some pictures I think would be of use to you."

"Oh, thanks," Elyse answered. "I can come pick them up within the hour if that's okay with you."

"That would be fine," he said. "I'll be at the museum for a few hours yet."

Elyse hung up the phone. Now she would finally see what Jacob looked like. After just reading about him, she wanted a face to put with the name. Maybe that would help her understand why her grandmother had been so secretive about the journal. So far, the journal didn't contain anything scandalous or unusual. But she had just started reading it, and while paging through it now, she noticed that several pages had been ripped from the book. In fact, they looked as if they had been torn out in haste. She wondered what those missing pages contained, or if they still even existed.

A clap of thunder interrupted Elyse's thoughts, and she went out to the sunporch facing the lake to look outside. Storms could appear out of nowhere on the lake. Just because it was a lake, and not an ocean, it didn't make it any less dangerous.

In 1933, the year before Uncle Joe was born, Elyse's great-grandfather had taken a new lighthouse boat to Green Island. A nor'easter had rolled in, which created a sudden squall, and he was hit by spray that filled his boat halfway with water.

Witnesses said it was a major battle for him to negotiate the waves between engine stops and starts. He finally ended up making the point above Stone's Dock on the other side of the island, where he and a man who had been watching him from the shore tied his boat out of harm's way.

Due to the impending storm, Elyse decided to call Sam back and promised to see him the next day, since she would be meeting Jack for brunch in the area. As soon as she hung up the phone, the lake changed from a burnished blue to an almost gray-green color. The white caps started slapping the ragged rocks and submerged the boulders at the edge of the lighthouse's shore in rapid succession, and the wind picked up considerably. Elyse turned on her radio to listen for any severe weather warnings. Torrents of rain poured down from the charcoal clouds, beating down the waves on the water and turning the property into swampland.

Elyse heard scratching and a loud "Meow!" from behind the door of the sunporch. She looked out the screen to see a dainty gray tabby cat looking up at her with imploring eyes. The downpour had pasted down her fur, and she lifted her right paw up as if to beg for entry into the dry home.

"By all means, please come in," she said as she opened the screen door. The soaked feline was a funny sight, and Elyse couldn't help but laugh out loud.

"I've been there myself a few times, my dear," she told her new furry friend. "Now, let's dry you off and get you something to eat."

Elyse was surprised to discover that the cat allowed her to dry off its fur with a towel, and even seemed to like the attention she gave it.

"I'll tell you what, kiddo, you can stay the night if you want. After that, it's up to you. I could use some company out here. Since you don't have a collar with a name, I'll give you one. How does Rainy sound?" The cat meowed in agreement. "Okay, then; Rainy it is. Let me get you something to eat. I hope tuna is to your liking," Elyse said as she proceeded to the kitchen with the cat happily switching its tail from side to side.

The storm ended as fast as it had started, and she decided to go back to sorting her grandmother's things. Rainy was fast asleep on the living room floor. *Cats are so adaptable*, she thought. *Why can't people just put things behind them? Why do we stay up nights worrying about what we cannot change? Cats are so in the moment, and when that moment is over, it's over for good.*

It was now darkening over the horizon. Elyse looked out the window to catch a glimpse of the calm lake, which just hours before had resembled a rollercoaster ride at nearby Cedar Point amusement park in Sandusky, Ohio. Now a soft rain was coming down, and the gulls were fishing for their dinner in the wind-whipped waves.

She suddenly felt melancholy as Leslie Bricusse's moving melody *When I Look In Your Eyes*, as sung by Diana Krall, began playing on the radio. She couldn't help but remember all the time she had wasted on Roger. He hadn't been worth the effort.

"Maybe Albert Schweitzer was right," Elyse said to the snoozing cat. "There are two means of refuge from the miseries of life: music and cats."

She turned around, and went into the kitchen. The mysterious, uninvited guest on the staircase stayed to listen to more of the song, but quickly departed when the cat raised her head and stared in its direction.

Chapter 5

Elyse was fast asleep when the cat jumped on her bed and meowed excitedly. "What in the world is wrong, Rainy?" she asked.

Then she heard it. Someone was whistling a song, and the sound was coming from the first floor. She was half-asleep, so at first she wondered if she were dreaming. Her mind raced with a million thoughts at once: *What if an intruder has broken into the place?* Then again, *What intruder whistles while he's ransacking your home?*

"I must have left the radio on," Elyse said to herself. She reached over to her nightstand and took out a small handgun that she had previously kept in her loft in New York City. Now she was glad she had brought it with her. Rainy slipped underneath the bed, and Elyse cautiously walked down the stairs.

The whistling had stopped. Maybe she had been dreaming after all. Then she heard it again, faint at first, then a little louder. The intruder was whistling *When I Look In Your Eyes. Had he been in the house since earlier that evening?* Then just as mysteriously as it started, the whistling stopped.

Elyse took the safety off her gun and shouted, "I have a gun, and I'm not afraid to use it! Come out where I can see you!"

The temperature of the room suddenly became frigid, and Elyse began to shiver. She looked across the hallway into the living room, saw the outline of a large man materialize within the beam of moonlight that illuminated the room, and thought, *I can't believe this is happening.*

"I see you now. What do you want?" Elyse quickly asked while watching her breath crystallize into frozen wisps of smoke as she pointed the gun at the intruder.

"I only wanted to see you again, Elyse," a deep, resonant voice replied.

"How do you know my name?" she asked with her heart pounding in her chest so hard that she could swear she was going to go into cardiac arrest at any minute.

"How could I not?" he replied.

"Well, I don't know you. I still can't see you. Come closer!" she demanded.

Then she saw him: a tall, handsome man dressed in captain's blues with dark-auburn hair and beard. His eyes were light in color, and he observed her with as much curiosity as she observed him.

"Have you forgotten me, Elyse?" he lamented.

As he walked toward her, Elyse could see that he wasn't of this world. He was transparent, yet three dimensional in nature: an apparition, a ghost if you will, and he was standing in her living room asking her questions. She was both terrified and intrigued by his presence.

Feeling as if she might faint, Elyse finally found the strength to ask, "Who are you and why are you here?"

"All I know is that I felt a strong longing to be here," he replied.

"Elyse was also my grandmother's name," she said.

"Is she still alive?" he pleaded.

"Why should I bother giving answers to someone who has yet to answer any of my questions and has obviously broken into my home?" Elyse remarked.

"If you are not my Elyse, then I have been dead too long," he said. The ghost seemed near tears as he swallowed hard and looked directly into Elyse's soul with eyes the color of a gray winter sky. "There is nothing for me here anymore," he began. "She was the reason for my coming."

"This is all too complicated to comprehend. Let me sit down and catch my breath," Elyse said as she sat down on one of the steps of the staircase and laid the gun by her side. It was obviously not needed anymore.

"I will answer your questions if you will answer mine first," the ghost continued. "If you truly are Elyse's granddaughter, then may I inquire as to who your grandfather was?" the ghost asked with curiosity.

"Okay, I'll play your little game for now. My grandfather's name was Patrick Dugan," Elyse replied.

"Patrick Dugan…I seem to remember a man by that name. Was he a *good* man?" he asked.

"Yes, he was *quite* honorable," Elyse answered.

The ghost looked disheartened by this news. Elyse couldn't figure out if he was glad her grandmother had been married or was distressed by it.

"I guess that is all that anyone can ask," he said.

By the questions he was asking, Elyse could tell that the ghost was experiencing some sort of memory loss. She was even beginning to wonder if he could even answer her initial questions.

"I need to find out the circumstances surrounding my death," he began again.

"You mean you don't remember *how* you died?" she asked.

"My spirit was taken from my body right before my death," he said. "It was most likely an unpleasant one; I had many enemies."

"You really don't know what year it is, do you?"

"My world is different than yours. If one dies before their time, whether it be an accident or by their own hand, they cannot move on until they reach the age when they *should* have died. Can you help me find the answers I seek?" he asked her with desperation in his voice.

"If that's the only way I can be sure you will leave here, then yes, I guess I have no choice but to help you. I can't sell this place if it's haunted," she said more to herself than him.

With that, the ghost's demeanor became surly. "I am not totally here by choice! I have been brought back here to discover the truth. I now believe it may be you I was meant to find and not your grandmother, and you cannot sell this place before finding out the answers!"

"It's strictly a business decision," she answered.

The ghost's eyes were now dark and dangerous, and she could feel his anger fill the room. Elyse suddenly grew silent. Her hand went toward the gun again, but then she remembered how futile that was and let it fall to her side.

"And what does a woman know about such things?" the ghost bellowed back.

"As you've just told me, things are different in *my* world."

"Different!" he shouted. "A man has his place and a woman hers. What kind of nonsense do you feed me, woman?"

"What a chauvinist you are. If you want my help, you've got to be less confrontational," Elyse shot back.

"And you are forbidden to use such gibberish in my presence," he countered. "The words you use are foreign to my ears."

Elyse was surprised at his candor, and he seemed just as surprised that she would dare debate him on the issue. "I believe I have answered all of your questions up to this point, so now it is my turn to get the answer to *my* main question: What is your name, sailor?"

"I am Jacob. Jacob Flannery."

Elyse gasped as she realized that she was actually in the presence of the legend himself. She could see why her grandmother had found him so attractive, despite his temper. He was passionate about everything. He deeply believed in what he was saying, and he didn't give a damn what you thought. "Politically correct" was certainly *not* in his vocabulary.

If he was this passionate about his love for her grandmother, then he must have been the greatest love of her life. After all, hadn't he traveled through time and space to see her grandmother one more time? Did she ever know how much he really loved her? Had her grandmother loved him as much?

"I will help you, Jacob Flannery, but mostly because it doesn't look like you are leaving until I do. My grandmother chose me to make sure the lighthouse was sold to a new owner, and I obviously owe her that more than I owe you anything. This won't be easy for either of us, so let's set a few ground rules right from the get-go: You cannot just appear out of thin air without warning. I'm not used to having a ghost as a roommate. Second, you must give me my privacy. Do not come into my bedroom or bathroom while I am in the house. If you can accept those terms, then I will do my best to help you."

"I will abide by your rules," Jacob said half-heartedly.

Elyse could see Jacob was mulling over the decision that he had just made. It must have been difficult for someone of his independent nature to rely on others to do anything for him.

"Why were you whistling that tune?" Elyse asked with curiosity.

"I found it to my liking."

"You say and do whatever you like, don't you?"

"I was never one to use words carefully. That is probably why I am before you now," he said matter-of-factly.

Elyse wondered exactly what Jacob meant by that, but was starting to grow weary. "I don't know how I'll manage it, but I've got to get some sleep. What will you do now, Jacob?"

"Wait for you to bring me the answers."

"And what if you don't like what I find?"

"What has come before cannot be changed; only what is yet to come can be rewritten," he answered.

"I hope I can help, Jacob, for both of our sakes." Elyse picked up her gun and put the safety back on. Then she got up to walk back up the stairs to her bedroom.

"Would you have used it if I were a real intruder?" the ghost asked.

"Yes, I would have."

"Then we are more alike than you know," Jacob replied with a sly smile before fading away into the shadows.

Elyse stood frozen on the stairs, thinking about everything she had just witnessed and experienced. Now her conversation with Uncle Joe on the day she'd arrived on the island took on a new meaning. He had mentioned that she should contact him if she heard anything unusual at the lighthouse. *Did he know the lighthouse was haunted?* She would have to confide in him tomorrow.

But for now, the image of the ghost was forever pressed into her memory like a faded flower in a book—a book exactly like her grandmother's journal. If she could only find the lost pages, then maybe Jacob could find his freedom.

Chapter 6

Morning came too soon for Elyse. Based on the time, she concluded that she'd inadvertently shut off the alarm clock next to her bed. Considering everything that had happened during the night, it was truly a miracle that she had slept at all! She looked out her bedroom window half-expecting to see Jacob sitting in one of the Adirondack chairs underneath the towering cedar trees.

Where had he gone? she wondered. If time wasn't the same for him as it was for her, then perhaps it had no beginning or end. Maybe he was living like her cat: in the present time only. He couldn't remember his past, and he couldn't move on to his future, whatever that might be. *Would the ghost ever be able to leave the lighthouse*? Elyse could see that she had her work cut out for her with this dilemma; between Jack and the ghost, she didn't know if she was coming or going.

Jack. Oh, my God, Elyse thought, *I had better get ready fast to meet him at Oak Point for brunch.* She decided to call a cab for the ride into town so she wouldn't be late. Then she quickly showered and dressed before bounding down the stairs to make another phone call.

"Hey, Uncle Joe, do you have a minute to talk?" Elyse asked.

"Sure, I've been enjoying my coffee off the bow," he began. "What's on your mind today, Little Bit?"

"Well, I just wanted to tell you that I *did* experience something very unusual at the lighthouse last night." Uncle Joe fell silent on the other side of the phone. "Uncle Joe, are you there?" she asked.

"Yes, I'm here. Are you okay, Elyse? Are you hurt?" he asked.

"No, I'm fine, but I feel odd even asking you this: did you know that the lighthouse is haunted?"

"I didn't know for sure," he began. "After your grandmother died, I took care of the lighthouse until you came into town. There were a few times when I thought I heard some strange noises, but I just brushed them off as my imagination."

"Did you ever *see* anything strange though?" Elyse asked.

"No, I never did," Uncle Joe replied, "but you saw something, didn't you?"

Elyse hesitated before she answered. She didn't want her uncle to think she was losing her mind, but if she didn't tell someone about it, she just *might* go crazy.

"Yes, I did," she began. "At first I thought I was dreaming, but then I saw him standing right before me as if he were still alive."

"Did you recognize him?"

"He told me that his name was Jacob Flannery."

"So the Devil still walks this earth!" Uncle Joe gasped. "Old stories about him still circulate the island to this day, maintaining he was a very manipulative man who was used to getting exactly what he wanted, regardless of the consequences to others. Maybe you should pack your things and stay here with me until the lighthouse is sold."

"I'll be okay, Uncle Joe. He doesn't mean me any harm," she said.

"But how can you be sure, Elyse? He can't be up to any good if he's come back to haunt you."

"That's just it, Uncle Joe, he's not haunting me at all; he's just lost and needs to find his way."

"Well, let him find it with someone else! You can't be serious about staying there, are you?"

"Yes, I am. It's something I have to do, maybe more for my soul than his."

"Just don't let him *take* your soul, Elyse. He was a powerful man in more ways than one."

"If I change my mind, I'll let you know. But for the time being, I feel safe here." Elyse was a stubborn woman, and she knew her uncle realized that fact. It was no use fighting with her when she had made up her mind.

"Please be careful, Little Bit. I love you," he said.

"I love you, too," she said before hanging up the phone.

The cab was honking its horn outside, and Elyse grabbed her backpack before locking the door to the sunporch with her grandmother's skeleton key.

The cab dropped her off at Oak Point. She walked over to the water's edge and looked across to the Stone Laboratory on Gibraltar Island. She was proud that The Ohio State University used the area for the Ohio Sea Grant Program, which happened to be the oldest freshwater biological field station and research lab in the United States.

Elyse thought Oak Point was the prettiest park on the island. It was small, but the views it offered were nothing short of spectacular. Towering high above the landscape to the right in the distance, she could see the 352-foot tall Doric column known as Perry's Monument. Uncle Joe had always told her that Put-in-Bay would probably be part of Canada now had Commodore Oliver Hazard Perry not won the Battle of Lake Erie (against the British Royal Navy) on September 10, 1813, during the War of 1812. Everyone who knew the story could still recite Commodore Perry's famous battle cry: "Don't give up the ship!" It made Elyse proud to realize that this battle had been such a pivotal event in our nation's history.

She heard the sound of rolling wheels behind her and turned around to see Jack piloting a tandem bicycle. He stopped right in front of her.

"I haven't ridden one of these things in years!" Elyse beamed as she touched the handlebars.

"Well, you're in luck today," Jack replied. "It was the last one left."

"You mean you didn't have one reserved in your name already?"

"I underestimated my competition."

"Never underestimate anyone."

"I'd never underestimate *you*," he responded before giving Elyse a sexy smile.

"What's for lunch?" she asked.

"It's my specialty. I hope you like it." Then he removed the wicker picnic basket from the back of the tandem, and Elyse pointed out a good location to set up shop. Jack opened the basket and took out a red-and-white checkered blanket. "This will serve two purposes," he said. "We can use it as our blanket and our tablecloth."

"A resourceful man, too! I'm impressed. What did you bring? Pâté, cheese, wine?" Elyse inquired as she peaked into the basket.

"Better than that. I've brought a couple of Roberto Rossi's famous chili dogs," Jack replied as he removed a warm carrying pouch from the basket.

She laughed loudly. "You're something else, Jacques LeClare! After the fabulous food I ate at your restaurant on Friday night, I wasn't quite sure what to expect today."

"This is the real me, Elyse. I told you before that I am not pretentious. I've also packed some chips, beer, fruit, and chocolate. If we aren't too full after lunch, maybe you could show me more of the island. I could use a tour guide."

"You're on," Elyse replied as she reached into the basket and took out napkins, utensils, a small pocket radio, and two cans of Molson beer. "I might have known it would be Canadian beer," she teased.

"Is there anything wrong with that?" Jack asked.

"Nothing at all; I love Canadian beer."

"I knew there was a reason why I liked you. Now all you have to do is tell me you like hockey and we're all set," he remarked.

Jack turned on the radio to Bobby Caldwell singing his song *The Girl I Dream About* and shot Elyse a quick glance when he thought she wasn't looking.

But she did see him and smiled to herself. She was doing the same thing to him after all. He was too good to be true: handsome, romantic, funny, and sweet all rolled into one big enchilada. How could she stop herself from falling in love with this one? It wouldn't be easy. She reminded herself that this was just a summer romance at best. In the fall, she would go back to New York City and her job as an editor for *Personality* magazine. Who needs to get hurt again? This guy would be hard to resist, though. He had her complete attention and was loving every minute of it. Then again, so was she.

They finished their chili dogs, chips, and beer while watching the boats slide in and out of the harbor. Elyse now knew what her dad had meant when he declared Put-in-Bay to be the "working man's Martha's Vineyard."

"Are you ready for dessert?" Jack asked her with a twinkle in his eye.

"Always, especially since you've already told me that chocolate is part of the equation," she answered.

Jack pulled out a bowl of ripe strawberries and a container of chocolate dipping sauce out of the basket and set everything on the tablecloth.

"Let me start one for you," he began as he dipped one of the berries in the dark, decadent pool of melted chocolate and put it up to Elyse's lips. She thought she would have a little fun with this, so instead of immediately taking a bite out of the strawberry, she slowly licked the chocolate sauce off from around the tip of the strawberry with her tongue before biting it off.

Jack's pupils grew wider, and his gaze became completely focused on Elyse as she prepared a chocolate-covered strawberry for his consumption. When she placed it before his lips, he looked directly at her with his intense eyes, and she knew she was in trouble. He took the strawberry out of her hand, and placed it on his plate, before he started kissing the nape of her neck with his roaming lips.

They locked in each other's arms and fell to the blanket, kissing full on the lips. She rolled on her back, and he lowered himself on her gently, all the while kissing and caressing her body with his soft touch. She opened her mouth to his tongue, and they explored each other's sensuality with more intensity.

Then he did it again: almost like clockwork, he stopped midstream, leaving Elyse breathless on the ground. He sat up and nervously pushed back his hair with his hand.

"I didn't mean for things to get out of hand," he said as she also sat up.

"You're not married, are you?" she asked him half-jokingly.

"Only to my work," he replied with a smile. "I don't want to rush you, Elyse. You've been through a lot lately."

Elyse grew silent and thought, *What did he mean by that last comment? Did he know about my grandmother's death or maybe my affair with Roger*? She decided to take this a step further and asked, "Why would you think I need space?"

"I heard that you lost your grandmother recently. It must have been a big blow," he replied.

So that's what he meant! Well, if he had been asking questions about her, it wouldn't have been too difficult to find someone who could answer them. Everyone on the island had known her grandparents. "You don't have to treat me with kid gloves," Elyse responded. "I'm a big girl now."

"Then we understand each other already," Jack replied.

She had never met anyone who was so careful with his emotions. What man would have the strength to turn off his libido as Jack had just done? She started to suspect he was keeping a deep, dark secret from her. Something, or someone, had a hold on him.

"Do you still want to give me a tour of the island?" he asked, changing the subject.

"I'm all yours," she answered with a double meaning.

They packed up the picnic basket, strapped it to the back of the bicycle, and boarded the bicycle built for two. He took the first seat, and she sat behind him. Elyse put on her Cleveland Indians' baseball cap and motioned for Jack to make a left turn into town.

They rode on the inside of the street past the docks, then the Put-in-Bay Yacht Club and Crew's Nest. They continued peddling past the yellow Victorian home with its turret until they reached the corner by the Doller building.

"Where should I go now?" he shouted back to Elyse.

"Let's go to the top of Perry's Monument," she answered.

They continued straight past the Boardwalk and DeRivera Park with its fountain enclosed by a rock wall and its white gazebo with a green-tiled roof.

The park itself was in the middle of the village. It was generously dotted with full-grown trees, lending a nice shady contrast to the downtown marina and the restaurants and shops encircling the area.

The road leading to the monument was narrow, and they stayed with the flow of traffic. To their left was a breakwall embracing the bay; the water was reflective and as clear as a looking glass, punctuated now and then by a pleasure boat soaking up the sun's rays.

When they reached the top of the monument, Jack put his right arm around Elyse to shield her from the wind. They looked out over the horizon, then into each other's eyes.

"Isn't it just beautiful up here?" she commented.

"Not as beautiful as you. Take me to your next attraction."

Elyse decided to direct him back into town to stop and see Sam at the museum, and then on to visit Tony's.

When they rode past the spot where the "Colonial" used to be, Elyse's heart sank. The two-story Colonial had been home to many things, including an 18,000 square foot dance hall, an eight-lane bowling alley, an ice cream shop, and a nineteenth-century-style saloon named The Bay 90s.

After the Colonial burned to the ground in 1988, a bar named the Beer Barrel Saloon was eventually built in its place. Elyse missed the familiar round rotunda and wished it could still be there as part of the scenery. She told Jack to hang a left at the corner, and they hugged the curb until they reached the museum.

"Is this another history lesson directed toward me, Ms. Montgomery?" he joked. "Just because I'm Canadian it doesn't mean that I'm totally clueless, you know."

"I wasn't inferring that in the least," she retorted. "You wouldn't mind looking around in here while I visit with a friend, would you?"

"No, it should prove to be interesting."

"I promise not to take too long," she said reassuringly.

Jack immediately began to explore the contents of the museum, while Elyse headed upstairs to find Sam. She didn't have to look very far, though, because he was camped out behind the computer.

"Oh, it's you, Ms. Montgomery. I'm glad you could make it," Sam said with a smile.

"So am I," Elyse answered. "You mentioned that you found something for me?"

"Yes, I have. It's pretty old, but you can still make out his features." He then reached into an envelope, pulled out a faded photograph, and handed it to Elyse.

She was taken aback by the likeness before her. There was Jacob—handsome and virile and full of life. He was standing next to a ship with ancient writing on it. Elyse couldn't quite make out the ship's name.

"Are you alright?" Sam asked with concern.

"Yes."

"Would you like to sit down? You look like you've just seen a ghost."

"Something like that," she answered as she sat down in a chair across from him. "Do you know what language that is on the side of the ship?"

"My only guess is that it may be Celtic in nature. Jacob was originally from Ireland," Sam replied.

"Would you mind if I keep this photograph for a while?"

"No, I trust you with it."

Elyse carefully slid the photo into her backpack and said, "I don't know how I can thank you, Sam."

"If it helps with your story, I guess that's thanks enough," he said.

Elyse stood up and shook Sam's hand before walking back down the stairs. *Yes, the ghost was telling the truth. He truly had been Jacob Flannery when he was alive.* Now that she had positively identified him, she needed to dig up some information about his ship. *Why wasn't the ship's name in English? Was this the same ship that Jacob may have taken with him to a watery grave?*

All Elyse knew was that she could use a cold drink about now. Jack was already waiting outside for her. "What's next?" he asked playfully.

"How about a game of pool and a tall cold one? I mean a beer, not a Lake Erie highball of plain H^2O," she added.

"Lead the way," he replied.

On their way to Tony's, Elyse's thoughts drifted to Jacob's comment the night before about having many enemies. Maybe that was the means to his end.

Chapter 7

When they reached the screen doors to Tony's, Elyse could already see customers sitting at the wooden bar on the right where the soda fountain had been when she was a girl. It looked like they still served ice cream. The game room contained a pool table, bowling machine, video games, jukebox, and red-metal tables with chairs.

There was also a toy wooden schooner with faded sails adorning a back wall that Elyse remembered from her youth. *The more things change, the more they stay the same,* she thought.

"I'll buy the first round," Jack said as she looked around the place, smiling.

"I'll rack up the balls," Elyse added. She readied the table for play and then sat down at one of the tables to wait for Jack.

"Here you are, Mademoiselle," he said as he placed a beer in front of her on the table and took a sip of his own beer before putting it down next to hers.

"How does a game of eight ball sound to you?" she asked.

"I think I can handle it," Jack answered.

"But can you handle my niece?" a voice interrupted from the bar area.

"Uncle Joe," Elyse said as she threw her arms around her uncle. "Jack, I'd like you to meet my uncle, Joe O'Reilly. Uncle Joe, this is Jack LeClare."

The two men shook hands heartily. "I hope you know that Elyse played pool here every summer vacation. In fact, she used to beat the pants off me now and then. I can't recall any other woman who could do that. She's a formidable opponent."

"I think I can give her a run for her money," Jack teased.

"Hey, speaking of money, some of the guys will be meeting me here soon for drinks. Would you mind if we put a wager on who will win?"

"Uncle Joe," Elyse scolded, "does everything in life come with odds?"

"Yes, I believe so. There's always a winner and a loser. Would it bother you much, my boy?" Uncle Joe asked.

"Actually, I think it would give us more of an edge to make it a contest," Jack responded as he looked over to Elyse.

"Okay, the best of three wins the contest. You ain't seen nothin' yet," Elyse said as she sashayed over to the pool table to choose her weapon.

"You may live to regret this," Uncle Joe whispered to Jack as he watched Elyse make her first move.

"You may be right," Jack joked.

The boys piled in just as Elyse applied billiard chalk to her cue stick.

"Hey, Big Joe, what kind of action do you have for us today?" Tom Parks asked as he took a seat at the bar with five other men.

"Well, my niece is back in town, and she is going to give this fine young man a run for his money," Uncle Joe replied.

"Is *that* little Elyse?" one of the men asked.

"Yep, sure is," Joe said proudly.

"Well she sure isn't little anymore," another man commented.

"Keep your eyes in your sockets, sailor," Uncle Joe remarked. "All bets are on!"

Uncle Joe, Tom, and two of the other men bet on Elyse, while the other three men bet on Jack. Elyse and Jack were asked to pick either heads or tails as Uncle Joe tossed a coin into the air, which landed on top of the bar.

"It's tails, Elyse. You go first," Uncle Joe shouted.

Elyse removed the ball rack, then took her stick and positioned it close to the cue ball. Her eyes focused on the back pockets as she skillfully divided the triangle of balls, dropping one ball into the left back pocket. Her supporters at the bar cheered, and Elyse took a bow. Jack laughed, and shook his head in disbelief.

Elyse's next shot wasn't so lucky, and she narrowly missed sinking another ball in a side pocket. "You're up," she smiled at Jack.

Jack seemed to go into a total mode of concentration and sank one ball. His supporters now cheered for him. His next shot was unsuccessful.

"I was just playin' with you until now, Mister," Elyse told Jack. "I'm all warmed up now."

"I bet you are," he responded with one of his smiles.

Elyse had a difficult time concentrating on her next shot after looking at Jack. It took her a few minutes to get her bearings, and then she was able to bank a ball off the side rail and sink the seven ball. The crowd roared, and she was on a roll. After sinking two more balls, and missing a third shot, it was Jack's turn.

There were ten balls on the table now. Jack's cheerleading section tried to spur him on with words of encouragement. He was able to sink one, and then had to sit down after missing his second shot.

Elyse bent down in front of Jack to adjust her sandal and purposely positioned her posterior right in front of his face. The boys at the bar chuckled. Jack slapped Elyse's behind, and she stood up abruptly.

"Hey, that's not fair!" she complained.

"You don't play fair, Ms. Montgomery," he answered.

"All is fair in love and pool," she responded as she sank another ball.

Elyse sank an additional ball after putting a spin on the cue ball, but couldn't make her next shot. Jack also sank two balls in a row before missing his next try. Now there were five numbered balls remaining.

"This deserves a little background music, don't you think?" Elyse asked him with a smile.

"Go ahead, be my guest," he answered.

Elyse went to the jukebox and put in her coin. When she came back to the table, Frank Loesser's song *Luck Be a Lady* by Frank Sinatra was already blaring from the speakers.

Jack laughed aloud, and then motioned for her to take her turn. Elyse swiveled her hips, and put on a little sideshow, while the boys at the bar whistled and laughed.

"You go get 'em, honey!" Uncle Joe chimed in.

Elyse missed her next shot. Now it was Jack's turn. He was eyeing up his options when Elyse whispered in his ear, "Your fly's open!" Jack made the shot anyway.

"You can't distract me from my goal, Elyse," he reminded her.

His next shot was also a good one, leaving only one more ball per player to go. Fortunately for Elyse, he missed his shot. She then sank her last ball easily, and took quite a while to set up her next shot. The audience was so quiet you could hear a drunk burp. Elyse lined up the cue ball to hit the eight ball on its left side, and sent it flying to the right side pocket.

The crowd cheered, and Jack stood up to shake Elyse's hand and concede victory. "Now, we'll play it *my* way," he added.

The second game was a bit dicier, and Jack won it. Elyse was starting to think that this man would be more of a challenge than she had originally thought.

"This is for all the marbles," Uncle Joe reminded them from the bar before they started the third game. "May the best player win."

Elyse took the first shot, and sent the balls flying in all directions. Unfortunately, none of them went in a pocket. Jack was luckier, and sank two balls before sitting down.

Elyse was determined to win now and sank three balls in a row before she took her seat, adding, "Looks like you've lost your touch, Jacques."

"My touch is never lost on you," he replied.

The guys at the bar laughed at his last comment, then held their collective breaths as Jack took center stage.

He was also able to sink three balls in row before missing his last shot. Now Elyse was worried. The only way she could make her next shot was to put the cue stick behind her back and bend over the table a little bit. It would be difficult, but she felt confident in her ability.

She looked over at Jack after she made the shot, and he had a big grin on his face. "Nice to know you're so flexible," he added.

Elyse missed her next shot, and Jack got up to take his turn. He made it easily, but couldn't sink another ball after that. Elyse looked over to her uncle, who gave her the thumbs up sign. She had Jack now; this was going to be cake.

She sank three balls, and then lined up her cue ball to bank the eight ball off one rail. It worked perfectly. Her uncle and his cohorts were jumping up and down in the bar as if they'd just won their bets on the World Series. Jack came up to her and offered his hand. She took it, and he pulled her closer before bending her backward and planting a big kiss on her lips. The crowd roared.

"To the winner goes the spoils," he whispered.

"Then remind me to win all the time," she replied.

Uncle Joe and his buddies eagerly shook their hands and offered congratulations to the winner.

"You had me worried there for a while," Uncle Joe told Elyse. "This boy knows how to shoot pool."

"I'm from Philly," Jack added.

"Oh, then that explains it," Joe laughed. "I've visited a few pool halls there myself. Can I get you a drink?"

"Another time, Joe," Jack replied. "If I don't get back to the restaurant soon, Pierre will send out a search party."

"But we were just getting acquainted," Uncle Joe said. "Bring him along anytime, Elyse. The boy's got 'balls,' if you know what I mean."

"I wouldn't have it any other way, Uncle Joe."

"It was nice meeting you, Joe; I'm sure I'll see you again soon," Jack added.

"You can count on it!" Uncle Joe said as he shook his hand good-bye.

"Let me walk you outside," Elyse said as she took Jack's hand.

Once they were outside, Jack gently kissed Elyse's hand like a proper gentleman and joked, "I hope you will not let the ugliness of this sporting event mar our relationship, Ms. Montgomery."

"Never!"

"Good, then may I ask you to join me tomorrow at the restaurant for dinner at sunset?"

"Won't you be too busy then to spend time with me?"

"No, the restaurant is closed all day tomorrow to prepare for an inspection."

"Wouldn't want to see LeClare's mentioned on the local news for anything but a good restaurant review, now would we?" Elyse joked.

"That's precisely the point, but it will also give us more time to get to know one another," Jack said. "That's what you want, isn't it?" he implored as his eyes burned his desire into her heart.

"Yes," she replied.

"Then, I look forward to our next meeting. *A demain*," he said as he jumped up on the bike and sped away.

Elyse sighed as Uncle Joe came out of the bar and gave her a knowing look. "He's a good match for you, my dear."

She snapped out of her daze and kissed Uncle Joe on the cheek. "Now, Uncle Joe, you know you're the only one for me."

"C'mon, Little Bit, let's join the boys for another round."

"Can't, Uncle Joe, I've got some work to do myself. Sam Smith found a picture of Jacob standing in front of a sailing vessel. I can't quite make out the name on it since it's in Celtic. I guess I'll be surfing the net this afternoon."

"Are you sure it was a sailing vessel, Elyse? I never knew that Jacob captained one."

"Positive. Here, take a look at it," she said as she handed the photograph to Uncle Joe.

"So, this is the Devil in the flesh. He looks mighty sure of himself. I wonder when this photo was taken," Uncle Joe remarked.

"That's precisely what I need to find out."

"Now don't forget; my invitation still stands if you change your mind about staying at the lighthouse. You don't need to be bothered by that sulking sailor. If you ask me, you'd be better off without him."

"I know you're there for me if I need you, Uncle Joe, but this is something I have to face alone."

"Maybe you should hang garlic bulbs around the place to keep that demon out," Uncle Joe added.

"That only works for vampires," Elyse teased.

"Don't trust him, Elyse. He had a strong soul."

"Possession only happens in the movies, Uncle Joe."

"I would beg to differ with you on that, Elyse. It seems Jack has already cast a spell on you."

Yes, Elyse thought, *he certainly has.*

Chapter 8

When Elyse got back to the lighthouse, she took off her sandals and poured herself a glass of lemonade. She took out the picture of Jacob that Sam had given to her earlier, and placed it next to her laptop computer while she explored the Internet.

First, she checked her email messages from Rachel and one from her attorney, Socrates Johnson. Socrates was a handsome black man in his mid-forties who always "dressed to the nines." Elyse had met him at a social function, where they spent the evening making up outlandish stories about the other "chi-chi" guests and what they were probably like in real life just to relieve their boredom.

Socrates fit his name; he was quite the philosopher. He graduated at the top of his class at Harvard, and was very involved in helping inner-city youth. His wife, Marcella, was also a dedicated woman who started a citywide reading program for underprivileged children.

Both were very good friends, so it was no surprise when Elyse chose Socrates to represent her at the upcoming contractual meeting with the 3R Corporation regarding the transfer of the lighthouse's deed. His email was short and sweet:

"Please contact me to confirm how much time you will need to straighten things out before I set a date for the meeting. Marcella and I miss you. Our love to you always. –Socrates."

The message from Rachel was a bit more entertaining:

"What's up? Just had to write and tell you that I bid for a table at Rao's for a charity event and got it! How in the hell will I explain a perpetual reservation at a restaurant to

our editor-in-chief? Don't worry, I'll think of something! Also, I contacted a source in Philly about your hot tamale. Seems like he is the real deal; hometown boy makes good and all that. Word is that he is being considered for the James Beard Foundation Award for Rising Star Chef of the year. My question to you is, does this guy "cook" in other areas as well? You're not one to kiss and tell, so my hopes are limited. That's it for now. I'll send more when I get more. Ciao, Rae"

Elyse smiled to herself as she imagined Rae trying to convince their new boss that she needed one of the ten coveted tables at Rao's for interviews. If anyone could do it, though, it was Rae. She was like a cat, always landing on her feet.

It was time to do some research before evening set in. She typed in the word "Celtic" and discovered various websites on pagan gods and goddesses, Celtic art and writing, and druids and bards. All this sounded like a class in history to her, which was just fine since she enjoyed such things.

She learned that the ancient Celts had created a form of writing called *ogham*. It was the writing of druids, who served as priests, and bards, who were highly trained poets. The *ogham* alphabet contained twenty letters, and was meant to be read from the bottom up. The letters were constructed using a combination of lines placed adjacent to or crossing a midline. A single letter may have contained from one to five vertical or angled strokes.

The Celts existed around the latter part of the fifth century B.C. and were not part of an empire. They were a mass of tribes or clans and were brave and warlike people skilled in arts and crafts. They viewed life as an eternal journey, and they believed in reincarnation.

Right up Jacob's alley, Elyse thought.

He sounded like someone who could have been a Celt in another lifetime. She looked at the markings on the side of the ship in the photo. She copied them down, and then remembering to read from the bottom up, looked up the letters in the key before her.

When she was done, she had spelled out the word *Rose.* Ships were often named after women, but why had he chosen this particular name? There was also a symbol at the very top of the letters. It looked like a fancy letter *S* with another curly-q sprouting from its middle, tucking under to its right side. She found out that this was called an "entry sign," and it centered on the concept of several returns or homecomings.

"Jacob," Elyse said aloud, almost expecting an answer, "you're much more complex than I'd imagined."

Did he consider his home to be Ireland or America? Did he plan to return to his homeland, or was he going to make the island his permanent home? Elyse wondered and knew she would have to ask him at his next appearance, which she now anticipated with great interest. He was someone to be reckoned with, that was sure, but he was also a complicated entity who possessed a thirst for life deeper than the depths he had navigated during his lifetime. She just couldn't shake the feeling that there was more to Jacob's story than anyone could have imagined. Being inquisitive by nature could sometimes be a curse, and she hoped she wouldn't regret helping him.

It was early evening now, and Elyse was ready to call it quits. What a day it had been. Jack had really been a good sport, and she was beginning to fall more in love with him every day. But she wondered about Jack's feelings for her:

Why does he continually pull away during our intimate encounters? What could he be hiding?

Maybe she would find out more tomorrow. After all, it would just be the two of them all evening long. Ah, how she liked the sound of that. Until then, she was hoping Jacob would show up soon so she could question him about the name of his ship. *It figures I'd get stuck with a ghost with amnesia*, she mused. Still, she had promised to help him find out how and why he died, and she always kept her promises.

Elyse fell asleep in the living room chair after doing her research, and was awakened by loud footsteps coming down the spiral staircase. When she opened her eyes, Jacob stood before her.

"Were you waiting for me?" he asked.

"In a matter of speaking," she responded as she threw the afghan on the back of the chair around her shoulders to ward off the room's sudden chill.

She imagined that he was accustomed to having women wait for him. After all, he had an air of confidence about him that was quite appealing.

"I was watching the moonlight dance on the water," he began, "then I suddenly grew very sad, for I remembered how it felt to dance with my Elyse. She could dance just like that moonlight, so graceful and free. Her hair smelled like jasmine, and her feet floated on clouds. It is her eyes that I miss the most, though. They were the deepest blue eyes I had ever seen. She spoke with those eyes without ever saying a word. She could never hide how she really felt about anything. It was always revealed in her eyes..."

Elyse sat mystified by Jacob's description of how it had been to dance with her grandmother. How could such a "man's man" also be so tender? He was truly a contradiction.

She decided to show him the secret letter that she'd found in the lighthouse.

"Jacob, I believe I can help you more if you see items that might hold some significance for you." He came closer as she showed him the letter and said, "Here's a letter that was hidden behind a brick in the wall of the lighthouse. Is it yours?"

"There is no date on this letter, but I know it is my writing. For some reason, I believe this may have been the last letter I ever wrote."

"Why do you say that?" Elyse asked.

"I did not sign my entire name at the bottom. I only used the first initial of my given name. Your grandmother was forbidden to see me the last time I returned to the island."

"How many times did you visit the island?" Elyse inquired.

"I was here several times, but the first time was when I was twenty-one years old," he began. "That is when I met Elyse. I was the first mate on a supply vessel that traveled the Great Lakes during the warmer months. I saw Elyse as much as I could during the time period before the lakes froze. Since I was the oldest of seven children, I had to return to Ireland for the winter months to work my family's farm and help my widowed mother. Then my mother died, and the other children were old enough to earn a living."

"When did you return to the island next?" she asked.

"Two years later," he said, "but this time I owned the shipping company that I had once worked for."

"That must have been quite an accomplishment," Elyse said in amazement.

"Some people should not consume liquor whilst playing cards," Jacob replied with a cocky demeanor. Elyse took this to mean that Jacob had won the shipping company in a card game. "I wanted Joseph to see that I was a respectable man and that I could take care of his daughter in the proper manner."

"Didn't he believe you could do that?" Elyse asked.

"No, he hated the ground I walked on," Jacob began. "I was the enemy due to the reputation that followed me from shore to shore: I liked to gamble and drink and be in the company of women. Once I met Elyse, though, I had no need for any other. She was the other half of my soul. Elyse was her father's little girl, but he failed to notice that she had become a woman. Then again, maybe he knew that fact but didn't want to admit it."

Elyse was struck by Jacob's admonishments. His love for her grandmother had been the real thing. *Then why hadn't she run off with him? Wasn't her love for him the same?*

"Jacob, let me show you a picture," Elyse said as she showed him the photo from Sam. When Jacob saw the picture, he placed his hand over his eyes and winced in pain. "Jacob," she shouted, "what's the matter?"

"This ship has something to do with my death, but I can tell you no more," he said abruptly. And just as suddenly as he had appeared, Jacob was gone, leaving Elyse with more questions than answers.

This was the most fascinating mystery she had ever probed, and Jacob was the most perplexing person she had ever encountered, dead or alive.

But the big question in her mind remained. *Why am I so drawn to Jacob?* Maybe he had been right about her that first night they'd met. Perhaps she was more like him than she wanted to admit.

Chapter 9

It was finally Monday morning, and Elyse was up early due to all the nagging questions occupying her mind of late. This was now more than an investigation to her. It was a quest. She was becoming increasingly intrigued by Jacob's secret life and saw another side of him: the side he kept hidden from most people except her grandmother. He was a true romantic in every sense of the word, and even though Sam Smith had hinted that he could charm the petticoat off any woman in his day, it was her grandmother he returned to whenever he had the chance.

Elyse kept meaning to ask him why the ship in the photograph was a sailing vessel and not a supply ship. If he owned a supply ship company, he should have, therefore, arrived on one. If Jacob hadn't been so upset about seeing the ship in the photo, she could have questioned him further. Now she would have to wait for their next meeting.

Elyse knew her day would be a busy one, since she was going to continue to sort through her grandmother's possessions. It looked like Socrates was eager to finalize things with the company bidding on the lighthouse and its surrounding property, but she knew he understood that she needed this time to grieve.

That was the first time she had labeled her feelings that way since she'd arrived on Put-in-Bay. She had kept her feelings surrounding her grandmother's death so shrouded that she hadn't allowed herself the time to unravel them in the appropriate manner.

She hadn't shed a tear at the funeral several months ago, but now she was feeling a little guilty, and also somewhat deprived, that she had not. She finally gave herself permission to mourn and cried alone in her room until she could cry no more.

When she went back downstairs, Rainy was meowing on the steps of the sunporch.

"I haven't been the best hostess in the world now, have I?" Elyse started. "After all, I left you in the house all day yesterday and outside the entire night. I promise to change my ways immediately."

Rainy meowed in response and then dashed into the kitchen to find her food bowl. Elyse looked out over the grounds and decided to have her morning tea and breakfast in one of the Adirondack chairs under a shade tree. Staring out onto the lake, she could envision how it had become Jacob's passion. It was so peaceful by the water. Most people she knew recharged their batteries by going to seaside resorts, and many planned to retire near a body of water.

Then again, it was anything but peaceful the night Jacob had died. Sam had told her that there had been a horrific thunderstorm that night. Was that the memory Jacob was having difficulty facing? Or was it something else that had happened before he left the island?

After breakfast, Elyse climbed up the stairs of the lighthouse tower. She saw a storage area in the wall and noticed that it was locked. On a hunch, she went back into the living room and grabbed the purple ribbon with the two keys.

The second key fit the lock exactly. She opened the door to find a clasped envelope. She sat down on the landing and opened it to discover four more pages of her grandmother's journal:

"Jacob will be visiting the island every week until the lake freezes over. Before winter arrives, he will take a sailing ship back to Ireland to be with his family. He wants

to see me when he returns. I am a little reluctant to do so, for I have recently heard some gossip about his many vices. He has assured me that it is totally unfounded, but father is still preaching to me to stay away from 'ne'er do wells' and concentrate on local boys. He is particularly fond of Patrick Dugan. I have known Patrick all my life, and we are very good friends. Since my own brother, Joseph, is just a child, I cannot talk to him like I can to Patrick. We like to swim and fish, and we also meet at church social functions. But I cannot dismiss the feelings I am having for the handsome sailor from Ireland. He is on my mind more and more. Do I dare spend time with him alone? I will let my heart decide."

Then Elyse read the second page from the journal:

"I saw Jacob in town again at the general store. He smiled and winked at me. This time I was with mother, so I was able to sneak outside whilst she spoke to Mrs. Baker. Jacob pushed a lock of my hair away from my eyes, and told me that we would have to find a secret place to meet when he was in port. I know I shouldn't have agreed to it, but I did. What has come over me? He told me that my eyes remind him of sapphires and that he will give me jewels to match them one day. He also asked me if there was some kind of "sign" we could use to signal that it was okay to meet. I suggested a kerosene lantern in the attic window of our home. He will be able to see it when his ship comes close to shore. As for our secret meeting place, we decided on East Point, which is on the opposite end of the island away from all of the docks. That way no one in town will see us together. There is a beach there, and we can be alone. I hope that I will have the courage to meet him there."

The third page continued on the same theme:

"I met Jacob at East Point as planned. I told mother that Patrick and I were going to visit a friend in town. I also

told Patrick about my plan in the event he is asked about my whereabouts. He is a dear friend, but today he almost acted jealous that I would dare meet with anyone but him! Jacob gave me a rose and kissed me on the cheek. We sat upon a blanket and talked about our dreams. Jacob is a dreamer like me. Whereas I dream of becoming a writer one day, Jacob dreams about having his own sailing vessel. He wants to see the world, and is also a wonderful poet. He showed me some of his writings, and I could not believe that he was capable of conveying that much feeling without much of an education. He told me that he reads a lot and would love to read my books one day. I told him that I would have to become published first! We are planning to meet every week at the same time and place. I hope I can convince Patrick that this is a good thing to do, for I cannot let father discover whom I am seeing."

The last entry was also about Jacob:

"I am going to tear out any pages of my journal that mention Jacob and hide them in various places around the house. One day I will retrieve all of the pages so that I may reread them. For the time being, I must be extremely careful about what I do or say in regards to Jacob. Patrick is still hiding my little secret, and the kerosene lantern is working fine as a signaling device to Jacob when he is near shore. I don't know where all this is leading, but I do know that Jacob is nothing like the person my father has described to me. He is sensitive and serious, and is a devoted son who sends most of his hard-earned wages back to Ireland to help out his mother and siblings. He is also the most beautiful man I have ever seen. He is now in my heart, forever etched like a drawing that cannot be erased by time or space. I dare say I am in love with Jacob Flannery."

“Wow,” was all Elyse could say when she put down the pages. Her grandmother had been as deeply in love with Jacob as he was with her. Then what could have happened to separate them? Surely her great-grandfather was an obstacle, but they had already circumvented that by meeting in a secluded place.

Elyse would have to look around the house for other pages from the journal, but now she decided to go back up to her grandparents’ bedroom and pack up her grandmother’s clothing for charity.

She folded swirling skirts and blouses, cardigans and coats. She took a hatbox out of the corner of the closet and tried on a few of the contents. She laughed at herself in the dresser mirror, and Rainy even came upstairs to investigate what was going on. She also tried on shawls and then packed them in boxes that she had brought upstairs.

When she got to the purses, she found a beautiful ivory-colored, beaded one that was much dressier than all the rest. She opened it up to find a ring box. When she tipped the lid, there was a brilliant sapphire ring surrounded by two delicate rubies set in a gold band. She never remembered seeing her grandmother wear this ring before and thought, *Why would she hide such a beautiful piece of jewelry in a purse in the back of her closet?* Elyse pulled up the bottom of the ring box to find a small note that read: “A promise kept. Forever in my heart.”

Elyse tried the ring on her finger, and it fit perfectly. She would wear it out to dinner tonight. It must have been a gift from Jacob to her grandmother. Hadn’t he promised her grandmother sapphires to match her eyes? This was by far the most surprising discovery of the day. Could this have been some sort of engagement ring, or was it a parting gift?

She would have to show it to Jacob the next time he appeared to her.

It was now afternoon and Elyse took a relaxing bubble bath to prepare for her date with Jack. She laid out her lingerie upon her bed and looked at the three dresses she had taken to the island. She decided on an ivory, sleeveless silk cocktail dress with hand-painted pansies.

Elyse applied her makeup and curled her hair into soft strands that she deftly restyled into an updo, leaving a few tendrils to circle the nape of her neck like silken spaghetti. When she looked in the mirror, she could definitely see a transformation.

Yes, Jack would like what he saw tonight, but would he like it enough to drop the armor he had been wearing up until now? Only time would tell, and Elyse felt certain that this was the night she and Jack would become lovers.

Chapter 10

The taxi transported Elyse to the dock by the Sonny S ferry. "Do you want me to come back later to drive you home?" the driver asked.

"I have a feeling that won't be necessary," she answered with a smile.

It was a gorgeous evening. The island seemed more lush and greener than usual after the week's heavy rains. The sun cast a golden glow over the water, and the boats on the lake resembled corks bobbing up and down in a rain barrel.

When Elyse reached the dock, she tipped the driver and bought a ticket for the ferry. When she turned around, Jean-Louis stood before her holding a beautiful bouquet of freshly cut flowers. "Mademoiselle Elyse, Monsieur Jacques wanted me to give these to you before I escort you to the island," he said.

"Why, thank you, Jean-Louis! They're exquisite," Elyse exclaimed as she took in a deep breath of the fragrant flowers.

"I grew them myself," he revealed proudly. "Jacques is putting a few last-minute touches on things before your arrival. Otherwise, he would have come himself."

"He wouldn't be a bit of a perfectionist, would he Jean-Louis?" Elyse asked.

"You have *no* idea," Jean-Louis began. "Actually, he is a good man. He is like a big brother to me."

Elyse was glad to hear that Jacques was beloved by his staff. Maybe that was the secret to his success: he was able to combine the rare talents of being a good manager with that of a friend.

When they arrived on the other side, Pierre and Fifi were there to greet them. Elyse was surprised to see Pierre was dressed in his full regalia, since it hadn't been a regular workday for him. "Mademoiselle, we are very pleased to see you again so soon," Pierre said with a twinkle in his eye.

Fifi even barked in agreement and wagged his tail as Pierre took Elyse's hand to help her out of the ferry. Since the restaurant was closed to the public, the other passengers hurried off to their condos on the island.

"Until we meet again," Jean-Louis said to Elyse as he kissed her hand before rushing back to work.

"That boy is picking up too much from the boss," Pierre said as he rolled his eyes.

"I'll say one thing about you French men: your reputation *is* warranted," Elyse said.

"It's a tough job, but we do it well," Pierre replied as Fifi took up the rear.

Once they were inside, Elyse could hear music playing softly in the background. The restaurant looked strange this empty, and she could smell something good simmering in the kitchen.

"I take it the inspection went well today, Pierre?" she inquired.

"*Oui*, we received the highest rating in all categories. Monsieur Jacques is a very particular person. He has very high standards. Apparently, that also applies to his taste in women."

"*Merci, beaucoup*," she replied.

Pierre led Elyse out to the terrace, which had been transformed into a tropical paradise. Baskets of brightly colored New Zealand impatiens had been hung from the overhead awning, while towering potted ferns with tiny white twinkling Christmas lights dotted the floor. In the middle of it all stood a magnificently set table with fine crystal and china and an ice bucket on a stand holding chilled champagne.

Pierre pulled the chair away from the table and motioned for Elyse to take her seat. He pushed in her chair and then bowed before leaving. Elyse placed her bouquet of flowers in the crystal vase before her.

She wondered where Jack was, when he appeared in the doorway wearing an expensive suit. He actually took her breath away; she had only seen him in casual clothes or his chef's jacket and was stunned at how elegant he looked. He easily could have been a model on the cover of *GQ*.

He sauntered over to the table and gently kissed Elyse on the cheek. "You grow even more beautiful to me every time we meet," he said.

"You clean up well, too," she joked.

"Why, thank you. I have planned a special dinner for the two of us. But before we begin, may I suggest we work up an appetite?"

Jack took her hand, and as if on cue, the staff turned up the volume on the stereo system so that saxophonist Warren Hill's *Do You Feel What I'm Feeling?* could be heard on the terrace.

Elyse took a single flower from the vase and put it between her teeth, put her hands on her hips, threw back her head, and stomped her feet in her best impression of a flamenco dancer. Jack laughed and placed the flower in her hair before twirling her around the terrace. Tonight was theirs as they circled the dance floor, completely in step and in tune with one another.

Before the song was finished, Jack dipped Elyse toward the floor before lifting her back up to end their dance in a dramatic fashion. "You sure can 'cut a rug' as they used to say," Elyse remarked.

"You're not so bad yourself."

"Do you have any more surprises up your sleeve tonight, Monsieur?"

"That depends what your expectations are," he whispered as he leaned closer in toward her.

"I expect nothing short of sheer surprise from you," she answered as Jack led her back to the table.

"Good, then I will describe our menu," he began. "We will start off with an appetizer of oysters on the half shell. Then I thought we'd have mixed baby greens with toasted pecans, feta cheese, and raspberry vinaigrette. Grilled orange-and-bourbon salmon and a side dish of fresh asparagus with foaming hollandaise sauce will follow. To top it off, we will go to heaven by eating a piece of mixed-berry and white-chocolate buttercream cake."

"Stop right there; you've sold me!"

"I'm glad you like my choices. You're still the best dish on the menu tonight," Jack said as he looked intensely at her. "May I interest you in some champagne?"

"Why, of course!"

Jean-Louis came out with the appetizer just as they finished their first glass of champagne. Jack was recounting one of his first experiences as a chef, which she found to be quite entertaining, as they finished their courses and shared their hopes and dreams.

"I want to thank you for one of the most lovely and romantic evenings of my life," Elyse remarked.

"You mean it's over already?" Jack asked.

"Not if you don't want it to be." Now she had played her trump card; it was up to him to make the next move.

"Follow me," he said as he took her hand and led her to the dance floor.

Jim Brickman's romantic piano ballad *Destiny* played softly in the background as Pierre and Jean-Louis peered at them from the doorway to the terrace.

"Should I plate-up their dessert?" Jean-Louis asked.

"I believe the kind of dessert they want is *not* on our menu, Jean-Louis," Pierre said, winking. "Let's close up shop. They will not even notice we are gone."

Jack gave Elyse a long, passionate kiss before leading her upstairs to his living quarters. Pierre had lit candles all around the room before his departure.

Elyse started to unzip her dress, and Jack helped her. There was no going back now. She then took the bobby pins from her hair and let her tresses cascade down.

He took off his suit jacket and placed it on the bed while she nuzzled his neck and unbuttoned his shirt. She gracefully backed up and lay down on top of the bed before he lay down on top of her.

His warm, wet lips kissed her face and neck, while his gentle hands rubbed her thighs up and down before removing her stockings from their garters. Then Elyse unbuttoned and unzipped his pants before Jack disposed of them on the floor. His well-toned body straddled hers, while he slid off her panties and unhooked her front-closure bra.

It was just the two of them now, and they pleasured each other into the night before finally falling asleep under the covers in each other's fantasies.

Chapter 11

When Elyse woke up the next morning, she almost forgot where she was. She smiled to herself and rolled over to touch Jack to assure herself that she wasn't dreaming. He wasn't there, so she threw on the dress shirt he'd left on the floor in their haste to undress the night before.

She could hear muffled talking coming from Jack's office. She decided to surprise him and was just about to knock on the door, when she overheard him say something puzzling: "I think I will need more time to investigate this matter," Jack said to someone on the other end of the call. Then there was a slight pause as he began again, "I know what you're looking for, but it will be more difficult than I'd originally thought. You must give me at least a few more weeks to come up with a plan."

Somehow Elyse didn't think Jack was talking about catering a party. This almost sounded like some kind of a secret mission to her. *What is he up to?*

"I am doing my best to rectify the situation. You can count on me to come through for you. I've got to go now. I have a busy day ahead of me. *Au revoir, Monsieur*," he said and hung up the phone.

Elyse decided to slip quietly back into bed and under the covers before Jack discovered her eavesdropping. She didn't know what he was doing, but somehow she sensed it wasn't legit. When he came out of the office, he was dressed in a pair of silk boxers with matching robe.

"Somehow I didn't imagine you in boxers," she teased.

"I, on the other hand, have often imagined you wearing nothing but my shirt," he retorted.

Elyse hit Jack with a pillow, and he jumped on the bed and landed on top of her. He gave her a kiss, and was just starting to take things further when there was a knock on the door.

"Monsieur Jacques, are you decent? We have a little surprise for you and your guest." It was Pierre, and no doubt most of the morning staff, judging by the laughter coming from the other side of the door.

"Well, Elyse, are you ready?" Jack asked.

"Is this part of the service here?" she joked.

"I guess it is now."

"Okay, send them in. I'm ready for anything!"

"Pierre, you may come in now."

Pierre, Jean-Louis, and two other staff members entered the room with a continental breakfast for two.

"Now, for your dining pleasure, we would like to serenade you with a little song," Pierre began. "Okay, boys, *commencer*!"

Then they all chimed in, singing Lerner and Loewe's *Thank Heaven for Little Girls*, while Elyse and Jack laughed. When the song was over, they clapped wildly.

"Don't quit your day job, guys. Maurice Chevalier you're not," Jack kidded.

"You were terrific," Elyse volunteered.

"I'm glad we met with your approval," Pierre began. "I have placed your messages on the breakfast tray, Jacques. Vitamix® called again about getting you to pose for them in their next ad."

"Pierre, tell them that I'll be glad to do it *after* Bobby Flay does. After all, I don't pose in the nude for just anyone," he said as he looked directly at Elyse.

"They want you to pose nude with a blender?" she asked.

"That's the general idea," he replied.

"I guess your field is becoming a little more *risqué* than I'd imagined!"

"It's all about image, but I'm not too sure I want to portray that kind of image."

"I think you'd look just fine, Jack. After all, a blender is bigger than a fig leaf," she added.

"You're right! My manhood wouldn't be compromised with something as big as a blender," he joked.

Elyse hit Jack with a pillow as Pierre and the staff laughed out loud.

"His goose is cooked," Jean-Louis whispered to Pierre.

"I couldn't have said it better myself," Pierre replied under his breath.

"Okay, the fun's over," Jack began. "Let's get back to work. We've got two private parties to cater today."

"We will leave you now, boss," Pierre said. "Enjoy your breakfast, Mademoiselle Elyse."

"Thanks, Pierre; Jean-Louis and the staff did an excellent job!"

"*Merci*, we aim to please," Pierre said as he placed the breakfast tray and its contents on the table.

"You know, Jean-Louis, I think I have corrupted you," Pierre commented to his sidekick as he shuffled the staff down the stairs.

When they were gone, Elyse looked lovingly at Jack and said, "You are one lucky, guy, Jacques LeClare. They really love you."

"I hope I can add one more person to that list this morning," he replied before giving her a passionate kiss.

"Are you hungry?" she asked.

"Only for you," he said as he kissed her again, and they sank back down into the silk sheets for another round of lovemaking.

After they had gotten their fill of one another, Jack put on his robe and got up to get the breakfast tray. Elyse couldn't help but notice that he took his pink message slips and deftly slipped them in his robe pocket.

"I can catch up on my calls later. Let's eat," he said.

Elyse wondered if the messages contained the name of the person Jack had been talking to earlier. *Why would he need to hide the messages from me? I have no interest in his clients.*

After they were finished with their breakfast in bed, Elyse gave Jack a big kiss on the check and said, "I don't mean to eat and run, but it is getting a bit late. I have to contact my attorney today about some pressing business."

"Oh, the lighthouse," he said matter-of-factly.

"When did I tell you about the lighthouse?" she inquired.

"You told me a lot about yourself last night, in words *and* in actions," Jack countered.

Elyse didn't recall telling Jack anything about selling the lighthouse, but she did drink her share of champagne, so anything was possible. "Then you know how important this is to me," she replied. "May I use your shower?"

"It's all yours," he answered. "I think I'll get dressed and check on the staff."

"You were wonderful," she whispered in Jack's ear.

"And you were better than that," he replied. "If you don't get out of this bed soon, Ms. Montgomery, I can't be held responsible for my actions."

Elyse jumped out of bed just as Jack tried to grab her. She took off his shirt and teasingly threw it at him. "Thanks for letting me borrow this," she said before walking stark naked to the bathroom and locking the door.

"You're going to give me my first coronary!" he shouted after her.

Elyse let the water run all over her body, which had been taken to new levels of excitement the night before. Jack had been a considerate and passionate lover, and she couldn't remember when she had felt so fulfilled. Now she would have to dress and get back to reality. It had truly been one enchanted evening.

After drying herself off, Elyse rolled her damp hair into an updo. She checked herself over in the mirror, and then went into the bedroom to finish dressing. Elyse accidentally knocked over a *Limoges* porcelain on the nightstand when she sat down to put on her shoes. A gold band rolled out onto the floor. Elyse picked it up and examined it carefully; it was a wedding ring. *Was this what he was hiding from me?*

She looked at it closely, and noticed the French phrase: *"A Ma Vie de Coeur Entier"* engraved on the outside of the ring. She was still looking at it when Jack quietly entered the room.

"You have my whole heart for my whole life," he said . "It is a French saying that dates back to the fifteenth century. That ring is a replica of a 'poesy,' or poetry, ring."

"I wasn't snooping around, Jack, honestly. I knocked the *Limoges* over by accident, and the ring just rolled out of it. Is it yours?" she asked sheepishly.

"No, it was my mother's wedding ring," he said. "I keep it by my bedside because it is all I have left from her."

"You'll want to put it back in its place then," she said as she handed it back to him.

"I promised her that I would keep it and give it to the woman I would marry one day," he began. "It was her dying wish. She didn't have much to give me after my father gambled away most of their savings. Her love was the greatest gift of all. It is with me still, in my soul."

"What a wonderful woman she must have been," Elyse responded.

"She would have liked you, too," Jack answered as he carefully placed the ring back into the delicate *Limoges*.

"Well, I think I've gotten into enough trouble for the day. Perhaps it's time for me to shove off."

"You don't have to leave yet, Elyse, do you? I still have to take my shower. You can join me and stay for lunch."

"If I don't get out of here soon, I'll be taking every meal of the day with you."

"That's precisely my plan," he teased as he gave her a quick kiss on the lips.

"I think I'll take a rain check on that lunch, if it's okay with you," she added.

"Not a problem. There's no expiration date on it for you, Mademoiselle."

"I guess I'll be seeing you around then, huh?" she asked.

"*Oui, chére*," he said as he gave her one last long, wet kiss.

Elyse sighed inside and waved good-bye before walking down the steps. She was definitely doomed as far as he was concerned. Uncle Joe had seen it written all over her face the day before at Tony's. Elyse didn't care who saw it anymore. She was in love.

Chapter 12

People at the dock gave Elyse a second look when she reached South Bass Island. She was in evening clothes, after all, and everyone else was casual. She didn't care, though, because she was still on cloud nine and didn't want to come down just yet. She looked at her watch and hailed down a taxi to drive her back to the lighthouse.

Rainy appeared out of nowhere while she was unlocking the door to the sunporch. "Hey, I see you finished the food I left out for you last night. Let's go inside and get your breakfast."

Elyse was pouring some food for Rainy when the cat suddenly stopped, arched her back, and hissed before running away. Elyse's back was turned, but she intuitively knew what had startled the cat, since the temperature of the room now felt like that of an icy tomb.

"You were not here last night," a deep, disgruntled voice said behind her.

Elyse was feeling too good to let a moody ghost spoil her morning. "I don't remember appointing you as my chaperone," she said as she turned around to face the ghost.

"Do you need one?" he asked sarcastically.

"Not since I was a little girl, Jacob, and that was a long time ago. I *do* have a life, you know."

She knew that last statement had been a mistake because Jacob truly looked wounded. Why did she have to remind him that he wasn't flesh and blood like her? It had been a careless thing to do on her part, so she decided to smooth things over.

"I'm sorry, Jacob, but sometimes I forget that you're…"

"Dead? I cannot go back to what should have been, or move forward to what will be. I am full of anger over what I've lost and what I can never have!"

She was stunned into silence by Jacob's tirade, and she could see the anger swelling up in him, waiting to explode like a lit grenade. Finally, she said, "Frustration can turn into anger, Jacob. Once we solve your puzzle, maybe you will be able to move on."

"I hope you are right, because I am growing weary of roaming these grounds. I cannot leave here! It is as if I am being punished for something," he answered.

"Or maybe it's me who's being punished," Elyse mused.

Jacob gave her that all-knowing smile of his that revealed that he had her all figured out. "How like your grandmother you are, to make light of a bad situation, just to see me smile."

"Do you think you could recall something more about the ship I showed you in the photograph the other night?"

"*The Rose*, that's what I christened her," he said. "She was a fine vessel with tall masts and sails. She was named after Elyse."

"So that was your pet name for my grandmother?"

"Yes, I called her my Irish rose. She loved roses, and she planted many on this land. I do not see them here anymore. Perhaps they died along with her memories of me."

Elyse could see that Jacob was starting to feel sorry for himself again, so she decided to change the subject. "Where did you go during those two years you stayed away from the island, Jacob?"

"I went back to Ireland first, to make sure that my mother and siblings were taken care of," he began. "My mother died of pneumonia not long afterward, and there was no need for me to stay since my brothers and sisters were of age. It was then that I decided to make some changes in my life and do things on my terms. I won the shipping company in a card game; then after six months, I decided to sell it to buy the sailing vessel."

"Why would you buy a sailing vessel at that point in your life?"

"I wanted to see the world and had the resources to do so. I spent some time in the Orient, and after I felt at peace with myself, I returned to the island to take Elyse back to Ireland with me."

"How did you find the peace within yourself?"

"It is not easy. First, you have to accept yourself the way you are. Then you must accept others the same way," Jacob said matter-of-factly.

She thought about that last statement awhile and believed she could see where Jacob was leading.

"There are those who are close minded and want to believe in one thing," he began. "I was not like that. I wanted to learn and explore other cultures and their beliefs. Maybe people who are afraid of doing what I did are satisfied just living their entire lives in a safe harbor. I, on the other hand, enjoyed the challenge of a storm now and then. How can one know the strength of an anchor if there is no storm? There is always a hidden danger associated with knowing too much. In the end, it makes you question your own beliefs. How many people are willing to risk that?"

"Were you always a risk taker?"

Jacob smiled, and his gray eyes gleamed in recognition of her observation. "There is no other way to be."

"Were you willing to risk everything for my grandmother?"

"If I would have been that way with your grandmother, then maybe our story would have ended differently," he replied.

"Were you afraid to tell her your feelings?" Elyse implored.

"She knew of my feelings for her, but in the end I was too proud to admit my mistakes and ask for her forgiveness."

"What do you mean by that?"

"I cannot remember that much yet. A cloud crosses my mind's eye when I try to seek the sun to guide me. Maybe *you* are that sun."

"I will try to light your way, Jacob."

"You already do," he said before vanishing right before her eyes.

Elyse stood there baffled again by Jacob's mysterious comments and revelations. So he *had* come back to the island to reclaim her grandmother's love. Had he been too late?

A telephone's shrill ring broke Elyse's concentration, and she ran over to pick up the receiver before the answering machine kicked in.

"Hey, stranger, how are things going on that oasis of yours?" the voice on the other side of the phone asked. It was Socrates; Elyse was happy to hear his voice. He was prompt as usual for their conference call regarding the sale of the lighthouse and its surrounding grounds.

"It's not exactly that way, Socrates. I've decided to research a story while I'm here," she said.

"Oh, just looking for another tax write-off, eh? I'm on to you, darlin'," he joked.

Elyse laughed out loud at Socrates' insinuation that she was all work and no play. "Actually, it's not like that at all. I'm really enjoying myself. Now when was the last time you heard me say that?"

"Can't remember, so I guess this has been a good break for you then. Marcella and I are looking forward to seeing you again once this meeting is arranged with 3R."

"Do you have a date set yet?" she asked.

"It will be approximately two weeks from now," he said. "Will that give you enough time to finish your personal business?"

"That should be about right. Just let me know the time and place so I can book a flight."

"No problem. Hey, what is Rachel doing at Rao's?" he asked.

Elyse laughed, for she had forgotten that Rachel had won a table at the impenetrable East Harlem restaurant that had its regulars and celebrities' names etched in stone.

"I guess she rates as much as you do now," she joked.

"What's the world coming to?" he laughed. "She told me that she tried calling you last night, but hung up when she got your machine."

"She knows I hate it when people do that. Do you know what she wanted?"

"Something about research you wanted her to do and that she had reached a dead end."

"Dead end, eh? Rachel never let that stop her before. I'll give her a call, Socrates."

"You do that, and don't go running off with some sailor while you're marooned on that island," he added.

"There's no way that will happen. You're stuck with me forever," she said.

"Good. I'll contact you with the particulars of the meeting in the near future. Take care of yourself, Elyse."

"You, too, Socrates. Give Marcella my love. *Ciao*!"

Elyse was very close to Socrates, but she didn't dare reveal what was going on at the lighthouse. How funny that he had mentioned running off with a sailor. If he only knew that a cantankerous, albeit *dead*, one was living with her right now…

She decided to change into something comfortable before calling Rachel. She went up to her bedroom and removed the comb from her hair. For the first time since moving in, she picked up her grandmother's brush on the dresser and used it to brush her shoulder-length hair. She studied her reflection in the mirror and could see a sharp resemblance to her grandmother through her nose and mouth. Her hair was also the same color as her grandmother's, but her eyes…her eyes did not look like anyone else's in her entire family.

Her grandmother had very dark blue eyes, and her grandfather had hazel eyes. Her mother had blue eyes, and her father had green eyes. But Elyse had light-blue eyes, the color of the water before it turns stormy and the whitecaps roll onto the shore.

She looked more closely at herself in the mirror and almost thought she saw Jacob staring back at her. She closed her eyes and shook her head, and when she looked in the mirror again, he was gone. Maybe his recent visitations were starting to get to her. A knock at the door had her flying down the steps to find out who was there.

A UPS man in the familiar brown uniform was waiting there with a small package for her. "Sign here," he said, holding out a clipboard and smiling.

Elyse thanked the man before closing the screen door. "Now, let me see who this is from," she said as she excitedly opened the box.

It was from Jack. It was the Jim Brickman CD they had been listening to the night before. Attached was a note that read, *"I hope every time you play our song, you will remember the magic in the air and in my heart. You, Elyse, are my destiny."*

Elyse couldn't believe how romantic this man was. How thoughtful of him to send this to her the morning after their rendezvous. *Could he be the man of my dreams, or is he just setting me up for another fall?* If she fell too hard this time, would her heart ever mend?

Jacob never got the chance to recover from his lost love for her grandmother. Had she forgotten to light the lantern and put it in the attic upon his return? Maybe the light he lost was not the one emanating from the lantern, but the one in her grandmother's heart. Only the missing pages of her grandmother's journal would provide the answer.

Chapter 13

It was almost evening, and Elyse decided to contact Rachel regarding 3R Corporation. Elyse knew all of Rachel's haunts, but guessed at around this time in the day she would still be at the office. She was right on the money, for Rachel picked up the receiver on the second ring.

"Queen of the Gossip Scene speaking," Rachel quipped.

"Since when?" Elyse joked.

"Hey, you! I was trying to reach you last night. Where the hell have you been? Late night?"

"*Very*!"

"You go, girl. Anything you want to share?" Rachel asked.

"It's still too early to say, but this may be *the* one."

"No way! That's great, Elyse. Say, does he have a brother?"

"Not that I know of, but of course you should know more about that than I do since you just dug up the dirt."

"Yeah, I did, didn't I?" Rachel began. "Well, one can always dream. I did contact several people about the 3R Corporation. They are based in Europe, but I couldn't find out anything more about them since they are a privately held corporation. There are three stockholders, so I'm guessing that is why the numeral three is in their name. As far as the individual parties involved are concerned, I haven't been able to unearth a thing. I'll keep searching though, since it means so much to you."

"I'd really appreciate it, Rae, and thanks for what you've done so far."

"It's all in a day's work. When is your meeting with Socrates? I ran into the man at Rao's last night—and in a new Brioni suit no less. He was with clients, so we couldn't kibitz too long."

"It looks like the meeting will be in a week. I'll email you all the details," Elyse said.

"Fair enough. I'll keep working on my leads, and you keep that cute chef of yours cookin'," Rachel joked.

"Don't you ever give up?"

"No, that's what got me where I am now. I'm one ambitious broad. Talk to you again soon!"

"Bye, Rae."

Elyse knew she needed to get back to the task of rummaging through her grandmother's belongings. It would be dark soon, so she decided to explore the attic with a flashlight.

The stairs up to the attic creaked under her feet like an old bordello mattress with tired box springs. When she finally reached the top of the stairs and flung open the door, she saw an archaic trunk caked with dust, plus an old floor lamp with a fringed shade, tables, chairs, and boxes of various shapes and sizes. The spiderwebs hanging in the rafters were as intricate as the snowflake ornaments Elyse's mother used to crochet for their Christmas tree.

Sunlight poured into the attic to unveil the entire area in such a way that it reminded Elyse of an ancient European cathedral that she had visited that would become completely illuminated when sunlight streamed through its stained glass windows.

When looking out the attic window out onto the lake, she imagined how it must have felt for her grandmother to secretly light the kerosene lantern and place it in front of this very window for Jacob to see upon his visits to the island.

How many times had this ritual been performed? she wondered. *And when did she perform it for the last time?*

The lake certainly looked inviting from this precipice, and Elyse could almost feel her grandmother's longing to be with Jacob on the water, sailing off to parts unknown with only each other as companions.

Elyse opened the dusty trunk first and found some of her grandmother's picture albums, paints, and brushes. She took a few minutes to page through the old albums and saw images of her great-grandparents, grandparents, and her own immediate family. She put these aside to take with her later.

She turned the flashlight toward what she believed was a folding table in one corner of the attic. The object was in an upright position and covered by a chenille throw. When she got closer to it, she flashed the light at the bottom and could make out splotches of paint underneath.

Elyse instinctively removed the throw and was awestruck at the sight before her: a portrait of Jacob in formal dress. He was wearing his captain's uniform, and his eyes were so penetrating that Elyse swore he could cast a spell on anyone. The portrait was obviously painted by her grandmother, but upon closer examination, she noticed that it had been slashed diagonally with a knife across the chest area by the heart. This didn't seem like something her grandmother would have done, so who did?

Elyse decided to take the canvas back downstairs with her to show Jacob later. Maybe he would know the story behind the painting. She placed the portrait in the living room behind the couch.

Outside she sat in an Adirondack chair and watched the wakes from the boats and ferries form crisscrosses on the placid water as the sun's light became more and more diffused by the impending dusk. Rainy meowed and circled Elyse's feet before curling up on the ground beside her chair.

"You better get used to seeing that transparent man around our house," she said to her feline friend. "He's not going *anywhere* until I can solve his dilemma. Sometimes I think *he's* more afraid of what I'll uncover than *I* am of his unpredictable behavior."

With that in mind, she got up and stretched before casually walking back to the house with Rainy by her side. It was a quiet evening, and Elyse decided to retire early after reading another chapter in a book about the Celts. Rainy curled up at the end of the bed as she opened the window in her room several inches to enjoy the refreshing lake breeze.

Unfortunately for Elyse, her time asleep was nothing like her quiet evening. She tossed and turned and moaned as her mind flashed images, sights, and sounds that converged into a fragmented collage of events.

In her nightmare, she stood outside the lighthouse during an approaching thunderstorm, while the raindrops drenched her hair and turned her cotton nightgown into parchment paper. She saw her grandmother as a young woman and her grandfather as a young man rushing out of the house into a waiting wagon as their horse nervously whinnied at each strike of lightning in the distance. Their wagon raced down the gravel road as the horse reared up and stopped seconds before lightning struck an enormous tree, sending it crashing to the ground.

Then Elyse was magically transported to the downtown dock, where she saw her grandmother kneeling on the dock with her grandfather comforting her. Her grandmother was crying hysterically and saying, "Now he'll never know!"

In the dream, Elyse could feel her grandmother's anguish and tried to reach out to touch her, but her grandmother didn't see her.

Suddenly, she was awake and abruptly sat up in bed with her sweat-soaked nightgown sticking to her skin. Her breath was heavy as the scene replayed over and over again in her mind. She was certain she had just witnessed actual events. Had she traveled back in time to experience the emotions her grandmother once felt? She took a few deep breaths before walking into the bathroom to splash cold water on her face.

She glimpsed her reflection in the mirror and cried, "I must be going crazy! Why is this happening to me?"

Back in the bedroom, she gazed out at the lake. It was so calm, just as it had been earlier that evening. Maybe it was the calm before the storm, as her grandfather used to say. Yes, something was definitely going to happen soon. She could feel it.

Chapter 14

The next morning, Elyse called Uncle Joe to see if he would meet her at Pasquale's Café, a small storefront restaurant located downtown. It had also been a restaurant when Elyse was a young girl, and she had often eaten breakfast there with her father. They would read the morning paper there together, and her father discussed its contents with her.

It was the only private time that she had with her father when they stayed on the island. He liked to see if she could debate him on current affairs and issues. They were truly father and daughter during those times, alike yet different. They respected each other's opinions, and knew when to agree to disagree.

"Hi, Uncle Joe, it's me. Do you think you could catch some grub with me at Pasquale's?"

"Don't see why not, my dear. I don't go on shift until the afternoon. Is something troubling you, Elyse?"

"Well, I did have one hell of a nightmare last night," she replied. "It was like watching a movie of Grandma's life."

"You don't say! Are you sure it wasn't something that Devil put in your drink?"

"Oh, Uncle Joe, he wouldn't harm me! He wasn't even in the dream."

"Well, just remember one thing: don't ever give the Devil a ride or he'll end up driving."

"He wasn't holding the steering wheel, or should I say reins, in this one. I'll tell you the rest at breakfast," Elyse said before putting down the receiver.

Yes, she thought, *someone was trying to give me a message about something. Maybe it wasn't Jacob this time, but my grandmother. After all, the dream focused on her. It was most likely about Jacob too, despite the fact that he didn't even have a cameo role.*

After Elyse took a quick shower and changed into street clothes, she put some food outside for Rainy and jumped on her bike. She was lucky to find a place for her bike outside the restaurant. Uncle Joe waved her down and was already slathering peanut butter on his pancakes as she walked in the door.

"You still putting that stuff on your pancakes?" she teased.

"Wouldn't have it any other way. I keep telling you to try it, but you've got your own bad habits. What about your bologna and crushed potato chip sandwiches? Are they still a staple of your diet?"

"You've got me there," Elyse responded. "So, I'm not exactly an orthodox eater either. We all have our strange food cravings."

"Is that chef of yours one of those cravings?"

"I think he could become even bigger than chocolate-covered pretzels," she answered while wiping some errant peanut butter off Uncle Joe's mouth with her napkin.

"Sounds pretty serious to me," Uncle Joe laughed.

"Do you need more peanut butter for those pancakes, Joe?" the waitress asked with a smile.

Uncle Joe stumbled nervously with his spoon as he stirred his coffee. "No, that's enough for today, Louise. Hey, have I introduced you to my niece, Elyse? She's staying over at the lighthouse for the summer."

"Nice to meet you, honey!" the petite, blond waitress said as she extended her hand.

Elyse placed her order with Louise before the waitress scurried off to fill more coffee cups. "Is there something going on here that I should know about, Uncle Joe?"

"Well, not exactly…Louise and I have an unspoken admiration for one another, if you know what I mean."

"Why don't you ask her out on a date, Uncle Joe?"

"A date? Why I wouldn't know the first thing about dating these days. Where would we go on this island, anyway?"

"Why don't you take Louise fishing?" Elyse volunteered.

"She does like to fish. Maybe I'll get up enough nerve to ask her one day."

"Uncle Joe, that day is now! I don't think you have to worry about her turning you down."

"What makes you say that, my dear?" "

"She's been back to our table to see if there is anything else you need more than she's been back to see all of her other customers' combined."

"Good point," Uncle Joe laughed. "Now tell me what this dream of yours was all about."

"It was the strangest thing, Uncle Joe," she began. "I was dressed in my nightgown watching Grandma and Grandpa race to the downtown dock in a horse-drawn wagon during a terrific thunderstorm. They were stopped in their tracks by a fallen tree, and then all of a sudden we were all at the dock with Grandma crying and Grandpa's arms shielding her. I could feel the intense pain welling up inside of her, and even though I reached out to touch her, she didn't know I was there."

"Gee, Elyse, I don't know what to tell you. I was much too young to have heard anything about that. It seems your grandmother was rushing to the dock to meet someone, and we *both* know who that probably was."

"Oh, I also found a portrait that I'm sure Grandmother painted of Jacob in the attic yesterday afternoon. It had been slashed with a knife or some other kind of pointed object. No doubt that's the cause of my nightmare. I guess I just have an overactive imagination."

"No, you don't," Uncle Joe said as his expression changed to a more somber one. "I was always aware that your grandmother had a secret she kept from the rest of the family. She may have taken it to her grave for all I know. But there is one way you can find out for sure."

Elyse was transfixed as Uncle Joe leaned in to whisper to her, "His name is Willie Anderson. He was the young assistant lighthouse keeper under your great-grandfather. I've heard rumors that he's still alive and living in a nursing home on the mainland. If this is true, then he might have witnessed what you've just described. That's assuming it happened at all…"

Elyse's eyes widened as she absorbed this piece of news. "You mean to tell me that he was working at the lighthouse before Grandma was married?" she asked.

"Yes, he was with your great-grandfather for quite a long time. He was a very loyal man. I don't think he ever talked about what went on at the lighthouse with anyone in town," Uncle Joe replied.

"That had to be difficult to do once Jacob was on the scene."

"That sure is an understatement if I've ever heard one. If you'll excuse the expression, I'll bet all hell broke loose once Jacob showed up at the place."

"What exactly did *you* hear about Jacob, Uncle Joe?" Elyse inquired.

"He was ruthless in business, unforgiving in fistfights, and a skirt-chasing rascal," he began. "Excuse my

French, but he sounded like a real son-of-a-gun to me. How your grandmother got mixed up with him, I'll never know. Your great-grandfather was the one who first compared him to the Prince of Darkness himself. Whatever he did, it must have been something unforgivable. Your great-grandfather cursed him until his dying day."

"If what you say is true, and this man is still alive, then maybe I do have a witness," Elyse said.

"I have a feeling Jacob won't like what he remembers," Uncle Joe remarked. "Does he appear to you as same age he is in your grandmother's portrait? If he's only aged in the painting, then maybe he's really still alive like in Oscar Wilde's novel *The Picture of Dorian Gray* that's been made into a movie many times."

"Uncle Joe, you've been watching way too many old movies. Believe it or not, he's as dead as a doornail, and he's not going to harm me in any way. He's looking for a solution to this problem as much as I am. If Willie Anderson is alive, I should be able to wrap this mystery up sooner than I thought."

"Do you think that's wise? I mean, some things might be better left buried. We all have a story to tell. If you change one part of the story, you may change the rest. Are you strong enough to accept whatever you learn? Is this worth risking everything you've ever known?"

"Well, Uncle Joe," Elyse said as she paid the bill and left a tip. "I asked someone else a question like that the other day, and his answer was yes."

"I hope you don't regret this, honey."

"There's no other way to be," she replied while walking out the door.

Now she was actually starting to sound like Jacob. God help her, maybe he was the Devil incarnate. A silver

Audi stopped next to Elyse as she put on her bike helmet. Her face lit up as she recognized the driver.

"Why, Mademoiselle, fancy meeting you here," Jack remarked as he leaned out the driver's side window.

"I was planning to call you later, Jack. Thank you for the thoughtful gift! May I return the favor by inviting you over for dinner tomorrow evening?" she asked.

"That suits me fine," he replied. "I haven't had an evening off in quite a while, and I'd really like to see what you can do with a saucepan."

"Is that a challenge, Monsieur?" Elyse joked.

"I just wondered if you excel in more than one thing," he joked before driving away.

Elyse blew him a kiss and then pointed to her posterior, as she saw him look in his rearview mirror and laugh. He got the message all right. *What a piece of work he is!*

Now it was time to do more investigative work on her part. She decided to go home and review her options before calling every nursing home in Sandusky and the surrounding areas to look for Willie Anderson.

If he had worked under her great-grandfather at the lighthouse, it meant he had also worked for the federal government. Perhaps she could track him down that way.

Chapter 15

Elyse spent the remainder of the day researching the whereabouts of Willie Anderson. It had been a tedious process due to the bureaucratic red tape. When it came down to it, all she really had to do was call Sam Smith from the very beginning. She guessed he might have something at the museum with identifying information on Willie, and she was right. Sam had a copy of Willie's driver's license, along with other things pertaining to his employment as the assistant lighthouse keeper.

The next morning, Elyse picked up copies of the pertinent paperwork at the museum and walked next door to the police station to see if she could get someone to track down her missing person.

"Hi, Bobby," she shouted over to a cute police officer sitting at a desk in the corner.

"Is that you, Elyse?" the police officer asked in surprise.

"None other!" She smiled.

"You can't be the same girl who used to swim with me at the bottom of the cliff on West Shore Boulevard. That girl didn't look anything like you," he commented.

"Hey, I was scrawny then, but I've filled out since."

"Are you here for a visit?"

"In a matter of speaking," she replied. "I'm handling my grandmother's estate. There are a few things in my way that I just don't have expertise in."

"And I'm guessing I do?" he laughed.

"Well, you are one of Put-in-Bay's finest. I'm sure it wouldn't be anything at all for you to, say, look up an address for an old friend?" she asked as she gave him her most beguiling look.

"Hand it over," he said as he reached out to grab the sheet of paper in Elyse's hand.

"Thanks, Bobby," she replied.

A few minutes later, he came back up to the counter with an address written on the back of the paper. "Now don't tell anyone how you got this, Elyse," he said. "I'm not supposed to run a check for every Tom, Dick, or Harriet who comes in here. This is the last known address of this person on the mainland. Hope it helps."

"I'm sure it will, Bobby. Thanks for all of your help. It was really nice to see you again," she added.

"Same here, Elyse. Would you like to meet at Tony's tonight for a beer?" Bobby inquired.

"I'm sorry, but I've made other plans," she replied with a smile.

"I should have tracked you down after you left the island. Take care of you
rself, Elyse," he said as she exited through the door.

With the address in hand, Elyse was now ready to make a few phone calls to the mainland to see if she could finally find the man who might hold the clue to the final hours of Jacob's life. She put the piece of paper in her backpack and got on her bike to head to the State Park. Uncle Joe would be waiting for her there in his little sixteen-foot fishing boat with all his fishing poles ready for action.

The park was located on the far west side of the island, and for the first time since her return, Elyse would have to pass the cemetery where her grandmother and grandfather were buried. Uncle Joe had been the one to make the lonely journey back to the island with the hearse for her grandmother's burial, while Elyse returned to New York

City immediately following the memorial service at the church.

Maybe I should have made that trip with him, Elyse thought to herself as she peddled past the tourists in golf carts and on buses along the way. It was just the two of them now. They didn't have any other family left. *How lonely it must have been for him to make that final trip.* Elyse had tried to rationalize with herself that she had no choice but to return to New York in order to reassign her workload and apply for family leave. In her heart, though, she knew that wasn't true. She still hadn't reconciled her feelings about her grandmother's treatment of her mother, and she wasn't ready to forgive her.

Elyse glided down the hill to the end of the road to the State Park. Uncle Joe was waiting for her at the dock. She could tell that he was just itching to get out on the water and "pitch those poles."

"Hey, Little Bit, over here!"

"I'm ready to catch that big one, Uncle Joe," Elyse remarked as she parked and locked her bike in a nearby stand.

"You better be, 'cause I've brought along four rods. Two for us and the other two will be dead in rod holders attached to *Old Bessie* here," he remarked as he affectionately patted the side of his aluminum boat.

"Well, let's shove off," she said as she stepped into the boat. "I've got some sandwiches and pop in my backpack for later."

"We've got it all covered then," Uncle Joe said over the hum of the boat's motor. "Let's get out further before we get started."

Elyse pulled her hair into a ponytail and pushed it through the back opening of her baseball cap as she sat down on the seat of the boat. She could feel the streams of sunlight caress her skin as she looked out over the horizon.

"This is the life, Uncle Joe: just the two of us and our fishing poles."

"You know it, my dear. Those walleye don't have a chance today. They spawn in the same places every year, so I'm betting I know where they'll be hiding based on last year's findings. We can only bag six fish this year, Elyse, so we better find some big ones."

"Are we jigging, rigging, or trolling today, Uncle Joe?"

"All the above. Why not stack the deck? We'll put a long rod out off the bow and another out the stern. I've tied on a bottom bouncer that's almost snag free because only the wire touches the bottom. Then I've attached a four-foot leader with a floating jig head. This will keep the bait off the bottom and allow us to keep bait in the fish zone without becoming snagged."

"You think of everything, don't you?"

"How smart can those fish be, Elyse? After all, they're fish."

"You say that every time. Then you change your tune when they don't bite."

"Well, a man's got to have confidence goin' in I say. It's not a good thing to blow the wind out of anyone's sails before they start out, now is it?"

"You're absolutely right there," Elyse laughed.

"Now, Elyse, here's your rod," Uncle Joe said as he handed her a fishing pole. "I've got it rigged just right. You can also watch the dead rod at the stern. Remember that walleye inhale bait rather than bite it. He'll ease up to within a few inches of the bait, then flare his gills and open his mouth at the same time and suck in the surrounding water and bait. Then he's ours."

"Sounds like you've researched this a bit, Uncle Joe."

"Sure have, it's all scientific nowadays. Actually, I have to admit that I cheated a little. The web page at *Walleye Central* has some pretty good ProPages attached to it. Hey, these guys are legends around these parts."

"You use the Internet, Uncle Joe?" she asked in amazement.

"Why not? It's free at the library."

"You never cease to amaze me!"

They spent a good twenty minutes before getting a tug on one of their lines. Elyse noticed the dead rod off the stern was slowly bending. She was able to reach the rod and set the hook in time to catch a respectable-sized walleye. Uncle Joe put the net under him, while she unhooked the fish before throwing him in the cooler packed with ice.

"Nice going, Elyse. Let's see if we can bag a few more while we're hot," he suggested.

Over the next hour, they caught two fish apiece before things got quiet. Elyse took the sandwiches from the bag, and handed one to Uncle Joe, who said, "Well, I'd say it's been a successful trip this time, Little Bit. What do you think?"

"Couldn't have been better, Uncle Joe," Elyse replied as she took a bite of her ham sandwich.

"Did you find out anything about Willie Anderson?" Uncle Joe asked with concern.

"Nothing concrete yet," she began. "I still have to make a few calls when I get back to the lighthouse."

"Is everything else okay up there, I mean, with 'what's his name' and all?"

"Yes, Uncle Joe, Jacob has been a regular guy."

"Well, maybe death agrees with him then."

"Uncle, Joe! That's pretty low, even for you."

"I just can't help myself, my dear. I've got to look out for you now. You're all I have left in this world."

Of course, he was right. Hadn't Elyse come to the same conclusion just a few hours earlier? She now felt the time was right to ask him the question that had entered her mind earlier that day: "Uncle Joe, did you mind it so much that I didn't follow you back to the island with Grandmother's body for her burial?"

"Nah, it wasn't all that bad. Some of my coworkers and the old timers met me at the dock and followed the hearse to the cemetery. The priest said a couple of words, and we all went to the Round House for drinks. There was nothing more to be said. Not many people around here still remember your grandmother."

"Still and all, I should have been there, Uncle Joe. Like you said, you're the only family that I have left."

"I understood your position, Elyse. You had to hurry back to the city to work things out with your company. I don't have the time or patience to sort through your grandmother's things."

"It's been perplexing. I still don't understand why Grandmother was so secretive. It's as if her life story was painted on pieces of a broken shell. It's frustrating as all hell, because I can only resolve it if the missing pieces wash up on shore."

"I'm sure you'll find out the answers to your questions in due time. You're a tenacious little cuss if I ever saw one. I'll never forget the first time I took you fishing: You wouldn't leave until you caught a fish. It was too small to keep, mind you, but you wouldn't give up until you caught one.

"Whatever happened between your grandmother and mother, Elyse, you can't blame yourself for what you're feeling now. When you're ready to forgive, you will. But until then, you have to work your feelings out in your way, whatever that may be."

"How did you get so smart, Uncle Joe?"

"Don't know; I guess all that bourbon didn't kill my brain cells after all."

They shared a laugh before finishing their lunch and decided to spend another hour out on the lake before packing it in for the afternoon. Elyse also wanted to leave enough time to get things ready for her dinner with Jack.

She was already daydreaming about seeing him again. Elyse was pleasantly surprised that Jack was becoming more and more a part of her heart and her dreams.

Chapter 16

When Elyse got back to the lighthouse, Rainy was sunning herself under the cedar tree overlooking the lake in the backyard. The cat got up and ran to her before she even had a chance to open the back porch door.

"I guess you know what I've got in this cooler then," Elyse teased. "You're right; it isn't canned tuna."

Elyse put the fish fillets in the refrigerator before going upstairs to take a shower. She still felt sticky from the intermingling of her sweat with sunscreen, and she wanted to smell fresh and clean again.

When she was done with her shower, she wrapped one towel around her body and another around her hair like a turban. When she entered the bedroom, she was startled to find Jacob staring at her from across the frigid room.

"Jacob, this is not part of our agreement!" she snapped.

"No it is not, but I just wanted to talk to you," said the ghost.

"And what is it that couldn't wait until after I was dressed?"

"The ring you wore the other night. May I see it?"

Elyse had almost forgotten about the ring she had on when she visited Jack the night before. Elyse took the ring from the dresser and showed it to Jacob.

"It is hers," he said. "She kept it then. Perhaps she did not forget me."

"Believe me, Jacob," Elyse began. "I don't think *anyone* could ever forget you."

"What do you mean? Am I not a charming sort?" he said with a sly smile.

"I'll give you that much, but you have to admit that you are a bit stubborn," she countered.

"Stubborn can be a good thing. It just means that you are passionate about your beliefs."

"That's a new one on me. You just make things up as you go along, don't you, Jacob?"

"It is called being resourceful."

"Did you give that ring to my grandmother as some sort of an engagement ring?"

"Yes, it could be called that. It was the last thing I did before I left for Ireland."

"Had she promised to go back with you when you returned?"

"In a matter of speaking. She was not of age at the time we first met. I figured I would come back when she was older, so it was more of a promise ring," Jacob replied.

"Is that why you stayed away exactly two years, Jacob?"

"Yes. I knew Joseph would not give us his blessing, so I wanted to make sure it was not needed."

"Why didn't she go with you when you came back for her?"

"That is something I do not recall. I know there was a fight, and then I remember leaving on the sailing vessel."

"Was the fight with my grandmother?"

Jacob looked confused. "I do not know. All I know is that she did not follow me."

"Are you sure? I mean, I dreamt of my grandmother the other night. She was hurrying to the downtown dock with my grandfather. Maybe she was rushing to find you."

Jacob's eyes widened as Elyse then recanted the entire dream to him. "Are you certain of this?" he asked

"Yes. I wouldn't lie to you," she replied.

"You have made me very happy. I will do my best to remember the rest for you. Keep the ring as a gift from me."

"Why, Jacob, I'm honored."

"It belongs to you now. You are part of Elyse."

"Can you do me a favor tonight, Jacob?"

"I will try."

"Please give me my privacy tonight, because I am expecting someone very special."

"If he is that special, then I will keep my distance."

"How did you know that I was expecting a man?"

"It is written all over your face," he answered before evaporating like morning mist over the lake.

"Damn him!" Elyse said before entering her closet to pick out some clothes. She decided on a cute pair of white sailor shorts and a light-blue, button-down shirt that she tied under her bust to reveal her midriff. Her sun-kissed skin was tan and glowing, and she slipped on her sandals before rushing down the stairs to the kitchen.

Rainy was meowing and circling her feet as she took the walleye fillets out of the refrigerator. Elyse opened a bottle of Great Lakes Brewing Company beer and poured about three-fourths of it into an egg and oil mixture, along with two-thirds of a cup of flour. Elyse took a swig of the remaining beer in the bottle before mixing the batter.

"Smooth," she said as she began heating the peanut oil in the cast-iron skillet.

It didn't take Elyse long to quickly dip the fish into a separate dish of seasoned flour, then the raised batter, before frying it up into a golden-brown consistency reminiscent of a Bit-O-Honey candy bar. She then put it on a cooling rack over a baking sheet and into the preheated oven to keep warm.

Elyse had already made her side dishes and set a folding table on the back porch with colorful picnic dinnerware and linens. She had to admit that she was truly looking forward to Jack's reaction to her culinary skills.

It wasn't long before Jack was knocking on the back-porch screen door. "Something smells good," he shouted.

"It better," she answered as she opened the porch door, "because Uncle Joe and I spent the better part of the afternoon catching it."

Jack gave Elyse a long, lustful kiss on the lips upon entering the back porch.

"You haven't even tried my food yet," she joked.

"I have missed you every minute of the day," he responded as he looked lovingly into her eyes.

"Same here. Would you like a quick tour of the place?" she asked quickly so they wouldn't become preoccupied with other things.

"Sure, why not," he replied.

Elyse proceeded to take Jack to every room of the lighthouse before ending up on the back porch where they started. "After dinner, I thought we would climb the staircase to the top of the tower," she began. "It's a breathtaking sight from up there."

"You have quite a place here, Elyse," he noted. "It is very much like you."

"What do you mean?"

"It's hauntingly beautiful and unique, but it is also remote and mysterious."

"You find me remote and mysterious, eh?" she chuckled.

"Only in a good way, of course," he laughed. "I don't think I will ever know everything you are thinking."

"That may be to my advantage. After all, my mother always told me to keep them guessing."

"She was right." Jack smiled, and Rainy was now in the room purring and circling around his feet.

"Monsieur Jacques, let me introduce you to my new acquaintance, Mademoiselle Rainy," Elyse said as she motioned toward the feline.

"*Enchanté, Mademoiselle*," Jacques replied as he knelt down to pet Rainy's head.

"I think she likes you. Either that or she figures she's found a sucker to feed her table scraps."

"I prefer to think that she has succumbed to my many charms."

"Okay, we'll have it your way," Elyse said as she poured beer into tall glasses on the table.

"Do you need any help in the kitchen?"

"No, believe it or not, I think I have it covered," she said while walking back to the kitchen.

Elyse watched Jack as he stood drinking his beer and looking out at the lake before him. "Here's the coleslaw and fries," she said as she placed the dishes on the table. "I'll be right back with the rest."

When Elyse returned with the main course, they sat down to a casual feast while soft jazz music played in the background.

"I could get used to this," Jack commented.

"Maybe now and then, Jack, but I can tell that you truly love your work."

"You're right. I would miss my staff and the work we do together," he began. "It is what keeps me going. It is my passion. What is your passion in life, Elyse?" He seemed interested in her answer.

"It used to be producing the best magazine in our genre, but now I just don't know anymore. I've changed since I've come back to the island, and that has me looking at my life in a different way. If I knew that I only had a few more years to live, I might take my life in another direction."

"What would you rather be doing then?"

"If I had my way, I would just write all day. It's what truly brings me joy. I can go anywhere in my dreams and put them down on paper to remember. I can express what is truly in my heart."

"Then why don't you do it?" he asked, adding, "What's stopping you?"

"My self-doubts, I guess. I'm not independently wealthy either. Most of all, I'm afraid of failure."

"Elyse, you've got to let go of that feeling. Do what is in your heart and success will follow. Don't die with your dreams still inside of you."

"Where were you, Jacques LeClare, when I was just starting out in my career?" she asked. "I feel like I've wasted so much time trying to be something I'm not."

"Time is never wasted. Everything you are today is a direct result of what you have experienced before. Don't you agree?"

"Yes, my experiences have made me what I am today. I do believe that, Jack. Now more than ever," she said as she unconsciously looked over in the direction of the portrait of Jacob that was still hidden behind the living room sofa. "Are you ready for that climb to the top of the tower now?"

"You lead the way," he said as he pulled her chair away from the table.

When they reached the outside of the lens tower, he put his arms around her to keep her warm since the night air was now cascading across the lake and bringing with it little bursts of wind.

"You were right, Elyse: this view is *magnifique*!"

"It isn't as famous as the view from the Eiffel Tower, but it's ours tonight."

Jack gently turned her face toward his with his hand and kissed her passionately on the lips. "I have to go away for a few days," he began. "It's for a charity event on the West Coast. I'll be leaving tomorrow at sunrise."

"Can you stay the night?"

"Yes. I will call Jean-Louis and have him meet me at the airport tomorrow morning with my things."

"I will miss you terribly, Jacques LeClare," Elyse whispered in his ear.

"I will miss you more."

They held onto each other tightly, looking out over the sparkling lake as the sunlight disappeared into the clouds. As God's brushstrokes transformed the day into night, their love for one another forever transformed their souls.

Chapter 17

The next morning, Jack lingered over his kiss with Elyse on the steps of the sunporch as the taxi waited for him in the driveway. He blew her one last kiss from the opened door of the taxi, and Elyse sighed.

"There he goes, Rainy," she said to her trusty companion. "I can't imagine my life without him now, and just a month ago I had sworn off men forever."

The ringing telephone broke Elyse's train of thought, and she ran into the house to answer it before the answering machine kicked in.

"Elyse, its Socrates. Did I wake you?" her trusted friend asked.

"Nah, I've been up for at least an hour. Are you calling about the meeting with 3R Corporation?"

"In fact, I am," he replied. "Mark your calendar for a week from now, my office, 10:00 a.m."

"Socrates, did you ever find out who the players are in this deal?"

"Does it really matter, Elyse? You wouldn't be having second thoughts, now, would you?"

"Well, the lighthouse is my second home in some respects, and I just wanted to make sure that whoever purchases it has its best interests in mind."

"You talk like that lighthouse has a soul of its own. It's just a structure. What the new owners do with it shouldn't matter to you at all."

Elyse knew in her heart that Socrates was wrong. The

lighthouse *did* have a soul. It held her memories, good and bad, and now it had imprisoned Jacob, who was roaming around aimlessly searching for the key to the invisible chains that kept him shackled to the shore for all eternity.

"I know it sounds crazy, Socrates, but I do think of this place as more than a house with a light tower in it. Maybe I'm just letting my emotions cloud the issue, but I can't deny what I'm feeling."

"Now you know that I will negotiate the best possible deal for you, don't you? Isn't that why you hired me?" he asked.

"That and you look pretty cute in running shorts."

"Is that why my business has picked up lately?" Socrates laughed.

"It couldn't hurt!"

"Now let's get back to business here. Are you ready to cut a deal or not, Elyse? Can I count on seeing you next week?"

She bit her bottom lip before answering, "Yes, count me in. I have some research to do on the mainland, so just email me if anything changes. Tell Marcella that I'm looking forward to some of her jambalaya when I'm in town next week."

"I'll give her your request. Marcella's so excited to see you that she's already planning a shopping trip to the off-price fashion houses on Seventh Avenue. That woman will die with a shopping bag in her hand."

"Now, Socrates, you're quite the fashion plate yourself, you know. I've never seen you in the same suit twice."

"And you never will if Marcella has anything to do with it. You take care now, Elyse. You're probably elated to be coming back home again."

She was actually taken aback by that last statement and thought, *Is New York City still my home, or is it Put-in-Bay?* She honestly couldn't answer that question anymore.

"I can't wait to see you, too. If you run into Rachel, tell her to answer her emails now and then, would you? I haven't heard from her in quite a while."

"If I see her, I'll relay the message. You'll need to wrap things up there soon, Elyse. I'll have my administrative assistant book your flight and mail your tickets this week."

"Thanks, Socrates. What would I do without you?"

"Probably get into more trouble than I could ever imagine."

"That's why I pay you the big bucks, buster. I'll see you next week," Elyse said as she hung up the receiver.

She decided to take one more trip down memory lane by searching the attic for more pages of her grandmother's journal. Time was of the essence now, and she just had to find out what transpired between her grandmother and Jacob on that fateful night.

When Elyse made it to the attic, she looked around, trying to figure out where her grandmother might have hidden the journal pages. Just at that moment, the sunlight from the attic window seemed to focus on an object she had overlooked the other day. It was dull and weather-beaten and resting on its side under an old comforter on a rocking chair.

Elyse pulled the comforter off the chair to find kerosene lamp. *Could this have been the very lamp my grandmother used to summon Jacob to South Bass Island's shores for their clandestine meetings?*

She picked it up and set it on a desk nearby. It was an older model Aladdin's lamp, and Elyse felt compelled to remove the chimney from the tarnished brass bowl underneath. That's when she discovered a piece of discolored paper folded and curled around the inside of the bowl. She pulled it out, and leaned against the desk as she began to read:

"Jacob is leaving the island tonight to go back to Ireland for a while. The other day I compared him to the thousands of Monarch butterflies that roost on the lighthouse grounds every spring and fall during their long migration south from Canada because he will soon be leaving me. He wiped away my tears, and reminded me that the butterflies always come back--as he will one day return for me. So that I will not forget his face, I have begun painting a portrait of him that I hope to show him upon his return. I already miss him terribly! Who will listen to my dreams now? He is my confessor, and I tell him everything that I am feeling and thinking. We are like one now, and I can even sense him approaching the shore before his boat is in view. He has told me that it is the same with him. When he returns, he told me that we will go on a journey around the world. We will sail the Seven Seas and visit foreign lands. Jacob will return for me when I am of age, since father does not approve of our love for one another. It will be difficult for me to leave this place, but I have no other choice. I must follow my heart, and that heart is now his."

Elyse couldn't believe what she had just read. Her grandmother *had* planned to go away with Jacob after all. *Then why didn't she?* This was the only piece of the puzzle still missing. She would have to contact Willie Anderson as soon as possible; it was her only mission in life now.

She folded the journal page up into a tiny square and put it in her shirt pocket. She planned to tell Jacob the good news tonight. It would verify everything she had guessed about her grandmother's feelings for him. Then Elyse put the chimney back on the base of the lamp and looked around the attic for a small, sturdy table to place it on. Finding one close by, she positioned the table in front of the attic window with the lamp in the middle. An eerie feeling came over her, and the hair on the back of her neck stood up. She stared at the lifeless lantern, its light now extinguished. It felt right placing it there. She knew Jacob would agree.

Elyse spent the rest of the day packing up the remaining things in the attic that she wanted to keep and hauling the boxes down the steps onto the porch behind the kitchen. Uncle Joe would have to put aside some time to go through the boxes with her in the near future.

She finally finished cleaning out the attic. There was nothing else to do now except sign the legal documents—and find the answer to the final question burning brighter than the lamp in her subconscious. As dusk came, the night blanketed the lake like a woolen cape as Elyse sipped tea on the living room sofa. Her back was a bit sore from lifting boxes that afternoon, so she planned to soak in the tub before retiring for the evening.

She walked out to the porch to look out at the lake while continuing to sip her tea. She was going to turn around and head upstairs, but was interrupted by Rainy carrying on outside as if she were possessed. "Rainy, what in the *world* is wrong with you?" Elyse said as she put her cup down before going outside to investigate the matter. Then she saw it: a bright light was emanating from the attic window. It was coming from the kerosene lantern that she had placed before the window earlier that day.

"Holy, Toledo," Elyse said as she looked up at the light. She hadn't been this spooked since the first night she had encountered Jacob. Elyse didn't sense any danger, so she rushed back inside the house to grab a flashlight before going upstairs to the attic. She swallowed hard as her trembling hand opened the attic door.

When she opened the door, there was Jacob, staring out at the lake. "Oh, my God, Jacob, it's just you." She sighed in relief.

"People never used my name after God's unless the phrase 'damn you' was in-between," Jacob mused.

"That I can believe," she remarked. "What are you doing up here?"

"I have never seen the lake from this side, and this is what your grandmother saw every time she lit this lantern," Jacob said sadly.

Elyse knew he was distressed and decided to give him the good news that she had just learned earlier in the day. "Jacob, I found something today that I think you should read."

"What is it, woman?"

"It's a page from my grandmother's journal. Let me read it to you." When she finished, tears were welling up in his eyes. She put the page down on the table by the lit lantern. *So the great Jacob Flannery could be brought to tears.* Elyse was stunned.

"I am deeply touched that you read this for me. You

did not have to. Do you feel disloyal to Patrick for doing so?" Jacob asked.

"No, because I know that my grandmother also loved my grandfather. You were the one that came before. I still don't know why she didn't end up leaving with you, but I intend to find out."

"What do you mean?"

"I have the name of an assistant lighthouse keeper who is still alive. He worked with my grandfather, and he may be able to help us."

"He must be very old now. Do you think he can still remember?"

"He has to, Jacob. How else can we solve this dilemma? I have looked high and low, trying to find the final pages of my grandmother's journal. All I know is that it always comes back to you. She hid the pages in places that reminded her of *you*, Jacob."

"That is your answer then. You need to be like your grandmother in thought and action. You must let her lead you to the answer."

"How will I do that, Jacob?"

"Have you asked for her help?"

"No, I haven't. What good would that do, she's dead?"

"So am I, but I can still see and hear you."

"Are you telling me that she can do the same?"

"Maybe she has been pointing you in the right direction all along…"

"Jacob, you may be right. After all, I didn't see the kerosene lantern until it practically ignited before me. I was drawn to it by the sunlight peering through the attic window. In fact, it was the only place in the room highlighted at the time. Funny, but I didn't realize that until now."

"You were not meant to realize anything then. Now that you are looking at things from another shore, you will find what you are seeking."

"I believe you are right, Jacob."

"Believing is only half the battle. Now you must find the strength within yourself to carry it through."

"Don't you think I can do this?"

"Oh, quite the contrary, I have all the faith in the world in you. I can see what others cannot. You are a truth seeker, and you will not rest until the truth is known."

"But will I like the truth I seek?" Elyse asked.

"That is for you to decide. I cannot give you more help than I already have. That is your fate," he answered.

"I now know that we have been brought together for a purpose, Jacob, but I'm not sure what it is yet."

"Whatever it is, I have been glad of our meeting. You are now the only light left for me on this earth." Jacob walked over to Elyse and stood directly in front of her. He kissed the first three fingertips of his own hand before tracing an arch on her forehead, and then he touched his own heart.

"What does that mean?" she asked with wonder.

"That was the secret sign language your grandmother and I would use with one another before parting. The arch represents the arch of this attic window and the hope that we will see one another soon. The kiss, followed by the touching of the heart, means 'forever in my heart.'"

Elyse recognized that same phrase from the small piece of paper hidden in the box that held Jacob's ring to her grandmother. The lantern suddenly grew dark, and Elyse turned on her flashlight and pointed it toward an empty space where Jacob had been standing just seconds before. He had vanished again in thin air!

"They don't make them any more dramatic than you, Jacob Flannery," Elyse said to the empty room before turning around to walk down the stairs.

Chapter 18

The next morning, Elyse awoke to a tiny yellow finch chirping loudly on her windowsill. She was planning to contact Willie Anderson today, and nothing was going to get in her way. Just as she finished zipping up her jeans, the telephone rang.

"Do you miss me yet?" a familiar voice asked.

"Actually, I was just being serenaded by a rather dapper looking fellow from my windowsill."

"He must be French," Jack joked.

"The answer to your question is *very much,"* she replied.

"Good, because I am coming home tomorrow night. Do you think you can meet me at the restaurant at midnight?"

"What do you have in mind, Jacques LeClare?"

"A moonlight swim perhaps? Just bring your swimsuit and plan on a midnight snack."

"Are we talking food here?"

"That's entirely up to you!"

"I will be there with bells on, Jacques LeClare."

"Then you'll forego the suit?"

"Now that would make an interesting fashion statement, wouldn't it?" she teased.

"It doesn't matter how you come. Just be there," his sexy voice responded.

Elyse melted inside and knew that wild horses couldn't keep her away at this point. "How are things going in California?"

"Fantastic! We have raised several million dollars for ALS research, and it was great to get together with my colleagues for some creative fun. We are usually a highly competitive bunch, but we put all that aside for the good of the cause."

"How noble of you. Are you often one to set aside your differences for a greater cause?"

"It's not anything you wouldn't do yourself, Elyse. You hold me to a higher standard."

"How do you know that I'm like that?" she asked with interest.

"It is something that I have sensed about you from the very beginning. You have a good soul, Elyse," he said.

She didn't quite know how to respond to that compliment, because it was the first time anyone had ever said something like that to her. "Why, thank you, Jack. You shouldn't think too highly of me, though. I have been known to burn soufflés," she joked.

"You? That is impossible. You are too perfect to do such a thing. I promise not to reveal your secret to anyone."

"You do that! I'm looking forward to seeing you tomorrow. Have a safe flight."

"I will only be happy when I can hold you in my arms again. *A tout a l'heure*, Elyse."

"See you later, too." Elyse repeated before hanging up the receiver. She closed her eyes and took in a deep breath before opening them again. *I must be dreaming,* she thought. *How could anyone be so perfect for me?*

She decided to get down to business now. She got out the piece of paper containing Willie Anderson's address and sat down by the phone with a pen and legal pad to record her findings. When Elyse dialed the telephone number, she was surprised to hear a voice that was younger than she had expected on the receiving end.

"Anderson residence," a man's voice replied.

"Hello, I'm a friend of Willie Anderson. Do you know where I can reach him?" she asked.

The person on the other end of the phone seemed hesitant to answer at first, because there was dead silence.

"Are you still there?" Elyse asked.

"How do you know Mr. Anderson?" the man asked.

"Actually, my great-grandfather was the lighthouse keeper at the South Bass Island lighthouse during the time Mr. Anderson was the assistant lighthouse keeper," she began. "My name is Elyse Montgomery."

"Glad to make your acquaintance, Ms. Montgomery," the man replied. "I'm Willie Anderson, Jr., and I live in my father's house now."

Elyse's heart sank. Maybe Bobby had picked up this gentlemen's name from the computer database, instead of his father's. What if the father had already died?

"Is your father still alive?" she asked hopefully.

"Yes, he lives just down the road at Sandusky Village. He's in his late nineties now, and since I'm no longer a young man myself, I had to place him in a nursing home," the man replied.

Elyse felt sorry for Willie Anderson, Jr. He almost seemed to be apologizing for his actions. "There are some things your father might be able to tell me about my grandmother, Mr. Anderson," she said. "Would it be possible for me to make an appointment to see him?"

"I don't see why not. He enjoys visitors. May I ask what it is that you're hoping to find out?"

"Your father was part of my great-grandfather's household back then, and now he's the only one left who can answer some questions I have about my grandmother in her youth," Elyse replied.

"I was sorry to hear that your grandmother died recently. Please accept my condolences, young lady. It's always a good idea to ask the questions that need to be asked when everyone's still alive. That way, you don't have to wonder about anything."

"I'm glad you understand. It's just that the lighthouse is up for sale, and I want to make sure that certain things are in place before I close the deal."

"Oh, you mean your *heart*," the older man responded.

"Come again?" she asked.

"Please don't think ill of me, miss, but it's in your voice," he said. "You're looking for something that means everything to you, aren't you?"

"Yes, Mr. Anderson, I believe I am. That is why I so desperately need to speak to your father. Can we arrange a meeting between all of us sometime soon?"

"Yes, I can meet you at the nursing home tomorrow

around lunchtime if you'd like. I often go to the home to feed him his meals. Would 11:30 a.m. be okay with you?"

"Yes, that sounds fine, Mr. Anderson. Should I meet you in the lobby?"

"That would work out well, Ms. Montgomery. I'll see you tomorrow then."

"Thanks for all of your help."

"No problem. It will be nice for my dad to see the relative of an old friend."

"I look forward to meeting you both then. Good-bye, Mr. Anderson."

"Good-bye."

Now that Elyse had an appointment to meet Willie Anderson she could finally breathe easier. Maybe she would get everything done before her meeting with 3R after all.

Chapter 19

Elyse spent the rest of the day cleaning the lighthouse and getting it ready for the inspection. A final offer wouldn't be made until the inspector took a look around the place and filed his report. When dusk came, she sat on the steps of the porch facing the lake with a pail of dirty water and a mop by her side. She wiped the sweat off her brow with the back of her palm as Rainy rubbed up against her legs.

"Housework is hell," Elyse complained to her furry feline. "At least I won't be the one cleaning this place much longer."

Then it hit Elyse like a ton of bricks. What would she do after she left the island? What would happen to her love affair with Jack? Could she ever go back to her former life now?

I've got to stop driving myself crazy, she thought to herself. *This island is just a page from my past; it's not who I am now.*

After her chores were complete, Elyse went into the living room and turned on the radio to some soothing music. When she turned around, Jacob was watching her with a puzzled look on his face. "Jacob, you startled me," she said as she caught her breath.

"Do you not know me by now?" he asked.

"I think the answer to that is 'not completely,'" she answered wryly.

"May I ask you a question?" he said. Elyse nodded her approval before he continued, "Why do you always surround yourself with noise?"

"What do you mean?"

"Every time you walk into the house, you turn on the picture box or that newfangled Victrola of yours."

"Jacob, it's the way I keep in touch with the world. Everyone lives in a global world now, and we can get the news about what's happening around the world in minutes."

"I think you surround yourself with these things because you are afraid," Jacob said as he slowly walked around the room, studying Elyse like a cat on the prowl.

"You mean I don't like silence?"

"No, you are afraid of something that you cannot escape. You are afraid of your feelings," Jacob said as he stopped in his tracks to look directly at her.

"Now Jacob, that's ridiculous," she protested.

Jacob stared at the radio, and it instantly turned off. Then he focused his steel-gray eyes on her and said, "Dreaming is more difficult when you cannot hear the beat of your heart."

"Do you think I'm avoiding something?"

"Not something, yourself." He continued, "There is music all around you. Listen to the water lapping up against the rocks, the wind whistling between the leaves of the cedars, and the gull's song. That is the real world, your world, not what you see in that picture box."

"Maybe I already know myself, Jacob. Maybe I don't have to search anymore."

Now he stood only a few feet away, watching her every move and nuance, waiting to pounce on her with words of wisdom. "Knowing oneself is the single most important thing a human being can do. Everyone has a purpose in life, and your search for that purpose is a journey. Your journey has only started, but mine has ended. My light was lost a long time ago, just like the light in this tower. Do not waste time, Elyse, for once a light is extinguished, it cannot be lit again."

Elyse paused for a few moments before answering, "If you sense that I'm being bombarded by a myriad of feelings, you are right. But I'm trapped by expectations put upon me by other people."

"In the end, you only have to answer to the Almighty. Do these other people hold more power than that?"

"No, of course they don't."

"Then, do what *you* feel is right. Why should the others answer for you?" he said matter-of-factly.

"I can't explain it to you, Jacob. Life isn't like that for me. I can't just sail around the world for two years and leave everyone and everybody guessing."

"You have already left that other world, Elyse, but you cannot see it yet. My only hope is that you will realize this fact before it is too late," he said with intensity.

"Is that what happened to you? Was there something that you left unfinished?"

"I cannot say for certain, but I do know that I will always regret what never was," he replied.

Jacob vanished before Elyse's eyes just as suddenly as he had appeared. She turned to look in the mirror over the walnut bureau in the hallway. It was almost as if Jacob could see right through her. He knew she was having second thoughts about leaving Jack, selling the lighthouse, and going back to her old life.

Why was he torturing her like this? She didn't have a choice. She couldn't possibly maintain this property by herself or afford to stay on Put-in-Bay indefinitely. No, she would have to move on, and the sooner the better. If she didn't, her heart might break.

Now in the stillness of the night, she could almost hear it cracking.

Chapter 20

The day had finally come to meet with Willie Anderson. Somehow, she knew this would be the day that would change everything. Even Rainy was acting unusually agitated as Elyse hitched a ride to Lime Kiln dock with Uncle Joe.

"Do you think you are doing the right thing, my dear?" Uncle Joe asked after she got into his truck.

"I am doing the only thing there is left to do, Uncle Joe. How can I go on without knowing the answers to my questions? Besides that, Jacob is depending on me to help him move on to another world."

"Seems to me that he would want to delay that voyage as long as possible, considering where he's going," Uncle Joe joked.

"Uncle Joe! If you only knew him the way that I do, you'd see things differently."

"I still wouldn't trust him, Elyse. You have much more to lose than he does. He's already lost his life; what could be worse than that?"

"Not recalling anything about the last day of your life. That's why he is still marooned on this island. He has no choice."

"But you do, Elyse. Just remember that at all costs. You still have free will."

Once the truck stopped in the parking lot, she gave Uncle Joe a quick kiss on the check. "Don't worry about me, Uncle Joe. I can handle this."

"I know you can, my dear, but I couldn't handle it if your heart gets broken. Good luck, and don't forget to call me when you return," he reminded her.

"I promise," Elyse said as she rushed off to buy her ticket for the ferry and a street map of Sandusky.

Once she reached the other side, she contacted a taxi company to drive her to a rental car agency. She took out the map and located the name of the street where she was heading before starting her rental car. As she turned into the parking lot of the nursing home, Elyse took a deep breath before gathering her belongings and walking to the front door.

"God help me," she whispered under her breath before going in.

A man in his seventies was seated in an upholstered chair in the lobby. He sat up to greet Elyse when she entered the lobby.

"Are you Ms. Montgomery?" he asked.

"Yes, I am. You must be Mr. Anderson," Elyse said as she extended her hand to shake his.

"I knew it was you. My father has some photographs of his tenure at the lighthouse. You are the spitting image of your grandmother."

"I guess there's no denying my genes. I'm so glad that you could meet me here, Mr. Anderson."

"It was no problem at all. I'm pretty much here every day anyway. Let's tell the nurses we're here. They'll be getting Dad's lunch ready about now."

They alerted the nursing station as to their intentions, and then proceeded to walk to the elder Mr. Anderson's room.

"He's a little hard of hearing, but his memory is as clear as a bell," Mr. Anderson added as he motioned for Elyse to enter the room before him.

When they got inside, Elyse saw a frail old man working a crossword puzzle with his glasses pushed down on his nose. "Hello, son," he began, "is this the young lady you told me about yesterday?"

"Yes, Dad, this is Ms. Montgomery. She is the granddaughter of Elyse O'Reilly, the lighthouse keeper's daughter."

The old man's eyes widened, as he almost seemed to recognize Elyse from another time and place.

"Did you say this is Elyse O'Reilly, son?"

"No, I said this is her *granddaughter*," the younger man repeated louder.

"I would have sworn she was the real McCoy. Sometimes I forget how long I've been alive. At my age, it seems like I've been around forever," the elder man said.

"You still look like you have a few good years left in you," Elyse commented.

"Hey, I like her already," Mr. Anderson said to his son.

"I was hoping you could answer some questions about the day a certain individual left the island for good, Mr. Anderson," Elyse said as she pulled up a chair close to the bedside before turning on her compact tape recorder.

"I don't see why not," he replied. "I can still remember those days like they were yesterday. Is the lighthouse still standing? It was such a beautiful sight back then."

"Yes, it's still there." Elyse smiled. "But there doesn't seem to be anyone on the island who can answer my questions for me. The lighthouse is up for sale, and before I sign it over, I need to know something about what transpired the night Jacob Flannery left the island for good."

Mr. Anderson looked at Elyse with eyes full of fear, and she put her hand on his arm to comfort him. "It's okay, Mr. Anderson, I'm not here to judge anyone. I just need to know what happened that night."

Mr. Anderson looked at his son, who nodded his approval before he began. "It was early in the evening, and I was in the barn brushing down the horses when I heard a terrible fight going on by the water's edge, so I walked outside to see what was happening."

"Who was involved in this fight, Mr. Anderson?" Elyse inquired.

"It was Mr. O'Reilly and the captain," the old man replied.

"By 'the captain,' do you mean Jacob Flannery?" she asked.

"Yes, it was him," Mr. Anderson said as he turned a paler shade of white. "I had long since learned to stay out of his way whenever he approached the grounds. Pardon me for saying so, but he didn't even want anyone to *look* at your grandmother. Since she was as beautiful as you are, that was a difficult thing for a young man to do, but I didn't want any part of Flannery. He was as strong as a bull with a temper to match."

"Do you remember what they fought about?" Elyse continued.

"He wanted to take your grandmother with him that night. He was leaving the island for good," he replied.

"Did my great-grandfather put up any resistance to this?" Elyse asked.

"Of course he did! He declared that she was home already and told the captain that she wanted no part of his pagan ways."

Elyse swallowed hard. She could only imagine the fury erupting out in the yard that day. Her great-grandfather had a bit of a temper himself, and he'd been a boxing champion to boot.

"What happened next?" she inquired.

"The captain told Mr. O'Reilly that he loved his daughter and she him. Then Mr. O'Reilly pushed the captain away from him and closer to the edge of the cliff."

"Did Jacob push him back?" Elyse asked.

"No, he didn't have the chance. Mr. O'Reilly yelled at Flannery to stay away from his daughter, and I'll never forget what he said next as long as I live."

Elyse could feel the apprehension in Mr. Anderson's voice, so she touched his hand again. "Go on," she said. "It happened a long time ago. Nothing you say can hurt anyone now."

"Mr. O'Reilly swore to God that he'd kill the captain if he didn't stay away from his daughter!"

Elyse gasped. She knew her great-grandfather had strong feelings about Jacob, but she didn't know how intense they really were. "What did Jacob say after that?"

"He told your great-grandfather that he already considered Elyse to be his wife. He didn't need his permission or that of his God to make it so."

Elyse knew her great-grandfather wasn't perfect, but she did know that he was very religious. In his eyes, Jacob had taken the name of God in vain.

"Did they get physical at all after that exchange?" Elyse asked.

"I'm sure it would have escalated to that point, but it never did. After the captain's tirade, Mr. O'Reilly clutched his chest and fell to the ground."

"Was he having a heart attack, Mr. Anderson?" she inquired.

"Yes, he was. Your grandmother must have seen what was going on from the lighthouse, because she rushed out to them."

"Did Jacob help my grandmother attend to her father?"

"No, not exactly. Your grandmother asked the captain what he had done, and all he could do was stand there in shock. She told him to leave and that she never wanted to see him again."

"Did he leave then?"

"Yes, he left like a scolded dog with his tail between his legs. It was then that your grandmother saw me standing by the barn and asked me to go into town to fetch Doctor Smith."

"Was that the last time you ever saw the captain at the lighthouse?"

"Yes, it was. He died that night in the storm. His ship sunk to the bottom of the lake. The average depth of the lake is around sixty feet, so when there's rough water, you run out of room to navigate a ship."

Elyse shut off the tape recorder. She had heard enough. She knew her great-grandfather did not die that night, but she also knew that Jacob had. After what she had just heard, she was almost glad that he did.

"Thank you for answering my questions, Mr. Anderson. I'll be leaving now so you may eat your lunch in peace." Elyse leaned over and kissed the old man on the forehead as the nurse brought in his lunch tray.

"I'll be back in a few minutes, Dad. I'll just walk Ms. Montgomery to the front door," the younger Mr. Anderson told his father.

As they walked to the door, Elyse was still in a state of shock from what she had just heard. Mr. Anderson's son must have sensed this, because he put his hand on her shoulder to comfort her. "I know my father is at peace with his life, Ms. Montgomery. He hasn't any regrets, and if the Lord comes to take him, he's ready. But I hope this news you've gotten today doesn't complicate your life in any way. It doesn't seem to have set well with you at all."

"You're right, Mr. Anderson, it was rather unsettling. But as a reporter, I know there are two sides to every story. I have to let the other side have their say too"

"How will you do that if Jacob Flannery is dead?" Mr. Anderson asked with a puzzled look on his face.

"It's a good thing he *is* dead, Mr. Anderson; that's the only thing that is going to protect him from me now," Elyse declared.

She slammed the door behind her, leaving a very confused soul on the other side.

Chapter 21

When Elyse got home that evening, she was beyond livid. She couldn't wait for Jacob to appear, so she decided to summon him herself. "Jacob Flannery, please show yourself this instant," she shouted so loudly that even Rainy ran for cover.

"What do you want, woman? How *dare* you make demands of me," Jacob bellowed back. He defiantly stood there before Elyse, throwing daggers at her with his eyes.

"What about the demands you've made of me?" she countered. "I haven't had one moment of peace since you've come into my life. Maybe my uncle was right about you all along. Perhaps I should call a priest and have this place exorcised. Then you can return to the darkness that matches your soul."

Jacob looked confused, and his eyes narrowed as he continued to study her. "I do not know what I have done, but we have been brought together for a single purpose, to discover a hidden truth that time cannot erase. You know this to be true, which is why you seek it also."

"All I know is that you left my great-grandfather to die before you sailed off to who knows what godforsaken place. You didn't even stick around long enough to see if he lived. How could you? Jacob, if you truly loved my grandmother as much as you claim, they why didn't you prove it to her by staying to help her?"

Jacob truly looked shocked at Elyse's revelation. "Who has told you these things?" he asked.

"I have just come from the mainland where I spoke to my great-grandfather's assistant lighthouse keeper. I have it all on tape. Do you want to hear it?" she challenged him.

"I believe in you, even if you do not believe in me," Jacob responded with a hurt look in his eyes.

"But the truth remains that you left my grandmother to tend to her seriously ill father herself. Didn't you think that she needed your help?" she asked.

"I cannot give you what you want," he answered with raw frustration in his voice. "If I knew the answer, I would not be standing before you now."

Elyse paused for a moment, for she could see the anger building up in Jacob like a steam boiler ready to explode. She had rehearsed what she would say to him on her return to the island and promised herself that he wouldn't get the best of her, no matter what. It was too late for that now, for she could feel the tears filling up her eyes. She closed them and turned her head away from Jacob so he would not see her cry.

"Do I cause you pain?"

"Yes, you do. You know, I thought you might have died as a result of your business dealings or one of your illicit affairs. I even looked into the possibility of someone sabotaging your ship. But you didn't need anyone to end your life for you. *You* were your own worst enemy, Jacob. Your pride kept you from admitting your mistakes. You built a fortress around your heart and never let it be penetrated. Then you lost both your one true love *and* your life."

Jacob walked closer to Elyse as she backed away from him in revulsion.

"Stay away from me, Jacob Flannery," she shouted.

"I will leave now if that is what you wish, but I still cannot abandon these grounds until the truth is known. Until then, I will be a permanent resident of this place. You have misjudged me, Elyse. Do not judge me by my mistakes. If you were judged by your mistakes, would others see *you* differently?"

"This is not a morality lesson, Jacob. We're talking about basic human decency here."

"Believe what you will, but I would not have left if I had known Joseph was still in danger."

"Can you verify this?"

"Not yet," Jacob responded with his eyes downcast.

"I'm beginning to think that your memory lapses are a convenient manipulation technique on your part. Please leave me now. I can't forgive you for what you've done, and I may not be able to forgive myself for wanting to help you."

Jacob stared at her with wounded eyes as he looked directly into her soul. "I only ask you this: why is it that God can forgive, but you cannot? Good-bye for now, Elyse."

Then he was gone from her view like a wisp of smoke blown away by the wind. He was gone in spirit, but not in her mind's eye. She would always see him and feel him here, because as he had said himself, he was now a part of this place forever.

Chapter 22

Elyse pulled herself together, and then decided to make an important call. "Uncle Joe," she started, "I'm back safely in one piece."

"No, you aren't," he remarked. Elyse could never pull one over on her uncle. He must have sensed the hesitation in her voice. "Don't kid a kidder, Little Bit. I know that something or someone is causing you grief."

"You're right on both accounts. I guess you were right about Jacob all along."

There was a long pause on the other side of the phone. "Did he hurt you, Elyse? Because if he did, I'll give him a piece of my mind. How dare that disciple of the Devil make you miserable!"

Elyse had never heard her uncle get angry with anyone before, but she had to admit it made her feel good that he was willing to defend her against Jacob, even if it was an impossible task.

"Uncle Joe, when I interviewed the assistant lighthouse keeper, he told me something that revealed Jacob's true character."

"What was that?"

"He told me that Jacob and your father were in a huge fight the day Jacob died. Jacob was trying to get Grandma to go away with him without Great-grandfather's permission."

"I'm sure that didn't go over too well!"

"No, you're absolutely right about that. Apparently, a big fight ensued, and Great-grandpa was felled to the ground by a heart attack."

"Wow," Uncle Joe remarked.

"But what really made me angry was what Jacob did next."

"And what was that, my dear?"

"Absolutely nothing. He showed his true colors, and as far as I'm concerned, he's a coward."

"I'm sorry, Elyse," Uncle Joe chimed in. "I won't add insult to injury and say I told you so."

"It really doesn't matter now, because I told Jacob to leave this place and never appear to me again."

"Can he do that?"

"Not really. He's stuck here, but at the moment I really don't give a damn."

"Now you're talking like an O'Reilly, Elyse! Don't let that scoundrel get the best of you. Let him live in limbo after what he did to our family."

"He *did* try to destroy our family, didn't he? What if your father would have died that night? Just think how different things would have been for everyone."

"Elyse, you must remember that families are more than a bunch of people living at the same address," he began. "They are all interconnected. Everyone's lives intersect, and the decisions we make affect more than our own solitary lives."

"Uncle Joe, tell me why life has to be so difficult."

"If it were easy, Little Bit, you wouldn't be able to tell the good times from the bad. You'd have no point of reference. When I'm out on the lake, I know where I'm going, and I know where I've been. The route is always the same, but the trip itself is always different. A smooth sea never made for a good sailor."

"Thanks for listening, Uncle Joe."

"Not a problem, my dear. Just keep your chin up, and good luck in New York City."

"I'll let you know how it all turns out. I probably won't be able to get back to you until I return though. I don't think the inspection tomorrow will be any problem at all, so I'm going to meet Jack tonight at his place."

"Glad to hear you're switching gears already. Don't let this news spoil the last few weeks you have on the island, Elyse. After all, you won't be around here much longer, you know."

"Yeah, I guess you're right about that. When I come back from the city, I promise to spend more time with you, Uncle Joe."

"Hey, don't worry about me. I took you up on that advice of yours. Louise and I are dating now."

"Why, Uncle Joe, you sly dog! And how long has this been going on?"

"I asked her out the other morning after you left the restaurant. I figured, hey, what do I have to lose? If she says no, she's still gotta serve me peanut butter on my pancakes if I order it, right?"

Elyse laughed loudly, which felt pretty good after her day so far. "You're truly one in a million, Uncle Joe!"

"I know, and now Louise knows it, too. Good-bye and good luck, Little Bit. Love you loads."

"Love you back," Elyse said before hanging up the phone's receiver.

Elyse poured herself a glass of wine and sat down on the steps of the sunporch to calm down. She stared out over the lake and tried to digest everything that had happened to her that day.

She still couldn't believe that Jacob had left her great-grandfather to die without even lending a helping hand. If she never saw that ghost again it would be too soon!

Her grandmother must have read him the riot act to cause him to leave so suddenly. It wasn't in her nature to be assertive, so maybe he hadn't known how to read her intentions. In the final analysis, though, he still should have stayed to help her great-grandfather and grandmother deal with their crisis.

Mr. Anderson had been right: Jacob had acted like a cowardly dog running away with his tail between his legs. Elyse had figured him to be more of a man than that. Yet something inside of her still questioned the accuracy of Anderson's story.

What if Jacob had known her great-grandfather was out of danger as he had claimed? How would she be able to research that if no one else was alive to answer her questions? She decided to do what Jacob had suggested weeks ago. She would visit her grandmother's gravesite and ask her for the answers to these questions.

This would have to wait until tomorrow, though, as the time was nearing for her to meet with Socrates in the city for the 3R Corporation meeting. She only had a few days to go. After the building inspector completed his final report, Elyse would be packing her bags for her flight the next day.

Since she hadn't heard from Rachel for quite a while, she made a mental note to contact her before she returned to the city. Maybe they could meet up somewhere. Rachel was always good for a few laughs, and she might have a solution to Elyse's romantic dilemma involving Jack.

Thinking about Jack was a welcome diversion to her at any time of the day. How she had missed him. Would she ever be able to leave here when it was becoming increasingly impossible to let a day go by without Jack's tender touch or loving voice calling her name?

Elyse put on a cute tankini that she'd received from Roger before their last trip together. He had bought it as a surprise gift before they left and had it delivered to her loft along with airline tickets to St. Barts. She had hoped he would tell her that he'd finally divorced his wife, but the subject was never broached. Instead, he spent seven glorious days romancing Elyse before unceremoniously dumping her upon their return to the city.

When she questioned him soon afterward about giving her the cold shoulder, he revealed that he had previously signed a prenuptial agreement with his wife that would render him penniless if he ever left her. Elyse couldn't believe it; she thought Roger loved her more than life itself. She then slapped his face and told him to go to hell. She could still see him holding his hand to his face for a long time before dropping it to his side. His eyes had been filled with pain, and he told her that she had already gotten her wish—he was already living there.

That seemed like years ago now, but it had only been a little over six months. What a blow he had been to her psyche. She had completely misread Roger's feelings for her. Was she now doing the same thing with Jack's feelings?

Elyse threw on some clothes over her swimsuit before grabbing her backpack and exiting out the door. "Good riddance to you, Jacob," she said under her breath as she looked back at the lighthouse one more time before entering the waiting cab.

Jean-Louis was waiting for Elyse in a speedboat by the dock. Elyse laughed out loud to see Jean-Louis in his PIB baseball cap, because he looked so terribly out of place. "Jean-Louis, I didn't know you were a sailor," she commented.

"Neither did I, Mademoiselle. Monsieur Jacques insisted I take boating instructions when I took the job on the island. I was always afraid of water. I guess he was worried I would be too afraid to come to work."

"Should I be worried about your abilities on the water then?" Elyse teased.

"*Non*," Jean-Louis scoffed. "Do you ever question my ability to help prepare the perfect dish for your consumption?"

"Never, Monsieur."

"Then you need not worry; I am a fast learner. You will be safe in my hands. Here, I have a hat for you, too," Jean-Louis said as he handed Elyse her own PIB baseball cap. She promptly placed it on her head.

The night air was warm and inviting. The boats in the harbor were lit up like tiny fireflies dancing on the water. Elyse held on to her cap as Jean-Louis turned up the throttle and sped toward Middle Bass Island's shore. He slowed down considerably before stopping the boat at the restaurant's private dock. He helped Elyse with her belongings, and they both walked to the back of the building to a private beach Elyse had never visited before. She smiled as she noticed Jack had been up to his old tricks again. Lighted bamboo torches were placed in the sand to simulate a beach party, and there was a beach blanket before her with a picnic basket to the side. The only thing missing was Jack.

"Is your boss still at work?" Elyse asked Jean-Louis.

"He should be here any minute, Mademoiselle, if he isn't here already," Jean-Louis replied with a sly smile. "I have to help Pierre. Please excuse me while I make a quick exit."

"Thanks for the ride," Elyse said as he smiled and hurried off into the darkness.

She put her backpack down on the blanket, and before she turned around, two hands were shielding her eyes. "That better be your hands, Jacques LeClare, or else there's a gigantic crab holding me hostage."

Jack turned her around to meet his face and then kissed her for a good solid minute before letting her catch her breath.

"I missed you, too," she said softly to him.

"I see you have come prepared?" he said as he pointed to her backpack.

"Yes, Clevelanders always have to be prepared for anything. If you don't like the weather one minute, just stick around for a few more and it will change."

Jack laughed. "I thought you were only going to bring yourself?" he teased as he leaned in closer for another kiss.

"Hold on a minute, Frenchie," she said as she playfully pushed him away, "I'm not that easy."

"Whatever it takes, I will win your love tonight," he joked.

"Don't you know that you already have it?" she said as she looked into his eyes.

"Come," he said while grabbing her arm, "I want to show you a little addition I made to the deck of the boathouse."

When Elyse walked down the beach, she could see a hot tub with Japanese lanterns woven in and out of the wooden rafters above. "Jack, you've really outdone yourself this time!"

"I thought you would like the added touches. Well, would you like to try it out?"

"Why not?" she said as she took off her top and shorts to reveal her tankini before gradually climbing inside the tub full of bubbling water.

Jack removed his shirt, but left on his jean shorts before entering the water.

"This feels heavenly," Elyse sighed as she sank down deeper into the water. "I don't know how you do it, but you really *do* make dreams come true, Jacques LeClare."

"I hope you will always remember me that way, Elyse," he said with a look of concern in his eyes.

"Hey, why the long face?"

"I guess I'm still suffering from jet lag. Let's not spoil the mood; I want to spend this entire evening alone with only you."

Elyse melted inside. How this man could make her swoon. "You seem unusually quiet tonight. Is there anything wrong?"

"Elyse, do you have any regrets in your life?"

"I guess we all do. There are a few I can think of right now, but they both seemed like a good idea at the time."

"Did one of them concern a lover?"

"Yes, it did."

"Did he break your heart?"

"At first I was devastated, but then I realized that it was the only way it could have ended. I try not to think about it anymore now. It's in my past."

"I'm glad to hear that you can bounce back so easily from a disappointment."

"Are you trying to let me down easy here, Jack?" she said teasingly

"No, nothing like that at all. I just need you to promise me that you will always remember our time together."

"I will *never* forget you, Jacques LeClare," she said as she leaned over to give him a kiss.

"Do you believe in true love?"

"Past research has shown me that there are roughly 10,000 people out there for every one person."

"Is that all?" he joked.

"No, really," she continued, "I guess it's a proven fact, but it doesn't matter what the statistics say, Jack. What do *you* believe?"

"Do you have a favorite song that you never grow tired of hearing, no matter how many times you hear it?"

"Yes, come to think of it, I do."

"That is like true love: someone who can keep the music playing forever in your heart."

"That's so beautiful," she said as Jack looked more seriously at her.

"If that music stops—perhaps something or someone has come between two people—do you believe that music can ever be heard again?" he asked.

"If both parties hear the music with the same intensity, then I believe it will *never* end," she replied. She was beginning to wonder what he was really trying to say, but she didn't want to take it further and ruin their evening either. "I know what will cheer you up!"

"What do you have in mind?"

"Cocktails in the buff," Elyse said as she deftly removed her tankini bottom and twirled it above her head before it landed on the deck below.

"I better unplug the lanterns before a boater sees you and crashes into the shore," Jack laughed.

"You better hurry up, Frenchie, because I'm turning into a prune in here."

He unplugged the lights and removed his shorts before jumping back into the hot tub and pulling Elyse down into the water as she succumbed to his many charms.

Chapter 23

The next morning, Elyse awoke in Jack's bed to see him sitting in a leather chair in a silk robe by the fireplace. He was drinking espresso from a small cup and smiled as he watched her stretch and yawn. "I didn't want to wake you," he said. "You looked like you needed some rest."

Elyse sat up in bed as she continued to stretch. "It was a long night, wasn't it?" "Not for me," he replied as he walked over to the bed to sit down next to her.

Elyse could see the open picnic basket on the floor with an empty bottle of wine resting inside. After their soak in the hot tub, they had decided to carry the basket back to Jack's place, where they had spent most of the night enjoying its contents and each other.

"We did eat, didn't we?" she asked.

"Yes, we did eventually. We were hungrier for each other though," he remarked.

Elyse put both of her arms around his neck and said, "You're good for a girl's diet, Jacques LeClare."

"You were pretty spry last night too, Ms. Montgomery," he said before giving her a loving kiss. Elyse took her arms away from Jack's neck, and gave him a little punch in one shoulder. "Love *does* hurt sometimes, doesn't it?" he teased.

She laughed and then decided to change the subject before Jack did something else to distract her. "Jack, I'm sorry, but since it's so late, I'm going to have to leave soon. I have important business to take care of tomorrow. Otherwise, wild horses couldn't drag me away. I hope you don't mind."

"No, I understand."

Elyse sensed that Jack was struggling with a problem he didn't know how to handle as she watched his expression change to one of concern.

"Now that you're awake, Elyse, there is something very important I must ask you: In all the time that you've known me, have you ever doubted the depth of my feelings for you?"

"I have always felt a connection with you, Jack."

"Good, then please remember that, no matter what else happens…" he began, then looked at her in a way that she had never seen him look at her before. "I have never said this to anyone, but I am hopelessly in love with you."

Elyse could feel her eyes tearing up as she replied, "And I with you, Jacques LeClare."

They passionately kissed as she lay back down on the bed with Jack on top of her. He pushed her hair away from her eyes and just stared at her. "You have the most amazing eyes. They change color with your moods. I can always tell what you are feeling just by looking in your eyes."

Elyse was suddenly taken aback: for just a minute there, Jack had sounded like Jacob. *How odd*, she thought.

"Did I say something wrong?" he asked.

"No, not at all, you could never say or do anything wrong," she replied.

After her last statement, Jack seemed uneasy again, so Elyse steered the conversation in another direction: "I guess this is good-bye for now. I'll be going to New York City to attend the contractual meeting regarding the sale of the lighthouse."

"Yes, I know," he said sadly.

"It's only a couple of days, though. When I come home, we can go back to where we left off, right?" she asked.

"I'll always be here for you," was all he said as he lovingly touched her face before getting out of bed and walking toward the stairs.

"Give me a minute to wash up, Jack, and I'll meet you downstairs."

"Take your time; I don't want to see you leave."

Elyse couldn't figure out why Jack wasn't his usual happy self this morning, so she just shrugged it off as possibly a morning hangover or leftover jet lag. When she got dressed and descended down the stairs, Jack was already dressed and serving up omelets on separate plates.

"Please sit down and join me for a quick breakfast," he implored. "The restaurant doesn't open until 11:00 a.m., and I gave the staff an extra hour off this morning."

She couldn't resist those deep blue eyes of his and replied, "Okay, I can stay for a little while."

They ate their breakfast in almost total silence and when they were done, Jack took her hand in his, kissed it, and said, "Never forget."

"I won't, I promise."

Then he walked her to the boat dock and kissed her one more time beneath the midmorning sun as she caught the first ferry back to South Bass Island. She waved to him from the ferry, and he waved back, but he still had that look of concern on his face. Elyse threw him a kiss, and he finally smiled that sexy smile of his and waved to her as the ferry floated out of sight.

She still didn't understand why Jack had acted so unusual that morning. Everyone is entitled to a bad day she reasoned, but Jack seemed almost remorseful.

He had told her that he was in love with her, and she had admitted the same to him. The verbal foreplay was over now, and all their cards were on the table. They couldn't just go back to being friends after what they had professed that morning. *Why didn't he seem happier*? she wondered.

Now she would have to decide what to do with her life. Should she relocate back to Ohio to be near Jack? Was their relationship serious enough to warrant such a step? As usual, she had more questions than answers, but she still needed to find out one thing before she left for New York.

She planned to stop by her grandmother's gravesite after the final inspection of the lighthouse. Maybe that's where she should have turned in the first place, for her grandmother was the only one who knew the answers.

Chapter 24

Just as Elyse had surmised, the inspection went well, and the inspector signed an official document that Elyse countersigned and dated.

"I guess you'll be vacating these premises then?" the inspector asked Elyse.

"Well, I actually have a few weeks left," she replied.

"It must have been quite interesting living here. I bet this place holds a lot of memories for you," he added.

"You have *no* idea," she said, half expecting Jacob to magically materialize behind the inspector to give him menacing looks.

"Good luck to you then. You must be eager to get back home," the inspector remarked.

Elyse gave him a half-hearted smile as she replied, "Yes, I guess so."

They shook hands good-bye, and he promised to fax a copy of the report to Socrates. Now it was almost over. Elyse's heart felt heavy, and she remembered her promised visit to her grandmother's gravesite, so she went in the backyard and picked wildflowers to put on the grave. She tied the flowers with a satin ribbon she'd found in her grandmother's sewing basket and placed them in her bike basket before peddling to the Crown Hill Cemetery situated on the hill up the road from the State Park.

Resting her bicycle against the fence surrounding the cemetery, she slowly took off her helmet before grabbing the bouquet of flowers. The time had finally come to make peace with her grandmother. When she saw the gravestone, there was nothing unusual about it at all. It was next to her grandfather's and was made of rose-hued granite stone. It had her grandmother's birth and death dates and her full name: "Elyse O'Reilly Dugan, Beloved Daughter, Wife, Mother, and Grandmother" along with a short inscription that read, "The light in her eyes shone brighter than the light from the beacon."

Elyse bent down to put her flowers on the grave and said the Lord's Prayer aloud. This wasn't a normal visitation; she sought her grandmother's help in solving a mystery that had shaken her world and turned it upside down. She knelt down on both knees, looked directly at the gravestone, and said, "Grandma, it's me. I guess you never thought you'd hear from me so soon. I have done what you've asked, and let me tell you, it was *no* easy feat. Not only did I have to get the lighthouse ready to sell, but I encountered someone you once knew."

Elyse took a deep breath before continuing. "His name is Jacob. I know all about your affair, and I also know that he was your first love. What I don't know is what happened between the two of you before he died. He told me to come to you for your help. I've tried to get the answers from everyone I could, but there is still a big piece of the puzzle missing.

"If you can give me the answer, it would help to solve the conflict within me. I still don't know why mother ran from the lighthouse the last summer we stayed with you, but now I know that you weren't to blame for her becoming ill after our return home. I'm sorry that I didn't see it at the time, but I didn't understand you then.

"After reading your journal pages and talking to Jacob, I've come to realize that you, indeed, were once just like me. You also had your hopes and dreams dashed by life's circumstances, but in the end, you finally accepted your fate and lived your life to the fullest without complaints or regrets. You were truly a lady, and I hope to follow in your footsteps as I learn to accept what fate is dealing me now. I didn't know about Jacob until now. He was your whole life, and you adeptly swept him under the carpet without any fanfare. It must have been so difficult for you. Now I also have to make a decision about someone who is everything to me, because I don't want to lose him like you lost Jacob so many years ago.

"I love you, Grandma, and I hope you will forgive me for my actions when I didn't know your story. Now you're gone, and I just hope that you can hear me. Jacob cannot leave the lighthouse until he knows what really happened on the night he died. You are the only one who can help me, and you are the only one who can free him. Please lead me to the answers I seek, for I cannot do this alone."

After she was done, Elyse got up and smiled. She felt relieved; she had spoken her peace, and now it was in God's hands. She said a quick prayer for her grandfather next and decided to add one last comment before she left: "Grandpa, I finally know what you meant about the lighthouse. I bet you have the same exact view as I do from the top of the tower from where you are now. It's all the same place, and you understood that before anyone else did!"

Now she was ready to go home and thought, *But wait, it's no longer my home.* She would pack her bags upon her return and then be on her way to the city tomorrow.

On the way back to the lighthouse, she felt tears rolling down her checks, but rationalized it as just the wind stinging her eyes. She couldn't possibly be crying about leaving this place: Look at the trouble it had brought her over the last six weeks, and that trouble could be spelled in one word: Jacob. Elyse wondered if he was still watching her, even though she had instructed him to leave the premises. It would be so like him to stay hidden, watching her every move and planning his next confrontation to give him the upper hand. What lies would he tell her then? Would he be able to remember the whole truth and not just bits and pieces? Did he even know *how* to tell the truth?

Elyse couldn't believe that she was actually thinking about that damn ghost again. She rode up to the sunporch to see Rainy sunning herself on the steps. She leaned down to pet Rainy's head, and then the two of them headed into the house for a snack.

Now that Elyse had nourished her soul with the light of forgiveness, she knew the knot in her stomach was a reminder to get something to eat and not a result of the unspoken feelings she had harbored in her heart for so long.

Chapter 25

Elyse left a message for Rachel on her voice mail stating that she would be in town the following day. Next was a quick call to Marcella; she wanted to know what Marcella had planned for their visit together. "Well, are you ready for one of our shopping excursions?" Elyse asked when she finally reached her friend.

"You know it," Marcella replied. "How are you doing all alone on that desolate island?"

"It hasn't been that bad. In fact, I've hardly had time to myself since I arrived here."

"Are you catching up with old friends?"

"Actually, I've recently met a wonderful man! It was so strange how we met, Marcella. It was almost as it were planned."

"God does work in mysterious ways, Elyse. Believe me, it *is* planned. I never would have met Socrates if my girlfriend hadn't become ill and given me her ticket for that charity event. His date cancelled too, so that just proves that it was meant to be."

"I guess you're right. Some things are simple destiny. I can't wait to tell you all about him. Now will I see you at the airport?"

"I would pick you up at the airport myself, but I have a prior commitment. I've contacted a limo company to send a driver to meet you at the airport. After your meeting, Socrates will drive you back to our apartment, and I'll catch up with you there later in the afternoon. Just make yourself comfortable like always; our home is your home."

"Thanks, Marcella. I'm sure I'll need to rest after the meeting. I didn't think it would be so emotionally draining to sell the lighthouse. After all, it was merely a summer getaway for me when I was growing up. Now it's taken on a new significance."

"You sound like you're having second thoughts about doing this."

"I seem to have lost a part of myself that I thought was so important along the way. I'm no longer the career-driven woman who thought she didn't need anyone to survive. Now I've found a part of myself that wants to connect with my family and live a much simpler life. It's not all about the money or the prestige; it's about loving and being loved. It's about being honest with yourself and other people about what you truly want. Games aren't part of the equation either, because if they were, you might roll the dice and be the big loser."

"I've never heard you talk like this before. Are you sure you're okay?"

"I've never felt better, Marcella. I'm in love again, and I never thought that I'd say *that* in a million years. I also feel closer to my family than I have in almost twenty years."

"You mean you can almost feel their presence there?" Marcella asked.

"It's much stronger than that," Elyse replied as her thoughts wandered back to Jacob and the unpleasant conversation they'd shared during their last encounter. "Maybe one day I can get more into depth with you about this, but, for right now, I have to finish packing."

"Okay, Elyse, just remember to bring your 'Bloomies' charge with you. They're having a dynamite sale this weekend, and we are going to be the first in line."

"I don't doubt it with you, Marcella. Give my love to that handsome husband of yours. Maybe you should stop dressing him in such fine clothes, because he makes too much of a lasting impression on other women."

"If that's all he does, then that's okay with me! His clients see the total package. He can't command high fees if he doesn't look the part, right?"

"Okay, I'll buy into that logic if it means we can spend tons of his money this weekend. I'll see you tomorrow."

"Have a safe flight."

Elyse packed her bags and spent the rest of the day walking around the grounds and enjoying the scenery. She wrestled with so many different feelings that she was beginning to grow weary. After the sun set, she decided to read a book on the living room couch while listening to the Jim Brickman CD Jack had given her. Rainy was on the floor, curled up on the rug, and Elyse was just soaking up her surroundings so she would never forget them.

She opened the windows to let in the lake breeze, and as Jim Brickman's piano melody *Bittersweet* started to play, she fell into a deep sleep. The song carried over into her subconscious and became a soundtrack in her dream, which opened with her grandmother and grandfather rushing back to the lighthouse in the horse-drawn wagon during a thunderstorm. Her grandmother was urging Patrick to run the horse faster so that she would be able to make it back to the lighthouse tower in time to catch Jacob's ship as it sailed past the shore.

Patrick frantically pulled the wagon into the yard; the elder Elyse bolted out of the wagon and into the lighthouse, leaving Patrick behind to hurriedly remove the reins from the horse and lead it into the barn. When Patrick arrived on the sunporch, he called out to Elyse's grandmother, but she did not answer. She had already gone up to the attic to light the kerosene lantern for Jacob to see before he circled the island to go out to sea.

The lightning grew more intense, and the thunder rumbled as Elyse's grandmother ran down the steps to the sunporch to see Patrick standing there with a worried look on his face. Then she grabbed a shawl before climbing up to the lighthouse tower. Patrick tried to grab her grandmother's hand before she started up the stairs, but he shook his head in disbelief before following her up to the lens tower.

When Patrick got up to the tower, in her dream, Elyse could see her grandmother outside on the platform with her shawl tightly wrapped around her head. Patrick rushed out there to be by her side, and he held her close as the wind whipped past them and the white caps on the lake swelled into waves larger than Elyse had never seen before. She saw her grandmother hold out her arms and shout Jacob's name several times, but of course there was no reply. Only the thunder and lightning answered her cries with their deafening crescendos.

Then Patrick took her grandmother back into the lens tower and dried her tears with his handkerchief before she fell into his arms and kept crying. But this time, her cries were more muffled and softer, more like those of a wounded animal that realizes its cries for help will never be heard.

Elyse awoke startled and turned around to see Jacob's covered portrait behind the couch still cloaked with the chenille throw. She removed the throw from the portrait and brought it from behind the couch to face her. She almost felt possessed by another soul as she turned the portrait over and feverishly tore off its backing. Then she saw an envelope sealed shut with her grandmother's embossed wax seal on the back of it.

Elyse opened the envelope and sat down on the couch to read its contents:

"If you are reading this letter, I pray that you have some connection to my family. If you do not, then you must see to it that my granddaughter, Elyse Montgomery, receives this letter posthaste:

Dear Elyse: I want to tell you what I told your mother the last time we spent the summer here at the lighthouse. Your mother did not want to hear the truth, but I know that you have always been one to search for it.

I want to tell you about a wonderful man, a man I had the privilege to know and love many years ago. His name was Jacob Flannery. I loved him before I fell in love with your grandfather and he was a man of many facets. He was strong, brave, and handsome, and he showed me a point of view of the world I had never known before. Even though my parents did not want me to see him, I could not keep myself from his arms. We were meant to be together, and I never doubted that he loved me with his whole being.

You may ask why I have this need to tell you about someone you will never know. I have my reasons for doing so. Jacob and I were more than friends; we were also lovers, and when he returned to the island for the second time from his native Ireland, we had planned to go away together. But that was not to be. My father had a heart attack after Jacob told him of our intentions, and I never got to say good-bye to Jacob before he sailed that night.

I tried to signal him to return to shore with a kerosene lantern that I used numerous times to welcome him to the island on his previous visits. The storm was too violent that night, and he never returned back to me because his ship sank that night in the storm.

Please believe me when I say that I deeply loved your grandfather. Patrick was the best thing that ever happened to me. But I never forgot Jacob. You see, I could not because every time I looked at your mother I saw him standing before me again. He was more than a passing fancy to me; he was the father of my child."

Elyse stopped reading for a minute and then continued on in shock.

"That is what I told your mother that day. She never forgave me for keeping it a secret from her all of those years. I thought I was protecting her from grief, but I only created sorrow. She loved Patrick deeply, and it was too much of a shock for her to learn the truth.

You are different though, my granddaughter, for you have always wanted to know the truth about everything. If you despise me for this, I will understand, but I cannot change what has already happened.

Patrick and I agreed to keep the secret from your mother because we felt it would do no one any good to dig up the past. Your mother would never have the chance to know her biological father, but it didn't matter. Patrick was the best father anyone could have asked for, and your mother believed he could do no wrong.

Jacob, on the other hand, was a wandering soul who was always searching for the answers. Much like yourself, don't you think? You have his eyes, Elyse. They aren't exactly the same color, but they have the same intensity and fire that his held.

I have said my peace. I cannot begin to tell you how many times I started to tell both you and your mother the truth, but could not. Now I know that it was wrong to keep a secret of such magnitude. The truth always comes out in the end, and I could not go to my grave without telling your mother the truth about Jacob.

That is all I have to say about the matter. My story has now been told. I know you will always think of Patrick as

your grandfather, as you rightfully should. But don't forget that there was another who came before him, one who gave your mother life and you a strong spirit. He would have loved you so much, Elyse, just as I have always loved you since the day you were born. Don't let anything get in the way of your dreams, my dear, for life is too brief a journey. I lived a long, happy life, and I wish the same for you. If you can love someone as deeply as I loved both Jacob and Patrick, then your journey will be all the sweeter.
My Love to You Forever, Grandma."

Elyse was in a state of shock after reading the letter, and she instinctively knew what she had to do next.

"Jacob, if you can hear my voice, please come to me now. I need to speak to you. There's something I have to tell you before I leave," she shouted.

Minutes later the temperature of the room took a familiar chilly turn as she watched Jacob materialize before her. "I am here because you asked," he responded.

"Jacob, my grandmother never got to tell you something important the night you died."

"How do you know this?" he asked with a puzzled look on his face.

Elyse didn't know any other way to tell him, so she spread her grandmother's letter out on the end table for Jacob to read and watched his facial expressions change several times while he read it. She could almost tell which sentence he was reading by the look in his eyes that changed from sorrow to joy in seconds. After he finished reading the entire letter, he walked closer to Elyse.

"You are a part of me; I should have seen it from the start. We are so alike. Did you not notice this yourself?" he inquired.

"If I look back on our meetings now, it is apparent. I should have guessed the truth sooner. I'm so sorry that you never had the chance to know it either."

"I did not know I had a daughter, but God granted me the privilege of meeting my granddaughter," he said as his eyes filled with tears.

A teardrop ran down Elyse's check as she smiled back at him. "I'm sorry I didn't even know you existed before I came back here."

"You do not have to acknowledge me in any other way but as a friend. I know that you loved Patrick, and I mean him no disrespect. How can I possibly thank someone who raised my child as his own? He was a much bigger man than I was in that respect. I will forever be grateful to him. He was your *true* grandfather."

"Jacob, can you remember anything else about that night after reading the letter?"

"When I do, I will come to you. Until then, know that I am here for you. After all, we are inextricably intertwined. We are family."

Then he disappeared into the darkness of the night and into Elyse's heart and mind forever.

Chapter 26

Elyse's alarm went off early the next morning. She hurriedly packed and got ready for her trip. She looked at herself in the mirror of the bureau and adjusted her tie belt before gathering her carry-on bag and suitcase. The cab was just pulling up the driveway as Elyse let Rainy out and locked the sunporch door. She was already in the cab when her phone rang and the answering machine turned on.

"Hi Elyse, it's Rae. For the love of God, pick up the phone! If you leave for New York City before you get this message, you'll never forgive yourself."

But Elyse did not hear the message, for she was already halfway to the dock. Her journey back to New York City was typical, and she was lucky there were no delays; the commuter plane was on time. She took out the book on Celtic culture and smiled as she realized that Jacob would be pleased to see her reading such a book.

When Elyse arrived at JFK Airport, a limo driver was holding up a sign with her last name on it. "Here in the flesh," she told the driver.

"Okay, lady, then we better get going," the driver replied.

Elyse entered the limo and took out the paperwork from her bag. Along with the original copy of the inspector's report, she had also taken photographs of the lighthouse and its grounds to be passed around the table for everyone to see.

When they finally made it into the city Elyse felt apprehensive. Returning home usually made her feel relieved, but this time was different. She wondered if she was letting her heart do all the thinking instead of her head. She tipped the limo driver before he sped off and wheeled her luggage into the lobby of the tower, stopping at the security guard's desk.

"Would you please tell Mr. Socrates Johnson that Elyse Montgomery has arrived?" she asked.

"Yes, Ms. Montgomery," the security guard began. "May I hold that luggage for you?"

"That would be very kind of you," she replied.

Before she knew it, Socrates was dashing out of the elevator, dapper as usual.

"New suit?" Elyse teased as she jokingly touched his lapel.

"No, but I'm sure I'll have at least a few more new ones after you and Marcella go shopping," he said, giving her a kiss on the cheek and standing back to admire her. "Did you arrive earlier and take in a spa treatment at the Red Door?" he asked.

"No, why do you ask?"

"Either that, or island life agrees with you. You look fantastic."

"That's good to know, considering what I *feel* like on the inside."

"That bad, huh?" Socrates asked.

"Actually, it's worse than you can imagine…"

"Okay, Elyse, you don't have to say or do anything at this meeting. Just nod your head when I acknowledge your presence. It doesn't look like anyone will be there except the two of us and counsel for the other side."

"That's good, Socrates, because I'm not sure I want to know who is on the buyer's end. What if I don't like them? I don't think I could sign the paperwork if I felt the new owners weren't legit."

"You've got to get over this, Elyse. Remember what we discussed before? This is just a piece of property, right?"

"I can't give you the same answer I gave you before. Things have changed, and this is going to be the most difficult thing I've ever done in my life."

"Okay, then take my hand. I'll hold it all the way up to the penthouse suite. You've got to settle down before we enter that room."

Socrates took Elyse's hand in his and led her to the elevators. He continued to hold her hand as he promised he would. Right before the elevator doors opened to their floor, he gave her a big hug. "It hasn't been easy for you, has it?" he whispered into her ear. "Don't worry. I'll make this as painless as possible."

Elyse's eyes filled with tears, and she wiped them away as the elevator doors opened. Then both she and Socrates greeted his assistant before entering the conference room to await the other party. Five minutes later, the telephone in the conference room rang.

"Mr. Johnson, counsel for the 3R Corporation is here to see you," Socrates' assistant announced to her boss.

"Send him in," Socrates responded. He shot Elyse one more glance, and she smiled back and nodded her head to let him know that she was fine.

Socrates rose to greet the other attorney. They shook hands, and then Socrates introduced the attorney to Elyse as he reached over to offer his hand to her next.

"Do you see any reason why this meeting will take longer than we'd originally planned?" Socrates asked the other attorney when everyone was seated.

"Well, actually, Mr. Johnson, I must ask you for a small favor. It seems that one of the owners of the 3R Corporation is stuck in traffic at this time, but would like to be present when the property is transferred," the attorney answered.

"I wasn't aware of this stipulation," Socrates began. "Is there a problem?"

"No, nothing like that," said the attorney, "just a personal request."

"Okay, we'll wait," Socrates said as he looked over to Elyse and smiled.

Ten more minutes passed before the telephone rang again. "Mr. Johnson, the other party has arrived," Socrates' assistant said.

"Please invite him in," Socrates said.

Both Socrates and the other attorney stood up, but since Elyse's knees were shaking, she decided to stay seated. When the door opened, Elyse's jaw dropped to the floor because standing before her, in all his glory, was none other than Roger Strong.

"Sorry I was late," he apologized. "Traffic, you know." Then he shot a glance at Elyse, who was still too stunned to say or do anything.

"I'd like to introduce you to my client, Mr. Johnson," the attorney said to Socrates. "Roger Strong, part owner of the 3R Corporation."

"I've already heard quite a lot about you," Socrates said to Roger as he looked him squarely in the eye and gave him a curt handshake.

"Nothing that's been said up to this point will match what I'll be doing here today, Mr. Johnson," Roger bragged. Then Roger turned his attention over to Elyse, who by this time was starting to get her bearings and was fit to be tied. "Why, Elyse, you look wonderful!" Roger began. "I guess that stress-free island life is just what the doctor ordered."

"Actually, Roger, never seeing you again was exactly what the doctor ordered," Elyse replied.

"It wasn't all that bad, was it? After all, we had a few laughs." Roger smirked.

"I'm still laughing," Elyse responded dryly.

The two attorneys just stood there dumbfounded. "Elyse, do you want to continue with this meeting, or should we cancel it right now?" Socrates asked with concern.

"No, let's see what 'Mr. 3R' has up his sleeve. Or should I say, *in* his sleeve. Maybe you should frisk him for a knife. He has a tendency to attack when one's back is turned," she remarked.

"Jolly good retort, Elyse," Roger chided. "I see your wit hasn't been dulled by the lack of excitement on that island."

"Not in the least," she said.

"Should we continue on then?" Socrates asked as he looked over at Elyse, who nodded in approval.

Roger's attorney handed Socrates a document, and he perused it carefully before placing it on the table before him. "After reading this document, I have ascertained that the parties involved are willing to make an offer of $10 million for the property in question. Is that correct?" Socrates asked the other attorney.

"Yes, that is the offer," the attorney responded.

"Is there any room for negotiation?" Socrates asked.

"No," Roger chimed in, "that's 3R's final offer."

"May I have a few minutes to confer with my client?" Socrates asked the other attorney.

"Go right ahead," the attorney answered.

Socrates smiled and led Elyse out to the office area and closed the door. "Did you have any idea that Roger was involved in this?" he asked.

"Are you kidding? If I had, I wouldn't even be here," she replied.

"I wonder what his *real* agenda is today?" Socrates mused.

"It's more than some kind of kinky thrill to get back at me, Socrates; he's up to something," Elyse said.

"Like what?" Socrates asked.

"Let's just go in there and ask him. Roger has always been one to brag about his accomplishments. I don't think he'll have any problem telling us exactly what he intends to do with the property once his name is on the deed."

"Okay, we'll ask him, but do you still want to go ahead with the sale? Is the asking price in your ballpark?"

"It was never about the money, Socrates; it's the principle. Now let's go in there and kick his behind."

Once everyone was seated in the conference room again, Socrates said to the other attorney, "My client has concerns about what will be done with the property in question after it is purchased by your client."

"I can't speak for my client, Mr. Johnson, for that is a private matter. If he wishes to address your concerns, he will do so on his own," the other attorney replied.

"That's quite okay, Phil," Roger began, "I don't mind telling Ms. Montgomery how the property will be transformed. In fact, I think she'll appreciate how my research led me to the decision to turn the site into a gambling casino and hotel."

Elyse could feel her blood pressure rising as she turned to ask, "What research was that, Roger?"

"South Bass Island used to be the location of a hotel called the Victory Hotel. In its heyday, the hotel was known for its gambling and gaming activities. Rattlesnake Island is also up for sale, and if I build townhouses and a marina there, it will only enhance the area."

"Roger, you don't know what you're doing here!" Elyse said as she raised her voice. "Put-in-Bay is *not* a theme park for high rollers. It's an island with people living on it who call it their home. If you put something like that on the island, it will change it forever. Families won't be able to afford to take their children there on vacation. Fishermen won't be able to fish the lake. Worst of all, it would become an island for the rich and famous, *not* the average man."

Socrates and the other attorney looked stunned after Elyse said her peace. "Perhaps I need to explain that this offer will only be extended on this day," Roger's attorney explained.

"Then I think that I will have to confer with my client in private one more time to determine whether or not she is willing to accept your offer," Socrates said.

Elyse and Socrates left the room for a second time.

"Elyse, this is the only offer we have on the property," Socrates began. "If we refuse it, I can't promise that you'll get another. If you want to kill this offer, just give me the word. But if you do, you've just bought yourself a white elephant."

"That's where you're wrong, Socrates. It's *not* a white elephant," Elyse declared. "It's been my home for the last six weeks, and I love it there. I don't think I really wanted to sell it anyway. Not now, not ever. I think I may have a solution to all of this. Here, let me write down the telephone number of a friend of mine. Have your assistant contact this person pronto, and then we'll take a break for lunch. When we come back, we should have our answer."

"Are you telling me that you have another buyer for the property?" Socrates asked.

"Not exactly a buyer, but a landlord," she replied. "You'll see what I mean later. In the meantime, just stall as long as you can."

"Okay, I can play the game as good as the next guy." Socrates laughed. "Maybe I've met my match in you today, though."

"You ain't seen nothin' yet," Elyse added. "That spineless coward in there doesn't have the faintest idea who he's dealing with here."

"You mean you're *not* the Elyse Montgomery I've come to know and love?" he teased.

"I became a different woman in many ways when I inherited that property, and I'm not going to let that jerk take it away from me…ever!"

"Let's go get 'em, Tiger," Socrates said as he led her back into the conference room.

"My client wants to cease negotiations until we contact a second party who has also expressed an interest in the property," Socrates bluffed.

"I wasn't aware of another bidder," Roger's attorney said as he turned to see a puzzled look on his client's face.

"It was a last-minute decision on their part," Socrates continued. "Why don't we all break for lunch, and then in a couple of hours we can reconvene at this location?"

Elyse looked over at Roger, who was now looking a bit baffled and agitated. She gave him her sweetest smile, and he just glared back at her.

"Since you cannot make a decision until all offers are on the table, I agree with your assessment of the situation. What do you think, Mr. Strong?" Roger's attorney asked him.

"Well, if we don't have any other choice, I guess I can wait a few hours," he replied.

"Good, then we'll all meet here again in two hours," Socrates continued.

Roger glanced at Elyse before leaving the room, and his attorney followed after him. Once they were gone, Elyse felt like a ton of bricks had been lifted off her shoulders. "Do you think there's a chance Roger might choke on a chicken bone?" Elyse joked.

Socrates laughed. "If he does, let's hope his attorney doesn't know the Heimlich maneuver. What do you say we strategize while we order in?" Socrates asked.

"Sounds good to me," Elyse replied. "I'm not that hungry anyway. Roger has a way of spoiling one's appetite."

"He's still got it bad for you, Elyse," Socrates remarked. "Why does he hate you so much?"

"He hates what he can't have, Socrates. His wife saw to it that we were kept apart. Now he's frustrated as all hell. He can't give her up, because she's the one with all the money and power."

"Do you think he ever loved her at all?"

"No, it was just a marriage of convenience. Her father was a mentor to Roger, and he wanted his daughter's holdings to be safe with someone who was a carbon copy of himself."

"I still don't know how you could have fallen for him. Sure, he's good looking for a guy and filthy rich, I'll grant you that, but he doesn't seem like he was meant for you in the first place."

"He used to be so different, Socrates. He was charming and witty and fun. I suppose the British accent didn't hurt either. He would surprise me with little gifts at a moment's notice, and I don't mean expensive ones either. He hid love poems in my desk at work; it was all so romantic. Every so often he would whisk me off somewhere for a long weekend, and we would talk for hours. He is so well read and intelligent. He knows something about everything. I just can't believe what a bitter man he's become."

"Life is bitter if there's nothing sweet in it," Socrates added. "*You* were that something sweet. You know, I think Jeannette should be back from lunch about now. I'll check to see if she's reached your friend yet."

"Good, because if my friend says what I think she will, Roger will experience his first real business failure."

Chapter 27

Elyse and Socrates were just starting to dive into their lunches when the telephone in the conference room rang. "Mr. Johnson, I have that party on the other line for Ms. Montgomery," his assistant announced.

"Just transfer the call, Jeannette, and go to lunch already. In fact, take an extra half-hour since you're leaving later than usual. Every place in town will be packed by now."

"Thanks, Mr. Johnson," Jeannette responded before transferring the call to Elyse.

Elyse picked up the receiver on the first ring. "Hi, Nancy? It's me, Elyse Montgomery. Sorry to drop this on you without any advance notice, but as the director of The Ohio State University's Ohio Sea Grant Program, I knew my offer would be too good for you to pass up."

Socrates sat back in his chair and watched in astonishment as Elyse closed a deal in a matter of minutes over the phone.

"You're something else," Socrates laughed. "I don't think Roger will know what hit him. How did you learn to negotiate like that?"

"My father was an attorney you know. Then there's this friend of mine, Socrates Johnson. Perhaps you've heard of him? He's one of the best in the business."

Socrates laughed a hearty laugh. "My, my, I can't wait to see the expression on Roger's face when he finds out that he's been outfoxed by the fox herself."

"It will be fun, won't it?" Elyse was proud of herself.

Lunch was over too soon, and Elyse excused herself to go to the restroom to freshen up a bit before the battle resumed. As she was leaving the restroom, she caught the scent of familiar cologne in the hallway. She looked up and saw Jack standing there dressed in a suit.

"Jack?" she asked, puzzled.

"Hello, Elyse," he said sheepishly.

Then before she could ask him what he was doing there, Roger and his attorney approached from the rear. "Oh, I see that you've met my protégé, Jacques LeClare," Roger said to Elyse. "Jacques, I think you already know Elyse Montgomery."

Jack wouldn't look Elyse straight in the eye. She couldn't believe this was happening to her.

"What's this all about, Jack?" Elyse asked.

"He's right, Elyse. I work for him," Jack responded. "Well, actually, he owns the restaurant. He and his wife, Renee, are two-thirds of the 3R Corporation. He made my adoptive father, Roberto Rossi, the third party per my request."

"Are you telling me that all this time you were working for that piece of dirt?" Elyse said as she glared at Roger.

"Yes, but it's not what you think; I didn't mean for it to become so complicated."

"A mere *complication*; is that all I was for you?" Elyse shouted. "Did Roger pay you to seduce me? Do you know what that makes you, Jack?"

"Yes, I do," he said sadly.

"He was the perfect foil, Elyse," Roger sneered. "After all, I needed someone to divert your attention away from my objective so I could purchase the lighthouse out from under your cute, little turned-up nose."

"Don't go counting your chickens before they've hatched," Elyse spit out.

"Still feisty I see. Well, you can't reject my offer," Roger added. "You can't possibly maintain that piece of property on your own, and you've had no time to find another buyer for the lighthouse. Jack saw to that. I think you and your hotshot attorney are bluffing."

"Go ahead, Roger, call my bluff," Elyse said as she got up close to his face.

"What on earth is going on here?" Socrates said as he rushed out of his office to see what all the yelling was about.

"It seems that your client is becoming verbally abusive with mine," Roger's attorney said to Socrates.

"Is this true, Elyse?" Socrates asked.

"I wasn't abusive in the least," she said. Then she hauled off and slapped Roger across the face. "It's called payback, and that's from my grandmother, my grandfather, and especially from me."

Everyone was too stunned to move. Elyse looked at Jack and turned her rage at him next: "The wound is too fresh for me to deal with you now, Jack. How could you? You and Roger probably had a lot of laughs on my expense. Was it all a lie? Did I just imagine it?"

Jack stood there silently watching her with a hurt expression in his eyes that made her want to cry. She wouldn't dare give any of them the satisfaction though. No, she would have the last laugh.

Elyse turned to her friend. "Socrates, I don't think there's any need to continue with these negotiations. After all, I have decided to donate the property to the OSU Ohio Sea Grant Program."

"You're doing *what*?" Roger gasped.

"They're going to use the property as part of their research program. You wouldn't want to look like the scoundrel you really are and fight them on this, would you,

Roger? What kind of press would that create for you? I can see the headlines now: *'Media Mogul Denies University Access to Research Grounds.'* You'd come out smelling like a piece of you know what."

"You can't do this to me." Roger was nearly foaming at the mouth.

"I not only can, I just did," Elyse said.

"Do you have verification of this deal?" Roger's attorney asked Socrates.

"Yes, in fact, I do. The university just faxed me a copy of a signed contract. It's a done deal. I was hoping to notify everyone at the same time," Socrates said to the beleaguered group before him.

"I guess there's no reason for us to stick around then," Roger said.

"I'll second that," Elyse said.

"Let's just part here," Socrates added. "There's no need to hold another meeting."

"If you don't mind, Socrates, I'm going to leave immediately," Elyse said.

"No, you go right ahead, I understand," he replied. Then Elyse gave Jack one more wounded look before she entered the elevator. "Well, gentlemen, I hope we can put this all behind us," Socrates said.

"You win some, you lose some," Roger remarked.

"You've lost quite a lot lately," Socrates said to Roger, knowing he would catch his drift that he was also referring to Elyse. All Roger could do was smirk back.

"I hope we can meet again under different circumstances," Roger's attorney told Socrates.

"Yes, much different," Socrates replied.

Then all hell broke loose. All this time Jack had been holding in his anger, and now it exploded like a cork from a shaken champagne bottle. "It's over, you self-centered son of a bitch. I'm getting out while I still have my name *and* my soul," Jack said to Roger.

"She'll never trust you now, Jack," Roger said. "I know Elyse better than you ever will."

"That's where you're wrong," Jack countered. "How can you say that when you never really loved her?"

"And you do?" Roger sneered. "So, is that what this is all about? You're in love with her, and that tart has weakened your resolve."

"She's no whore," Jack attacked him right back. "And you should talk: *you've* been living off your wife's millions for years. I can't believe Elyse willingly slept with you."

"Don't kid yourself, Jacques, she went willingly each and every time," Roger began. "Come to think of it, *you* did too—figuratively speaking of course. You're in bed with me now."

"You know I had no other choice," Jack said. "Roberto needed that money for his cancer treatments. He could never afford health insurance because he and his wife spent every last penny on my education. I owed them."

"Elyse will never believe you now," Roger said.

"You English are so damn smug. You're so 'anal' that you don't even *need* an asshole."

"Your career is over, Jack," Roger said. "I've grown tired of you and that Eurotrash staff of yours."

Socrates and the other attorney watched in the wings, observing every nuance, but they hadn't counted on what Jack would do next: He formed a tight fist and knocked Roger out cold. "The thing about trash, Roger," Jack said to the belittled billionaire, "is that it always ends up on the floor."

Then Jack got on the elevator, leaving both Socrates and the other attorney to stare at Roger sprawled out on the floor.

"I suppose it would have happened to him sooner or later," Roger's attorney said to Socrates.

"I need a drink," Socrates replied.

"I'd leave him here, but he's one of my biggest clients," Roger's attorney said.

"Too bad we can't choose clients like we choose our friends," Socrates added.

"The only trouble with that is most of my friends can't afford my fees," the attorney added as he got down on both knees to try and revive Roger.

"Why don't you two go into my office and take it easy," Socrates told him. "There's something I have to do right away. My assistant, Jeannette, will be back from lunch any minute. She'll assist you in any way she can."

"Go ahead. He's not going anywhere," Roger's attorney said as he began to fan Roger with a piece of paper.

"That guy had one mean right hook. What's his name again?" Socrates asked.

"That was Jacques LeClare. He's the chef who was working for Mr. Strong in his restaurant on Middle Bass Island," replied the attorney.

"It all makes sense now…" Socrates said as he rushed off to catch the elevator before the doors closed.

Chapter 28

Elyse was still in a state of shock when she exited the elevator on the main floor. "Ms. Montgomery," the security guard at the front desk called out to her, "do you want your luggage now?"

Elyse didn't hear him because she was overwhelmed with emotions that numbed her senses. Once she got outside on the street, she started walking and didn't care where she went. She only knew that she was pierced to the core of her very being. *How could Jack do this to me? Was everything we had experienced together just a one-act play to him? How could I have let myself fall in love with such abandon?* Living on that island had cost her that edge that she had developed while living in the city. How could she be so gullible?

Since Elyse was heading toward Greenwich Village, where Rachel lived, she decided to signal a cab to her friend's apartment. She knocked on Rachel's door and saw a bloodshot eyeball examining her from the peephole before the door swung open wide.

"It's too late, isn't it?" Rachel asked.

Once Elyse saw her friend's face, she could no longer hold in the tears. Rachel put her arms around her, and led her into her apartment. "Here, sit down on the couch while I get you a year's worth of tissues."

Rachel's comment made Elyse smile a little bit, but it couldn't stop the tears from flowing. "Don't try to make me smile, Rae," Elyse began. "It hurts too much to laugh."

"Now dry those tears," Rachel began. "I knew I should have come home on an earlier flight and skipped that party. Then I would have been able to call you the night *before* you left. What was I thinking? Well, never mind, I know what I was thinking; it's not important. What's important is that we put you back together again. You're falling to pieces."

"It was my worst nightmare. Both Roger and Jack were scheming behind my back to steal the lighthouse out from under me."

"Are you sure that Jack was involved?"

"He even admitted it to my face, Rae. He's no saint in my book."

"No man's a saint, Elyse. I wasn't a saint myself last night, but that doesn't mean I'm a bad person. Maybe he had a good reason for what he did."

"A good reason?" He had a good reason all right, money and power. Isn't that what it always boils down to? He signed his soul over to the Devil himself. The blood probably isn't even dry on the contract yet."

"I don't know, honey. I'd give the guy a chance. I know that you're upset right now, but you told me that he's something special. If he's that special to you, you couldn't have been *that* wrong about him."

"I've lost my touch, Rae, that's what happened. I used to be able to smell a rat a mile away. I fell in love, and I couldn't see the writing on the wall. He was just using me to get the property." Elyse blew her nose and threw the crumbled tissue on the floor in a pile that was starting to resemble a snowdrift.

"Let me make us some tea, and we'll try to put some facts together," Rachel said. "The only way a man like Jack would get involved with a man like Roger is if he were desperate."

"Didn't we cover this already?" Elyse asked.

Rae filled her teakettle with water and placed it on a lit gas burner on her stovetop. "I don't think that your Jack would become allies with Roger unless it meant that someone or something would benefit."

"Isn't it obvious, Rae, *he's* the beneficiary."

"No, it's never that easy, Elyse. We're both journalists, and we know you've got to dig to find the ulterior motive behind *why* an individual said or did what they did. It's never black or white; you know that."

Elyse stopped crying and sat back on the couch to collect her thoughts. "You may be right, Rae, but why didn't Jack explain his part right there and then?"

"Fear could be a factor. Maybe Roger has Jack in such a tight spot that he can't squeeze out. You know yourself how powerful Roger is. He's a one-man conglomerate. Jack must have some unpaid loans with Big Shot's name on them."

"No, for some reason I don't think it involves money. It has to be something else."

"Then why don't you let me do some more research on it for you?" Rachel added. "I'm not going anywhere for a few weeks. I'll even take a vacation day to look into it if I have to."

Rae poured the boiling water into two teacups, and added a tea bag to each one before placing the cups with saucers on the coffee table.

"I love you, Rae," Elyse said as she hugged her friend.

"The feeling is mutual!"

"Oh, boy, I just remembered that I left my luggage at the front desk in the lobby at Socrates' office building," Elyse exclaimed.

"Does Socrates know where you are now?"

"No, he doesn't; I was supposed to go to his apartment to meet up with him and Marcella later. I guess I better call his cell phone."

"*That* would be a good idea. Here, use my cell," she added as she threw her phone to Elyse.

"What would I ever do without you?" Elyse said as she caught the phone.

"Let's not go there now. I'm just glad your mental homing device brought you straight to me, and that I decided to work at home today. Things happen for a reason, Elyse, and we're not capable of getting the gist of it at the get-go. Sometimes it doesn't all become clear for days, weeks, or even years. I didn't find out why Matt Shapiro threw that salamander down my shirt in Biology class until last year at our twentieth high school reunion. But I promise you this: between the two of us, we'll solve this one soon. We've got to because I don't think I've ever seen you this distraught before. You've got it bad, honey, and all I want is for you to be happy."

"The funny thing is, I thought I *was* happy. By the way, why *did* Matt Shapiro throw that salamander down your shirt?"

"He just wanted to see my boobs. Hell, all he had to do was ask!"

Elyse laughed and Rachel chimed in. She had gone to the right place after all. Rachel had made her forget her troubles, if even for a second, and now she felt like she could swallow her pride and get down to the business at hand.

Chapter 29

Elyse sipped her tea as she looked out Rae's window at the street down below. Rae had just left to get some groceries, and Elyse was mentally reviewing her options. She hadn't been able to contact Socrates for reasons yet unknown, so she left a voice mail for him and Marcella at their apartment.

"Now where does Rae keep some paper?" she said to herself as she went over to Rae's desk and searched the drawers. She found some stationery and envelopes and began to write:

"Dear Rae: I love you dearly, so I hope you won't be too hard on yourself about what happened today. None of it was your fault. I would have found out eventually, and I guess it was better sooner than later.

I'm sorry that I couldn't stay here any longer, but I need to get back home and face my demons. Then I'll know in which direction I'm headed. Right now I'm in limbo, and you know how crazy that makes me! Thanks for your sage advice, and I will be in touch with you in a few days."

Then she wrote a second note:

"Dear Marcella and Socrates: Sorry about today, Socrates. It wasn't the meeting we had in mind, but you have to admit that things are never boring when the two of us get together! Thanks for handling the contract with the OSU Ohio Sea Grant Program. I know they will take good care of the property.

Please forgive me for skipping out on you, Marcella. I need to get back to the island as soon as possible. Remember our conversation the other day? I have to find out what my destiny is. Put that shopping trip on hold; I may be in need of some therapeutic shopping after all. Give me a few days to collect my thoughts, and then I'll give you two a call."

Elyse signed both letters, and addressed them to her friends. Then she called the airport and booked the next flight back to Ohio before locking the door behind her.

She made it to the airport just in time to catch her flight. She didn't want to go back to the lighthouse just yet. That would be the first place anyone would look for her. No, she would go to Uncle Joe's. He had an unlisted phone number and would cover for her while she pulled herself together.

She needed time to sort through her thoughts the same way she'd sorted through her grandmother's belongings. She didn't want to throw anything away that was worth saving. If she never spoke to Jack again, how would she ever know his side of the story? Then again, could she even recognize the truth if he told it to her?

Her plane landed smoothly on the runway, and Elyse thought about all the changes in her life over the last six weeks. She felt glad to be back again. Her home base had now been permanently changed, and at least she knew where she wanted to stay. She still had to tell Uncle Joe about Jacob's real identity, and she was hoping to discover that Jacob had remembered the last day of his life so his spirit could finally rest.

What will happen next? she thought as she left the plane. She headed right over to a solitary landline and called Uncle Joe.

"Hello," said the voice on the other end.

"It's just me."

"Little Bit! Aren't you home a few days too soon?"

"I need to spend some time alone, Uncle Joe. If anyone, and I mean *anyone,* asks you where I am just tell them that you don't know."

"What's wrong, Elyse?"

"Nothing's right. I'll tell you everything when I get to your place."

"Okay, dear, just take a deep breath and relax. I'm always here if you need me."

"Thanks, Uncle Joe. You're the one thing that's still right with this world." Then she hung up the receiver and was on her way back home again to Put-in-Bay.

Chapter 30

Uncle Joe was waiting for her at Lime Kiln dock when her ferry rolled in. Elyse was so relieved to see him that she threw her arms around him. "Whoa," he exclaimed. "The last time you hugged me like that was when you thought your dog Sport had run away. This can't be good news."

"You're right, Uncle Joe, it isn't."

"Don't you have any luggage for me to carry?"

"No, not this time around. I kind of left in a hurry."

"This story is getting better and better," he remarked as they both got into his pickup truck and drove off to the Ship House.

"Okay, Little Bit, if I'm going to be considered an accessory to a crime by hiding a known felon, let me know right now."

"It's nothing *that* bad," Elyse said as she gave Uncle Joe a half-hearted smile. "I just need some space for a while."

"Does this involve your chef?"

"Yes, it unfortunately does. I can't believe I didn't see it coming, Uncle Joe. He was working for Roger Strong all this time, trying to divert my attention away from the sale of the lighthouse so Roger could go behind my back and swoop it out from under me."

"No!"

"It only gets worse from there… He even admitted it to my face back at the meeting in the city. He played me for a fool, Uncle Joe."

"I can't believe we're talking about the same man here, Elyse."

"Well, believe me, we are, and no one was more surprised than me."

"Did they get the lighthouse?"

"No, I donated it to OSU by contacting its director of the Ohio Sea Grant Program, and the university will officially take ownership of it in a few weeks. Until then, I guess I'll be staying there," Elyse replied.

"Good for you," Uncle Joe blurted out. "You've got your dad's brains, your mom's looks, and your uncle's chutzpah."

Then Elyse remembered the other thing that she had to tell Uncle Joe—Jacob's relationship to her mother.

Uncle Joe parked his truck and they climbed up the ladder of the ship. Once inside, Elyse felt the time was right to tell him the big secret: "That's not the only reason I've been out of sorts."

"Aren't you feeling well?" he asked with concern.

"No, it's not that at all. It involves something I discovered while I was at the lighthouse." Elyse sat down on the couch and Uncle Joe followed suit. "Uncle Joe, you were right about Grandma. She had been seriously involved with Jacob Flannery."

"I knew it," Uncle Joe remarked matter-of-factly.

"But it goes much deeper than that: You see, she was hopelessly in love with him and he with her. They had planned to sail away together the second time he came to the island, but Great-grandpa put a stop to it."

"Did he beat Jacob to a bloody pulp?"

"He didn't have the chance because your father had a heart attack after a very vocal confrontation with Jacob on the lighthouse grounds. I confirmed this when I interviewed the former assistant lighthouse keeper. After he had the heart attack, Grandma rushed to his side. She was so upset with Jacob that she banished him from the grounds."

"Well, wasn't that the end of it then?" Uncle Joe asked. "Didn't Jacob die soon afterward?"

"Yes, in fact, he died that evening in a terrible thunderstorm. His ship, *The Rose*, sank, and Jacob's body was never found."

"Wow! Wouldn't that make a darn good script for a movie?"

"It's a little more complicated than a movie plot, though, because Jacob left behind a legacy that has carried over to this day."

"And what's that, my dear?"

"Me," Elyse blurted out. "I'm his granddaughter. Grandmother was pregnant with my mother when Jacob died. He never knew she was expecting his child. Maybe if he had known, things would have been different. All I know is that Grandmother grew to love Patrick in time, but she never forgot Jacob in her heart."

"I can't believe it: my sister and that rabble-rouser were lovers! Well she sure kept everything a big secret from me. Who would have guessed?"

"It's all true. I found a letter written by Grandmother behind a portrait of Jacob she had painted that revealed everything. I couldn't believe it at first myself, but now it all makes perfect sense."

Uncle Joe shook his head in disbelief. "Did your mother know about this?"

"Yes, she found out the last summer we stayed at the lighthouse. I guess that's why she ran out of the lighthouse, sobbing. It was too much of a shock for her. She had just lost her beloved father a year earlier, and she didn't want to hear that he wasn't her biological father. They had always been so close."

"Have you told *him* about this?" Uncle Joe asked.

"Yes, I've told Jacob everything. He was a bit shocked at first, but I think it made him happy in a strange kind of way."

"What do you mean?"

"After he died, Grandmother married Patrick in quite a rush. Jacob thought that she had forgotten him, but it wasn't that way at all. She wanted to give the baby a name, and Patrick was willing to do so because he had always been in love with her himself."

"Has this information filled in the blanks for the ghost?"

"Not entirely; he still needs to remember more about the night he died. Once he does, I think he'll be free to move on."

"You've got a monumental task in front of you then."

"I know, which is why I came here. I just want to stare at the lake and soak in the sun's rays. I need to figure out what to do about Jack and how I can help Jacob. I'm a basket case, Uncle Joe."

"Elyse, just remember this: the Bible says that faith is the hope of things to come and the evidence of things not seen. You've got to have faith, Little Bit."

"If you're starting to quote the Bible, Uncle Joe, then I *know* I'm in trouble," Elyse said. "Would you mind if I take a shower?"

"Go ahead. I'll head over to the lighthouse and pick up some of your clothes when I feed the cat."

"That would be great. Thanks so much."

"I've got to go into town right now, but I'll be back by dinner time," he added. "We can grill some steaks and knock back a few beers. It looks like you need it."

"That sounds wonderful."

"Okay, I'll be off then. You just relax and take it easy. After the news you gave me today, I think *I* need those beers even more than you."

They laughed, which helped to diffuse the tension that Elyse had been feeling.

After her shower, Elyse threw on one of her uncle's oxford shirts. She opened a beer and walked barefoot out to the bow to catch the last rays of the afternoon sun that had turned the horizon into a reddish glow.

"Red sky at night, sailor's delight," she said aloud as the sun kissed her face and she closed her eyes to drink in its warmth. She sat down in a deck chair, and turned on a nearby pocket radio to hear Bobby Caldwell sing Charlie Chaplin's song *Smile*. She would make a decision about Jack in the morning. For now, she didn't want anything, or anybody, to ruin this sunset.

Chapter 31

Jack was across the street when he saw Uncle Joe come out of the grocery store with two bags. It appeared the old man was stocking up on supplies. He just had to cross the street and ask him the inevitable: "Joe, have you seen Elyse?"

"I can't tell you anything, my boy. That's up to Elyse," Uncle Joe replied.

"She's here, isn't she? Is she at the lighthouse?"

"Listen, Jack," Uncle Joe started, "if you love my niece, you'd better come up with a pretty good reason why you were in cahoots with her ex. Otherwise, it's a lost cause."

"There is a *very* good reason," Jack said.

"Then don't tell me, tell her!"

"If you see her, Joe, tell her to remember the last thing I said to her before she left for the city. Also tell her that I'll be leaving tonight."

"I will tell her *if* I see her," Uncle Joe replied before getting into his truck and driving off.

Jack stood there watching Joe's truck drive away before running to the dock to catch the ferry to Middle Bass Island. The first person he saw when he entered the restaurant was Jean-Louis.

"Jean-Louis, crack out that bottle of single malt scotch and bring it to me upstairs," Jack told his friend.

"Okay, Jacques," he replied with a concerned look.

Jack walked upstairs to his apartment, and turned on the radio. Jean-Louis knocked on the half-opened door and Jack motioned for him to come inside, saying, "You can just leave the bottle here."

"If you wish," Jean-Louis replied before leaving.

Jack was now left to his deepest, darkest thoughts as the radio station played Bobby Caldwell's melancholy jazz tune *Tomorrow*.

"Sing it, Bobby," Jack mumbled as he took out a tumbler, filled it with ice, and poured himself a double shot of scotch. He wondered if all the liquor in the world could ever numb the pain in his heart at this very moment. The door moved slightly, and Jack looked up to see Fifi adorned with a pink bow, examining him with his head cocked sideways.

"Want to join me for a drink?" he asked the poodle. Fifi barked in response to his invitation and wagged his tail. "Fifi, I think I'm having an identity crisis. Hell, why am I talking to you? You think you're a girl!"

Fifi barked again, which brought Pierre up the stairs to see what was going on. "Fifi, what is the matter?" he asked the dog.

"He was just keeping a broken man company, Pierre," said Jack

"*Mon Dieu*!" Pierre exclaimed. "This is worse than I thought; you are actually drinking scotch."

"It does the trick, Pierre."

"Not for me. Only French wine will touch *these* lips. Look at you, Jacques: you are a mess. What is troubling you?"

"Life, Pierre, life! I just decked my boss, betrayed my woman, and now I'm having a conversation with a dog that has a gender-identity disorder…"

"Fifi, go back downstairs," Pierre ordered the dog. "Have Jean-Louis give you a treat!"

The dog turned around and obeyed his master's orders.

"It could be worse, you know," Pierre continued. "You must live your life as if everything you do will be known. You need to take control of the situation."

"I thought that's what I *was* doing, Pierre. I'm in complete control of the amount of alcohol I'm consuming," Jack said sarcastically.

"Not *that* way. Don't let things stay like this. You can change them," Pierre explained.

"Let's face the facts here, Pierre. My career is over as the executive chef of this place, and Elyse will never speak to me again. What could be worse?"

"If *you* never speak to Elyse again," Pierre replied reasonably. Jack put his drink back down on his desk and looked directly at Pierre. "Good, now I have your attention. Jacques, I have never seen you so miserable, and this can only mean one thing."

"And what's *that*?"

"Why, you're in love, of course. When my Margot was alive, I used to fall asleep every night holding her little hand in mine. It was our private ritual. No matter how angry she had been with me during the day, she always showed her love for me by performing that one gesture. Since she died, I still sometimes find myself reaching for her hand in the middle of the night. Reach your hand out to Elyse. If she takes it, then you will have your answer."

Jack's eyes brightened as he sat up in his chair. "You may be right, Pierre. If I don't go to her, I won't know how she feels about me."

"That's the spirit, Boss. Now let's sober you up. A shower, shave, and espresso are in order here."

"You know those irises in the garden out back?"

"*Oui*, I do," Pierre replied.

"Please send Jean-Louis out to gather a bouquet for me. Oh, and find me as many candles as you can."

"Candles?" Pierre asked with a puzzled look on his face.

"I have something special in mind," Jack replied as he leapt to his feet.

"If anyone can change her mind, it is you. After all, you have French blood in your veins!"

"Right now that blood is a bit tainted with alcohol. I'm going to take that shower after all," he said as he began to remove his shirt.

"What about that trip to the Chef's Garden in Huron tonight?" Pierre asked.

"I almost forgot about that," he replied. "I'll be able to make it there and back before the end of the day. I guess it will be my last official act as the chef here."

"Did you at least put out Mr. Strong's lights?" Pierre asked.

"I cleaned his clock, and you know what, Pierre? I'd do it again in a New York minute!"

"That's my boy," Pierre said under his breath as he turned around and smiled before leaving the room.

Chapter 32

Elyse was still outside watching the sunset when Uncle Joe came back from the store. "Let me come down and help you with that load," she shouted to him.

"Much obliged, my dear," he replied.

She climbed down the ladder and grabbed one of the grocery bags Uncle Joe held before the two of them headed back up the ladder to the deck of the ship.

"Here are some of your clothes, Elyse. I hope these things go together; I'm no fashionista."

"Did you run into anyone while you were out?" she asked on a hunch.

"Yes, I did, in fact. Jack met me outside the grocery store and asked if you were on the island."

"You didn't tell him that I was here, did you?"

"No, I kept my word. But he wanted me to give you a message. He said that he wanted you to remember what he told you the night before you left for New York City. He also said that he was leaving tonight."

"Leaving?" Elyse said as her thoughts instantly flashed back to their last intimate interlude together. "Did he happen to say where he was going?"

"No, but if you want my opinion, that boy looked like a piece of road kill. He's in love with you, Elyse, and this whole thing is just eatin' him alive."

"I don't know if I can face him again, Uncle Joe. How can I trust him after what he did?"

"Couldn't you at least give the guy a chance? I mean, if he looks that torn apart on the outside, his heart must be mush."

"Okay, I'll see him one more time before he leaves. Let's see what you brought home in that bag of yours. I'll get dressed and go over to the restaurant before he leaves."

"You really should leave on the outfit that you're wearing now."

"But this is your shirt, Uncle Joe!"

"How come it never looks that good on me?"

Elyse quickly changed, and was off and running. "Here's a kiss for good luck," Uncle Joe said as he gave his niece a quick kiss on the check before she went over the side of the ship and down the ladder. "Oh, and here's the keys to the truck," he added as he threw them down to her.

"I love you, Uncle Joe," Elyse shouted up to him on the bow.

"That goes double for me! Now go get him, Little Bit."

*   *

Elyse didn't know that Jack was already on his way to the lighthouse when she left for the restaurant. Noticing a storm brewing from the northeast and that the lake was already forming white caps, he knew that he only had a short window of opportunity before he left for Huron, but he just had to see Elyse.

He rolled up his window as the sky darkened and the raindrops fell and turned on the radio to get the local weather report:

"A small craft advisory has been issued for the rest of the evening. Waves on the lake could reach eight to ten feet. This could be a potentially dangerous storm with torrential downpours and damaging winds. Keep tuned to this channel for further updates."

After the report was over, Diane Warren's song *Show Me the Way Back to Your Heart*, as sung by Brian McKnight, started to play on the radio. Jack turned up the volume since the words fit so perfectly with what he was feeling inside.

When Jack pulled up to the lighthouse, he thought he saw someone watching him from the attic window. When he got out of the car and looked up, though, the figure had vanished. The rain was coming down more heavily now, and Jack hadn't brought a jacket or umbrella. If it was Elyse he had seen in the window, then maybe he could plead with her to give him another chance. He didn't care how it looked, he was going to get down on his knees and beg for her forgiveness.

"Elyse," he shouted through the pouring rain, "if you're here, please listen to me. I never meant to hurt you. Roger lied to me, too. He didn't tell me about you until much later. He had already paid my father's medical bills, and I had no choice. But if I had to do it over again, I wouldn't have agreed to it. I would have found another way. Look at me, Elyse: I'm on my knees. Please forgive me for what I've done; I love you with all of my heart!"

Now Jack was soaking wet, and when he stood up, he definitely saw a shadowy figure move away from the attic window.

"Okay, I deserve this treatment," he continued. "If you don't believe me now, maybe you will tomorrow, or the next day, or the day after that. I don't care how long it takes, but I'm going to *make* you believe me. All I know is that I can't live without you. You breathe life into my soul, and I can't go on if you're not by my side."

Jack stood there waiting for a reply, but none came. He knew there was little time left before his flight, so he decided to add one more thing: "I'll be back, Elyse, you can count on it. I know you can't stay angry with me forever. I'll *never* give up on our love!"

Then he got back into his car, devastated and drenched, as Jacob secretly watched the car meander down the driveway until it was out of sight.

Chapter 33

Elyse had a premonition that she should go to the lighthouse before heading out to the restaurant. She was hoping that Jack might stop there before he left, so she hurriedly drove up to the house, parked the truck, and unlocked the door of the sunporch. Once inside, she began to shake the rain off her clothes when Rainy began circling her feet.

"Hi, Rainy," she said as she bent down to pet her cat. "It looks like Uncle Joe has added a few pounds to your waistline. I missed you, too."

Elyse went over to her answering machine and saw three messages. The first one was from Rachel, the message she had missed that fateful day. The second one was also from her friend:

"Hey, Elyse, it's just me. You left in a hurry, so I hope everything is okay. Thanks for the note. I was feeling kinda guilty. Please take care of yourself, and call me as soon as you can."

The next message was from Socrates:

"Please call me as soon as you receive this message. It's vitally important! Marcella and I understand your need to straighten things out. Good luck!"

Elyse was getting ready to pick up the receiver and call Socrates when Rainy suddenly darted out of the room as the temperature indoors plummeted.

"Jacob?" she called out as she stood up.

"He was here," the familiar deep voice resounded as Jacob's form materialized before her.

"How long ago?"

"I cannot judge time the same way you can, but I believe it was not too long ago."

"Did he see you?"

"No, he did not," Jacob replied as he walked closer to Elyse. "I will swear by this though: he is as much in love with you as I was with your grandmother."

"How do you know that?"

"My God, woman, he was outside on his knees begging for your forgiveness," Jacob bellowed back.

"In this weather?"

"He looked like a drowned rat," Jacob continued. "*Is* he?"

"I'm not sure," Elyse replied.

"He said that he was sorry for his actions. Were these actions unforgivable?"

"Perhaps, but he hasn't given me a good reason why I should dismiss them."

"Have you tried listening?"

"I haven't been able to reach him!"

"Then you must try harder," Jacob added. "There is an old Chinese saying that goes, *'If you do not change the way you are going, you will most likely end up there.'*"

"Do you have some kind of 'magical' compass I can use to point me in the right direction?" she asked him sarcastically.

"It is not a compass that you need. Use your intuition. When I was alive, I was neither a white knight nor a dark devil. Can you truly say you are one or the other? If the truth be told, you are neither, but part of each one is within you. In the future, you will save yourself a lot of sorrow if you realize now that love is a never-ending act of forgiveness."

Elyse thought long and hard about what Jacob said before answering, "I haven't been a saint myself."

Jacob raised his eyebrows in mock surprise. "So, then you are *not* perfect?" he teased.

"No, Jacob, I've made mistakes too."

"No two artists paint the same picture. If you choose to use a darker brush, then that is what you shall see. The choice is yours. Ask yourself what you choose to see, and that will be your reality."

Then the ghost vanished just as quickly as he had appeared. Elyse knew what she had to do next: call the restaurant to see if Jack had left the island yet. "Pierre?" she began. "Hi, it's Elyse. Jack ran into my uncle earlier today and told him he was leaving tonight. Is he still there?"

"Mademoiselle Elyse, he *so* wanted to speak to you before his departure," Pierre responded. "Apparently you were not at home when he called on you. I am sorry, but his flight was scheduled to leave fifteen minutes ago."

Elyse felt her heart sink to her stomach. "Do you know when he'll return?" she asked.

"He intends to return around midnight," Pierre answered.

"Would you mind if I waited for him at the restaurant?" Elyse asked.

"Why of course not," Pierre exclaimed. "I know he needs to speak to you about something important."

"Okay, then," Elyse said, "I'll see you in about an hour."

"Good," Pierre replied, "I will have Jean-Louis pick you up at the dock, island-side."

"*Merci beaucoup*, Pierre."

"*Je vous en prie, Mademoiselle*."

The call to Socrates was next on her list. *What news could he possibly have that is so earth shattering*? Socrates never used words like "vitally important" unless he meant them. After all, he was an attorney, and words were his weapon.

"Socrates, it's Elyse. Did you get my note?"

"Yes, I did, and that was some disappearing act you performed today. I left my cell phone at the office in my rush to find you. My first instinct was to check for you back at my apartment, and when you weren't there, I went directly over to Rachel's to find that you had already left. But that's not the only reason why I called, Elyse. Something happened after you walked out today that I think you should know about."

"And what's that?" she asked.

"Jacques LeClare stood up to Roger Strong and broke all ties with him. He even broke his nose! He belted him so hard that Jeannette told me it took twenty minutes to revive him. I've never seen a man defend someone so valiantly. Jacques told Roger that he only took his money in order to pay his father's medical bills. That man's career is over now, Elyse. He defended your honor, and I believe that he is deeply in love with you."

"Wow," was all she could say, "I guess I missed all the fireworks!"

"If Jacques has to change careers, he'd make a hell of a middle weight," Socrates laughed.

"I wish I would have known all this earlier, Socrates. Jack has gone to the mainland on business, and I won't be able to see him until later."

"Don't let this one go, Elyse."

"Is that the trusted counsel or my friend talking here?"

"Friend."

"Thanks, Socrates."

"Any time."

After hanging up the telephone, she decided to gather her rain slicker and umbrella since the weather outside was getting worse by the minute. The rain was coming down in buckets, and the white caps outside her door were the size of ocean waves. This didn't bode well for Jack. He was traveling in a small plane, and the winds were not letting up.

The lights started to flicker in the room, so Elyse went into the kitchen to look for a flashlight when the lighthouse went completely dark. Rainy screeched and ran for cover as she finally found one. Her heart was starting to pound faster now as she thought, *What if I don't ever get the chance to talk to Jack again?* Would those searing words that she'd spoken to him back in New York be the last ones he would ever hear from her?

She turned around and screamed as Jacob suddenly materialized before her.

"Jacob, don't *ever* do that to me again!"

"I remember, Elyse. I remember it all."

"You know what happened the night you died?" she asked in astonishment.

"Yes. The storm raging outside right now is the twin of the one that took my life. Come," he told her as she followed him out to the sunporch.

The glare of the lightning caused Elyse to shield her eyes a few times as she held the lit flashlight in front of her as a guide.

"We were halfway out on the lake when it happened," Jacob began as he stopped and pointed out to the water. "I made sure that we sailed past the lighthouse so I might catch a glimpse of Elyse one more time, but the storm was too fierce. Once I believed I heard her calling out my name, but it must have been the gale-force wind echoing in my ears. The lightning struck the main mast, and the sail caught fire. I told my crew to abandon ship as I tried to put out another fire on deck with a pail of water. But it was too late to save her; *The Rose* was damaged beyond repair, and most of the crew had gone overboard. My first mate begged me to follow him off the vessel, but I was too proud. I did not want to lose the only thing I had left in this world. After he left, another bolt of lightning hit the mast and split it in two. When the mast fell, it hit me in the head and rendered me unconscious. Not long after that, the ship went down."

"That must have been a horrible way to die," Elyse said.

"As I said when we first met, I do not remember being in any pain at all. I believe my spirit was lifted from my body before I drowned."

"You *were* right about one thing, Jacob. An entry in Grandmother's journal mentions that she had called out to you that night. Perhaps you really did hear her voice. At least I'd like to believe that you did."

"That is not all I remember, either. I now know what happened concerning the fight with Joseph." Elyse waited for his recollection with great anticipation as Jacob began:

"I had secretly met with Elyse two months before that night. One of my crew was able to get a message to her, asking that she meet me on the mainland where we were stocking up on supplies for the long journey home. That is when it happened. She surrendered herself to me that night, and it was glorious. I had never felt closer to anyone, but we both knew that we would have to wait before we could be together forever.

"Two months later, I returned to the island for the last time. When I had that fight with Joseph, he revealed that he had found the portrait his daughter had painted of me, along with the numerous letters I had written to her from abroad. He admitted to slashing the portrait in front of Elyse and forbidding her from seeing me ever again. He also threatened me. Of course, I refused to obey his wishes. Your grandmother was old enough to make her own decisions, and that is what he feared most of all. If he had not taken ill that day, I believe Elyse would have left with me the following morning as we had planned.

"Patrick came to see me at the docks before I left that night. I had not planned to leave after the fight, but when he told me that Joseph was on the mend, I saw no earthly reason why I should stay. Still, he begged me to stay and speak to Elyse. He called me an arrogant fool and remarked that he wished Elyse would look at him with half as much love as she looked at me. But I would not listen due to my pride. I told him that he should be happy because the path was now open for him. He called me a coward for wanting to leave so quickly and told me that I was making a mistake.

"I told him that I never made mistakes, only bad choices, which I eventually learned to live with. He could not believe I would give up Elyse so easily. I said that I could not love her more than I did, yet I could also not prove it more than I already had. That is when I gave him the poem for Elyse that you found hidden in the lighthouse tower. I then bid him farewell and wished for his God to be with him. The last thing he told me was that he thought I needed his God more than he did."

"I'm sorry, Jacob," Elyse said apologetically.

"Why should you be sorry? I lived a full life. I did more than most people do in a lifetime. My time was short, but it was *remarkable*. My life would have been fuller if I had lived longer and spent more time with Elyse, but at least I was allowed the privilege of knowing her at all. The fact that we recognized the depth of our love early on was a blessing in disguise, for who knew how little time we would have together. Now I can see there is no distance on this earth as far away as yesterday."

Elyse could feel her eyes welling up with tears as Jacob reached his hand over to her face, as if to wipe away the first teardrop that fell on her cheek. "Do not make the same mistake I did," he advised. "If you love that man, you must tell him. Your pride should not overtake you. When all is said and done, in the end, the only thing that ever matters is love."

"Will I ever see you again?"

"People meet and part; and they have sorrow and joy, just like the moon that wanes and waxes. Some may say that I sowed the wind and then reaped the whirlwind. Perhaps I got what I deserved. I only hope that you will not think of me as someone who sinned, but rather as one who was saved. I am thankful for the help you gave me, but I can no longer stay on this earth. I was a part of your life for a little while, but you will be part of my heart forever."

Jacob stood directly in front of Elyse as he kissed the end of the fingertips of his one hand before tracing an arch on her forehead. Then he touched his heart again with the same hand.

"Forever in my heart," he said to Elyse with tears in his eyes.

"Forever in my heart," she repeated before he smiled, turned around, and walked toward the door. Then he abruptly stopped and turned his head to one side as if he had seen someone he recognized.

"I see them both now: my Elyse and Patrick. She is motioning for me to follow her. She looks the same as when I last saw her. Patrick is also young and smiling, and they have both forgiven me. I can feel their love, and it is lighting my way. It is done, and now I understand it all. My voyage is complete," Jacob said as he continued to walk through the doorway and into eternity.

After he left, the lights turned on again. There seemed to be a lull in the storm at this point. Elyse knew she had to hurry if she wanted to meet Jean-Louis at the dock. She wiped a tear from her eye as she accidentally left the door to the sunporch unlocked behind her.

Before leaving, she looked up into the star-kissed sky and said, "I'll never forget you, Jacob Flannery," before getting into the truck and driving away.

Somewhere, someplace, Jacob must be smiling down on me, she thought.

Chapter 34

The storm subsided, but Uncle Joe had always told Elyse that a storm has three waves. One violent episode had passed, so Elyse knew that two more would follow. When she pulled up to the dock, Jean-Louis was already waiting for her.

"Mademoiselle Elyse," he shouted. "Let's hurry before the storm resumes. It's a good thing we are on the bay side, because I don't think I could have driven this boat with my eyes closed."

"I appreciate your effort, Jean-Louis," she said as she stepped carefully inside the craft.

They sped off to the other side of the bay, and once they reached Middle Bass Island, Jean-Louis tied up the boat to the dock as they rushed into the restaurant before the clouds cried down on them.

"*Vite! Vite!*" Pierre said as he opened the door. "You made it just in time. Jean-Louis, don't forget to check that leak in the kitchen roof. I have put a bucket beneath it."

"I will see what I can do," he said as he smiled at Elyse before hurrying off to the kitchen.

"Have you heard from Jack?" Elyse asked.

"*Non*, I have not, Mademoiselle," Pierre replied as Fifi came up to Elyse wagging his tail.

"I'm worried about him," she said as she bent down to pet the dog.

"Perhaps we should call the airline, Mademoiselle," Pierre suggested. "Let's use the phone in the kitchen."

Pierre led Elyse to the back of the restaurant with Fifi close behind. Jean-Louis was mopping the floor as they entered the room. Just as Elyse was walking over to the telephone, all of the electricity on the island turned off. Now she knew Jack was in trouble.

"Are you okay, Mademoiselle Elyse?" Pierre called out to her in the dark.

"Yes, this is only the second time this has happened to me tonight," she exclaimed.

"Jean-Louis, are you still with us?" Pierre shouted.

"I am not *dead* yet, Pierre," Jean-Louis joked.

"Do you remember where we keep the emergency candles?" Pierre asked Jean-Louis.

"*Oui*," he replied.

"*Tres bien*," Pierre continued, "then you will be able to find some and bring them back upstairs." Elyse and Pierre sat down on the chairs encircling the kitchen's island as they waited for Jean-Louis to return.

"Pierre," Jean-Louis shouted up to his coworker, "I cannot find the candles!"

"Jean-Louis," Pierre responded as he stood up, "do not use the words 'cannot,' 'will not,' or 'never' in front of me. Your grandfather was in the French Resistance; surely you can find a few candles down there."

"I will keep looking then," Jean-Louis replied.

"Oh, I almost forgot," Elyse said, "I brought a flashlight just in case the storm gets rough again."

"Never mind, Jean-Louis," Pierre shouted down to his protégé. "It seems Mademoiselle has thought to bring a flashlight with her."

Jean-Louis trudged up the stairs carrying a bottle of wine. "I thought this would help pass the time…"

"What an excellent idea," Pierre chimed in as he took out three wine goblets and poured a glass for each of them.

"To Monsieur Jacques," he said as he held up his goblet.

Elyse and Jean-Louis followed suit, and they toasted the only person who was missing from all of their hearts.

"Do you think he's okay?" Elyse asked Pierre with concern.

"You cannot believe otherwise," Pierre warned. "To think of the alternative is unbearable for us all."

"I know what he wanted to tell me," Elyse told him.

"Then you must also know that he never meant to hurt you, Mademoiselle."

"There are too many broken hearts in the world," she said to Pierre. "Several people I love and trust have advised me to forgive Jack if I truly love him."

"And *do* you?" he asked.

"More than you know," she answered.

"The feeling is mutual for him, Mademoiselle," Pierre began. "Believe me, I saw the condition he was in after he arrived home from New York. He was heartbroken and wanted more than anything to apologize for his actions in person. That is why he took the time to go to the lighthouse before he left."

"I wish I would have been there," Elyse proclaimed.

"Me, too," he responded sadly.

"Do you have a battery-operated radio?" she asked.

"*Oui*, Monsieur Jacques keeps one in his quarters," Jean-Louis chimed in. "Would you like me to get it for you?"

"Yes," she answered, "maybe we can get a handle on when this storm will end." Elyse then handed Jean-Louis the flashlight before he hurried up the stairs to Jack's apartment.

When he returned, Pierre took the radio from Jean-Louis and tuned the radio's dial to the weather station:

"The storm seems to be waning in intensity. Winds have blown the storm off course, but have done extensive

damage on shore. The Coast Guard has informed us that there is a small plane down in the waters by Put-in-Bay. They are presently searching for survivors."

"*Ce n'est pas vrai*," Pierre exclaimed.

"I'm afraid it *is* true," Elyse responded. "I just pray it wasn't Jack's plane!"

"What will we do now?" Jean-Louis asked.

"We must go to the airport," Pierre replied. "They are the only ones who can tell us if Monsieur Jacques was on that plane or not. Jean-Louis, get the boat ready. Mademoiselle Elyse, I will stay behind and man the station in case I hear from him. If I do, I will leave word at the airport."

"You would have made a good general, Pierre," Elyse remarked to her friend. "Let's go," she said as she grabbed Jean-Louis' hand. Pierre and Fifi stood watch at the open door of the restaurant as they ran outside.

"*Bonne chance*," Pierre shouted to them as he picked up his dog. "Fifi, I'm afraid they will need all the luck in the world this night. Let us pray for everyone's safe return."

Elyse waved good-bye to Pierre as Jean-Louis untied the boat and jumped in and started the engine. Before Elyse knew it, they were speeding across the bay as the lights on Middle Bass Island reawakened, as did the lights on Put-in-Bay.

Chapter 35

When Elyse and Jean-Louis reached South Bass Island's shore, Elyse gave him a quick kiss on the cheek and said, "Thanks for being such a good friend to Jack *and* me."

"As usual, the pleasure was all mine," Jean-Louis said as he helped her out of the boat.

"When I find out where he is, I'll give you and Pierre a call," Elyse promised.

"Are you sure you want to go alone?" Jean-Louis asked with concern.

"Yes, this is something I must do myself." Then Elyse got into the truck and drove away as Jean-Louis waved good-bye.

Trees were down on the island roads everywhere. The storm had definitely left its mark. It seemed like hours before Elyse reached the airport and got out of the truck.

"Can you tell me if Jacques LeClare was on the plane that's missing?" Elyse anxiously asked the man behind the desk.

"Oh, you mean that chef?" the man replied.

"Yes, that's him."

"He was supposed to be on that plane, but for some reason he let another man take his place."

"You mean he never left?" she asked in surprise.

"No, he stayed here during the first blackout, but then he must have changed his mind because he said he'd prefer to wait out the storm at another location," the man added. "I'm sorry, lady, but I don't have an address or anything to give you. "

"Never mind, I *know* the address," Elyse said as she rushed out to the truck.

If Elyse's instincts were correct, she knew exactly where Jack had gone to wait out the storm. When she made it back to the driveway leading up to the lighthouse, she abandoned her truck due to a fallen tree that was blocking her path.

Her heart was pounding faster and faster as she ran toward the lighthouse. When she saw it, her face lit up like the lost light once housed in its tower. There were a dozen luminarias containing lit votive candles on either side of the steps leading up to the sunporch. The full moon illuminated the sky, which cast a romantic glow on the entire scene.

Elyse walked up the steps of the sunporch and opened the door. A table had been set for two with a bottle of champagne in a wine cooler and a crystal vase containing irises. Lit candles were everywhere, and the CD Jack had bought her was playing Jim Brickman's beautiful love song *Your Love* in the background.

Elyse was overcome with emotion, and her eyes filled with tears. Then she saw him. He was standing several feet in front of her, begging her to take him back with his eyes. She could stand it no longer and ran into his outstretched arms; they kissed each other as if they'd been separated for years.

"I thought you were dead," she cried.

"What are you talking about?" he asked.

"Your plane, the one you were supposed to be on tonight—it crashed."

"You've got to be kidding!"

"Don't *ever* do that to me again, Jacques LeClare."

"I would never hurt you on purpose, Elyse. When you left me back in the city, the music stopped playing for me. *You* are the one who keeps it playing," Jack said as he looked deeply into her eyes.

"I know everything, Jack. You can fill me in on all the details later. I'm just glad that you're alive!"

"There is only one more thing I need to do," he said to her as he pulled a ring box out of his pocket and got down on bended knee.

Elyse watched him as he removed its contents, his mother's wedding ring. He looked up at Elyse as he held the ring in his hand. "*A ma vie de coeur entier*," he recited to her with tears in his eyes.

"You *never* had to ask, Jacques LeClare," she said as he stood up and placed the ring on the third finger of her left hand before taking her in his arms again.

Now that their love had totally transformed them that magical night, Elyse swore she could hear Jacob's voice in the shadows softly saying:

"*Always remember, let love light your way…*"

Epilogue

Elyse Montgomery married Jack LeClare, and The Ohio State University made them both the new caretakers of the South Bass Island lighthouse and the surrounding property. Elyse quit her job at *Personality* magazine and wrote a best-selling novel about Jacob and her grandmother, entitled *Lost Light*. Six months after their wedding, Elyse announced to Jack that they would be the proud parents of twin boys, whom they decided to name Jacob and Patrick.

Jacques LeClare won the James Beard award for the "Rising Star Chef of the Year" and got his own show on the Food Network with **Jean-Louis** as his sidekick and **Pierre** as his talent agent.

Jean-Louis posed nude for the Vitamix® blender campaign and got rave reviews.

Uncle Joe married **Louise**, and they spend most of their free time fishing and hosting weekly poker parties for their friends.

Rachel dated *Personality* magazine's "Sexiest Guy of the Year."

Socrates entered the field of politics with his loyal wife, **Marcella**, at his side.

Roger Strong's wife dumped him for a much younger man—and left him absolutely nothing.

Elyse memorialized **Jacob Flannery** with a boulder, or cairn, that she placed on the lighthouse grounds facing the lake. She also planted rose bushes on the property in memory of her grandmother. Jacob's portrait was restored and donated to the island's museum.

Fifi got his own website and became the mascot on Jacques' show.

Rainy became the proud mother of three kittens named Porcini, Portobello (Bella), and Button.

And everything is as it was always meant to be!

Acknowledgments

I would like to thank my loving husband, Steve, and daughter, Heather, for believing in me enough to let me pursue my dream. I would also like to thank my parents, Peggy and Ken, for instilling in me the belief that I can do whatever I set out to accomplish. You are all *"forever in my heart"*.

A million thanks to North Coast Litho in Cleveland, OH for the printing of this novel.

Then there is my friend, Priscilla, for taking time out of her hectic schedule to edit the first draft of my book. I also could not have done this without my editor, Jill Welsh, whose expertise was essential to the completion of this project.

A big "thank you" to Nancy Cruickshank with The Ohio State University's Ohio Sea Grant Program for research materials, and the artist Donna Elias who gave me permission to use her beautiful watercolor print of the lighthouse as my cover art.

Thanks also go to Uncle Earl for introducing me to Put-in-Bay in the first place, as well as Debbie Kennedy for designing the book's cover.

You have *all* been instrumental in helping me get this story to print, and I will be eternally grateful!

About the Author

J. M. Halis lives in a suburb of Cleveland, Ohio with her husband, daughter, and Beagle/Jack mixed-breed dog named Siena Bella. She works in the medical field, but her true love has always been creative writing. Put-in-Bay has been her "summer island" from the time she was ten years old, and this book is her love letter to the island. *Lost Light* is her first novel.

THE ORIGINS OF THE ISLAMIC STATE

BEING A TRANSLATION FROM THE ARABIC
ACCOMPANIED WITH ANNOTATIONS
GEOGRAPHIC AND HISTORIC NOTES OF THE

KITÂB FUTÛḤ AL–BULDÂN

OF

al-Imâm abu-l 'Abbâs Aḥmad **ibn-Jâbir al-Balâdhuri**

BY

PHILIP KHÛRI HITTI, PH.D.
On the permanent staff of the Syrian Protestant College, Beirût, Syria
Gustav Gottheil Lecturer in Columbia University

Beirut
KHAYATS
1966

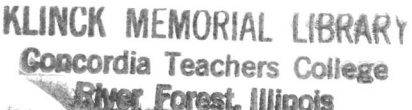

KHAYATS Oriental Reprint No. 11
Reprinted from the original edition of 1916
by Permission of Columbia University Press

Published by KHAYATS
90-94 Rue Bliss, Beirut, Lebanon

To

My Teacher, Friend and Colleague,

PROFESSOR RICHARD J. H. GOTTHEIL, Ph.D.

of Columbia University

FOREWORD

Interest in the Nearer East has increased our desire to know as accurately as is possible the beginnings of the faith and of the various states that have played so important a part in its history. The Arabs themselves have had, from the earliest times, a keen sense for historical tradition and an equally keen desire to preserve that tradition in writing. There is, perhaps, no people of earlier times that has left us so large an amount of documentary evidence as to its beginnings as they have. The evidence, of course, needs sifting and sorting according to the canons of criticism we have learned to employ in all such cases. But, this work cannot be done by Oriental scholars alone, whose time is often taken up largely with the philological and literary examination of the texts that have come down to us. It is, therefore, eminently a part of their duty to render these texts accessible to students of history who are not masters of the Arabic language.

Dr. Ḥitti has undertaken this task in connection with the record of one of the earliest Arab historians whose work has been preserved. Since its publication in 1866 by Professor de Goeje, al-Balâdhuri's "Futûḥ al-Buldân" has been recognized as one of our chief authorities for the period during which the Arab state was in process of formation. This task of translating has not been a simple one: proof is that the attempt has not been made before this. The style of al-Balâdhuri is often cryptic and unintelligible. This is perhaps due to the fact that the work, as it has reached us, is a shortened edition of a much larger one which, though existent up to the seventeenth century, has not been found in any of the collections of manuscripts to which we have access. In its present form, the work mentions often men and matters that probably were treated of in the longer recension, but of which now we know nothing. Dr. Ḥitti's translation is, therefore, in a certain sense also, a commentary and an exposition. As such, I trust that it will be found useful to Orientalists as well as to students of history. His fine sense for the niceties of Arabic expression has often enabled him to get through a thicket that is impenetrable to us Westerners.

RICHARD GOTTHEIL.

COLUMBIA UNIVERSITY, JANUARY, 1916.

CONTENTS

PAGE

FOREWORD ....

INTRODUCTION
Arabic Historiography with Special Reference to al-Balâdhuri. 1

PART I—ARABIA

CHAPTER I
Al-Madînah 15

CHAPTER II
The Possessions of the banu-an-Naḍîr 34

CHAPTER III
The Possessions of the banu-Ḳuraiẓah 40

CHAPTER IV
Khaibar 42

CHAPTER V
Fadak 50

CHAPTER VI
Wâdi-l-Ḳura and Taimâ' 57

CHAPTER VII
Makkah 60

CHAPTER VIII
The Wells of Makkah 77

CHAPTER IX
The Floods in Makkah 82

CHAPTER X
Aṭ-Ṭâ'if 85

CHAPTER XI
Tabâlah and Jurash 91

CHAPTER XII
Tabûk, Ailah, Adhruḥ, Maḳna and al-Jarbâ' 92

CHAPTER XIII
Dûmat al-Jandal 95

PAGE

CHAPTER XIV
The Capitulation of Najrân 98

CHAPTER XV
Al-Yaman 106

CHAPTER XVI
'Umân 116

CHAPTER XVII
Al-Baḥrain 120

CHAPTER XVIII
Al-Yamâmah 132

CHAPTER XIX
The Apostasy of the Arabs in the Caliphate of abu-Bakr aṣ-Ṣiddîḳ 143

CHAPTER XX
The Apostasy of the banu-Walî'ah and al-Ash'ath ibn-Ḳais ibn-Ma'dikarib ibn-Mu'âwiyah-l-Kindi 153

CHAPTER XXI
Al-Aswad al-'Ansi and those in al-Yaman who Apostatized with him 159

PART II—SYRIA

CHAPTER I
The Conquest of Syria 165

CHAPTER II
The Advance of Khâlid ibn-al-Walîd on Syria and the Places he Reduced on his Way 169

CHAPTER III
The Conquest of Buṣra 173

CHAPTER IV
The Battle of Ajnâdîn (or Ajnâdain) 174

CHAPTER V
The Battle of Fiḥl in the Province of the Jordan 176

CHAPTER VI
The Province of the Jordan 178

CHAPTER VII
The Battle of Marj aṣ-Ṣuffar 182

CHAPTER VIII
The Conquest of Damascus and its Province 186

CHAPTER IX
Ḥimṣ 200

PAGE

CHAPTER X
The Battle of al-Yarmûk 207

CHAPTER XI
Palestine 213

CHAPTER XII
The Province of Ḳinnasrîn and the Cities called al-'Awâṣim 223

CHAPTER XIII
Cyprus 235

CHAPTER XIV
The Samaritans 244

CHAPTER XV
Al-Jarâjimah 246

CHAPTER XVI
The Frontier Fortresses of Syria 253

PART III—MESOPOTAMIA

CHAPTER I
The Conquest of Mesopotamia [al-Jazîrah] 269

CHAPTER II
The Christians of the banu-Taghlib ibn-Wâ'il 284

CHAPTER III
The Fortifications of the Mesopotamian Frontier 287

CHAPTER IV
Arabic made the Language of the State Registers 301

PART IV—ARMENIA

CHAPTER I
The Conquest of Armenia 305

PART V—NORTHERN AFRICA

CHAPTER I
The Conquest of Egypt and al-Maghrib [Mauritania] 335

CHAPTER II
The Conquest of Alexandria 346

CHAPTER III
The Conquest of Barḳah and Zawîlah 352

CHAPTER IV
The Conquest of Tripoli 355

PAGE

CHAPTER V
The Conquest of Ifriḳiyah ... 356

CHAPTER VI
The Conquest of Ṭanjah [Tangiers] ... 362

PART VI—ANDALUSIA

CHAPTER I
The Conquest of Andalusia ... 365

PART VII—ISLANDS IN THE SEA

CHAPTER I
The Conquest of Certain Islands in the Sea ... 375

PART VIII—NUBIA

CHAPTER I
Terms made with Nubia ... 379

CHAPTER II
The Ḳarâṭîs ... 383

PART IX—AL-'IRÂḲ AND PERSIA

CHAPTER I
The Conquest of as-Sawâd ... 387
The Caliphate of abu-Bakr aṣ-Ṣiddiḳ.

CHAPTER II
The Caliphate of 'Umar ibn-al-Khaṭṭâb ... 401

CHAPTER III
The Battle of Ḳuss an-Nâṭif, or the Battle of al-Jisr ... 403

CHAPTER IV
The Battle of Mihrân or an-Nukhailah ... 405

CHAPTER V
The Battle of al-Ḳâdisîyah ... 409

CHAPTER VI
The Conquest of al-Madâ'in ... 417

CHAPTER VII
The Battle of Jalûlâ' ... 420

CHAPTER VIII
The Founding of al-Kûfah ... 434

PAGE

CHAPTER IX
Wâsiṭ al-'Irâḳ ... 449

CHAPTER X
Al-Baṭâ'iḥ ... 453

CHAPTER XI
Madînat as-Salâm ... 457

CHAPTER XII
Arabic made the Language of the Register ... 465

PART X—MEDIA [AL-JIBÂL]

CHAPTER I
Ḥulwân ... 469

CHAPTER II
The Conquest of Nihâwand ... 471

CHAPTER III
Ad-Dînawar, Mâsabadhân and Mihrijânḳadhaf ... 478

CHAPTER IV
The Conquest of Hamadhân ... 481

CHAPTER V
Ḳumm, Ḳâshân and Iṣbahân ... 485

CHAPTER VI
The Death of Yazdajird ibn-Shahriyâr ibn-Kisra ibn-Abarwîz ibn-Hurmuz ibn-Anûshirwân ... 490

INDEX ... 495

ERRATA ... 517

INTRODUCTION

Arabic Historiography with Special Reference to al-Balâdhuri

Although rudimentary elements of historiography can be traced back to the description of the " days ", *i. e.,* the battles between the tribes, and such stories as the " Ma'rib dam ", " the owners of the elephant " and the digging of the " Zamzam well "—all of pre-Islamic antiquity—, yet Arabic historical writing, in the strict sense of the term, is a branch of Islamic literature. Interest in Muḥammad necessitated the compilation of traditions (Ar. *ḥadîth*) relating to the life and campaigns of the Prophet and his companions. The communistic theocracy of warriors under the early caliphs, and particularly 'Umar's system of assigning state pensions to Moslems according to their kinship to the Prophet, gave impetus to the study of genealogy in which even pagan Arabs, who attached special importance to descent, were interested. The elucidation of passages in poetry, one of the earliest and most fully-developed modes of expression among the Arabs, and the necessity of determining persons and places referred to in their religious literature made philologists apply themselves to historical research. The three sources of Arabian history therefore are: (1) pre-Islamic stories, (2) traditions relative to the life and campaigns of the Prophet and the companions, and (3) genealogical lists and poetical compositions. The earliest books of history are: biography (*sîrah*), books of campaigns (*maghâzi*), and books of genealogy and classes (*ansâb wa-ṭabaḳât*).

The domains of theology, law and history in their early rise overlap and are not sharply defined from one another.

No student of Arabic literature fails to be impressed with the fact that the bearers of the torch of learning among the Arabs were in most cases of foreign and particularly of Persian stock. This is to be explained by the fact that public opinion considered it contemptible for the Arab to busy himself with the pursuit of knowledge to the neglect of the noble art of warring. To this general tendency, however, studying anecdotes, transmitting traditions, and remembering stories—especially if they commemorated the deeds of heroes, orators and poets, formed a conspicuous example. We read in al-Mas'ûdi [1] that Mu'âwiyah the founder of the Umaiyad dynasty "devoted one-third of the night to the reading of the news and battles of the Arabs and non-Arabs." We also read in *al-Bayân* [2] that al-Manṣûr the Abbasid caliph after long hesitation decided to put abu-Muslim al-Khurâsâni to death as a result of hearing an anecdote about Sapor the Persian king. One of the favorite sayings in early Islam was the following found in *al-'Iḳd al-Farîd* [3]: "For kings the study of genealogy and histories, for warriors the study of battles and biography, and for merchants the study of writing and arithmetic."

The chief source from which history writing flowed was tradition (*ḥadîth*). It was a pious custom that when Moslems met, one should ask for news (*ḥadîth*), and the other should relate a saying or anecdote of Muhammad. Each event is related in words of eyewitnesses or contemporaries and transmitted to the final narrator through a chain of intermediate reporters. The authenticity of the reported fact

[1] Vol. v, p. 77, Paris, 1869.

[2] al-Jâḥiz, vol. ii, pp. 154-155, Cairo, 1313 A. H.

[3] Vol. i, p. 198, Cairo, 1293 A. H.

depends on (1) the continuity of the chain and (2) the confidence in each reporter. Thus would al-Balâdhuri start his narrative regarding the campaign of the Prophet against Najrân:[1] "Bakr ibn-al-Haitham related to me, that 'Abdallâh ibn-Ṣâliḥ related to him, on the authority of al-Laith ibn-Sa'd, on the authority of Yûnus ibn-Ziyâd al-Aili, on the authority of az-Zuhri, who said.

This form of historic composition is unique in the case of the Arabs and meets the most essential requirements of modern historiography, namely, "back to the source" and "trace the line of authorities." The system, however, has its drawbacks in that it crystallized the record of events and rendered deviation from the trodden path sacrilegious. Aside from the use of judgment in the choice of *isnâd*—the series of authorities—the Arabian authors exercised very little power of analysis, criticism, comparison or inference, their golden rule being "what has been once well said need not be told again." Aṭ-Ṭabari, in the introduction to his great work, gives expression to that principle, where, conscious of the exception that many of his readers might take to some of his reports, he pleads,[2] "We only transmit to others what has been transmitted to us."

Another way of handling traditions is that in which the compiler combines different traditions into one continuous whole, prefixing a statement of his authorities or contenting himself by interrupting the narrative, wherever need may be, by citing the particular authority. While al-Balâdhuri is an exponent of the former type and spares no pains in basing every fact, whenever possible, on an independent *isnâd*, yet he sometimes resorts to the other method as he himself acknowledges in the first lines of his *Futûḥ* (p. 15):

[1] *Futûḥ al-Buldân*, p. 98.

[2] Vol. i, p. 7, ed. De Goeje, Leiden, 1879-1881.

"I have been informed by certain men learned in tradition, biography and the conquest of the lands whose narratives I transmitted, abridged and pieced up together into one whole," etc. Where his store of authorities fails him, al-Balâdhuri introduces his narratives by "they said," or "he said," or "it was said."

On a geographical basis, Moslem tradition may be grouped into two categories: (1) that of al-Madînah as represented by Muḥammad ibn-Isḥâḳ and al-Wâḳidi, and (2) that of al-'Irâḳ. Notwithstanding the fact that al-Balâdhuri lived in Baghdâd, the tradition of al-Madînah, which for obvious reasons is more reliable than that of al-'Irâḳ, forms the basis of his works.

History, whose domain in the time of the first four caliphs was not sharply defined, made its full appearance, and was recorded for the first time under the sway of the Umaiyads. According to *al-Fihrist,*[1] Mu'âwiyah ibn-abi-Sufyân[2] summoned from al-Yaman one, 'Âbid ibn-Sharyah, and asked him about past events, histories of the Arabs and foreign kings and "ordered that the answers be recorded." This "book of the kings and past events," however, is lost.

The early favorite forms of writing history were biography, genealogy and description of campaigns. The oldest biography is *Sîrat Rasûl Allâh* written for al-Manṣûr by ibn-Isḥâk (d. 151/767). This we do not possess in its original form but only in the recension of ibn-Hishâm (d. 213/834). Genealogy borders on biography and, calling for elucidation, both lead on to history. Genealogical books were first written in the Umaiyad period. The genealogical list served as an army roll. The study of tradition

[1] p. 89, ed. Flügel. [2] caliph 41-60/661-680.

necessitated the study of the life and character of the reporter on whom the authenticity of the report depends. Thus the reporters were classified into classes (*ṭabaḳât*). The most famous writer of *ṭabaḳât* was ibn-Sa'd (d. 230), the secretary of al-Wâḳidi and the compiler of *Kitâb aṭ-Ṭabaḳât al-Kabîr*.

Campaigns playing an important rôle in the life of Muḥammad and the early caliphs soon began to assert their claim for special attention and were treated in special books. Besides, the necessity of recording and studying the campaigns arose from the fact that in levying a tax (*kharâj*) on the conquered land, those in authority were first confronted with the task of determining whether it was taken "by peace", "by capitulation", or "by force", and what the terms in each case were. This gave rise to many books on campaigns (*maghâzi*), one of the oldest of which is al-Wâkidi's (d. 207/822). Some books were issued treating of the conquest of one city, most of which books have been lost. Given a number of books on the conquest of different cities, the next step would be to compile them into one whole. That step was taken by al-Balâdhuri—the last great historian of Moslem campaigns.

Before the Abbasid period no books on general history were attempted. In the golden age of the Abbasid caliphate and under Persian influence, historiography flourished and developed a new form of composition. The translation of such books as the Pehlevi *Khuday-Nama* by ibn-al-Muḳaffa' into the Arabic *Kitâb al-Mulûk*, coupled with the fact that the Moslem commonwealth was now richly recruited by Persian converts, made the idea of chronological collocation of events, for which the school of al-Madinah had paved the way, develop to the plan of a complete series of annals. The first to undertake such a history was aṭ-Ṭabari. Thus the historian who at the rise of Islam was a traditionist or reporter becomes now a chronicler. The annalistic method of aṭ-Ṭabari was followed by ibn-al-Athîr and abu-l-Fida.

Al-Mas'ûdi inaugurated a new system of writing history. Instead of grouping events around years as center, he grouped them around kings, dynasties and races. His system was followed among others by ibn-Khaldûn, but did not win so much favor as that of aṭ-Ṭabari.

The first record we have regarding the life of al-Balâdhuri is that of *al-Fihrist.*[1] Other sources for his life are Yâḳût, *Mu'jam al-Udabâ'*, (pp. 127-132),[2] and al-Kutubi, *Fawât al-Wafayât* (Vol. I, pp. 8-9, Bûlâḳ, 1283). Ibn-Khallikân refers to him on more than one occasion but does not give his biography.[3] From these sources we learn that Aḥmad ibn-Yaḥya ibn-Jâbir al-Balâdhuri was a native of Baghdâd descended from Persian stock. His grandfather, Jâbir, was secretary to al-Khaṣîb, minister of the finances of Egypt under the caliph ar-Rashîd. Aḥmad was an intimate friend of the caliphs al-Mutawakkil and al-Musta'în and tutored 'Abdallâh, the brilliant son of al-Mu'tazz. He distinguished himself in poetry—especially satires, tradition and genealogy. The year 279/892 saw his death, mentally deranged as a result of drinking the juice of the anacardia (*balâdhur*); hence his surname al-Balâdhuri. Besides writing *Futûḥ al-Buldân*, which is a digest of a larger work that has been lost, he wrote *Ansâb al-Ashrâf*,[4] of which only two volumes are preserved, one in the Schefer collection of the

[1] p. 113, ed. Flügel.

[2] Leiden, 1907, ed. Margoliouth.

[3] See also de Goeje's introduction to al-Balâdhuri; and Hamaker, *Specimen Catalogi*, p. 7 *seq.*

[4] *Lineage of Nobles.* See Ḥâjji Khalîfah, vol. i, pp. 455 and 274, ed. Flügel, Leipzig, 1835.

Bibliothèque Nationale,[1] and the other has been autographed by Ahlwardt.[2] Al-Mas'ûdi [3] quotes al-Balâdhuri's *ar-Radd-'ala ash-Shu'ûbîyah* (Refutation of ash-Shu'ûbîyah),[4] which book is also lost.

Of the works of al-Balâdhuri the one that claims our special attention is *Futûḥ al-Buldân*.[5] The book shares with other books of Arabic history the advantage of tracing the report back to the source. Being a synopsis of a larger work, its style is characterized by condensation whereby it gains in conciseness but loses in artistic effect and clearness. Certain passages are mutilated and ambiguous. It is free from exaggeration and the flaws of imagination. Throughout the work the sincere attempt of the author to get to the fact as it happened and to record it as it reached him is felt. The chapters on colonization, soldier's pay, land tax, coinage and the like make it especially valuable.

The book does not escape the weaknesses common to Arabian histories. The "*ipse dixit*" which was a source of strength was also a source of weakness. Once the words supposed to have been uttered by a contemporary or eye-witness are ascertained, the author feels his duty fulfilled, and his function as a historian degenerates into that of a reporter. The personal equation is not only reduced but the personality of the author is almost eliminated, appearing only as a recipient of a tradition. Scarcely an opinion or remark is made. The intellect is not brought to bear on the data.

[1] De Goeje, *ZDMG*, XXXVIII, 382-406.

[2] Greifswald, 1883. *Cf.* Nöldeke, *GGA*, 1883, p. 1096 *seq.*; Thorbecke, Lbl. Or. Phil., vol. i, pp. 155-156.

[3] Vol. iii, pp. 109-110.

[4] Goldziher, *Muhammedanische Studien*, vol. i, p. 166.

[5] ed. De Goeje, Leiden, 1866. See Nöldeke, *GGA*, 1863, 1341-1349.

A weak characteristic of Arabic historians is their utter disregard of the social side of national life. Political history to them is history *par excellence*. It should, however, be said, to the credit of al-Balâdhuri, that while from a modern standpoint he is defective in that respect, still he stands superior to other historians.

As one reads *Futûḥ al-Buldân* and is struck by the fact that a long chapter is devoted to the "digging of the wells of Makkah",[1] whereas the conquest of Tripoli, Africa, is dismissed with a few words,[2] he cannot help feeling his sense of proportion suffer. Most of the two chapters entitled "The Founding of al-Kûfah"[3] and "of al-Baṣrah"[4] are devoted to the explanation of the names given to baths, canals and castles and only a small part relates to actual colonization.

One might also add that Arabic historians were not very sensitive on the question of indecency of language. In general the language of *Futûḥ* is clean, with the exception of the case of al-Mughîrah, the governor of al-Baṣrah under 'Umar.[5]

According to Hâji Khalfa,[6] the first writers on biography and campaigns were, among others, 'Urwah ibn-az-Zubair (d. 93) and Wahb ibn-Munabbih (d. 114); and we read[7] that Muḥammad ibn-Muslim az-Zuhri wrote a book of campaigns. These works are all lost and the first biography we have is that of ibn-Hishâm (d. 213) based on ibn-Isḥâḳ (d. 151). Az-Zubair and az-Zuhri, as well as ibn-Isḥâḳ, are among the sources of al-Balâdhuri.

That in most cases the same tradition that underlies the

[1] pp. 77-82. [2] pp. 355.
[3] pp. 434-448. [4] pp. 346-372 in De Goeje's edition.
[5] pp. 344-345 in De Goeje's edition. [6] Vol. v, p. 646.
[7] In vol. v, pp. 154 and 647.

life of Muḥammad according to ibn-Hishâm is made use of by al-Balâdhuri in the first chapters of his *Futûḥ* is made evident by a comparison of the chapters on the banu-an-Naḍîr, Khaibar and Tabûk.[1] Al-Balâdhuri makes no mention of ibn-Hishâm but quotes ibn-Isḥâḳ eleven times. The *isnâd* in Balâdhuri being longer, it might be conjectured that he did not get his material at first hand from ibn-Isḥâḳ's work but through subsequent reporters. Al-Madâ'ini lived from 135-215 (753-830). He wrote a "history of the caliphs" and a book of "campaigns", both of which are lost and are known only by excerpts through al-Balâdhuri, aṭ-Ṭabari and Yâḳût. Of these, al-Balâdhuri alone has over forty citations from him.

Al-Wâḳidi (d. 207/823) wrote 28 books recorded in *al-Fihrist*,[2] only a few of which have come down to us. Having lived at Baghdâd his works were certainly accessible to al-Balâdhuri, who quotes him on 80 different occasions and more than any other source. Most of the quotations are made through ibn-Sa'd, the secretary of al-Wâḳidi, and one of al-Balâdhuri's teachers. A comparison between the campaigns against banu-an-Naḍîr [3] and banu-Ḳuraiẓah [4] in al-Balâdhuri, and the corresponding ones in al-Wâḳidi's *Kitâb al-Maghâzi*,[5] shows many points of contact but no absolute interdependence.

Ibn-Sa'd (d. 230) being the disciple of al-Wâḳidi and the professor of al-Balâdhuri acted as a connecting link between the two. In his *Futûḥ*, al-Balâdhuri has 48 citations from him, many of which were communicated by word of mouth and were recorded verbatim by al-Balâdhuri. In his book

[1] *Cf.* Hishâm, p. 652 and Balâdhuri, p. 34; Hishâm, p. 779 and Balâdhuri, p. 42.

[2] p. 99.

[3] p. 34.

[4] p. 40.

[5] pp. 353 and 371, ed. von Kremer, Calcutta, 1856.

aṭ-Ṭabakât (*the Book of Classes*), many striking similarities to the traditions of al-Balâdhuri are noticed.

Ad-Dînawari (d. 282/896) was another contemporary of al-Balâdhuri. He wrote a number of books of which only one of importance has come down to us, *i. e., al-Akhbâr aṭ-Tiwâl.*[1] Contrary to al-Balâdhuri, al-'Irâḳ tradition is the basis of his work. It is probable that neither of the two authors was familiar with the work of the other.

In addition to these, al-Balâdhuri quotes many other authorities of whom the most favorite ones are: Ḥammâd ibn-Salamah, Bakr ibn-al-Haitham, 'Âmir ash-Sha'bi, Sufyân ibn-Sa'îd ath-Thauri, 'Amr ibn-Muḥammad an-Nâḳid and Hishâm ibn-al-Kalbi, most of whose works are either unknown to us or have entirely disappeared.

The most illustrious writer on history after al-Balâdhuri was aṭ-Ṭabari (d. 310). According to *al-Fihrist* and ibn-Khallikân, he traveled in Egypt, Syria and al-'Irâk in quest of learning and died in Baghdâd. Aṭ-Ṭabari makes no mention of al-Balâdhuri.

In the introduction to his remarkable work, *Murûj adh-Dhahab*, al-Mas'ûdi (d. 346) cites scores of books from which he drew his material, and among which he mentions al-Balâdhuri's paying it a high tribute in these words, "We know of no better work on the history of the Moslem conquests".[2]

Not only did later historians draw freely from al-Balâdhuri but subsequent geographers used him extensively as a source. Ṭhe remarkable work of Yâḳût, *Mu'jam al-Buldân*, reproduces a great part of the book. Muḳaddasi quotes him,[3] and so al-Hamadhâni,[4] and al-Mas'ûdi.[5]

[1] ed. Vladimir Guirgass, Leiden, 1888.

[2] al-Mas'ûdi, p. 14, Paris, 1861.

[3] *Aḥsan at-Taḳâsîm*, 313.

[4] *Kitâb al-Buldân*, 303, 321.

[5] *Kitâb at-Tanbîh*, 358, 360.

The above-sketched attempt to view al-Balâdhuri in his historic setting warrants the conclusion that the tradition recorded by him was mostly communicated to him by word of mouth and partly through books that have mostly been lost, and that it was a source for al-Mas'ûdi and Yâḳût, and through them for many subsequent Arabic historians and geographers.

PART I

ARABIA

CHAPTER I

Al-Madînah

In the name of Allah, the compassionate, the merciful, whose help I solicit! 2

The Prophet in al-Madînah. Says Aḥmad ibn-Yaḥya ibn-Jâbir:—

I have been informed by certain men learned in tradition, biography, and the conquest of the lands, whose narratives I transmitted, abridged and pieced up together into one whole, that when the Messenger of Allah emigrated from Makkah to al-Madînah he was entertained as the guest of Kalthûm ibn-Hidm ibn-Amru'i-l-Ḳais ibn-al-Ḥarîth ibn-Zaid ibn-'Ubaid ibn-Umaiyah ibn-Zaid ibn-Mâlik ibn-'Auf ibn-'Amr ibn-'Auf ibn-Mâlik ibn-al-Aus [1] in Ḳubâ'.[2] So much, however, of his discourse was carried on in the home of Sa'd ibn-Khaithamah ibn-al-Ḥârith ibn-Mâlik of [the tribe of] banu-as-Sâlim ibn-Amru'i-l-Ḳais ibn-Mâlik ibn-al-Aus that some thought he was the guest of the latter.[3]

Ḳubâ' Mosque. Of the *Companions* of the Prophet, the early *Emigrants* together with those of the *Anṣâr* [4] who had joined him had already built a mosque at Ḳubâ' to pray in, prayer at that time being directed towards Bait-al-Maḳdis [Jerusalem]. Now, when the Prophet arrived in

[1] Ibn-Ḥajar, *Kitâb al-Iṣâbah*, vol. iii, pp. 613-614.

[2] A suburb of al-Madînah; see Yâḳût, *Mu'jam al-Buldân*, vol. iv, pp. 23-24.

[3] Ibn-Hishâm, *Sîrat Rasûl Allâh*, p .334.

[4] The Helpers—originally applied to the early converts of al-Madînah.

Ḳubâ', he led them in prayer in it. That is why the people of Ḳubâ' say that it is the one meant by Allah when he says: "There is a mosque founded from its first day in piety. More worthy that thou enter therein."[1] Others report that the "mosque founded in piety" is that of the Prophet [in al-Madînah].

Abu-'Âmir ar-Râhib. 'Affân ibn-Muslim aṣ-Ṣaffâr from 'Urwah[2] who gave the following explanation to tne text:
" There are some who have built a mosque for mischief and 3
for infidelity, and to disunite the 'Believers,' and in expectation of him who, in time past, warred against Allah and his Messenger":—The mosque of Ḳubâ' was built by Sa'd ibn-Khaithamah and its site was owned by Labbah[3] where she used to tie up her donkey. The dissenters therefore said: "Should we pray on a spot where Labbah used to tie up her donkey? Never. Rather shall we select for ourselves some other place for prayer until abu-'Âmir[4] comes and leads our service." Now, abu-'Âmir had fled from the face of Allah and his Prophet to Makkah and thence to Syria where he was converted to Christianity. Hence the text revealed by Allah: "There are some who have built a mosque for mischief and for infidelity and to disunite the 'Believers,' and in expectation of him who, in time past, warred against Allah and his Messenger"—referring to abu-'Âmir.

Rauḥ ibn-'Abd-al-Mu'min al-Maḳri from Sa'id ibn-Jubair:—Banu-'Amr ibn-'Auf erected a mosque in which the

[1] Koran, 9: 109.

[2] The series of authorities introducing a tradition have been cut short throughout the translation, only the first and last authorities being mentioned.

[3] "Lajja" in F. Wüstenfeld, *Geshichte der Stadt Medina*, p. 131.

[4] Ibn-Hishâm, pp. 561-562; and *Geschichte der Stadt Medina*, p. 53.

Prophet led them in prayer. This aroused the jealousy of their brothers banu-Ghanm ibn-'Auf who said, "If we, too, could erect a mosque and invite the Prophet to pray in is as he prayed in our friends'! Abu-'Âmir, too, may pass here on his way from Syria and lead us in prayer." Accordingly, they erected a mosque and sent an invitation to the Prophet to come and pray in it. But no sooner had the Prophet got up to start, than the following text was revealed to him: "There are some who have built a mosque for mischief and for infidelity and to disunite the 'Believers,' and in expectation of him who, in time past, warred against Allah and his Messenger," the one meant being abu-'Âmir, "never set thou foot in it. There is a mosque founded from its first day in piety. More worthy it is that thou enter therein. Therein are men who aspire to purity and Allah loveth the purified. Which of the two is best? He who hath founded his building on the fear of Allah and the desire to please him," etc., referring to the mosque of Ḳubâ'. 4

Muhammad ibn-Ḥâtim ibn-Maimûn from al-Ḥasan:—When the text, "Therein are men who aspire to purity" was revealed, the Prophet communicated with those who prayed in the mosque of Kubâ' asking about the meaning of the purity mentioned in connection with their name, and they replied, "We, Prophet of Allah, wash after voiding excrement and urine."

"*The mosque founded in piety.*" Muhammad ibn-Ḥâtim from 'Âmir:—Some of the people of Kubâ' used to wash with water the place of exit of the excrement.[1] Hence the text, "They aspire to purity."

'Amr ibn-Muhammad an-Nâkid and Ahmad ibn-Hishâm from Sahl ibn-Sa'd:—Two men in the time of the Prophet disagreed regarding the "mosque founded in piety," the one

[1] *Cf.* az-Zamakhshari, *Kashshâf*, vol. i, p. 564 (ed. Lees).

contending it was the Prophet's mosque, the other, the Ḳubâ' mosque. They finally came and asked the Prophet to which he replied, "It is this mosque of mine." [1]

'Amr ibn-Muḥammad from ibn-'Umar:—The "mosque founded in piety" is the mosque of the Prophet.

Muḥammad ibn-Ḥâtim from Ubai ibn-Ka'b:—In answer to a question directed to the Prophet regarding the "mosque founded in piety," the Prophet replied: "It is this my mosque."

Hudbah ibn-Khâlid from Sa'îd ibn-al-Musaiyib who said regarding the "mosque founded in piety" that the great mosque of the Prophet is the one meant. 5

A tradition to the same effect is reported by 'Ali ibn-'Abdallâh al-Madîni on the authority of Khârijah ibn-Zaid ibn-Thâbit and by 'Affân on the authority of Sa'îd ibn-al-Musaiyib, and by Muḥammad ibn-Ḥâtim ibn-Maimûn as-Samîn on the authority of 'Abd-ar-Raḥmân ibn-abi-Sa'îd al-Khudri's father.

Ḳubâ' mosque was later enlarged and added to. When 'Abdallâh ibn-'Umar entered it for prayer, he always turned his face to the "polished column" [2]; and that was the place where the Prophet always prayed.

The Prophet arrives at al-Madînah. The Prophet spent in Ḳubâ' Monday, Tuesday, Wednesday, and Thursday, riding away on Friday for al-Madînah. Friday prayer he performed in a mosque erected by banu-Sâlim ibn-'Auf ibn-'Amr ibn-'Auf ibn-al-Khazraj, that being the first Friday on which he led public prayer. Then the Prophet passed by the houses of the *Anṣâr* one by one [3] and each one of them offered to entertain him. He kept his way, however, until

[1] Baiḍâwi, *Anwâr at-Tanzîl,* vol. i, p. 401.

[2] *Geschichte der Stadt Medina,* p. 65.

[3] Ibn-Hishâm, p. 336.

he arrived at the site of his mosque in al-Madînah where his camel knelt.[1] He dismounted. Then came abu-Aiyûb Khâlid ibn-Zaid . . .[2] ibn-al-Khazraj who took off the saddle of the Prophet's camel. The Prophet took up his abode at abu-Aiyûb's.[3] Certain Khazrajis invited the Prophet, but he retorted, "Man is where his camel's saddle is." He remained at abu-Aiyûb's for seven months. He took up his residence there after [Friday-] prayer, one month since his departure [from Makkah]. The *Anṣâr* presented to the Prophet all the unoccupied parts of their lands, saying, "O Prophet of Allah, take our own dwellings if thou wish." 6
But he said, "No!"

The mosque of the Prophet. Abu-Umâmah[4] As'ad ibn-Zurârah ibn-'Udas ibn-'Ubaid ibn-Tha'labah ibn-Ghanm ibn-Mâlik ibn-an-Najjâr, *Naḳîb*-in-chief,[5] used to conduct Friday prayers for his Moslem followers in a mosque of his own in which the Prophet, too, used to pray. The Prophet, thereafter, requested As'ad to sell him a piece of land contiguous to this mosque. The land was in the hands of As'ad but belonged to two orphans in his custody whose names were Sahl and Suhail sons of Râfi' ibn-abi-'Amr ibn-'Â'idh ibn-Tha'labah ibn-Ghanm.[6] As'ad proposed to offer it to the Prophet and to pay its price to the orphans himself. But the Prophet refused and paid for its price ten *dînârs*,[7]

[1] Ibn-Sa'd, *Kitâb aṭ-Ṭabaḳât*, vol. i¹, p. 160.

[2] In this and in other cases to come, the genealogical table has been cut short in the translation.

[3] Ad-Diyârbakri, *al-Khamîs*, vol. i, p. 386.

[4] *Geschichte der Stadt Medina*, p. 60.

[5] *Naḳîb* is the superintendent of a people who takes cognizance of their actions and is responsible for them; ibn-Ḥajar, vol. i, pp. 61-63.

[6] Ibn-Hishâm, p. 503.

[7] A gold coin worth about ten shillings.

which money he secured from abu-Bakr aṣ-Ṣiddîḳ. By the Prophet's orders, bricks were prepared and used for building the mosque. Its foundations were laid with stones; its roof was covered with palm branches; and its columns were made of trunks of trees.[1] When abu-Bakr became caliph he introduced no changes in the mosque. When 'Umar was made caliph he enlarged it and asked al-'Abbâs ibn-'Abd-al-Muṭṭalib to sell his house that he might add it to the mosque. Al-'Abbâs offered the house as a gift to Allah and the Moslems; and 'Umar added it to the mosque.

In his caliphate, 'Uthmân ibn-'Affân reconstructed the mosque with stone and gypsum, making its columns of stone, and its roof of teak-wood. 'Uthmân also added to the mosque and carried to it small pebbles from al-'Aḳîḳ.[2] The first caliph to plant in it *maḳṣûrah*[3] was Marwân ibn-al-Ḥakam ibn-abi-l-'Âṣi ibn-Umaiyah who made his *maḳṣûrah* of carved stones. No change was thereafter introduced in the mosque until al-Walîd ibn-'Abd-al-Malik ibn-Marwân succeeded his father. This al-Walîd wrote to his *'âmil* [lieutenant, governor] in al-Madînah, 'Umar ibn-'Abd-al-'Azîz, ordering him to destroy the mosque and reconstruct it.
Meanwhile, he forwarded to him money, mosaic, marble, and 7
eighty Greek and Coptic artisans from Syria and Egypt. Accordingly, the *'âmil* rebuilt it and added to it, entrusting the supervision of its work and the expenditure for it to Ṣâliḥ ibn-Kaisân, a freedman of Su'da, a freedmaid of the family of Mu'aiḳib ibn-abi-Fâṭimah ad-Dausi. This took place in the year 87, some say 88.[4] After this, no caliph

[1] Al-Hamadhâni, *Kitâb al-Buldân*, p. 24.

[2] Hamadhâni, *Kitâb al-Buldân*, p. 25.

[3] See *JAOS.*, vol. xxvii, pp. 273-274, Gottheil, "a distinguished family of Fatimite Cadis"; and *Geschichte der Stadt Medina*, p. 71.

[4] *Geschichte der Stadt Medina*, p. 73.

made changes in the mosque down to the time of al-Mahdi's caliphate.

According to al-Wâkidi, al-Mahdi sent 'Abd-al-Malik ibn-Shabîb al-Ghassâni and another[1] descended from 'Umar ibn-'Abd-al-'Azîz to al-Madînah to reconstruct its mosque and increase it in size. The governor of al-Madînah was at that time Ja'far ibn-Sulaimân ibn-'Ali. It took these two one year to carry out the undertaking. One hundred cubits [Ar. *dhirâ'*] were added to the rear, making its length 300 cubits and its width 200.

According to 'Ali ibn-Muhammad al-Madâ'ini, al-Mahdi appointed Ja'far ibn-Sulaimân to the governorship of Makkah, al-Madînah and al-Yamâmah. Ja'far enlarged the mosques of Makkah and al-Madînah, the work in the latter being completed in the year 162. Al-Mahdi had visited Makkah before the pilgrimage season, in the year [1]60, and ordered that the *maksûrah* be supplanted and that it be put on the same level with the mosque.

In the year 246, caliph Ja'far al-Mutawakkil ordered that the mosque of al-Madînah be repaired. Much mosaic was subsequently carried to it; and the year 247 marked the completion of the work.

'Amr ibn-Hammâd ibn-abi-Ḥanîfah from 'Â'ishah:—The Prophet said: "All districts or cities were conquered by force, but al-Madînah was conquered by the Koran."

The inviolability of al-Madînah. Shaibân ibn-abi-Shaibah-l-Ubulli from al-Ḥasan:—The Prophet said: "Every prophet can make a place inviolable, so I have made al-Madînah inviolable as Abraham had made Makkah. Between its two *Harrahs,*[2] its herbage shall not be cut, its trees 8

[1] 'Abdallâh ibn-'Âsim; De Goeje's edition of Balâdhuri, p. 7, note b.

[2] The word means tracts of black stones, i. e., the volcanic region in the vicinity of al-Madînah.

shall not be felled,[1] nor should weapons be carried in it for fight. He, therefore, who does that or harbors in his home one who has done so, may be cursed of Allah and his angels and all men. From him no repentance or ransom shall be accepted."

Rauḥ ibn-'Abd-al-Mu'min al-Baṣri-l-Maḳri from abu-Hurairah:—The Prophet said: "My Lord, Abraham was thy servant and messenger, and so am I thy servant and messenger. And I have made inviolable all that lies between its two stony tracts as Abraham had made Makkah inviolable." Abu-Hurairah used to say: "By him who holds my life in his hands, even if I should find the deer in Baṭiḥân [2] I would not care for them."

Shaibân ibn-abi-Shaibah from Muḥammad ibn-Ziyâd's grandfather (a freedman of 'Uthmân ibn-Maẓ'ûn and the holder of a piece of land belonging to the Maẓ'ûn family in *Harrah*) who said:—" 'Umar ibn-al-Khaṭṭâb with his robe on his head would sometimes call on me at midnight, take a seat and converse with me. I would then bring him cucumbers and vegetables. But one day he said: 'Go not: I have made thee superintendent of this place. Let no one beat a tree with a stick [that its leaves may fall] or cut off a tree (referring to the trees of al-Madînah); and if thou find anyone doing it, take away his rope and ax.' When I asked him, 'Shall I take his robe?' he answered, 'No'."

Abu-Mas'ûd ibn-al-Ḳattât from Ja'far ibn-Muḥammad's father:—The Prophet declared inviolable all trees growing between Uḥud and 'Air, allowing [only] the driver of the water-carrying camel to cut *al-ghaḍa* [3] trees and use them for repairing his ploughs and carts.

[1] Al-Bukhâri, *al-Jâmi' aṣ-Ṣaḥîḥ*, vol. i, p. 40.

[2] Also Baṭḥân or Buṭḥân; see al-Hamdâni, *Ṣifat Jazîrat al-'Arab*, p. 124, line 9.

[3] "Of the genus Euphorbia with a woody stem, often 5 or 6 ft. in height, and innumerable round green twigs"—Palgrave's *Travels*, vol. i, p. 38.

Ḥima ar-Rabadhah. Bakr ibn-al-Haitham from Zaid ibn-Aslam's father who said:—"I heard 'Umar ibn-al-Khaṭṭâb say to one[1] whom he placed in charge of *Ḥima*[2] ar-Rabadhah and whose name Bakr forgot, 'Stretch not thy wing[3] to any 9
Moslem. Beware the cry of the oppressed, for it is answered. Admit [to the *Ḥima*] the owner of the small herd of camels and sheep but keep off the cattle of ibn-'Affân and ibn-'Auf; for if their cattle should perish they resort to sowing, whereas if the cattle of this poor man perish, he comes to me crying, "O, *commander of the believers!* O, *commander of the believers!*" To offer grass is easier for the Moslems than to offer money in gold and silver.[4] By Allah, this is their land for which they fought in pre-Islamic time and which was included in their terms when they became Moslem. They would, therefore, certainly feel that I oppress them; and had it not been for the cattle [secured by declaring a place *Ḥima*] to be used in the cause of Allah, I would never make a part of a people's land *Ḥima*'."

Ḥima an-Naḳî'. Al-Ḳâsim ibn-Sallâm abu-'Ubaid from ibn-'Umar:—The Prophet declared an-Naḳî' *ḥima* and reserved it for the Moslem cavalry.[5] Abu-'Ubaid told me that it is an an-Naḳî' [and not al-Baḳî', as some have it] and that the *ḥandaḳûḳ* plant [sweet trefoil] grows in it.

Mus'ab ibn-'Abdallah az-Zubairi from Sa'd ibn-abi-

[1] Whose name was Hunai; Bukhâri, vol. ii, p. 263.

[2] Reservation, pasture land reserved for the public use of a community or tribe to the exclusion of everyone else. Rabadhah was a district and a village 5 miles from al-Madînah.

[3] Treat leniently, see ibn-al-Athîr, *an-Nihâyah*, vol. iii, p. 26.

[4] i. e., it is easier to let the owner of the little herd feed his flock on the *Ḥima* than to give him money for sustaining his children.

[5] *Geschichte der Stadt Medina*, p. 155; Wâḳidi, *Kitâb al-Maghâzi*, pp. 183-184. Naḳî' lay 20 parasangs from Madînah.

Wakkâṣ:—The latter once found a young servant felling trees in the *ḥima* [reserved land]. He beat the servant and took his ax. The servant's mistress, or a woman of his kin, went to 'Umar and accused Sa'd. 'Umar ordered that the ax and the clothes be returned. But Sa'd refused saying, "I will not give up spoils given me by the Prophet whom I heard say, 'Whomever ye find cutting trees in the *ḥima,* ye should beat and deprive of what he has.'" From the ax Sa'd made a shovel which he used in his property to the end of his life.

Al-Ghâbah. Abu-l-Ḥasan al-Madâ'ini from ibn-Ju'dubah and abu-Ma'shar:—When the Prophet was at Ẓuraib (probably on his return from the expedition of dhu-Kard) banu-Ḥârithah of the *Anṣâr* said to him referring to the site of al-Ghâbah [forest], "This is the place for our camels to go loose, and for our sheep to graze, and for our women to go out." The Prophet then ordered that he who had cut off a tree should replace it by planting a small shoot. Thus was al-Ghâbah planted with trees.

Wâdi-Mahzûr. 'Abd-al-A'la ibn-Hammâd an-Narsi from abu-Mâlik ibn-Tha'labah's father:—The Prophet decreed in 10
the case of Wâdi-Mahzûr [1] that the water be shut off on the the surface until it rises to the two ankles, at which it should be conducted to the other place, thus preventing the owner of the higher property from holding the water from the owner of the lower one.

Ishâk ibn-abi-Isrâ'îl from 'Abd-ar-Rahmân ibn-al-Ḥârith:—The Prophet decreed in the case of the Mahzûr torrent that the owner of the higher property should hold the water until it rises to the two ankles, at which he must let it go to the holder of the lower land.

[1] One of the valleys of Madînah, see al-Bakri, *Kitâb Mu'jam Ma-sta'jam,* vol. ii, p. 562.

'Amr ibn-Hammâd ibn-abi-Hanîfah from 'Abdallah ibn-abi-Bakr ibn-Muḥammad ibn-'Amr ibn-Hazm al-Ansâri's father:—The Prophet decreed in the case of Mahzûr torrent and Mudhainîb [1] that the water be shut in until it reaches the two ankles, then the upper supplies the lower. According to Mâlik, the Prophet passed a similar judgment in the case of Batihân torrent.

Al-Ḥusain ibn-al-Aswad al-'Ijli from abu-Mâlik ibn-Tha'labah ibn-abi-Mâlik's father:—The Prophet was called upon to decide in the case of Mahzûr, the valley of banu-Kuraizah, upon which he decreed that water rising above the two ankles cannot be shut in by the higher owner from the lower owner.

Al-Ḥusain from Ja'far ibn-Muḥammad's father:—The Prophet decreed in the case of Mahzûr torrent that the owners of palm trees have right to the ankle-high water, sowers have right to the water as high as the two straps of the sandal, after which the water is sent to the lower owners.

Hafs ibn-'Umar ad-Dûri from 'Urwah:—The Prophet 11
said: "Batihân is one of the channels of Paradise."

'Ali ibn-Muhammad al-Madâ'ini abu-l-Ḥasan from Ju'dubah and others:—In the caliphate of 'Uthmân, al-Madînah was threatened with destruction by the Mahzûr torrent, which necessitated the erection of a dam by 'Uthmân. Abu-l-Hasan added that in the year 156 the torrent brought a terrifying volume of water. The governor at that time. 'Abd-as-Samad ibn-'Ali ibn-'Abdallâh ibn-al-'Abbâs, sent 'Ubaidallâh ibn-abi-Salamah-l-'Umri who, with a big crowd, started after the afternoon prayer to see the torrent which had, by that time, covered the *ṣadaḳah*-lands [2] of the Prophet. An old woman from al-'Âliyah-

[1] "Mudhainib" in al-Bakri, pp. 518, 562.

[2] Mawardi, *al-Ahkâm as-Sulṭânîyah*, p. 292. *Sadakah* is a portion which a man gives from his property to the poor by way of propitiation. It is primarily superogatory, whereas *zakât* is obligatory.

region [1] pointed out to them a spot to which she had often heard people refer. There they dug and the water found exit through which it passed to *Wâdi*-Baṭiḥân. From Mahzûr to Mudhainîb is a water-course which empties its water in it.

The Prophet calls al-Madînah Ṭaybah. Muḥammad ibn-Abân al-Wâsiṭi from al-Ḥasan: — The Prophet invoked Allah's blessing on al-Madînah and its inhabitants calling it Ṭaybah.[2]

Abu-'Umar Ḥafṣ ibn-'Umar ad-Dûri from 'Â'ishah, *the mother of the believers*:—When the Prophet emigrated to al-Madînah, a disease spread among the Moslems in it. Among those taken seriously ill were abu-Bakr, Bilâl and 'Âmir ibn-Fuhairah. During his illness, abu-Bakr often repeated the following verse: [3]

> "One in the morning may lie amidst his family
> and death may be nearer to him than his sandal's strap." [4]

Bilâl often repeated the following:

> "O, would I that I spent a night
> at Fakh where *idhkhir* and *jalîl* [5] plants surround me!
> And would that I some day visit Majannah-water to drink it,
> and see Shâmah and Ṭafîl [Mts.]!"

'Âmir ibn-Fuhairah used to repeat the following:

> "I have found death before I tasted it, 12
> verily the death of the coward comes from above.[6]
> [Man struggles according to his own ability,]
> like the bull that protects his skin with his horn." [7]

[1] Yâḳût, *s.v.* 'Âliyah.

[2] Al-Hamadhâni, *Kitâb al-Buldân*, p. 23; *Geschichte der Stadt Medina*, p. 10.

[3] Hishâm, p. 414; Azraḳi, *Akhbâr Makkah*, p. 383.

[4] *Cf.* Freytag, *Arabum Proverbia*, vol. i, p. 492, no. 63.

[5] *Idhkhir* a small plant of sweet smell used for roofing houses. *Jalîl* a weak plant with which the interstices of houses are stopped up.

[6] Freytag, *Proverbia*, vol. i, p. 7, no. 10.

[7] Az-Zamakhshari, *al-Fâ'iḳ*, vol. ii, pp. 5-6.

This was reported to the Prophet and he prayed: "Make al-Madînah, O Allah, wholesome for us as thou hast made Makkah for us, and bless for us its *ṣâʿ* and *mudd* [1] [grain measures]!"

The water-course of al-Ḥarrah. Al-Walîd ibn-Ṣâliḥ from 'Urwah:—One of the *Anṣâr* had a dispute with az-Zubair ibn-al-'Auwâm regarding the water-courses that run from al-Ḥarrah to the plain. The Prophet said, "Zubair, use the water, then turn it to thy neighbor." [2]

Al-'Aḳîḳ as fief. Ḥusain ibn-'Ali ibn-al-Aswad al-'Ijli from Hishâm ibn-'Urwah's father:—As 'Umar was parcelling al-'Aḳîḳ into fiefs, he came to a part of it regarding which he remarked, "I never gave such a land in fief." To this Khauwât ibn-Jubair replied, "Give it out to me." And 'Umar did.

Al-Ḥusain from Hishâm ibn-'Urwah's father:—'Umar gave al-'Aḳîḳ in fief from its upper to its lower end.

Al-Ḥusain from Hishâm ibn-'Urwah:—'Umar accompanied by az-Zubair set out to distribute fiefs, and as 'Umar was giving them out, he passed by al-'Aḳîḳ and said: "Where are the seekers of fiefs? I have not yet today passed by a more fertile land." Az-Zubair said: "Give it out to me." And 'Umar did.

A similar tradition was communicated by al-Ḥusain from Hishâm ibn-'Urwah's father.

Khalaf ibn-Hishâm al-Bazzâr from Hishâm ibn-'Urwah's father who said:—"'Umar ibn-al-Khaṭṭâb gave out as fief to Khauwât ibn-Jubair al-Anṣâri a piece of dead land. This we bought from him."

A similar tradition was communicated to me by al-Ḥusain ibn-al-Aswad on the authority of Hishâm's father.

---

[1] Wâḳidi, *al-Maghâzi*, p. 14; al-Azraḳi, p. 382.

[2] One tradition occurring here and defining certain terms in the previous tradition has been omitted in the translation. Evidently it is a gloss.

Other fiefs. Al-Husain from 'Urwah:—Abu-Bakr gave out as fief to az-Zubair the land lying between al-Jurf [1] and Ḳanâh.[2] Abu-l-Hasan al-Madâ'ini told me that Kanâh is a valley stretching from at-Tâ'if to al-Arhadîyah and Karkarat al-Kudr and thence it comes to Sudd-Ma'ûnah from which it runs by the end of al-Kadûm and ends at the head of *Ḳubûr ash-Shuhadâ'* [martyrs' tombs] at Uḥud.

Abu-'Ubaid al-Kâsim ibn-Sallâm from certain learned men:—The Prophet gave out as fief to Bilâl ibn-al-Hârith al-Muzani certain mines [3] in the Furu' district.

'Amr an-Nâkid and ibn-Sahm al-Antâki from abu-'Ikrimah the freedman of Bilâl ibn-al-Hârith al-Muzani:—The Prophet gave out as fief to Bilâl a piece of land having a mountain and mines. The sons of Bilâl sold a part of it to 'Umar ibn-'Abd-al-'Azîz in which one mineral (or he may have said two) appeared. The sons of Bilâl thereupon said: "What we sold thee is not the minerals but the tillable land." Then they brought forth a statement written for them by the Prophet on a palm leaf which 'Umar kissed and with which he rubbed his eye saying to his steward: "Find out what the income and the expenses are, retain what thou hast expended, and give them back the balance."

Abu-'Ubaid from Bilâl ibn-al-Hârith:—The Prophet gave out all al-'Akîk as fief to Bilâl.

The zakât on the metals. Mus'ab az-Zubairi from Mâlik ibn-Anas:—The Prophet assigned as fief to Bilâl ibn-al-Ḥârith certain mines in the Furu' district. On this, all 14
our learned men agree. Nor do I know of any disagree-

[1] Called 'Arsat al-Bakal in al-Wâkidi's days, see Wâḳidi, tr. Wellhausen, pp. 103-104.

[2] A valley near Mount Thaib, one day's journey from Madînah.

[3] The mines of al-Kabaliyah, see al-Mutarrizi, *Kitâb al-Mughrib*, vol. ii, p. 108.

ment among our followers regarding the fact that in the case of mines the *zakât* is one-fourth of the tithe. It is reported that az-Zuhri often repeated that in the case of mines *zakât* is binding. It is moreover reported that he said that the *zakât* is one-fifth. That is what the people of al-'Irâḳ say who at present impose on the mines of al-Furu', Najrân, dhu-l-Warwah, Wâdi-l-Ḳura and others one-fifth in accordance with the view of Sufyân ath-Thauri, abu-Ḥanîfah, abu-Yûsuf and the school of al-'Irâḳ.[1]

'Ali's fiefs. Al-Ḥusain ibn-al-Aswad from Ja'far ibn-Muḥammad:—The Prophet assigned to 'Ali as fief four pieces of land, i. e., the two Fuḳairs, Bi'r-Ḳais, and ash-Shajarah.[2]

A similar tradition was communicated to me by al-Ḥusain on the authority of Ja'far ibn-Muḥammad.

'Amr ibn-Muḥammad an-Nâḳid from Ja'far ibn-Muḥammad's father:—'Umar ibn-al-Khaṭṭâb assigned to 'Ali as fief Yanbu',[3] and another piece was added to it.

A similar tradition was communicated to me by al-Ḥusain on the authority of Ja'far ibn-Muḥammad's father.

The well of 'Urwah, the reservoir of 'Amr and the canal of Banât-Nâ'ilah, etc. The next tradition was communicated to me by one in whom I trust on the authority of Mus'ab ibn'Abdallâh az-Zubairi:—The well of 'Urwah ibn-az-Zubair is named after 'Urwah ibn-az-Zubair; the 'Amr reservoir is named after 'Amr ibn-az-Zubair; the canal of Banât-Nâ'ilah is named after children of Nâ'ilah, daughter of al-Farâfiṣah-l-Kalbîyah and wife of 'Uthmân ibn-'Affân ('Uthmân had taken possession of this canal and conveyed

[1] Mâlik ibn-Anas, *al-Mudauwanah*, vol. ii, p. 47; ash-Shâfi'i, *Kitâb al-Umm*, vol. ii[2], p. 36.

[2] Yâḳût, vol. iii, pp. 260-261.

[3] Yâḳût, vol. iv, pp. 1038-1039.

its water to a piece of land at al-'Arṣah [1] which he cultivated and worked); the land of abu-Hurairah is ascribed to abu-Hurairah ad-Dausi; and aṣ-Ṣahwah in Mt. Juhainah is the *ṣadaḳah* of 'Abdallah ibn-'Abbâs.

Ḳaṣr-Nafîs. It is said that the Nafîs castle is ascribed to Nafîs at-Tâjir [the merchant] ibn-Muḥammad ibn-Zaid ibn-'Ubaid ibn-al-Mu'alla ibn-Laudhân ibn-Ḥârithah ibn-Zaid of al-Khazraj, the allies of banu-Zuraiḳ ibn-'Abd-Ḥârithah of al-Khazraj. This castle stands in Ḥarrat-Wâḳim at al-Madînah. 'Ubaid ibn-al-Mu'alla died as martyr 15
in the battle of Uḥud. Others say it is Nafîs ibn-Muḥammad ibn-Zaid ibn-'Ubaid ibn-Murrah, Mu'alla's freedman. This 'Ubaid and his father were among the captives of 'Ain at-Tamr. 'Ubaid ibn-Murrah died in the battles of al-Ḥarrah. His surname was abu-'Abdallâh.

'Â'ishah well. The 'Â'ishah well is ascribed to 'Â'ishah ibn-Numair ibn-Wâḳif, 'Â'ishah being a man's name of al-Aus.

Al-Muṭṭalib well and al-Murtafi' well. Al-Muṭṭalib well on the 'Irâḳ road is ascribed to al-Muṭṭalib ibn-'Abdallâh ibn-Ḥanṭab ibn-al-Ḥârith ibn-'Ubaid ibn-'Umar ibn-Makhzûm. Ibn-al-Murtafi' well is ascribed to Muḥammad ibn-al-Murtafi' ibn-an-Naḍîr al-'Abdari.

The Sûḳ in al-Madînah. Muḥammad ibn-Sa'd from 'Aṭâ ibn-Yasâr, the freedman of Maimûnah, daughter of al-Ḥârith ibn-Ḥazn ibn-Bujair of al-Hilâl tribe:—When the Prophet wanted to found a market in al-Madînah he said: "This is your market and no *kharâj* will be assessed on it."

The 'Arim dam. Al-'Abbâs ibn-Hishâm al-Kalbi from his grandfather and Sharḳi ibn-al-Ḳuṭâmi-l-Kalbi:—When Nebuchadnezzar destroyed Jerusalem,[2] expelled of the

[1] See Yâḳût, *al-Mushtarik*, p. 159.

[2] Bait al-Maḳdis or al-Bait al-Muḳaddas. See ibn-Khurdâdhbih, *Kitâb al-Masâlik*, pp. 78 and 79.

Israelites those whom he expelled, and carried away those whom he carried into captivity, some Israelites fled away to al-Ḥijâz and settled in Wâdi-l-Ḳura, Taima', and Yathrib. At that time there lived in Yathrib a tribe of Jurhum and a remnant of al-'Amâliḳ who lived on date-planting and wheat-growing. Among these, the Israelites settled and associated with them, and kept increasing in number, as Jurhum and al-'Amâlik were decreasing, until the former drove the latter from Yathrib and established their authority over it, taking possession of their cultivated and pasture lands. This was their condition for a long time. Then it came to pass that those of the people of al-Yaman descended from Saba ibn-Yashjub ibn-Ya'rub ibn-Ḳaḥṭân were filled with the spirit of oppression and tyranny and ignored the grace of their God in regards to the fertility and luxury he bestowed on them. Consequently, Allah created rats that began to bore the dam, which stood between two mountains and had pipes which the people could open when they wished and get as much water as they wanted. This is the 'Arim
dam.[1] The rats went on working on the dam until it was 16
broken through. Thus did Allah let their gardens sink and their trees disappear, changing them into *khamt*,[2] tamarisk and some few jujube trees.[3]

The wanderings of al-Azd. Seeing what happened, Muzaiḳiyah i. e. 'Amr ibn-'Âmir . . . ibn-Amru'i-l-Ḳais . . . ibn-Ya'rub ibn-Ḳaḥṭân sold all the property and cattle he possessed, summoned the Azd and started together to the land of the tribe of 'Akk. There they settled. 'Amr remarked: " To seek herbage before knowledge is weakness." The tribe of 'Akk were distressed at the fall of their best

[1] Koran, 34: 15.

[2] A tree with bitter fruit.

[3] *GGA*, 1863, p. 1348.

lands into the hands of al-Azd and asked the latter to evacuate the land. Thereupon a one-eyed and deaf man of al-Azd, named Jidh', made an attack on a 'Akk party and destroyed them. This resulted in a war between al-Azd and 'Akk. The Azd, after being defeated, returned and charged, in reference to which Jidh' composed the following verse:

> "We are the descendants of Mâzin—there is no doubt,
> the Ghassân of Ghassân versus the 'Akk of 'Akk,
> and they shall see whether we or they are the weaker."

(Previous to this al-Azd had settled near a spring called Ghassân. Hence their name, Ghassân.)[1] Al-Azd now set off until they arrived in the land of Ḥakam ibn-Sa'd al-'Ashîrah . . . ibn Ya'rub ibn-Kaḥtân. There they fought and won the victory over Ḥakam. But it occurred to them to move, and they did, leaving a small band behind. The next place they came to was Najrân. Here they met resistance from the inhabitants of the place but finally won the victory. After settling in Najrân they departed with the exception of a few who had special reasons to stay Al-Azd then arrived in Makkah which was populated with the Jurhum tribe. They made their abode in Batn-Marr. Tha'labah the son of 'Amr Muzaiḳîya demanded of Jurhum that the plain of Makkah be given to his people. This request having been refused, a battle ensued in which Tha'labah got control of the plain. Tha'labah and his people, however, realized after this that the place was unwholesome, and found it hard to make their living in it; so they dispersed, one band of them leaving for 'Umân, another for as-Sarât, another for al-Anbâr and al-Ḥîrah, another for Syria and 17
one band chose Makkah for abode. This made Jidh' say: "Every time ye go to a place, ye al-Azd, some of you

[1] Near Sudd-Ma'rib in al-Yaman; Hishâm, p. 6.

detach[1] themselves from the rest. Ye are on the point of becoming the tail among the Arabs." That is why those who settled in Makkah were called Khuzâ'ah.[2] Then came Tha'labah ibn-'Amr Muzaiḳîya with his son and followers to Yathrib whose people were Jews. They settled outside the city where they grew and increased in number and became so strong as to drive the Jews from Yathrib. Thus they came to live inside the city and the Jews outside of it.

Al-Aus and al-Khazraj. Al-Aus and al-Khazraj are the sons of Ḥârithah ibn-Tha'labah[3] ibn-'Amr Muzaiḳîya ibn-'Âmir, and their mother was Ḳailah, daughter of al-Arḳam. Some say she was a Ghassanide of al-Azd tribe, others say she was of 'Udhrah tribe.

In pre-Islamic times, the Aus and the Khazraj saw many battles which made them trained in warfare. They became so used to fighting that their valor spread far, their courage became well known, their bravery was often cited and their name became a source of terror in the hearts of the Arabs, who feared them. Their possessions were well guarded against encroachment, and their neighbor was well protected; and all that was preparatory to the fact that Allah wanted to have them support his Prophet and to honor them by lending him aid.

It is reported that at the arrival of the Prophet in al-Madînah he wrote an agreement and made a covenant with the Jews of Yathrib.[4] The Jews of Ḳainuḳâ', however, were the first to violate the covenant, and the Prophet expelled them from al-Madînah. The first land that the Prophet conquered was that of the banu-an-Naḍîr.

[1] Ar. *inkhaza'a*, see *an-Nihâyah* under *khaza'a*.

[2] Azraḳi, p. 55.

[3] Hishâm, p. 140; *Geschichte der Stadt Medina*, p. 56.

[4] One of the names of Madînah.

CHAPTER II

The Possessions of the banu-an-Naḍîr

Banu-an-Naḍîr besieged. The Prophet once accompanied by abu-Bakr, 'Umar and Usaid ibn-Ḥuḍair came to the banu-an-Naḍîr who were Jews and solicited their aid for raising the bloodwit of two men of the banu-Kilâb ibn-Rabî'ah who had made peace with him and who were killed by 'Amr ibn-Umaiyah aḍ-Ḍamri.[1] The Jews intended to drop a stone on him but the Prophet left them and sent them word ordering 18
them to evacuate his city [Yathrib] because of their perfidy and violation of covenant. The Jews refused to comply, and announced hostility.[2] Upon this the Prophet marched and besieged them for fifteen days, at the close of which they capitulated, agreeing to evacuate his town and to be entitled to whatever the camels could carry with the exception of coats of mail and armor, the Prophet taking their land, palm-trees, coats of mail and other arms. Thus did all the possessions of the banu-an-Naḍîr become the property of the Prophet. The Prophet used to sow their land planted with palm-trees and thus provided for his family and wives for one year. With what could not be consumed, he bought horses and arms.

Fiefs assigned. Of the land of banu-an-Naḍîr, the Prophet gave fiefs to abu-Bakr, 'Abd-ar-Raḥmân ibn-'Auf, abu-

[1] Hishâm, p. 652; Ibn-Sa'd, vol. ii2, p. 40; Al-Wâḳidi, al-*Maghâzi*, p. 353.

[2] Al-Ya'ḳûbi, *Ta'rîkh*, vol. ii, p. 49.

Dujânah [1] Simâk ibn-Kharashah as-Sâ'idi and others. This occurred in the year 4 of the Hegira.

Mukhairiḳ. According to al-Wâḳidi, one of the banu-an-Naḍîr, Mukhairiḳ, was a learned rabbi and he believed in the Prophet and offered him all that he possessed, which was seven palm-gardens surrounded with walls. This the Prophet set apart as *ṣadaḳah*-land. The seven gardens are: al-Mîthab, aṣ-Ṣâfiyah, ad-Dalâl, Ḥusna,[2] Barḳah, al-A'wâf, Mashrabat umm-Ibrâhîm,[3] Ibrâhîm being the son of the Prophet and his mother being Mâriyah, the Copt.

Other versions of the conquest. Al-Ḳâsim ibn-Sallâm from az-Zuhri:—The attack on the banu-an-Naḍîr, the Jews, took place six months after the battle of Uḥud. The Prophet pressed the siege until they agreed to evacuate the city stipulating that they take with them whatever utensils their camels could carry with the exclusion of the coats of mail. Hence the text revealed by Allah: "All that is in the heavens and all that is on the earth praiseth Allah! And He is the mighty, the wise! He it is who caused the unbelievers among the people of the Book", etc.,[4] to "put the wicked to shame."

The next tradition was communicated to us by al-Ḥusain ibn-al-Aswad on the authority of Muḥammad ibn-Isḥâḳ [5] regarding the above text which Allah hath revealed to his Messenger:—Those referred to are banu-an-Naḍîr. By "Ye pressed not towards it with horse or camel. But Allah giveth his Messengers authority over whomsoever He willeth",[6] Allah showed that it is wholly assigned to the

[1] Ya'ḳûbi, vol. ii, p. 50.

[2] "Al-Ḥasna" in *Geschichte der Stadt Medina*, p. 150.

[3] Wâḳidi, tr. Wellhausen, p. 166.

[4] Koran, 59: 1.

[5] Hishâm, pp. 654 and 655.

[6] Baiḍâwi, vol. ii, pp. 322-323.

Prophet and to no one else. The Prophet then parcelled 19
out the land among the *Emigrants*. But when Sahl ibn-Ḥunaif and abu-Dujânah mentioned their poverty, he gave them a share. As for the text: "The spoil taken from the people of the villages and assigned by Allah to his Messenger, it belongeth to Allah and to the Messenger," etc., to the end of the text, it means that Allah made another division among the Moslems.

According to a tradition I received from Muḥammad ibn-Ḥâtim as-Samîn on the authority of ibn-'Umar, the Prophet burnt and cut down the palm-trees of the banu-an-Nadîr in reference to which Ḥassân ibn-Thâbit says:

> "The leading men of the banu-Lu'ai would have regarded it easy,
> to bring about the great fire at Buwairah."[1]

According to ibn-Juraij, it was in this connection that Allah revealed the text: "Whatever palm-trees ye have cut down or left standing on their stems was by Allah's permission and to put the wicked to shame."

A similar tradition was communicated to us by abu-'Ubaid on the authority of ibn-'Umar.

Abu-'Amr ash-Shaibâni, among other reporters, holds that the above-quoted verse was composed by abu-Sufyân ibn-al-Ḥârith ibn-'Abd-al-Muṭṭalib and that its wording is as follows:

> "The leading men of the banu-Lu'ai would have regarded it hard,
> to bring about the great conflagration of Buwairah."

(According to other reports it is Buwailah [and not Buwairah]).[2] Ḥassân ibn-Thâbit in answer to that wrote the following:

[1] Al-Bakri, under Buwairah; Ibn-Hishâm, pp. 712-713.

[2] Yâḳût, vol. i, p. 765.

"May Allah perpetuate the conflagration
and make the fire rage in its parts.
They were given the Book but they lost it.
Thus with respect to the Taurât they are blind and erring."[1]

The Prophet's special share. 'Amr ibn-Muḥammad an-Nâḳid from Mâlik ibn-Aus ibn-al-Ḥadathân:—It was stated by 'Umar ibn-al-Khaṭṭâb that the possessions of the banu-an-Naḍîr were assigned by Allah to the Prophet, the Moslems having not "pressed toward them with horse or camel." 20
Thus they were wholly his property. The Prophet used to spend their annual income on his family and invest what was left in horses and arms to be used in the cause of Allah.

Hishâm ibn-'Ammâr ad-Dimashḳi from Mâlik ibn-Aus ibn-al-Ḥadathân:—'Umar ibn-al-Khaṭṭâb told him [Mâlik] that the Prophet had three special shares which he appropriated for himself; namely, the possessions of the banu-an-Naḍîr, Khaibar and Fadak. The possessions of the banu-an-Naḍîr he reserved for use in case of misfortunes that might befall him. Those of Fadak were reserved for wayfarers. Those of Ḳhaibar he divided into three portions, two of which he divided among the Moslems and the third he reserved for his and his family's expenses, distributing what was left after the expenses to the needy among the *Emigrants*.

Al-Ḥusain ibn-al-Aswad from az-Zuhri:—The possessions of the banu-an-Naḍîr were among the things that Allah assigned to his Prophet. The Moslems "pressed not towards them with horse or camel." They were therefore wholly the property of the Prophet; and he divided them among the *Emigrants*, giving nothing of them to the *Anṣâr* with the exception of two persons who were needy, i. e., Simâk ibn-Kharashah abu-Dujânah, and Sahl ibn-Ḥunaif.

[1] *Cf.* Ḥassân ibn-Thâbit, *Dîwân*, p. 46.

Al-Ḥusain from al-Kalbi:—When the Prophet secured the possessions of the banu-an-Naḍîr, who were the first he made to evacuate the land, Allah said: "He it is who caused the unbelievers among the 'People of the Book' to quit their homes and join those who had evacuated previously." [1] Thus these possessions were among the spoils towards which the Moslems "pressed not with horse or camel." The Prophet then said to the *Anṣâr*: "Your brethren, the *Emigrants* have no possessions. If ye therefore desire, I will divide these [newly acquired possessions] and what ye already possess among you and the *Emigrants.* But if ye desire, keep ye your possessions and I will divide these [newly acquired ones] among the *Emigrants* alone." To this the *Anṣâr* replied: "Divide these among them and give them from our possessions whatever thou wishest." Because of this the text was revealed: "They prefer them before themselves, though poverty be their own lot." [2] Thereupon abu-Bakr said: "May Allah give you the good recompense, ye *Anṣârs* your case and ours is like that referred to by al-Ghanawi where he said,

'May Allah recompense in our behalf the Ja'far,
who when our feet slipped in al-Waṭ'atain and we fell,
took ungrudging care of us
although our mothers would have murmured if they were in their place.
The rich are many and every hungry man
goes to places kept warm and sheltered.'"

The fief of az-Zubair. Al-Ḥusain from Hishâm ibn-'Urwah's father:—The Prophet assigned as fief to az-Zubair ibn-'Auwâm a piece of the banu-an-Naḍîr's land planted with palm-trees.

Al-Ḥusain from Hishâm ibn-'Urwah's father:—The Pro-

[1] Koran, 59:2. [2] Kor., 59:9.

phet gave out of the land of the banu-an-Naḍîr in fief and he gave a fief to az-Zubair.

Muḥammad ibn-Sa'd,[1] the secretary of al-Wâkidi, from Anas ibn-'Iyâḍ, and 'Abdallâh ibn-Numair from Hishâm ibn-'Urwah's father:—The Prophet assigned as fief to az-Zubair a piece of the banu-an-Naḍîr's land planted with palm-trees. Abu-Bakr assigned to az-Zubair as fief al-Jurf. Anas in his tradition says the land was dead. 'Abdallâh ibn-Numair says in his tradition that 'Umar gave az-Zubair as fief all of al-'Aḳîḳ.

[1] Ibn-Sa'd, vol. ii2, p. 41.

CHAPTER III

THE POSSESSIONS OF THE BANU-ḲURAIẒAH

The subjection of the banu-Ḳuraiẓah. The Prophet besieged banu-Ḳuraiẓah for a few days in dhu-l-Ḳa'dah, and a few days in dhu-l-Ḥijjah, of the year 5, the whole time being fifteen days.[1] These banu-Ḳuraiẓah were among those who had assisted in the fight against the Prophet in the battle of al-Khandaḳ [the moat] also called battle of al-Aḥzâb [the confederates]. Finally they surrendered and he installed Sa'd ibn-Mu'âdh al-Ausi as their ruler. The latter decreed that every adult[2] be executed, that women and children be carried as captives and that all that they possessed be divided among the Moslems.[3] The Prophet approved of the decree saying: "What thou hast decreed is in accordance with the decree of Allah and his Prophet."

Gabriel appears to the Prophet. 'Abd-al-Wâḥid ibn-Ghiyâth from 'Â'ishah:—When the Prophet was done with 22
the battle of al-Aḥzâb, he went into the wash-room in order to wash. There Gabriel appeared to him and said, "Muḥammad, thou hast laid down thy arms; but we have not yet. Hasten against the banu-Ḳuraiẓah." 'Â'ishah upon this said to the Prophet: "O Prophet of Allah, I have seen him [Gabriel] through a hole in the door with the dust around his head!"[4]

[1] Dhu-l-Ka'dah 23—dhu-l-Ḥijjah 9; *cf.* Wâḳidi, tr. Wellhausen, p. 210; Ṭabari, vol. i, p. 1487.

[2] Literally "every one on whose beard the razor could be used."

[3] Wâḳidi, *Maghâzi*, p. 373.

[4] Wâḳidi, *Maghâzi*, p. 371; Ibn-Sa'd, vol. ii[1], p. 55; Ibn-Hishâm, p. 684.

The adults executed. 'Abd-al-Wâḥid ibn-Ghiyâth from Kathîr ibn-as-Sâ'ib:—Banu-Ḳuraiẓah were presented to the Prophet with the result that those of them who had attained to puberty [1] were executed and those who had not attained to puberty were spared.

Ḥuyai ibn-Akhṭab put to death with his son. Wahb ibn-Baḳîyah from al-Ḥasan:—Ḥuyai ibn-Akhṭab made a covenant with the Prophet agreeing never to assist anyone against him and mentioned Allah as surety for the covenant. When he and his son were brought before the Prophet on the day of Ḳuraiẓah, the Prophet remarked: "The one mentioned as surety has done his part." By the order of the Prophet the heads of the man and his son were cut off.[2]

The division of the booty. Bakr ibn-al-Haitham from Ma'mar who said:—I once asked az-Zuhri whether the banu-Ḳuraiẓah had any lands, to which he replied directly, "The Prophet divided it among the Moslems into different shares."

Al-Ḥusain ibn-al-Aswad from ibn-'Abbâs:—The Prophet divided the possessions of the banu-Ḳuraiẓah and Khaibar among the Moslems.[3]

The conquest according to az-Zuhri. Abu-'Ubaid al-Ḳâsim ibn-Sallâm from az-Zuhri:—The Prophet pressed the siege against banu-Ḳuraiẓah until they surrendered to Sa'd ibn-Mu'âdh who decreed that their men be executed, their children be taken as captives and their possessions be divided. Accordingly, a certain number of men were put to death on that day.

[1] Literally every one who "had the dreams and hair" that mark adolescence.

[2] Ṭabari, vol. i, p. 1494.

[3] Wâḳidi, Wellhausen, pp. 220-221.

CHAPTER IV

KHAIBAR. 23

The capitulation of Khaibar. The Prophet invaded Khaibar[1] in the year 7. Its people contended with him, delayed him and resisted the Moslems. So the Prophet besieged them for about one month.[2] They then capitulated on the terms that their blood would not be shed, and their children be spared, provided that they evacuate the land, which he permitted the Moslems to take together with the gold and silver and arms—except what was on the person of the banu-Khaibar, and that they keep nothing secret from the Prophet. They then told the Prophet, "We have special experience in cultivation and planting palm-trees," and asked to be allowed to remain in the land. The Prophet granted them their request and allowed them one-half of the fruits and grains produced saying: "I shall keep you settled so long as Allah keeps you."

'Umar expels the people of Khaibar. During the caliphate of 'Umar ibn-al-Khaṭṭâb, a pestilence spread among them and they mistreated the Moslems. 'Umar, thereupon, made them evacuate the land, dividing what they had among those of the Moslems who already had a share in it.

The terms made. Al-Ḥusain ibn-al-Aswad from Muḥammad ibn-Isḥâḳ who said:—"I once asked ibn-Shihâb about Khaibar and he told me that he was informed that the

[1] Yâḳût, vol. ii, p. 503.

[2] Diyârbakri, *Ta'rîkh al-Khamîs,* vol. ii, p. 47.

Prophet captured it by force after a fight, and that it was included among the spoils which Allah assigned to his Prophet. The Prophet took its fifth and divided the land among the Moslems. Those of its people who surrendered did [1] so on condition that they leave the land; but the Prophet asked them to enter into a treaty, which they did."

Ḥuyai hides a bag full of money. 'Abd-al-A'la ibn-Ḥammâd an-Narsi from ibn-'Umar:—The Prophet came to the people of Khaibar and fought them until he drove them to their castle and captured their land and palm-trees. They then capitulated on the terms that their blood be not shed, that they evacuate the land and be entitled to all that their camels could carry, and that the Prophet be entitled to the gold and silver and arms.[2] The Prophet made it a condition for them that they hold nothing secret or hidden from him, otherwise they are no more within his protection or covenant. They, however, hid a leather bag in which were kept money and jewels belonging to Ḥuyai ibn-Akhṭab.
This bag Ḥuyai had brought to Khaibar on the occasion 24
of the expulsion of the banu-an-Naḍîr. The Prophet asked Sa'yah ibn-'Amr saying, "What has become of the bag which Ḥuyai brought from the banu-an-Naḍîr?" To this Sa'yah answered, "Wars and expenses have emptied it." But the Prophet remarked, "It was a short time and a big sum of money. Moreover, Ḥuyai was killed before that." The Prophet then turned Sa'yah over to az-Zubair and the latter put him to the torture. At last Sa'yah said: "I saw Ḥuyai roaming about in a deserted place yonder." Search was made in the deserted place and the bag was found. The Prophet, thereupon, put the two sons of abu-l-Ḥuḳaiḳ to death, one of whom was the husband of Safîyah,[3] the daugh-

[1] Hishâm, p. 779. [2] Ibn-Sa'd, vol. ii², pp. 79-80.

[3] who became one of the wives of Muhammad, see an-Nawâwi, *Tahdhîb al-Asmâ'*, pp. 846-847.

ter of Ḥuyai ibn-Akhṭab. Moreover, he captivated their children and women and divided their possessions because of their breach of faith.

'Abdallâh ibn-Rawâḥah estimates the produce. The Prophet also wanted to expel the banu-Khaibar from the land but they said, "Let us stay in the land to repair it and manage it." The Prophet and his companions having no slaves to manage it, and they having no time to do it themselves, he gave them Khaibar on condition that they have one-half of every palm-tree or plant . . . [1] as it occurred to the Prophet. 'Abdallâh ibn-Rawâḥah used to come every year and estimate by conjecture the quantity of dates upon the palm-trees and rent them one-half. Banu-Khaibar accused him to the Prophet charging him with partiality in estimation and offered to bribe him. To this he ['Abdallâh] replied saying, "Do ye enemies of Allah mean to give me unlawful money? [2] By Allah, I have been sent to you by one whom of all men I love best. As for you, I hate you more than monkeys and pigs. My hatred to you and love to him, however, shall never stand in the way of my being just to you." They then said, "Through this [justice] have heavens and earth been established!"

The green spot in the eye of Safîyah, the Prophet's wife. Once the Prophet, noticing a green spot in the eye of Ṣafîyah, daughter of Ḥuyai, asked her about it, and she said, "As my head lay in the lap of ibn-abi-l-Ḥuḳaiḳ, I saw in my sleep as if a moon fell in my lap. When I told him of what I saw he gave me a blow saying, 'Art thou wishing to have the king of Yathrib?' " [3] Ṣafîyah added, "Of all men the Prophet was the one I disliked most, for he had killed

[1] Text not clear.

[2] Kor., 5:67 and 68.

[3] Ṭabari, vol. i, p. 1582.

my husband, father and brother. But he kept on saying, 'Thy father excited the Arabs to unite against me and he did this and that,' until all hatred was gone away from me."

The Prophet used to give annually each of his wives 80 25
camel-loads of dates and 80 loads of barley from Khaibar.

'Umar divides Khaibar. It was stated by Nâfi' that during the caliphate of 'Umar ibn-al-Khaṭṭâb, the people of Khaibar mistreated the Moslems and deceived them and broke the hands of the son of 'Umar [1] by hurling him from the roof of a house. Consequently, 'Umar divided the land among those of the people of Ḥudaibiyah who had taken part in the battle of Khaibar.

The forts of Khaibar. Al-Ḥusain ibn-al-Aswad from Abdallâh ibn-abi-Bakr ibn-Muḥammad ibn-'Amr ibn-Ḥazm:—The Prophet besieged the people of Khaibar in their two fortresses—al-Waṭîḥ and Sulâlim. When they felt that their destruction was sure, they requested the Prophet to let them off and spare their lives. This he did. The Prophet had already taken possession of all their property [2] including ash-Shiḳḳ, an-Naṭât and al-Katîbah together with all their forts except what was in the above-mentioned two.

"Speedy victory." The following tradition regarding the text: [3] "And rewarded them with a speedy victory" was transmitted by al-Ḥusain ibn-al-Aswad on the authority of 'Abd-ar-Raḥmân ibn-abi-Laila:—Khaibar and another are meant who could not be subdued by the Persians and Greeks.

The division of Khaibar. 'Amr an-Nâkid from Bushair ibn-Yasâr:—The Prophet divided Khaibar into thirty-six shares and each share into a hundred lots. One-half of the shares he reserved for himself to be used in case of

[1] Hishâm, p. 780.

[2] Six fortresses mentioned by Ya'ḳûbi, vol. ii, p. 56.

[3] Kor., 48: 18.

accident or what might befall him, and the other half he distributed among the Moslems. According to this, the Prophet's share included ash-Shiḳḳ with an-Naṭât and whatever was included within them. Among the lands turned into *waḳf* [1] were al-Katîbah and Sulâlim. When the Prophet laid his hands on these possessions, he found that he had not enough *'âmils* [2] for the land. He therefore turned it over to the Jews on condition that they use the land and keep only one-half of its produce. This arrangement lasted throughout the life of the Prophet and abu-Bakr. But when 'Umar was made caliph, and as the money became abundant in the lands of the Moslems, and the Moslems became numerous enough to cultivate the land,
'Umar expelled the Jews to Syria and divided the property 26
among the Moslems.

Bakr ibn-al-Haitham from az-Zuhri:—When the Prophet conquered Khaibar the fifth share of it [reserved for himself] was al-Katîbah; as for ash-Shiḳḳ, an-Naṭât, Sulâlim and al-Waṭîḥ they were given to the Moslems. The Prophet left the land in the hands of the Jews on condition that they give him one-half of the produce. Thus the part of the produce assigned by Allah to the Moslems was divided among the Moslems until the time of 'Umar who divided the land itself among them according to their shares.

Abu-'Ubaid from Maimûn ibn-Mihrân:—The Prophet besieged the inhabitants of Khaibar between twenty and thirty days.

Al-Ḥusain ibn-al-Aswad from Bushair ibn-Yasâr:—The Prophet divided Khaibar into thirty-six shares—eighteen for the Prophet to meet the expenses of accidents, visitors,

[1] Unalienable legacy to the Moslem general community.

[2] Governors whose chief function it was to collect taxes and conquer more lands.

and delegates, and the remaining eighteen shares to be divided each among one hundred men.[1]

Al-Ḥusain from Bushair ibn-Yasâr :—Khaibar was divided into thirty-six shares, each one of which was subdivided into one hundred lots. Eighteen of these shares were divided among the Moslems including the Prophet, who had in addition eighteen shares to meet the expenses of visitors and delegates and accidents that might befall him.

'Abdallâh ibn-Rawâḥah estimates the produce. 'Amr an-Nâḳid and al-Ḥusain ibn-al-Aswad from ibn-'Umar:— The Prophet sent ibn-Rawâḥah to Khaibar who made a conjectural estimation of the palm-trees and gave the people their choice to accept or refuse, to which they replied: "This is justice; and upon justice have heaven and earth been established."

The sons of abu-l-Ḥuḳaiḳ put to death. Isḥâḳ ibn-abi-Isrâ'îl from an inhabitant of al-Madînah:—The Prophet 27
made terms with the sons of abu-l-Ḥuḳaiḳ stipulating that they conceal no treasure. But they did conceal; and the Prophet considered it lawful to shed their blood.

Abu-'Ubaid from Maimûn ibn-Mihrân:—The people of Khaibar were promised security on their lives and children on condition that the Prophet get all that was in the fort. In that fort were the members of a family strongly opposed to the Prophet. To them the Prophet said: "I am aware of your enmity to Allah and to his Prophet, but this is not to hold me from granting you what I granted your companions. Ye, however, have promised me that if ye conceal a thing your blood will become lawful to me. What has become of your utensils?" "They were all"—they replied, "used up during the fight." The Prophet then gave word to

[1] *Cf.* Wâḳidi, tr. Wellhausen, p. 285; Ṭabari, vol. i, p. 1588; Athîr, vol. ii, p. 171.

his *Companions* to go to the place where the utensils were. The vessels were disinterred and the Prophet struck off their heads.

Abdallâh ibn-Rawâḥah. 'Amr an-Nâḳid and Muḥammad ibn-aṣ-Ṣabbâḥ from ibn-'Abbâs:—The Prophet turned Khaibar over with its soil and palm-trees to its inhabitants allowing them half of the produce.

Muḥammad ibn-aṣ-Ṣabbâḥ from ash-Sha'bi:—The Prophet turned Khaibar over to its inhabitants for one-half of the produce and sent 'Abdallâh ibn-Rawâḥah to estimate the dates (or perhaps he said the palm-trees). This he estimated and divided into two halves and asked them to choose whichever one they wanted. Upon this they said, "It is by this that heavens and earth have been established."

A certain friend of abu-Yûsuf from Anas:—'Abdallâh ibn-Rawâḥah said to the people of Khaibar, "If ye wish, I will estimate and let you choose; otherwise, ye estimate and let me choose." Upon this they said, "It is by this that heavens and earth have been established."

The division of Khaibar. Al-Ḳâsim ibn-Sallâm from az-Zuhri:—The Prophet took Khaibar by force as a result of a fight; and after taking away one-fifth, he divided the remaining four-fifths among the Moslems.

The Jews of Khaibar expelled. 'Abd-al-A'la ibn- 28
Ḥammâd an-Narsi from ibn-Shihâb:—The Prophet said: "There can be no two religions at the same time in the Arabian peninsula."[1] 'Umar ibn-al-Khaṭṭâb investigated until he found it certain and assured that the Prophet had said, "There can be no two religions at the same time in the Arabian peninsula." Accordingly, he expelled the Jews of Khaibar.

[1] Gottheil, "*Dhimmis and Moslems in Egypt*," in *O. T. and Semitic Studies*, vol. ii, p. 351.

The Prophet gives his share. Al-Walîd ibn-Şâliḥ from al-Wâḳidi's *sheikhs*:—The Prophet assigned his share in Khaibar as a means of subsistence, bestowing on each one of his wives 80 camel-loads of dates and 20 loads of barley; on his uncle al-'Abbâs ibn-'Abd-al-Muṭṭalib 200 loads; and on abu-Bakr, 'Umar, al-Ḥassân, al-Ḥusain and others including the banu-al-Muṭṭalib ibn-'Abd-Manâf a certain number of loads. To this end, he drew up for them a document.

Al-Walîd from Aflaḥ ibn-Ḥumaid's father who said:—"I was made by 'Umar ibn-'Abd-al-'Azîz governor of al-Karîbah; and we used to give the heirs of the recipients of the Prophet's bestowals their due, those heirs being numbered and recorded by us.

'Umar divides Khaibar. Muḥammad ibn-Ḥâtim as-Samîn from Nâfi':—The Prophet turned Khaibar over to the hands of its people on condition that they give him one-half of the produce. Thus they held it during the life of the Prophet, abu-Bakr and the early part of the caliphate of 'Umar. Then 'Abdallâh ibn-'Umar visited them for some purpose and they attacked him in the night. He ['Umar], therefore, turned them out of Khaibar and divided it among those of the Moslems who were present [in its battle] giving a share to the Prophet's wives. To the latter he said, "Whichever of you likes to have the fruit can have it, and whichever likes the estate can have it, and whatever ye choose will be yours and your heirs' after you."

Al-Ḥusain ibn-al-Aswad from ibn-'Abbâs:—Khaibar was divided into 1580 shares. The Moslems were 1580 men, of whom 1540 had taken part in the battle of al-Ḥudaibiyah and forty were with Ja'far ibn-abi-Ṭâlib in Abyssinia.

The fief of az-Zubair. Al-Ḥusain ibn-al-Aswad from
ibn-'Urwah's father:—The Prophet gave as fief to az-Zubair 20
lands in Khaibar planted with palm- and other trees.

CHAPTER V

FADAK

The capitulation of Fadak. As the Prophet departed from Khaibar, he sent to the people of Fadak [1] Muḥaiyiṣah ibn-Mas'ûd al-Anṣâri inviting them to Islam. Their chief was one of their number named Yûsha' ibn-Nûn the Jew. They made terms with the Prophet, agreeing to give up one-half of the land with its soil.[2] The Prophet accepted. Thus one-half was assigned wholly to the Prophet because the Moslems "pressed not against it with horse or camel." [3] The Prophet used to spend the income on the wayfarers.

'Umar expels the inhabitants. The inhabitants of Fadak remained in it until 'Umar ibn-al-Khaṭṭâb became caliph and expelled the Jews of al-Ḥijâz. On that occasion he sent abu-l-Haitham Mâlik ibn-at-Taiyihân (some say an-Naiyihân), Sahl ibn-abi-Ḥaithamah al-Anṣâri, and Zaid ibn-Thâbit al-Anṣâri, who estimated justly the value of one-half of its soil. This value 'Umar paid to the Jews and expelled them to Syria.

Sa'îd ibn-Sulaimân from Yaḥya ibn-Sa'îd:—The people of Fadak made terms with the Prophet agreeing to give one-half of the land and the palm-trees. When 'Umar expelled them, he sent some one to estimate their share in land and palm-trees and he gave them their value.

[1] Yâḳût, vol. iii, pp. 856-857.

[2] Not only the produce.

[3] Athîr, vol. ii, p. 171; Mas'ûdi, *Kitâb at-Tanbîh*, p. 258.

Bakr ibn-al-Haitham from az-Zuhri:—'Umar ibn-al-Khaṭṭâb gave the people of Fadak the price of one-half of their land and palm-trees.

Al-Ḥusain ibn-al-Aswad from az-Zuhri, 'Abdallâh ibn-abi-Bakr and certain sons of Muḥammad ibn-Maslamah:—Only a remnant of the Khaibar was spared. They betook themselves to the fortifications and asked the Prophet to save their lives and let them go off. The people of Fadak having heard of that surrendered on the same conditions.[1]
Thus Fadak became the special share of the Prophet, for the 30
Moslems "pressed not against it with horse and camel."

A similar tradition was transmitted to us by al-Ḥusain from 'Abdallâh ibn-abi-Bakr, with one addition, that among those who were intermediary between the two parties was Muḥaiyiṣah ibn-Mas'ûd.

Al-Ḥusain from 'Umar:—The Prophet had three portions appropriated to himself exclusive of his men: the land of banu-an-Naḍîr which was unalienable and to meet the expenses of the accidents that might befall him, Khaibar which he divided into three parts, and Fadak the income of which was reserved for wayfarers.

The wives of the Prophet demand an inheritance. 'Abdallâh ibn-Ṣâliḥ al-'Ijli from 'Urwah ibn-az-Zubair:—The wives of the Prophet delegated 'Uthmân ibn-'Affân to ask abu-Bakr to give them their inheritance from the share of the Prophet in Khaibar and Fadak. But 'Â'ishah said to them, "Do ye not fear Allah? and have ye not heard the Prophet say—'What we leave as *ṣadaḳah* cannot be inherited?' This property therefore is the property of the people of Muḥammad to meet the expenses of the accidents and guests, and when I die it goes to the one in authority after me." On hearing this, the other wives desisted from their request.

[1] Diyârbakri, vol. ii, pp. 57 and 64.

A similar tradition was communicated to us by Aḥmad ibn-Ibrâhîm ad-Dauraḳi on the authority of 'Urwah.

The banu-Umaiyah confiscate Fadak. Ibrâhîm ibn-Muḥammad ibn-'Ar'arah from al-Kalbi: — The banu-Umaiyah confiscated Fadak and violated the law of the Prophet in regard to it. But when 'Umar ibn-'Abd-al-'Azîz became caliph, he reinstated the land in its old condition.

Fâṭimah demands Fadak. 'Abdallâh ibn-Maimûn al-Mukattib from Mâlik ibn-Ja'wanah's father:—Fâṭimah said to abu-Bakr, "The Prophet assigned to me Fadak; thou shouldst therefore give it to me." [1] 'Ali ibn-Abi-Ṭâlib acted as a witness in her favor. But abu-Bakr asked for another witness; and umm-Aiman testified in her favor.
Abu-Bakr, thereupon, said "Thou, daughter of Allah's Pro- 31
phet, knowest that no evidence can be accepted unless it is rendered by two men or a man and two women." Upon this she departed.

Rauḥ al-Karâbîsi from one supposed by Rauḥ to have been Ja'far ibn-Muḥammad:—Fâṭimah said to abu-Bakr, "Give me Fadak, the Prophet has assigned it to me." Abu-Bakr called for evidence and she presented umm-Aiman and Rabâḥ, the Prophet's freedman, both of whom testified in her favor. But abu-Bakr said, "In such a case no evidence could be accepted unless it be rendered by a man and two women."

Ibn-'Â'ishah at-Taimi from umm-Hâni:—Fâṭimah, the Prophet's daughter, called on abu-Bakr and asked: "Who will inherit thee when thou art dead?" to which he replied, "My son and family." "Why then," asked she, "hast thou —and not we—inherited the Prophet's possessions?" "Daughter of Allah's Prophet," answered abu-Bakr, "by Allah, I have inherited from thy father neither gold nor

[1] Bukhâri, vol. iii, p. 131.

silver, neither this nor that." "But," said she, "thou hast inherited our share in Khaibar and our *ṣadaḳah* in Fadak." To this abu-Bakr replied, "Daughter of Allah's Prophet, I heard Allah's Prophet say, 'This is but something assigned by Allah as a means of subsistence to use during my life; on my death it should be turned over to the Moslems.'"

'Uthmân ibn-abi-Shaibah from Mughîrah:—'Umar ibn-'Abd-al-'Azîz once summoned the banu-Umaiyah and addressed them saying: "Fadak belonged to the Prophet and by the income from it he met his own expenses, supplied the needy among the banu-Hâshim and helped the unmarried among them to marry. Fâṭimah asked him to bestow it on her, but he refused. After the Prophet's death, abu-Bakr used it in the same way. And so did 'Umar when he became caliph. And now I am going to put it back to its original use; and ye will be my witnesses."

Ḳura 'Arabîyah. The following tradition was transmitted to us by Suraij ibn-Yûnus from az-Zuhri in explanation of the text, "Against which ye pressed not with horse or camel": [1]—The places referred to are Ḳura 'Arabîyah [2] that belong to the Prophet, i. e., Fadak, and this and that.

'Umar expels the Jews of Fadak. Abu-'Ubaid from az- 32
Zuhri or someone else:—'Umar expelled the Jews of Khaibar and they evacuated the place. As for the Jews of Fadak, they retained half the fruits [produced] and half the soil, in accordance with the conditions on which they made terms with the Prophet. 'Umar paid them the price of half the products and half the soil in gold, silver and pack-saddles, and then expelled them.

The khuṭbah of 'Umar ibn-'Abd-al-'Azîz. 'Amr an-Nâḳid from abu-Burḳân:—The following is taken from the

[1] Kor., 59:6.

[2] Bakri, pp. 657-658; Wâḳidi, *Maghâzi*, p. 374.

speech of 'Umar ibn-'Abd-al-'Azîz on his installment in the caliphate: "Fadak was among the spoils that Allah assigned the Prophet and the 'Moslems pressed not against it with horse and camel.' When Fâṭimah asked him to give her the land, he said, 'Thou hast nothing to demand from me, and I have nothing to give thee.' The Prophet used to spend the income from it on wayfarers. Then came abu-Bakr, 'Umar, 'Uthmân and 'Ali who put it to the same use as the Prophet. But when Mu'âwiyah became caliph he gave it as fief to Marwân ibn-al-Ḥakam; and the latter bestowed it on my father and on 'Abd-al-Malik. Thus it was handed down to al-Walîd, Sulaimân and myself. When al-Walîd became caliph, I asked him to give me his share, which he did. In like manner, I asked Sulaimân for his share and he gave it. Thus I brought it into one whole again. And nothing that I possess is dearer to me than it! Be ye therefore my witnesses, that I have restored it to what it was."

Al-Ma'mûn gives Fadak to the descendants of Fâṭimah. In the year 210, the *commander of the believers* al-Ma'mûn 'Abdallâh ibn-Hârûn ar-Rashîd ordered that Fadak be delivered to the children of Fâṭimah. To that effect he wrote to his *'âmil* in al-Madînah, Ḳutham ibn-Ja'far, saying, "Greetings!—*The commander of the believers,* in his position in the religion of Allah and as caliph [successor] of his Prophet and a near relative to him, has the first right to enforce the Prophet's regulations and carry out his orders and deliver to him, whom the Prophet granted something or gave it as *ṣadaḳah,* the thing granted or given as such. In Allah alone does the success as well as the strength of the *commander of the believers* lie, and to do what makes him win His favor is his [the commander's] chief desire.

The Prophet had given Fâṭimah, his daughter, Fadak and bestowed it as *ṣadaḳah* on her. That was an evident and

well-known fact on which there was no disagreement among 33
the relatives of the Prophet, who do not cease to lay claim on what was given to Fâṭimah as *ṣadaḳah* and to which she is entitled. Consequently, the *commander of the believers* has deemed it right to return it to the heirs of Fâṭimah and deliver it to them, seeking thereby to win the favor of Allah by establishing his right and justice, and of Allah's Prophet by carrying out his command and his wish regarding his *ṣadaḳah*. This the *commander of the believers* ordered recorded in his registers and sent in writing to his *'âmils*. And since, after the death of the Prophet, it has been customary on every *mausim* [1] to have any person claim a grant, or *sadakah* or promise,[2] and to have his claim accepted, then Fâtimah's claim on what the Prophet has bestowed on her should—above that of every one else—be accepted as true.

The *commander of the believers* has written to al-Mubârik at-Ṭabari, his freedman, ordering him to give Fadak back to the heirs of Fâṭimah, the Prophet's daughter, with all its boundaries and the rights attached to it, and including its slaves and products and other things, all to be delivered to Muḥammad ibn-Yaḥya ibn-al-Ḥusain ibn-Zaid ibn-'Ali ibn-al-Ḥusain ibn-'Ali ibn-abi-Ṭâlib and to Muhammad ibn-'Abdallâh ibn-al-Hasan ibn-'Ali ibn-al-Ḥusain ibn-'Ali ibn-abi-Ṭâlib, both of whom the *commander of the believers* has put in charge of the land in behalf of its owners.

Know therefore that this is the opinion of the *commander of the believers* and what Allah has inspired him to do as His will, and what He has enabled him to do in the way of winning His favor and His Prophet's favor. Let those under thee know it; and treat Muḥammad ibn-Yaḥya

[1] Meeting time of the pilgrims, see *an-Nihâyah,* vol. iv, p. 211, and Muṭarrizi, *al-Mughrib*, vol. ii, p. 250.

[2] Ar. *'idat,* see Bukhâri, vol. ii, p. 285; vol. iii, p. 168.

and Muḥammad ibn-'Abdallâh as thou hast treated al-Mubârik aṭ-Ṭabari; and help them in any way that makes for the fertility, interest and productivity of the land. May it be Allah's will, and peace be unto thee.

Written on Wednesday, two days after the beginning of dhu-l-Ḳa'dah, year 210."

Al-Mutawakkil restores Fadak to its old condition. When al-Mutawakkil, however, became caliph, he ordered that the land be reinstated in the condition in which it had been before al-Ma'mûn.

CHAPTER VI

WÂDI-L-ḲURA AND TAIMÂ'

Wâdi-l-Ḳura taken by assault. When the Prophet departed from Khaibar, he came to Wâdi-l-Ḳura [1] and invited its people to Islam. They refused and started hostilities. 34
The Prophet reduced the place by force; and Allah gave him as booty the possessions of its inhabitants. To the lot of the Moslems fell pieces of furniture and other commodities of which the Prophet took away one-fifth. The Prophet left the land with its palm-trees in the hands of certain Jews on the same rent terms which he had made with the people of Khaibar.[2] Some say that 'Umar expelled its Jews and divided it among those who fought for its conquest. Others, however, say that 'Umar did not expel them, for it is not included in al-Ḥijâz. Today it is annexed to the administrative district of al-Madînah and is included among its suburbs.

Mid'am condemned to fire. I was informed by certain scholars that the Prophet had a slave, named Mid'am, whom Rifâ'ah ibn-Zaid al-Judhâmi had presented to him. During the invasion of Wâdi-l-Ḳura, Mid'am was shot by an arrow from an unknown quarter as he was putting down the saddle of the Prophet's camel. When someone remarked, "Blessed, O prophet of Allah, is thy slave, for he was shot by an arrow and suffered martyrdom," the Pro-

[1] Yâḳût, vol. iv, p. 678.

[2] Wâḳidi, tr. Wellhausen, p. 292.

phet replied, "Nay, the mantle he took from the spoils on the day of Khaibar shall verily burn on him like fire." [1]

Shaibân ibn-Farrûkh from al-Ḥasan:—Someone remarked to the Prophet, "Thy lad, so and so, has suffered martyrdom," to which the Prophet replied, "Rather he is dragged to fire in a mantle he unlawfully took from the spoils."

'Abd-al-Wâḥid ibn-Ghiyâth from al-Ḥasan:—Some one remarked to the Prophet, "Happy art thou, for thy lad, so and so, has suffered martyrdom!" to which he replied, "Rather he is dragged to fire in a mantle he unlawfully took from the spoils." [2]

Taimâ' capitulates. When the people of Taimâ' heard how the Prophet had subjugated the people of Wâdi-l-Ḳura, they made terms with him, agreeing to pay poll-tax, and they settled in their homes with their lands in their possession.[3] The Prophet assigned 'Amr ibn-Sa'îd ibn-al-'Âṣi ibn-Umaiyah as governor to Wâdi-l-Ḳura, and assigned Yazîd ibn-abi-Sufyân after its conquest, the latter having become Moslem on the day of the conquest of Taimâ'.

'Umar expels the inhabitants. 'Abd-al-A'la ibn-Ḥammâd an-Narsi from 'Umar ibn-'Abd-al-'Azîz:—'Umar ibn-al-Khaṭṭâb expelled the people of Fadak, Taimâ' and 35
Khaibar. The fight between the Prophet and the people of Wâdi-l-Ḳura took place in Jumâda II, year 7.

The fief of Ḥamzah ibn-an-Nu'mân. Al-'Abbâs ibn-Hishâm al-Kalbi from his grandfather:—The Prophet gave as fief to Ḥamzah ibn-an-Nu'mân ibn-Haudhah-l-'Udhri his whip's throw [4] in Wâdi-l-Kura. This Hamzah was the

[1] Hishâm, p. 765.
[2] Bukhâri, vol. iii, pp. 129-130.
[3] Diyârbakri, vol. ii, p. 65.
[4] Mawardi, p. 330.

chief of the banu-'Udhrah and the first of the people of al-Ḥijâz to offer the Prophet the *ṣadaḳah* of banu-'Udhrah.

The fief of 'Abd-al-Malik ibn-Marwân. 'Ali ibn-Muhammad from al-'Abbâs ibn-'Âmir's uncle:—'Abd-al-Malik ibn-Marwân called on Yazîd ibn-Mu'âwiyah and said, "O *commander of the believers,* Mu'âwiyah in his caliphate bought from certain Jews a piece of land in Wâdi-l-Ḳura and made many improvements in it. Thou hast let that land fall into negligence. It is therefore lost, and its income has decreased. Give it therefore as fief to me, and I shall take care of it." To this Yazîd replied: "We are not stingy in big things, nor can a trifling escape our eye." 'Abd-al-Malik then said, "Its income is so much . . . " "Thou canst have it," said Yazîd.[1] When 'Abd-al-Malik departed Yazîd remarked, "It is said that this is the man that will rule after us. If that is right, we would have done him favor and expect to receive something in repay; if it is false, we have granted him a gift."

[1] L. Caetani, *Annali dell Islâm,* vol. ii, p. 50, note 7.

CHAPTER VII

Makkah

The cause of its invasion. When the Prophet made arrangements with the Ḳuraish in the year of al-Ḥudaibiyah and wrote down the statement of the truce[1] to the effect that he who desires to make a covenant with Muḥammad can do so, and he who desires to make a covenant with Ḳuraish can do so; and that he of the *Companions* of the Prophet who comes to Ḳuraish should not be returned, and he of the banu-Ḳuraish or their allies who comes to the Prophet should be returned, then those of Kinânah who were present rose and said, "We will enter into a covenant with Ḳuraish, and accept their terms"; but Khuzâ'ah said, "We will enter into the covenant of Muḥammad and his contract." Since between 'Abd-al-Muṭṭalib and Khuzâ'ah an old alliance existed, 'Amr ibn-Sâlim ibn-Ḥaṣîrah-l-Khuzâ'i composed the following verse:

> "O Allah! I am seeking from Muḥammad
> the hereditary alliance of our father and his."[2] 36

One of the clan of Khuzâ'ah hearing one of the clan of Kinânah sing a poem satirizing the Prophet, attacked him and crushed his head. This incident provoked evil and fighting between the two parties. Ḳuraish reinforced banu-Kinânah and together they attacked Khuzâ'ah in the night time, thus violating the covenant and the arrangement.

[1] Wâḳidi, *Maghâzi*, p. 387; Hishâm, pp. 746-747, 803.

[2] Hishâm, p. 806; Wâḳidi, *Maghâzi*, p. 402; Fâkihi, p. 42.

Thereupon, 'Amr ibn-Ṣâlim ibn-Ḥaṣîrah-l-Khuzâ'i came to the Prophet and solicited his aid. This led the Prophet to invade Makkah.

The following is taken from a long tradition communicated to us by abu-'Ubaid al-Ḳâsim ibn-Sallâm on the authority of 'Urwah:—Ḳuraish made terms with the Prophet, stipulating that both parties promise each other security against treachery and stealth,[1] so that a man coming on pilgrimage to Makkah or to visit there, or passing on his way between al-Yaman and aṭ-Ṭâ'if is safe; and he of the "polytheists" who passes through al-Madînah on his way to Syria and the East is safe. In this covenant the Prophet included banu-Ka'b; and Ḳuraish included in their covenant their allies of the banu-Kinânah.

Abu-Sufyân as an envoy. 'Abd-al-Wâḥid ibn-Ghiyâth from 'Ikrimah:—The banu-Bakr of Kinânah were included in the peace terms of Ḳuraish, and the Khuzâ'ah were included in the peace terms of the Prophet. But a fight took 37
place between the banu-Bakr and Khuzâ'ah at 'Arafah.[2] Ḳuraish provided banu-Bakr with arms, and gave them water to drink, and shelter. Some of the Ḳuraish objected saying, "Ye have violated the covenant," yet the others replied, "We have not. By Allah, we did not fight. We only gave them provision, water, and shelter."

They, thereupon, said to abu-Sufyân ibn-Ḥarb, "Go and renew the alliance and reconcile the parties" Abu-Sufyân proceeded to al-Madînah where he met abu-Bakr and said to him, "Abu-Bakr, renew the alliance and reconcile the parties."

Abu-Bakr asked him to see 'Umar. Accordingly he met 'Umar and said, "Renew the alliance and reconcile the

[1] Hishâm, p. 747; Caetani, vol. ii, p. 106; Wâḳidi, tr. Wellhausen, p. 257, note 1; and *Fâ'iḳ*, vol. ii, p. 114.

[2] Hishâm, p. 803; Fâkihi, pp. 49 and 144-145; Yâḳût, vol. iii, p. 646.

parties," to which 'Umar replied, "May Allah cut off the alliance what is still connected and wear out what is still new." Abu-Sufyân then said, "By Allah I never saw a worse head of a tribe than thou!" Thence he went to Fâṭimah who asked him to meet 'Ali. This he did and made the same request. 'Ali replied, "Thou art the *sheikh* of Ḳuraish and its chief. Renew therefore the alliance and reconcile the parties." Abu-Sufyân then clapped his right hand against the left saying, "I have renewed the alliance and reconciled the parties."

He then left and came to Makkah. The Prophet had said, "Abu-Sufyân is coming. He returns satisfied without having effected any result." When he returned to the people of Makkah he told them what had happened and they said, "By Allah we know none more foolish than thou. Thou dost bring us neither war that we may be warned, nor peace that we may feel safe."

Khuzâ'ah then came to the Prophet and complained of what had befallen them. The Prophet said, "I was ordered to secure one of the two towns Makkah or aṭ-Ṭâ'if." Thereupon, the Prophet ordered that the march be commenced. Thus he set out with the *Companions* saying, "O Allah, strike upon their ears [with deafness] that they may not hear,[1] so that we may take them by surprise!" The Prophet pressed the march until he camped at Marr aẓ-Ẓahrân. Ḳuraish had asked abu-Sufyân to return. When he [abu-Sufyân] got to Marr aẓ-Ẓahrân and saw the fires and the tents he said, "What is the matter with the people? They seem like the people celebrating the night of 'Arafah." Saying this, he was surrounded by the Prophet's horsemen, who took him prisoner; and he was brought before the Prophet. 'Umar came and wanted to execute him, but al-

[1] *Cf.* Kor., 18: 10.

'Abbâs prevented him and he [abu-Sufyân] embraced Islâm and presented himself before the Prophet. When the time for morning prayer came, the Moslems bestirred themselves for ablution before prayer. "What is the matter?" said
abu-Sufyân to al-'Abbâs ibn-'Abd-al-Muṭṭalib, "Do they 38
mean to kill me?" "No," answered al-'Abbâs, "they have risen for prayer." As they began to pray, abu-Sufyân noticed that when the Prophet knelt they knelt; when he prostrated himself, they prostrated themselves; upon which he remarked, "By Allah I never saw, as I did to-day, the submissiveness of a people coming from here and there—not even in the case of the noble Persians, or the Greeks who have long fore-locks." [1]

Al-'Abbâs asked the Prophet saying, "Send me to the people of Makkah that I may invite them to Islâm." No sooner had the Prophet sent him than he called him back saying, "Bring my uncle back to me, that the 'polytheists' may not kill him." Al-'Abbâs, however, refused to return until he came to Makkah and made the following statement: "O ye people, embrace Islâm and ye shall be safe. Ye have been surrounded on all sides. Ye are confronted by a hard case that is beyond your power.[2] Here is Khâlid in the lower part of Makkah, there is az-Zubair in the upper part of it, and there is the Prophet of Allah at the head of the *Emigrants, Anṣâr* and Khuzâ'ah." To this Ḳuraish replied, "And what are Khuzâ'ah with their mutilated noses!"

The entrance into Makkah. 'Abd-al-Wâḥid ibn-Ghiyâth from abu-Hurairah:—The spokesman of Khuzâ'ah repeated the following verse before the Prophet:

[1] Fâkihi, p. 155; Wâḳidi, *Maghâzi*, p. 405.

[2] Fâkihi, p. 150; *Fâ'iḳ*, vol. i, p. 338.

"O Lord, I am seeking from Muḥammad
the hereditary alliance between our father and his.
Reinforce therefore, with Allah's guidance, a mighty victory,
and summon the worshippers of Allah, and they will come for help." [1]

Ḥammâd states on the authority of 'Ikrimah that Khuzâ'ah called the Prophet as he was washing himself, and the Prophet replied, "Here I am!"

According to al-Wâḳidi among others, a band of Ḳuraish took up arms on the day of the conquest [of Makkah] saying, "Never shall Muḥammad enter the city except by force." Accordingly, Khâlid ibn-al-Walîd led the fight against them and was the first to receive the order of the Prophet to enter.[2] So he killed twenty-four men from [the tribe of] Ḳuraish and four from [the tribe of] Hudhail. Others state that twenty-three men from Ḳuraish were
killed on that day and the rest took to flight seeking refuge 39
in the mountain heights which they climbed. Of the *Companions* of the Prophet, Kurz ibn-Jâbir al-Fihri, and Khâlid al-Ash'ar al-Ka'bi suffered martyrdom on that day. According to Hishâm ibn-al-Kalbi, however, the latter of the martyrs was Ḥubaish al-Ash'ar ibn-Khâlid al-Ka'bi [3] of the tribe of Khuzâ'ah.

Abu-Hurairah describes the conquest. Shaibân ibn-abi-Shaibah-l-Ubulli from 'Abdallâh ibn-Rabâḥ:—A number of deputations came to call on Mu'âwiyah. It was in Ramaḍân, and we used to prepare food for one another. Abu-Hurairah was one of those who often invited us to his dwelling-place. I [ibn-Rabâḥ] therefore prepared a meal and invited them. Then abu-Hurairah asked, "Shall I, O *Anṣâr*, amuse you with a narrative concerning you?" and

[1] Ṭabari, vol. i, pp. 1621-1622.

[2] Fâkihi, p. 153, *seq.*

[3] "Khunais ibn-Khâlid" in Hishâm, p. 817.

he went on to describe the conquest of Makkah as follows: "The Prophet advanced until he came to Makkah. At the head of one of the two wings of the army, he sent az-Zubair, at the head of the other, Khâlid ibn-al-Walîd, and of the infantry abu-'Ubaidah ibn-al-Jarrâḥ. The way they took was through the bottom of the valley. The Prophet was at the head of his cavalry detachment. On seeing me the Prophet called, 'Abu-Hurairah,' and I replied, 'Here I am, Prophet of Allah.' 'Summon the *Anṣâr*,' said he, 'and let no one come but my *Anṣâr*.' I summoned them and they came around. In the meantime, Ḳuraish had gathered their mob and followers saying, 'Let us send these ahead. If they win, we will join them; and if defeated, we shall give whatever is demanded.' 'Do ye see' said the Prophet, 'the mob of Ḳuraish?' 'We do,' answered the *Anṣâr*. He then made a sign with one hand over the other as if to say, 'kill them.' To this the Prophet added, 'Meet me at aṣ-Ṣafa.' Accordingly we set out, each man killing whomever he wanted to kill, until abu-Sufyân came to the Prophet saying, 'O Prophet of Allah, the majority of Ḳuraish is annihilated. There is no more Ḳuraish after this day.' [1] The Prophet thereupon announced, 'He who enters the house
of abu-Sufyân is safe, he who closes his own door is safe, 40
and he who lays down his arms is safe.' On this the *Anṣâr* remarked one to the other, 'The man is moved by love to his relatives and compassion on his clan.' The Prophet at this received the inspiration which we never failed to observe whenever it came. He therefore said: 'O ye *Anṣâr*, ye have said so and so . . . ' 'We have, Prophet of Allah,' replied the *Anṣâr*. 'Nay,' said the Prophet, 'I am the slave of Allah and his Prophet. I have immigrated to Allah and to you. 'My life is your life; my death is your death!'

[1] Fâkihi, p. 154.

Hearing this, the *Anṣâr* began to weep saying, 'By Allah, we said what we said only in our anxiety to spare the Prophet of Allah.' The people then crowded to the house of abu-Sufyân and closed its doors laying down their arms. The Prophet proceeded to the ' stone ' and laid hold of it. He then made the circuit of the ' House ' and came, with a bow in his hand held at its curved part, to an idol at the side of the Ka'bah. He began to stab the eye of the idol saying, 'Truth has come and falsehood has vanished, it is the property of vanity to vanish.' [1] When the circuit was done, he came to aṣ-Ṣafa, climbed it until he could see the ' House,' and he raised his hand praising Allah and praying."

The Prophet's orders. Muḥammad ibn-aṣ-Ṣabbâḥ from 'Ubaidallâh ibn-'Abdallâh ibn-'Utbah:—On the occasion of the conquest of Makkah, the Prophet made the following statement, " Slay no wounded person, pursue no fugitive, execute no prisoner; and whosoever closes his door is safe."

Ibn-Khaṭal proscribed. Al-Wâḳidi states that the invasion in which the conquest was effected was carried on in the month of Ramaḍân in the year 8. On that occasion the Prophet remained in Makkah to the time of the festival at the end of Ramaḍân, after which he proceeded to invade Ḥunain. To the governorship of Makkah he assigned 'Attâb ibn-Asîd ibn-abi-l-'Îṣ ibn-Umaiyah, and ordered the demolishing of the idols and the effacement of the pictures that stood in the Ka'bah. He also said, "Put ibn-Khaṭal to death, even if ye find him holding the curtains of the Ka'bah." Accordingly, abu-Barzah[2]-l-Aslami put him to death. According 41
to abu-al-Yaḳẓân, however, the name of ibn-Khaṭal was Ḳais, and the one who put him to death was abu-Shiryâb al-Anṣâri. This ibn-Khaṭal had two female slave-

[1] Kor., 17: 83.

[2] Al-Wâḳidi, p. 414, calls him abu-Bardah; *cf.* ibn-Duraid, *Kitâb al-Ishtiḳâḳ*, p. 66; Nawâwi, *Tahdhîb al-Asmâ'*, p. 788; Hishâm, p. 819.

singers who always sang poems satirizing the Prophet. One of them was killed, and the other lived to the time of 'Uthmân when a rib of hers was broken and caused her death.

Miḳyas ibn-Ṣubâbah proscribed. Numailah ibn-'Abdallâh al-Kinâni killed Miḳyas ibn-Ṣubâbah-l-Kinâni, the Prophet having announced that whosoever finds him may kill him. The Prophet did this for the following reason: Miḳyas had a brother, Hâshim ibn-Ṣubâbah ibn-Ḥazn, who embraced Islâm and witnessed with the Prophet the invasion made on al-Muraisî'. Hâshim was mistaken by one of the *Anṣâr* for a "polytheist" and killed. Miḳyas thereupon came to the Prophet and the Prophet decreed that the relatives of the slayer responsible for the bloodwit should pay it. Miḳyas received the bloodwit and became Moslem. Later he attacked his brother's slayer, slew him and took to flight, after which he apostatised from Islam and said:

"My soul has been healed by having him lie,
 deep in the blood flowing from his veins his clothes soaked,
I took revenge on him by force leaving it,
 for the leaders of banu-an-Najjâr, the high in rank, to pay his bloodwit,
thereby I attained my ambition, and satisfied my vengeance,
 and I was the first to forsake Islâm."[1]

Al-Ḥuwairith proscribed. 'Ali ibn-abi-Ṭâlib killed al-Ḥuwairith ibn-Nuḳaidh ibn-Bujair[2] ibn-'Abd ibn-Ḳuṣai, the Prophet having declared that whosoever finds him may kill him.

Ibn-Khaṭal's slave-singers. Bakr ibn-al-Haitham from al-Kalbi:—A female slave-singer owned by Hilâl ibn-'Abdallâh, i. e., ibn-Khaṭal al-Adrami of the banu-Taim, came to the Prophet in disguise. She embraced Islâm and acknowl-

[1] Mawardi, pp. 229-230.

[2] Hishâm, p. 819.

edged the Prophet as chief. Not knowing who she was, the Prophet did not molest her. The other singer of Hilâl was killed. Both singers, however, used to sing satires against the Prophet.

Ibn-az-Ziba'ra embraces Islam. Ibn-az-Ziba'ra as-Sahmi embraced Islâm before the Moslems had chance to kill him, and sang poems in praise of the Prophet. On the day of 42
the conquest of Makkah the Prophet declared his blood lawful, but he was not molested.

The Prophet's khuṭbah. Muḥammad ibn-aṣ-Ṣabbâḥ al-Bazzâz from al-Ḳâsim ibn-Rabî'ah:—On the day of the battle of Makkah the Prophet delivered the following *khuṭbah* [speech]: " Praise be to Allah who made his promise true, and gave his army victory[1] and all alone defeated the 'confederates.' Verily every privilege of pre-Islamic time and every blood and every claim lie under my feet with the exception of the custody of the 'House'[2] and the providing of the Pilgrims with beverage."

Khalaf al-Bazzâr from 'Abdallâh ibn-'Abd-ar-Raḥmân's *sheikhs*:—On the day of the conquest of Makkah the Prophet asked Ḳuraish, "What think ye?"[3] to which they replied, "What we think is good, and what we say is good. A noble brother thou art, and the son of a noble brother. Thou hast succeeded." The Prophet then said, "My answer is that given by my brother Joseph,[4] 'No blame be on you this day. Allah will forgive you; for he is the most merciful of the merciful.' Verily every debt, possession, and privilege of pre-Islam lie under my feet with the exception of the custody of the 'House' and providing the pilgrims with beverage."

[1] Hishâm, p. 821.

[2] The sanctuary at Makkah; Azraḳi, p. 17 *seq.*

[3] Ṭabari, vol. i, p. 1642.

[4] Kor., 12:92.

Shaibân from 'Abdallâh ibn-'Ubaid ibn-'Umair:—The Prophet said in his *khuṭbah,* "Yea, all Makkah is inviolable. What is between its two rugged mountains was not lawful for any one before me, nor will it be made for any after me. To me it was made lawful for only one hour on one day. Its fresh herbage shall not be cut, its thorny trees shall not be felled, its game shall not be chased, what is found [1] in it shall not be kept unless previous announcement has been made of the find." Al-'Abbâs said, "From this should be excluded the *idhkhir* plant [2] to be used by our jewelers, blacksmiths and as a means of cleansing [3] our houses." The Prophet then added, "The *idhkhir* is excluded."

Yûsuf ibn-Mûsa-l-Ḳaṭṭân from ibn-'Abbâs:—The Prophet said, "The fresh herbage of Makkah shall not be cut, its trees shall not be felled." "With the exception of the 43
idhkhir plant," remarked al-'Abbâs, "which is for the blacksmiths [4] and for the cleansing of the houses." This the Prophet allowed.

'Umar advised not to confiscate the treasure. Shaibân from al-Ḥasan:—'Umar wanted to seize the treasure of the Ka'bah to use it in the cause of Allah. But Ubai ibn-Ka'b al-Anṣâri turned to him and said: "Before thee, 'Commander of the Believers' came thy two *companions*; [5] who would have surely done so, if it were an act of virtue." [6]

Makkah inviolable. 'Amr an-Nâḳid from Mujâhid: [7]—

[1] Abu-Isḥâḳ ash-Shirâzi, *at-Tanbîh,* p. 156.

[2] A sweet rush resembling papyrus used for roofing houses.

[3] Ar. *ṭuhûr,* according to other readings *ẓuhûr* "and for the roofs." See Wâḳidi, tr. Wellhausen, pp. 338-339.

[4] Ar. *ḳuyûn*; Azraḳi, p. 85, has *ḳubûr* "graves".

[5] Muḥammad and abu-Bakr.

[6] Caetani, vol. ii, p. 129, note 1.

[7] ibn-Jabr; see an-Nawâwi, p. 540.

" Makkah is inviolable," said the Prophet, " It is not legal either to sell its dwellings or to rent its houses."

The dwelling places of Makkah not to be rented. Muḥammad ibn-Ḥâtim al-Marwazi from 'Â'ishah who said, " Once I said to the Prophet, ' Build for thee, Prophet of Allah, a house in Makkah that will protect thee against the sun,' to which he replied, ' Makkah is the dwelling place only of those who are already in it.' "

Khalaf ibn-Hishâm al-Bazzâr from ibn-Juraij who said, " I have read a letter written by 'Umar ibn-'Abd-al-'Azîz in which the renting of houses in Makkah is prohibited."

Abu-'Ubaid from ibn-'Umar:—The latter said: " The whole of *al-Ḥaram* is a place of worship." [1]

'Amr an-Nâḳid from 'Abd-al-Malik ibn-abi-Sulaimân: —A message written by 'Umar ibn-'Abd-al-'Azîz to the chief of Makkah reads: " Let not the inhabitants of Makkah receive rent for their houses because it is not legal for them."

The following tradition regarding the text, "Alike for those who abide therein and for the stranger [2] " was communicated to us by 'Uthmân ibn-abi-Shaibah from 'Abd-ar-Raḥmân ibn-Sâbit:—By the stranger is meant the pilgrims and visitors who go there and who have equal right in the buildings, being entitled to live wherever they want, provided none of the natives of Makkah goes out of his home.

The following tradition regarding the same text was communicated to us by 'Uthmân on the authority of Mujâhid:—The inhabitants of Makkah and other people are alike so far as the dwellings are concerned.

'Uthmân and 'Amr from Mujâhid:—'Umar ibn-al-Khaṭṭâb 44
once said to the people of Makkah, " Make no doors for your houses that the stranger may live wherever he wants."

[1] Azraḳi, p. 5 *seq.*

[2] Kor., 22:25.

'Uthmân ibn-abi-Shaibah and Bakr ibn-al-Haitham from abu-Ḥaṣîn.—The latter said, " I once told Sa'id ibn-Jubair in Makkah that I wanted to 'abide therein' to which he replied, 'Thou art already abiding therein' and he read, 'Alike for those who abide therein and for the stranger.' "

The following tradition in explanation of the same text was communicated to us by 'Uthmân on the authority of Sa'îd ibn-Jubair :—All people in it are alike whether they are the inhabitants of Makkah or of some other place.

Muhammad ibn-Sa'd from al-Wâḳidi :—Many cases were brought before abu-Bakr ibn-Muhammad ibn-'Amr ibn-Hazm regarding the rents of the houses of Makkah, and abu-Bakr in each case judged against the tenant. This too is the view of Mâlik and ibn-abi-Dhi'b. But according to Rabî'ah and abu-az-Zinâd, there is no harm in taking money for renting houses or for selling dwellings in Makkah.[1]

Al-Wâḳidi said, " I saw ibn-abi-Dhi'b receiving the rent of his house in Makkah between aṣ-Ṣafa and al-Marwah."

It was said by al-Laith ibn-Sa'd, " Whatever has the form of a house its rent is legal for its proprietor. As for the halls, the roads, the courts, and the abodes that are in a state of ruins, he who comes to them first can have them first without rent."

A tradition to the same effect was transmitted to me by abu-'Abd-ar-Rahmân al-Awdi on the authority of ash-Shâfi'i.

Said Sufyân ibn-Sa'id ath-Thauri: " To rent a house in Makkah is illegal " ; and he insisted on that.

According to al-Auzâ'i, ibn-abi-Laila and abu-Hanîfah, if the rent is made during the nights of the Pilgrimage it is void, but if it is in other nights, whether the one who hires is a neighbor or not, it is all right.

[1] *Cf.* Ḳuṭb-ad-Din, *al-I'lâm*, p. 17.

According to certain followers of abu-Yûsuf, its rent is absolutely legal. The one "abiding therein" and the "stranger" are alike only as regards making the circuit of the "House."

The plants of the Ḥaram. Al-Ḥusain ibn-'Ali ibn-al-
Aswad from 'Abd-ar-Raḥmân ibn-al-Aswad:—The latter
found no harm in gathering vegetables, cutting, eating or
making any other use of anything else planted by man in 45
Makkah be it palm-trees or otherwise. He only disapproved
of this being done with trees and plants that grow of their
own accord without the agency of man. From this category *al-idhkhir* was excluded. According to al-Ḥasan ibn-
Ṣâliḥ, 'Abd-ar-Raḥmân allowed it in the case of rotten trees
that have decayed and fallen to pieces.

According to the view of Mâlik and ibn-abi-Dhi'b, as stated by Muḥammad ibn-'Umar al-Wâḳidi, regarding the legality or illegality of felling a tree of the Ḥaram, it is wrong at all events; but if the man who does it is ignorant he should be taught and receive no penalty; if he knows but is impious, he should be punished without paying the value of the trees. He who cuts it may have it for his use. According to abu-Sufyân ath-Thauri and abu-Yûsuf, he should pay the value of the tree he cuts and cannot have the wood for his use. The same view is held by abu-Ḥanîfah.

According to Mâlik ibn-Anas and ibn-abi-Dhi'b, there is no harm in cutting the branches of the *thumâm* plant and the ends of the senna plant from the Ḥaram to be used as medicine or tooth-picks.

According to Sufyân ibn-Sa'îd, abu-Ḥanîfah, and abu-Yûsuf, whatever in the Ḥaram is grown by man or was grown by him can be cut with impunity; whatever is grown without the agency of man, its cutter should be responsible for its value.

"I once," said al-Wâḳidi," asked ath-Thauri and abu-Yûsuf regarding the case of one who plants in the Ḥaram something that is not ordinarily grown and which he tends until it grows high, would it be right for him to cut it. They answered in the affirmative. Then I asked about the case of a tree that may grow of its own accord in his garden and that does not belong to the category of trees planted by man, and they said, 'He can do with it whatever he likes.'"

Muḥammad ibn-Sa'd from al-Wâḳidi:—The latter said, "It has been reported to us that ibn-'Umar used to eat in Makkah vegetables grown in the Ḥaram."

Muḥammad ibn-Sa'd from Mu'âdh ibn-Muḥammad:—The latter said, "I have seen on the table of az-Zuhri vegetables grown in the Ḥaram."

"No pilgrim or visitor of the Ḥaram," said abu-Ḥanîfah, "shall have his camel graze in the Ḥaram, nor shall he cut grass for it." The same view is held by Zufar. But Mâlik, ibn-abi-Dhi'b, Sufyân, abu-Yûsuf and ibn-abi-Sabrah are of the opinion that there is no harm in having the animals graze, but the man should not cut the grass for them. Ibn-abi-Laila, however, holds that there is no harm in having someone cut the grass.

'Affân and al'Abbâs ibn-al-Walîd an-Narsi from Laith:— 46
'Aṭâ' found no harm in using the vegetables of the Ḥaram as well as what is planted therein including the branches and the tooth-picks, but Mujâhid disapproved of it.

The history of the Ḥaram-mosque. The Ḥaram-mosque at the time of the Prophet and abu-Bakr had no wall to surround it. When 'Umar, however, became caliph and the number of the Moslems increased, he enlarged the mosque and bought certain houses which he demolished to increase its size. Certain neighbors of the mosque refused to sell their houses and 'Umar had to demolish their houses, the prices of which he deposited in the treasury of al-Ka'bah until they took them later.[1] Moreover he raised around the mosque a low wall not higher than a man's stature. On this wall the lamps were put. When 'Uthmân ibn-'Affân became caliph, he purchased certain dwellings and thereby enlarged the mosque. Certain people whose dwellings he seized after depositing their prices, met him near the "House" with loud protests, upon which 'Uthmân addressed them as follows: "It is only my compassion on you and my leniency in dealing with you that made you venture to do this against me. 'Umar did exactly what I am doing but ye kept silent and were satisfied." He then ordered them to jail where they remained until 'Abdallâh ibn-Khâlid ibn-Asîd[2] ibn-abi-l-'Îṣ spoke to him on their behalf and they were released.

It is reported that 'Uthmân was the first to erect the porches of the mosque, which he did on the occasion of enlarging it.

In the days of Abraham, Jurhum and the 'Amâliḳ, the bottom of the door of the Ka'bah was level with the ground until it was built by Ḳuraish, at which time abu-Ḥudhaifah ibn-al-Mughîrah said, "Raise, people, the door of the Ka'bah, so that no one may enter without a ladder. Then would no man whom ye do not want to enter be able to do so. In case some one ye hate should come, ye may throw him down, and he will fall injuring those behind." The suggestion was followed by Ḳuraish.

When 'Abdallâh ibn-az-Zubair ibn-al-'Auwâm fortified himself in the Ḥaram-mosque, taking refuge in it against al-Ḥuṣain ibn-Numair as-Sakûni who was fighting with a Syrian army, one of 'Abdallâh's followers carried one day

[1] Azraḳi, p. 307.

[2] or Usaid; see Azraḳi, p. 307.

burning fibres of a palm-tree on the top of a lance. The wind being violent, a spark flew and attached itself to the curtains of the Ka'bah and burnt them. As a result, the walls were cracked, and turned black. This took place in the year 64. After the death of Yazîd ibn-Mu'âwiyah and the departure of al-Ḥuṣain ibn-Numair to Syria. ibn-az-Zubair ordered that the stones that had been thrown into it[1] 47
be removed, and they were removed. He then demolished the Ka'bah, and rebuilt it on its old foundation, using stones in the building. He opened two doors on the ground, one to the east, and the other to the west; one for entrance and the other for exit. In building it he found that the foundation was laid on *al-Ḥijr.*[2] His object was to give it the shape it had in the days of Abraham, as it had been described to him by 'Â'ishah, *the mother of the believers,* on the authority of the Prophet.[3] The doors of the Ka'bah, ibn-az-Zubair plated with gold, and its keys he made of gold. When al-Ḥajjâj ibn-Yûsuf fought on behalf of 'Abd-al-Malik ibn-Marwân and killed ibn-az-Zubair, 'Abd-al-Malik wrote to al-Ḥajjâj ordering him to rebuild the Ka'bah and the Ḥaram-mosque, the stones hurled at it having made cracks in the walls. Accordingly, al-Ḥajjâj pulled the Ka'bah down and rebuilt it according to the shape given it by Ḳuraish, removing all stones thereof. After this 'Abd-al-Malik often repeated, "I wish I had made ibn-az-Zubair do with the Ka'bah and its structure what he voluntarily undertook to do!"[4]

The cover of the Ka'bah. In pre-Islamic times the cover

[1] *Cf.* Ḳuṭb-ad-Dîn, p. 81.

[2] The space comprised by the curved wall al-Ḥaṭîm, which encompasses the Ka'bah on the north-west side.

[3] Ḳuṭb-ad-Dîn, p. 81.

[4] *Ibid.*, p. 84.

of the Ka'bah consisted of pieces of leather and *ma'âfir*[1] cloth. The Prophet covered it with Yamanite cloths, 'Umar and 'Uthmân clothed it in Coptic cloths, and Yazîd ibn-Mu'âwiyah clothed it in Khusruwâni silk.[2] After Yazîd, ibn-az-Zubair and al-Ḥajjâj clothed it in silk. The Umaiyads during a certain part of their rule, clothed it in robes offered as tribute by the people of Najrân. The Umaiyads used to strip[3] the Ka'bah of its old covers when the cloths of silk were put on. At last came al-Walîd ibn-'Abd-al-Malik who amplified the Ḥaram-mosque and conveyed to it columns of stone and marble, and mosaic. According to al-Wâkidi, al-Manṣûr added to the mosque during his caliphate and rebuilt it. This took place in the year 139.

The reconstruction of the two mosques. It has been stated by 'Ali ibn-Muḥammad ibn-'Abdallâh al-Madâ'ini, that Ja'far ibn-Sulaimân ibn-'Ali ibn-'Abdallâh ibn-al-'Abbâs was made by al-Mahdi governor over Makkah, al-Madînah and al-Yamâmah. Ja'far enlarged the two mosques of Makkah and al-Madînah and rebuilt them.

Al-Mutawakkil—Ja'far ibn-abi-Isḥâḳ al-Mu'taṣim-Billâh 48
ibn-ar-Rashîd Harûn ibn-al-Mahdi—renewed the marble of the Ka'bah, made a belt of silver around it, plated its walls and ceiling with gold—which act was unprecedented—, and clothed its pillars with silk.[4]

[1] A tribe in al-Yaman. See *Nihâyah,* vol. iii, p. 109; and *cf.* Yâḳût, vol. iv, p. 282.

[2] *Cf.* Azraḳi, p. 176; Ḳuṭb-ad-Dîn, p. 68.

[3] Azraḳi, p. 180.

[4] Ḳuṭb-ad-Dîn, p. 54.

CHAPTER VIII

THE WELLS OF MAKKAH

BEFORE Ḳuṣai brought Ḳuraish together, and before they entered Makkah, they used for drinking purposes reservoirs, rain-water tanks on mountain tops, a well called al-Yusairah dug by Lu'ai ibn-Ghâlib outside the Ḥaram and another well called ar-Rawa dug by Murrah ibn-Ka'b and which lay just beyond 'Arafah. Later, Kilâb ibn-Murrah[1] dug outside of Makkah three wells Khumm, Rumm and Jafr; and Ḳuṣai ibn-Kilâb dug another which he called al-'Ajûl and prepared a drinking place in connection with it.[2]

After the death of Ḳuṣai a certain man of the banu-Naṣr ibn-Mu'âwiyah fell into al-'Ajûl well and it was no more used.

Badhdhar was a well dug by Hâshim ibn-'Abd-Manâf. It lies close to Khandamah at the mouth of abu-Ṭâlib's water-course. This Hâshim also dug Sajlah[3] which Asad ibn-Hâshim gave to 'Adi ibn-Naufal ibn-'Abd-Manâf abu-l-Muṭ'im. It is asserted by some, however, that he sold it to him, and by others that it was 'Abd-al-Muṭṭalib who gave it to him when he dug Zamzam and the water became abundant in Makkah. This Sajlah was later included in 49
the Mosque.

'Abd-Shams ibn-'Abd-Manâf dug out aṭ-Ṭawi which lay in the upper part of Makkah. He dug out another for his

[1] Azraḳi, pp. 436, 439, 496; Hishâm, p. 95.

[2] A few verses composed in regard to this and other wells have been omitted from the translation.

[3] Bakri, p. 766; Fâkihi, p. 120.

special use called al-Jafr. Maimûn ibn-al-Ḥaḍram, an ally of the banu-'Abd-Shams ibn-'Abd-Manâf, dug his own well which was the last to be dug in Makkah during the pre-Islamic period. Near by this well, lies the tomb of al-Manṣûr the "Commander of the Believers." The first name of al-Ḥaḍrami was 'Abdallâh ibn-'Imâd.[1] Besides, 'Abd-Shams dug two wells which he called Khumm and Rumm[2] after Kilâb ibn-Murrah's wells. Khumm lay near the dam, and Rumm near Khadîjah's house.

Banu-Asad ibn-'Abd-al-'Uzza ibn-Ḳuṣai dug a well called Shufiyah, the well of the banu-Asad.[3]

Umm-Aḥrâd was one dug by the banu-'Abd-ad-Dâr ibn-Ḳuṣai.

Banu-Jumaḥ dug as-Sunbulah well which is the same as 50
the well of Khalaf ibn-Wahb al-Jumaḥi.

Banu-Sahm dug the well called al-Ghamr which is the well of al-'Âṣi ibn-Wâ'il.

Banu-'Adi dug al-Ḥafîr.

Banu-Makhzûm dug as-Suḳya, the well of Hishâm ibn-al-Mughîrah ibn-'Abdallâh ibn-'Umar ibn-Makhzûm.

Banu-Taim dug ath-Thuraiya which is the well of 'Abdallâh ibn-Jud'ân ibn-'Amr ibn-Ka'b ibn-Sa'd ibn-Taim.

The banu-'Âmir ibn-Lu'ai dug an-Naḳ'.

Jubair ibn-Muṭ'im had a well—the banu-Naufal well, which has lately been included in Dâr al-Ḳawârîr erected by Ḥammâd al-Barbari in the caliphate of Harûn ar-Rashîd.[4]

In the pre-Islamic period, 'Aḳîl ibn-abi-Ṭâlib had dug a well which is now included in the house of ibn-Yûsuf.[5]

Al-Aswad ibn-abi-l-Bakhtari ibn-Hâshim ibn-al-Ḥârith ibn-Asad ibn-'Abd-al-'Uzza had at al-Aswad gate near by al-

[1] Nawâwi, p. 432.

[2] Bakri, pp. 318, 437-438.

[3] Azraḳi, p. 438.

[4] Azraḳi, p. 437.

[5] Azraḳi, p. 441.

Ḥannâṭîn [embalmers'] a well that was later added into the Mosque.

'Ikrimah well was named after 'Ikrimah ibn-Khâlid ibn-al-'Âsi ibn-Hâshim ibn-al-Mughîrah; 'Amr well, as well as 'Amr water-course, after 'Amr ibn-'Abdallâh ibn-Ṣafwân ibn-Umaiyah ibn-Khalaf al-Jumaḥi. Aṭ-Ṭalûb, which lay in the lower part of Makkah, was the property of 'Abdallâh ibn-Ṣafwân. Ḥuwaiṭib well was named after Ḥuwaiṭib ibn-'Abd-al-'Uzza ibn-abi-Ḳais of banu-'Âmir ibn-Lu'ai, and 51
it lay in the court of his house at the bottom of the valley. Abu-Mûsa well belonged to abu-Mûsa-l-Ash'ari and lay at al-Ma'lât. Shaudhab well was named after Shaudhab, Mu'âwiyah's freedman, and was later added to the Mosque. Some say that this Shaudhab was the freedman of Ṭâriḳ ibn-'Alkamah ibn-'Uraij ibn-Jadhîmah-l-Kinâni, others that he was the freedman of Nâfi' ibn-'Alḳamah ibn-Safwân ibn-Umaiyah . . . ibn-Shiḳḳ al-Kinâni, a maternal uncle of Marwân ibn-al-Ḥakam ibn-abi-l-'Âṣi ibn-Umaiyah. Bakkâr well was named after a man from al-'Irâḳ who lived in Makkah, and it lay in dhu-Ṭuwa; Wardân well after Wardân, a freedman of as-Sâ'ib[1] ibn-abi-Wadâ'ah ibn-Dubairah as-Sahmi. Sirâj drinking place lay in Fakh and belonged to Sirâj, a freedman of the banu-Hâshim. Al-Aswad well was named after al-Aswad ibn-Sufyân . . . ibn-Makhzûm and lay near the well of Khâliṣah, a freed-maid of al-Mahdi the "Commander of the Believers." Al-Barûd which lay in Fakh belonged to Mukhtarish[2] al-Ka'bi of [the tribe of] Khuzâ'ah.

Certain houses and gardens in Makkah. According to ibn-al-Kalbi, the owner of ibn-'Alḳamah house in Makkah was Ṭâriḳ ibn-'Alḳamah ibn-'Uraij ibn-Jadhîmah-l-Kinâni.

[1] Azraḳi, p. 442, gives al-Muṭṭalib; *cf.* Hishâm, p. 462.

[2] Azraḳi, p. 442, gives Khirâsh.

According to abu-'Ubaidah Ma'mar ibn-al-Muthanna, 'Abd-al-Malik ibn-Ḳuraib al-Aṣma'i and others, ibn-'Âmir garden was the property of 'Umar ibn-'Ubaidallâh . . . ibn-Lu'ai and was by mistake called ibn-'Âmir or the banu-'Âmir garden. In reality, it is ibn-Ma'mar's garden. Others say that it was so called after ibn-'Âmir al-Ḥaḍrami; still others, after ibn-'Âmir ibn-Kuraiz, and all that is mere guessing.

I was told by Mus'ab ibn-'Abdallâh az-Zubairi that Makkah in pre-Islamic times was called Ṣalâḥ.

Ibn-Sibâ' jail. The following was told to me by al-'Abbâs 52
ibn-Hishâm al-Kalbi:—A certain Kindi inquired in writing from my father about the one after whom ibn-Sibâ' jail of al-Madînah was named, about the story of Dâr an-Nadwah, Dâr al-'Ajalah, and Dâr al-Ḳawârîr in Makkah. My father wrote back the following answer: "As for ibn-Sibâ' jail, it was a house for 'Abdallâh ibn-Sibâ' ibn-'Abd-al-'Uzza ibn-Naḍlah ibn-'Amr ibn-Ghubshân al-Khuzâ'i. Sibâ' was surnamed abu-Niyâr and his mother was a midwife in Makkah. In the battle of Uḥud, he was challenged by Ḥamzah ibn-'Abd-al-Muṭṭalib who cried, 'Come, thou son of the female circumciser!'[1] and killed him. As Ḥamzah stooped on his victim to take his armor, he was thrust with a spear by Waḥshi. The mother of the poet Ṭuraiḥ ibn-Ismâ'il ath-Thaḳafi was the daughter of 'Abdallâh ibn-Sibâ', an ally of the banu-Zuhrah.

Dâr an-Nadwah. As for an-Nadwah [council-chamber], it was built by Ḳuṣai ibn-Kilâb, and people used to meet in it and have the cases decided.[2] Later, Ḳuraish used to assemble in it to consult about war and general affairs, to assign the standard-bearers and to contract marriages. This was the first house established in Makkah by Ḳuraish.

[1] "An expression of contumely used by the Arabs whether the mother is really a female circumciser or not." (*Tâj al-'Arûs.*)

[2] Azraḳi, pp. 65, 66; Diyârbakri, vol. i, p. 175; Ṭabari, vol. i, p. 1098; Iṣṭakhri, p. 16.

Dâr al-'Ajalah. Then comes Dâr al-'Ajalah which belonged to Sa'îd ibn-Sa'd ibn-Sahm. The banu-Sahm claim that it was built before an-Nadwah; but this is a false claim. An-Nadwah remained in the hands of the banu-'Abd-ad-Dâr ibn-Ḳuṣai until it was sold by 'Ikrimah ibn-Hâshim ibn-'Abd-Manâf ibn-'Abd-ad-Dâr ibn-Kusai to Mu'âwiyah ibn-abi-Sufyân, and the latter converted it into a governor's house.

Dâr al-Ḳawârîr. Dâr al-Kawârîr belonged to 'Utbah ibn-Rabî'ah ibn-'Abd-Shams ibn-'Abd-Manâf, then to al-'Abbâs ibn-'Utbah ibn-'Abd-Shams ibn-'Abd-al-Muttalib, and later to Ja'far's mother, Zubaidah, daughter of abu-l-Faḍl ibn-al-Manṣûr the "Commander of the Believers." Because earthen jars were partly used in making its pavement and walls, the hall was called al-Ḳawârîr [the jar building]. It was built by Ḥammâd al-Barbari in the caliphate 53
of ar-Rashîd.

Ku'aiki'ân and Ajyâd. It was related by Hishâm ibn-Muhammad al-Kalbi that 'Amr ibn-Muḍâḍ al-Jurhumi fought with another Jurhum man named as-Sumaida'. 'Amr appeared carrying arms that were rattling. Hence Ku'aiki'ân [rattling] the name of the place from which he appeared. As-Sumaida' appeared with bells covering his horses' necks. Hence Ajyâd [necks] the name of the place whence he appeared. According to ibn-al-Kalbi, it was said that he appeared with horses that were marked, hence the name Ajyâd [steeds]. The common people of Makkah, however, call it "Jiyâd aṣ-Ṣaghîr" and "Jiyâd al-Kabîr."

Al-Walîd ibn-Sâlih from Kathîr ibn-'Abdallâh's grandfather, who said:—"We accompanied 'Umar ibn-al-Khattâb on his visit in the year 17, and on the way were met by the owners of the wells, who asked 'Umar for permission to build dwelling places between Makkah and al-Madînah where, up to that time, no houses stood. 'Umar granted them permission, but imposed the condition that the wayfarer should have the first claim on the water and shade."

CHAPTER IX

THE FLOODS IN MAKKAH

Umm-Nahshal flood. Al-'Abbâs ibn-Hishâm from ibn-Kharrabûdh al-Makki and others:—Makkah was visited by four floods. One was umm-Nahshal flood which took place in the days of 'Umar ibn-al-Khaṭṭâb.[1] This flood rose so high that it penetrated into the Mosque from the highest part of Makkah. 'Umar therefore made two dams, the higher of which extended between the house of Babbah (so called by its occupants, the house being that of 'Abdallâh ibn-al-Ḥârith ibn-'Abd-al-Muṭṭalib ibn-'Abd-Manâf who ruled al-Baṣrah at the time of the insurrection of ibn-az-Zubair) and the house of Abân ibn-'Uthmân ibn-'Affân. The lower dam lay at al-Ḥammârîn; and it is the one known as Âl-Âsîd dam. Thus was the flood kept back from the Ḥaram mosque. According to the same tradition umm-Nahshal, the daughter of 'Ubaidah[2] ibn-Sa'îd ibn-al-'Âṣi
ibn-Umaiyah, was carried away by the flood from the higher 54
part of Makkah and therefore was the flood named after her.

Al-Juḥâf w-al-Jurâf. Another flood was that of al-Juḥâf w-al-Jurâf which took place in the year 80 in the time of 'Abd-al-Malik ibn-Marwân. It overtook the pilgrims on a Monday morning and carried them away together with their baggage, and surrounded the Ka'bah. About this the poet said:

[1] Azraḳi, pp. 394-398.

[2] Azraḳi, pp. 394-395: "'Ubaid".

"Ghassân never saw a day like Monday,
when so many were saddened and so many eyes wept;
and when the flood carried away the people of al-Miṣrain [1]
and made the secluded women run astray climbing the mountains." [2]

On this occasion, 'Abd-al-Malik wrote to his *'âmil* in Makkah, 'Abdallâh ibn-Sufyân al-Makhzûmi — others say that the poet al-Hârith ibn-Khâlid al-Makhzûmi was his *'âmil*—ordering him to build walls without clay around the houses that bordered on the valley, and around the Mosque, and to erect dams at the openings of the roads, so that the houses should be secure. To this effect, he sent a Christian who made the walls and set up the dam known as the banu-Kurâd's or banu-Jumah's. Other dams were constructed in lower Makkah. A poet says:

"One drop of tears I shall keep, the other I shall pour forth,
if I pass the dam of the banu-Ḳurâd."

Al-Mukhabbil. Another flood was the one called al-Mukhabbil. When it came, many were afflicted with a disease in their body and palsy in their tongues. Hence the name al-Mukhabbil [rendering some limb crippled].

Abu-Shâkir. Still another flood came later in the caliphate of Hishâm ibn-'Abd-al-Malik in the year 120. It is known as abu-Shâkir flood after Maslamah ibn-Hishâm, who in that year had charge of the fair [of the pilgrims].

Wâdi-Makkah. The flood of Wâdi-Makkah comes from a place known as Sidrat 'Attâb ibn-Asîd ibn-abi-l-Îṣ.

The flood in the caliphate of ar-Rashîd. It was reported by 'Abbâs ibn-Hishâm that a great flood took place in the caliphate of al-Ma'mûm 'Abdallâh ibn-ar-Rashîd; and its water rose almost as high as the "stone." [3]

[1] Al-Baṣrah and al-Kûfah.

[2] *Cf.* Azraki, p. 396.

[3] The "black stone" of al-Ka'bah; Azraḳi, p. 397.

The limits of al-Haram. Al-‘Abbâs from ‘Ikrimah:—A
part of the limits set to al-Ḥaram having been obliterated in
the days of Mu‘âwiyah ibn-abi-Sufyân, he wrote to Marwan 55
ibn-al-Hakam, his *‘âmil* in al-Madînah, ordering him to ask
Kurz ibn-‘Alkamah-l-Khuzâ‘i, if he were still alive, to establish the limits of al-Ḥaram, since he was familiar with
them. Kurz was still alive; and he established the limits
which are today the marks of al-Ḥaram. According to al-
Kalbi, this was Kurz ibn-‘Alḳamah ibn-Hilâl ibn-Juraibah
ibn-‘Abd-Nuhm ibn-Hulail ibn-Ḥubshîyah-l-Khuzâ‘i, the one
who followed the steps of the Prophet to the cave in which
the Prophet, accompanied by abu-Bakr as-Siddîk, had disappeared, when he wanted to take the Hegira to al-
Madînah. Kurz saw on the cave a spider web, and below it,
the Prophet's foot-print which he recognized saying, " This
is the Prophet's foot, but here the track is lost."

CHAPTER X

AṬ-ṬÂ'IF

The Prophet lays siege to aṭ-Ṭâ'if. When the Hawâzin were defeated in the battle of Hunain, and Duraid ibn-aṣ-Ṣimmah was slain, the surviving remnant came to Awtâs. The Prophet sent them abu-'Âmir al-Ash'ari who was put to death. Then abu-Mûsa 'Abdallâh ibn-Ḳais al-Ash'ari took the command and the Moslems advanced on Awṭâs. Seeing that, the chief of the Hawâzin at that time, Mâlik ibn-'Auf ibn-Sa'd of banu-Duhmân ibn-Naṣr ibn-Mu'âwiyah ibn-Bakr ibn-Hawâzin, fled to at-Ṭâ'if, whose people he found ready for the siege with their fortress repaired and the provisions gathered therein. Here he settled. The Prophet led the Moslems until they got to at-Tâ'if. Thakîf hurled stones and arrows on the Moslems, and the Prophet set a ballista on the fortress. The Moslems had a mantelet[1] made of cows' skins on which Thakîf threw hot iron bars and burnt it, killing the Moslems underneath. The siege of at-Tâ'if by the Prophet lasted for fifteen days,[2] the invasion having begun in Shauwâl, in the year 8.

Certain slaves surrender. Certain slaves from aṭ-Ṭâ'if presented themselves before the Prophet. Among them were abu-Bakrah ibn-Masrûḥ,—[later] the Prophet's freed- 56

[1] Ar. *dabbâbah*—a machine made of skins and wool, men enter into it and it is propelled to the lower part of a fortress where the men, protected from what is thrown upon them, try to make a breach. See Zaidân, *Ta'rîkh at-Tamaddun al-Islâmi,* vol. i, p. 143.

[2] *Cf.* Hishâm, p. 872.

man, and whose [first] name was Nufai'—, and al-Azraḳ—after whom the Azâriḳah were named, who was a Greek blacksmith and slave, and whose [full] name was abu-Nâfi' ibn-al-Azraḳ al-Khâriji. For doing so, these slaves were set free.[1] It is claimed by others, however, that Nâfi' ibn-Azraḳ al-Khâriji was of the banu-Ḥanîfah and that the al-Azraḳ who came from aṭ-Ṭâ'if was another man.

The terms of capitulation. Then the Prophet left for al-Ji'rânah to divide the captives and the booty of Ḥunain.[2] Thaḳîf, fearing lest he should return, sent a deputation with whom he made terms stipulating that they become Moslem, and keep what they possess in the form of money or buried treasures.[3] The Prophet imposed a condition on them that they would neither practise usury nor drink wine. They were addicted to usury. To this end, he wrote them a statement.

The old name of aṭ-Ṭâ'if was Wajj. When it was fortified and surrounded by a wall it was called aṭ-Ṭâ'if.

The Jews in aṭ-Ṭâ'if. Al-Madâ'ini from certain *sheikhs* from aṭ-Ṭâ'if:—In the district of aṭ-Ṭâ'if lived some Jews driven from al-Yaman and Yathrib, who had settled there for trade. On them poll-tax was imposed. It was from some of them that Mu'âwiyah bought his possessions aṭ-Ṭâ'if.

The land of aṭ-Ṭâ'if is included in the district of Makkah. Al-'Abbâs ibn-'Abd-al-Muṭṭalib had a piece of land in aṭ-Ṭâ'if from which grapes were taken and made into the beverage used for the Pilgrims. The men of Ḳuraish had possessions in aṭ-Ṭâ'if to which they came from

[1] *Cf.* Hishâm, p. 874.

[2] Tabari, vol. i, p. 1670; abu-l-Fida, *al-Mukhtaṣar*, vol. i, p. 147 (Cairo, 1325).

[3] Ar. *ar-rikâz,* treasures buried in pre-Islamic days; Bukhâri, vol. i, p. 381; Mawardi, p. 207.

Makkah to repair. The conquest of Makkah and the conversion of its people to Islam made Thaḳîf covet and lay hold on these possessions, but with the conquest of aṭ-Ṭâ'if, they were again put in the hands of the Makkans, and in fact all the land of aṭ-Ṭâ'if became one of the districts of Makkah.

Abu-Sufyân loses his eye. It was in the battle of aṭ-Ṭâ'if that abu-Sufyân ibn-Ḥarb lost his eye.[1]

The zakât from Thaḳîf on grapes and dates. Al-Walîd ibn-Ṣâliḥ from 'Attâb ibn-Asîd:—The Prophet ordered that the vine-trees of Thaḳîf be estimated as in the case of dates and that the *zakât* [legal alms] be taken in the form of raisins, as in the case of dates.

According to al-Wâḳidi, abu-Ḥanîfah says: "The vine-trees are not estimated, but when the produce, whether large 57
or small, is gathered the *zakât* is taken."

According to Ya'ḳûb: "If the produce is gathered and the weight of it is five *wasḳs* [loads] then its *zakât* is one-tenth or half of one-tenth." The same view is held by Sufyân ibn-Sa'îd ath-Thauri. The *wasḳ* is equal to 60 *ṣâ's*.[2]

Mâlik ibn-Anas and ibn-abi-Dhi'b state that according to the commended practice [Ar. *sunnah*] the *zakât* on grape is taken by estimation as in the case of dates.[3]

The zakât on honey. Shaibân ibn-abi-Shaibah from 'Amr ibn-Shu'aib:—A *'âmil* of 'Umar ibn-al-Khaṭṭâb in aṭ-Ṭâ'if wrote to 'Umar, "Those who own honey fail to contribute to us what they used to contribute to the Prophet, i. e., one vase out of each ten." 'Umar wrote back to him, "If they would contribute, thou shouldst protect their valleys, otherwise do not."

[1] Diyârbakri, vol. ii, p. 124.

[2] Yaḥya ibn-Âdam, *Kitâb al-Kharâj*, p. 100.

[3] Mâlik ibn-Anas, *al-Muwaṭṭa*, pp. 116-117; and *cf.* Shâfi'i, *Kitâb al-Umm*, vol. ii², p. 27.

'Amr ibn-Muhammad an-Nâkid from 'Abd-ar-Rahmân ibn-Ishâk's grandfather:—'Umar assessed one-tenth in the case of honey.

Dâ'ûd ibn-'Abd-al-Ḥamîd the *ḳâḍi* of ar-Rakkah from Khasîf:—'Umar ibn-'Abd-al-'Azîz wrote to his *'âmils* in Makkah and aṭ-Ṭâ'if, " There is *ṣadaḳah* on the bee-hives. Therefore, take it thereof." According to al-Wâkidi, it has been reported that ibn-'Umar said, " There is no *sadakah* on hives." According to Mâlik and ath-Thauri, no *zakât* is taken on honey though it may be in great quantities.[1] The same is the view of ash-Shâfi'i.[2] According to abu-Ḥanîfah, if the honey is raised in a tithe-land the tithe is taken whether the honey is much or little; but if it is raised in the *kharâj*-land, nothing is to be taken, because both *zakât* and *kharâj* cannot be taken from one and the same man.

Al-Wâḳidi states that he was told by al-Ḳâsim ibn-Ma'n and Ya'ḳûb that abu-Hanîfah said: " If honey is raised in the land of a *dhimmi* there is no tithe on it, but there is *kharâj* on the land. And if it is produced in the land of a Taghlabi[3] one-fifth is taken thereof." The same view is held by Zufar. According to abu-Yûsuf,[4] if the honey is produced in the *kharâj*-land; it is exempt of everything; but if in the tithe land, one *raṭl*[5] is taken out of ten.

According to Muhammad ibn-al-Ḥasan, no *ṣadaḳah* what- 58
ever is taken on what is less than five *faraḳs*.[6] The same view is held by ibn-abi-Dhi'b.

[1] *Muwaṭṭa*, p. 121.

[2] *Umm*, vol. ii², p. 33.

[3] Banu-Taghlib were Christian Arabs on whom 'Umar-ibn al-Khaṭṭâb doubled the tax. See abu-Yûsuf, *Kitâb al-Kharâj*, p. 68.

[4] Yûsuf, p. 40.

[5] A *raṭl* is about 5 pounds.

[6] A *faraḳ* is 16 *raṭls*. *Nihâyah*, vol. iii, p. 196.

It was reported by Khâlid ibn-'Abdallâh aṭ-Ṭaḥḥân that ibn-abi-Laila said, "Whether it is produced in the tithe-or *kharâj*-land, one *raṭl* is due on every ten. The same view is held by al-Ḥasan ibn-Sâlih ibn-Ḥai.

A tradition reported to me by abu-'Ubaid on the authority of az-Zuhri states that the latter held that one vase [Ar. *zikk*] [1] is due on every ten.

The tithe on fruits and grains. Yaḥya ibn-Âdam from Bishr ibn-'Âṣim and 'Uthmân ibn-'Abdallâh ibn-Aus:—Sufyân ibn-'Abdallâh ath-Thakafi wrote to 'Umar ibn-al-Khaṭṭâb, whose *'âmil* he was in at-Tâ'if, stating that before him was the case of a garden in which vine-trees grow, as well as plum and pomegranate trees and other things that are many folds more productive than vines, and soliciting 'Umar's orders regarding the taking of its tithe. But 'Umar wrote back, "No tithes on it."

It was stated by Yaḥya ibn-Âdam that he heard Sufyân ibn-Sa'îd (whose view is the following) say:—"There is no *ṣadakah* except on four of the products of the soil, i. e., wheat, barley, dates and raisins, provided the product measures five *wasks*." [2] But abu-Ḥanîfah's view is that whatever the tithe-land produces is subject to the tithe, though it be a bundle of vegetables. The same view is held by Zufar. But according to the view of Mâlik, ibn-abi-Dhi'b and Ya'kûb, vegetables and the like are not subject to *sadakah*. Nor is there *ṣadakah* on what is less than five *wasḳs* of wheat, barley, maize, husked barley, tare, dates, raisins, rice, sesame, peas and the grains that can be measured and stored, including lentils, beans, Indian peas and millet. If any of these measure five *wasks*, then it is subject to *ṣadakah*. The same view, according to al-Wâkidi, is held by Rabî'ah ibn-

[1] A receptacle of skin for holding wine and the like.

[2] Yaḥya ibn-'Âdam, *Kitâb al-Kharâj*, pp. 109-110.

abi-'Abd-ar-Raḥmân. According to az-Zuhri all spices and pulse [1] is subject to *zakât*. Mâlik holds that no *ṣadaḳah* is due on pears, plums, pomegranates or the rest of the fresh fruits. The same view is held by ibn-abi-Laila. According to abu-Yûsuf, there is no *ṣadaḳah* except on what can 59
be measured by *al-ḳafîz*.[2] Abu-az-Zinâd ibn-abi-Dhi'b and ibn-abi-Sabrah hold that no *ṣadaḳah* is taken on vegetables and fruits, but there is *sadakah* on their prices the moment they are sold.

A tradition was communicated to me by 'Abbâs ibn-Hishâm on the authority of his grandfather to the effect that the Prophet assigned 'Uthmân ibn-abi-l-'Âsi ath-Thakafi as his *'âmil* in at-Tâ'if.

[1] Seed of a leguminous plant that is cooked.

[2] Adam, p. 101.

CHAPTER XI

TABÂLAH AND JURASH

BAKR ibn-al-Haitham from az-Zuhri:—The people of Tabâlah and Jurash [1] accepted Islam without resistance.[2] The Prophet left them on the terms agreed upon when they became Moslems, imposing on every adult of the "People of the book" [3] among them one *dînâr*, and making it a condition on them to provide the Moslem wayfarers with board and lodging. Abu-Sufyân ibn-Ḥarb was assigned by the Prophet as the governor of Jurash.

1 Cities in al-Yaman; Bakri, pp. 191 and 238; Hamdâni, *Jazîrat al-'Arab*, p. 127, line 19; Yâḳût, vol. i, p. 817 and vol. ii, p. 60.

2 Ṭabari, vol. i, p. 1730.

3 Jews and Christians.

CHAPTER XII

Tabûk, Ailah, Adhruh, Makna and al-Jarbâ'

Tabûk makes terms. When in the year 9 the Prophet marched to Tabûk in Syria for the invasion of those of the Greeks, 'Âmilah, Lakhm, Judhâm and others whom he learnt had assembled against him, he met no resistance.[1] So he spent a few days in Tabûk, whose inhabitants made terms with him agreeing to pay poll-tax.

Ailah makes terms. During his stay at Tabûk, there came to him Yuhanna ibn-Ru'bah, the chief of Ailah, and made terms, agreeing to pay on every adult in his land one *dînâr per annum* making it 300 *dînârs* in all. The Prophet made it a condition on them that they provide with board and lodging whomsoever of the Moslems may pass by them. To this effect he wrote them a statement[2] that they may be kept safe and protected.

Muhammad ibn-Sa'd from Talhah-l-Aili:—'Umar ibn-'Abd-al-'Azîz never raised the tax of the people of Ailah above 300 *dînârs*.[3]

Adhruh makes terms. The Prophet made terms with the people of Adhruh[4] stipulating that they pay 100 *dînârs* in Rajab of every year.

Al-Jarbâ' makes terms. The people of al-Jarbâ'[5] made

[1] Ibn-Sa'd, vol. ii[1], p. 118; Hishâm, p. 893; Ṭabari, vol. i, p. 1692.

[2] Hishâm, p. 902.

[3] Wellhausen, *Das Arabische Reich*, p. 173.

[4] Yâḳût, vol. i, p. 174; Iṣṭakhri, p. 58; Muḳaddasi, p. 54.

[5] Yâḳût, vol. ii, p. 46.

terms and agreed to pay poll-tax. To this effect the Prophet wrote them a statement.

Maḳna makes terms. The people of Maḳna made terms 60
with the Prophet, agreeing to offer one-fourth of what they fish and spin, one-fourth of their horses and coats of mail, and one-fourth of their fruits. The inhabitants of Maḳna were Jews.[1] An Egyptian told me that he saw with his own eye the statement that the Prophet wrote them on a red parchment, the writing on which was partly effaced, and which he copied and dictated to me as follows:

"In the name of Allah, the compassionate, the merciful. From Muhammad, the Messenger of Allah, to the banu-Ḥabîbah and the inhabitants of Makna: peace be with you. It has been revealed unto me from above that ye are to return to your village. From the time this my letter reaches you, ye shall be safe; and ye have the assurance of security from Allah and from his Messenger. Verily, the Messenger of Allah has forgiven you your sins and all blood for which ye have been pursued. In your village, ye shall have no partner but the Messenger of Allah or the Messenger's messenger. There shall be no oppression on you nor hostility against you. Against whatever the Prophet of Allah protects himself, he will protect you. Only to the Prophet of Allah shall belong your cloth-stuff, slaves, horses[2] and coats of mail, save what the Prophet or the Prophet's messenger shall exempt. Besides that, ye shall give one-fourth of what your palm-trees produce, one-fourth of the product of your nets, and one-fourth of what is spun by your women; but all else shall be your own; and God's Prophet has exempted you from all further poll-tax or forced labor. Now, if ye

[1] Wâḳidi, tr. Wellhausen, p. 405.

[2] Ar. *kurâ'*, see *Nihâyah*, vol. iv, p. 16; and Muṭarrizi, vol. ii, p. 148; Margoliouth translates "camp-followers" in Zaidân's *Umayyads and Abbasids*, p. 121.

hear and obey, it will be for the Prophet to do honor to the honorable among you and pardon those among you who do the wrong. Whosoever of the banu-Habîbah and the inhabitants of Makna bethinks himself to do well to the Moslems, it shall be well for him; and whosoever means mischief to them, mischief shall befall him. Ye are to have no ruler save of your number of the family of the Prophet. Written by 'Ali-ibn-abu-Ṭâlib [1] in the year 9."

[1] *Sic!* Being genitive, it should be "abi". See note in De Goeje's edition, p. 60.

CHAPTER XIII

DÛMAT AL-JANDAL

Khâlid ibn-al-Walîd captures Ukaidir. The Prophet 61
sent Khâlid ibn-al-Walîd ibn-al-Mughîrah-l-Makhzûmi to Ukaidir ibn-'Abd-al-Malik al-Kindi, later as-Sakûni, at Dûmat al-Jandal.[1] Khâlid took him captive, killed his brother, robbed him of a silk cloak[2] interwoven with gold, and brought Ukaidir before the Prophet. Ukaidir accepted Islam,[3] upon which the Prophet wrote for him and the people of Dûmat the following statement:—

"This is a statement from Muhammad, the Prophet of Allah, to Ukaidir as he accepted Islâm and forsook the objects of worship and idols, and to the people of Dûmat:— To us shall belong the water-places outside the city, the untilled lands, the deserts and waste lands, as well as the defensive and offensive weapons, the horses, and the fortress; and to you shall belong the palm-trees within the city, and the running water. Your cattle which are pasturing shall not, for the purpose of taking the *ṣadaḳah*, be brought together [but shall be numbered on the pasture-land], and what is above the fixed number of animals from which a *ṣadaḳah* is required shall not be taken into consideration.[4] Your herds shall graze wherever ye want, and ye shall ob-

[1] Yâḳût, vol. ii, p. 625.

[2] Ṭabari, vol. i, pp. 1702-1703.

[3] Diyârbakri, vol. ii, p. 142; Athîr, vol. ii, p. 214.

[4] *Cf.* Sprenger, *Das Leben und die Lehre des Mohammad*, vol. iii, p. 419.

serve prayer in its time, and pay the *zakât* as it is due. To this effect, I give you the covenant of Allah and his promise, and ye are entitled to our sincerity as regards the fulfillment of the terms. Witnessed by Allah and those of the Moslems who are present."

Ukaidir violates the covenant. Al-'Abbâs ibn-Hishâm 62
al-Kalbi from his grandfather:—The Prophet sent Khâlid ibn-al-Walîd to Ukaidir. Ukaidir was brought by Khâlid before the Prophet; he became a Moslem, and the Prophet wrote him a statement. But no sooner had the Prophet been dead, than Ukaidir stopped the payment of the *ṣadaḳah,* violated the covenant and left Dûmat al-Jandal for al-Ḥîrah, where he erected a building and called it Dûmat after Dûmat al-Jandal. His brother, however, Ḥuraith [1] ibn-'Abd-al-Malik embraced Islam and thereby entered into possession of the property held by his brother.[2]

Ḥuraith's daughter marries. Yazîd ibn-Mu'âwiyah married the daughter of Ḥuraith, Ukaidir's brother.

Abu-Bakr sends Khâlid against Ukaidir. Al-'Abbâs from 'Awânah ibn-al-Hakam:—Abu-Bakr wrote to Khâlid ibn-al-Walîd, when the latter was at 'Ain at-Tamr, ordering him to go against Ukaidir, which he did, killing Ukaidir and capturing Dûmat. After the death of the Prophet, Ukaidir left Dûmat and then returned to it. Having killed him, Khâlid went to Syria.

Laila daughter of al-Jûdi a captive. According to al-Wâkidi, on Khâlid's way from al-'Irâḳ to Syria, he passed through Dûmat al-Jandal, which he captured, carrying away many captives, among whom were Laila, the daughter of al-Jûdi-l-Ghassâni. Others say Laila was carried away by
Khâlid's horsemen from a Ghassân settlement stationed by 63

[1] Ibn-Ḥajar, vol. i, p. 773, by mistake gives "Ḥuraib".

[2] One verse omitted.

a watering-place [*hâdir*]. It was this daughter of al-Jûdi whom 'Abd-ar-Rahmân ibn-abi-Bakr aṣ-Ṣiddik had fallen in love with, and the one whom he meant when he said:

> "I thought of Laila with as-Samâwah[1] intervening between;
> and what has the daughter of al-Jûdi to do with me?"

Thus did he win her hand and marry her. But such a hold had she on him that he gave up all his other wives. At last, however, she was affected with such a severe disease that her looks were changed and he no more liked her. He was advised to give her what is usually given at divorce[2] and send her to her own people, which he did.

Al-Wâkidi's version of the conquest. According to al-Wâkidi, the Prophet led the invasion against Dûmat al-Jandal in the year 5 and met no resistance. In Shauwâl, year 9, he sent Khâlid ibn-al-Walîd to Ukaidir, twenty months after the former had embraced Islam.

The reconstruction of Dûmat al-Jandal. I heard it said by someone from al-Hîrah that Ukaidir and his brothers used to go to Dûmat al-Hîrah and visit their uncles of the Kalb tribe and spend some time with them. One day as they were together on a hunting trip, there arose before their view a city in ruins with only few walls standing. The city was built of stones [Ar. *jandal*]. This city they rebuilt, planted in it olive- and other trees, and called it Dûmat al-Jandal in distinction from Dûmat al-Ḥîrah.[3]

Az-Zuhri's version of the conquest. 'Amr ibn-Muḥammad an-Nâkid from az-Zuhri:—The Prophet sent Khâlid ibn-al-Walîd ibn-al-Mughîrah to the people of Dûmat al-Jandal who were some of the Christians of al-Kûfah. Khâlid captured Ukaidir, their chief, and arranged to receive poll-tax from him.

[1] A desert from Dûmat to 'Ain at-Tamr; Istakhri, p. 23.

[2] Ar. *mut'ah. Muwatta,* p. 208.

[3] Caetani, vol. ii, p. 263.

CHAPTER XIV

THE CAPITULATION OF NAJRÂN

The terms agreed upon. Bakr ibn-al-Haitham from az-Zuhri:—There came to the Prophet the military chief and the civil chief,[1] delegated by the people of Najrân in al-Yaman, and asked for terms which they made on behalf of the people of Najrân, agreeing to offer two thousand robes —one thousand in Ṣafar and one thousand in Rajab—each one of which should have the value of one ounce [*aukiyah*], the ounce weighing 40 *dirhams*. In case the price of the robe delivered should be more than one ounce, the surplus would be taken into consideration; and if it were less, the deficiency should be made up. And whatever weapons, horses, camels or goods they offered, should be accepted instead of the robes, if they are the same value. Another condition was made that they provide board and lodging for the Prophet's messengers for a month or less, and not detain them for more than a month. Still another condition was that in case of war in al-Yaman, they are bound to offer as loan thirty coats of mail, thirty mares and thirty camels, and whatever of these animals perish, the messengers [of the Prophet] guarantee to make up for them. To this effect, the Prophet gave them Allah's covenant and his promise. Another condition was that they be not allured to change their religion or the rank they hold in it, nor should they be called upon for military service or made to pay the tithe.[2] The

[1] Hishâm, p. 401.

[2] *Cf.* Yûsuf, pp. 40-41.

Prophet made it a condition on them that they neither take nor give usury.

The two monks of Najrân and the Prophet. Al-Ḥusain ibn-al-Aswad from al-Ḥasan:—There came to the Prophet two monks from Najrân.[1] The Prophet proposed Islâm to them, and they replied, "We embraced Islâm before thou didst." To this the Prophet replied, "Ye have told a lie. Three things keep you from Islâm: pork eating, cross-worship and the claim that Allah has a son." "Well then," said they, "who is 'Îsa's father?" Al-Ḥasan adds that the Prophet was never too quick but always waited for Allah's command. Hence the text revealed by his Lord:[2] "These signs and this wise warning do we rehearse to thee. Verily, Jesus is as Adam in the sight of Allah. He created him of dust: He then said to him, 'Be'—and he was," etc. to "on those who lie."

This the Prophet repeated to them and then asked them to join with him in imprecating the curse of Allah upon whichever of them was wrong,[3] taking hold of the hands of Fâṭimah, al-Ḥasan and al-Ḥusain. At this, one of the two monks said to the other, "Climb the mountain and do not join with him in imprecating the curse, for if thou shouldst, thou wouldst return with the curse on thee." "What shall we do then?" asked the other. "I believe," said the former, "we had better give him the *kharâj* rather than join with him in imprecating the curse."[4]

A statement of the treaty. Al-Ḥusain from Yaḥya ibn-
Âdam who said:—"I copied the statement of the Prophet 65
to the people of Najrân from that of a man who took it from al-Ḥasan ibn-Ṣâliḥ. These are the words:

[1] Yâḳût, vol. iv, pp. 751-757.

[2] Kor., 3:51.

[3] *Cf.* Kor., 3:54.

[4] *mubâhalah.* Bukhâri, vol. iii, pp. 167-168; abu-l-Faraj, *Aghâni*, vol. x, p. 144.

'In the name of Allah, the compassionate, the merciful. The following is what the Messenger of Allah, Muḥammad, wrote to Najrân, at whose disposal [1] were all their fruits, their gold, silver and domestic utensils, and their slaves, but which he benevolently left for them, assessing on them two thousand robes each having the value of one *aukiyah*, one thousand to be delivered in Rajab of every year, and one thousand in Ṣafar of every year. Each robe shall be one *aukiyah*; and whatever robes cost more or less than one *aukiyah*, their overcost or deficiency shall be taken into consideration; and whatever coats of mail, horses, camels or goods they substitute for the robes shall be taken into consideration. It is binding on Najrân to provide board and lodging for my messengers [2] for one month or less, and never to detain them for more than a month. It is also binding on them to offer as loan thirty coats of mail, thirty mares and thirty camels, in case of war in al-Yaman due to their rebelling. Whatever perishes of the horses or camels, lent to my messengers, is guaranteed by my messengers and is returned by them. Najrân and their followers [3] are entitled to the protection of Allah and to the security of Muḥammad the Prophet, the Messenger of Allah, which security shall involve their persons, religion, lands and possessions, including those of them who are absent as well as those who are present, their camels, messengers and images.[4] The state they previously held shall not be changed, nor shall any of their religious services or images be changed. No attempt shall be made to turn a bishop from his office as a bishop, a monk from his office as a monk, nor the sexton

[1] The text here is probably corrupt; *cf.* Wellhausen, *Skizzen und Vorarbeiten*, vol. iv, pp. 25 and 132; Yûsuf, p. 41.

[2] Sent to bring the *kharâj*.

[3] Ar. *ḥâshiyah* = Jews. Sprenger, vol. iii, p. 502.

[4] *amthilah* = crosses and pictures used in churches.

of a church from his office, whether what is under the control of each is great or little. They shall not be held responsible for any wrong deed or blood shed in pre-Islamic time. They shall neither be called to military service nor compelled to pay the tithe. No army shall tread on their land. If some one demands of them some right, then the case is decided with equity without giving the people of Najrân the advantage over the other party, or giving the other party the advantage over them. But whosoever of them has up till now [1] received usury, I am clear of the responsibility of his protection.[2] None of them, however, shall be held responsible for the guilt of the other. And as a guarantee to what is recorded in this document, they are entitled to the right of protection from Allah, and to the security of Muḥammad the Prophet, until Allah's order is issued, and so long as they give the right counsel [to Moslems] and render whatever dues are bound on them, provided they are not asked to do anything unjust. Witnessed
by abu-Sufyân ibn-Ḥarb, Ghailân ibn-'Amr, Mâlik ibn-'Auf 66
of banu-Naṣr, al-Aḳra' ibn-Ḥâbis al-Ḥanẓali and al-Mughîrah. Written by—' "[3]

Yaḥa ibn-Âdam adds, "I have seen in the hands of the people of Najrân another statement whose reading is similar to that of this copy, but at the close of it the following words occur: Written by 'Ali ibn-abu-Ṭâlib.'[4] Concerning this I am at a loss to know what to say."

'Umar expels them. When abu-Bakr aṣ-Ṣiddîḳ became caliph he enforced the terms agreed upon and issued another statement similar to that given by the Prophet. When

[1] Ya'ḳûbi, vol. ii, p. 62, has "after this year".

[2] Caetani, vol. ii, p. 352; Sprenger, vol. iii, p. 502; Athîr, vol. ii, p. 223.

[3] 'Abdallâh ibn-abi-Bakr; abu-Yûsuf, p. 4; see H. Lammens' comment on this protocol, *Mélanges de la Faculté Orientale,* vol. v², p. 346.

[4] And not "abi" as required by the rules of the Arabic grammar.

'Umar ibn-al-Khaṭṭâb became caliph, they began to practise usury, and became so numerous as to be considered by him a menace to Islâm. He therefore expelled them and wrote to them the following statement:

"Greetings! Whomever of the people of Syria and al-'Irâḳ they happen to come across, let him clear for them tillable land; and whatever land they work, becomes theirs in place of their land in al-Yaman." Thus the people of Najrân were dispersed, some settling in Syria and others in an-Najrânîyah in the district of al-Kûfah, after whom it was so named. The Jews of Najrân were included with the Christians in the terms and went with them as their followers.

The Najranites under 'Uthmân. When 'Uthmân ibn-'Affân became caliph, he wrote to his *'âmil* in al-Kûfah, al-Walîd ibn-'Uḳbah ibn-abi-Mu'aiṭ, as follows:

"Greetings! The civil ruler, the bishop and the nobles of Najrân have presented to me the written statement of the Prophet and showed me the recommendation [1] of 'Umar. Having made inquiry regarding their case from 'Uthmân ibn-Ḥunaif, I learned that he had investigated their state and found it injurious to the great landlords [2] whom they prevented from possessing their land. I have, therere, reduced their taxation by 200 robes—for the sake of Allah and in place of their old lands. I recommend them to thee as they are included among the people entitled to our protection."

Another source for 'Umar's statement. I heard it said by one of the learned that 'Umar wrote them the following statement:—"Greetings! Whomsoever of the people of Syria or al-'Irâḳ they pass by, let him clear for them tillable land". Another I heard say, "waste land".

[1] Lammens, *MFO*, vol. v², p. 677.

[2] *dihḳâns*; Âdam, pp. 42-43.

One reason for their expulsion. 'Abd-al-A'la ibn-Ḥammâd an-Narsi from 'Umar ibn-'Abd-al-'Azîz: — The Prophet said during his illness, "There shall not remain two religions in the land of Arabia." Consequently, when 'Umar ibn-al-Khaṭṭâb became caliph, he expelled the people of Najrân to an-Najrânîyah and bought their properties and 67
possessions.

Al-'Abbâs ibn-Hishâm al-Kalbi from his grandfather:— The Najrân of al-Yaman received their name from Najrân ibn-Zaid ibn-Saba ibn-Yashjub ibn-Ya'rub ibn-Ḳaḥṭân.

'Umar and 'Ali refuse to reinstate them in the land. Al-Ḥusain ibn-al-Aswad from Sâlim ibn-abi-l-Ja'd:—The people of Najrân having increased in number to 40,000, became jealous of one another and came to 'Umar ibn-al-Khaṭṭâb saying, "Transplant us from the land". 'Umar had considered them a menace to the Moslems, so he took this opportunity and expelled them from the land. Later, however, they repented, and returning to 'Umar said, "Reinstate us in the land", but 'Umar refused. When 'Ali ibn-abi-Ṭâlib became caliph, they came to him and said, "We plead with thee by thy right-hand writing and thy intermediacy on our behalf with thy Prophet that thou mayst reinstate us in the land." To this 'Ali replied: "'Umar was a man of sound judgment, and I hate to act differently." [1]

The number of robes received by Mu'âwiyah. Abu-Mas'ûd al-Kûfi from al-Kalbi:—The chief of an-Najrânîyah at al-Kûfah used to send his messengers to all the people of Najrân who were in Syria and other districts and to gather money assessed evenly on them for raising the required robes. When Mu'âwiyah (or Yazîd ibn-Mu'âwiyah) came to power, they complained to him because of their dispersion, the death of some of them, and the conversion to Islâm of

[1] Âdam, p. 9.

others. They also presented the statement issued by 'Uthmân ibn-'Affân for the reduction of the number of robes. To this they added, "And now we have still more decreased, and become weaker." He then reduced the number by another 200 robes, thus reducing the original number by four hundred.

Al-Ḥajjâj restores the number. When al-Ḥajjâj ibn-Yûsuf was made governor of al-'Irâḳ and ibn-al-Ash'ath revolted against him, the former charged the non-Arab landlords and the people of Najrân with siding with the latter, and, therefore, he raised the number to 1,800 robes, and ordered that the robes be of the kind adorned with figures.

'Umar ibn-'Abd-al-'Azîz reduces the number. When 'Umar ibn-'Abd-al-'Azîz came to power, they complained to him that they were in danger of extinction, that they were decreasing in number, that the continuous raids of the Arabs overburdened them with heavy taxes for revictualling them, and that they suffered from the unjust treatment of al-Ḥajjâj. By 'Umar's orders their census was taken, and it was found that they were reduced to one-tenth of their original number, upon which 'Umar said, "I consider that the terms of this capitulation impose a tax on their heads and not on their lands. The poll-tax of the dead and the Moslems, however, is annulled." He therefore held them responsible for 200 robes of the value of 8,000 *dirhams*.

Yûsuf ibn-'Umar restores the original tax. In the time of al-Walîd ibn-Yazîd, when Yûsuf ibn-'Umar was made 68
governor of al-'Irâḳ, he [Yûsuf], moved with partisanship to al-Ḥajjâj, charged them the original tax.

Abu-l-'Abbâs reduces the number of robes. When abu-l-'Abbâs was proclaimed caliph, they met him on the way as he appeared in al-Kûfah and strewed myrtle branches on the road and threw some on him as he was going home from the mosque. With this the caliph was greatly pleased. Later they brought their case before him and told him of their paucity in number and of their treatment by 'Umar ibn-'Abd-al-'Azîz and Yûsuf ibn-'Umar. To this they added, "We are somehow related to thy uncles (on the mother's side), the banu-l-Ḥârith ibn-Ka'b." 'Abdallâh ibn-ar-Rabî' al-Ḥârithi spoke in their favor; and al-Ḥajjâj ibn-Arṭât confirmed what they claimed. Therefore, abu-l-'Abbâs held them responsible only for the 200 robes previously given by them, having a value of 8,000 *dirhams*.

Ar-Rashîd writes them a favorable statement. Abu-Mas'ûd said, "When ar-Rashîd Hârûn became caliph and started for al-Kûfah on his way to the Pilgrimage, they brought their case before him and complained of the harsh treatment of the *'âmils*. By the caliph's orders there was written to them a statement fixing the number at 200 robes. The statement I myself saw. Moreover the caliph ordered that they be freed from dealing with the *'âmils,* and that they pay the dues directly to the treasury."

'Amr an-Nâḳid from ibn-Shihâb az-Zuhri:—The following text was revealed against the unbelievers among the Ḳuraish and the Arabs,[1] "Fight therefore against them until there is no more civil discord, and the only worship be that of Allah," and the following against the "People of the Book."[2] "Make war upon such of those to whom the Book has been given as believe not in Allah, or in the last day, and who forbid not that which Allah and his Messenger have forbidden, and who profess not the profession of the truth," etc. to "humbled." Thus the first among the "People of the Book" to pay poll-tax, so far as we know, were the people of Najrân who were Christian. Then, the people of Ailah, Adhruḥ and Adhri'ât paid it in the battle of Tabûk.

[1] Kor., 2:189.

[2] Kor., 9:29.

CHAPTER XV

AL-YAMAN

The people of al-Yaman embrace Islâm. When the news of the rise of the Prophet and the success of his righteous cause reached the people of al-Yaman, they sent their envoys, and the Prophet gave them a written statement confirming 69
them in the possession of whatever property, lands, and buried treasures were included in their terms when they became Moslems. Thus they accepted Islâm; and the Prophet sent them his messengers and *'âmils* to acquaint them with the laws of Islâm and its institutes and to receive their *ṣadaḳah* and the poll-tax of those among them who still held to Christianity, Judaism or Magianism.

The Prophet's letter. Al-Ḥusain ibn-al-Aswad from al-Ḥasan:—The Prophet wrote to the people of al-Yaman, "Whosoever repeats our prayer, turns his face to the *ḳiblah* as we do,[1] and eat what we slaughter, such a one is a Moslem and has the security of Allah and the security of his Prophet. But whosoever refuses to do so, tax is binding upon him."

A similar tradition was communicated to me by Hudbah on the authority of al-Ḥasan.

The governor of Ṣan'â'. It is reported by al-Wâḳidi that the Prophet sent Khâlid ibn-Sa'îd ibn-al-'Âṣi as a commander over Ṣan'â' and its land. Al-Wâḳidi adds that some say that the Prophet assigned al-Muhâjir ibn-abi-Umaiyah ibn-al-Mughîrah-l-Makhzûmi to be governor of Ṣan'â, in which position he died. Still others say, according

[1] Turning the face towards Makkah during prayer.

to al-Wâkidi, that the one who made al-Muhâjir governor over Ṣan'â' was abu-Bakr aṣ-Ṣiddîk, who also assigned Khâlid ibn-Sa'îd over the provinces of upper al-Yaman.

Al-Muhâjir as governor of Kindah and aṣ-Ṣadif. According to Hishâm ibn-al-Kalbi and Haitham ibn-'Adi the Prophet assigned al-Muhâjir over Kindah and aṣ-Ṣadif. On the death of the Prophet, abu-Bakr wrote to Ziyâd ibn-Labîd al-Bayâḍi-l-Anṣâri assigning to him the governorship of Kindah, aṣ-Ṣadif and other places in addition to what he already ruled over in Ḥaḍramaut. Al-Muhâjir he assigned over Ṣan'â' and later asked him in writing to reinforce Ziyâd ibn-Labîd, without dismissing him from the governorship of Ṣan'â'.

Ziyâd, governor of Ḥaḍramaut. It is agreed by all that the Prophet assigned Ziyâd ibn-Labîd to Ḥaḍramaut.

The governors of Zabîd, Rima', 'Adan, al-Janad and Najrân appointed. The Prophet assigned abu-Mûsa-l-Ash'ari to Zabîd, Rima', 'Adan and the coast region, and assigned Mu'âdh ibn-Jabal to al-Janad, made him *kâḍi* and charged him with collecting *ṣadakah* in al-Yaman. He then assigned to Najrân 'Amr ibn-Ḥazm al-Anṣâri; and, according to other reports, he assigned abu-Sufyân ibn-Ḥarb to Najrân after 'Amr ibn-Ḥazm.

The letter of the Prophet to Zur'ah sent with Mu'âdh. 'Abdallâh ibn-Ṣâliḥ al-Mukri' from 'Urwah ibn-az-Zubair:
—The Prophet wrote to Zur'ah ibn-dhi-Yazan as follows: 70

"Greetings! On the arrival of my messenger Mu'âdh ibn-Jabal and his companions, gather all your *ṣadakah* and poll-tax and deliver them to him. Mu'âdh is the chief of my messengers, and one of the righteous among my immediate companions. I have been informed by Mâlik ibn-Murârah[1] ar-Rahâwi that thou wert the first to desert

[1] Hishâm, p. 956, gives "Murrah"; and Nawâwi, p. 539, "Marârah".

Ḥimyar and embrace Islâm. Therefore, good times lie before thee. And I order you, all Ḥimyar,[1] not to exhibit perfidy or deviation, for verily is the Prophet of Allah the lord of both the rich and the poor among you. As for the *sadakah,* it is not legal for Muhammad or any of his relatives to take; it is rather *zakât* through which ye are purified, and which goes to the poor among the Moslems and the Believers. It was Mâlik that conveyed the information and kept the secret. As for Mu'âdh, he is one of the righteous among my immediate companions and one of their coreligionists. I, therefore, order you to treat him well, for he is highly esteemed. And peace be unto you!"[2]

The Prophet orders Mu'âdh to take the tithe. Al-Ḥusain ibn-al-Aswad from Mûsa ibn-Ṭalḥah:—The Prophet sent Mu'âdh ibn-Jabal[3] to collect the *ṣadaḳah* of al-Yaman ordering him to take on dates, wheat, barley and grapes (perhaps he said, raisins) one-tenth and one-half of a tenth.

Instructions to 'Amr ibn-Ḥazm. Al-Ḥusain from Muḥammad ibn-Isḥâḳ:—The Prophet wrote the following to 'Amr ibn-Ḥazm when he sent him to al-Yaman:

"In the name of Allah, the compassionate, the merciful. This is a declaration from Allah and his Prophet. All ye that have believed! be faithful to your compacts:[4] this is an ordinance from the Prophet Muḥammad, the Messenger of Allah, to 'Amr ibn-Ḥazm when he delegated him to al-Yaman. He ordered him to fear Allah in whatever he performs, and to take from the spoils the fifth that belongs to Allah as well as what is prescribed as *ṣadaḳah* on the property of the Believers which is one-tenth in case it is

[1] Hishâm, p. 957.

[2] *Cf.* Ṭabari, vol. i, p. 1719.

[3] Bukhâri, vol. iii, p. 156; Diyârbakri, vol. ii, p. 158.

[4] Kor., 5: 1.

watered by flowing water or rain, and one-half of a tenth if it is watered by means of the bucket."[1]

The Prophet's letter to the kings of Ḥimyar. Al-Ḥusain from Muḥammad ibn-Isḥâk:—The following is what the Prophet wrote to the kings of Ḥimyâr:

"In the name of Allah, the compassionate, the merciful. From the Prophet Muḥammad, the Messenger of Allah, to 71
al-Hârith ibn-'Abd-Kulâl, Nu'aim ibn-'Abd-Kulâl, and Sharh ibn-'Abd-Kulâl, to an-Nu'mân Ḳail dhi-Ru'ain, Ma'âfir and Hamdân. Greetings! Allah will guide you by his own guidance if ye act well, obey Allah and his Prophet, observe the prayer, pay the *zakât*, give out of the spoils the fifth that belongs to Allah, the share of his Prophet, and the portion which belongs to him as chief exclusive of his companions, and deliver what is prescribed by Allah to the Believers in the form of *ṣadaḳah* on the property, which is one-tenth in case the land is watered by spring, or rain water, and half of the tenth if watered by means of the bucket."[2]

According to Hishâm ibn-Muḥammad al-Kalbi the letter of the Prophet was addressed to 'Arîb and al-Ḥârith, the sons of 'Abd-Kulâl ibn-'Arîb ibn-Liyashraḥ.[3]

The Prophet's letter to Mu'âdh. Yûsuf ibn-Mûsa-l-Ḳaṭṭân from al-Ḥakam:—The Prophet wrote to Mu'âdh ibn-Jabal, when the latter was in al-Yaman, stating that one-tenth is to be assessed on what is watered by rain or flowing water, and half of a tenth on what is watered by means of the bucket and water-wheel; that on every adult one *dînâr* or its equivalent in clothes is to be assessed; and that no Jew is to be enticed to leave Judaism.[4]

[1] *Cf.* Ṭabari, vol. i, p. 1727.

[2] *Cf.* Ṭabari, vol. i, p. 1718.

[3] Ibn-Duraid, *al-Ishtiḳâḳ*, p. 308: "*Yalyashraḥ*"; see *ZDMG*, vol. xx, p. 237.

[4] Here is omitted the explanation of certain words in the tradition.

The instructions given to Mu'âdh. Abu-'Ubaid from Masrûḳ:—The Prophet delegated Mu'âdh to al-Yaman giving him orders to take a one-year-old cow out of every thirty cows; one full-grown cow, of every forty; and one *dînâr*, or its equivalent in clothes, from every adult.

The Magians taxed. Al-Ḥusain ibn-al-Aswad from al-Ḥasan:—The Prophet collected poll-tax from the Magians of Hajar and the Magians of al-Yaman, and assessed one *dînâr* or its equivalent in clothes on every adult or female from the Magians of al-Yaman.

The people of al-Yaman taxed. 'Amr an-Nâḳid from 72
'Amr ibn-Shu'aib's grandfather: — The Prophet assessed one *dînâr* as tax on every adult among the people of al-Yaman.

Shaibân ibn-abi-Shaibah-l-Ubulli from Yaḥya ibn-Saifi or from ibn-'Abbâs:—When the Prophet delegated Mu'âdh ibn-Jabal to al-Yaman he said, "When thou comest to any of the 'People of the Book,' tell them, 'Allah made it obligatory on you to pray five times per day and night'. If they obey, tell them, 'Allah made it obligatory on you to fast during the month of Ramaḍân of every year'. If they obey, tell them, 'Allah made it obligatory on him of you who can afford it to undertake a pilgrimage to Makkah'. If they obey, tell them, 'Allah has made it obligatory on you to offer *ṣadaḳah* on your possessions to be taken from the rich among you and turned over to the poor among you.' If they obey, then avoid their choice possessions and beware of the imprecation of the oppressed, for between his imprecation and Allah there is no veil or screen."[1]

Products subject to ṣadaḳah. Shaibân from al-Mughîrah ibn-'Abdallâh:—Al-Ḥajjâj said, "Give *ṣadaḳah* on every leguminous plant." Regarding this abu-Burdah ibn-abi-

[1] Bukhâri, vol. iii, p. 157.

Mûsa said, " He is right ", which made Mûsa ibn-Ṭalḥah say to abu-Burdah, " This man [al-Ḥajjâj ?] now claims that his father was among the Prophet's *Companions.* The Prophet sent Mu'âdh ibn-Jabal to al-Yaman and gave him instructions to collect *ṣadaḳah* on dates, wheat, barley and raisins."

'Amr an-Nâḳid from Mûsa ibn-Ṭalḥah ibn-'Ubaidallâh who said :—" I have read the letter of Mu'âdh ibn-Jabal when the Prophet sent him to al-Yaman, and there occurred in it the following statement, ' Take *ṣadaḳah* on wheat, barley, dates and corn.' " 73

Why more tax on the Syrians. 'Ali ibn-'Abdallâh al-Madîni from ibn-abi-Najîḥ who said, " I once asked Mujâhid, ' Why did 'Umar levy on the people of Syria a heavier poll-tax than on the people of al-Yaman ?' and he replied, ' Because they were people of means.' "

Nothing on al-awḳâṣ. Al-Ḥusain ibn-'Ali ibn-al-Aswad from Ṭâ'ûs :—When Mu'âdh arrived in al-Yaman, there was brought before him a medial number of cows and a medial amount [1] of honey, on which he said, " I have no instructions to take anything on this."

The salt of Ma'rib. Al-Ḥusain ibn-al-Aswad from Abyaḍ ibn-Ḥammâl :—The latter asked the Prophet to give him as fief the salt in Ma'rib ; but hearing someone say, " It is like perennial water," [2] the Prophet refused to assign it.

A tradition to the same effect was communicated to me by al-Ḳâsim ibn-Sallâm and others on the authority of Abyaḍ ibn-Ḥammâl.

The Prophet gives a fief in Ḥaḍramaut. According to a

[1] Ar. *awḳâṣ* = what is between one *farîḍah* and the next ; as, for instance when camels amount in number to five, one sheep or goat is to be given for them ; and nothing is to be given for such as exceed that number until they amount to ten ; thus what is between the five and ten is termed *waḳṣ*, pl. *awḳâṣ*.

[2] Having an unfailing and continuous output.

tradition communicated to me by Ahmad ibn-Ibrâhim ad-Dauraki on the authority of 'Alkamah ibn-Wâ'il al-Ḥaḍrami's father, the Prophet gave out as fief to the latter ['Alkamah's father] a piece of land in Hadramaut.

Muhammad ibn-Yûsuf severe on al-Yaman. 'Ali ibn-Muhammad ibn-'Abdallâh ibn-abi-Saif, a freedman of Kuraish, from Maslamah ibn-Muhârib:—When Muhammad ibn-Yûsuf, the brother of al-Ḥajjâj ibn-Yûsuf, was the governor of al-Yaman, he misbehaved, oppressed the people and took pieces of land from certain men without paying their prices. Among the lands he thus wrested was al-Harajah. Morever he levied on the people of al-Yaman a *kharâj* which he gave the form of an assessed rate of land-tax. When 'Umar ibn-'Abd-al-'Azîz came to power, he wrote to his *'âmil* instructing him to abolish that assessed land-tax and take nothing more than the tithe saying, "Though I may not get from al-Yaman more than a handful of *katam*,[1] I would rather have that than the passing of such a tax." However, when Yazîd ibn-'Abd-al-Malik came to power he reinstated it.

Ṣadaḳah on plants, grains and vegetables. Al-Ḥusain ibn-Muhammad az-Za'farâni from abu-'Abd-ar-Rahmân Hishâm ibn-Yûsuf, the *kâdi* of San'â':—The people of 74
Khufâsh presented a statement from abu-Bakr as-Siddik on a parchment ordering them to pay *ṣadaḳah* on a piece of land planted with *wars*.[2]

According to Mâlik, ibn-abi-Dhi'b, all the canonists of al-Ḥijâz, Sufyân ath-Thauri and abu-Yûsuf there is no *zakât* on *wars*, *wasmah*,[3] *kirt*,[4] *katam*, *hinna*[5] and roses.

[1] A plant product used for dyeing the hair black.

[2] A certain plant like sesame existing in al-Yaman only, used for dyeing.

[3] A plant with the leaves of which one tinges or dyes.

[4] A kind of leek.

[5] A plant used for dyeing the hands and feet.

Abu-Ḥanîfah, however, holds that there is *zakât* on these, whether in large or small quantities. Mâlik holds that the *zakât* on saffron is five *dirhams*, if its price amounts to 200 *dirhams* and if it is sold. The same is the view of abu-az-Zinâd who is reported by others to have said, "Nothing on saffron." According to abu-Ḥanîfah and Zufar there is *zakât* on it whether it is in large or small quantities. Abu-Yûsuf and Muḥammad ibn-al-Ḥasan claim, "If its price amounts to the lowest price for which five *wasḳs* of dates, wheat, barley, corn or any other kind of grains sell, then there is *ṣadaḳah* on it." According to ibn-abi-Laila, there is nothing on vegetables. The same view is held by ash-Sha'bi.[1] According to 'Aṭâ' and Ibrâhîm an-Nakha'i, whatever the tithe-land produces, be it in great or small quantities, is subject to the tithe or half the tithe.

Al-Ḥusain ibn-al-Aswad from ibn-abi-Rajâ' al-'Uṭâridi who said:—"In al-Baṣrah, ibn-al-'Abbâs used to collect our *ṣadaḳahs* even from the bundles of leek."

Al-Ḥusain from Ṭâ'ûs and 'Ikrimah:—The latter asserted that there is no *zakât* on *wars* and cotton.

The tax on the dhimmis. The following is the view of abu-Ḥanîfah and Bishr:—In case of the *dhimmis* who are in possession of lands included in the tithe-land, like for instance al-Yaman whose people accepted Islâm and made terms on their lands, al-Baṣrah which was cultivated by the Moslems, and other lands given out as fiefs by the caliphs to which no Moslem or "man of the covenant" has claim, it is binding on these people to pay tax on their person and *kharâj* on their lands according to what their lands can bear. Whatever is received from them follows the course of the money received as *kharâj*. If, however, any one of them becomes Moslem, he is exempt from the poll-tax but

[1] Yaḥya ibn-Âdam, p. 107.

remains always subject to the *kharâj* on his land, as it is the case in as-Sawâd. The same view is held by ibn-abi-Laila. According to ibn-Shubrumah and abu-Yûsuf, tax is 75
levied on their heads, and they should pay double what the Moslems pay on their lands, which would be a fifth or a tenth. This they said on the analogy of the case of the Christian banu-Taghlib. Abu-Yûsuf added that whatever is taken from them should follow the course of the money received as *kharâj*. In case a *dhimmi* becomes Moslem or his land goes to a Moslem, then it becomes tithe-land. The same view is reported to have been held by 'Aṭâ' and al-Ḥasan.

According to ibn-abi-Dhi'b, ibn-abi-Sabrah, Sharîk ibn-'Abdallâh an-Nakha'i, and ash-Shâfi'i, there is tax on their heads, but no *kharâj* or tithe on their land, because they are not included in those on whom *zakât* is binding, nor is their land a *kharâj*-land. The same opinion is held by al-Ḥasan ibn-Ṣâliḥ ibn-Ḥai-l-Mamdâni.

According to Sufyân ath-Thauri and Muḥammad ibn-al-Ḥasan, there is tithe on them but not in a doubled form, because that which counts is the land, and the possessor is not to be taken into consideration. According to al-Auzâ'i and Sharîk ibn-'Abdallâh, if they are *dhimmis* like the Jews of al-Yaman, whose people became Moslem while they were still in the land, then nothing is taken but the poll-tax, and you should not let the *dhimmi* buy the tithe-land or possess it.

The case of a Jew who holds tithe-land. Al-Wâḳidi said, "I once asked Mâlik about the case of a Jew from al-Ḥijâz who buys land in al-Jurf and plants it. Mâlik said, 'The tithe is taken from him'. I then replied, 'Didst thou not claim that there is no tithe on the land of a *dhimmi* if he acquires it from the tithe-land?' 'That', said Mâlik, 'holds true, if he stays in his own country; but in case he leaves his country, then that becomes a question of trade.' "[1]

A man of the banu-Taghlib who uses a tithe-land. Abu-az-Zinad, Mâlik ibn-Anas, ibn-abi-Dhi'b, ath-Thauri, abu-Ḥanîfah and Ya'ḳûb said regarding the case of one of the banu-Taghlib who plants a piece of the tithe-land that he should pay a double-tithe. If he rents a tithe-farm then—according to Mâlik, ath-Thauri, ibn-abi-Dhi'b and Ya'ḳûb—the one who plants the farms should pay the tithe. Abu-Ḥanîfah, however, maintains that the owner of the land should pay it; and Zufar shares the same view.

The case of one who is behind in payment of the tithe. According to abu-Ḥanîfah, in case a man fails to pay the tithe for two years, then the authorities [Ar. *sulṭân*] take only one tithe as he begins again to pay. The same is true of the *kharâj*-land. But abu-Shimr holds that the authorities take the arrears, because it is justly due to them.

[1] *Cf.* abu-Yûsuf, p. 69.

CHAPTER XVI

ʻUmân

The Prophet sends abu-Zaid al-Anṣâri to ʻUmân. The al-Azd were in ascendency in ʻUmân,[1] although it had in its deserts[2] many other peoples. In the early part of the year 8, the Prophet delegated to them abu-Zaid al-Anṣâri of al-Khazraj, who was one of those who compiled the Koran in the time of the Prophet. His [full] name, according to al-Kalbi, was Ḳais ibn-Sakan ibn-Zaid[3] ibn-Ḥarâm; according to some Baṣrah philologists, his name was ʻAmr ibn-Akhṭab, the grandfather of ʻUrwah ibn-Thâbit ibn-ʻAmr ibn-Akhṭab; and according to Saʻîd ibn-Aus al-Anṣâri, it was Thâbit ibn-Zaid. The Prophet also sent ʻAmr ibn-al-ʻÂṣi as-Sahmi with a letter to ʻAbd[4] and Jaifar, the two sons of al-Julanda, calling them to Islâm.[5] The Prophet said, "If these people accept the witness of truth and pledge obedience to Allah and his Prophet, ʻAmr will be the commander and abu-Zaid will officiate in prayer, propagate Islâm, and teach the Koran and the institutes of the Prophet." 76

On the arrival of abu-Zaid and ʻAmr at ʻUmân, they found that ʻAbd and Jaifar were at Ṣuḥâr on the sea-coast. They carried the letter of the Prophet to them, and they

[1] Yâḳût, vol. iii, p. 717.

[2] Ar. *bâdiyah*; see *MFO*, vol. iv, p. 98.

[3] Hishâm, p. 504, gives "Ḳais ibn-Zaʻûra" for Zaid.

[4] Hishâm, p. 971: "ʻIyâdh"; adh-Dhahabi, *al-Mushtabih*, p. 133: "ʻAbbâd"; *cf.* Athîr, vol. ii, p. 177.

[5] Yaʻḳûbi, vol. ii, p. 85; Sprenger, vol. iii, p. 382.

both accepted Islâm and invited the Arabs to it. The Arabs then responded and showed special interest in it. 'Amr and abu-Zaid stayed in 'Umân until the death of the Prophet. It is said by some, however, that abu-Zaid returned to al-Madînah before that.

Al-Azd and other tribes apostatize. Consequent upon the death of the Prophet, al-Azd apostatized from Islâm under the leadership of Laḳîṭ ibn-Mâlik dhu-at-Tâj and left for Dabba [1] (some say for Damma in Dabba), Abu-Bakr, thereupon, dispatched against them Ḥudhaifah ibn-Miḥṣan al-Makhzûmi, who in a battle with Laḳîṭ and his companions killed him and took from the people of Dabba many captives whom they sent to abu-Bakr. At this, al-Azd returned to Islâm. Other clans from 'Umân, however, apostatized and 77
went as far as ash-Shiḥr. These 'Ikrimah followed and overpowered, carrying away a large booty and killing many of their number. Then some of the tribe of Mahrah ibn-Ḥaidân ibn-'Amr ibn al-Ḥâfi ibn-Ḳuḍâ'ah massed a body of men, against whom 'Ikrimah came; but they offered no resistance and paid *ṣadaḳah*.

Ḥudhaifah made governor. Abu-Bakr assigned Ḥudhaifah ibn-Miḥṣan as governor over 'Umân. When abu-Bakr died, Ḥudhaifah was still over it; but he was later dismissed and sent to al-Yaman.

'Îsa ibn-Ja'far abuses the people. The state of 'Umân continued in a fair way, its people paying *ṣadaḳah* on their property, and poll-tax being taken from those among them who were *dhimmis* until the caliphate of ar-Rashîd who made 'Îsa ibn-Ja'far ibn-Sulaimân ibn-'Ali ibn-'Abdallâh ibn-al-'Abbâs its ruler. The latter left for 'Umân with some troops from al-Baṣrah, who began to violate women, and rob

[1] Ṭabari, vol. i, p. 1981: "Daba".

the people, and make public use of musical instruments.[1] The people of 'Umân, who were mostly Shurât,[2] having learned that, fought against him and held him back from entering the city. Finally, they succeeded in killing and crucifying him. Then they broke with the caliph[3] and refused to do him homage, making one of their own their ruler.

Some assert that the Prophet sent abu-Zaid carrying his letter to 'Abd and Jaifar, the two sons of al-Julanda of al-Azd, in the year 6, and sent 'Amr in the year 8, a short time after his conversion to Islâm, which took place, together with the conversion of Khâlid ibn-al-Walîd and 'Uthmân ibn-Ṭalḥah-l-'Abdi in Ṣafar, year 8. 'Amr had come from Abyssinia to the Prophet.[4] The Prophet said to abu-Zaid, "From the Moslems, take *ṣadaḳah*; but from the Magians, take poll-tax."

The letter of 'Umar ibn-'Abd-al-'Azîz to 'Adi. Abu-l-Ḥasan al-Madâ'ini from al-Mubârak ibn-Fuḍâlah:—The following is what 'Umar ibn-'Abd-al-'Azîz wrote to 'Adi ibn-Arṭât al-Fazâri, his *'âmil* in al-Baṣrah:

"Greetings! I have previously written to 'Amr ibn-'Abdallâh asking him to distribute whatever he received in 'Umân as date or grain tithes among the poor of its inhabitants, the nomadic people who may descend on it and those whom need, poverty, or obstruction of the way may compel to stay in it. Regarding this, he wrote to me that having asked thy representative who came before him to
'Umân about those articles of food and dates, he was told 78

[1] *Cf.* Salîl ibn-Râziḳ, *History of Imâms and Seyyids of Oman*, tr. Badger, p. 11.

[2] Schismatics commonly known as *Khawârij*. They say that they owe their name to Koran, 2:203.

[3] The word used is *sulṭân*.

[4] Hishâm, pp. 716-717.

that thy representative had sold them and delivered the price to thee. Return to 'Amr, therefore, what thy representative in 'Umân had carried to thee as the price of dates and grains, that 'Amr may invest it where I instructed him, and spend it as I told him. May this be the will of Allah, and peace be unto thee!"

CHAPTER XVII

AL-BAḤRAIN

Al-Mundhir ibn-Sâwa, governor of al-Baḥrain. The land of al-Baḥrain formed a part of the Persian kingdom. In its desert lived a great many Arabs from the tribes of 'Abd-al-Ḳais, Bakr ibn-Wâ'il and Tamîm. At the time of the Prophet, the one who ruled the Arabs in it in the name of the Persians was al-Mundhir ibn-Sâwa [1] one of the sons of 'Abdallâh ibn-Zaid ibn-'Abdallâh ibn-Dârim ibn-Mâlik ibn-Ḥanẓalah. This 'Abdallâh ibn-Zaid was surnamed al-Asbadhi after a village in Hajar called al-Asbadh. Others claim that he was named after the al-Asbadhi people, who were worshippers of horses in al-Baḥrain.

Al-'Alâ' delegated by the Prophet. At the beginning of the year 8, the Prophet delegated al-'Alâ ibn-'Abdallâh ibn-'Imâd al-Ḥaḍrami, an ally of the banu-'Abd-Shams, to al-Baḥrain, giving its people the choice between following Islâm or paying tax. With him, the Prophet sent a letter to al-Mundhir ibn-Sâwa and Sibukht the satrap [2] of Hajar,[3] giving them the choice between following Islâm or paying tax. They both were converted and, together with them, all the Arabs living there and a few Persians. The rest of the population, however, including Magians, Jews and

[1] Ḥajar, vol. iii, p. 943.

[2] *marzubân*; Ibn-Ḥajar, vol. i, p. 213, in quoting al-Balâdhuri gives his name thus: "Usaikhit (Usaikhib)"; *cf.* Ibn-Sa'd in Wellhausen, *Skizzen*, vol. iv, p. 15; Yâḳût, vol. i, p. 508.

[3] Another name for Baḥrain, hence the Greek: Gerrha; Caetani, vol. ii, p. 194.

Christians made terms with al-'Alâ' and this is a copy of the statement written between the two parties:

"In the name of Allah, the compassionate, the merciful. These are the terms agreed upon between al-'Alâ' ibn-al-Ḥaḍrami and the people of al-Baḥrain. It is agreed that they will save us [the Moslems] the trouble of work, and divide with us the dates; and whosoever of them fails to keep this may the curse of Allah, the angels, and the world altogether be upon him." As for the poll-tax, al-'Alâ' assessed one *dînâr* on every adult. 79

The letter of the Prophet. 'Abbâs ibn-Hishâm from ibn-'Abbâs:—This is what the Prophet wrote to the people of al-Baḥrain:

"Greetings! If ye observe prayer, give *zakât*, remain loyal to Allah and his Prophet, pay the tithe of the dates and half the tithe of the grains, and do not bring up your children as Magians, then ye will be treated according to the terms agreed upon when ye became Moslem, with the exception of the fire-temple that is to be delivered to Allah and his Prophet. If, however, ye refuse, then tax will be incumbent on you."

The Magians and Jews prefer tax. The Magians and Jews, however, refused Islâm and preferred the payment of poll-tax. Upon this, the hypocrites among the Arabs remarked, "The Prophet pretended that he would accept poll-tax from none outside the 'People of the Book', but, here he is accepting it from the Magians of Hajar who are not 'People of the Book.'" On this occasion the text was revealed—"O ye that have believed! take heed to yourselves. He who erreth shall not hurt you when ye have the guidance."[1] According to certain reports, the Prophet sent al-'Alâ' at the time he sent his envoys to the kings in the year 6.[2]

[1] Kor., 5: 104.

[2] Ya'ḳûbi, vol. ii, p. 84.

Al-'Alâ' as a wall between them. Muḥammad ibn-Muṣaffa al-Ḥimṣi from al-'Alâ' ibn-al-Hadrami who said: "The Prophet sent me to al-Bahrain (or perhaps he said 'Hajar') and I used to come as a wall between brothers [i. e. try to create discord] some of whom have been converted. From the Moslem among them, I would take the tithe, and from the 'polytheist,' *kharâj*."[1]

The Prophet's letter. Al-Ḳasim ibn-Sallâm from 'Urwah ibn-az-Zubair:—The Prophet wrote to the people of Hajar as follows:—[2]

"In the name of Allah, the compassionate, the merciful. From Muḥammad the Prophet to the people of Hajar: ye are in peace. I praise Allah on your behalf, beside whom there is no god. Then I admonish you by Allah and by yourselves that ye do not go astray after having been guided, nor be misled after having the right pointed out to you. What ye have done has reached me, and now the offense of the guilty shall not be charged to him among you who behaves himself. When my commanders come to you obey
them, reinforce them and help them in carrying out Allah's 80
plan and his cause, for whosoever among you does the good deed, his deed shall not be lost before Allah or before me. Your delegation has come to me, and I did nothing for them but what was pleasing to them; although if I were to enforce all my right on you, I would expel you from Hajar. Thus did I accept intercession for the absent among you, and bestow favor on the present. Remember the grace of Allah upon you."

The tax imposed on al-Baḥrain. Al-Ḥusain ibn-al-Aswad from Ḳatâdah:—In the time of the Prophet, no fight took place in al-Bahrain, for some of the people accepted Islâm,

[1] Yâḳût, vol. i, p. 509; Ḥajar, vol. iii, p. 943; Caetani, vol. iii, p. 202.

[2] Wellhausen, *Skizzen*, vol. iv, pp. 15-16.

and others made terms with al-'Alâ', agreeing to give half the grains and dates.

Al-Husain from az-Zuhri:—The Prophet took poll-tax from the Magians of Hajar.

What the Prophet wrote to the Magians. Al-Husain from al-Ḥasan ibn-Muhammad:—The Prophet wrote to the Magians of Hajar, inviting them to Islâm and providing that if they are converted, they will have the rights we have, and be under the obligations we are under; but those who refuse Islâm will have to pay the tax, and we will not eat what they slaughter nor marry their women.

Al-Ḥusain from Sa'îd ibn-al-Musaiyib:[1]—The Prophet exacted tax from the Magians of Hajar, 'Umar exacted it from those of Persia, and Uthmân from the Berbers.

A similar tradition was communicated by al-Ḥusain on the authority of az-Zuhri.

'Amr an-Nâḳid from Mûsa ibn-'Ukbah:—The Prophet wrote to Mundhir ibn-Sâwa as follows:—

"From Muhammad the Prophet to Mundhir ibn-Sâwa:—thou art at peace. I praise Allah in thy behalf, beside whom there is no god. Thy letter I received, and its contents I heard. Whosoever repeats our prayer, faces the 81
ḳiblah as we do [in prayer] and eats what we slaughter, such one is a Moslem; but whosoever refuses will have to pay tax."

'Abbâs ibn-Hishâm al-Kalbi from ibn-'Abbâs:—The Prophet having written to al-Mundhir ibn-Sâwa, the latter accepted Islâm and called the people of Hajar to it, some of whom accepted and others did not. As for the Arabs, they became Moslems, but the Magians and Jews accepted the tax and it was exacted from them.

Al-'Alâ' sends 80,000 dirhams. Shaibân ibn-Farrûkh from Ḥumaid ibn-Hilâl:—Al-'Alâ' ibn-al-Ḥadrami sent

[1] Duraid, p. 62: "Musaiyab".

from al-Baḥrain to the Prophet a sum of money amounting to 80,000 [*dirhams*], more than which sum the Prophet never received either before or after. The Prophet gave a part of it to his uncle al-'Abbâs.

Hishâm ibn-'Ammâr from 'Abd-al-'Azîz ibn-'Ubaidallâh:—The Prophet communicated with those in Hajar whom Kisra had settled there as hostages [*waḍâ'i'*], but they refused Islâm and tax was laid on them, one *dînâr* on every man.

Abân ibn-Sa'îd made governor and succeeded by abu-Hurairah. The Prophet dismissed al-'Alâ' and assigned to al-Baḥrain Abân ibn-Sa'îd ibn-al-'Âṣi ibn-Umaiyah. According to other reports, al-'Alâ' was assigned to one district of al-Baḥrain, a part of which was al-Ḳaṭîf, and Abân to another in which lay al-Khaṭṭ. The former report, however, is the more authentic. On the death of the Prophet, Abân left al-Baḥrain and came to al-Madînah. The people of al-Baḥrain, thereupon, asked abu-Bakr to send al-'Alâ' back to them. This he did. Thus, according to this report, al-'Alâ' held the governorship of al-Baḥrain until he died in the year 20. Then 'Umar assigned to his place abu-Hurairah ad-Dausi. Others say that 'Umar assigned abu-Hurairah before the death of al-'Alâ', who, thereupon, left for Tauwaj in Persia, intending to settle in it. Later, however, he returned to al-Baḥrain where he died. Abu-Hurairah often repeated, "After we buried al-'Alâ', we wanted to lift a brick from the tomb. On lifting it we found al-'Alâ' missing from the coffin."

'Uthmân ibn-abi-l-'Âṣi made governor. Abu-Mikhnaf asserted that 'Umar ibn-al-Khaṭṭâb wrote to al-'Alâ' ibn-al-Ḥaḍrami, his *'âmil* in al-Baḥrain, calling him back, and assigned 'Uthmân ibn-abi-l-'Âṣi ath-Thaḳafi to al-Baḥrain and 'Umân. On the arrival of al-'Alâ' in al-Madînah, he was assigned by 'Umar to the governorship of al-Baṣrah, in 82

the place of 'Utbah ibn-Ghazwân. No sooner had he arrived there, than he died. This took place in the year 14, or the beginning of 15. Then 'Umar assigned Ḳudâmah ibn-Maẓ'ûn al-Jumaḥi for the collection of taxes from al-Baḥrain, and gave abu-Hurairah authority over the military guard and charge of the conduct of prayer. Later he dismissed Ḳudâmah, inflicted on him the legal punishment for drinking wine,[1] and gave abu-Hurairah authority over the military guard and charged him with the conduct of prayer. At last, he dismissed abu-Hurairah and confiscated a part of his wealth. Then he assigned Uthmân ibn-abi-l-'Âṣi to al-Baḥrain and 'Umân.

Abu-Hurairah made governor after Ḳudâmah. Al-'Umari[2] from al-Haitham:—Ḳudâmah ibn-Maẓ'ûn had charge of tax-collecting and the military guard, and abu-Hurairah acted as leader of prayer and *ḳâḍi*. The latter gave witness against Ḳudâmah, and 'Umar assigned him to al-Baḥrain after Ḳudâmah. Later 'Umar dismissed him, confiscated a part of what he possessed and ordered him to return. This he refused to do 'Umar, thereupon, assigned 'Uthmân ibn-abi-l-'Âṣi as governor, who still held the office at the death of 'Umar. When 'Uthmân was in Persia, his substitute over 'Umân and al-Baḥrain was his brother, Mughîrah ibn-abi-l-'Âṣi, others say Ḥafṣ ibn-abi-l-'Âṣi.

'Umar confiscates abu-Hurairah's wealth. Shaibân ibn-Farrûkh from abu-Hurairah who said:—" 'Umar made me his *'âmil* over al-Bahrain. There I gathered 12,000 [*dirhams*]. On my return to 'Umar, he addressed me saying: 'O thou the enemy of Allah and of the Moslems (he may have said 'and of his Book'), thou hast stolen the money of Allah!' To this I replied, 'Neither am I the enemy of

[1] Flogging with 80 stripes; see *Muwaṭṭa*, p. 357.

[2] *i. e.*, abu-'Umar Ḥafṣ ibn-'Umar ad-Dûri.

Allah, nor of the Moslems, (he may have said 'nor of his Book'): rather am I the enemy of him who has enmity against them. The money, I have got from horses that multiplied in number and from different shares that mounted up.' 'Umar then took from me 12,000. In my morning prayer I repeated, 'Lord forgive 'Umar.' After this, 'Umar used to take from the people of al-Baḥrain and give them back more than what he would take. At last 'Umar asked me, 'Wouldst thou not act as *'âmil,* abu-Hurairah?' and I replied 'No,' to which he answered, 'And why not? Better men than thou were made *'âmils,* for instance Joseph,[1] who said, "Set me over the granaries of the land."' To this I replied, 'Joseph was a prophet and the son of a prophet, whereas I am abu-Hurairah, son of Umaimah, and I am afraid of three things and of two things that thou mayest bring upon me.' 'And why,' said 'Umar, 'didst thou not say five?' 'I fear that thou dost whip my back, defame my honor, and take my money; and I hate to speak
without meekness and to rule without knowledge.'" 83

Al-Ḳasim ibn-Sallâm and Rauḥ ibn-'Abd-al-Mu'min from abu-Hurairah:—When abu-Hurairah returned from al-Baḥrain, 'Umar said to him, "O thou enemy of Allah and enemy of his Book; hast thou stolen the money of Allah?" "Neither am I", replied abu-Hurairah, "the enemy of Allah, nor of his Book; rather am I the enemy of him who has enmity against them. I did not steal the money of Allah." "How then," said 'Umar, "did 10,000 *dirhams* come to thee?" "Through horses" said abu-Hurairah, "that reproduced and stipends that came in successions and shares that mounted up." 'Umar took the money from him. The rest of the tradition is similar to what is reported by abu-Hilâl.[2]

[1] Kor., 12:55.

[2] One of the intermediate authorities of the preceding tradition whose final authority is abu-Hurairah himself.

The apostasy of al-Ḥuṭam. On the death of al-Mundhir ibn-Sâwa, a little after the death of the Prophet, those in al-Baḥrain descended from Ḳais ibn-Tha'labah ibn-'Ukâbah apostatized under al-Ḥuṭam from Islâm. This al-Ḥuṭam was Shuraiḥ ibn-Ḍubai'ah ibn-'Amr ibn-Marthad, one of the sons of Ḳais ibn-Tha'labah. He was nicknamed Ḥuṭam for saying,

> "The night found her in the company of a strong driver who does not drive gently [Ar. *ḥuṭam*]".[1]

Together with these there apostatized from Islâm in al-Baḥrain all the Rabî'ah tribe with the exception of al-Jârûd, i. e. Bishr ibn-'Amr al-'Abdi[2] and those of his people who followed him. For a leader, they chose a son of an-Nu'mân ibn-al-Mundhir, named al-Mundhir. Al-Ḥuṭam followed the Rabî'ah and joined them with his men. Having received this information, al-'Alâ' ibn-al-Ḥaḍrami marched at the head of the Moslems until he came to Juwâtha, which was the fortification of al-Baḥrain. As Rabî'ah advanced towards him, he set out towards them with his Arabs and non-Arabs and led a heavy fight against them. Then the Moslems took refuge in the fortification where they were besieged by the enemy. It was in reference to this occasion that 'Abdallâh ibn-Ḥadhaf al-Kilâbi said:

> "Wilt thou carry this message 84
> to abu-Bakr and all the youths of al-Madinah?
> Hasten to the aid of some young men of your number,
> who are invested as captives in Juwâtha."[3]

At last al-'Alâ' made a sally with the Moslems and fell upon the Rabî'ah during the night. A fierce battle ensued in which al-Ḥuṭam was killed.

[1] Ṭabrîzi, *Ḥamâsah*, vol. i, p. 173.

[2] Hishâm, p. 944; Duraid, pp. 186 and 197.

[3] Ṭabari, vol. i, p. 1962.

According to other authorities, al-Ḥuṭam came to the Rabî'ah as they were in Juwâtha, whose inhabitants had all forsaken Islâm, and had chosen for leader al-Mundhir ibn-an-Nu'mân. Al-Ḥuṭam took up his abode with them. Al-'Alâ' pressed the siege until he reduced Juwâtha and dispersed the crowd, killing al-Ḥuṭam. Of the two reports, however, the former is more authentic. Describing the death of al-Ḥuṭam, Mâlik ibn-Tha'labah-l-'Abdi says:

"We left Shuraiḥ with the blood covering him
like the fringe of a spotted Yamanite garment.
It was we that deprived unum-Ghaḍbân of her son,
and broke our lance in Ḥabtar's eye.
It was we that left Misma' prostrate on the ground,
at the mercy of hyenas and eagles that will attack him."

Al-Mundhir ibn-an-Nu'mân. It is reported that al-Mundhir ibn-an-Nu'mân was nicknamed al-Gharûr, but when the Moslems won the victory he said, "I am not al-Gharûr [1] [the deceitful] but al-Maghrûr [the deceited]." This al-Mundhir went with the remnant of Rabî'ah as far as al-Khaṭṭ, which al-'Alâ' moved against and conquered, killing al-Mundhir and those in his company. According to others, al-Mundhir escaped, entered al-Mushaḳḳar and let in the water around him, making it impossible to be reached. Finally he made terms, agreeing to leave the city, which he did. He then joined Musailimah with whom he was killed. Some claim that al-Mundhir was killed in the battle of Juwâtha; others that he surrendered and then fled away but was pursued and put to death. Al-'Alâ' having written to abu-Bakr for reinforcement, the latter wrote to Khâlid ibn-al-Walîd ordering him to hasten from al-Yamâmah to the reinforcement of al-'Alâ'. Al-Ḥuṭam,

[1] Hishâm, p. 945; Ṭabari, vol. i, p. 1970; Ḥajar, vol. iii, p. 385; Athîr, vol. ii. p. 281.

however, was killed[1] before the arrival of Khâlid. So Khâlid with al-'Alâ' laid siege to al-Khaṭṭ. Later, Khâlid received a letter from abu-Bakr ordering him to leave for al-'Irâḳ, to which he started from al-Baḥrain, in the year 12.

Al-Wâḳidi says, "According to our companions, Khâlid came first to al-Madînah, whence he started for al-'Irâḳ."

'Abdallâh ibn-Suhail suffers martyrdom. 'Abdallâh ibn- 85
Suhail ibn-'Amr of the banu-'Âmir ibn-Lu'ai, whose surname was abu-Suhail and whose mother was Fâkhitah daughter of 'Âmir ibn-Naufal ibn-'Abd-Manâf, suffered martyrdom at Juwâtha. This 'Abdallâh was one of those who came with the "infidels" to the battle of Badr, but then he joined the Moslem side and embraced Islâm. He took part with the Prophet in the battle of Badr. On the receipt of the news of his death, his father, Suhail ibn-'Amr, said, "I expect Allah's renumeration for his loss." On a pilgrimage to Makkah Suhail was met by abu-Bakr who consoled him, and Suhail replied, "I am informed that the Prophet said, 'A martyr can intercede for seventy of his relatives,' and it is my hope that my son will begin with no one before me." When 'Abdallâh suffered martyrdom, he was 38 years of age.

'Abdallâh ibn-'Abdallâh suffers martyrdom. Another martyr of the battle of Juwâtha was 'Abdallâh ibn-Abdallâh ibn-Ubai. According to others than al-Wâḳidi, his martyrdom took place during the battle of al-Yamâmah.

Al-'Alâ' reduces az-Zârah, as-Sâbûn and Dârîn. Al-Muka'bar al-Fârisi,[2] who was the friend of Kisra and was once sent by him to annihilate the banu-Tamîm for interfering with his camels (and whose full name was Fairûz ibn-Jushaish[3]), fortified himself in az-Zârah. There, many

[1] *Aghâni*, vol. xiv, p. 48.

[2] Nöldeke, *Geschichte der Perser und Araber*, pp. 259 *seq.*

[3] Perhaps Jushnas, see *Skizzen*, vol. vi, p. 33, note 2; Nöldeke, *Perser*, p. 110, note 3; Athîr, vol. ii, p. 256.

Magians who had assembled in al-Ḳaṭif [1] and had refused to pay tax joined him. Al-'Alâ' invested az-Zârah but failed to reduce it in the caliphate of abu-Bakr. In the early part of the caliphate of 'Umar, however, he reduced it. In the course of the caliphate of 'Umar, al-'Alâ' conquered by force as-Sâbûn [2] and Dârîn where there is [today] a spot known as Khandaḳ al-'Alâ' [the trench of al-'Alâ'].

According to Ma'mar ibn-al-Muthanna, al-'Alâ' with 'Abd-al-Ḳais invaded, in the caliphate of 'Umar ibn-al-Khaṭṭâb, certain villages in as-Sâbûn and reduced them. He then invaded the city of al-Ghâbah and killed those in it who were Persians. Thence he moved to az-Zârah in which al-Muka'bar stayed, and besieged him. The satrap of az-Zârah challenged him to a duel, and Barâ' ibn-Mâlik accepted the challenge and killed him, taking spoils from him which amounted to 40,000 [*dirhams*]. Under safe conduct, one of the people of az-Zârah came forth to point out the drinking water, and showed al-'Alâ' the spring that issues from az-Zârah. This spring al-'Alâ' filled up. The people seeing that, came to terms, agreeing to offer him one-third of the city and one-third of the gold and silver 86
in it, together with one-half of what they owned outside the city. Then came al-Akhnas al-'Âmiri to al-'Alâ' and said, "They have not made terms regarding their children who are now in Dârîn." Karrâz an-Nukri pointed out to al-'Alâ' the ford by which he could cross over to them. Thus did al-'Alâ' with a band of Moslems plunge into the sea; and the first thing the people of Dârîn knew of was the exclamation, "Allah is great!" The people of Dârîn sallied forth and attacked them from three sides, but the Moslems killed their fighters and gained possession of the children

[1] Yâḳût, vol. iv, p. 143.

[2] Yâḳût gives "as-Sâbûr".

and captives. Seeing that, al-Muka'bar became Moslem. On this occasion Karrâz said:

> "Al-'Alâ' feared the basin of the sea as he plunged into it,
> but I have of old crossed it over to the 'unbelievers' of Dârîn."

Khalaf al-Bazzâr and 'Affân from Muḥammad ibn-Sîrîn:—In the duel between Barâ' ibn-Mâlik and the satrap of az-Zârah, the former stabbed the latter above his spine, and he fell dead. Then Barâ' went down and cut off his hands and took his bracelets, a furred coat he had on, and a belt. This booty, being so large, 'Umar took one-fifth of it. It was the first booty in Islâm of which the fifth was taken.

CHAPTER XVIII

Al-Yamâmah

The origin of the name. Al-Yamâmah was first called Jau but was later named after a woman, al-Yamâmah, daughter of Murr [from the tribe] of Jadî, who was crucified at its gate. Allah knows whether this is true.

The envoys to the Prophet. When the Prophet wrote to the kings of the world in the year 7 (or 6 as it is said), he wrote to Haudhah ibn-'Ali-l-Ḥanafi and the people of al-Yamâmah summoning them to Islâm. His letter to this effect he forwarded with Salîṭ ibn-Ḳais ibn-'Amr al-Anṣâri [1] (later al-Khazraji). The people of al-Yamâmah, thereupon, sent to the Prophet their delegation, one of whom was Mujjâ'ah 87
ibn-Murârah. To Mujjâ'ah and in accordance with his request, the Prophet gave out as fief a piece of unutilized land. Another delegate was ar-Rajjâl [2] ibn-'Unfuwah who became Moslem and read the "*Sûrah* of the Cow" and other *Sûrahs* of the Koran. He, however, apostatized from Islâm after a time. Among the delegates was one, Musailimah, the false Prophet,[3] Thumâmah ibn-Kabîr ibn-Ḥabîb,[4] who said to the Prophet, "If it be thy will, we will leave all authority in thy hand and swear allegiance to thee, with the understanding that after thee, all will return to us [Musaili-

[1] *Cf.* Hishâm, p. 971.

[2] Raḥḥal, see ibn-Sa'd in *Skizzen*, vol. iv, p. 46.

[3] Bukhâri, vol. iii, p. 167.

[4] Ibn-Duraid, p. 209; Nawâwi, p. 554; Hishâm, p. 945.

mah]." "No," said the Prophet, "by no means, and may Allah smite thee!" Previous to this, Haudhah ibn-'Ali-l-Ḥanafi had written to the Prophet asking that after the Prophet, the authority might be delegated to himself, and promising to become Moslem and come to the reinforcement of the Prophet. "No; nor anything else," answered the Prophet, "and may Allah let me get rid of him!" Before long Haudhah was dead.

Musailimah, the false Prophet. When the delegation of the banu-Ḥanîfah returned to al-Yamâmah, Musailimah, the false Prophet,[1] asserted his claim as a prophet, and ar-Rajjâl ibn-'Unfuwah testified that the Prophet gave him [Musailimah] a share in the authority with him.[2] Banu-Ḥanîfah and others in al-Yamâmah followed him. He then wrote the following message to the Prophet and forwarded it through 'Ubâdah ibn-al-Ḥârith of the banu-'Âmir ibn-Ḥanîfah, whose surname was ibn-an-Nauwâḥah,[3] and who was [later] killed in al-Kûfah by 'Abdallâh ibn-Mas'ûd who heard that he and his companions believed in the false claims of Musailimah:

"From Musailimah, the Messenger of Allah, to Muḥammad, the Messenger of Allah. Greetings! To us half the land belongs, and to Ḳuraish the other half, but Ḳuraish do not act equitably; and peace be unto thee. Written by 'Amr ibn-al-Jârûd al-Ḥanafi."

To this the Prophet replied:

"In the name of Allah, the compassionate, the merciful. From Muḥammad, the Prophet, to Musailimah, the false Prophet. Greetings! 'For the earth is Allah's: to such of his servants as he pleaseth doth he give it as a heritage' [4];

[1] Ar. *al-Kadhdhâb*, the impostor.

[2] Diyârbakri, vol. ii, p. 175.

[3] Nawâwi, p. 374.

[4] Kor., 7: 125.

and peace be to those who follow the true guidance! Written by Ubai ibn-Ka'b." [1]

Khâlid ibn-al-Walîd goes against Musailimah. When, at 88
the death of the Prophet, abu-Bakr was proclaimed caliph and, in a few months, destroyed those of the people of Najd and its environs who apostatized from Islâm, abu-Bakr sent Khâlid ibn-al-Walîd ibn-al-Mughîrah-l-Makhzûmi to al-Yamâmah giving him orders to fight against Musailimah, the false Prophet. As Khâlid came within sight of al-Yamâmah, he met a group of the banu-Ḥanîfah among whom was Mujjâ'ah ibn-Murârah ibn-Sulmi.[2] He killed them and spared Mujjâ'ah whom he carried off in chains. Khâlid put up his camp one mile from al-Yamâmah. Banu-Ḥanîfah came out to him, and among them were ar-Rajjâl and Muḥakkim ibn-aṭ-Ṭufail ibn-Subai', nicknamed the Muḳakkim al-Yamâmah. Khâlid, seeing something glittering among them, turned to his men and said, "Know ye Moslems that Allah has spared you the trouble of your enemy. Do ye not see how they have drawn the swords one against the other? I suppose there is discord among them, and their force will be used on themselves." Mujjâ'ah, fettered in his chains, shouted, "No, these are Indian swords which they, for fear of being broken, hold up to the sun in order render the blades flexible." They then met. The first to meet the Moslems was ar-Rajjâl ibn-'Unfuwah, who was immediately killed by Allah's help. Many of the distinguished men and "Koran-readers" among the Moslems fell martyrs. The Moslems then returned and went back, but Allah favored them with a victory and made the people of al-Yamâmah take to flight. The Moslems pursued them,

[1] *Cf.* Ya'ḳûbi, vol. ii, p. 146; ibn-Sa'd in *Skizzen*, vol. iv, pp. 13-14; Athîr, vol. ii, pp. 228-229; Sprenger, vol. iii, p. 306.

[2] *Cf.* Ibn-Duraid, p. 23.

inflicting horrible death on them. Muḥakkim was hit by an arrow shot by 'Abd-ar-Raḥmân ibn-abi-Bakr aṣ-Ṣiddîḳ, the brother of 'Â'ishah through her father, and he fell dead. The " infidels " took refuge in al-Ḥadîḳah which was since that day called " Ḥadîḳat al-Maut." [1] In al-Ḥadîḳah, Musailimah was killed by Allah's help. Banu-'Amr ibn-Lu'ai ibn-Ghâlib said that he was killed by Khidâsh ibn-Bashîr ibn-al-Aṣamm of the banu-Ma'îṣ ibn-'Âmir ibn-Lu'ai; but certain *Anṣâr* say that he was killed by 'Abdallâh ibn-Zaid ibn-Tha'labah of the banu-l-Ḥârith ibn-al-Khazraj, who was shown a vision of the call for prayer.[2] Still others assert that he was killed by abu-Dujânah Simâk ibn-Kharashah who later fell as martyr; and others, by 'Abd-allâh ibn-Zaid ibn-'Âṣim, a brother of Ḥabîb ibn-Zaid of the 89
banu-Mabdhûl of the banu-an-Najjâr. This Ḥabîb had his hands and feet once cut off by Musailimah. Waḥshi ibn-Ḥarb al-Ḥabashi, the murderer of Ḥamzah, claimed that he was the one who killed Musailimah, and used to say, " I killed the best of all people and the worst of all people." Some believe that all those mentioned above took part in killing Musailimah. Among those who claimed having killed Musailimah, was Mu'âwiyah ibn-abi-Sufyân and the banu-Umaiyah credited him for it.

Abu-Ḥafṣ ad-Dimashḳi quotes from one who was present when 'Abd-al-Malik ibn-Marwân asked a man of the banu-Ḥanîfah who witnessed the battle of al-Yamâmah as to who was the one who killed Musailimah, to which the latter replied, " He was killed by one whose description is as follows :—" " By Allah ", exclaimed 'Abd-al-Malik, " thou hast decided the question of his killing in favor of Mu'âwiyah."

According to a report, when the false Prophet was seized

[1] " The park of death."

[2] Hishâm, p. 308; ibn-Duraid, pp. 268-269.

by the throat, he shouted, "O banu-Ḥanîfah, fight for your relatives!" which he repeated until Allah brought about his death.

'Abd-al-Wâḥid ibn-Ghiyâth from Hishâm ibn-'Urwah's father:—The Arabs forsook the true faith, and abu-Bakr sent Khâlid ibn-al-Walîd who met them and said, "By Allah, I shall never cease until I come face to face with Musailimah!" The *Anṣâr* objected saying, "This idea is of your own and was not given out by abu-Bakr; take us back to al-Madînah that we may give rest to our horses." "I shall, by Allah, never cease," repeated Khâlid," until I come face to face with Musailimah!" Consequently, the *Anṣâr* left him. They then said to themselves, "What is this that we have done? If our friends win the victory, we will be reviled; and if they are defeated, we would be the cause of their defeat." Thus they returned and joined Khâlid. The Moslems and the "polythesists" met, and the former took to flight until they got to their place of abode where as-Sâ'ib ibn-al-'Auwâm stood up and addressed them saying, "Ye have reached, O people, your place of abode; and after his own place of abode, man has no place to flee to!" [1] Finally, Allah caused the defeat of the "polytheists," and Musailimah was killed. Their watchword on that occasion was "O people of the '*Sûrah* of the Cow'!"

I was told by one of the inhabitants of al-Yamâmah that some one, who was under the protection of the banu-Ḥanîfah, repeated the following verse when Muḥakkim was killed:

> "If I escape from it, I escape from that which is a calamity; 90
> otherwise out of the same vessel I shall drink."

Mujjâ'ah makes terms. By this time, the Moslems were

[1] An Arabic proverb.

worn out by war and entirely exhausted. But Mujjâ'ah said to Khâlid, "Most of the people of al-Yamâmah did not go out to fight you, and what ye have killed is only the small minority. In spite of that they have exhausted your utmost effort as I see. Nevertheless I am ready to make terms with you on their behalf." Accordingly, he made terms with Khâlid, agreeing to give one-half of the captives, gold, silver, coats of mail and horses. Having trusted him, Khâlid sent him back to his men. As soon as he entered al-Yamâmah he ordered the boys, women and aged men of al-Yamâmah to put on their arms and hold the forts. As Khâlid and the Moslems looked toward them, they entertained no doubt that they were fighters, and they said, "Mujjâ'ah has told us the truth." Then Mujjâ'ah came out to the Moslems' camp and said, "The people refused the terms which I made with you, and there are the fortifications of al-'Irḍ manned to their fullest capacity. But I kept urging them until they agreed to make terms on one-fourth of the captives and one-half of the gold, silver, coats of mail and horses." Both parties agreed on these terms, and Khâlid accepted them and signed his name. Mujjâ'ah then came with Khâlid to al-Yamâmah. Seeing those left in it, Khâlid turned to Mujjâ'ah and said, "Thou hast cheated me, Mujjâ'ah." The people of al-Yamâmah at last accepted Islâm, and the *ṣadaḳah* was taken from them.

Khâlid reinforces al-'Alâ'. Khâlid received the message of abu-Bakr directing him to reinforce al-'Alâ' ibn-al-Ḥaḍrami. Accordingly, he started for al-Baḥrain and left in his place over al-Yamâmah Samurah ibn-'Amr al-'Anbari. The conquest of al-Yamâmah was effected in the year 12.

A description of Musailimah. I was told by abu-Rabâḥ al-Yamâmi, on the authority of certain *sheikhs* from al-Yamâmah, that Musailimah, the false Prophet, was short, exceedingly pale, with a camois and flat nose. He was nicknamed abu-Thumâmah, and according to others, abu-Thumâlah. His *muezzin* [1] was one, Ḥujair, who in calling to prayer used to chant, "I testify that Musailimah *claims* to be the Prophet of Allah." Remarking on this, some one said, "Ḥujair has expressed it eloquently," which phrase has since become a proverb.

Those who fell martyrs in al-Yamâmah. Among those who suffered martyrdom in al-Yamâmah were abu-Ḥudhaifah ibn-'Utbah ibn-Rabî'ah ibn-'Abd-Shams, whose first name was Hushaim, and some say Mihsham; [2] Sâlim, a freedman of abu-Ḥudhaifah surnamed abu-Abdallâh, and who was a freedman [3] of Thubaitah daughter of Ya'âr [4] of 91
the *Anṣâr* (and others say Nubaithah who was a woman); Khâlid ibn-Asîd ibn-abi-l-'Îṣ ibn-Umaiyah; 'Abdallâh, i. e., Al-Ḥakam ibn-Sa'ıd ibn-al-'Âṣi ibn-Umaiyah, who, according to others, was killed in the battle of Mu'tah; Shujâ' ibn-Wahb al-Asadi, an ally of the banu-Umaiyah, whose surname was abu-Wahb; aṭ-Ṭufail ibn-'Amr ad-Dausi of al-Azd; Yazîd ibn-Rukaish al-Asadi, an ally of the banu-Umaiyah; Makhramah ibn-Shuraiḥ al-Ḥaḍrami, an ally of the banu-Umaiyah, as-Sâ'ib ibn-al-'Auwâm, a brother of az-Zubair ibn-al-'Auwâm; al-Walîd ibn-'Abd-Shams ibn-al-Mughîrah-l-Makhzûmi; as-Sâ'ib ibn-'Uthmân ibn-Maẓ'ûn al-Jumaḥi; and Zaid ibn-al-Khaṭṭâb ibn-Nufail, a brother of 'Umar ibn-al-Khaṭṭâb, who, according to some, was killed by abu-Maryam al-Ḥanafi whose proper name was Ṣubaiḥ ibn-Muḥarrish. According to ibn-al-Kalbi, Zaid was killed by Labîd ibn-Burghuth al-'Ijli, who later came to 'Umar and 'Umar said to him, "Thou art the sacks" (his name, Labîd,

[1] The chanter who calls to prayer from the minaret.

[2] Hishâm, p. 165.

[3] Hishâm, pp. 422 and 486.

[4] *Ibid.*, p. 322.

meaning sacks). The surname of Zaid was abu-'Abd-ar-Raḥmân, and he was the senior of 'Umar. According to some, the proper name of abu-Maryam was Iyâs ibn-Ṣubaiḥ, and he was the first in the time of 'Umar to hold the position of *ḳâḍi* in al-Baṣrah. He died in Sanbîl which lies in al-Ahwâz. Other martyrs were abu-Ḳais ibn-al-Ḥârith ibn-'Adi ibn-Sahm; 'Abdallâh ibn-al-Ḥârith ibn-Ḳais; Salîṭ ibn-'Amr, a brother of Suhail ibn-'Amr of the banu-'Amr ibn-Lu'ai; and Iyâs ibn-al-Bukair al-Kinâni. Among the *Anṣâr*, the following suffered martyrdom: 'Abbâd ibn-al-Ḥârith ibn-'Adi of the banu-Jaḥjaba of al-Aus; 'Abbâd ibn-Bishr ibn-Waḳsh al-Ashhali of al-Aus, surnamed abu-ar-Rabî', and according to others, abu-Bishr; Mâlik ibn-Aus ibn-'Atîk al-Ashhali; abu-'Aḳîl ibn-'Abdallâh ibn-Tha'labah ibn-Baiḥân al-Balawi, an ally of the banu-Jaḥjaba, and whose proper name was 'Abd-al-'Uzza, but who was called by the Prophet "'Abd-ar-Raḥmân the enemy of the idols"; 92
Surâḳah ibn-Ka'b ibn-'Abd-al-'Uzza an-Najjâri of al-Khazraj; 'Umârah ibn-Ḥazm ibn-Zaid ibn-Laudhân an-Najjâri (who is supposed by others to have died in the time of Mu'âwiyah); Ḥabîb ibn-'Amr ibn-Miḥṣan an-Najjâri; Ma'n ibn-'Adi ibn-al-Jadd ibn-al-'Ajlân al-Balawi of the Ḳuḍâ'ah, and an ally of the *Anṣâr*; Thâbit ibn-Ḳais ibn-Shammâs ibn-abi-Zuhair the *khaṭîb* of the Prophet and who was of the banu-l-Ḥârith ibn-al-Khazraj (whose surname was abu-Muḥammad, and who at that time was the commander of the *Anṣâr*); abu-Ḥannah ibn-Ghuzaiyah ibn-'Amr one of the banu-Mâzin ibn-an-Najjâr; al-'Âṣi ibn-Tha'labah ad-Dausi of al-Azd, an ally of the *Anṣâr*; abu-Dujânah Simâk ibn-Aus ibn-Kharashah ibn-Laudhân as-Sâ'idi of al-Khazraj; abu-Usaid Mâlik ibn-Rabî'ah as-Sâ'idi (others say he died in al-Madînah, year 60); 'Abdallâh ibn-'Abdallâh ibn-Ubai ibn-Mâlik (whose first name was al-Ḥubâb but who was given by the Prophet his father's name. His

father played the hypocrite in religion. He is the one called ibn-Ubai ibn-Salûl, Salûl being the mother of Ubai and of [the clan of] Khuzâ'ah, and he bears her name. His father was Mâlik ibn-al-Ḥârith of the banu-l-Khazraj (others say he suffered martyrdom in the battle of Juwâtha at al-Baḥrain); 'Uḳbah ibn-'Âmir ibn-Nâbi' of the banu-Salimah of al-Khazraj; and al-Ḥârith ibn-Ka'b ibn-'Amr of the banu-an-Najjâr. The Prophet had sent Ḥabîb ibn-Zaid ibn-Âṣim of the banu-Mabdhûl ibn-'Amr ibn-Ghanm ibn-Mâzin ibn-an-Najjâr, together with 'Abdallâh ibn-Wahb al-Aslami to Musailimah. Musailimah did not molest 'Abdallâh, but cut off the hands and feet of Ḥabîb. The mother of Ḥabîb was Nusaibah, daughter of Ka'b. According to al-Wâḳidi, the two men [sent by the Prophet] came from 'Umân in the company of 'Amr ibn-al-'Âṣi. Musailimah drove them back. 'Amr and all those in his company escaped, with the exception of these two who were captured. In the battle of al-Yamâmah, Nusaibah took part in the fight and returned with a number of wounds inflicted on her. She is the mother of Ḥabîb and 'Abdallâh, the sons of Zaid. She also took part in the battle of Uḥud, and was one of the two women who 93
"swore allegiance" in the day of al-'Aḳabah.[1] Other martyrs of the battle of al-Yamâmah were 'Â'idh ibn-Mâ'iṣ az-Zuraḳi of al-Khazraj and Yazîd ibn-Thâbit al-Khazraji, a brother of Zaid ibn-Thâbit, the authority on "The Laws of Heritage."[2]

Regarding the number of those that fell as martyrs in al-Yamâmah, there is no agreement. The minimum estimate mentioned is 700, the maximum 1,700, while others assert that they were 1,200.

[1] Hishâm, pp. 312 *seq.*

[2] Ḥajar, vol. ii, pp. 40 *seq.*; Ibn-Khallikân, *Wafayât al-A'yân*, vol. i, p. 372, note 2.

Mujjâ'ah is assigned al-Ghûrah and other fiefs. Al-Ḳâsim ibn-Sallâm from Hishâm ibn-Ismâ'îl:—There came to the Prophet Mujjâ'ah-l-Yamâmi to whom the Prophet gave a fief and wrote the following statement: "In the name of Allah, the compassionate, the merciful. This statement is written by Muḥammad, the Messenger of Allah, to Mujjâ'ah ibn-Murârah ibn-Sulmi. I give thee as fief al-Ghûrah, Ghurâbah,[1] and al-Ḥubal. If any one objects, refer him to me." (Al-Ghûrah is the chief village of al-Ghurâbât and is close to Ḳârât). After the death of the Prophet, Mujjâ'ah came to abu-Bakr, who assigned him as fief al-Khiḍrimah. Later he came to 'Umar, who assigned to him ar-Raiya. After that he came to 'Uthmân, who assigned to him another fief "the name of which," says al-Ḥârith,[2] "I do not remember."

Furât ibn-Ḥaiyân gets a fief. Al-Ḳâsim ibn-Sallâm from 'Adi ibn-Ḥâtim:—The Prophet assigned to Furât ibn-Ḥaiyân al-'Ijli a piece of land in al-Yamâmah.

The "park of death." Muḥammad ibn-Thumâl al-Yamâmi from certain *sheikhs*:—The Ḥadîḳah was called Ḥadîḳat al-Maut [the park of death] because of the great number of people that were slain in it. In the time of al-Ma'mûn, Isḥaḳ ibn-abi-Khamîṣah, a freedman of Ḳais, built in it a cathedral mosque. The Ḥadîḳah before that time was known as Ubâḍ.

According to Muḥammad ibn-Thumâl, the Ḳaṣr al-Ward[3] was named after al-Ward ibn-as-Samîn ibn-'Ubaid al-Ḥanafi. According to another, the fortification was called Mu'tiḳ [i. e., emancipator] because of its strength, indicat- 94

[1] Bakri, vol. ii, p. 703: "'Awânah".

[2] Ibn-Murrah-l-Ḥanafi, one of the intermediary reporters of this tradition.

[3] Yâḳût, *Marâṣid*, under *Ward*.

ing thereby that he who takes refuge in it is safe from his enemy.

Ar-Raiya spring. Ar-Raiya was a spring from which the aṣ-Ṣa'fûḳah, as well as al-Khuyaibah and al-Khiḍrimah, got their drinking water, aṣ-Ṣa'fûḳah[1] being a crown-land thus called after one of the agents over it, whose name was Sa'fûḳ.

[1] Bakri, p. 607.

CHAPTER XIX

The Apostasy of the Arabs in the Caliphate of abu-Bakr aṣ-Ṣiddîḳ

Abu-Bakr threatens those who withhold ṣadaḳah. When abu-Bakr was proclaimed caliph, certain Arab tribes apostatized from Islâm and withheld the *ṣadaḳah*. Some of them, however, said, "We shall observe prayer but not pay *zakât*." In reference to that abu-Bakr said, "If they refuse me a one-year *ṣadaḳah*,[1] I shall surely fight against them." According to other reports he said, "If they refuse me a two-year *ṣadaḳah*."

'Abdallâh ibn-Ṣâliḥ al-'Ijli from ash-Sha'bi:—'Abdallâh ibn-Mas'ûd said, "After the death of the Prophet we found ourselves in a state in which we would have perished had not Allah favored us with abu-Bakr. By the consensus of opinion, we agreed not to fight on a female camel that had entered on its second year or a male camel that had entered on its third year, but appropriate for ourselves the income of Ḳura 'Arabîyah[2] and worship Allah until the right course is revealed unto us." Allah gave orders to abu-Bakr to fight them. Then, by Allah, abu-Bakr was not satisfied by anything but one of two:—a humiliating plan or an evacuating war. As for the humiliating plan, it was that they acknowledge that those of their number who were killed went to hell, and that our property that fell into their hands should be returned to us; and the evacuating war was that they leave their homes.

[1] Ar. *'iḳâl*, see an-Nasâ'i, *Sunan*, vol. i, p. 335.

[2] Yaḥya ibn-Adam, p. 122; Bakri, p. 657.

The delegation of Buzâkhah. Ibrâhîm ibn-Muḥammad from Ṭârik ibn-Shihâb:—A delegation from Buzâkhah came to abu-Bakr and he gave them their choice between 95 "the evacuating war" or "the humiliating peace". To this they replied, "'The evacuating war' we have known what it is, what is then 'the humiliating peace?'" "It is," said abu-Bakr, "that we deprive you of the coats of mail and horses, and keep the booty we took from you; and that ye return the booty ye took from us, pay bloodwit for those of us who were slain and consider those of you who were slain to be in hell-fire."

Shujâ' ibn-Mukhallad al-Fallâs from 'Â'ishah the "mother of the Believers":—The latter said, "After the death of the Prophet, what befell my father [1] would have softened the firm mountains if it had befallen them. Hypocrisy in al-Madînah exalted itself, and the Arabs apostatized from their faith. By Allah, not a point they disagreed upon, which my father did not cause to disappear as something without which Islam could do [?]."

Abu-Bakr dispatches an army. Abu-Bakr set out to al-Ḳaṣṣah [2] in the land which belongs to Muḥârib in order to direct the armies marching against the apostates. He was accompanied by the Moslems. Those who went against the Moslems were Khârijah ibn-Ḥiṣn ibn-Ḥudhaifah ibn-Badr al-Fazâri [3] and Manẓûr ibn-Zabbân ibn-Saiyâr al-Fazâri of the banu-l-'Usharâ', who were joined with the tribe of Ghaṭafân. The fight raged fiercely but the "polytheists" were put to flight, and abu-Bakr sent Ṭalḥah ibn-'Ubaidallâh at-Taimi in their pursuit. Ṭalḥah fell upon them at the lower part of Thanâya 'Ausajah where he killed

[1] Abu-Bakr.

[2] Ṭabari, vol. i, p. 1870: "dhu-l-Ḳaṣṣah."

[3] Ibn-Sa'd, vol. iii[1], p. 37.

only one of them, all the rest having fled away, and he could not catch up with them. This made Khârijah ibn-Ḥiṣn repeat, "Woe to the Arabs because of ibn-abi-Ḳuḥâfah [i. e. abu-Bakr]."

While abu-Bakr was at al-Ḳaṣṣah, he set Khâlid ibn-al-Walîd ibn-al-Mughîrah al-Makhzûmi in command over the people,[1] and sent over the *Anṣâr* Thâbit ibn-Ḳais ibn-Shammâs al-Anṣâri, who was one of those that [later] suffered martyrdom in the battle of al-Yamâmah. Thâbit, however, was subordinate to Khâlid. Abu-Bakr ordered Khâlid to direct his course towards Ṭulaiḥah ibn-Khuwailid al-Asadi, who had claimed to be a prophet[2] and was then at Buzâkhah. This Buzâkhah is a spring belonging to the banu-Asad ibn-Khuzaimah. Khâlid set out against him and sent before him 'Ukkâshah ibn-Miḥṣan al-Asadi, an ally of 96
the banu-'Abd-Shams, together with Thâbit ibn-Aḳram al-Balawi, an ally of the *Anṣâr*. Ḥibâl ibn-Khuwailid[3] met them and was slain by them. Having heard the news, Ṭulaiḥah with his brother, Salamah, set out and, meeting 'Ukkâshah and Thâbit, slew them both. Regarding this event Ṭulaiḥah sang:

"As I saw their faces I thought of my brother Ḥibâl
and was sure that I was going to avenge his death.
It was on the evening of that day that I left ibn-Aḳram in his grave,
together with 'Ukkâshah al-Ghanmi, by the battlefield."

The Moslems and their enemy at last met and a fierce battle was fought. With Ṭulaiḥah in the fight was 'Uyainah ibn-Ḥiṣn ibn-Ḥudhaifah ibn-Badr at the head of 700 men of the banu-Fazârah. When 'Uyainah saw the swords of the

[1] Ya'ḳûbi, vol. ii, p. 145.

[2] He imitated Muḥammad by composing *saj'* or rhyming prose, see Ṭabari, vol. i, p. 1738; and Goldziher, *Muhammedanische Studien*, vol. ii, p. 4001.

[3] Hishâm, p. 453.

Moslems butchering the "polytheists," he came to Ṭulaiḥah asking, "Canst thou not see what the army of abu-l-Faṣîl[1] is doing, and did not Gabriel bring thee any message?" "Yes" said Ṭulaiḥah, "Gabriel came to me and said 'Thou wilt have a grinding stone as he has, and a day that thou wilt never forget!'"[2] "By Allah," cried 'Uyainah, "I believe that thou wilt have a day which thou wilt never forget. O banu-Fazârah, this is a false prophet." Saying this, he left Ṭulaiḥah's army which was soon after defeated. The Moslems were victorious. 'Uyainah ibn-Ḥiṣn was taken captive and brought to al-Madînah. Abu-Bakr spared his life and set him free. Ṭulaiḥah ibn-Khuwailid took to flight and entered a tent of his, where he took a bath and went out. Then he rode on his horse, intending to visit the sacred places, and came to Makkah, then to al-Madînah professing Islâm. According to others, he came to Syria, was taken hold of by those of the Moslems who were on a campaign, and sent to abu-Bakr in al-Madînah, where he became Moslem. Later, he distinguished himself in the conquest of al-'Irâḳ and Nihâwand. One day, 'Umar said to him, "Didst thou kill the faithful servant 'Ukkâshah ibn-Miḥṣan?" And he replied, "I have been the means of bringing about the welfare of 'Ukkâshah ibn-Miḥṣan; and he has been the means of bringing about[3] my misery. I beg Allah's pardon upon me."

Dâ'ûd ibn-Ḥibâl al-Asadi told me on the authority of
certain *sheikhs* among his people that 'Umar ibn-al- 9
Khaṭṭâb said to Ṭulaiḥah, "Thou didst lie before Allah when thou didst claim that he revealed to thee the text, 'Allah has nothing to do with the dust on your faces and

[1] Khâlid's surname was abu-Sulaimân, see Nawâwi, p. 224; and ibn-Ḳutaibah, *Kitâb al-Ma'ârif*, p. 90.

[2] Ṭabari, vol. i, p. 1897; Athîr, vol. ii, p. 264.

[3] *Cf.* Ṭabari, vol. i, p. 1898.

the ugliness of your hinder parts. When ye therefore mention Allah, be abstemious and stand upright, for, verily, froth is on the surface of what is pure.' "[1] "'Commander of the Believers'", replied Ṭulaiḥah, "this is one of the corruptions of unbelief which has altogether been destroyed by Islâm. I am not, therefore, to be scolded for holding a part of it." 'Umar remained silent.

Khâlid in Rammân and Abânain. Khâlid ibn-al-Walîd came to Rammân [2] and Abânain [3] where the remnant of the army of Buzâkhah stood. They refrained from fighting against him and swore allegiance before him to abu-Bakr.

Banu-'Âmir ibn-Sa'ṣa'ah embrace Islâm. Khâlid ibn-al-Walîd sent Hishâm ibn-al-'Âṣi ibn-Wâ'il as-Sahmi, a brother of 'Amr ibn-al-'Âṣi, one of the early Moslems and one of the *Emigrants* to Abyssinia, to the banu-'Âmir ibn Ṣa'ṣa'ah. Banu-'Âmir did not resist him and professed Islâm and practised the call to prayer. So he left them.

Ḳurrah's life spared. Ḳurrah ibn-Hubairah-l-Ḳushairi, having refused to pay *ṣadaḳah* and reinforced Ṭulaiḥah, was taken by Hishâm ibn-al-'Âṣi to Khâlid. The latter carried him to abu-Bakr to whom Ḳurrah said, "By Allah I never forsook my faith since I became a believer. As 'Amr ibn-al-'Âṣi on his way back from 'Umân passed by me, I treated him hospitably and was loyal to him." 'Amr was questioned by abu-Bakr regarding that, and he corroborated the statement. Consequently, abu-Bakr spared Ḳurrah's life.

Others assert that Khâlid advanced to the land of the banu-'Âmir, took Ḳurrah captive and sent him to abu-Bakr.

The battle of al-Ghamr. Then Khâlid ibn-al-Walîd ad-

[1] Freytag, *Prov.*, vol. i, p. 174, no. 80, and p. 731, no. 63.

[2] Yâḳût, vol. ii, p. 815; Bakri, p. 412.

[3] or Abânân; Yâḳût, vol. i, p. 75; Bakri, p. 63.

vanced to al-Ghamr[1] where a band of the banu-Asad, Ghaṭafân and others had gathered under the leadership of Khârijah ibn-Ḥiṣn ibn-Ḥudhaifah. According to others, they had on different days different leaders, and each party had its own leader drawn from its own ranks. They fought against Khâlid and the Moslems, with the result that some of them were killed and the others took to flight. With reference to the battle of al-Ghamr says al-Ḥuṭai'ah-l-'Absi:

> "Yea, may all short and humble lances be sacrificed,
> in favor of the horsemen's lances at al-Ghamr!"[2]

Khâlid meets abu-Shajarah. Thence Khâlid moved to Jau Ḳurâḳir.[3] Others say he moved to an-Nuḳrah. There
a crowd was gathered by the banu-Sulaim and put under the 98
leadership of abu-Shajarah 'Amr ibn-'Abd-al-'Uzza as-Sulami whose mother was al-Khansâ'. They fought against Khâlid, and one of the Moslems fell a martyr. By Allah's help at last, the "polytheists'" troops were dispersed, and Khâlid had on that day the apostates burned. When abu-Bakr was told about it, he said, "I shall not sheathe a sword that Allah had unsheathed against the 'unbelievers.'" Abu-Shajarah accepted Islâm, and coming to 'Umar found him distributing alms among the poor, so he begged for some. 'Umar asked him, "Art thou not the one who said:

> 'I quenched my lance's thirst on Khâlid's troops,
> and I hope after this that my life will be prolonged'?"

Saying this, he lashed him with the whip.[4] "Islâm, O 'Commander of the Believers,'" replied abu-Shajarah, "has blotted all this out."

[1] *Skizzen*, vol, vi, p. 11, note 1.

[2] Bakri, p. 696, and p. 718, line 12.

[3] *Cf.* Yâḳût, vol. ii, p. 161, lines 12-13.

[4] Ṭabari, vol. i, p. 1907.

Al-Fujâ'ah put to death by fire. There came to abu-Bakr one, al-Fujâ'ah, whose proper name was Bujair ibn-Iyâs ibn-'Abdallâh as-Sulami, and said to him, "Give me horse and arms that I may fight against the apostates." Abu-Bakr gave him horse and arms. Al-Fujâ'ah began to molest the people, killing both Moslems and apostates. He, moreover, gathered a large body of men. Abu-Bakr wrote to Ṭuraifah ibn-Ḥâjizah, a brother of Ma'n ibn-Ḥâjizah, ordering him to go against him. This, ibn-Ḥâjizah did and captured him. He then sent him to abu-Bakr, who ordered him burned in the neighborhood of al-Muṣalla [place of prayer]. Others say that abu-Bakr wrote to Ma'n concerning al-Fujâ'ah, and Ma'n directed against him his brother, Ṭuraifah, who captured him.

Khâlid in al-Buṭâḥ and al-Ba'ûḍah. Later, Khâlid set out against those of the banu-Tamîm who were in al-Buṭâḥ [1] and al-Ba'ûḍah. They fought against him, but he dispersed them [2] killing Mâlik ibn-Nuwairah, a brother of Mutammam ibn-Nuwairah. This Mâlik was the Prophet's *'âmil* for the *ṣadaḳahs* of the banu-Ḥanẓalah. When the Prophet died Mâlik held whatever was in his keeping and said to banu-Ḥanẓalah, "Keep your own money."

Mâlik beheaded. According to other reports, Khâlid met nobody in either al-Buṭâḥ or al-Ba'ûḍah, but he sent detachments among the banu-Tamîm, one of which was under Ḍirâr ibn-al-Azwar al-Asadi. Ḍirâr met Mâlik and, as a result of the conflict which ensued, Ḍirâr took Mâlik and some others captive, and brought them before Khâlid. In accordance with Khâlid's orders, their heads were cut off,[3] Ḍirâr with his own hand cutting off that of Mâlik. Ac-

[1] Yâḳût, vol. i, p. 661.

[2] Ṭabari, vol. i, p. 1924.

[3] *Cf.* Ḥajar, vol. iii, p. 722; abu-l-Fida, *al-Mukhtaṣar*, vol. i, p. 158, (Cairo, 1325).

cording to certain reports, Mâlik said to Khâlid, "By Allah, I did not apostatize!" And abu-Ḳatâdah-l-Anṣâri gave witness that the banu-Ḥanẓalah had laid down their arms and made the public call to prayer. Hearing this, 'Umar 99
ibn-al-Khaṭṭâb said to abu-Bakr, "Thou hast sent a man who kills Moslems and tortures by fire!"

It is reported that Mutammam ibn-Nuwairah once came to 'Umar ibn-al-Khaṭṭâb who asked him, "How far did thy sorrow over they brother, Mâlik, carry thee?" "I wept over him for one year," said Mutammam, "until my sound eye envied the one that had gone; and never did I see fire without feeling as if my grief was strong enough to kill me, because he always left his fire burning till the morning, lest a guest should come and fail to locate his place." 'Umar then asked for a description of him, and Muttamam said, "He used to ride a restive steed and lead a slow-paced camel, while he would be between two water bags exuding water in the chilly night, wrapped up in a loose garment, and armed with a long lance. Thus would he go through the night until the morn. His face was a fragment of a moon." [1] "Sing me," said 'Umar, "some of what thou hast composed regarding him." And Mutammam repeated the elegy in which he said:

> "For a long time we were boon companions like the two fellow-drinkers of Jadhîmah,
> that people said, 'They will never be separated!'" [2]

"If I could write good poetry" remarked 'Umar, "I would have written an elegy on my brother, Zaid." "It is not a parallel case, 'Commander of the Believers'", answered Mutammam, "had my brother met the same death that thy brother has met, I would not have mourned over him."

[1] *Cf.* De Slane, Ibn-Khallikân, vol. iii, pp. 651-652.

[2] *Aghâni,* vol. xiv, pp. 70-71.

"Nobody did ever console me," said 'Umar, "as well as thou didst." [1]

Sajâḥ the Prophetess. Umm-Ṣâdir Sajâḥ, daughter of Aus ibn-Ḥiḳḳ ibn-Usâmah ibn-al-Ghanîz ibn-Yarbû' ibn-Ḥanẓalah ibn-Mâlik ibn-Zaid Manât ibn-Tamîm (others say she was Sajâḥ, daughter of al-Ḥârith ibn-'Uḳfân ibn-Suwaid ibn-Khâlid ibn-Usâmah), claimed to be a prophetess and a soothsayer.[2] She was followed by some of the banu-Tamîm and some of her uncles on her mother's side of the banu-Taghlib. One day she composed the following rhyming sentences: "The Lord of heavens orders you to carry out against ar-Ribâb [3] invasions." She invaded them but was defeated by them, they being the only ones who fought against her.[4] She then came to Musailimah-l-Kadhdhâb [the false Prophet] at Ḥajar and married him,[5] making her religion one with his. When he was killed, she returned 100
to her brethren and there she died. According to ibn-al-Kalbi, however, Sajâḥ accepted Islâm and emigrated to al-Baṣrah and remained a good Moslem. 'Abd-al-A'la ibn-Ḥammâd an-Narsi heard it said by certain *sheikhs* of al-Baṣrah that Samurah ibn-Jundab al-Fazâri led her funeral service as he was the governor of al-Baṣrah under Mu'âwiyah before the arrival of 'Abdallâh ibn-Ziyâd from Khurâsân to assume the office of governor of al-Baṣrah. Ibn-al-Kalbi added that the *muezzin* of Sajâḥ was al-Janabah [6] ibn-Ṭâriḳ ibn-'Amr ibn-Ḥauṭ ar-Riyâḥi, and others say [7] it was Shabath ibn-Rib'i ar-Riyâḥi.

[1] Ibn-Ḳutaibah, *Kitâb ash-Shi'r*, pp. 193-194.

[2] Ar. *kâhin*; see *Skizzen*, vol. iii, p. 130; Goldziher, *Abhandlungen zur Arabischen Philologie*, vol. i, pp. 107-108; Zaidân, vol. iii, pp. 16-18; J. G. Frazer, *Golden Bough*, vol. i, p. 230.

[3] The confederate tribes of Ṭai, 'Adi and 'Uḳl.

[4] *Skizzen*, vol. vi, p. 14.

[5] *Aghâni*, vol. xii, p. 157; abu-l-Fida, vol. i, p. 157 (Cairo, 1325).

[6] Dhahabi, *Mushtabih*, p. 141.

[7] Duraid, p. 137.

The insurrection of Khaulân. Khaulân in al-Yaman having apostatized, 'Umar sent against them Ya'la ibn-Munyah (Munyah, his mother, was of the banu-Mâzin ibn-Manṣûr ibn-'Ikrimah ibn-Khaṣafah ibn-Ḳais ibn-'Ailân ibn-Muḍar, and his father was Umaiyah ibn-abi-'Ubaidah, one of the sons of Mâlik ibn-Ḥanẓalah ibn-Mâlik, an ally of the banu-Naufal ibn-'Abd-Manâf) who won a great victory over them and carried away booty and captives. According to others, however, he met no resistance, and all of them returned to Islâm.

CHAPTER XX

The Apostasy of the banu-Walî'ah and al-Ash'ath ibn-Ma'dikarib ibn-Mu'âwiyah-l-Kindi

The cause of the insurrection of Kindah. The Prophet sent Ziyâd ibn-Labîd al-Bayaḍi of the *Anṣâr* as governor to Ḥaḍramaut; later extending his power over the Kindah. According to others, it was abu-Bakr aṣ-Ṣiddîḳ who extended his power over the Kindah. This Ziyâd ibn-Labîd was a resolute and sturdy man, and took young she-camels as *ṣadaḳah* from a certain man of the banu-Kindah. The Kindah man asked him to return them and take something else, but having marked them with the *ṣadaḳah* brand, Labîd refused his request. Labîd was approached by al-Ash'ath ibn-Ḳais, but still he refused saying, " Never will I return a thing that has been branded with the mark." This caused an uprising of all Kindah against him with the exception of as-Sakûn who still adhered to his side. Hence the verse of their poet:

"It was we that came to the rescue of the faith, 101
when our people miserably went astray and we supported ibn-umm-Ziyâd.
From the right claim of al-Bayâḍi we sought not to deviate,
and the piety of Allah was our best provision."

Banu-'Amr gathered against Labîd. Against Labîd were assembled the banu-'Amr ibn-Mu'âwiyah ibn-al-Ḥârith al-Kindi. Labîd, at the head of the Moslems, attacked them during the night time and killed many, among whom were Mikhwas, Mishraḥ, Jamad and Abḍa'ah the sons of Ma'dikarib ibn-Walî'ah ibn-Shuraḥbîl ibn-Mu'âwiyah ibn-Ḥujr al-Ḳarid (Ḳarid in their dialect means horse) ibn-al-Ḥârith al-Wallâdah ibn-'Amr ibn-Mu'âwiyah ibn-al-Ḥârith. These four brothers were in possession of so many valleys that they were called the "four kings." Previous to this, they had presented themselves before the Prophet, but later on they apostatized. Their sister, al-'Amarradah, was killed by one who mistook her for a man.

Ziyâd fights against al-Ash'ath. As Ziyâd returned with captives and booty, he passed by al-Ash'ath ibn-Ḳais and his people. Seeing him, the women and children began to cry [1] which made al-Ash'ath burn with indignation, and set out with a band of his men.[2] He fell upon Ziyâd and his companions, and many Moslems were lost. The Moslems were then defeated, and all the great men of Kindah rallied to the support of al-Ash'ath ibn-Ḳais. Seeing this, Ziyâd wrote to abu-Bakr asking for reinforcement. Abu-Bakr wrote to al-Muhâjir ibn-abi-Umaiyah, ordering him to reinforce Ziyâd. Ziyâd and al-Muhâjir, at the head of the Moslems, met al-Ash'ath and dispelled his men, and attacking his companions, made a fearful slaughter among them. Thence al-Ash'ath's men took refuge in a fortification of theirs, an-Nujair, where the Moslems besieged them. The siege was pressed until they were exhausted and al-Ash'ath sought safety for a certain number of his men. He did not include himself in that number because al-Jifshîsh [3] al-Kindi, whose name was Ma'dân ibn-al-Aswad ibn-Ma'dikarib, holding him by the waist, said, "Include me in that number." [4] Thus al-Ash'ath excluded himself in favor of al-Jifshîsh. Al-Ash'ath presented himself before Ziyâd ibn-

[1] Ṭabari, vol. i, p. 2005.

[2] Ya'ḳûbi, vol. ii, p. 149.

[3] Jafshîsh in Fairûzâbâdi, *al-Ḳâmûs*, vol. ii, p. 276.

[4] *Cf.* Ṭabari, vol. i, p. 2009.

Labîd and al-Muhâjir who sent him to abu-Bakr. The latter favored him by giving to him in marriage his sister umm-Farwah,[1] daughter of abu-Ḳuḥâfah, who later gave birth to Muḥammad, Isḥâḳ, Ḳuraibah, Ḥubâbah and 102
Ja'dah. According to others, abu-Bakr gave him in marriage his sister Ḳuraibah; and when he married her, he came to the market, and every slaughtered camel he saw, he cut its two heel-tendons, paid its price and gave it to the people to eat. After living in al-Madînah, he set out on a razzia to Syria and al-'Irâḳ. His death took place at al-Kûfah where his funeral service was conducted by al-Ḥasan ibn-'Ali ibn-abi-Ṭâlib, after the latter had been reconciled with Mu'âwiyah. This al-Ash'ath was surnamed abu-Muhammad and nicknamed " 'Urf an-Nâr " [the fire-crest].

The insurrection of the banu-Walî'ah and al-Ash'ath. According to other reports, the banu-Walî'ah apostatized before the Prophet's death. When Ziyâd ibn-Labîd heard of his death, he called the people to swear allegiance to abu-Bakr, which they all did with the exception of the banu-Walî'ah. Ziyâd fell upon them in the night time and killed them. Al-Ash'ath apostatized and fortified himself in an-Nujair where he was besieged by Ziyâd ibn-Labîd and al-Muhâjir who joined hands against him. Abu-Bakr sent 'Ikrimah ibn-abi-Jahl, after his departure from 'Umân, to reinforce them; but on his arrival, an-Nujair was already reduced. Abu-Bakr requested the Moslems to share the booty with him, which they did.

Ath-Thabjâ' and Hind severely punished. It is reported that certain women at an-Nujair having rejoiced at the death of the Prophet, abu-Bakr wrote ordering that their hands and feet be cut off. Among these women were ath-Thabjâ' al-Ḥaḍramîyah, and Hind, daughter of Yamîn, the Jewess.

[1] *Cf.* Ṭabari, vol. i, p. 2012.

The Prophet assigns governors to Ṣan'â', Kindah, Ḥaḍramaut and aṣ-Ṣadif. Bakr ibn-al-Haitham from certain *sheikhs* of al-Yaman:—The Prophet made Khâlid ibn-Sa'îd ibn-al-'Âṣi governor of Ṣan'â', but he was driven out of it by al-'Ansi, the false Prophet. Over the Kindah, he assigned al-Muhâjir ibn-abi-Umaiyah; over Ḥaḍramaut and aṣ-Ṣadif, Ziyâd ibn-Labîd al-Anṣâri. Aṣ-Ṣadif were the descendants of Mâlik ibn-Muratti' ibn-Mu'âwiyah ibn-Kindah.[1] They were called Ṣadif because Muratti' married a woman from Ḥaḍramaut and made it a condition that she would take up her abode with him, and in case she bore a child he would not force her to remain away from her people's home. She did bear a child, Mâlik, and the judge decided that Murratti' should send her back to her people. When Mâlik left him with her, Murratti' said, "Mâlik turned away [Ar.-*ṣadafa*] from me." Hence the name aṣ-Ṣadif.

The insurrection of the banu-'Amr. 'Abd-ar-Razzâḳ said that he was told by certain *sheikhs* from al-Yaman that 103
abu-Bakr wrote to Ziyâd ibn-Labîd and to al-Muhâjir ibn-abi-Umaiyah-l-Makhzûmi who was then over Kindah, ordering them to come together and work hand in hand and with one accord in order to secure for him the caliphate and fight against him who refrains from paying *ṣadaḳah*, and that they should get the help of the Believers against the Unbelievers and of the obedient against the disobedient and transgressors. Once they took as *ṣadaḳah* from a Kindah man a youthful she-camel. He asked them to change it for another. Al-Muhâjir allowed it, but Ziyâd insisted on keeping the camel saying, "Never will I return it after being stamped with the *ṣadaḳah* brand." Therefore, the banu-'Amr ibn-Mu'âwiyah gathered a large body of men.

[1] Khallikân, vol. iv, pp. 595-596.

Then said Ziyâd ibn-Labîd to al-Muhâjir, "Thou dost see this crowd. It is not wise to have us all leave our position. Separate, therefore, thyself with a band of men from the main army, and that will keep our plans concealed. Then I will attack these 'unbelievers' in their homes at night." Ziyâd was resolute and sturdy. He went against the banu-'Amr and, under the cover of the night, fell upon them and some of them began to kill the others. At last Ziyâd and al-Muhâjir met accompanied by the captives and prisoners. They were intercepted by al-Ash'ath ibn-Ḳais and the leading men of Kindah, who fought a fierce battle against them. At last the Kindis fortified themselves in an-Nujair, where the siege was pressed against them until they were exhausted and greatly damaged and al-Ash'ath surrendered. Some say that the Ḥaḍramaut had come to reinforce the Kindah but were met by Ziyâd and al-Muhâjir who defeated them.

The apostasy of Khaulân. Now Khaulân apostatized, and abu-Bakr directed against them Ya'la ibn-Munyah who fought against them until they yielded and agreed to give *ṣadaḳah.* Then al-Muhâjir received abu-Bakr's letter conferring on him the governorship of Ṣan'â' and its adjoining districts, making his province border on what Ziyâd already held.[1] Thus was al-Yaman divided among three: al-Muhâjir, Ziyâd and Ya'la. The land between the extreme limit of al-Ḥijâz and the extreme limit of Najrân was assigned to abu-Sufyân ibn-Ḥarb.

The story of al-Ash'ath. Abu-Naṣr at-Tammâr from Ibrâhîm an-Nakha'i:—Al-Ash'ath ibn-Ḳais al-Kindi, together with some of the Kindah tribe, apostatized and were 104
besieged. Al-Ash'ath secured safety for 70 of his men but did not include himself among them. He was therefore brought before abu-Bakr who said to him, "We shall cer-

[1] Caetani, vol. ii, p. 804.

tainly kill thee, as thou art under no safe conduct, having excluded thyself from that group." "Nay," answered al-Ash'ath, "Thou, successor of the Messenger of Allah, wilt rather favor me with a wife." This abu-Bakr did, giving him his own sister in marriage.

Three things abu-Bakr wished he had done. Al-Ḳâsim ibn-Sallâm abu-'Ubaid [1] from abu-Bakr aṣ-Ṣiddîḳ:—The latter said, " I wish I had done three things that I did not do: —I wish I had cut off the head of al-Ash'ath ibn-Ḳais when he was brought before me, because it seemed to me there was no sort of evil to be done which he would not attempt to do or help to bring about; I wish I had killed rather than burnt al-Fujâ'ah when he was brought before me; and I wish I had directed 'Umar ibn-al-Khaṭṭâb to al-'Irâḳ as I had directed Khâlid to Syria, and thus would have extended both my right and left arms in the cause of Allah." [2]

The captives of an-Nujair ransomed. 'Abdallâh ibn-Ṣâliḥ al-'Ijli from ash-Sha'bi:— Abu-Bakr returned the captives of an-Nujair by ransom receiving 400 *dirhams* for each head. In order to pay for them, al-Ash'ath ibn-Ḳais had to borrow from the merchants of al-Madînah. After paying the ransom of the captives, he returned the loan. Al-Ash'ath ibn-Ḳais wrote the following elegy for Bashîr ibn-al-Audaḥ, who was one of the delegates to the Prophet and who later apostatized, Yazîd ibn-Amânât and those slain in the battle of an-Nujair:—

" By my life—and life is not an insignificant thing to me—
   I had the greatest right to hold tenaciously to those who fell dead.
There is no wonder except when they divide their captives;
   and the world after them is not safe for me.
I am like the camel that lost her young and her milk flows,
   when she longs for them and comes to the bag, stuffed with straw.
Let the tears of my eyes, therefore, flow
   for the loss of the noble ibn-Amânât and the generous Bashîr."

[1] Bakri, p. 747, line 14.
[2] Ya'ḳûbi, vol. ii, pp. 155-156; Mas'ûdi, vol. iv, pp. 184-185.

CHAPTER XXI

AL-ASWAD AL-'ANSI AND THOSE IN AL-YAMAN WHO APOSTATIZED WITH HIM 105

Al-Aswad al-'Ansi claims to be a prophet. Al-Aswad ibn-Ka'b ibn-'Auf al-'Ansi played the soothsayer [Ar. *kâhin*] and claimed to be a prophet. He was followed by the 'Ans tribe which was named after Zaid ibn-Mâlik ibn-Udad ibn-Yashjub ibn-'Arîb [1] ibn-Zaid ibn-Kahlân ibn-Saba, who was the brother of Murâd ibn-Mâlik, Khâlid ibn-Mâlik and Sa'd al-'Ashîrah ibn-Mâlik, together with others outside the 'Ans tribe. Al-Aswad took for himself the name of "Raḥmân [the merciful of] al-Yaman," as Musailimah had taken the name of "Raḥmân al-Yamâmah." [2] He had a trained donkey that would bow on hearing his injunction, "Bow before thy Lord," and that would kneel on hearing "Kneel". Therefore, al-Aswad was called "dhu-l-Ḥimâr [3] [he of the donkey]. Others say he was called "dhu-l-Khimâr" [the veiled one] because he always appeared with a veil and turban.[4] I was told by others from al-Yaman that he was called al-Aswad because the color of his face was black, his proper name being 'Aihalah.

The Prophet invites him to Islâm. In the year in which the Prophet died, he sent Jarîr ibn-'Abdallâh al-Bajali, who

[1] Wüstenfeld, *Register*, p. 86.

[2] Hishâm, p. 200, line 3.

[3] Mas'ûdi, *at-Tanbîh*, pp. 276-277.

[4] Diyârbakri, vol. ii, p. 173.

had in that same year accepted Islâm, against al-Aswad, inviting him to Islâm. But al-Aswad refused. Other reports deny that the Prophet sent Jarîr to al-Yaman.

Al-Aswad as governor of Ṣan'â'. Al-Aswad moved against Ṣan'â' and reduced it, driving Khâlid ibn-Sa'îd ibn-al-'Âṣi from it. Others say he rather drove al-Muhâjir ibn-abi-Umaiyah, and took quarters with Ziyâd ibn-Labîd al-Bayaḍi, with whom he remained until he received a message from abu-Bakr ordering him to go to the aid of Ziyâd. When the work of Ziyâd and al-Aswad was done, abu-Bakr conferred on the latter the governorship of Ṣan'â' and its provinces. Al-Aswad, however, was haughty and he oppressed al-Abnâ', i. e., the descendants of the Persians who were originally sent to al-Yaman by Kisra in the company of ibn-dhi-Yazan and under the leadership of Wahriz. Al-Aswad made them serve him and compelled them to do things against their will. Moreover, he married al-Marzubânah, the wife of Bâdhâm their king, who was their governor under Abarwîz.[1] This made the Prophet direct against him Ḳais ibn-Hubairah-l-Makshûḥ al-Murâdi (called al-Makshûḥ because he was cauterized on his side on account of a disease) instructing him to win over to his side
al-Abnâ'. With al-Makshûḥ, the Prophet sent Farwah ibn- 106
Musaik al-Murâdi. No sooner had they arrived at al-Yaman, than the news of the death of the Prophet reached them. Ḳais left on al-Aswad the impression that he concorded with his opinion, and so he got his consent to enter Ṣan'â'. Accordingly, Ḳais entered Ṣan'â' with a group of men including among others men of [the clan of] Madhḥij and some from Hamdân. He then won over to his side one of al-Abnâ', Fairûz ibn-ad-Dailami, who had accepted Islâm. Ḳais and Fairûz then brought the chief of al-Abnâ' (whose

[1] "Barwîz" in Caetani, vol. iv, p. 490.

name according to some was Bâdhâm, and according to others, Bâdhâm was dead by this time and his successor was one Dâdhawaih.[1] The latter view is more authentic). Dâdhawaih accepted Islâm.

Al-Aswad slain. Ḳais met Thât ibn-dhi-l-Ḥirrah[2]-l-Ḥimyari and won him over to his side. Many missionaries were sent by Dâdhawaih among al-Abnâ' who accepted Islâm and conspired to take al-Aswad unawares and slay him. They plotted with his wife who hated him, and she pointed out a gutter leading to his place. Through this they entered before daybreak. Some say they dug a hole through the wall of his house, through a crack,[3] and found him sleeping under the influence of drink. Ḳais slew him and he began to bellow like a bull, so much so that his guard scared by the noise asked, "What is the matter with Raḥmân al-Yaman?'" "The inspiration," answered his wife, "is upon him." Thus they were quieted. Ḳais severed his head, and, early in the morning, climbed the city wall and shouted, "Allah is great! Allah is great! I testify that there is no god but Allah and that Muḥammad is the Prophet of Allah, and that al-Aswad, the false Prophet, is the enemy of Allah!" As the followers of al-Aswad gathered, Ḳais cast the head to them and they dispersed with the exception of a few. At this the men of Ḳais opened the door and put the rest of the followers of al-'Ansi to the sword, and none escaped except those who accepted Islâm.

According to some reports, however, it was Fairûz ibn-ad-Dailami who killed al-Aswad, Ḳais only giving the last stroke and severing his head. Certain scholars assert that

1 "Dâdhûwaih" in Nawâwi, p. 232.

2 Ḥajar, vol. i, p. 345: "Bâb ibn-dhi-l-Jirrah".

3 Caetani, vol. ii, p. 683; Ṭabari, vol. i, p. 1865; Fida, vol. i, p. 155; Diyârbakri, vol. ii, p. 173.

the death of Ḳais took place five days before the expiration of the Prophet, who on his death-bed said: "Allah has brought about the death of al-Aswad al-'Ansi through the righteous man Fairûz ibn-ad-Dailami," and that the
news of the conquest came to abu-Bakr ten days after 107
he had been proclaimed caliph.

Bakr ibn-al-Haitham from an-Nu'mân ibn-Burzuj, one of al-Abnâ':—The Prophet's *'âmil*, whom al-Aswad drove out of Ṣan'â', was Abân ibn-Sa'îd ibn-al-'Âṣi; and the one who killed al-Aswad was Fairûz ibn-ad-Dailami.[1] When both Ḳais and Fairûz at al-Madînah claimed having killed him, 'Umar pointed to Fairûz saying, "It was this lion who killed him!"

Ḳais suspected of the murder of Dâdhawaih. Ḳais was charged with having killed Dâdhawaih, and abu-Bakr received the information that he was intent on expelling al-Abnâ' from Ṣan'â'. Abu-Bakr's anger was thereby aroused, and he wrote to al-Muhâjir ibn-abi-Umaiyah at his entry to Ṣan'â' as abu-Bakr's *'âmil*, instructing him to bring Ḳais before him. When Ḳais was brought before abu-Bakr, he was requested by him to swear fifty oaths near the Prophet's pulpit that he did not kill Dâdhawaih. This he did, and was consequently set free by abu-Bakr, who directed him to Syria with those of the Moslems summoned for the invasion of the Greeks.[2]

[1] Mirkhondi, *Rauḍat aṣ-Ṣafa,* vol. ii, p. 679.

[2] Ar. *ar-Rûm* = the East Romans, the Byzantines.

PART II

SYRIA

CHAPTER I

The Conquest of Syria

The "tying of the three banners." When abu-Bakr was done with the case of those who apostatized, he saw fit [1] to direct his troops against Syria. To this effect he wrote to the people of Makkah, aṭ-Ṭâ'if, al-Yaman, and all the Arabs in Najd and al-Ḥijâz calling them for a "holy war" and arousing their desire in it and in the obtainable booty from the Greeks. Accordingly, people, including those actuated by greed as well as those actuated by the hope of divine remuneration, hastened to abu-Bakr from all quarters, and flocked to al-Madînah. Abu-Bakr gave three banners [2] to three men [appointed them commanders] namely: Khâlid ibn-Sa'îd ibn-al-'Âṣi ibn-Umaiyah, Shuraḥbîl ibn-Ḥasanah, an ally of the banu-Jumaḥ and 'Amr ibn-al-'Âṣi ibn-Wâ'il as-Sahmi. (Shuraḥbîl, according to al-Wâḳidi, was the son of 'Abdallâh ibn-al-Muṭâ' al-Kindi, Ḥasanah being his mother and a freedmaid of Ma'mar ibn-Ḥabîb ibn-Wahb ibn-Ḥudhâfah ibn-Jumaḥ. But according to al-Kalbi, Shuraḥbîl was the son of Rabî'ah ibn-al-Muṭâ' descended from Ṣûfah, i. e., al-Ghauth ibn-Murr ibn-Udd ibn-Ṭâbikhah.) [3] The tying of these banners took place on 108
Thursday the first of Ṣafar, year 13, after the troops had camped at al-Jurf throughout the month of Muḥarram with abu-'Ubaidah ibn-al-Jarrâḥ leading their prayers. Abu-

[1] *Cf.* Ya'ḳûbi, vol. ii, p. 149.

[2] Zaidân, vol. i, pp. 135-136.

[3] Ṭabari, vol. i, p. 2079.

Bakr wanted to give a banner to abu-'Ubaidah; but the latter begged to be relieved. Others claim that he did give one to him, but that report is not confirmed. The fact is that when 'Umar became caliph, he conferred on him the governorship of all Syria.

Abu-'Ubaidah commander-in-chief. Abu-Mikhnaf states that 'Umar said to the commanders, "If ye altogether are to lead a fight, your commander will be abu-'Ubaidah 'Âmir ibn-'Abdallâh ibn-al-Jarrâḥ al-Fihri, otherwise Yazîd ibn-abi-Sufyân." [1] Others assert that 'Amr ibn-al-'Âṣi acted only as a reinforcement for the Moslems and commanded only those who joined him.

Abu-Bakr replaces Khâlid by Arwa. The assignment of Khâlid ibn-Sa'id by abu-Bakr to the leadership displeased 'Umar who approached abu-Bakr with a view to dismissing him, charging him with being "a vain-seeking man who tries to make his way through dispute and bigotry." [2] Accordingly abu-Bakr dismissed Khâlid and directed abu-Arwa ad-Dausi to take the banner from his hand. Abu-Arwa met him at dhu-l-Marwah where he received the banner from him and carried it back to abu-Bakr. Abu-Bakr handed it to Yazîd ibn-abi-Sufyân [3] who left, with his brother Mu'âwiyah carrying the banner before him. Others say that the banner was delivered to Yazîd at dhu-l-Marwah whence he started at the head of Khâlid's army. Khâlid went with the army of Shuraḥbîl for the divine remuneration.[4]

Abu-Bakr gives instructions to the commanders. Abu-Bakr instructed 'Amr ibn-al-'Âṣi to follow the way of Ailah

[1] Abu-Ismâ'il al-Baṣri, *Futûḥ ash-Shâm*, p. 5; Ḥajar, vol. iii, pp. 1352-1353.

[2] *Skizzen*, vol. vi, p. 62, note 1; *Ya'ḳûbi*, vol. ii, p. 149.

[3] Mas'ûdi, vol. iv, pp. 186-187.

[4] As a volunteer.

with Palestine [1] for objective. Yazîd he instructed to follow the way of Tabûk. To Shuraḥbîl, he wrote to follow the way of Tabûk, too. At the outset each one of the commanders had three thousand men under his leadership, but abu-Bakr kept on sending reinforcements until each one had 7,500. Later the total was increased to 24,000.

It is reported on the authority of al-Wâḳidi that abu-Bakr assigned 'Amr to Palestine, Shuraḥbîl to the Jordan, and Yazîd to Damascus saying, "When ye all fight together, your commander is the one in whose province ye are fighting." It is also reported that to 'Amr he gave oral instructions to lead the prayers in case the armies are united, and
to have each commander lead the prayer of his own army 109
when the armies are separate. Abu-Bakr ordered the commanders to see that each tribe flies a banner of its own.

Abu-Bakr directs Khâlid ibn-al-Walîd to Syria. On his arrival in the first district of Palestine, 'Amr ibn-al-'Âṣi sent a message to abu-Bakr informing him of the great number of the enemy, their great armament, the wide extent of their land and the enthusiasm of their troops. Abu-Bakr, thereupon, wrote to Khâlid ibn-al-Walîd ibn-al-Mughîrah-l-Makhzûmi—who was at that time in al-'Irâḳ—directing him to go to Syria. According to some, he thereby made him a commander over the commanders in the war. According to others, Khâlid only commanded his men who accompanied him; but whenever the Moslems met for a battle, the commanders would choose him as their chief for his valor and strategy and the auspiciousness of his counsel.

The battle of Dâthin. The first conflict between the Moslems and the enemy took place in Dâthin,[2] one of the

[1] Ar. *Philasṭîn.* For a description of these provinces see al-Ya'ḳûbi *Kitâb al-Buldân*, p. 325 *seq.*; Yâḳût, vol. iii, p. 913.

[2] Ṭabari, vol. i, p. 2108: "ad-Dâthinah, and some say ad-Dâthin"; *cf.* Caetani, vol. ii, pp. 1138-1139.

villages of Ghazzah, which lay on the way between the Moslems and the residence of the patrician [1] of Ghazzah. Here the battle raged furiously, but at last Allah gave victory to his friends and defeat to his enemies whom he dispersed. All this took place before the arrival of Khâlid ibn-al-Walîd in Syria.

The battle of al-'Arabah. Thence Yazîd ibn-abi-Sufyân went in quest of the partrician, but hearing that a large host of Greeks were gathered in al-'Arabah, which lay in Palestine, he directed against them abu-Umâmah aṣ-Ṣudai ibn-'Ajlân al-Bâhili, who, falling upon them, put most of them to the sword and went his way. Regarding this battle of al-'Arabah, abu-Mikhnaf reports that six of the Greek leaders at the head of 3,000 men camped at al-'Arabah when abu-Umâmah with a body of Moslems advanced against them and defeated them, killing one of their leaders. Thence he pursued them to ad-Dubbiyah (i. e. ad-Dâbiyah) [2] where he inflicted another defeat on them, and the Moslems carried off a large booty.

According to a tradition communicated by abu-Ḥafṣ ash-Shâmi on the authority of certain *sheikhs* from Syria, the first conflict of the Moslems was the Battle of al-'Arabah before which no fighting at all took place since they left al-Ḥijâz. In no place between al-Ḥijâz and al-'Arabah did they pass without establishing their authority and taking possession of it without resistance.

[1] A leader of an army, from the Latin "*patricius*".

[2] De Goeje, *Mémoire sur la Conquête de la Syrie*, p. 31.

CHAPTER II

The Advance of Khâlid ibn-al-Walîd on Syria and 110
the Places he reduced on his Way

Khâlid takes 'Ain at-Tamr and Sandaudâ' by force. When Khâlid ibn-al-Walîd received abu-Bakr's letter at al-Ḥîrah, he left in his place al-Muthanna ibn-Ḥârithah ash-Shaibâni over the district of al-Kûfah, and set out at the head of 800 men in Rabî' II, year 13. (Some give 600 and others 500 as the number of men.) On his way, he passed through 'Ain at-Tamr and reduced it by force. (According to others, he received abu-Bakr's message in 'Ain at-Tamr after having subdued it.) From 'Ain at-Tamr Khâlid made his way to Ṣandaudâ'[1] in which lived some of the Kindah and Iyâd tribes and non-Arabs.[2] These people fought against him; but Khâlid won the victory and left in the city Sa'd ibn-'Amr ibn-Ḥarâm al-Anṣâri whose descendants still live in it. Khâlid, having learnt that a body of the banu-Taghlib ibn-Wâ'il at al-Muḍaiyaḥ and al-Ḥuṣaid had apostatized and were led by Rabî'ah ibn-Bujair, made his way to them. They fought against him; but he put them to flight and took captives and booty. The captives he sent to abu-Bakr, and among them was umm-Ḥabîb aṣ-Ṣahbâ', daughter of Ḥabîb ibn-Bujair, and [later] the mother of 'Umar ibn-'Ali ibn-abi-Ṭâlib.

Khâlid crosses the desert to Suwa. Then Khâlid made an incursion on Ḳurâḳir which was a spring belonging to the

[1] Baṣri, p. 59: "Ṣandawa"; Ṭabari, vol. i, p. 2109.

[2] Ar. *'Ajam*; see *Muh. Stud.*, p. 101 *seq.*

Kalb tribe, and thence crossed the desert to Suwa[1] which was also a spring held conjointly by the Kalb and some men of the Bahrâ'. Here Khâlid killed Ḥurḳûṣ ibn-an-Nu'mân al-Bahrâni of the Ḳuḍâ'ah tribe and swept off all their possessions. When Khâlid wanted to cross the desert, he gave the camels all the water they could drink and then thrust into the camels' lips spears, which he left for them to drag,[2] lest they should ruminate and get thirsty again. The quantity of water he carried along, though big, was exhausted on the way. So Khâlid had to slay the camels one after the other and drink with his men the water from their bellies. Khâlid had a guide named Râfi' ibn-'Umair aṭ-Ṭâ'i whom the poet meant when he said:

"How wonderful has Râfi' been, 111
who succeeded in finding the way from Ḳurâḳir to Suwa,
to the water from which the coward who attempts to reach it returns before attaining it.
No human being before thee ever did that!"

When the Moslems arrived in Suwa they found Ḥurḳûṣ and a band of men drinking and singing. Ḥurḳûṣ himself was saying:

"Again give me to drink before abu-Bakr's army is on,
our death may be at hand while we are unaware." [3]

As the Moslems killed him, his blood flowed into the basin from which he had been drinking; and some report that his head, too, fell therein. It is claimed by others,[4] however, that the one who sang this verse was one of those of the banu-Taghlib whom Khâlid had attacked with Rabî'ah ibn-Bujair.

[1] Baṣri, p. 63: "Shuwa".

[2] Ṭabari, vol. i, p. 2123: "He muzzled their mouths", and so Diyârbakri, vol. ii, p. 257; Caetani, vol. ii, p. 1196.

[3] *Cf.* Ṭabari, vol. i, p. 2124; *Mémoire*, p. 46; Diyârbakri, vol. ii, p. 25.

[4] Baṣri, p. 62 *seq.*

Khâlid in Ḳarḳîsiya. According to al-Wâḳidi, Khâlid started from Suwa to al-Kawâthil thence to Ḳarḳîsiya whose chief met him with a large host. Khâlid left him alone, turned to the mainland and went his way.

Arakah makes terms. Another place to which Khâlid came was Arakah [1] (i. e. Arak) whose people he attacked and besieged. The city surrendered and made terms, offering a certain sum for the Moslems.

Dûmat al-Jandal, Ḳuṣam, Tadmur and al-Ḳaryatain taken. Dûmat al-Jandal [2] he then reached and conquered. Then he came to Ḳuṣam in which the banu-Mashja'ah ibn-at-Taim ibn-an-Namir ibn-Wabarah ibn-Taghlib ibn-Ḥulwân ibn-'Imrân ibn-al-Ḥâfi ibn-Ḳuḍâ'ah came to terms with him. Khâlid wrote them a promise of security and advanced to Tadmur [3] [Palmyra]. Tadmur's inhabitants held out against him and took to their fortifications. At last they sought to surrender and he wrote them a statement guaranteeing their safety on condition that they be considered *dhimmah* people,[4] that they entertain Moslems and that they submit to them. Khâlid then pushed to al-Ḳaryatain, 112
whose people resisted him but were defeated, losing a large booty.

Ḥûwârîn reduced. Khâlid proceeded to Ḥûwârîn [5] in Sanîr and made a raid on its cattle. Its inhabitants, having been reinforced by the inhabitants of Ba'labakk and of Buṣra (the capital of Ḥaurân) stood out against him. The victory was won by Khâlid who took some as captives and killed others.

[1] Baṣri, p. 67; Ṭabari, vol. i, p. 2109; Yâḳût, vol. i, p. 21.

[2] Balâdhuri, part I, chap. XIII.

[3] Guy Le Strange, *Palestine under the Moslems,* pp. 540-542.

[4] Christians, Jews and Sabians with whom a covenant has been made, who pay a poll tax and for whose security Moslems are responsible.

[5] Baṣri, p. 68.

Ghassân attacked. Thence he came to Marj Râhiṭ and led an incursion against Ghassân on their Easter day—they being Christians. He took some captive and killed others.

Thanîyat al-'Uḳâb. Khâlid then directed Busr ibn-abi-Arṭât al-'Âmiri of the Ḳuraish and Ḥabîb ibn-Maslamah-l-Fihri to the Ghûṭah [1] of Damascus where they attacked many villages. Khâlid arrived at Thanîyat in Damascus, the Thaniyat al-'Uḳâb of to-day, and stood there for one hour, spreading his banner. This banner was the one the Prophet used, and was black in color; and because the Arabs call a banner "*'uḳâb,*" the Thanîyat was known since as Thanîyat al-'Uḳâb. Others say that it was thus called because a vulture [Ar. *'uḳâb*] happened to descend on it at that time. But the first explanation is more reliable. I heard it said by some that at that place stood a stone image of a vulture. But there is no truth in that statement.

Khâlid meets abu-'Ubaidah. Khâlid camped at the East [Sharḳi] gate of Damascus; and according to others, at the Jâbiyah gate. The bishop of Damascus offered him gifts and homage and said to Khâlid, "Keep this covenant [2] for me." Khâlid promised to do so. Then Khâlid went until he met the Moslems who were at Ḳanât Buṣra. According to others, however, he came to the Jâbiyah where abu-'Ubaidah was with a band of Moslems. Here they met and went together to Buṣra.

[1] A place in Damascus noted for its orchards; ibn-Jubair, *Riḥlah,* p. 261; Le Strange, p. 33.

[2] What covenant is meant is not clear. This tradition may have been confused with one that comes later and speaks of the agreement between Khâlid and the bishop. *Cf.* Caetani, vol. ii, pp. 1204-1205.

CHAPTER III

The Conquest of Buṣra

Buṣra comes to terms. When Khâlid ibn-al-Walîd at the head of the Moslems arrived in Buṣra,[1] all the Moslems gathered against it and put Khâlid in chief command. 113
They drew close to it and fought its patrician until he was driven with his armed men inside the town. Others assert that since Buṣra lay within the district of Damascus and, consequently under the rule and commandership of Yazîd ibn-abi-Sufyân, it was he who held the chief command. At last its people came to terms stipulating that their lives, property and children be safe, and agreeing to pay the poll-tax. According to some reporters, the inhabitants of Buṣra made terms agreeing to pay for each adult one *dînâr* and one *jarîb* [2] of wheat.

Thus the Moslems conquered all the region of Ḥaurân [Auranitis] and subdued it.

Ma'âb surrenders. Abu-'Ubaidah ibn-al-Jarrâḥ, at the head of a heavy detachment composed of the commanders' troops that had joined him, led the way to Ma'âb [Moab] in the district of al-Balḳâ' where the enemy was massed. Ma'âb surrendered and made terms similar to those made by Buṣra. According to others, however, the conquest of Ma'âb was effected before that of Buṣra. Still others assert that abu-'Ubaidah conquered Ma'âb when he was the commander of all the Moslem forces in Syria in the days of 'Umar.

[1] Eski-Shâm or Old Damascus; Baedeker, *Palestine and Syria*, p. 201 (ed. 1894).

[2] Mawardi, p. 265, says that *al-jarîb* is a measure of land 10 x 10 rods. It is also a measure of wheat that varies in different localities.

CHAPTER IV

The Battle of Ajnâdîn (or Ajnâdain)

The enemy routed. The battle of Ajnâdîn [1] ensued. In this battle about 100,000 Greeks took part, the majority of whom were massed one band after the other by Heraclius [Hiraḳl], the rest having come from the neighboring districts. On that day, Heraclius was in Ḥimṣ [Emesa]. Against this army, the Moslems fought a violent battle, and Khâlid ibn-al-Walîd particularly distinguished himself. At last, by Allah's help, the enemies of Allah were routed and shattered into pieces, a great many being slaughtered.

The martyrs. Those who suffered martyrdom on that day were 'Abdallâh ibn-az-Zubair ibn-'Abd-al-Muṭṭalib ibn-Hâshim, 'Amr ibn-Sa'îd ibn-al-'Âṣi ibn-Umaiyah, his brother Abân ibn-Sa'îd (according to the most authentic report. Others, however, claim that Abân died in the year 29), Ṭulaib ibn-'Umair ibn-Wahb ibn-'Abd ibn-Ḳuṣai (who fought a duel with an "unbeliever" who gave him a blow that severed his right hand making his sword fall down with
the palm. In this condition he was surrounded and killed 114
by the Greeks. His mother Arwa, daughter of 'Abd-al-Muṭṭalib, was the Prophet's aunt. His surname was abu-'Adi), and Salamah ibn-Hishâm ibn-al-Mughîrah. According to others, Salamah was killed at Marj aṣ-Ṣuffar. Other martyrs were: 'Ikrimah ibn-abi-Jahl ibn-Hishâm al-Makhzûmi, Habbâr ibn-Sufyân ibn-'Abd-al-Asad al-Makhzûmi (who, according to others, was killed in the battle of

[1] *Mémoire*, p. 50 *seq.*; *Skizzen*, vol. vi, p. 54.

Mu'tah), Nu'aim ibn-'Abdallâh an-Naḥḥâm al-'Adawi (who, according to others, was killed in the battle of al-Yarmûk), Hishâm ibn-al-'Âṣi ibn-Wâ'il as-Sahmi (who is also supposed by others to have been slain in the battle of al-Yarmûk), Jundub ibn-'Amr ad-Dausi, Sa'îd ibn-al-Ḥârith, al-Ḥârith ibn-al-Ḥârith, and al-Ḥajjâj ibn-al-Ḥârith ibn-Ḳais ibn-'Adi as-Sahmi. According to Hishâm ibn-Muḥammad al-Kalbi, an-Naḥḥâm was killed in the battle of Mu'tah.

Sa'îd ibn-al-Ḥârith ibn-Ḳais was slain in the battle of al-Yarmûk; Tamîm ibn-al-Ḥârith, in the battle of Ajnâdîn; his brother, 'Ubaidallâh ibn 'Abd-al-Asad, in al-Yarmûk; and al-Ḥârith ibn-Hishâm ibn-al-Mughîrah, in Ajnâdîn.

Heraclius flees to Antioch. When the news of this battle came to Heraclius, his heart was filled with cowardice and he was confounded. Consequently, he took to flight to Antioch [Anṭâkiyah] from Ḥimṣ [Emesa]. It was mentioned by someone that his flight from Ḥimṣ to Antioch coincided with the advance of the Moslems to Syria. This battle of Ajnâdîn took place on Monday twelve days before the end of Jumâda I, year 13. Some, however, say two days after the beginning of Jumâda II, and others two days before its end.

After that, the Greeks massed an army at Yâḳûṣah which was a valley with al-Fauwârah at its mouth. There the Moslems met them, dispelled them and put them to flight with a great slaughter. Their remnants fled to the cities of Syria. The death of abu-Bakr took place in Jumâda II, year 13, and the Moslems received the news in al-Yâḳûṣah.[1]

[1] *Mémoire*, p. 64.

CHAPTER V

The Battle of Fiḥl in the Province of the Jordan

Abu-'Ubaidah commander-in-chief. The battle of Fiḥl [1] in the province of the Jordan was fought two days before the end of dhu-l-Ḳa'dah and five months after the proclamation of 'Umar ibn-al-Khaṭṭâb as caliph. The commander-in-chief was abu-'Ubaidah ibn-al-Jarrâḥ, to whom 'Umar had sent a letter with 'Âmir ibn-abi-Waḳḳâṣ, a brother of Sa'd ibn-abi-Waḳḳâṣ, conferring on him the governorship of Syria and the chief command.[2]

Some say that the appointment of abu-'Ubaidah to the governorship of Syria was received when Damascus was under siege. Khâlid being the chief commander in time of war, abu-'Ubaidah concealed the appointment from him for many days.[3] When asked by Khâlid for the reason, abu-'Ubaidah said, " I hated to dishearten thee and weaken thy position as thou stoodst facing an enemy."

Terms made after the victory. The way this battle came about was that when Heraclius came to Antioch he summoned the Greeks and the inhabitants of Mesopotamia to go forth to war, putting them under the command of one of his men in whom he trusted. These met the Moslems at Fiḥl in the province of the Jordan and a most fierce and bloody battle ensued, which ended, by Allah's help, in the victory of the Moslems. The Greek patrician with about

[1] Faḥl or Fiḥl, ancient Pella; *Mémoire*, p. 73.

[2] *Ibid.*, p. 106.

[3] Ṭabari, vol. i, pp. 2146 and 2147.

10,000 men was slaughtered, and the rest of the army distributed themselves in the cities of Syria, some of them joining Heraclius. The inhabitants of Fiḥl took to the fortifications where they were besieged by the Moslems until they sought to surrender, agreeing to pay tax on their heads and *kharâj* on their lands. The Moslems promised them the security of life and property, agreeing not to demolish their walls. The contract was made by abu-'Ubaidah ibn-al-Jarrâḥ, but according to others, by Shuraḥbîl ibn-Ḥasanah.

CHAPTER VI

The Province of the Jordan

Tiberias makes terms. Ḥafṣ ibn-'Umar al-'Umari from al-Haitham ibn-'Adi:—Shuraḥbîl conquered all the province 116 of the Jordan [al-Urdunn] by force, with the exception of Tiberias, whose inhabitants came to terms, agreeing to give up one-half of their homes and churches.[1]

'Amr ibn-al-'Âṣi and then abu-'Ubaidah in chief command. Abu-Ḥafṣ ad-Dimashḳi from abu-Bishr — the *muezzin* of the mosque at Damascus—and others:—When the Moslems arrived in Damascus, each commander used to direct his forces to a special region which he would make the object of his incursions. Thus 'Amr ibn-al-'Âṣi used to go against Palestine, Shuraḥbîl against the Jordan province and Yazîd ibn-abi-Sufyân against the province of Damascus. In case the enemy was massed in one group, they would all combine against him, each [commander] hastening to the support and the reinforcement of the other. In the early days of abu-Bakr, when they would join forces, the commander-in-chief would be 'Amr ibn-al-'Âṣi. This was the case until the arrival of Khâlid ibn-al-Walîd, who became the commander of the Moslems in every battle. Abu-'Ubaidah ibn-al-Jarrâḥ later assumed the chief command in the whole of Syria, and the commanders acknowledged him as their chief for war and peace in behalf of 'Umar ibn-al-Khaṭṭâb. This was brought about when 'Umar was

[1] Ṭabari, vol. i, p. 2159.

proclaimed caliph and wrote to Khâlid dismissing him and assigning abu-'Ubaidah.

Shuraḥbîl and then 'Amr seizes Tiberias. Shuraḥbîl ibn-Ḥasanah took Tiberias [Ṭabaraiyah] by capitulation after a siege of some days. He guaranteed for the inhabitants the safety of their lives, possessions, children, churches and houses with the exception of what they should evacuate and desert, setting aside a special spot for a Moslem mosque. Later, in the caliphate of 'Umar, the people of Tiberias violated the covenant and were joined by many Greeks and others. Abu-'Ubaidah ordered 'Amr ibn-al-'Âṣi to attack them, so he marched against them at the head of 4,000 men. 'Amr took the city by capitulation, the terms being similar to those of Shuraḥbîl. According to others, however, it was Shuraḥbîl also who conquered it the second time.

Shuraḥbîl subdues all the Jordan province. In addition to that, Shuraḥbîl took easy possession of all the cities of the Jordan with their fortifications, which, with no resistance, capitulated on terms similar to those of Tiberias. Thus did he take possession of Baisân, [Bethshean, Scythopolis] Sûsiyah, Afîḳ, Jarash, Bait-Râs, Ḳadas, and al-Jaulân, and subdue the district of the Jordan and all its land.

According to abu-Ḥafṣ on the authority of al-Waḍîn ibn-'Aṭâ', Shuraḥbîl conquered Acre, Tyre and Ṣaffûriyah.

The sea-coasts reduced. It is stated by abu-Bishr, the *muezzin,* that abu-'Ubaidah directed 'Amr ibn-al-'Âṣi to 117
the sea-coasts of the province of the Jordan. There the Greeks became too numerous for him being recruited by men from the district under Heraclius who was then at Constantinople. 'Amr, therefore, wrote to abu-'Ubaidah asking for reinforcements. The latter sent Yazîd ibn-abi-Sufyân who went forth, having his brother, Mu'âwiyah, in the van of the army. The littoral of the Jordan was conquered by Yazîd and 'Amr to whom abu-'Ubaidah wrote regarding its con-

quest. In that campaign Mu'âwiyah distinguished himself and left a great impression.

Mu'âwiyah transplants people. Abu-Alyasa' al-Anṭâki from certain *sheikhs* from Antioch and the Jordan:—A body of Persians were transplanted in the year 42 by Mu'âwiyah from Ba'labakk, Ḥimṣ and Antioch to the sea-coasts of the Jordan, i. e., Tyre, Acre and other places; and he transplanted in the same year, or one year before or after, certain Asâwirah [1] from al-Baṣrah and al-Kûfah and certain Persians from Ba'labakk and Ḥimṣ to Antioch. One of the Persian leaders was Muslim ibn-'Abdallâh, grandfather of 'Abdallâh ibn-Ḥabîb ibn-an-Nu'mân ibn-Muslim al-Anṭâki.

Mu'âwiyah makes repairs in Acre and Tyre. According to a tradition communicated to me by Muḥammad ibn-Sa'd on the authority of al-Wâḳidi, and by Hishâm ibn-al-Laith aṣ-Ṣûri on the authority of certain *sheikhs* from Syria, when Mu'âwiyah came to sail from Acre to Cyprus he made repairs in Acre ['Akka] and in Tyre [Ṣûr]. Later both cities were rebuilt by 'Abd-al-Malik ibn-Marwân, after having fallen into ruins.

Hishâm ibn-al-Laith from our *sheikhs* who said, "When we took up our abode in Tyre and the littoral, there were Arab troops and many Greeks already there. Later, people from other regions came and settled with us, and that was the case with all the sea-coast of Syria."

Artisans settled along the sea-coast. Muḥammad ibn-Sahm al-Anṭâki from contemporaneous *sheikhs*:—In the year 49 the Greeks left for the sea-coast. Industry at that time was confined to Egypt. Consequently, and in accordance with Mu'âwiyah ibn-abi-Sufyân's orders, certain artisans and carpenters were gathered and settled along the coast. As for the industry of the Jordan province it was all confined to Acre.

[1] Persian armed cavalry.

Hishâm moves the industry to Tyre. Abu-l-Khaṭṭâb al-Azdi mentioned the case of a descendant of abu-Mu'aiṭ who lived in Acre and ran mills and workshops. Hishâm ibn-'Abd-al-Malik wanted him to sell them to him; but the man refused. Hishâm therefore moved the industry [1] to Tyre where he ran an inn and a workshop. 118

Tyre a naval base. According to al-Wâḳidi, the ships used to be in Acre until the time of the banu-Marwân who moved them to Tyre, where they are until to-day.[2] In the year 247, al-Mutawakkil gave orders that the ships be stationed in Acre and all along the coast, and he manned them with fighters.

[1] Ar. *ṣinâ'ah*; Ya'ḳûbi, p. 327: "*dâr aṣ-ṣinâ'ah*" which means arsenal. The reference may be to the industry of making ships. *Cf.* Le Strange, p. 342 *seq.*

[2] Ibn-Jubair, p. 305.

CHAPTER VII

THE BATTLE OF MARJ AṢ-ṢUFFAR

The "unbelievers" put to flight. The Greeks met in great numbers and were reinforced by Heraclius. The Moslems encountered them at Marj aṣ-Ṣuffar on their way to Damascus on the first of Muḥarram, year 14.[1] The battle that ensued was so violent that blood flowed along with water and turned the wheels of the mill. Of the Moslems about 4,000 were wounded. At last the "unbelievers" took to flight and were dispersed, disregarding everything until they came to Damascus and Jerusalem. On that day, Khâlid ibn-Sa'îd ibn-al-'Âṣi ibn-Umaiyah (surnamed abu-Sa'îd) fell a martyr. In the evening previous to the day in the morning of which the battle was fought, he was married to umm-Ḥakîm, the daughter of al-Ḥârith ibn-Hishâm al-Makhzûmi, and the wife of 'Ikrimah ibn-abi-Jahl.[2] Hearing the news of his death, umm-Ḥakîm pulled out the post of the tent and fought with it. On that day, according to some report, she killed seven and had her face still covered with the ointment perfumed with saffron[3] [with which women anointed themselves on the first night of matrimony].

According to the report of abu-Mikhnaf, this battle of Marj took place twenty days after the battle of Ajnâdîn;

[1] *Mémoire*, pp. 79-80.

[2] Ibn-Sa'd, vol. iv[1], p. 71.

[3] Ṭabari, vol. i, p. 3169; *Aghâni*, vol. vi, pp. 6-7; Caetani, vol. iii, p. 322.

the conquest of Damascus followed it, and after the conquest of Damascus the battle of Fiḥl took place. The report of al-Wâḳidi, however, is more authentic.

It was regarding the battle of Marj that Khâlid ibn-Sa'îd ibn-al-'Âṣi said:

> "Isn't there a horseman who, tired of stabbing,
> would lend me his lance for the battle of Marj aṣ-Ṣuffar?"

Referring to this battle, 'Abdallâh ibn-Kâmil ibn-Ḥabîb ibn-'Amîrah ibn-Khufâf ibn-Amru'i-l-Ḳais ibn-Buhthah ibn-Sulaim said:

> "The tribes of Mâlik took part, but 'Amîrah disappeared
> from my sight in the battle of Marj aṣ-Ṣuffar,"

meaning Mâlik ibn-Khufâf. 119

The story of the Samṣâmah sword. According to Hishâm ibn-Muḥammad al-Kalbi, in the battle of Marj, Khâlid ibn-Sa'îd suffered martyrdom with his sword aṣ-Ṣamṣâmah hanging down from his neck. The Prophet had sent him as *'âmil* to al-Yaman, and on his way he passed by the kindred of 'Amr ibn-Ma'dikarib az-Zubaidi of Madhḥij and attacked them, taking as captives the wife of 'Amr and other kinsmen. 'Amr proposed that Khâlid grants them their liberty and they would accept Islâm. And so it was. 'Amr offered Khâlid his own sword, aṣ-Ṣamṣâmah,[1] saying:

> "A friend whom I offered as present not because of any hatred
> but because presents are for those of noble birth.
> A friend whom I did not betray and who did not betray me,
> and so my qualities and fellow-drinkers did not.
> I bestowed it on a nobleman of Ḳuraish
> who was pleased with it and by which he was protected against the evil men."

This sword Mu'âwiyah took from the neck of Khâlid when

[1] *Aghâni*, vol. xiv, pp. 27, 31, 32.

he fell martyr in the battle of Marj. Mu'âwiyah kept it, but its possession was later disputed by Sa'îd ibn-al-'Âṣi ibn-Sa'îd ibn-al-'Âṣi ibn-Umaiyah. 'Uthmân decided the case in favor of the latter, who kept it until the battle of ad-Dâr in which Marwân was struck on the nape of the neck and Sa'îd fell unconscious by a blow. A Juhainah man took the Ṣamṣâmah. The Juhainah man kept it, and one day he gave it to a polisher to polish it. The polisher could not believe that one of the Juhainah could possess such a sword, so he took it to Marwân ibn-al-Ḥakam, the governor of al-Madînah, who asked the Juhainah man for an explanation, and he told its story. "By Allah," exclaimed Marwân, "in the battle of ad-Dâr, my sword was stolen from me, and so was that of Sa'îd ibn-al-'Âṣi." Then came Sa'îd and recognizing his sword took it, carved his name on it, and sent it to 'Amr ibn-Sa'îd al-Ashdaḳ, the governor of Makkah. Sa'îd perished, and the sword was left with 'Amr ibn-Sa'îd. When 'Amr ibn-Sa'îd was killed at Damascus and his belongings were stolen, his brother on the father's side, Muḥammad ibn-Sa'îd, took the sword, which later passed to Yaḥya ibn-Sa'îd. At the death of Yaḥya, it passed to 120
'Anbasah ibn-Sa'îd ibn-al-'Âṣi and then to Sa'îd ibn-'Amr ibn-Sa'îd. When the last perished, the sword went to Muḥammad ibn-'Abdallâh ibn-Sa'îd whose descendants live now in Bâriḳ. Then it went to Abân ibn-Yaḥya ibn-Sa'îd who decked it with an ornament of gold and kept it with the mother of a child [concubine] of his. At last Aiyûb ibn-abi-Aiyûb ibn-Sa'îd sold it to al-Mahdi the "Commander of the Believers" for over 80,000 [*dirhams*]. Al-Mahdi put the ornament of gold back on it. When it came finally into the possession of Mûsa-l-Hâdi, the "Commander of the Believers," he admired it and ordered the poet abu-l-Haul to describe it, upon which the latter said:

"He who acquired the Ṣamṣâmah of 'Amr az-Zubaidi
is the best of all men—Mûsa-l-Amîn.
It is the sword of 'Amr which as we know
is the best that a scabbard ever sheathed.
Green in color between the edges of which is a garment
of poison in which death is clad.
If one unsheathes it, its brilliancy dazzles
that of the sun, so that the sun would scarcely be seen.
When the one to be smitten is at hand,
it does not matter whether the left or the right hand applies it.
What a good sword it is for him, who wants to defend his honor,
to smite with in the battle, and what a good companion!" [1]

Later on, al-Wâthiḳ-Billâh, the "Commander of the Believers," called a polisher and ordered him to temper it. On doing so, the sword was changed.

[1] *Cf.* De Slane, ibn-Khallikân, vol. iii, p. 637.

CHAPTER VIII

The Conquest of Damascus and its Province

The positions taken by the different generals. When the Moslems were done with the fight against those who were gathered at al-Marj, they stayed there for fifteen days at the end of which they returned [*sic*] to Damascus [Dimashḳ]. This took place fourteen days before the end of Muḥarram, year 14. Al-Ghûṭah and its churches the Moslems took by force. The inhabitants of Damascus betook themselves to the fortifications and closed the gate of the city. Khâlid ibn-al-Walîd at the head of some 5,000 men whom abu-'Ubaidah had put under his command, 121
camped at al-Bâb ash-Sharḳi [the east gate]. Some assert that Khâlid was the chief commander but was dismissed when Damascus was under siege. The convent by which Khâlid camped was called Dair Khâlid.[1] 'Amr ibn-al-'Âṣi camped at the Tûma gate; Shuraḥbîl, at the Faradîs gate, abu-'Ubaidah at the Jâbiyah gate, and Yazîd ibn-abi-Sufyân from the Ṣaghîr gate to the one known as Kaisân gate.[2] Abu-ad-Dardâ' appointed 'Uwaimir ibn-'Âmir al-Khazraji commander of a frontier garrison settled in the fortification [3] at Barzah.[4]

The statement written by Khâlid. The bishop [5] who had

[1] Diyârbakri, vol. ii, p. 259.

[2] H. Lammens, *MFO,* vol. iii[1], p. 256; Kremer, *Topographie von Damaskus,* the chart next to page 36.

[3] *Mémoire*, p. 90.

[4] Jubair, p. 274; Yâḳût, vol. i, p. 563.

[5] Caetani, vol. iii, p. 364, note 2.

provided Khâlid with food at the beginning of the siege was wont to stand on the wall. Once Khâlid called him, and when he came, Khâlid greeted him and talked with him. The bishop one day said to him, "Abu-Sulaimân, thy case is prospering and thou hast a promise to fulfil for me; let us make terms for this city." Thereupon, Khâlid called for an inkhorn and parchment and wrote:—

"In the name of Allah, the compassionate, the merciful. This is what Khâlid would grant to the inhabitants of Damascus, if he enters therein: he promises to give them security for their lives, property and churches. Their city-wall shall not be demolished; neither shall any Moslem be quartered in their houses. Thereunto we give to them the pact of Allah and the protection of his Prophet, the caliphs and the 'Believers'. So long as they pay the poll-tax, nothing but good shall befall them."

The Moslems enter the city. One night, a friend of the bishop came to Khâlid and informed him of the fact that it was the night of a feast [1] for the inhabitants of the city, that they were all busy and that they had blocked the Sharḳi gate with stones and left it unguarded. He then suggested that Khâlid should procure a ladder. Certain occupants of the convent, by which Khâlid's army camped, brought him two ladders on which some Moslems climbed to the highest part of the wall, and descended to the gate which was guarded only by one or two men. The Moslems co-operated and opened the door. This took place at sunrise.

In the meantime, abu-'Ubaidah had managed to open the Jâbiyah gate and sent certain Moslems over its wall. This made the Greek fighters pour to his side and lead a violent fight against the Moslems. At last, however, the Greeks took to flight. Then abu-'Ubaidah at the head of

[1] Ṭabari, vol. i, p. 2152.

the Moslems opened the Jâbiyah gate by force and made their entrance through it. Abu-'Ubaidah and Khâlid ibn- 122
al-Walîd met at al-Maksalât which was the quarter of the coppersmiths in Damascus. The same spot is mentioned in a poem by Ḥassân ibn-Thâbit under the name of al-Barîṣ:

> "He who calls at al-Barîṣ for a drink,
> [is given the water of Barada mixed with dainty wine]."[1]

According to other reports, one night the Greeks carried out through the Jâbiyah gate a corpse. A number of their brave and armed men accompanied the funeral. The rest of them stood at the gate to prevent the Moslems from opening it and entering until their Greek comrades should have returned from the burial of the dead man, thus taking advantage of the Moslems' state of unmindfulness. But the Moslems knew of them and fought with them at the gate a most fierce and bloody conflict which ended in the opening of the gate by the Moslems at sunrise. Seeing that abu-'Ubaidah was on the point of entering the city, the bishop hurried to Khâlid and capitulated. He then opened the Sharki gate and entered with Khâlid, with the statement which Khâlid had written him unfolded in his hand. Regarding that, certain Moslems remarked, "By Allah, Khâlid is not the commander. How could his terms then be binding?" To this, abu-'Ubaidah replied, "Even the lowest of the Moslems can make binding terms on their behalf." And sanctioning the capitulation made by Khâlid, he signed it, not taking into account the fact that a part of the city was taken by force.[2] Thus all Damascus was considered as having capitulated. Abu-'Ubaidah wrote to 'Umar regarding that and forwarded the message. Then

[1] Ḥassân, *Dîwân*, p. 17.

[2] Ya'kûbi, vol. ii, p. 159; Lammens, *MFO*, vol. iii[1], p. 250.

the gates of the city were opened and all the Moslems met within.

According to the report of abu-Mikhnaf and others, Khâlid entered the city by assault, whereas abu-'Ubaidah entered it by capitulation, and they both met at the Zaiyâtîn 123
[market of oil-dealers]. The former report however, is more authentic.

Al-Haitham ibn-'Adi claimed that the people of Damascus capitulated agreeing to give up one-half of their homes and churches. Muḥammad ibn-Sa'd reported that abu-'Abdallâh al-Wâḳidi said, "I have read the statement issued by Khâlid ibn-al-Walîd to the people of Damascus and found no mention in it of 'half the homes and churches'. I do not know where the one who reported it got his information. The fact is that when Damascus was taken possession of, a great number of its inhabitants fled to Heraclius who was then at Antioch, leaving many vacant dwellings behind that were later occupied by the Moslems."

Some one reported that it was abu-'Ubaidah who had his quarters at the Sharḳi gate, and Khâlid at the Jâbiyah gate; but this view is erroneous.

The date of the conquest. According to al-Wâḳidi, the conquest of Damascus was effected in Rajab, year 14,[1] but the date which Khâlid's statement of capitulation bears was Rabî' II, year 15. The explanation is that Khâlid wrote the statement with no date, but when the Moslems were preparing to set out against those gathered for their fight in al-Yarmûk, the bishop came to Khâlid asking him to renew the statement and add as witnesses abu-'Ubaidah and the Moslems. Khâlid granted the request and inserted the names of abu-'Ubaidah, Yazîd ibn-abi-Sufyân, Shuraḥbîl ibn-Ḥasanah and others as witnesses. The date he put was the one in which the statement was renewed.

[1] Ya'ḳûbi, vol. ii, p. 159.

The city considered as having capitulated. Al-Ḳâsim
ibn-Sallâm from Sa'îd ibn-'Abd-al-'Azîz at-Tanûkhi:— 124
Yazîd entered Damascus by capitulation through the Sharḳi gate. At al-Maḳsalât the two Moslem commanders met, and the whole city was considered as having capitulated.

The siege conducted for four months. Al-Ḳâsim from abu-l-Ash'ath aṣ-Ṣan'âni or abu-'Uthmân aṣ-Ṣan'âni:— Abu-'Ubaidah spent at the Jâbiyah gate four months [1] conducting the siege.

The case of a church. Abu-'Ubaid from Rajâ' ibn-abi-Salamah:—Ḥassân ibn-Mâlik presented to 'Umar ibn-'Abd-al-'Azîz the case of a church that one of the commanders had bestowed on him as fief, and the possession of which was contested by the non-Arabs of Damascus. Regarding that, 'Umar said, "If it is included in the fifteen churches mentioned in their covenant, thou hast no claim on it."

The following was stated by Ḍamrah on the authority of 'Ali ibn-abi-Ḥamalah, "The non-Arabs of Damascus disputed with us the right to a church at Damascus that was assigned by someone as fief to the banu-Naṣr, and the case was presented to 'Umar ibn-'Abd-al-'Azîz who took the church from us and returned it to the Christians. When Yazîd ibn-'Abd-al-Malik, however, came to power he gave it back to the banu-Naṣr."

The poll-tax. Abu-'Ubaid from al-Auzâ'i who said:— "At the outset, the poll-tax in Syria consisted of one *jarîb* and one *dînâr* per head. 'Umar ibn-al-Khaṭṭâb made it four *dînârs* on those who had gold and forty *dirhams* on those who had silver, arranging them in ranks according to the wealth of the rich, the poverty of the poor and the medium possessions of the middle class."

Hishâm heard it said by our *sheikhs* that the Jews were

[1] Ya'ḳûbi, *Buldân*, p. 325: "one year".

for the Christians as *dhimmis* paying *kharâj* to them, and were, therefore, included in the capitulation.

According to certain reports, one of the terms imposed by Khâlid ibn-al-Walîd on the inhabitants of Damascus, when they capitulated, was that every man should give as poll-tax one *dînâr* and one *jarîb* of wheat, together with vinegar and oil for feeding the Moslems.

'Amr an-Nâḳid from Aslam, the freedman of 'Umar ibn- 125
al-Khaṭṭâb:—'Umar wrote to the commanders of the provinces of Syria [Ar. *ajnâd*] instructing them to levy a tax on every adult, making it forty *dirhams* on those who possessed silver, and four *dînârs* on those who possessed gold. Morever, he ordered that in the way of providing the Moslems with wheat and oil, they have to give every Moslem in Syria and Mesopotamia [Ar. al-Jazîrah] two *modii* [1] of wheat and three *ḳisṭs* [1] of oil per month. He also assessed on them grease and honey, the quantity of which I do not know; and for every Moslem in Egypt per month one *irdabb* [1] [of wheat], clothing, and the right of being entertained as guest for three days.

'Amr ibn-Ḥammâd ibn-abi-Ḥanîfah from Aslam:—'Umar assessed as poll-tax four *dînârs* on those who possessed gold, and forty *dirhams* on those who possessed silver, in addition to offering the Moslems a subsistence tribute and providing them with three-days' entertainment.

A similar tradition was communicated to me by Muṣ'ab on the authority of Aslam.

The cathedral of St. John. It is reported that when Mu'âwiyah ibn-abi-Sufyân came to power, he desired to add the church of St. John to the mosque [2] in Damascus; but the

[1] Ar. *mudi*, Latin *modius*, is 17 *sâ's*; a *ḳisṭ* is half a *sâ'*; an *irdabb* is 24 *sâ's*.

[2] Al-Maḳḳari, *Nafḥ aṭ-Ṭib*, vol. i, p. 368.

Christians refused. So he refrained. Later, when 'Abd-al-Malik ibn-Marwân was in power, he made the same request for the enlargement of the mosque offering them money in exchange; but they refused to deliver the church to him. In his turn, al-Walîd ibn-'Abd-al-Malik called the Christians and offered them large sums for the church, and when they refused, he threatened them saying, "If ye do not agree, I will surely tear it down." To this someone replied, "He, 'Commander of the Believers', who tears down a church will lose his wits and be affected with some blight." Al-Walîd, being angered at what was said, ordered that a spade be brought and began demolishing the walls with his own hand, while he had a robe of yellow silk on him. He then called workmen and house-razers and they pulled the church down. Thus it was included in the mosque. When 'Umar ibn-'Abd-al-'Azîz became caliph, the Christians complained of what al-Walîd had down for their church. 'Umar wrote to his *'âmil* ordering him to return to the Christians that part which he had added to the mosque from their church. The people of Damascus disliked the idea saying, "Shall we destroy our mosque after we have called to prayer and held service in it? And can a Christian church be returned [to its former owners]?" Among the Moslems were at that time Ṣulaimân ibn-Ḥabîb al-Muḥâribi and other canonists. They then came to the Christians and proposed to turn over to them all the churches of al-Ghûṭah that had been taken by force and were in the hands of the Moslems, provided they give up the church
of St. John and cease to assert their claim on it. The 12
Christians rather seemed to favor the proposition and consented to it. 'Umar's *'âmil* communicated the news to 'Umar who was pleased and signed the agreement. Next to the tower of the Mosque of Damascus at the southern porch stands an inscription on marble near the roof which was

part of that which was built by the order of al-Walîd the "Commander of the Believers" in the year 86.

The wall of Damascus. I myself heard Hishâm ibn-'Ammâr say, "The wall around the city of Damascus remained standing until it was demolished by 'Abdallâh ibn-'Ali ibn-'Abdallâh ibn-al-'Abbâs after the question between Marwân and the banu-Umaiyah had been settled."

Buṣra, Adhri'ât, al-Bathanîyah and other places reduced. Abu-Ḥafṣ ad-Dimashḳi from the *muezzin* of the Damascus Mosque and other men:—At the arrival of Khâlid, the Moslems gathered their forces against Buṣra, and it capitulated. They then were dispersed throughout all Ḥaurân which they subdued. The chief of Adhri'ât came to them offering to capitulate on the same terms on which the people of Buṣra had capitulated and agreeing to make all the land of al-Bathanîyah [1] a *kharâj* land. The request was granted, and Yazîd ibn-abi-Sufyân entered the city and made a covenant with its people. Thus the two districts of Ḥaurân and al-Bathanîyah came under the full control of the Moslems. Thence they came to Palestine and the Jordan, invading what had not yet been reduced. Yazîd marched against 'Âmmân and made an easy conquest of it, making terms of capitulation similar to those of Buṣra. Besides, he effected the complete conquest of the province of al-Balḳâ'. When abu-'Ubaidah came to power, all that was already conquered. At the conquest of Damascus, abu-'Ubaidah was the commander-in-chief; but the terms of capitulation were made by Khâlid, abu-'Ubaidah concurring.

'Arandal, ash-Sharât and the sea-coast reduced. During the governorship of abu-'Ubaidah, Yazîd ibn-abi-Sufyân went and took possession of 'Arandal [2] by capitulation. He

[1] Modern Nuḳrah in Ḥaurân.

[2] The correct form is Gharandal; Ya'ḳûbi, *Buldân*, p. 326; Baedeker, p. 150.

also subdued the province of ash-Sharât with its mountains. It is stated by Sa'îd ibn-'Abd-al-'Azîz on the authority of al-Waḍîn that after the [second] conquest of Damascus Yazîd came to Sidon, 'Irḳah,[1] Jubail, and Bierût (which lie on the sea-coast)[2] with his brother, Mu'âwiyah, leading the van of the army. These cities he conquered with great facility, expelling many of their inhabitants. The conquest of 'Irḳah was effected by Mu'âwiyah himself when Yazîd was governor. Toward the close of the caliphate of 12
'Umar ibn-al-Khaṭṭâb or the beginning of the caliphate of 'Uthmân ibn-'Affân, the Greeks restored some of these coast-towns, and Mu'âwiyah again marched against those towns and conquered them. He then made repairs in them and stationed garrisons in them among whom he distributed the fiefs.

Tripoli captured. When 'Uthmân was made caliph and Mu'âwiyah became governor of Syria, the latter directed Sufyân ibn-Mujîb al-Azdi to Tripoli [Aṭrâbulus] which was a combination of three cities.[3] Sufyân erected on a plain a few miles from the city a fort which was called Ḥiṣn Sufyân [Sufyân fort], intercepted the recruits from the sea as well as from the land and laid siege to the city. When the siege was pressed hard against them, the inhabitants of Tripoli met in one of the three fortifications and wrote to the king of the Greeks asking for relief through reinforcement or ships on which they might escape and flee to him. Accordingly, the king sent them many ships which they boarded in the night time and fled away. When Sufyân arose in the morning—he having been accustomed to sleep

[1] "'Arḳah" in Hamadhâni, *Buldân*, p. 105; Caetani, vol. iii, p. 801; "Correggi: 'Arqaq".

[2] *Journal Asiatique,* 1859, vol. i, p. 120, note 1.

[3] As its Greek name designates.

every night in his fort, and fortify the Moslems in it, and to rise up in the morning against the enemy—he discovered that the fortification in which the people of Tripoli were was vacant. Immediately he entered it and sent the news of the conquest to Mu'âwiyah. Mu'âwiyah made it a dwelling-place for a large body of Jews. It is this fortification in which the harbor of the city is to-day. Later 'Abd-al-Malik built it and made it stronger.

Mu'âwiyah used to send every year to Tripoli a large body of troops to guard the city and used to assign it to a different *'âmil*; but in case the sea was closed, the *'âmil* with a small band would stay and the rest would return. This state of affairs lasted until 'Abd-al-Malik began to rule. In the days of the latter, one of the Greek patricians with a large body of men came to the city and asked for a promise of safety, agreeing to settle therein and pay *kharâj*. His request was granted. He had not been there two years or two years and a few months when he took advantage of the absence of the troops from the city, shut its gate and killed the *'âmil*, taking his soldiers and many Jews as captives. He then made his way together with his followers to the land of the Greeks [Asia Minor]. Later the Moslems caught him on the sea going to a Moslem coast-town with a large number of ships, and killed him. Others say they took him captive and sent him to 'Abd-al-Malik who killed and crucified him. I heard someone say that 'Abd-al-Malik
sent someone who besieged him in Tripoli until he surren- 128
dered and was carried before 'Abd-al-Malik who killed and crucified him. Some of his followers took to flight and got as far as the land of the Greeks.

'Ali ibn-Muḥammad al-Madâ'ini related on the authority of 'Attâb ibn-Ibrâhîm that Tripoli was conquered by Sufyân ibn-Mujîb, that its inhabitants violated the covenant in the days of 'Abd-al-Malik and that it was reduced by al-Walid ibn-'Abd-al-Malik in his reign.

The Mediterranean littoral reduced. Abu-Ḥafs ash-Shâmi from al-Waḍîn:—At first Yazîd ibn-abi-Sufyân directed Mu'âwiyah against the littoral of the province of Damascus excluding Tripoli whose possession he did not covet. Mu'âwiyah sometimes spent on the reduction of the fort a few days—two or more—in the course of which he was resisted either slightly or strongly before he could take it.

When the Moslems conquered a city, whether so situated as to overlook a wide territory or on the coast, they would station in it whatever number of Moslems was necessary; and if the enemy in it should start a revolt the Moslems would flock to it for reinforcement. But when 'Uthmân ibn-'Affân became caliph he wrote to Mu'âwiyah instructing him to fortify the coast-cities and man them, and to give fiefs to those whom he settled in them. Mu'âwiyah did accordingly.

Abu-Ḥafṣ from Sa'îd ibn-'Abd-al-'Azîz who said:—"I heard it said by some that after the death of his brother Yazîd, Mu'âwiyah wrote to 'Umar ibn-al-Khaṭṭâb describing the condition of the coast-towns. 'Umar wrote back ordering that their fortifications be repaired, that garrisons be stationed in them, that watchmen be posted on their towers and that means be taken for lighting the fire on the towers to announce the approach of the enemy. 'Umar gave Mu'âwiyah no permission to carry out a naval campaign. But Mu'âwiyah insisted so much that 'Uthmân allowed him to carry out a sea expedition and instructed him to keep ready in the coast-cities troops in addition to those already in them, whether he wanted to set out on the campaign in person or send some one else on it. He also instructed him to give the garrison lands and distribute among them whatever houses had been evacuated, and to establish new mosques and enlarge those that had been established before his caliphate."

According to al-Wadîn, after that, men from all quarters moved to the coast cities.

'Alkamah nominated governor of Ḥaurân. Al-'Abbâs ibn-Hishâm al-Kalbi from Ja'far ibn-Kilâb al-Kilâbi:—'Alḳamah ibn-'Ulâthah ibn-'Auf ibn-al-Ahwas ibn-Ja'far ibn-Kilâb was assigned by 'Umar ibn-al-Khattâb to the governorship of Ḥaurân and he was made responsible to Mu'â- 129
wiyah. This position he held until his death. Before his death he heard that al-Hutai'ah-l-'Absi was coming to visit him; so 'Alḳamah bequeathed to him in his will a share equal to one of his sons' shares. Hence the poem of al-Ḥuṭai'ah:[1]

> "Between me and becoming rich—had I only reached thee, when thou wert still living—
> there would have been an interval of only a few nights."

Ḳubbash farm. I was told by certain learned men among whom was a neighbor of Hishâm ibn-'Ammâr that abu-Sufyân ibn-Harb possessed in the pre-Islamic period, in which he carried on trade with Syria, a village in al-Balkâ' called Ḳubbash. This village passed into the possession of Mu'âwiyah and his son, and at the beginning of the [Abbasid] dynasty, it was confiscated and possessed by certain sons of al-Mahdi, the "Commander of the Believers." Then it passed into the hands of certain oil-sellers of al-Kûfah known as the banu-Nu'aim.

The Prophet gives fief to Tamîm and Nu'aim. 'Abbâs ibn-Hishâm from his grandfather:—Once came Tamîm ibn-Aus of the banu-ad-Dâr ibn-Hâni' ibn-Habîb of [the tribe of] Lakhm, surnamed abu-Rukaiyah, with his brother Nu'aim ibn-Aus, to the Prophet who gave them as fief Ḥibra, Bait-'Ainûn[2] and Masjid Ibrâhîm, and to that end he wrote

[1] Goldziher: "Der Dîwân des Ǵarwal b. Aus al-Ḥuṭej'a" in *ZDMG*, vol. xlvi, p. 30.

[2] Ibn-Duraid, p. 226.

a statement. When Syria was subdued, all that was restored to them. When Sulaimân ibn-'Abd-al-Malik used to pass near this land he would not stop in it saying, " I am afraid the curse of the Prophet will follow me."

'Umar gives stipends to diseased Christians. Hishâm ibn-'Ammâr told me he heard it said by certain *sheikhs* that on his way to al-Jâbiyah in the province of Damascus, 'Umar ibn-al-Khaṭṭâb passed by certain Christians smitten with elephentiasis [1] and he ordered that they be given something out of the *ṣadaḳahs* and that food stipends be assigned to them.

Dair Khâlid. Hishâm reported that he heard it said by al-Walîd ibn-Muslim that Khâlid ibn-al-Walîd made a condition in favor of the convent known as Dair Khâlid, when its occupants offered him a ladder to climb to the city wall, to the effect that their *kharâj* be reduced. The condition was enforced by abu-'Ubaidah.

The terms with Ba'labakk. When abu-'Ubaidah was
done with Damascus, he advanced to Ḥimṣ. On his way, 13
he passed through Ba'labakk whose inhabitants sought to secure safety and capitulate. Abu-'Ubaidah made terms guaranteeing the safety of their lives, possessions and churches. To that end he wrote the following statement:

" In the name of Allah, the compassionate, the merciful. This is a statement of security to so and so, son of so and so, and to the inhabitants of Ba'labakk—Greeks, Persians and Arabs—for their lives, possessions, churches and houses, inside and outside the city and also for their mills. The Greeks are entitled to give pasture to their cattle within a space of 15 miles, yet are not to abide in any inhabited town. After Rabî' and Jumâda I shall have passed, they are at

[1] Ar. *mujadhdhamîn*, see *Ḳâmûs, Tâj al-'Arûs* and *Nihâyah;* Caetani, vol. iii, p. 933, translates: " mutilati ".

liberty to go where they will. Whosoever of them adopts Islâm, shall have the same rights as we and be bound by the same obligations; and their merchants are entitled to go whither they will in the countries that have become ours through capitulation. Those of them who do not adopt Islâm [1] are bound to pay poll-tax and *kharâj*. Allah is witness and his witness is sufficient."

[1] *Cf:* Zaidân, vol. iv, p. 122, Margoliouth's translation.

CHAPTER IX

Ḥimṣ

The inhabitants capitulate. 'Abbâs ibn-Hishâm from abu-Mikhnaf: — When abu-'Ubaidah was through with Damascus, he sent ahead of him Khâlid ibn-al-Walîd and Milḥân ibn-Zaiyâr aṭ-Ṭâ'i and then he followed them. When they met in Ḥimṣ [Emesa],[1] the people of the city resisted them, but finally sought refuge in the city and asked for safety and capitulation. They capitulated to abu-'Ubaidah agreeing to pay 170,000 *dînârs*.[2]

As-Simṭ captures Ḥimṣ. According to al-Wâḳidi and others, as the Moslems stood at the gates of Damascus there appeared a dense band of the enemy's horsemen. The troops of the Moslems set out and met them between Bait-Lihya and ath-Thanîyah. The enemy was defeated and took to flight in the direction of Ḥimṣ via Ḳâra. The Moslems pursued them to Ḥimṣ but found that they had turned away from it. The people of Ḥimṣ saw the Moslems and, being scared because Heraclius had run away from them and because of what they heard regarding the Moslems' power,
valor and victory, they submitted and hastened to seek the 131
promise of security. The Moslems guaranteed their safety and refrained from killing them. The people of Ḥimṣ offered them food for their animals and for themselves and the Moslems camped on the Orontes [al-Urunṭ, or al-Urund] (the river which empties its water in the sea near

[1] Yâḳût, vol. ii, p. 335; *Skizzen*, vol. vi, p. 60.

[2] Ya'ḳûbi, vol. ii, p. 160.

Antioch). The commander of the Moslems at that time was as-Simṭ ibn-al-Aswad al-Kindi.

When abu-'Ubaidah was through with Damascus, he left over it in his place Yazid ibn-abi-Sufyân, came to Ḥimṣ via Ba'labakk, and encamped at the Rastan gate. The people of Ḥimṣ capitulated, and he guaranteed the safety of their lives, possessions, city-wall, churches, and wells excluding one-fourth of St. John's Church which was to be turned into a mosque. He made it a condition on those of them who would not embrace Islâm to pay *kharâj*.[1]

According to certain reports, it was as-Simṭ ibn-al-Aswad al-Kindi who made the terms with the people of Ḥimṣ. When abu-'Ubaidah arrived, he caused the terms to take effect. As-Simṭ divided the city into lots, each marked for one Moslem to build his house. He also made them settle in every place whose occupants had evacuated it and in every yard that was deserted.

The terms with Hamâh, Shaizar, Fâmiyah and other places. Abu-Ḥafṣ ad-Dimashḳi from Sa'id ibn-'Abd-al-'Azîz:—When abu-'Ubaidah ibn-al-Jarrâḥ effected the conquest of Damascus, he left over it as his lieutenant Yazîd ibn-abi-Sufyân; over the province of Palestine, 'Amr ibn-al-'Âṣi; and over the province of the Jordan, Shuraḥbîl. He then advanced to Ḥimṣ whose people capitulated on the same terms as those of Ba'labakk. Leaving over Ḥimṣ 'Ubâdah ibn-aṣ-Ṣâmit al-Anṣâri, he pushed towards Ḥamâh [Epiphania] whose people met him offering their submission. He made terms with them, stipulating that they pay tax on their heads and *kharâj* on their land. Thence he proceeded towards Shaizar. The people of Shaizar [Larissa] went out to meet him bowing[2] before him and

[1] Nöldeke, *ZDMG*, vol. xxix, p. 76 *seq;* Caetani, vol. iii, p. 432, note 2.

[2] Ar. *kaffara*; see *GGA*, 1863, p. 1348; *Kashshâf*, vol. i, p. 22.

accompanied by players on the tambourines and singers. They agreed to terms similar to those made with the people of Ḥamâh. Abu-'Ubaidah's horsemen reached as far as az-Zarrâ'ah and al-Ḳasṭal. He then passed through Ma'-arrat Ḥimṣ [Ma'arrat an-Nu'mân] which was named after an-Nu'mân ibn-Bashîr.[1] Its people came out playing on tambourines and singing before him. Thence he came to Fâmiyah whose people met him in the same way and consented to pay poll-tax and *kharâj*. Thus was the question of Ḥimṣ brought to an end, and Ḥimṣ and Ḳinnasrîn became parts of one whole.[2]

The "Junds" and "'Awâṣim." There is a disagreement regarding the name "Jund"[3] [as applied to the military districts of Syria]. According to some, Palestine was called 132
"Jund" by the Moslems because it was a collection of many provinces, and so was each of Damascus, Jordan, Ḥimṣ and Ḳinnasrîn. According to others, each district which had an army that received its monthly allowance in it was called "Jund." Thus Mesopotamia belonged to Ḳinnasrîn; but 'Abd-al-Malik ibn-Marwân made it a separate "Jund," that is, made its army take its allowance from its *kharâj*. 'Abd-al-Malik was asked to do so by Muḥammad ibn-Marwân. Down to the time of Yazîd ibn-Mu'âwiyah, Ḳinnasrîn and its districts were included in the province of Ḥimṣ; but Yazîd constituted Ḳinnasrîn, Antioch, Manbij and their districts as one "Jund." When ar-Rashîd Hârûn ibn-al-Mahdi was made caliph, he set Ḳinnasrîn apart and made of it and its districts one "Jund." He also separated Manbij, Dulûk, Ra'bân, Ḳûrus, Antioch and Tîzîn and called them "al-'Awâṣim"[4] because these were

[1] Yâḳût, *al-Mushtarik*, p. 401.

[2] *Cf.* Caetani, vol. iii, p. 790, line 7.

[3] The same word is commonly used for "troops".

[4] Zaidân, vol. i, p. 153; the word means "those that give protection."

the cities to which the Moslems resorted after making an invasion and leaving the frontier cities, and where they were safe and protected. The chief city of "al-'Awâṣim" he made Manbij [Hierapolis]. In this city 'Abd-al-Malik ibn-Ṣâliḥ ibn-'Ali lived in the year 173 and erected many buildings.

Al-Lâdhiḳîyah entered. Abu-Ḥafṣ ad-Dimashḳi from Sa'îd ibn-'Abd-al-'Azîz, and Mûsa ibn-Ibrâhîm at-Tanûkhi from certain *sheikhs* of Ḥimṣ:—Abu-'Ubaidah appointed in his place over Ḥimṣ 'Ubâdah ibn-aṣ-Ṣâmit al-Anṣâri who left for al-Lâdhiḳîyah.[1] Its people resisted him and the city had a massive gate that could be opened only by a number of men. Seeing how difficult it was to reduce the city, 'Ubâdah encamped at a distance from it and ordered that trenches like canals be dug, each one large enough to conceal a man with his horse. The Moslems made special effort and got the work done. They then pretended to be returning to Ḥimṣ; but no sooner had the night fallen with its darkness, than they returned to their camp and trenches, while the people of al-Lâdhiḳîyah were negligent of them being under the impression that the Moslems had 133
left them. Early in the morning, they opened their gate and drove forth their cattle; but how terrified they were to meet the Moslems and see them enter through the gate! Thus was the city taken by force. 'Ubâdah entered the fort and then climbed its wall and called "Allah is great" etc. Certain Christians of al-Lâdhiḳîyah fled to al-Yusaiyid, and later sought to surrender, agreeing to return to their lands. They were assigned to lands, and a fixed *kharâj*[2] was assessed to be paid by them every year whether they should increase or decrease in number. Their church was left for

[1] Laodicea; Yâḳût, vol. iv, p. 338.

[2] *Kharâj muḳâṭa'ah.* See Berchem, *La Propriété Territoriale*, p. 45.

them. The Moslems, following the order of 'Ubâdah, erected in al-Lâdhiḳîyah a cathedral mosque that was later enlarged.

Al-Lâdhiḳîyah destroyed and rebuilt. In the year 100, when 'Abd-al-'Azîz was caliph, the Greeks made a descent by sea on the coast of al-Lâdhiḳîyah. They destroyed the city and took its inhabitants prisoners. 'Umar ordered that it be rebuilt and fortified and asked the [Greek] " tyrant "[1] to accept ransom for the Moslem prisoners. But this was not carried out till after his death in the year 101. The city was completed and garrisoned by the order of Yazîd ibn-'Abd-al-Malik.

According to a tradition communicated by one from al-Lâdhiḳîyah, 'Umar ibn-'Abd-al-'Azîz fortified the city and finished its work before he died. All what Yazîd ibn-'Abd-al-Malik did was to repair the city and increase its garrison.

Baldah taken by assault. Abu-Ḥafṣ ad-Dimashḳi from Sa'îd ibn-'Abd-al-'Azîz and Sa'îd ibn-Sulaimân al-Ḥimṣi:— 'Ubâdah with the Moslems appeared at the coast and took by assault a city called Baldah lying two parasangs from Jabalah. The city was later destroyed and its inhabitants evacuated it. Jabalah, which was a fortification for the Greeks and was deserted by them when the Moslems conquered Ḥimṣ, was established by Mu'âwiyah ibn-abi-Sufyân and guarded by a garrison.

The fort of Jabalah. Sufyân ibn-Muḥammad al-Bahrâni from certain *sheikhs*:—Mu'âwiyah erected for Jabalah[2] a fort outside the older Greek fort which was now inhabited by monks and others devoted to religious exercises.

[1] Ar. *ṭâghıyah,* an appellation of the Byzantine emperor used by the Arabian writers.
[2] Gabala, Gibellus Major, or Zibel; Le Strange, pp. 459-460.

Anṭarṭûs reduced. Sufyân ibn-Muḥammad from his father and *sheikhs*:—'Ubâdah with the Moslems conquered Anṭarṭûs [Tortosa] which was a fortified town and which was evacuated by its holders. Mu'âwiyah built Antartûs and fortified it [1] giving the fiefs to the holders of the fort. The same thing he did with Maraḳîyah and Bulunyâs.

Guards stationed in the littoral towns. Abu-Ḥafṣ ad- 134
Dimashḳi from his *sheikhs*: — Abu-'Ubaidah effected the conquest of al-Lâdhiḳîyah, Jabalah and Anṭarṭûs through 'Ubâdah ibn-as-Sâmit and used to put them in charge of a guard until the time in which the sea was closed.[2] When Mu'âwiyah stationed garrisons in the coast cities and fortified them, he put garrisons in, and fortified these cities, too, and treated them as the other littoral towns.

Salamyah. It was reported to me by a *sheikh* from Hims that close to Salamyah [Salaminias] lay a city called Mu'takifah which one day was completely destroyed by an earthquake and only one hundred of its inhabitants survived. The survivors erected one hundred houses and lived in them. This new settlement was called *Silm Mi'ah* [3] which name was corrupted into Salamyah. Later there came to this place Sâlih ibn-'Ali ibn-'Abdallâh ibn-'Abbâs, fortified it and lived in it with his sons. Many of his descendants still have their abode in it. According to ibn-Sahm al-Antâki, however, Salamyah is an ancient Greek name.

Marwân destroys the wall of Ḥimṣ. I was told by Muḥammad ibn-Muṣaffa-l-Ḥimṣi that the wall of Hims was destroyed by Marwân ibn-Muhammad, because in his retreat before the people of Khurâsân, he passed by the

[1] Yâḳût, vol. i, p. 388.

[2] The guard was posted in them so long as the sea was open for navigation, *i. e.*, until winter time.

[3] "The safety of one hundred."

people of Ḥimṣ, who had broken off from their allegiance, and they carried away some of his baggage, property and armories.

Al-Faḍl ibn-Ḳârin and Mûsa ibn-Bugha as governors of Ḥimṣ. The city of Ḥimṣ had stones for pavement. In the days of Aḥmad ibn-Muḥammad ibn-abi-Isḥâḳ al-Mu'taṣim-Billâh, the people rose against his *'âmil* over them, al-Faḍl ibn-Ḳârin aṭ-Ṭabari, a brother of Mayazdiyâr ibn-Ḳârin,[1] and in accordance with his orders the pavement was removed. They rebelled again, repaved the city and fought against al-Faḍl ibn-Ḳârin until they worsted him. After robbing him of his money and wives, they put him to death and crucified him. Al-Mu'taṣim directed against them Mûsa ibn-Bugha-l-Kabîr [the Elder] his freedman, and the inhabitants including a large number of Christians and Jews, fought against him. After a fearful slaughter, Mûsa put the survivors to flight, pursued them to the city and entered it by force. This took place in the year 250.

Ḥimṣ is the seat of a large granary that receives wheat and oil from the cities of the coast and other places that were given out as fiefs for their holders and recorded for them as such in special record books.

[1] *Cf.* Athîr, vol. vii, p. 88.

CHAPTER X 135

THE BATTLE OF AL-YARMÛK

A description of the battle. Heraclius gathered large bodies of Greeks, Syrians, Mesopotamians and Armenians numbering about 200,000.[1] This army he put under the command of one of his choice men [2] and sent as a vanguard Jabalah ibn-al-Aiham al-Ghassâni at the head of the "naturalized" Arabs [*musta'ribah*] of Syria of the tribes of Lakhm, Judhâm and others, resolving to fight the Moslems so that he might either win or withdraw to the land of the Greeks [3] and live in Constantinople. The Moslems gathered together and the Greek army marched against them. The battle they fought at al-Yarmûk was of the fiercest and bloodiest kind.[4] Al-Yarmûk [Hieromax] is a river. In this battle 24,000 Moslems took part. The Greeks and their followers in this battle tied themselves to each other by chains, so that no one might set his hope on flight. By Allah's help, some 70,000 of them were put to death, and their remnants took to flight, reaching as far as Palestine, Antioch, Aleppo, Mesopotamia and Armenia. In the battle of al-Yarmûk certain Moslem women took part and fought violently. Among them was Hind, daughter of 'Utbah and

[1] De Goeje, *Mémoire sur la Conquête de la Syrie*, p. 107.

[2] Ṭabari, vol. i, p. 2347.

[3] *i. e.*, Asia Minor; Arabic—*Bilâd ar-Rûm*.

[4] Al-Baṣri, *Futûḥ ash-Shâm*, p. 130 *seq.*; Pseudo-Wâḳidi, *Futûḥ ash-Shâm*, vol. ii, pp. 32-35.

mother of Mu'âwiyah ibn-abi-Sufyân, who repeatedly exclaimed, "Cut the arms of these 'uncircumcised' with your swords!" Her husband abu-Sufyân had come to Syria as a volunteer desiring to see his sons, and so he brought his wife with him. He then returned to al-Madînah where he died. year 31, at the age of 88. Others say he died in Syria. When the news of his death was carried to his daughter, umm-Ḥabîbah, she waited until the third day on which she ordered some yellow paint and covered with it her arms and face saying, "I would not have done that, had I not heard the Prophet say, 'A woman should not be in mourning for more than three days over anyone except her husband.'" It is stated that she did likewise when she received the news of her brother Yazîd's death. But Allah knows best.

Those who lost an eye or suffered martyrdom. Abu-Sufyân ibn-Ḥarb was one-eyed. He had lost his eye in the battle of aṭ-Ṭâ'if. In the battle of al-Yarmûk, however, al-Ash'ath ibn-Ḳais, Hâshim ibn-'Utbah ibn-abi-Waḳḳâṣ az-Zuhri (i. e. al-Mirḳâl) and Ḳais ibn-Makshûḥ, each lost 136
an eye. In this battle 'Âmir ibn-abi-Waḳḳâṣ az-Zuhri fell a martyr. It is this 'Âmir who once carried the letter of 'Umar ibn-al-Khaṭṭâb assigning abu-'Ubaidah to the governorship of Syria. Others say he was a victim of the plague; still others report that he suffered martyrdom in the battle of Ajnâdîn; but all that is not true.

Habîb ibn-Maslamah pursues the fugitives. Abu-'Ubaidah put Ḥabîb ibn-Maslamah-l-Fihri at the head of a cavalry detachment charged with pursuing the fugitive enemy,[1] and Ḥabîb set out killing every man whom he could reach.

The story of Jabalah. Jabalah ibn-al-Aiham sided with the *Anṣâr* saying, "Ye are our brethren and the sons of our

[1] Athîr, vol. i, p. 179.

fathers," and professed Islâm. After the arrival of 'Umar ibn-al-Khaṭṭâb in Syria, year 17, Jabalah had a dispute with one of the Muzainah and knocked out his eye. 'Umar ordered that he be punished, upon which Jabalah said, "Is his eye like mine? Never, by Allah, shall I abide in a town where I am under authority." He then apostatized and went to the land of the Greeks. This Jabalah was the king of Ghassân [1] and the successor of al-Ḥârith ibn-abi-Shimr.

According to another report, when Jabalah came to 'Umar ibn-al-Khaṭṭâb, he was still a Christian. 'Umar asked him to accept Islam and pay *ṣadaḳah*; but he refused saying, "I shall keep my faith and pay *ṣadaḳah*." 'Umar's answer was, "If thou keepest thy faith, thou hast to pay poll-tax." The man refused, and 'Umar added, "We have only three alternatives for thee: Islâm, tax or going whither thou willest." Accordingly, Jabalah left with 30,000 men to the land of the Greeks [Asia Minor]. 'Ubâdah ibn-aṣ-Ṣâmit gently reproved 'Umar saying, "If thou hadst accepted *ṣadaḳah* from him and treated him in a friendly way, he would have become Moslem."

In the year 21, 'Umar directed 'Umair ibn-Sa'd al-Anṣâri at the head of a great army against the land of the Greeks, and put him in command of the summer expedition[2] which was the first of its kind. 'Umar instructed him to treat Jabalah ibn-al-Aiham very kindly and to try and appeal to him through the blood relationship between them, so that he should come back to the land of the Moslems with the understanding that he would keep his own faith and pay the amount of *ṣadaḳah* he had agreed to pay. 'Umair marched until he came to the land of the Greeks and proposed to

[1] Nöldeke: "Die Ghassânischen Fürsten" in *Abhandlungen der Königlichen Akademie der Wissenschaften* (Berlin), 1887, No. II, p. 45 *seq.*

[2] Zaidân, vol. i, p. 155; Ḳudâmah, *Kitâb al-Kharâj* in ibn-Khurdâdhbih, *Kitâb al-Masâlik*, p. 259.

Jabalah what he was ordered by 'Umar to propose; but Jabalah refused the offer and insisted on staying in the land of the Greeks. 'Umair then came into a place called al-Ḥimâr—a valley—which he destroyed putting its inhabi- 137
tants to the sword. Hence the proverb, "In a more ruined state than the hollow of Ḥimâr." [1]

Heraclius' adieu to Syria. When Heraclius received the news about the troops in al-Yarmûk and the destruction of his army by the Moslems, he fled from Antioch to Constantinople, and as he passed ad-Darb [2] he turned and said, "Peace unto thee, O Syria, and what an excellent country this is for the enemy!" [3]—referring to the numerous pastures in Syria.

The battle of al-Yarmûk took place in Rajab, year 15.[4]

Ḥubâsh loses his leg. According to Hishâm ibn-al-Kalbi, among those who witnessed the battle of al-Yarmûk was Ḥubâsh ibn-Ḳais al-Ḳushairi, who killed many of the 'uncircumcised" and lost his leg without feeling it. At last he began to look for it. Hence the verse of Sauwâr ibn-Aufa:

> "Among us were ibn-'Attâb and the one who went seeking his leg; and among us was one who offered protection to the quarter,"

—referring to dhu-l-Ruḳaibah.[5]

Christians and Jews prefer Moslem rule. Abu-Ḥafṣ ad-Dimashḳi from Sa'îd ibn-'Abd-al-'Azîz:—When Heraclius massed his troops against the Moslems and the Mos-

[1] Bakri, vol. i, p. 254. Freytag, *Proverbia,* vol. i, p. 231, no. 66.

[2] The pass of Taurus.

[3] Ṭabari, vol. i, pp. 2395 and 2396.

[4] The date of the Yarmûk is confused by some Arabian historians with that of Ajnâdîn, Jumâda ii, year 13; see Athîr, vol. ii, p. 315.

[5] *Kâmûs*: "his name was Mâlik".

lems heard that they were coming to meet them at al-Yarmûk, the Moslems refunded to the inhabitants of Ḥimṣ the *kharâj* [1] they had taken from them saying, "We are too busy to support and protect you. Take care of yourselves." But the people of Ḥimṣ replied, "We like your rule and justice far better than the state of oppression and tyranny [2] in which we were. The army of Heraclius we shall indeed, with your *'âmil's* help, repulse from the city." The Jews rose and said, "We swear by the Thorah, no governor of Heraclius shall enter the city of Ḥimṣ unless we are first vanquished and exhausted!" Saying this, they closed the gates of the city and guarded them. The inhabitants of the other cities—Christian and Jew—that had capitulated to the Moslems, did the same, saying, "If Heraclius and his followers win over the Moslems we would return to our previous condition, otherwise we shall retain our present state so long as numbers are with the Moslems." When by Allah's help the "unbelievers" were defeated and the Moslems won, they opened the gates of their cities, went out with the singers and music players who began to play, and paid the *kharâj*.

Abu-'Ubaidah reduces Ḳinnasrîn and Antioch. Abu-'Ubaidah marched against the province of Ḳinnasrîn and Antioch and reduced it.

Shuraḥbîl transferred to Ḥimṣ. Al-'Abbâs ibn-Hishâm al-Kalbi from his grandfather:—As-Simṭ ibn-al-Aswad al-Kindi distinguished himself as a fighter in the battle of 138
al-Yarmûk and particularly in Syria and Ḥimṣ. It was he who divided the houses of Ḥimṣ among its people. His son Shuraḥbîl was in al-Kûfah disputing the leadership over the Kindah tribe with al-Ash'ath ibn-Ḳais al-Kindi. Now,

[1] Yûsuf, p. 81.

[2] Barhebraeus, *Chron. Eccles.*, vol. i, p. 274.

as-Simt appeared before 'Umar saying, " 'Commander of the Believers', I see thou dost not separate even captives from one another, yet thou hast separated me from my son. Change his position, if thou pleasest, to Syria, or mine to al-Kûfah." "Well," said 'Umar, "I shall change his position to Syria." Accordingly, Shurahbîl took up his abode in Ḥimṣ with his father.

CHAPTER XI

PALESTINE

Places conquered by 'Amr ibn-al-'Âṣi. Abu-Hafs ad-Dimashki from learned *sheikhs* :—The first conflict between Moslems and Greeks took place in the caliphate of abu-Bakr in the province of Palestine, the one in chief command over the Moslems being 'Amr ibn-al-'Âṣi. Later on in the caliphate of abu-Bakr, 'Amr ibn-al-'Âṣi effected the conquest of Ghazzah, then Sabastiyah [1] and Nâbulus [Neapolis] with the stipulation that he guaranteed to the inhabitants the safety of their lives, their possessions and their houses on condition that they pay poll-tax, and *kharâj* on their land. He then conquered Ludd [Lydda] and its district, and then Yubna [Jabneh or Jabneel], 'Amawâs [Emmaus] and Bait-Jabrîn [2] [Eleutheropolis] where he took for himself an estate [3] which he named 'Ajlân after a freedman of his. He then conquered Yâfa [Jaffa] which according to others was conquered by Mu'âwiyah. 'Amr also conquered Rafah and made similar terms with it.

The conquest of Jerusalem. As 'Amr was besieging Îliyâ', *i. e.,* Jerusalem in the year 16, abu-'Ubaidah after reducing Ḳinnasrîn and its environs, came to him, and according to a report, sent him from Jerusalem to Antioch whose people had violated the covenant. 'Amr reduced the

[1] *i. e.,* Samaria; abu-l-Fida, vol. i, p. 160.

[2] Athîr, vol. ii, p. 390.

[3] Yâkût, vol. i, p. .9, line 12.

city and returned [to Jerusalem]. Only two or three days after his return, the inhabitants of Jerusalem asked to capitulate to abu-'Ubaidah on the same terms as those of the cities of Syria as regards tax and *kharâj*, and to have 139
the same treatment as their equals elsewhere, provided the one to make the contract be 'Umar ibn-al-Khaṭṭâb in person, Abu-'Ubaidah communicated this in writing to 'Umar who came first to al-Jâbiyah in Damascus and then to Jerusalem. He made the terms of capitulation with the people of Jerusalem to take effect and gave them a written statement. The conquest of Jerusalem took place in the year 17.

A different account has been reported regarding the conquest of Jerusalem.

Al-Ḳâsim ibn-Sallâm from Yazîd ibn-abi-Ḥabîb:—Khâlid ibn-Thâbit al-Fahmi was sent by 'Umar ibn-al-Khaṭṭâb, who was at that time in al-Jâbiyah, at the head of an army to Jerusalem. After fighting with the inhabitants, they agreed to pay something on what was within their fortified city and to deliver to the Moslems all what was outside. 'Umar came and concurred, after which he returned to al-Madînah.[1]

Hishâm ibn-'Ammâr from al-Auzâ'i: — Abu-'Ubaidah reduced Ḳinnasrîn and its districts in the year 16; after which he came to Palestine and camped in Jerusalem, whose people asked him to make terms with them, which he did in the year 17, with the stipulation that 'Umar would come in person, put the terms into effect and write a statement of them to the people.

'Umar welcomed by the people of Adhri'ât. Hishâm ibn-'Ammâr from 'Abdallâh ibn-Ḳais:—The latter said, " I was one of those who went with abu-'Ubaidah to meet 'Umar as he was coming to Syria. As 'Umar was passing,

[1] Ṭabari, vol. i, p. 2360.

he was met by the singers and tambourine players of the inhabitants of Adhri'ât [1] with swords and myrtle. Seeing that, 'Umar shouted 'Keep still! Stop them!' But abu-'Ubaidah replied, 'This is their custom (or some other word like it), "Commander of the Believers," and if thou shouldst stop them from doing it, they would take that as indicating thy intention to violate their covenant.' 'Well, then, said 'Umar, 'let them go on.'"

The plague of 'Amawâs. The plague of 'Amawâs [Emmaus] occurred in the year 18. To it a great many Moslems fell victim, among whom was abu-'Ubaidah ibn-al-Jarrâḥ (who was 58 years old and a commander in the army) and Mu'âdh ibn-Jabal of the banu-Salimah of al-Khazraj who was surnamed abu-'Abd-ar-Raḥmân and who died in the district of al-Ukḥuwânah in the province of the Jordan, aged 38. This Muâdh, abu-'Ubaidah on his death-bed had appointed as his successor. According to others he appointed 'Iyâḍ ibn-Ghanm al-Fihri. Some others say he appointed 'Amr ibn-al-Âṣi who appointed his own son as 140
successor and departed for Egypt. Al-Faḍl ibn-al-'Abbâs ibn-'Abd-al-Muṭṭalib, surnamed abu-Muḥammad, fell, according to some, as martyr in Ajnâdin; but the fact is that he was a victim to the plague at 'Amawâs. Other victims were Shuraḥbîl ibn-Ḥasanah, surnamed abu-'Abdallâh (who died 69 years old); Suhail ibn-'Amr of the banu-'Âmir ibn-Lu'ai, surnamed abu-Yazîd; and al-Ḥârith ibn-Hishâm ibn-al-Mughîrah-l-Makhzûmi (who, according to others, fell a martyr in the battle of Ajnâdin).

Yazîd ibn-abi-Sufyân governor of Syria. When 'Umar ibn-al-Khaṭṭâb received the news of the death of abu-'Ubaidah, he wrote to Yazîd ibn-abi-Sufyân appointing him in his place as governor of Syria, and ordering him to

[1] Edrei of Numbers xxi: 33.

invade Ḳaisârîyah [Caesarea]. According to others, however, Yazîd was appointed by 'Umar as governor of the Jordan and Palestine; abu-ad-Dardâ', of Damascus; and 'Ubâdah ibn-aṣ-Ṣâmit, of Ḥimṣ.

The conquest of Ḳaisârîyah. Muḥammad ibn-Sa'd from al-Wâḳidi:—There is difference of opinion regarding the conquest of Ḳaisârîyah [Caesarea]. Some say Mu'âwiyah subdued it; others, 'Iyâḍ ibn-Ghanm, after the death of abu-'Ubaidah whose successor he was; and still others 'Amr ibn-al-'Âṣi. According to some, 'Amr ibn-al-'Âṣi left for Egypt and appointed his son 'Abdallâh to succeed him. The truth in all that, on which scholars agree, is that the first to lay siege to the city was 'Amr ibn-al-'Âṣi who made his descent on it in Jumâda I, year 13. 'Amr would camp around it as long as he could, and whenever the Moslem forces wanted to combine against their enemy, he would go to them. Thus he witnessed the battles of Ajnâdîn, Fiḥl, al-Marj, Damascus and al-Yarmûk. He then returned to Palestine and after taking Jerusalem laid siege to Ḳaisârîyah. From Ḳaisârîyah he left for Egypt. After abu-'Ubaidah, Yazîd ibn-abi-Sufyân became governor of Syria, and he appointed his brother to press the siege. Smitten by the plague, Yazîd returned to Damascus where he died.

Other than al-Wâkidi state that 'Umar appointed Yazîd ibn-abi-Sufyân to the governorship of Palestine together with the other provinces of Syria and ordered him to invade Ḳaisârîyah which had already been besieged. Yazîd went against it with 17,000 men. Its people resisted; and 141
he laid the siege. In the last part of the year 18, he fell ill and departed for Damascus leaving his brother Mu'âwiyah in his place at Ḳaisârîyah. Mu'âwiyah reduced the city [1]

[1] Ya'ḳûbi, vol. ii, p. 172.

and wrote to Yazîd to that effect, and the latter communicated the news to 'Umar.

Mu'âwiyah nominated governor of Syria. At the death of Yazîd ibn-abi-Sufyân, 'Umar wrote to Mu'âwiyah making him governor in his [Yazîd's] place, upon which abu-Sufyân thanked 'Umar saying, "May the tie of relationship be made stronger by thy kind behavior!"

Hishâm ibn-'Ammâr from Tamîm ibn-'Aṭîyah:—'Umar made Mu'âwiyah ibn-abi-Sufyân governor of Syria after Yazîd, and appointed with him two men of the Prophet's Companions for conducting prayer and performing the duties of *ḳâḍi*: abu-ad-Dardâ' to act as *ḳâḍi* and to conduct prayer at Damascus and the Jordan, and 'Ubâdah to act as *ḳâḍi* and conduct prayer at Ḥimṣ and Ḳinnasrîn.

Mu'âwiyah besieges Ḳaisârîyah. Muḥammad ibn-Sa'd from al-Wâḳidi:—When 'Umar ibn-al-Khaṭṭâb made Mu'âwiyah governor of Syria, the latter besieged Ḳaisârîyah until he reduced it, the city having been under siege for seven years. Its conquest took place in Shauwâl, year 19.

Muḥammad ibn-Sa'd from 'Abdallâh ibn-'Âmir:—Mu'âwiyah besieged Ḳaisârîyah until he lost all hope of reducing it. Previous to this, the city had been besieged by 'Amr ibn-al-'Âṣi and his son. When Mu'âwiyah at last took it by storm, he found in it 700,000 [*sic!*] soldiers with fixed stipends, 30,000 Samaritans and 20,000 Jews. He found in the city 300 markets, all in good shape. It was guarded every night by 100,000 men stationed on its wall. The city was reduced in the following way:—A Jew named Yûsuf came to the Moslems at night and pointed out to them a road through a tunnel the water in which would reach a man's waist; in consideration for which information, safety was guaranteed him and his relatives. Mu'âwiyah sanctioned the conditions [made to Yûsuf] and the Moslems entered the city by night, calling "Allah is great!"

The Greeks seeking to flee through the tunnel found it occupied by Moslems. The Moslems opened the city gate and Muʻâwiyah with his men went in. Many Arabs were in the city [as prisoners?]. One of them was a woman, Shaḳrâ', whom Ḥassân ibn-Thâbit referred to when he said:

> "Shaḳrâ says, 'If thou shouldst relinquish wine, thou wouldst become rich in number.'[1]"

Others say her name was Shaʻthâ'.

The captives from Ḳaisârîyah. Muḥammad ibn-Saʻd from al-Wâḳidi: — The prisoners from Ḳaisârîyah [Caesarea] amounted to 4,000. When Muʻâwiyah sent them to ʻUmar ibn-al-Khaṭṭâb the latter gave orders that they be settled in al-Jurf. They were then distributed among the orphans of the *Anṣâr*, and some were used as clerks and manual laborers for the Moslems. The daughters of abu-Umâmah Asʻad ibn-Zurârah, having been given by abu-Bakr two servants from the prisoners of ʻAin at-Tamr who were now dead, ʻUmar assigned to the daughters two of the captives of Ḳaisârîyah to take the place of the two dead servants.

Muʻâwiyah forwarded two men of the Judhâm to carry the news of the conquest to ʻUmar. Fearing that they might not hasten enough, he forwarded a man of the Khathʻam who exerted all effort in walking by day and by night repeating:

"The two brothers of Judhâm have brought insomnia on me,
  the brother of Hishm and the brother of Ḥarâm.
How can I sleep so long as they are ahead of me?
They are going along and the midday heat is becoming vehement."[2]

At last he got ahead of them and presented himself before

---

[1] *Cf.* Ḥassân ibn-Thâbit, *Dîwân*, p. 61; al-Mubarrad, *al-Kâmil*, p. 148.
[2] Ṭabari, vol. i, p. 2397.

'Umar who, hearing the news of the conquest, exclaimed "Allah is great!"

Hishâm ibn-'Ammâr from one whose name I do not remember:—Ḳaisârîyah was taken by storm in the year 19. Hearing the news of its capture, 'Umar exclaimed, "Ḳaisârîyah is taken by storm. Allah is great!" and so did the rest of the Moslems. The city was besieged for seven years and was finally reduced by Mu'âwiyah.

The death of Yazîd ibn-abi-Sufyân took place at the end of the year 18, in Damascus.

The date of the conquest of Ḳaisârîyah. Those who claim that Mu'âwiyah reduced Ḳaisârîyah in the days of his brother believe that it was not reduced before the end of the year 18; but those who claim that it was reduced while he was governor of Syria believe that it was reduced in the year 19. Of the two views, the latter is the tenable one. According to still other reports, the city was reduced in the early part of the year 20.

'Asḳalân reduced. 'Umar ibn-al-Ḳhaṭṭâb wrote to Mu'âwiyah instructing him to follow up the conquest of what was left in Palestine. Accordingly, Mu'âwiyah conquered 'Asḳalân [Ascalon] which capitulated after some resistance. According to others, however, it was 'Amr ibn-al-'Âṣi who first conquered the city. Later, its inhabitants violated the covenant and were reinforced by the Greeks. It was then that Mu'âwiyah reduced it, settled garrisons of cavalry in it and put it in charge of a guard. 143

'Abd-al-Malik makes repairs in 'Asḳalân, Ḳaisârîyah and other places. Bakr ibn-al-Haitham from certain *sheikhs* of 'Asḳalân:—The Greeks destroyed 'Asḳalân and expelled its inhabitants in the days of ibn-az-Zubair. When 'Abd-al-Malik ibn-Marwân became ruler, he rebuilt the city and fortified it, and made repairs in Ḳaisârîyah, too.

Muḥammad ibn-Muṣaffa from abu-Sulaimân ar-Ramli's

father:—In the days of ibn-az-Zubair the Greeks went out against Ḳaisârîyah and devastated it and razed its mosque to the ground. When 'Abd-al-Malik ibn-Marwân was settled in his rule, he made repairs in Ḳaisârîyah, restored its mosque and left a garrison in it. Moreover, he built Tyre and outer Acre which had shared the same fate as Ḳaisârîyah.

Sulaimân ibn-'Abd-al-Malik builds ar-Ramlah. The following tradition was communicated to me by certain men well versed in the conditions of Syria:—Al-Walîd ibn-'Abd-al-Malik made Sulaimân ibn-'Abd-al-Malik governor of the province of Palestine. Sulaimân took up his abode in Ludd and then founded the city of ar-Ramlah and fortified it.[1] The first thing he built in it was his palace and the house known as Dâr aṣ-Ṣabbâghîn [the house of the dyers] in the middle of which he made a cistern. He then planned the mosque and began its construction, but he became caliph before its completion. After becoming caliph, he continued its construction which was completed by 'Umar ibn-'Abd-al-'Azîz who reduced the original plan, saying, "The inhabitants of ar-Ramlah should be satisfied with the size thereof to which I have reduced it."

After having erected a house for himself, Sulaimân permitted the people to build their houses, which they did. He dug for the inhabitants of ar-Ramlah their canal which is called Baradah, and he dug also wells. The one he appointed to oversee the expenses of his palace in ar-Ramlah and of the cathedral mosque[2] was one of his clerks, a certain Christian of Ludd named al-Batrik ibn-an-Naka.[3]

[1] Ar. *maṣṣara*—"to make a city a boundary line between two things;" see *an-Nihâyah*; Le Strange, p. 303, translates: "made it his capital."

[2] Mukaddasi, p. 164.

[3] "Ibn-Baka" in Hamadhâni, *Buldân*, p. 102.

Before Sulaimân there was no such city as ar-Ramlah, and its site was sand [Ar. *raml*].

The Dâr aṣ-Ṣabbâghîn passed to the hands of the heirs of Sâlih ibn-'Ali ibn-'Abdallâh ibn-al-Abbâs, because it was confiscated with the possessions of the banu-Umaiyah.

The expenses of the wells and canal of ar-Ramlah, after the time of Sulaimân ibn-'Abd-al-Malik, were met by the banu-Umaiyah. But when the banu-l-Abbâs assumed the caliphate, they paid the expenses. The order for these ex- 144
penses was issued yearly by every caliph; but when al-Mu'taṣim became caliph, he gave a permanent decree for these expenses, thereby doing away with the necessity of issuing an order every time by the caliph. It became thereafter a current expense which the *'âmils* paid and kept an account of.

"Reduction" and "restoration" in the kharâj. There are in Palestine special places containing documents from the caliphs, set aside from the records of the *kharâj* of the common people and containing a statement of the "reduction" and "restoration", the explanation of which is the following:—Certain estates having been abandoned in the caliphate of ar-Rashîd and deserted by their occupants, ar-Rashîd sent Harthamah ibn-A'yan to cultivate them. Harthamah asked some of their old tenants and farmers to go back to them with the understanding that he would reduce their *kharâj* and would deal with them more leniently. Those who went back are those to whom the "reductions" were made. Others came after that and their old lands were restored to them. These are the ones to whom the "restorations" were made.

Fiefs in 'Askalân. The following tradition was related to me by Bakr ibn-al-Haitham:—"I met a man of the Arabs in 'Askalân who said that his grandfather was one of those settled in 'Askalân by 'Abd-al-Malik and was given a fief in it as one of the garrison of cavalry to whom fiefs were assigned. He also showed me a piece of land, saying, 'This is one of the fiefs given by 'Uthmân ibn-'Affân'. I heard Muḥammad ibn-Yûsuf al-Fâryâbi [1] say:—' Here in 'Askalân are fiefs which were given out by the orders of 'Umar and 'Uthmân, and it matters not who takes possession of them.' "

[1] "Firyâbi" in Ṭabari, vol. iii, p. 2557.

CHAPTER XII

The Province of Ḳinnasrîn and the Cities called al-'Awâṣim

Ḳinnasrîn capitulates. Abu-'Ubaidah ibn-al-Jarrâḥ, after being through with al-Yarmûk, went to the province of Ḥimṣ and passed from one place to the other examining it.[1] Then he went to Ḳinnasrîn [Chalcis] with Khâlid ibn-al-Walîd commanding the van of his army.[2] The inhabitants of the city of Ḳinnasrîn resisted at first, then they sought refuge in their stronghold and asked to capitulate. Abu-'Ubaidah made terms with them similar to those of Ḥimṣ. Thus the Moslems effected the conquest of the land of Ḳinnasrîn with its villages. The Ḥâḍir[3] Ḳinnasrîn had been settled by the Tanûkh tribe since they came to Syria and pitched their tents in it. They later built their 145
houses in it. These, abu-'Ubaidah summoned to Islâm. Some of them accepted it, but the banu-Salîḥ ibn-Ḥulwân ibn-'Imrân ibn-al-Ḥâfi ibn-Ḳuḍâ'ah remained Christian.[4]

Certain sons of Yazîd ibn-Ḥunain aṭ-Ṭâ'i-l-Anṭâki from their *sheikhs*:—A group of men from this Ḥâḍir Ḳinnasrîn embraced Islâm in the caliphate of al-Mahdi who inscribed on their hands in green color the word "Ḳinnasrîn."

[1] Ar. *istaḳrâha*, Caetani, vol. iii, p. 790, translates: "rinovo con gli abitanti il primitive trattato."

[2] Ṭabari, vol. i, p. 2393.

[3] "A place where people alight and take up their abode by a constant source of water," *T. 'A. Cf.* Wâḳidi, *Futûḥ*, vol. ii, pp. 35-39.

[4] *Cf.* Yâḳût, vol. iv, p. 184.

Kinnasrîn violates the covenant. Thence abu-'Ubaidah departed bent upon Aleppo [Ḥalab], but hearing that the people of Ḳinnasrîn had violated the covenant and proved perfidious, he directed against them as-Simṭ ibn-al-Aswad al-Kindi who reduced the city after besieging them.

Hishâm ibn-'Ammâr ad-Dimashḳi from 'Abd-ar-Raḥmân ibn-Ghanm:—" We kept our post against Ḳinnasrîn with as-Simṭ (or, perhaps he said Shuraḥbîl ibn-as-Simṭ) as our leader. When he reduced the city, he carried off cows and sheep as booty. One part of the booty he distributed among us and the remaining part was treated according to the laws governing the spoils [Ar. *maghnam* [1]]."

The Ḥâḍir Ṭaiyi'. The Ḥâḍir Ṭaiyi' [2] was of old origin. It dates back to the disastrous war termed Ḥarb al-Fasâd [3] which tore up the tribe of Ṭaiyi' some of whom then came and established themselves on the two mountains [*al-Jabalain, i. e.,* Aja and Salma]. Under these circumstances a large body of the Ṭaiyi' were dispersed over the country and some came and settled [near Ḳinnasrîn]. When abu-'Ubaidah came to them, some became Moslems and many made terms agreeing to pay poll-tax, a little after which they all accepted Islâm with the exception of a few.

The Ḥâḍir of Aleppo. Close by the city of Aleppo stood a settlement called the Ḥâḍir Ḥalab in which different Arab tribes including Tanûkh lived. Abu-'Ubaidah made terms with them in which they agreed to pay poll-tax. Later they embraced Islâm and lived with their descendants in the same place until a little after the death of ar-Rashîd. The inhabitants of this Ḥâḍir once fought against the people of

[1] Mawardi, p. 240 *seq.*

[2] *Mushtarik,* p. 118.

[3] In which many atrocities were committed by both parties. See "*Annotations on al-Ḳâmûs,*" by Muḥammad ibn-aṭ-Ṭaiyib al-Fâsi.

the city of Aleppo and tried to drive them out of their city. The Hâshim tribe of the people of Aleppo wrote to all the Arab tribes of the vicinity asking for help. The first to come to their support and aid was al-'Abbâs ibn-Zufar ibn-'Âṣim al-Hilâli (according to his maternal pedigree, because umm-'Abdallâh ibn-al-'Abbâs was Lubâbah, daughter 146
of al-Ḥârith ibn-Ḥazn ibn-Bujair ibn-al-Huzam of the Hilâl tribe). The people of that Ḥâḍir could not resist this al-'Abbâs and his men. They were therefore expelled from their Ḥâḍir, and that at the time of the insurrection of Muḥammad ibn-ar-Rashîd; and their Ḥâḍir was destroyed. They moved to Ḳinnasrîn whose people met them with food and clothing. No sooner had they entered the city, than they attempted to subjugate it and were therefore driven out. Thus they were dispersed over the land, some settling in Takrît (whom I myself have seen) and others in Armenia and various other regions.

Al-'Abbâs ibn-Zufar in Aleppo. I was told by al-Mutawakkil that he heard a *sheikh* of the banu-Ṣâliḥ ibn-'Ali ibn-'Abdallâh ibn-'Abbâs say to al-Mu'taṣim, in the year in which the latter invaded 'Ammûrîyah',[1] that when al-'Abbâs ibn-Zufar al-Hilâli arrived in Aleppo for the support of the Hashimites, some of their women called him saying, "Our hope, uncle, is in Allah and in thee!" To this al-'Abbâs answered, "There is no danger, if it be the will of Allah; may Allah disappoint me, if I should disappoint you!"

Ḥiyâr bani-l-Ka'ḳâ'. Ḥiyâr bani-l-Ḳa'ḳâ' was a well-known town in pre-Islamic time. In it was the stopping place of al-Mundhir ibn-Mâ' as-Samâ' al-Lakhmi, the king of al-Ḥîrah. It was also settled by the banu-l-Ḳa'ḳâ' ibn-Khulaid . . . ibn-Baghîḍ, who chose it for their abode and after whom it was thus called.

[1] *Mushtarik*, p. 317; *Yâḳût*, vol. iii, p. 730.

'Abd-al-Malik ibn-Marwân had given to al-Ḳa'ḳâ' a part of this Ḥiyâr as fief, and to al-Ḳa'ḳâ's uncle, al-'Abbâs ibn-Jaz' ibn-al-Ḥârith other fiefs which he exempted from the *kharâj* [1] and assessed it on al-Yaman. They were also exempt after he died. All or most of them were waste land. The daughter of this al-'Abbâs, Wallâdah, lived with 'Abd-al-Malik and brought forth al-Walîd and Sulaimân.

Abu-'Ubaidah reduces Aleppo. Abu-'Ubaidah set out for Aleppo sending before him 'Iyâḍ ibn-Ghanm al-Fihri. (The name of the latter's father was 'Abd-Ghanm; but when 'Iyâḍ accepted Islâm, he hated to be called 'Abd-Ghanm,[2] so he said, "I am 'Iyâḍ ibn-Ghanm"). Abu-'Ubaidah, finding the people in a fortified position, camped around the city; but no sooner had he done so, than they sought to capitulate and make terms regarding the safety 14
of their lives, their possessions, city wall, churches, homes and the fort. All this was granted them with the exception of a site for the mosque. The one to make the terms was 'Iyâḍ; and abu-'Ubaidah sanctioned them.

Some reporters claim that they capitulated, agreeing to share with the Moslems half of their homes and churches provided their lives be spared. Others assert that abu-'Ubaidah found nobody in Aleppo, its inhabitants having moved to Antioch. From there they agreed in writing with abu-'Ubaidah on the terms of peace. When the terms were concluded, they returned to Aleppo.

Antioch reduced by abu-'Ubaidah. Abu-'Ubaidah set out from Aleppo for Antioch [Anṭâkiyah] in which a large body of men from the province of Ḳinnasrîn had fortified themselves. On his arrival at Mahrûbah, which lay about

[1] Ar. *aughara.* See Zaidân, vol. ii, p. 133.

[2] One of the pre-Islamic gods.

two parasangs from Antioch, the troops of the enemy met him; and he dispersed them and forced them to seek refuge in the city. Abu-'Ubaidah invested the city at all its gates, most of the army being at the Bâb Fâris and Bâb al-Baḥr [sea gate]. At last they capitulated, agreeing to pay poll-tax or evacuate the place. Some of them did leave; but others remained, and to the latter abu-'Ubaidah guaranteed safety, assessing one *dînâr* and one *jarîb* [of wheat] on every adult. Later, they violated the contract, which made abu-'Ubaidah send against them 'Iyâḍ ibn-Ghanm and Ḥabîb ibn-Maslamah, who reduced the city and made terms identical with the previous ones. Some say, however, that they violated the contract after abu-'Ubaidah's return to Palestine. So he sent from Jerusalem 'Amr ibn-al-'Âṣi who reduced it and returned to Jerusalem whose people, after a short time, sought to capitulate and make peace.

A garrison stationed in Antioch. Muḥammad ibn-Sahm al-Antâki from certain *sheikhs* of the frontier cities:—Antioch was highly esteemed by 'Umar and 'Uthmân. When it was therefore reduced, 'Umar wrote to abu-'Ubaidah saying, " Station in Antioch Moslems of strong determination and good management. Let them be its garrison, and never stop their allowances." When he made
Mu'âwiyah governor, 'Umar wrote to him something to that 148
effect. Later 'Uthmân instructed Mu'âwiyah to station in it troops that would never leave and to assign them fiefs, which Mu'âwiyah did. The following was said by abu-Sahm, " As a child, while I was standing on the bridge of Antioch spanning the Orontes [Ar. al-Urunṭ] I heard an aged man of Antioch say, ' This piece of land is a fief from 'Uthmân to certain men that were in the army sent by abu-'Ubaidah. It was allotted them in the time in which Mu'âwiyah was, according to 'Uthmân's assignment, the governor of Syria.' "

Muslim ibn-'Abdallâh loses his life. Mu'âwiyah ibn-abi-Sufyân transplanted to Antioch in the year 42 some Persians and others from Ba'labakk, Ḥimṣ, al-Baṣrah and al-Kûfah.[1] One of those transplanted was Muslim ibn-'Abdallâh, the grandfather of 'Abdallâh ibn-Ḥabîb ibn-an-Nu'mân ibn-Muslim al-Antâki. This Muslim was killed at one of the gates of Antioch which is known to-day as Bâb Muslim. His death was brought about when the Greeks started from the coast and set up their camp against Antioch and one of the "uncircumcised" threw a stone on Muslim, who was then on the city wall, and killed him.

Seleucia given as fief. According to a tradition communicated to me by certain *sheikhs* from Antioch, among whom was ibn-Burd al-Faḳîh, al-Walîd ibn-'Abd-al-Malik gave as fief to some of the troops of Antioch the land of Seleucia [Ar. Salûḳîyah] lying at the sea-coast. Moreover, he fixed the tax on a *filthur* (i. e., *jarîb*) one *dînâr* and one modius [2] of wheat. They cultivated the land; and the terms were carried into effect. He also built the fort of Seleucia.

Baghrâs. The land of Baghrâs [Pagrae] belonged to Maslamah ibn-'Abd-al-Malik who gave it as an unalienable legacy [3] to be used in the cause of righteousness. The same man owned 'Ain as-Sallaur with its lake and al-Iskandarîyah [Alexandria] which latter passed as fief into the hands of Rajâ', a freedman of al-Mahdi, to be inherited by his [al-Mahdi] sons Manṣûr and Ibrâhîm, later to Ibrâhîm ibn-Sa'îd al-Jauhari, then by purchase to Aḥmad ibn-abi-Duwâd al-Iyâdi, and lastly to al-Mutawakkil, "the Commander of the Believers."

[1] "Misrân" used for the last two localities.

[2] De Goeje, gloss. to *Biblio. Geog. Arab.*, vol. iv, pp. 352-353; C. H. Becker, *Papyri Schott-Reinhardt*, vol. i, p. 31.

[3] Ar. *waḳf*.

Maslamah gives fiefs to Rabî'ah. According to a tradition communicated to me by ibn-Burd al-Antâki and others, certain men of the Rabî'ah tribe were assigned fiefs by Maslamah ibn-'Abd-al-Malik, which were later confiscated, passed to al-Ma'mûn and put in charge of Sâlih al-Khâzin, the proprietor of the "Dâr[-Sâliḥ]" in Antioch.

Abu-'Ubaidah reduces Ma'arrat Miṣrîn and other places. Abu-'Ubaidah, hearing that a large body of Greeks were 149
assembled between Ma'arrat Misrîn [1] and Aleppo, met them and killed many patricians, dispersing the whole army and carrying away captives and booty. Thus he effected the conquest of Ma'arrat Miṣrîn and made terms similar to the terms of Aleppo. His cavalry roamed about until they got to Bûka and reduced the villages of al-Jûmah, Sarmîn,[2] Martahwân [3] and Tîzîn.[4] The occupants of the convents of Ṭabâya [5] and al-Fasîlah capitulated, agreeing to entertain whomever of the Moslems passed by them. The Khunâsirah Christians, too, came to abu-'Ubaidah and made terms. Thus did all the land of Kinnasrîn and Antioch fall into the hands of abu-'Ubaidah. I learnt from al-'Abbâs ibn-Hishâm on the authority of his father that the Khunâsirah were thus called after one, Khunâsir ibn-'Amr ibn-al-Hârith al-Kalbi — later al-Kinâni — who was their chief.

Butnân Habîb was so called after Ḥabîb ibn-Maslamah-l-Fihri who was sent from Aleppo either by abu-'Ubaidah or Iyâḍ ibn-Ghanm to Butnân, where he reduced a fort that later bore his name.

[1] Known also as Ma'arrat Ḳinnasrîn and Ma'arrat Nasrîn. Yâkût, vol. iv, p. 574.

[2] *Ibid.*, vol. iii, p. 83.

[3] Lammens, *MFO*, vol. i, p. 242; Yâḳût, vol. iv, p. 487.

[4] or Tûzîn. Yâkût, vol. i, p. 907.

[5] ? No diacritical points.

The treaty with Ḳûrus. Abu-'Ubaidah set out bent upon Ḳûrus[1] [Cyrrhus], sending at the head of the vanguard 'Iyâḍ. The latter was met by one of the monks of Ḳûrus, who asked to capitulate on behalf of its people. 'Iyâḍ sent the monk to abu-'Ubaidah, who was now between Jabrîn[2] and Tall A'zâz.[3] Abu-'Ubaidah accepted the capitulation and proceeded to Ḳûrus where he signed a covenant with its people, granting them the same rights granted to the people of Antioch. To the monk, he wrote a special statement regarding a village that he owned called Sharḳina.[4] He then distributed his cavalry and subdued all the province of Ḳûrus to the end of the frontier of Niḳâbulus (Nicepholis).

Ḳûrus a frontier garrison for Antioch. Ḳûrus was for Antioch the seat of a garrison that kept watch on the enemy. To it came every year a detachment[5] from the Antioch army to act as garrison. Later, one of the four divisions into which the army of Antioch was divided[6] was moved to it; and the periodical detachments were no more sent there.

Salmân fort. Salmân ibn-Rabî'ah-l-Bâhili was in the army of abu-'Ubaidah, together with abu-Umâmah aṣ-Ṣudai ibn-'Ajlân, a Companion of the Prophet. This Salmân occupied a fort in Ḳûrus which was called after him Ḥiṣn [fort] Salmân. He then returned from Syria, together with others, to reinforce Sa'd ibn-abi-Waḳḳâṣ in al-'Irâḳ. 15
According to others, Salmân ibn-Rabî'ah had led an invasion

[1] Ya'ḳûbi, *Buldân,* p. 363; Rustah, p. 107.

[2] Jibrîn or Jibrîn Ḳurasṭâya. Yâḳût, vol. ii, p. 19.

[3] or Tall 'Azâz. Yâḳût, vol. iii, p. 667.

[4] The word is uncertain, *cf.* "Ṣorqanié, Surkanyâ" in Lammens, "Villages Yézidis," *MFO,* vol. ii, p. 382.

[5] Ar. *ṭâli'ah,* 1,500-2,000 men who came in spring and returned in winter.

[6] Zaidân, vol. i, p. 120.

against the Greeks after the conquest of al-'Irâḳ and before he started for Armenia. On setting out from the district of Mar'ash, he encamped near this fort and it was called after him. This Salmân together with Ziyâd [1] were among the Slavs whom Marwân ibn-Muḥammad stationed in the frontier fortresses.[2] I heard someone say that this Salmân was a Slav and that the fort was named after him.

Manbij, Dulûk and Ra'bân make terms. Abu-'Ubaidah advanced to Ḥalab as-Sâjûr [3] and sent before him 'Iyâḍ to Manbij [Hierapolis]. When abu-'Ubaidah came up to 'Iyâḍ, he found that the people of Manbij had capitulated on terms similar to those of Antioch. Abu-'Ubaidah carried the terms into effect and sent 'Iyâḍ ibn-Ghanm to the region of Dulûk and Ra'bân, whose inhabitants capitulated on terms similar to those of Manbij. One condition imposed on them was that they search for news regarding the Greeks and forward it in writing to the Moslems. To every district abu-'Ubaidah conquered, he assigned a *'âmil* and sent with him some Moslems. But in the dangerous places he posted garrisons.

Bâlis and Ḳâṣirîn captured. Abu-'Ubaidah proceeded until he got to 'Arâjîn.[4] The van of the army he sent to Bâlis [Barbalissus]; and to Ḳâṣirîn he sent an army under Ḥabîb ibn-Maslamah. Bâlis and Ḳâṣirîn [2] belonged to two brothers of the Greek nobility to whom were given as fiefs the adjacent villages and who were made guardians of the Greek towns of Syria that lay between Bâlis and Ḳâṣirîn. When the Moslem armies reached these towns, their inhabi-

[1] The one after whom Hisn Ziyâd was named; Yâḳût, vol. ii, p. 276.

[2] Ar *thughûr*; Zaidân, vol. i, pp. 153-155.

[3] Yâḳût, vol. i, p. 315; *Mush'tarik*, p. 142.

[4] Sometimes 'Arshîn; Lammens, *MFO*, vol. i, p. 240, note 3.

[5] Yâḳût, vol. iv, p. 16.

tants capitulated, agreeing to pay poll-tax or evacuate the places. Most of them left for the Byzantine Empire, Mesopotamia and the village of Jisr Manbij [or Ḳal'at an-Najm]. At this time there was no bridge [Ar. *jisr*]. It was first put up for the summer expeditions in the days of 'Uthmân ibn-'Affân. Others claim that it is of ancient origin.

Abu-'Ubaidah stationed in Bâlis a body of fighting men and settled in the city some Arabs, who were in Syria and who, after the advent of the Moslems to Syria, had accepted Islâm, together with others who were not among the forces sent to the frontiers, but who had emigrated from the deserts and belonged to the Ḳais tribe. In Ḳâṣirîn, he settled others who, either themselves or their descendants, refused to stay in it. Abu-'Ubaidah reached as far as the Euphrates and then returned to Palestine. 151

Maslamah canal. Bâlis and the villages attached to it on its upper, middle, and lower extremities were tithe-lands watered only by rain. When Maslamah ibn-'Abd-al-Malik ibn-Marwân led an expedition against the Greeks from the side of the Mesopotamian frontier fortresses, he camped at Bâlis whose inhabitants, together with those of Buwailis, Ḳâṣirîn, 'Âbidîn, and Ṣiffîn (which were villages attached to Bâlis) came to him, together with the inhabitants of the upper extremity, and they all asked him to dig for them a canal from the Euphrates to irrigate their land, agreeing to offer him one-third of the produce of the land, after taking away the usual tithe for the government.[1] Maslamah consented and dug the canal called Nahr Maslamah; and the people lived up to their promise. Moreover, Maslamah repaired and strengthened the city wall. According to others, Maslamah himself started the idea and proposed the terms.

[1] Ar. *Sulṭân*.

Bâlis and its villages as fief. At the death of Maslamah, Bâlis with its villages passed into the hands of his heirs, who held them until the appearance of the "blessed dynasty" [Abbasid], at which time 'Abdallâh ibn-'Ali confiscated the possessions of the banu-Umaiyah, including Bâlis and its villages. Abu-l-'Abbâs the "Commander of the Believers," assigned Bâlis and its villages as fief to Sulaimân ibn-'Ali ibn-'Abdallâh ibn-al-'Abbâs, from whom they passed to his son, Muḥammad ibn-Sulaimân. Muḥammad's brother, Ja'far ibn-Sulaimân, repeatedly calumniated his brother to ar-Rashîd, the "Commander of the Believers," stating that he used to spend many times the income of the possessions and [crown-] domains he held, for the purpose of attaining his ambition,[1] and upon the slaves and other dependents he kept. He added that it was legal for the "Commander of the Believers" to appropriate the money of his brother. These letters ar-Rashîd ordered preserved. Now, when Muḥammad died, Ja'far's letters were brought out and used as an argument against him. Muḥammad had no other brother from his father and mother than Ja'far. The latter acknowledged that they were his letters; and so the possessions passed to ar-Rashîd, who gave Bâlis and its villages as fief to al-Ma'mûn, after whom they passed to his son.

Mu'âdh advises against the division of the land. Hishâm ibn-'Ammâr from 'Abdallâh ibn-Ḳais al-Hamdâni:—When 'Umar ibn-al-Khaṭṭâb came to al-Jâbiyah and wanted to divide the land among the Moslems, on the ground that it was taken by force, Mu'âdh ibn-Jabal objected saying, "By Allah, if thou dividest the land, the result will certainly be unfavorable. The great part will be in the hands of these people, who will pass away, and the whole will 152
become the possession of one man. Others will come after

[1] The caliphate; Athîr, vol. vi, p. 82.

them, who will bravely defend Islâm, but find nothing left. Seek therefore some plan that suits those who come first as well as those who come last." 'Umar acted according to the suggestion of Mu'âdh.

The chief of Buṣra tells a lie regarding the tax. Al-Ḥusain ibn-'Ali ibn-al-Aswad al-'Ijli from Salamah-l-Juhani's uncle:—The chief of Busra recounted that he had capitulated to the Moslems, agreeing to offer food, oil and vinegar. 'Umar asked that a statement be written down to that effect; but abu-'Ubaidah showed that the chief of Busra was telling an untruth and said, "The fact is that we made terms by which certain things should be sent to the winter quarters of the Moslems." Then 'Umar decreed that a poll-tax be assessed graded according to the various classes,[1] and that *kharâj* be imposed upon the land.

'Umar fixes the tax. Al-Husain from Aslam, a freedman of 'Umar:—'Umar wrote to the tax-collectors instructing them to levy poll-tax only on those who were adult, and he fixed it at four *dînârs* on those who possessed gold. He also assessed on them a subsistence tax by which each Moslem in Syria and Mesopotamia would receive two modii of wheat, and three *kists* of oil, and the right to be entertained as a guest for three days.

The tithe-lands of Syria. Abu-Ḥafs ash-Shâmi from Makḥûl[2]:—Every piece of "tithe-land" in Syria is one whose people had evacuated it, and which had been given as fief to the Moslems, who, by the permission of the governors, cultivated it after it had lain as waste land claimed by no one.

[1] De Goeje, *Mémoire*, p. 150.

[2] Ḥajar, vol. iii, p. 935.

CHAPTER XIII

Cyprus

The first conquest of Cyprus. According to al-Wâḳidi and others, the first expedition against Cyprus was led in sea by Mu'âwiyah ibn-abi-Sufyân. This was the first time the Moslems sailed in the Mediterranean. Mu'âwiyah had asked 'Umar's permission to lead a naval expedition, but 'Umar refused.[1] When 'Uthmân ibn-'Affân became caliph, Mu'âwiyah wrote again asking permission to invade Cyprus, informing him about its proximity and the ease of acquiring it. In answer to this, 'Uthmân wrote, " I have seen the
answer 'Umar gave when thou madest the request from him 153
to lead a sea-expedition." In the year 27, Mu'âwiyah again wrote to 'Uthmân, referring to the ease with which the sea could be crossed to Cyprus. 'Uthmân wrote back this time saying, " If thou sailest with thy wife, we allow thee to do so; otherwise, not." Accordingly, Mu'âwiyah embarked from Acre with a large number of ships, accompanied by his wife Fâkhitah daughter of Ḳaraẓah[2] ibn-'Abd-'Amr ibn-Naufal ibn-'Abd-Manâf ibn-Ḳuṣai. Likewise, 'Ubâdah ibn-aṣ-Ṣâmit took his wife umm-Ḥarâm of the *Anṣâr,* daughter of Milḥân. This took place in the year 28, after the cessation of the rainy season; others say, in the year 29. When the Moslems arrived in Cyprus and landed on its shore (Cyprus being an island 80 x 80 parasangs), its

[1] Ṭabari, vol. i, pp. 2820-2821.

[2] Duraid, p. 55.

Archon [Urkûn] demanded to make terms of capitulation, which was considered unavoidable by the people. Mu'âwiyah made terms with them on 7,200 *dînârs* to be paid annually by them. Similar terms had been made with them by the Greeks. Thus the people of Cyprus pay two tributes. It was made a condition that the Moslems would not prevent them from paying the tribute to the Greeks; on the other hand the Moslems made it a condition that they would not fight [1] those who may come after them to subjugate the Cyprians, and that the Cyprians would keep the Moslems informed regarding the movement of their enemy—the Greeks. Thus when the Moslems used to undertake an expedition by sea, they did not molest the Cyprians. They were not supported by the Cyprians; nor did the Cyprians support any one against them.

The second invasion by Mu'âwiyah. In the year 32, however, the Cyprians offered ships as an aid to the Greeks in an expedition in the sea. Consequently, Mu'âwiyah invaded them in the year 33 with 500 ships. He took Cyprus by force, slaughtering and taking prisoners. He then confirmed them in the terms that were previously made, and sent to the island 12,000 men of those whose names were recorded in the register [Ar. *dîwân*] [2] and erected mosques in it. Moreover, Mu'âwiyah transplanted from Ba'labakk a group of men, and erected a city on the island, whose inhabitants were assigned special stipends until the death of Mu'âwiyah. His son Yazîd, who succeeded him, sent the troops back and ordered the city destroyed.

According to other reports, the second invasion of Cyprus by Mu'âwiyah was carried out in the year 35.

Why Yazîd withdrew the troops. Muhammad ibn-Musaffa-l-Ḥimṣi from al-Walîd:—Yazîd ibn-Mu'âwiyah

[1] Athîr, vol. iii, p. 74.

[2] And therefore received stipends; al-Muṭarrizi, *al-Mughrib*, p. 187.

was offered a large and considerable sum of money as bribe; and that was why he withdrew the troops from Cyprus, upon which the Cyprians destroyed their city and Mosques. 154

Umm-Ḥarâm dies in Cyprus. Muḥammad ibn-Sa'd from 'Abd-as-Salâm ibn-Mûsa's father:—When Cyprus was invaded for the first time, umm-Ḥarâm, daughter of Milḥân, sailed with her husband, 'Ubâdah ibn-aṣ-Ṣâmit. On their arrival in Cyprus, she disembarked and was offered a mule to ride upon. As she was riding, the mule stumbled; and she was killed. Her tomb in Cyprus is called "the Tomb of the Righteous Woman."[1]

Some of those who took part in the campaign. Among those who joined the campaign with Mu'âwiyah were the following:—Abu-Aiyûb Khâlid ibn-Zaid ibn-Kulaib al-Anṣâri, abu-ad-Dardâ', abu-Dharr al-Ghifâri, 'Ubâdah ibn-aṣ-Ṣâmit, Faḍâlah ibn-'Ubaid al-Anṣâri, 'Umair ibn-Sa'd ibn-'Ubaid al-Anṣâri, Wâthilah ibn-al-Aṣka' al-Kinâni, 'Abdallâh ibn-Bishr al-Mâzini, Shaddâd ibn-Aus ibn-Thâbit (a nephew of Ḥassân ibn-Thâbit), al-Miḳdâd, Ka'b al-Ḥabr ibn-Mâti'[2] and Jubair ibn-Nufair al-Ḥaḍrami.

Mu'âwiyah makes permanent peace. Hishâm ibn-'Ammâr ad-Dimashḳi from Ṣafwân ibn-'Amr:—Mu'âwiyah ibn-abi-Sufyân personally carried out the invasion of Cyprus and was accompanied by his wife. Its conquest, effected by Allah, was complete; and the booty he brought to the Moslems was great. The raids of the Moslems were repeated until Mu'âwiyah in his caliphate concluded permanent terms with the Cyprians to the effect that they pay 7,000 *dînârs* and give advice and warnings to the Moslems regarding their enemy, the Greeks. This or something like it was agreed upon.

[1] *JRAS*, 1897, pp. 81-101.

[2] Nawâwi, p. 523; ibn-Ḳutaibah, *Kitâb al-Ma'ârif*, p. 219.

The Cyprians expelled and returned. Al-Walîd ibn-Yazîd ibn-'Abd-al-Malik expelled many of the Cyprians to Syria, because of a charge of suspicion brought against them. When the Moslems disapproved of the act, Yazîd ibn-al-Walîd ibn-'Abd-al-Malik returned them to their home. In the caliphate of ar-Rashîd, an invasion was led against them by Ḥumaid ibn-Ma'yûf al-Hamdâni because of a rebellion they had started; and many were carried off as prisoners. Later they behaved properly towards the Moslems; and, by ar-Rashîd's orders, their prisoners were returned.

The tax increased. Muḥammad ibn-Sa'd from al-Wâḳidi:—The terms between Mu'âwiyah and the Cyprians were kept in force until the time of 'Abd-al-Malik ibn-Marwân who added 1,000 *dînârs* to their tax. That was the case until the caliphate of 'Umar ibn-'Abd-al-'Azîz who cancelled the addition. When Hishâm ibn-'Abd-al-Malik, 155
however, came to power, he restored it; and it was kept until the caliphate of abu-Ja'far al-Manṣûr, who expressed himself as follows: "We shall, above everyone else, do justice to them, and not enrich ourselves by oppressing them." Accordingly, he restored the terms made by Mu'âwiyah.

'Abd-al-Malik wants to annul the treaty. The following was communicated to me by certain Syrian scholars and abu-'Ubaid al-Ḳâsim ibn-Sallâm:—During the governorship of 'Abd-al-Malik ibn-Ṣâliḥ ibn-'Ali ibn-'Abdallâh ibn-'Abbâs over the frontier cities [Ar. *thughûr*], the Cyprians started a rebellion; and he, therefore, desired to break the covenant made with them. The canonists were numerous, among whom were the following whose opinions he sought: al-Laith ibn-Sa'd, Mâlik ibn-Anas, Sufyân ibn-'Uyainah, Mûsa ibn-A'yan, Ismâ'îl ibn-'Aiyâsh, Yaḥya ibn-Ḥamzah, abu-Isḥâḳ al-Fazâri, and Makhlad ibn-al-Ḥusain. They all answered him.

The opinion of al-Laith. The following is a quotation from the letter of al-Laith ibn-Sa'd: "The Cyprians are being constantly charged by us with infidelity to Moslems and loyalty to Allah's enemies, the Greeks. Allah himself has said:[1] 'Or if thou fear treachery from any people, cast off their treaty in like manner.' He did not say, 'cast not off their treaty until thou art sure of their treachery.' I, therefore, consider it best that thou castest off their treaty and givest them a respite of one year for enforcing the law. Those of them who desire to go and settle in a Moslem land and become *dhimmis,* paying the *kharâj,* may do so; those who desire to emigrate to the land of the Greeks may do so; and those who desire to remain in Cyprus, with the understanding they are hostile, may do so and be considered an enemy to be fought and attacked. To give them a respite of one year would be enough to refute any protest they may make, and to prove our loyalty to the covenant."

The opinion of Mâlik. The following statement was written by Mâlik ibn-Anas:—"Our peace with the Cyprians is of old standing and carefully observed [? Ar. *mutaẓâhar*] by the governors placed over them, because they considered the terms a humiliation and belittlement to the Cyprians, and a source of strength to the Moslems, in view of the tax paid to them and the chance they had of attacking their enemy. Yet I know of no governor who broke their terms or expelled them from their city. I, therefore, consider it best to hesitate in breaking their covenant and casting off their treaty until the evidence [of disloyalty] is well established against them, for Allah says:[2] 'Observe, therefore, the engagement with them through the whole time of their treaty.' If, after that, they do not behave properly and 156
abandon their deceit, and thou art convinced of their perfidy,

[1] Kor., 8:60.

[2] Kor., 9:4.

then thou mayest attack them. In that case, the attack would be justified and would be crowned with success; and they would suffer humiliation and disgrace, by Allah's will."

The opinion of Sufyân ibn-'Uyainah. This is what Sufyân ibn-'Uyainah wrote: "We know of no one who made a covenant with the Prophet and violated it, without having the Prophet consider it legal to put him to death, except the people of Makkah. Their case was a favor on the part of the Prophet. Their violation consisted in rendering aid to their allies against the Khuzâ'ah, the Prophet's allies. One of the terms stipulated against the people of Najrân was not to practise usury; but when they did practise it, 'Umar decreed that they be expelled. Thus by 'the consensus of opinion' [Ar. *ijmâ'*], he who violates a covenant forfeits the right of being entitled to security."

The opinion of Mûsa ibn-A'yan. Mûsa ibn-A'yan wrote:—"Similar cases took place in the past, but in each case the governors would grant a period of respite; and so far as I know, none of the early men ever broke a covenant with the Cyprians or any other people. It may be that the common people and the mass among the Cyprians had no hand in what their leaders did. I, therefore, consider it best to abide by the covenant and fulfil the conditions thereof, in spite of what they have done. I have heard al-Auzâ'i say regarding the case of some, who, after making terms with the Moslems, conveyed information about their secret things and pointed them out to the 'unbelievers': 'If they are *dhimmis*, they have thereby violated their covenant and forfeited their claim on security, making it right for the governor to kill or crucify them, if he so desires; but if they had been taken by capitulation and are not entitled to the Moslem's security, then the governor would cast off their treaty, for Allah loveth not the machinations of the deceivers.'[1]"

[1] *Cf.* Kor., 12: 52.

Ismâ'îl ibn-'Aiyâsh's opinion. The following is what Ismâ'îl ibn-'Aiyâsh wrote: "The people of Cyprus are humiliated and oppressed and they are subjugated, together with their wives, by the Greeks. It is therefore proper for us to defend and protect them. In the covenant of the people of Taflîs, Ḥabîb ibn-Maslamah wrote, 'In case something should arise to divert the attention of the Moslems from you and some enemy should subjugate you, that would not be a violation of your covenant, so long as ye keep loyal to the Moslems.' I, therefore, consider it best that they be left on their covenant and the security promised them, especially because when al-Walîd ibn-Yazîd expelled them to Syria, the Moslems considered the act outrageous, and the canonists disapproved of it; so much so that when Yazîd ibn-al-Walîd ibn-'Abd-al-Malik came to power, he restored them to Cyprus, which act was approved of by the Moslems and considered just."

Yaḥya ibn-Ḥamzah's opinion. The following was the statement issued by Yaḥya ibn-Ḥamzah: "The case of Cyprus is parallel to that of 'Arbassûs[1] in which it has a 157
good example and a precedent to be followed. This is the case of 'Arbassûs: 'Umair ibn-Sa'd once came to 'Umar ibn-al-Khaṭṭâb saying, 'There lies between us and the Greeks a city called 'Arbassûs, whose people disclose to our enemy our secrets, but do not disclose to us our enemy's.' 'Umar replied, 'When thou goest there, propose to give them for every ewe they possess two; for every cow, two; and for everything, two. If they consent, give that to them, expel them from the city and raze it to the ground. But if they refuse, then cast off their treaty to them and give them one year at the expiration of which thou mayest destroy the city.' 'Umair went to the city; and its people refused the

[1] Yâkût, vol. iii, p. 633.

offer. He, therefore, gave them one year at the expiration of which he destroyed it. The people of 'Arbassûs had a covenant similar to that of the people of Cyprus. To leave the Cyprians on the terms made with them and to have the Moslems use in their own cause what they receive [as tax] from the Cyprians is preferable. All holders of covenant, for the sake of whom the Moslems are not supposed to fight and on whom the Moslem regulations are not binding, are not *dhimmis* but 'people of tribute'[1] to be spared so long as they are worthy, to be treated according to the covenant so long as they abide by it and consent to it, and to be forgiven so long as they pay their dues. It is reported that Mu'âdh ibn-Jabal always hated to have the enemy capitulate on definite terms unless the Moslems were by the force of circumstances compelled to make terms, because no one could tell whether such capitulation would be of value and strength for the Moslems."

The opinion of abu-Isḥâḳ and Makhlad. Abu-Isḥâḳ al-Fazâri and Makhlad ibn-al-Ḥusain wrote as follows:—"We can find nothing more similar to the case of Cyprus than the case of 'Arbassûs and the decision of 'Umar ibn-al-Khaṭṭâb regarding it. 'Umar gave them two alternatives to choose from: a double fold of what they possessed and the evacuation of the city, or a respite of one year after casting off their treaty. Having rejected the former proposition, they were given one year at the end of which the city was destroyed. Al-Auzâ'i repeated a tradition to the effect that when Cyprus was conquered, the *status quo* of the people was kept, and terms were made on 14,000 *dînârs* of which 7,000 should go to the Moslems and 7,000 to the Greeks: and it was stipulated that the Cyprians should not

[1] Ar. *ahl fidyah*, who are governed by their own laws and pay something to be let alone. For *fidyah* see at-Tahânawi, *Kashf Iṣṭilâḥât al-Funûn*, vol. ii, p. 1157.

disclose to the Greeks the condition of the Moslems.[1] Al-Auzâ'i used to say, 'The Cyprians did not abide by the terms they made with us.' But we consider them as 'people bound to us by covenant,' whose terms of peace involve rights to them and obligations on them, and the 158
violation of which is legal only if they do some thing that shows their perfidy and treachery."

[1] Evidently there is a mistake in the text. The negative particle "*la*" is superfluous.

CHAPTER XIV

THE SAMARITANS

The terms made by abu-'Ubaidah. Hishâm ibn-'Ammâr from Ṣafwân ibn-'Amr: — Abu-'Ubaidah ibn-al-Jarrâḥ made terms with the Samaritans in the provinces of the Jordan and Palestine, who acted as spies and guides for the Moslems, stipulating that they pay tax on their persons but nothing on their lands. When Yazîd ibn-Mu'âwiyah, however, assumed power he assessed *kharâj* on their lands.

The tax imposed by Yazîd. I was informed by certain men well versed in the conditions of the Jordan and Palestine that Yazîd ibn-Mu'âwiyah assessed *kharâj* on the lands of the Samaritans in the Jordan, and levied on every man two *dînârs* as poll-tax. He also assessed *kharâj* on their lands in Palestine and levied five *dînârs* on every man.

Sects. The Samaritans are Jews and are divided into two classes, one is called ad-Dustân [Dositheans] and the other al-Kûshân.[1]

Their lands become crown-land. There was in Palestine in the early part of the caliphate of ar-Rashîd a devastating plague which in some cases would attack all the members of a household. As a result, their land was rendered waste and useless. Ar-Rashîd put it in charge of some who cultivated it and [by gifts] attracted the farmers and tenants into it, thus making it crown domains. In these places the

[1] *Cf.* Al-Makrîzi, *al-Khiṭaṭ*, vol. iv, p. 371; *The Jewish Encyclopaedia*, *s. v.* "Samaritans"; J. A. Montgomery, *History of the Samaritans*, p. 253 *seq.*; De Sacy, *Chrestom.*, vol. i, pp. 305, 341-344.

Samaritans lived. One of those villages called Bait-Mâma, which lay in the district of Nâbulus and whose inhabitants were Samaritans, made a complaint in the year 246 to the effect that they were poor and unable to pay the five-*dînâr kharâj*, upon which al-Mutawakkil gave orders that it be reduced again to three.

Mu'âwiyah spares the hostages. Hishâm ibn-'Ammâr
from Ṣafwân ibn-'Amr and Sa'îd ibn-'Abd-al-'Azîz:— 159
The Greeks made peace with Mu'âwiyah with the stipulation that he pay them a certain sum of money. Mu'âwiyah took hostages from them and held them in Ba'labakk. The Greeks proved perfidious to Mu'âwiyah, but still the Moslems did not consider it legal to put the hostages in their hands to death; and so they set them free, saying, "Loyalty against perfidy is better than perfidy against perfidy." According to Hishâm, al-Auzâ'i, among other authorities, maintains the same view.

CHAPTER XV

Al-Jarâjimah

The treaty with al-Jarâjimah. I am informed by certain *sheikhs* from Antioch that al-Jarâjimah [1] were the inhabitants of a town called al-Jurjûmah [2] lying between Baiyâs and Bûḳa on mount al-Lukâm [Amanus] near Ma'din az-Zâj [vitriol pit]. While the Greeks held the authority over Syria and Antioch, the Jarâjimah were under the rule of the patrician and governor of Antioch. When abu-'Ubaidah came and reduced Antioch, they confined themselves to their city and, in their anxiety to save their lives, they tried to go and join the Greeks. The Moslems took no note of them, nor did any one call their attention to them. When later the people of Antioch violated their covenant and acted treacherously, abu-'Ubaidah sent and conquered Antioch once more, after which he made Ḥabîb ibn-Maslamah-l-Fihri its governor. Ḥabîb attacked al-Jurjûmah, whose people did not resist but immediately sought for peace and capitulation. Terms were made providing that al-Jarâjimah would act as helpers to the Moslems, and as spies and frontier garrison in Mount al-Lukâm. On the other hand it was stipulated that they pay no tax, and that they keep for themselves the booty [3] they take from the enemy in case they fight with the Moslems. In these terms were in-

[1] Less correctly Jurâjimah. They are identical with the Mardaites; Lammens, *MFO*, vol. i, p. 17.

[2] *Encyclopaedia of Islâm*, vol. i, *s. v.*, "Djarâdjima".

[3] Ar. *nafl*. See Muṭarrizi, p. 80.

cluded besides the Jarâjimah all those who lived in their city, as well as the merchants, employees and dependents, whether Nabateans or not, together with the inhabitants of the villages. These were called "*ar-Rawâdîf*"[1] because they were included in the terms with the Jarâjimah though not of their number. Others say they were so called because they came riding behind al-Jarâjimah when the latter presented themselves in the Moslem camp. On certain occasions, al-Jarâjimah acted properly with respect to the [Moslem] governors; but on others, they deviated from the right path and held friendly communications with the 160
Greeks.

'Abd-al-Malik agrees to pay them a certain sum. In the days of ibn-az-Zubair, when Marwân ibn-al-Ḥakam died and 'Abd-al-Malik, who was appointed by Marwân as heir-apparent, wished to succeed Marwân in the caliphate and was ready to leave for al-'Irâḳ to fight against al-Muṣ'ab ibn-az-Zubair, certain Greek horsemen went forth to Mt. al-Lukâm under a Greek leader and started for the Lebanon, after having been joined by a large body of al-Jarâjimah, Nabateans, and runaway slaves once possessed by the Moslems. Under these conditions, 'Abd-al-Malik had to make terms with them, agreeing to pay 1,000 *dînârs* per week. He also made terms with the Greek "tyrant," agreeing to pay him a sum of money, because 'Abd-al-Malik was too busy to fight against him, and because he feared that in case the "tyrant" came to Syria, he might overpower him. In this, he followed the precedent of Mu'âwiyah who, being engaged in the fight in al-'Irâḳ, agreed to pay something to them [the Greeks], and took hostages from them, whom he held in Ba'labakk. All this synchronized with the attempt made by 'Amr ibn-Sa'îd ibn-al-'Âṣi to secure the caliphate

[1] Followers, dependents.

and his closing the gates of Damascus immediately after
'Abd-al-Malik had left the city, which made Abd-al-Malik
still more busy. This took place in the year 70.

Suḥaim slays the Greek general. After that, 'Abd-al-
Malik sent to the Greek leader Suhaim ibn-al-Muhâjir
who, in disguise and through gentle behavior, succeeded in
reaching him. Suḥaim played the act of a friend and won
the favor of the leader by censuring 'Abd-al-Malik. cursing him and dwelling on his weak points, so much so that
the leader put full confidence in Suḥaim and was wholly
deceived. At the favorable moment, however, Suḥaim fell
upon him with a band of troops and freedmen of 'Abd-al-
Malik, who had been previously prepared for the attack and
stationed in a convenient place, and killed him together with
the Greeks who were with him. Suhaim thereupon announced publicly a promise of security to those who had
joined the Greek leader. Accordingly, the Jarâjimah were
partly scattered among the villages of Ḥimṣ and Damascus;
but the majority returned to their city on al-Lukâm. In
like manner, the Nabateans returned to their villages, and
the slaves to their masters.

Maimûn al-Jurjumâni. One of these slaves was Maimûn
al-Jurjumâni, a Greek slave, who belonged to the banu-umm-
al-Hakam (umm-al-Ḥakam being the sister of Mu'âwiyah
ibn-abi-Sufyân) who were of the tribe of Thakîf. The
slave was named after al-Jarâjimah, because he mixed with
them and rebelled with them in Mt. Lebanon. Hearing
of his strength and valor, 'Abd-al-Malik asked his masters
to set him free, which they did. He was then put by 'Abd-
al-Malik at the head of a regiment of troops and stationed
at Antioch. With 1,000 men from Antioch, he and Maslamah ibn-'Abd-al-Malik led an invasion to aṭ-Ṭuwânah.[1]

[1] Yâkût, vol. iii, p. 554.

After fighting valiantly and standing gallantly, he fell a martyr. This so much grieved 'Abd-al-Malik that he sent a large army against the Greeks to avenge his death.

Al-Walîd makes terms with them. In the year 89, al-Jarâjimah gathered themselves into their city and were joined by a host of Greeks from Alexandretta [Iskandarûnah] and Rûsis.[1] Consequently, al-Walîd ibn-'Abd-al-Malik sent against them Maslamah ibn-'Abd-al-Malik, who fell upon them with a host of Moslems and reduced their city on the following terms: Al-Jarâjimah may settle wherever they wished in Syria, each one of them receiving eight *dînârs*, and each family receiving the fixed provisions of wheat and oil, *i. e.*, two modii of wheat and two *ḳisṭs* of oil; neither they nor any of their children or women should be compelled to leave Christianity; they may put on Moslem dress; and no poll-tax may be assessed on them, their children or women. On the other hand, they should take part in the Moslem campaigns and be allowed to keep for themselves the booty from those whom they kill in a duel; and the same amount taken from the possession of the Moslems should be taken [as tax] from their articles of trade and from the possessions of the wealthy among them. Then Maslamah destroyed their city and settled them in Mt. al-Ḥûwâr, Sunḥ al-Lûlûn [?] and 'Amḳ Tîzîn. Some of them left for Ḥimṣ. The patrician of al-Jurjûmah accompanied by a body of men, after taking up his abode in Antioch fled to the Byzantine Empire.

Al-Wâthiḳ cancels the poll-tax. When a certain *'âmil* held al-Jarâjimah of Antioch responsible for poll-tax, they brought their case before al-Wâthiḳ-Billâh at the time of his caliphate, and he ordered it cancelled.

Al-Mutawakkil levies tax. I was informed by a writer

[1] Yâḳût, vol. ii, p. 840.

in whom I have full confidence that al-Mutawakkil ordered that poll-tax be levied on these Jarâjimah and that the regular allowance for food be given them, because, among other things, they were of value in the frontier garrisons.

Al-Jarâjimah molest the summer expeditions. It is claimed by abu-l-Khaṭṭâb al-Azdi that in the days of 'Abd-al-Malik, the people of al-Jurjûmah used to make razzias against the villages of Antioch and al-'Amḳ; and whenever 162
the summer expedition was carried out, al-Jarâjimah would cut off those who lagged behind or followed, together with any whom they could cut off at the rear of the army. They went so far against the Moslems that, by 'Abd-al-Malik's orders, certain people from Antioch and some Nabateans were given stipends, placed as garrisons and set behind the armies of the summer expeditions in order to repel al-Jarâjimah from the rear. Therefore those set behind the armies of the summer expedition were called *rawâdîf, i. e.*, followers, and to every one of them eight *dînârs* were assigned. The former account is more authentic.

Az-Zuṭṭ. Abu-Ḥafs ash-Shâmi from Makḥûl:—Mu'âwiyah transplanted in the year 49 or 50 to the sea-coast some of the Zuṭṭ and Sayâbijah [1] of al-Baṣrah, and made some of them settle in Antioch. According to abu-Ḥafṣ, there is in Antioch a quarter known by the name of az-Zuṭṭ. Some of their descendants are in Bûḳa in the province of Antioch and are known by the name of az-Zuṭṭ.

Some of the Zuṭṭ of as-Sind [2] were carried by Muḥammad ibn-al-Ḳâsim to al-Ḥajjâj, who sent them to Syria, and were later transplanted by al-Walîd ibn-'Abd-al-Malik to Antioch.

Lebanon rebels. Muḥammad ibn-Sa'd from al-Wâḳidi:—

[1] *Kâmil*, p. 41, line 3; p. 82, line 17; De Goeje, *Mémoires sur les Migrations des Tsiganes*, pp. 1-32, 86-91.

[2] Ḥauḳal, p. 226.

Some people in Lebanon rebelled, complaining of the collector of the *kharâj* of Ba'labakk. This made Ṣâliḥ ibn-'Ali ibn-'Abdallâh ibn-'Abbâs send against them troops who destroyed their fighting power, and the rest were allowed to retain their [Christian] faith. Ṣâliḥ sent the latter back to their villages and expelled some of the natives of Lebanon. Al-Ḳâsim ibn-Sallâm related to me on the authority of Muḥammad ibn-Kathîr that Ṣâliḥ received a long communication from al-Auzâ'i, of which the following extract has been preserved: "Thou hast heard of the expulsion of the *dhimmis* from Mt. Lebanon, although they did not side with those who rebelled, and of whom many were killed by thee and the rest returned to their villages. How didst thou then punish the many for the fault of the few and make them leave their homes and possessions in spite of Allah's decree:[1] 'Nor shall any sinning one bear the burden of another,' which is the most rightful thing to abide by and follow! The command worthy of the strictest observance and obedience is that of the Prophet who says, 'If one oppresses a man bound to us by covenant and charges him with more than he can do, I am the one to overcome him by arguments.'"[2] To this he added other citations.

The frontier and littoral towns fortified. Muḥammad ibn-Sahm al-Anṭâki from abu-Isḥâḳ al-Fazâri:—The banu- 163
Umaiyah used to direct their summer and winter campaigns against the Greeks beyond the frontier cities of Syria and Mesopotamia by means of Syrians and Mesopotamians, and they used to station the ships for the invasion and to post the guard on the coast, giving up or delaying the invasion at the time in which the enemy was strong and wide awake [?]. When abu-Ja'far al-Manṣûr began his rule, he examined the

[1] Kor., 6: 164.

[2] As-Suyûti, *Kanz al-'Ummâl*, I, 270.

forts and cities of the coast, peopled and fortified them, and rebuilt those of them that were in need of being rebuilt. The same thing he did with the frontier cities. When al-Mahdi became caliph, he carried the work in the remaining cities and forts to completion and strengthened the garrisons. Mu'âwiyah ibn-'Amr states, "What we saw of the efforts of Hârûn the 'Commander of the Believers' in conducting invasions, and of his penetrating insight in carrying on the holy war was really great. The industries he established were not established heretofore. He distributed possessions in the frontier and coast cities. He brought distress on the Greeks and humiliated them." Caliph al-Mutawakkil ordered in the year 247 that ships be stationed on all the sea-coast and that garrisons be posted on it.

CHAPTER XVI

The Frontier Fortresses[1] of Syria

Moslem razzias beyond the frontiers. I was informed by certain *sheikhs* from Antioch and bv others that in the days of 'Umar and 'Uthmân, and after their time, the frontier cities of Syria included Antioch and other cities called later al-'Awâṣim by ar-Rashîd. The Moslems used to lead their raids beyond these cities as they now raid what is beyond Ṭarsûs. Between Alexandretta and Ṭarsûs lay Greek forts and frontier garrisons, similar to those through which the Moslems now pass, and the inhabitants of which would sometimes, because of fear, leave them and flee to the Byzantine Empire, and sometimes, Byzantine fighters would be brought and stationed in them. It is said that when Heraclius left Antioch, he joined to himself the people of these towns, so that the Moslems might not be able to go between Antioch and the land of the Byzantines through a cultivated land.

Ibn-Ṭaibûn[2] al-Baghrâsi from certain *sheikhs*:—The latter said, "What is known to us is that Heraclius moved the 164
men from these forts, which he shattered. So, when the Moslems made their raids, they found them vacant. In certain cases the Greeks would make an ambush by these forts and take by surprise those of the army who were held back or cut off. Thus the leaders of the summer and winter campaigns, on entering the Greek land, would leave heavy troops in these forts until their return."

[1] Ar. *thughûr*; see Iṣṭakhri, pp. 55-56.

[2] ? Lacking in diacritical points.

The first to pass through ad-Darb. Regarding the first one to cross ad-Darb,[1] *i. e.*, Darb Baghrâs [2] there is a disagreement. Some assert that the first was Maisarah ibn-Masrûḳ al-'Absi who was despatched by abu-'Ubaidah ibn-al-Jarrâḥ and who met a host of Greeks accompanied by the "naturalized" [*musta'ribah*] Arabs of the Ghassân, Tanûkh and Iyâd, trying to follow Heraclius [in Asia Minor]. Maisarah fell upon them and wrought a bloody massacre among them. He was later joined by Mâlik al-Ashtar an-Nakha'i sent as a reinforcement by abu-'Ubaidah from Antioch.

According to others, the first to cross ad-Darb was 'Umar ibn-Sa'd al-Anṣâri, when he was sent in connection with the case of Jabalah ibn-al-Aiham.

According to abu-l-Khaṭṭâb al-Azdi, abu-'Ubaidah himself led the summer expedition passing through al-Maṣṣîṣah and then through Ṭarsûs whose people, together with those of the fortified cities lying beyond, had evacuated their places. Thus abu-'Ubaidah entered the land of the [Greek] enemy and carried his campaign as far as Zandah. According to others, abu-'Ubaidah did not himself go, but sent Maisarah ibn-Masrûḳ, who reached as far as Zandah.

Mu'âwiyah and the forts. Abu-Ṣâliḥ al-Farrâ' from one supposed by him to have been 'Ubâdah ibn-Nusai:—When Mu'âwiyah in the year 25 invaded 'Ammûriyah [Amorium], he found the forts between Antioch and Tarsûs all vacant. He therefore left in those forts some men from Syria, Mesopotamia and Ḳinnasrîn until he had finished his expedition. One or two years later, he sent Yazîd ibn-al-Ḥurr al-'Absi at the head of the summer expedition and

[1] "Gr. *Derbe* near the Cilician gates which were the chief mountain pass from the direction of the countries occupied by the Arabs into the territory of the Greeks"—Lane. See Caetani, vol. iii, p. 805.

[2] Perhaps Bailân pass of to-day.

instructed him to do the same thing, which Yazîd did. All the governors used to do the same.

The same authority says, "I read in the book of *Maghâzi Mu'âwiyah* [Mu'âwiyah's campaigns] that Mu'âwiyah in the year 31 led an invasion setting out from near al-Maṣṣîṣah and penetrating as far as Daraulîyah. On his return, he destroyed all the fortresses [belonging to the 165
Greeks] between the latter place and Antioch.

Al-Maṣṣîṣah. Muḥammad ibn-Sa'd from al-Wâkidi and others:—In the year 84, 'Abdallâh ibn-'Abd-al-Malik ibn-Marwân led the summer campaign, entered through the Darb Anṭâkiyah and reached al-Maṣṣîṣah [Mopsuestia], where he rebuilt the fort on its old foundations. In this city, he caused troops to settle, among whom were 300 chosen from those known to be among the most valorous and strong. The Moslems had never lived in this town before. He also built a mosque in it over Tall al-Ḥiṣn [the hill of the fort], and then led his army to the invasion of Sinân fort, which he reduced. He then sent Yazîd ibn-Ḥunain aṭ-Ṭâ'i-l-Anṭâki who led an incursion and returned.

Abu-l-Khaṭṭâb al-Azdi holds that the first Moslem to build the fort of al-Maṣṣîṣah[1] was 'Abd-al-Malik ibn-Marwân through his son 'Abdallâh in the year 84 on its old foundation. Its building and manning were completed in the year 85. In this fortified town stood a church which was converted into a granary. The troops [Ar. *ṭawâli'*] from Antioch, numbering 1,500-2,000, used to go up to it every year and spend the winter in it, at the end of which they would leave.

When 'Umar ibn-'Abd-al-'Azîz came to the granary of al-Maṣṣîṣah, he wanted to destroy the town together with the forts that lay between it and Antioch saying, "I hate

[1] Hamadhâni, p. 112.

to see the Greeks besieging its people." When he, however, learned that the town was built to check the Greek advance on Antioch, and that, in case it was destroyed, nothing would remain to stop the enemy from taking Antioch, he desisted and erected for its people a cathedral mosque in the Kafarbaiya quarter. In the mosque, he made a cistern whereon his name was inscribed. In the caliphate of al-Mu'tasim-Billâh, the mosque, which was called Masjid al-Ḥiṣn [the fort mosque], fell into ruins.

Hishâm ibn-'Abd-al-Malik built the part outside the city wall [Ar. *rabaḍ*]; and Marwân ibn-Muhammad built, to the east of Jaihân,[1] al-Khusûs [wood houses], around which he erected a wall with a wooden gate, and dug a moat.

When abu-l-'Abbâs became caliph, he assigned stipends for 400 men to be added to the garrison at al-Maṣṣiṣah, and distributed fiefs among them. When al-Mansûr became 166
caliph, he assigned stipends for 400 men at al-Maṣṣiṣah. In the year 139, al-Mansûr ordered that the city of al-Massîsah, the wall of which had become shattered by earthquakes and whose population within the walls had become few in number, be well populated. Accordingly, in the year 140, he built the wall of the city, made its inhabitants settle in it and called it al-Ma'mûrah. Moreover, al-Manṣûr erected a cathedral mosque in it on the site of a heathen temple, and made it many times the size of the mosque of 'Umar. Al-Ma'mûn enlarged the mosque in the governorship of 'Abdallâh ibn-Tâhir ibn-al-Husain over al-Maghrib. Al-Manṣûr assigned stipends for 1,000 men of its inhabitants. Besides, he transplanted [into it] the inhabitants of al-Khusûs, who were Persians, Slavs and Christian Nabateans—all of whom were settled in al-Khusûs by Marwân—gave them in it lots marked for dwell-

[1] Pyramus river.

ings in exchange for and of the same measure as their old homes, pulled down their old dwellings and helped them to build the new ones. To these soldiers, who received stipends, al-Manṣûr gave fiefs and dwellings.

When al-Mahdi became caliph, he assigned stipends for 2,000 men at al-Maṣṣîṣah but gave them no fiefs, because the city was already manned with troops and volunteers. The periodical contingents [*ṭawâli'*] used to come from Antioch every year until the city was governed by Sâlim al-Barallusi, who assigned in their place[1] stipends for 500 fighters, making a special rate of 10 *dînârs* for each. Thus the people of the city were multiplied and strengthened. This took place when al-Mahdi held the caliphate.

Muḥammad ibn-Sahm from the *sheikhs* of the frontier region:—In the days of the "blessed dynasty", the Greeks pressed the inhabitants of al-Maṣṣîṣah so hard that they left the city. After that Ṣâliḥ ibn-'Ali sent to it Jabrîl ibn-Yaḥya-l-Bajali who peopled it and made Moslems settle in it in the year 140. Ar-Rashîd[2] built Kafarbaiya; but according to others it was begun in the caliphate of al-Mahdi, and ar-Rashîd changed the plan of its construction and fortified it with a moat. Its inhabitants complained to al-Ma'mûn concerning the rent[3] paid for the houses therein, and he abolished it. The houses were like inns. By order of al-Ma'mûn, a wall was commenced around the city and raised high, but not completed before his death. Al-Mu'taṣim-Billâh ordered that the wall be finished and raised to its proper height.

Al-Muthaḳḳab. Al-Muthaḳḳab[4] was fortified by Hishâm

[1] Read *mauḍi'aha* in place of *mauḍi'ahu.*

[2] Mas'ûdi, vol. viii, p. 295.

[3] Ar *ghallah, i. e.*, rent due for houses built on the state property.

[4] Iṣṭakhri, p. 63; Ḥauḳal, p. 121.

ibn-'Abd-al-Malik, who entrusted the work to Ḥassân ibn-Mâhawaih al-Anṭâki. As the moat was being dug, a leg-bone of extraordinary length was found and sent to Hi-shâm. 167

Ḳaṭarghâsh, Mûrah and Baghrâs. Hishâm also had Ḳaṭarghâsh fort built by 'Abd-al-'Azîz ibn-Ḥaiyân al-Anṭâki. He also had Mûrah fort erected by a man from Antioch. This last fort was built because the Greeks had interfered with one of his messengers at Darb al-Lukâm near al-'Aḳabah-l-Baiḍa. In this fort, he stationed forty men and a body of al-Jarâjimah. In Baghrâs [Pagrae] he established a garrison of fifty men and built a fort for it. Hishâm, moreover, built the Bûḳa fort in the province of Antioch, which was recently renewed and repaired.

After the Greeks had made a raid on the littoral of the province of Antioch in the caliphate of al-Mu'taṣim-Billâh, a fort was built on that littoral by Muḥammad ibn-Yûsuf al-Marwazi, surnamed abu-Sa'îd.

'Umar intends to destroy al-Maṣṣîṣah. Dâ'ûd ibn-'Abd-al-Ḥamîd, the *ḳâḍi* of ar-Raḳḳah, from a grandfather of his:—'Umar ibn-'Abd-al-'Azîz intended to destroy al-Maṣṣîṣah and move its inhabitants because they suffered so much from the Greeks; but he died before he could accomplish it.

'Aḳabat an-Nisâ'. I was informed by certain men from Antioch and Baghrâs that when Maslamah ibn-'Abd-al-Malik invaded 'Ammûriyah, he took his wives with him; and other men in his army did the same. The banu-Umaiyah used to do that in order to infuse enthusiasm in the army by making them jealous for their harem. As Maslamah was passing through 'Akabat [1] Baghrâs on a narrow road that bordered on a valley, a stretcher in which a woman was carried fell down to the foot of the mountain. This made

[1] A place difficult of ascent.

Maslamah order that all women should go on foot. So they did; and that 'Aḳabat was, therefore, called "'Aḳabat an-Nisâ'" [the women's 'Akabat]. Previous to this, al-Mu'taṣim had built on the edge of that road a low stone wall.

The roads of Antioch cleared of lions by means of buffaloes. It was stated by abu-an-Nu'mân al-Anṭâki that the road between Antioch and al-Maṣṣîṣah was frequented by lions which molested the passers-by. When al-Walîd ibn-'Abd-al-Malik came to rule, the complaint was made to him, and he sent 4,000 buffaloes by which the required result was attained through Allah's help.

Muḥammad ibn-al-Ḳâsim ath-Thaḳafi, the *'âmil* of al-Ḥajjâj over as-Sind, had sent from as-Sind thousands of buffaloes to al-Hajjâj, who gave al-Walîd 4,000 of them, 168
and left the rest in the jungles of Kaskar.[1] When Yazîd ibn-al-Muhallab was deposed and killed, and the possessions of the banu-l-Muhallab were confiscated by Yazîd ibn-'Abd-al-Malik, the latter carried away 4,000 buffaloes, which were in the districts of Dijlah[2] and Kaskar. These, too, Yazîd sent to al-Massîsah together with az-Zuṭṭ sent there. Thus the buffaloes at al-Massîsah were originally 8,000. At the time of the insurrection of Marwân ibn-Muḥammad ibn-Marwân the people of Antioch and Ḳinnasrîn brought under their control and took possession of many of these animals; but when al-Manṣûr became caliph he ordered that they be restored to al-Massîṣah. As for the buffaloes of Antioch, they were first brought by az-Zutt, and so were the first ones of Bûka.

Jisr al-Walîd. According to abu-l-Khaṭṭâb, the bridge on the road of Adhanah [Adana] from al-Massîsah lay nine

[1] Hamadhâni, *Buldân,* p. 196; ibn-Khurdâdhbih, p. 7.

[2] Yâḳût, vol. iii, p. 745.

miles from the latter, was built in the year 125, and was called Jisr al-Walîd after al-Walîd ibn-'Abd-al-Malik, who was slain.

Adhanah. According to abu-an-Nu'mân al-Anṭâki and others, Adhanah was built in the year 141 or 142 as the Khurâsân troops under Maslamah ibn-Yaḥya-l-Bajali, and the Syrian troops under Mâlik ibn-Adham al-Bâhili (all sent by Ṣâliḥ ibn-'Ali) were camping in it.

Saiḥân castle. In the year 165, al-Mahdi sent his son Hârûn ar-Rashîd on an expedition to the Greek Empire. After camping at al-Khalîj, ar-Rashîd went forth and repaired al-Maṣṣîṣah and its mosque, increasing its garrison and arming its inhabitants. He also built the castle which lay by Saiḥân [Saruṣ river] near Adhanah bridge. Previous to this, al-Manṣûr had sent Ṣâliḥ ibn-'Ali on an invasion to the Greek Empire, and the latter sent Hilâl ibn-Daigham, at the head of a group of men from Damascus, the Jordan and other places, who built this castle; but the structure not being firm, ar-Rashîd dismantled the castle and rebuilt it.

Abu-Sulaim rebuilds Adhanah. In the year 194[1] abu-Sulaim Faraj al-Khâdim built Adhanah well and strong, fortified it, and chose men from Khurâsân and others to live in it, giving them an increase of stipends. All that was done by the order of Muḥammad ibn-ar-Rashîd. He also made repairs in Ḳaṣr Saiḥân. When ar-Rashîd died in the year 193, his *'âmil* for collecting tithes from the frontier fortresses was abu-Sulaim who was now confirmed in his position by Muḥammad [ibn-ar-Rashîd]. To this abu-Sulaim belonged the residence in Antioch [that bears his 16
name].

Tarsûs and al-Hadath. Muḥammad ibn-Sa'd from al-

[1] "193" in Yâḳût, vol. i, p. 179, line 19.

Wâkidi:—In the year 162, al-Ḥasan ibn-Ḳaḥṭabah aṭ-Ṭâ'i invaded the land of the Greeks at the head of an army of the people of Khurâsân, Mauṣil,[1] and Syria, reinforced by men from al-Yaman and volunteers from al-'Irâḳ and al-Ḥijâz. He started near Ṭarsûs and called the attention of al-Mahdi to the great troubles spared to Islâm, and the good chance it afforded to frustrate and avert the enemies' intrigues and plans by building Ṭarsûs, fortifying it and stationing a garrison in it. In that campaign, al-Ḥasan distinguished himself and subdued the land of the Greeks, and was therefore called ash-Shaiṭân [the devil]. Among his men in the invasion were Mandal al-'Anazi—the traditionist of the school of al-Kûfah—and Mu'tamir ibn-Sulaimân al-Baṣri.

Muḥammad ibn-Sa'd from Sa'd ibn-al-Ḥasan:—When al-Ḥasan left the land of the Greeks, he camped at Marj [plain of] Ṭarsûs from which he rode to the city, which was then in ruins. After examining it, he went around it in all directions and estimated that it could be inhabited by one hundred thousand.[2] When he appeared before al-Mahdi, he described the condition of the city and referred to the strength that Islâm and the Moslems would acquire, and to the anger and disappointment that will ensue to the enemy, if the city were rebuilt and manned with a garrison. He also told al-Mahdi something about al-Ḥadath that encouraged him to build it. Accordingly, al-Mahdi ordered him to build Ṭarsûs and start with al-Ḥadath, which was immediately built. Al-Mahdi then ordered that Ṭarsûs be built. In the year 171, ar-Rashîd heard that the Greeks had enjoined one another to set forth to Ṭarsûs in order to fortify it and station troops in it. He therefore sent in the year 171 Harthamah ibn-A'yan as commander of the summer campaign and ordered him to build Ṭarsûs, settle people

[1] Hamadhâni, *Buldân*, pp. 26-27, 128.

[2] *Ibid.*, p. 113.

in it and make it a fortified boundary town [1] between the two countries. Harthamah did so, putting the work, in accordance with ar-Rashîd's orders, in charge of Faraj ibn-Sulaim al-Khâdim. Faraj put someone in charge, went to Madînat as-Salâm [2] and sent the first garrison, numbering 3,000, whom he chose from among the people of Khurâsân. The garrison came to Ṭarsûs. He then sent the second garrison that numbered 2,000 men, 1,000 of whom were from al-Maṣṣîṣah and 1,000 from Antioch, promising each man an increment of ten *dînârs* on his original stipend. The second garrison camped with the first at al-Madâ'in near Bâb al-Jihâd, from the beginning of Muḥarram in the year 172, until the construction of the city of Ṭarsûs with its fortification and mosque was completed. Faraj measured the land between the two rivers and found it to be 4,000 lots, each lot being twenty *dhirâ'*s square. These lots he gave as fiefs to the inhabitants of Ṭarsûs. In Rabî' II, 172, the two garrisons settled in the city.

Yazîd ibn-Makhlad governor of Ṭarsûs. 'Abd-al-Malik ibn-Ṣâliḥ appointed Yazîd ibn-Makhlad al-Fazâri as *âmil* over Ṭarsûs. Those of the inhabitants who came from Khurâsân were afraid of him, because he belonged to the clan of al-Hubairîyah, and drove him from the city. He appointed abu-l-Fawâris to succeed him and 'Abd-al-Malik ibn-Ṣâliḥ confirmed abu-l-Fawâris in his position. This took place in the year 173.

Sîsîyah. Muḥammad ibn-Sa'd from al-Wâḳidi:—In the year 194 or 193, the inhabitants of Sîsîyah [or Sîs, later Little Armenia] evacuated their homes and went as far as the mountainous region of the Greeks.[3] This Sîsîyah was

[1] Ar. *miṣr*.

[2] City of peace, *i. e.*, Baghdâd.

[3] Yâḳût, vol. iii, p. 217, gives the date 93 or 94 and reads *a'âli ar-Rûm* instead of *a'la ar-Rûm*.

the city of Tall 'Ain-Zarbah and was rebuilt in the caliphate of al-Mutawakkil by 'Ali ibn-Yaḥya-l-Armani [the Armenian]. It was later ruined by the Greeks.

Antioch burnt. The one who burnt Antioch—condemned as it was to burning [1]—in the land of the Greeks was 'Abbâs ibn-al-Walîd ibn-'Abd- al-Malik.

Tall Jubair. Tall Jubair was so called after a Persian from Antioch who fought a battle in it. The Tall lies less than 10 miles from Ṭarsûs.

Dhu-l-Kilâ'. The name of the fort known as dhu-l-Kilâ' is really a corruption of dhu-l-Ḳilâ' [the fort of the castles], which name was given to it because it was made up of three castles. The explanation of its name in the Greek tongue is "the fortress with the stars."

Kanîsat aṣ-Sulḥ. Kanîsat aṣ-Ṣulḥ [the church of peace] was so called because when the Greeks came to ar-Rashîd to capitulate, they made it their headquarters.

Marj Husain. Marj Ḥusain was named after Ḥusain ibn-Muslim al-Anṭâki who fought a battle in it and defeated the enemy.

Ḍamâlu. In the year 163, al-Mahdi sent on a campaign his son, Hârûn ar-Rashîd, who laid siege to Ḍamâlu (colloquial Samâlu). Its people asked a promise of security for ten of their nobility including the Comes.[2] Ar-Rashîd consented. One of their terms stipulated that they be never separated from one another. Therefore they were settled in Baghdâdh near Bâb ash-Shammâsîyah.[3] Their quarter

[1] Hamadhâni, *Buldân*, p. 37: Said Makḥûl, "Four cities are of the cities of Paradise; Makkah, al-Madînah, Îliyâ' [Jerusalem] and Damascus; and four of the cities of fire: Antioch, aṭ-Ṭuwânah, Constantinople and San'â'."

[2] Ar. *al-Ḳûmis* = a leader of two hundred; Zaidân, vol. i, p. 118; Ḳudâmah, pp. 255-256.

[3] Le Strange, *Baghdâd*, p. 202.

they called Samâlu, and it is still known as such. Others say that they surrendered to al-Mahdi who spared their lives and gathered them in that place, ordering that it be called 171
Samâlu. According to ar-Rashîd's orders, those who were left in the fort were sold publicly.

One Abyssinian, who was heard cursing ar-Rashîd and the Moslems, was crucified on one of the towers of the fort.

'Ain Zarbah and al-Hârûnîyah. Aḥmad ibn-al-Ḥârith al-Wâsiṭi from al-Wâḳidi:—In the year 180, ar-Rashîd ordered that the city of 'Ain Zarbah [Anazarbus] be built and fortified. He summoned to it a regiment from Khurâsân and others, to whom he gave houses as fiefs. In the year 183, he ordered al-Hârûnîyah built. It was accordingly built and manned with a garrison and with volunteers that emigrated to it. The city was named after him. Others say that Hârûn started its erection in the caliphate of al-Mahdi, but completed it in his own caliphate.

Kanîsat as-Saudâ'. The city of Kanîsat as-Saudâ' [black church] had been built by the Greeks of black stone since the earliest of days, and had an old fort that was destroyed in the general havoc. Ar-Rashîd ordered that this city be rebuilt and fortified. He also summoned to it troops, allowing them larger stipends. I was told by 'Azzûn ibn-Sa'd, one of the inhabitants of the frontier region, that the Greeks once invaded it—as al-Ḳâsim ibn-ar-Rashîd was staying in Dâbiḳ—and carried away its cattle and a number of prisoners. They were pursued by the people of al-Maṣṣîṣah and its volunteers, who saved all that had been carried away and killed many of the Greeks, sending the rest of them back in distress and disorder. Then al-Ḳâsim sent some one to fortify the city, make repairs in it and increase its garrison. For this purpose some of az-Zuṭṭ, previously transplanted by al-Mu'taṣim to 'Ain Zarbah and its environs from al-Baṭâ'ih, which lay between Wâsiṭ and al-Baṣrah, and which they had conquered, were available.

Abu-Isḥâḳ al-Fazâri's opinion on the land of ath-Thaghr. I was informed by abu-Ṣâliḥ al-Anṭâki that abu-Isḥâḳ al-Fazâri hated to buy land in the frontier region [*ath-Ṭhaghr*] because he said, "Those who first wrested this land from the Greeks did not divide it among themselves, and it later passed to others. Thus it had been transmitted to others and attached to itself a suspicion that the wise man would do well to avoid."

Tithe-exemptions annulled by al-Mutawakkil. In *ath-Thaghr,* so many pieces of land were exempt from the tithe that the total income of tithes was diminished to such an extent that it could not meet the expenses. By al-Mutawakkil's orders, therefore, all these exemptions were in the year 243 abolished.

PART III

MESOPOTAMIA

CHAPTER I

The Conquest of Mesopotamia [al-Jazîrah] 172

'Iyâḍ its governor. Dâ'ûd ibn-'Abd-al-Ḥamîd the *ḳâḍi* of ar-Raḳḳah from Maimûn ibn-Mihrân:—All of Mesopotamia was conquered by 'Iyâḍ ibn-Ghanm who, after the death of abu-'Ubaidah, was made its ruler by 'Umar ibn-al-Khaṭṭâb. Abu-'Ubaidah had appointed 'Iyâḍ to be his successor over Syria, but 'Umar ibn-al-Khaṭṭâb appointed first Yazîd ibn-abi-Sufyân then Mu'âwiyah over Syria, and ordered 'Iyâḍ [1] to invade Mesopotamia.

Al-Ḥusain ibn-al-Aswad from Sulaimân ibn-'Aṭâ' al-Ḳurashi:—Abu-'Ubaidah sent 'Iyâḍ ibn-Ghanm to Mesopotamia, and died while 'Iyâḍ was still there. 'Umar then assigned 'Iyâḍ after abu-'Ubaidah as governor of Mesopotamia.

The terms with ar-Ruha. Bakr ibn-al-Haitham from Sulaimân ibn-'Aṭâ':—When 'Iyâḍ ibn-Ghanm, who was sent by abu-'Ubaidah, reduced ar-Ruha [2] [Edessa, modern Urfa], he stood at its gate riding on a brown horse; and the inhabitants made terms stipulating that they should keep their cathedral and the buildings around it, and agreeing not to start a new church other than what they already had, to give succor to the Moslems against their enemy, and to forfeit their right of protection in case they fail to keep any of these conditions. Similar terms to those of ar-Ruha were made by the people of Mesopotamia.

[1] R. Duval, "Histoire d'Édesse," in *Journal Asiatique*, Juillet-Août, 1891, pp. 106 *seq.*

[2] Ṭabari, vol. i, p. 2505.

The version of al-Wâkidi. Muhammad ibn-Sa'd states on the authority of al-Wâkidi that the most authentic report he heard regarding 'Iyâd was that abu-'Ubaidah, in the year 18, fell victim to the plague of Emmaus ['Amawâs] after appointing 'Iyâd as his successor [over Syria]. 'Iyâd received a letter from 'Umar, conferring upon him the governorship of Hims, Kinnasrîn and Mesopotamia. On Thursday the middle of Sha'bân, year 18, he marched to Mesopotamia at the head of 5,000 men, the van of the army being led by Maisarah ibn-Masrûk al-'Absi, the right wing by Sa'îd ibn-'Âmir ibn-Hidhyam al-Jumahi and the left by Safwân ibn-al-Mu'attal as-Sulami. Khâlid ibn-al-Walîd was on the left wing. Others assert that after Abu-'Ubaidah, Khâlid never marched under any man's flag but re- 173
mained in Hims, where he died in the year 21 after designating 'Umar to execute his will.[1] Some claim that he died in al-Madînah; but that he died in Hims is the more authentic report.[2]

The terms with ar-Rakkah. The van of 'Iyâd's army arrived in ar-Rakkah [3] and made a raid on its environs, where Beduin Arabs were encamped with a group of peasants, carrying off much booty. Those who escaped took to flight and entered the city of ar-Rakkah. 'Iyâd advanced with his troops until he arrived, with his troops in military array,[4] at Bâb ar-Ruha—one of the gates of the city. For an hour the Moslems were shot at, and some of them were wounded. In order to escape the enemy's stones and arrows, 'Iyâd withdrew, and, after going round the city on

[1] Hajar, vol. i, pp. 853-854.

[2] Yâkût, vol. ii, pp. 74-75.

[3] Athîr, vol. ii, p. 439.

[4] Ar. *ta'bi'ah.* See Wüstenfeld, "Die Taktik des Aelianus," in *Abhandlungen des Gesellschaft der Wissenschaften*, Göttingen, 1880.

horseback, he stationed horse-guards at its gates. He then returned to the main army and sent bands of soldiers[1] who went around, bringing back with them prisoners from the villages and large quantities of food. It was the proper time for reaping the harvest. This condition having lasted for five or six days the patrician of the city asked for peace from 'Iyâḍ, who made terms with him, guaranteeing for the population the security of their lives, children, possessions and city. 'Iyâḍ said, "The land is ours; we have subdued and secured it". However, he left it in their hands on the *kharâj* basis. That part of the land which was not wanted and rejected by the *dhimmis*, he turned over to the Moslems on the tithe basis. Moreover, 'Iyâḍ assessed poll-tax to the amount of one *dînâr* per annum on every man, holding women and boys exempt. In addition to the *dînâr*, he levied on them *ḳafîzes*[1] of wheat, and some oil, vinegar and honey. When Mu'âwiyah came to power, he laid that as a regular tax upon them. The people then opened the city gates and established a market for the Moslems at the Ruha gate. The following is the statement issued by 'Iyâḍ:

"In the name of Allah, the compassionate, the merciful. This is what 'Iyâḍ ibn-Ghanm gave to the people of ar-Raḳḳah when he entered the city. He gave them security for their lives and possessions. Their churches shall not be destroyed or occupied, so long as they pay the tax assessed on them and enter in no intrigue. It is stipulated that they build no new church or place of worship, or pub-

[1] Ar. *sarâya* who, according to al-Mas'ûdi, *Kitâb at-Tanbîh*, p. 279, were bands of soldiers varying between 3 and 500 persons, that go forth at night.

[2] A measure of capacity consisting of ten *makkûks*; *cf.* Mawardi, p. 265.

licly strike clappers,[1] or openly celebrate Easter Monday[2] or show the cross in public. Thereunto, Allah is witness and Allah is a sufficient witness. Signed by 'Iyâḍ's own signature."

Others report that 'Iyâḍ assessed four *dînârs* on every adult of ar-Rakkah; but the fact is that 'Umar wrote after 174
this to 'Umair ibn-Sa'd, his governor, instructing him to assess four *dînârs* on every man, as it was the case with those who possessed gold.

The terms with ar-Ruha. 'Iyâḍ then advanced against Ḥarrân and encamped at Bâjuddah, whence he sent forth the van of the army. The people of Ḥarrân closed the city gates, shutting the troops out. 'Iyâḍ followed up the van and when he camped at Ḥarrân, the Ḥarnânîyah from among its inhabitants sent him a word saying that they had under their control a part of the city and asking him to go to ar-Ruha, promising to accept whatever terms he may make with it, and leaving him free to negotiate with the Christians of Ḥarrân. Hearing that, the Christians sent him word, consenting to what had been proposed and offered by al-Ḥarnânîyah. Accordingly, 'Iyâḍ advanced to ar-Ruha whose people gathered against and shot at the Moslems for an hour. The fighters made a sally, but the Moslems put them to flight and forced them to seek refuge in the city. No sooner had that taken place than they offered to capitulate and make peace. To this, 'Iyâḍ consented and wrote them the following statement:[3]

"In the name of Allah, the compassionate, the merciful.

[1] Ar. *nâḳûs*.

[2] Ar *bâ'ûth*, used to-day for the Christian festival of Monday after Easter, is defined by *Ḳâmûs, Tâj al-'Arûs* and *Lisân al-'Arab* as corresponding to the Moslem prayer in which a petition for rain is offered. *Cf.* S. Fraenkel, *Die Aramäischen Fremdwörter im Arabischen*, p. 277.

[3] *Cf.* Yûsuf, p. 23.

This is a statement from 'Iyâḍ ibn-Ghanm to the bishop of ar-Ruha. If ye open before me the city gate and agree to offer to me for every man one *dînâr* and two modii of wheat, then I grant you safety for your persons, possessions and those dependent on you. It is incumbent on you to guide the one who goes astray, to repair the bridges and roads, and give good counsel to the Moslems. Thereunto, Allah is witness; and he is sufficient."

Dâ'ûd ibn-'Abd-al-Ḥamid from a grandfather of his:—The statement of 'Iyâḍ to the inhabitants of ar-Ruha ran as follows:—

"In the name of Allah, the compassionate, the merciful. This is a statement from 'Iyâḍ ibn-Ghanm and his accompanying Moslems to the inhabitants of ar-Ruha. I have granted them security for their lives, possessions, offspring, women, city and mills, so long as they give what they rightly owe. They are bound to repair our bridges, and guide those of us who go astray. Thereunto, Allah and his angels and the Moslems are witnesses."

Harrân and Sumaisâṭ capitulate. 'Iyâḍ then came to Ḥarrân and directed Ṣafwân ibn-al-Mu'aṭṭal and Ḥabîb ibn-Maslamah-l-Fihri to Sumaisâṭ.[1] With the people of Ḥarrân, he made terms similar to those of ar-Ruha. Its inhabitants opened the city gates for him, and he assigned a governor over it. He then came to Sumaisâṭ and found Ṣafwân ibn-al-Mu'aṭṭal and Ḥabîb ibn-Maslamah directing their operations against it, after having reduced many 175
of its villages and forts. The people of Sumaisâṭ made terms similar to those of ar-Ruha. 'Iyâḍ used to make incursions from ar-Ruha and return to it.

All Mesopotamia reduced by 'Iyâḍ. Muḥammad ibn-Sa'd from az-Zuhri:—In the days of 'Umar ibn-al-Khaṭṭâb, not

[1] Samosata; Iṣṭakhri, p. 62.

a foot was left in Mesopotamia unsubdued by 'Iyâḍ ibn-Ghanm who reduced Ḥarrân, ar-Ruha, ar-Raḳḳah, Ḳarḳîsiya [Circesium] Naṣîbîn [Nisibis] and Sinjâr.

Muḥammad [ibn-Sa'd] from Thâbit ibn-al-Ḥajjâj:—'Iyâḍ effected the conquest of ar-Raḳḳah, Ḥarrân, ar-Ruha, Naṣîbîn, Maiyâfâriḳin, Ḳarḳîsiya, and all the villages and towns of the Euphrates by capitulation; but all the open fields by force.

Muḥammad [ibn-Sa'd] from Râshid ibn-Sa'd:—'Iyâḍ effected the conquest of Mesopotamia and its towns by capitulation; but its land, by force.

The terms with Harrân. Someone reported that when 'Iyâḍ came to Ḥarrân from ar-Raḳḳah, he found it deserted, its inhabitants having moved to ar-Ruha. When ar-Ruha was captured, the people of Ḥarrân in it made terms regarding their city similar to those of ar-Ruha.

Sarûj and other places subdued by 'Iyâḍ. Abu-Aiyûb ar-Raḳḳi-l-Mu'addab from al-Ḥajjâj ibn-abi-Manî' ar-Ruṣâfi's[1] grandfather:—'Iyâḍ captured ar-Raḳḳah, then ar-Ruha, then Ḥarrân, and then Sumaisâṭ on the same terms of capitulation. Thence he came to Sarûj,[2] Râs-kîfa[3] and al-Arḍ al-Baiḍâ', subdued their land, and made terms with the holders of their forts similar to those of ar-Ruha. The people of Sumaisâṭ after that rebelled, which made him, on hearing it, return and besiege the city until he reduced it. Having heard that the inhabitants of ar-Ruha had broken their covenant, he camped around the city, upon which they opened their city gates. He entered the city and left in it his *'âmil* with a small band. Thence he came to the villages of the Euphrates[4] which are

[1] Dhahabi, *Mushtabih*, p. 225; *Mushtarik*, p. 206.

[2] Baṭnân; see *ZDMG*, vol. xxx, p. 354.

[3] R. Payne Smith, *Thesaurus Syriacus*, cols. 3902 and 2910.

[4] *Ḳuraiyât* or *Ḳaryât al-Furât*; *cf.* Hamadhâni, *Buldân*, p. 136.

Jisr Manbij and its dependents, which he reduced on similar terms. 'Ain al-Wardah or Ra's al-'Ain [1] to which he came next held out against him; so he left it. He then came to Tall Mauzin [2] and took it on the same terms as ar- 176
Ruha. That took place in the year 19. Against Ḳarḳisiya, 'Iyâḍ directed Ḥabib ibn-Maslamah-l-Fihri who took the city by a capitulation similar to that of ar-Raḳḳah. 'Iyâḍ captured Âmid without fighting and on terms similar to those of ar-Ruha. He captured Maiyâfâriḳin on the same terms. He also reduced the fort of Kafartûtha.[3] After a conflict, he reduced Naṣibin and the terms concluded were similar to those of ar-Ruha. Ṭûr 'Abdîn,[4] Ḥiṣn Mâridîn and Dâra [5] he took on the same terms. Ḳarda and Bâzabda he conquered on the same terms as those of Naṣibîn. The patrician of az-Zawazân came to 'Iyâḍ and made terms regarding his lands, agreeing to pay tax. All that took place in the year 19 and in a part of Muḥarram, year 20. He then advanced to Arzan and took possession of it on terms similar to those of Naṣibîn. He then passed through ad-Darb into Badlîs which he left for Khilâṭ with whose patrician he made terms. Finally, he got to al-'Ain al-Ḥâmiḍah in Armenia beyond which he did not go. On his way back, he made the chief of Badlis responsible for the *kharâj* of Khilâṭ with its poll-tax and what was due on its patrician. He then proceeded to ar-Raḳḳah, and on to Ḥimṣ whose governorship had been entrusted to him by 'Umar. In the year 20, he died. 'Umar after that appointed Sa'îd ibn-'Âmir ibn-Ḥidhyam, who died after a short time. 'Umar

[1] Hoffman, *Syrische Akten Persischer Märtyrer*, p. 183.

[2] Hoffman, *op. cit.*, p. 224, note 1778.

[3] R. Payne Smith, *op. cit.*, col. 1801.

[4] R. Payne Smith, *op. cit.*, col. 1451.

[5] Hoffman, *op. cit.*, p. 46.

then appointed 'Umair ibn-Sa'd al-Anṣâri, who succeeded in capturing 'Ain al-Wardah after a severe conflict.

'Ain al-Wardah or Ra's al-'Ain captured. Al-Wâkidi from abu-Wahb al-Jaishâni Dailam ibn-al-Muwassa':—'Umar ibn-al-Khaṭṭâb wrote to 'Iyâḍ instructing him to send 'Umair ibn-Sa'd to 'Ain al-Wardah. This he did. The van of the army went ahead, assailed a group of peasants and carried away some of the enemy's cattle as booty. The inhabitants of the city closed their gates and set up the mangonels[1] on them. Many Moslems were killed by stones and arrows. Then one of the patricians of the city appeared and cursed the Moslems saying, "We are different from what ye have met heretofore!" At last the city was taken by capitulation.

Amr ibn-Muḥammad from a grandfather of al-Ḥajjâj ibn-abi-Manî':—Ra's al-'Ain[2] held out against 'Iyâḍ ibn-Ghanm; but 'Umair ibn-Sa'd, who was 'Umar's governor over Mesopotamia, reduced it after a fierce resistance on 177
the part of its inhabitants. The Moslems entered by force; but terms of capitulation were drawn up stipulating that the land be held by them and the tax be imposed on their persons to the amount of four *dînârs* per head. Their women and children were not taken as captives.

The following statement was made by al-Ḥajjâj: "I heard it said by certain *sheikhs* from Ra's al-'Ain that when 'Umair entered the city he shouted, 'Never mind; never mind; [come] to me! [come] to me!' and that constituted a guarantee of security for them."

It is claimed by al-Haitham ibn-'Adi that 'Umar ibn-al-Khaṭṭâb sent abu-Mûsa-l-Ash'ari to 'Ain al-Wardah, which

[1] Ar. *'arrâdah;* see *Ḥamâsah* (ed. Freytag), p. 307.

[2] Another name for 'Ain-al-Wardah. See al-Mas'ûdi, *Tanbîh*, p. 54; Yâkût, vol. iii, p. 764.

he invaded with the troops of Mesopotamia after the death of 'Iyâḍ. The fact is that 'Umair captured it by force and did not take any captives. He only imposed *kharâj* and poll-tax. The view of Haitham is not shared by any other authority.

According to al-Ḥajjâj ibn-abi-Manî', a part of the inhabitants of Ra's al-'Ain having vacated it, the Moslems utilized their lands and cultivated them according to the fief system.

Sinjâr captured. Muḥammad ibn-al-Mufaḍḍal al-Mauṣili from certain *sheikhs* of Sinjâr:—Sinjâr[1] was held by the Greeks. Kisra—[Chosroes] known as Abarwîz—wanted to put to death one hundred Persians who were brought before him because of rebellion and disobedience. Someone having interceded in their behalf, he ordered them sent to Sinjâr, which he was then attempting to reduce. Two of them died, and 98 arrived there, joined the troops who were encamped against the city, and were the first to capture it. There they settled and multiplied. When 'Iyâḍ was through with Khilâṭ and was going to Mesopotamia, he sent an expedition to Sinjâr, took the city by capitulation, and settled it with Arabs.

Mauṣil. Some reports claim that 'Iyâḍ reduced one of the forts of Mauṣil, but that is not confirmed.

According to ibn-al-Kalbi, 'Umair ibn-Sa'd, the *'âmil* of 'Umar is identical with 'Umar ibn-Sa'd ibn-Shuhaid ibn-'Amr one of al-Aus; but according to al-Wâḳidi, he is 'Umair ibn-Sa'd ibn-'Ubaid whose father, Sa'd, was killed in the battle of al-Ḳâdisîyah. This Sa'd, according to the Kufite school, is one of those who compiled the Koran in the time of the Prophet.

Khâlid dismissed. Al-Wâḳidi states that some reports

[1] Yâḳût, vol. iii, p. 158.

claim that Khâlid ibn-al-Walîd ruled in 'Umar's name a part of Mesopotamia; and once as he was in a bath, at Âmid [Diyârbakr], or at some other place, he daubed himself 178
with a substance containing wine, which made 'Umar dismiss him. This, however, is not confirmed.

The tax on Mesopotamia. 'Amr an-Nâķid from Maimûn ibn-Mihrân:—For some time, oil and vinegar and food were taken for the benefit of the Moslems in Mesopotamia, which tax was later reduced through the sympathy of 'Umar and fixed at 48, 24, and 12 *dirhams.* In addition to the poll-tax, every one had to provide two *mudds* of wheat two *ķisṭs* of oil and two *ķisṭs* of vinegar.

Mosques erected. I was informed by a number of the inhabitants of ar-Raķķah that when 'Iyâḍ died and Sa'îd ibn-'Âmir ibn-Ḥidhyam became governor of Mesopotamia, the latter erected the mosque of ar-Raķķah and that of ar-Ruha, after which he died. The mosques in Diyâr Muḍar and Diyâr Rabî'ah were erected by 'Umair ibn-Sa'd.

Mu'âwiyah settles Arab tribes. When Mu'âwiyah ruled over Syria and Mesopotamia in the name of 'Uthmân ibn-'Affân, he was instructed by him to settle the Arabs in places far from the cities and villages, and allow them to utilize the lands unpossessed by anyone. Accordingly, he caused the banu-Tamîm to settle at ar-Râbiyah; and a promiscuous multitude of Ķais and Asad and others, in al-Mâziḥin and al-Mudaibir.[1] The same thing he did in Diyâr Muḍar. In like manner, he stationed the Rabî'ah in their Diyâr. The cities and villages and frontier garrisons he put in charge of some, who received stipends in order to guard them and protect them, and whom he put there with his *'âmils.*

Scorpions in Naṣîbîn. Abu-Ḥafṣ ash-Shâmi from Ḥam-

[1] Ķudâmah, p. 246.

mâd ibn-'Amr an-Naṣibi:—The *'âmil* of Naṣibîn wrote to Mu'âwiyah, 'Uthmân's governor over Syria and Mesopotamia, complaining that some of the Moslems in his company had fallen victim to the scorpions. Mu'âwiyah wrote back instructing him to demand of the inhabitants in each quarter of the city a fixed number of scorpions to be brought every evening. This he did. They used to bring the scorpions before him, and he would order that they be killed.

Ḳarḳîsiya, the Euphrates forts and other places reduced. Abu-Aiyûb al-Mu'addab ar-Raḳḳi from abu-'Abdallâh al-Ḳarḳasâni's *sheikhs*:—When 'Umair ibn-Sa'd captured Ra's al-'Ain he made his way across and beyond al-Khâbûr [1] to Ḳarḳîsiya whose people had violated the covenant. With them he made terms similar to those made before, 179
and then advanced against the forts along the course of the Euphrates one after the other, which he reduced all on the same terms as Ḳarḳîsiya. In none of them did he meet severe resistance. Some of them would sometimes throw stones at him. When he was through with Talbas [2] and 'Ânât, [3] he came to an-Na'ûsah, Âlûsah [4] and Hît where he found out that 'Ammâr ibn-Yâsir, the *'âmil* of 'Umar ibn-al-Khaṭṭâb over al-Kûfah, had sent an army for the invasion of the region above al-Anbâr, under the leadership of Sa'd ibn-'Amr ibn-Ḥarâm al-Anṣâri. The holders of these forts had come to Sa'd and demanded peace, which he arranged with them, retaining one-half of the church of Hît. 'Umair, therefore, kept on his way to ar-Raḳḳah.

I learned from certain scholars that the one who went against Hît and the forts beyond in al-Kûfah was Midlâj

[1] A tributary of the Euphrates; *Tanbîh,* p. 54.

[2] Vowels uncertain; Caetani, vol. iv, p. 222.

[3] Hoffman, *op. cit.,* p. 137, note 1162.

[4] Yâḳût, vol. i, p. 65.

ibn-'Amr as-Sulami, an ally of the banu-'Abd-Shams and one of the Companions, who effected their capture. This Midlâj built al-Ḥadîthah on the Euphrates. His descendants were at Hît. The memory of one of them, surnamed abu-Hârûn, still lives there. Others assert that Midlâj was sent by Sa'd ibn-'Amr ibn-Ḥarâm; but Allah knows best.

Nahr Sa'îd. In the place of Nahr Sa'ịd—the canal named after Sa'îd ibn-'Abd-al-Malik ibn-Marwân (who was nicknamed Sa'îd al-Khair and who practised asceticism)—once stood a jungle frequented by lions. Al-Walîd gave it to him [Sa'îd] as fief, and he dug out the canal and erected the buildings that stand there. According to others, it was 'Umar ibn-'Abd-al-'Azîz who gave it as fief.

Ar-Râfiḳah. There is no trace that ar-Râfiḳah is an old city. It was built by al-Manṣûr the "Commander of the Believers" in the year 155, according to the plan of his city in Baghdâdh. Al-Manṣûr stationed in it an army of the people of Khurâsân and entrusted it to al-Mahdi, who was at that time the heir-apparent. Later, ar-Rashîd built its castles. Between ar-Raḳḳah and ar-Râfiḳah lay a wide tract of sown land to which 'Ali ibn-Sulaimân ibn-'Ali moved the markets of ar-Raḳḳah when he came as governor to Mesopotamia. Previous to this, the greatest market of ar-Raḳḳah was called Sûḳ Hishâm al-'Atîḳ [the old market of Hishâm]. When ar-Rashîd visited ar-Raḳḳah, he increased the number of these markets, whose income together with that from the confiscated towns, is still collected to-day.

Ruṣâfat Hishâm and al-Hani wa-l-Mari. As for Ruṣâfat Hishâm,[1] it was built by Hishâm ibn-'Abd-al-Malik who 180
previous to its building, used to stop at az-Zaitûnah. Hi-

[1] or ar-Ruṣâfat bi-ash-Shâm; Yâḳût, vol. ii, p. 784. Ruṣâfat means causeway.

shâm dug out al-Hani wa-l-Mari [canals], thus making the crown-land known as al-Hani-wa-l-Mari tillable land. He founded in it Wâsiṭ ar-Raḳḳah.[1] This same land was confiscated at the beginning of the [Abbasid] dynasty and passed into the hands of umm-Ja'far Zubaidah, daughter of Ja'far ibn-al-Manṣûr, who built in it the fief house that bears her name, and settled more people in it.

Ar-Raḥbah. There is no trace that ar-Raḥbah, which lies below Ḳarḳîsiya, is an old city, it having been built by Mâlik ibn-Ṭauḳ ibn-'Attâb[2] at-Taghlabi in the caliphate of al-Ma'mûn.

Adhramah. Adhramah in Diyâr Rabî'ah was an old village which al-Ḥasan ibn-'Umar ibn-al-Khaṭṭâb at-Taghlabi took from its chief and in which he built a castle, thus fortifying it.

Kafartûtha. Kafartûtha[3] was an old fort that was occupied by the offspring of abu-Rimthah, who made a town of it and foritfied it.

Diyâr Rabî'ah and al-Barrîyah. Mu'âfa ibn-Ṭâ'ûs from his father:—The latter said, "I asked certain *sheikhs* regarding the tithes of Balad and Diyâr Rabî'ah and al-Barrîyah[4] and was told that they were the tithes of lands held by the Arabs when they embraced Islâm, or reclaimed by them from waste lands unpossessed by any one or given up by the Christians, and which have consequently become waste and covered with brushwood. These lands were given to the Arabs as fiefs."

'Ain ar-Rûmîyah. Abu-'Affân ar-Raḳḳi from certain *sheikhs* of the writers of ar-Raḳḳah and others:—'Ain ar-

[1] Yâḳûṭ, vol. iv, p. 889.

[2] *Cf.* Maḥâsin, vol. ii, p. 34.

[3] R. Payne Smith, col. 1801.

[4] The desert part of Mesopotamia. Yâḳût, vol. i, p. 601; Bakri, p. 566.

Rûmîyah together with its spring belonged to al-Walîd ibn-'Ukbah ibn-abi-Mu'aiṭ who gave it to abu-Zubaid aṭ-Ṭâ'i from whom it passed to abu-l-'Abbâs the "Commander of the Believers." Abu-l-'Abbâs gave it as fief to Maimûn ibn-Ḥamzah, the freedman of 'Ali ibn-'Abdallâh ibn-'Abbâs, from whose heirs ar-Rashîd bought it. It lies in the district of ar-Rakkah.

Ghâbat ibn-Hubairah. Ghâbat ibn-Hubairah [the forest of ibn-Hubairah] was first given as fief to ibn-Hubairah, but later confiscated and assigned as fief to Bishr ibn-Maimûn, the builder of aṭ-Ṭâkât [1] [archways or arcades] at Baghdâdh in the vicinity of Bâb ash-Shâm [the Syrian gate]. This Ghâbat was later bought by ar-Rashîd. It lies in the province of Sarûj.

'Â'ishah fief. The fief which was given by Hishâm to his daughter, 'Â'ishah, at Râskîfa and which bore her name was also confiscated.

Sala'ûs and Kafarjadda. 'Abd-al-Malik and Hishâm owned a village called Sala'ûs and half of another called 181
Kafarjadda which lay in the province of ar-Ruha.

Tall 'Afrâ', Tall Madhâba, al-Muṣalla and Rabaḍ Harrân. In Ḥarrân, al-Ghamr ibn-Yazîd owned Tall 'Afra', the land of Tall Madhâba,[2] and Arḍ al-Muṣalla [place of prayer], together with the confiscated lands and the workshops in Rabaḍ Ḥarrân.

Marj 'Abd-al-Wâḥid. Before al-Ḥadath and Zibaṭrah were built, Marj [3] 'Abd-al-Wâḥid was a pasturing place reserved for the Moslems [4]; but when these two were built, the Moslems could do without the Marj, which was peopled

[1] *Cf.* Le Strange, *Baghdâd during the Abbasid Caliphate*, p. 130.

[2] Lacking in diacritical points.

[3] The word means meadow.

[4] Ar. *ḥima*; see Mawardi, p. 324.

and later added by al-Ḥusain al-Khâdim in the caliphate of ar-Rashîd to al-Aḥwâz. After that, some people unjustly took possession of it and of its farms, in which condition it remained until 'Abdallâh ibn-Ṭâhir came to Syria and returned it to the crown-lands. Abu-Aiyûb ar-Raḳḳi heard it said that 'Abd-al-Wâḥid, after whom the Marj was named, was 'Abd-al-Wâḥid ibn-al-Ḥârith ibn-al-Ḥakam ibn-abi-l-'Âṣi, a cousin of 'Abd-al-Malik. He owned the Marj, but turned it into a pasture land exclusively for the Moslems. He is the one whom al-Ḳaṭâmi lauded, saying:

"If fate would overlook only 'Abd-al-Wâḥid,
let not the case of all the other inhabitants of the city grieve thee."

CHAPTER II

THE CHRISTIANS OF THE BANU-TAGHLIB IBN-WÂ'IL

'Umar doubles their ṣadaḳah. Shaibân ibn-Farrûkh from as-Saffâḥ ash-Shaibâni:—'Umar ibn-al-Khaṭṭâb wanted to collect the poll-tax from the Christian tribe, banu-Taghlib; but they took to flight and some of them went to a distant land. An-Nu'mân ibn-Zur'ah (or Zur'ah ibn-an-Nu'mân) addressed 'Umar saying: "I plead in Allah's name for the banu-Taghlib. They are a body of Arabs too proud to pay poll-tax, but severe in warfare. Let not thy enemy, therefore, be enriched by them to thy disadvantage."[1] Thereupon 'Umar called them back and doubled the *ṣadaḳah* laid on them.

Neither Moslems, nor of the "people of the Book." Shaibân from ibn-'Abbâs:—The latter said, "What is slaughtered by the Christians of the banu-Taghlib shall not be eaten, and their women shall not be taken as wives [by 182
us]. They are neither of us nor of the 'people of the Book.'"

'Umair consults 'Umar. 'Abbâs ibn-Hishâm from 'Awânah ibn-al-Ḥakam and abu-Mikhnaf:—'Umair ibn-Sa'd wrote to 'Umar ibn-al-Khaṭṭâb informing him that he had come to the regions on the Syrian slope of the Euphrates and captured 'Ânât and the other forts of [*i. e.*, along the course of] the Euphrates; and that when he wished to constrain the banu-Taghlib of that region to accept Islâm, they refused and were on the point of leaving for some Byzantine territory; no one on the Syrian slope of the Euphrates whom he wished to constrain to Islâm had before the banu-

[1] *Cf.* Yûsuf, p. 68.

Taghlib showed such tenacity and asked permission to emigrate. 'Umair asked 'Umar's advice on this matter. 'Umar wrote back ordering him to double on all their pasturing cattle [1] and land the amount of *ṣadaḳah* ordinarily taken from Moslems; and if they should refuse to pay that, he ought to war with them until he annihilates them or they accept Islâm. They accepted to pay a double *ṣadaḳah* [2] saying, "So long as it is not the tax of the 'uncircumcized,' we shall pay it and retain our faith." [3]

The terms with the banu-Taghlib. 'Amr an-Nâḳid from Dâ'ûd ibn-Kurdûs:—After having crossed the Euphrates and decided to leave for the land of the Greeks, the banu-Taghlib made terms with 'Umar ibn-al-Ḳhaṭṭâb, agreeing not to immerse [baptize] a child or compel him to accept their faith, and to pay a double *ṣadaḳah*. Dâ'ûd ibn-Kurdûs used to repeat that they had no claim to security [*dhimmah*], because they used immersion in their ritual—referring to baptism.

Only they pay double ṣadaḳah. Al-Ḥusain ibn-al-Aswad from az-Zuhri:—None of the "people of the Book" pay *ṣadaḳah* on their cattle except the Christian banu-Taghlib or—he perhaps said—the Christian Arabs, whose whole possessions consist of cattle. These pay twice what the Moslems pay.

Zur'ah intercedes in their behalf. Sa'îd ibn-Sulaimân Sa'dawaih from Zur'ah ibn-an-Nu'mân:—The latter interceded with 'Umar in favor of the Christians of the banu-Taghlib, saying, "They are Arabs too proud to pay the poll-tax, and are possessors of tillable land and cattle." 'Umar had decided to take tax from them and they became dispersed in the whole country. At last, 'Umar made terms

[1] *Cf.* Yûsuf, p. 68.

[2] *Cf.* ibn-Anas, *al-Mudauwanah-l-Kubra*, vol. ii, p. 42.

[3] *MFO*, vol. iii, pp. 159, 162.

with them, stipulating that they pay double what the Moslems pay in the form of *ṣadaḳah* on the land and cattle, and that they do not christen their children. 183

What 'Ali would do. According to Mughîrah, 'Ali used to repeat, "If I should have the time to deal with the banu-Taghlib, I would have my own way with them. Their fighters I would surely put to death, and their children I would take as captives, because by christening their children they violated the covenant and are no more in our trust [*dhimmah*]."

What Ziyâd said. Abu-Naṣr at-Tammâr from Ziyâd ibn-Ḥudair al-Asadi:—The latter said, "I was sent by 'Umar to the Christians of the banu-Taghlib in order to collect from them half the tithe on their possessions, and was warned against collecting tithes from a Moslem, or from a *dhimmi* that pays *kharâj*."

'Uthmân withdraws his word. Muḥammad ibn-Sa'd from Muḥammad ibn-Ibrâhîm ibn-al-Ḥârith:—'Uthmân gave orders that nothing be accepted from the banu-Taghlib as tax except the tithe on gold and silver. Having, however, learned the fact that 'Umar took from them a double *ṣadaḳah*, he withdrew his word.

The tax on banu-Taghlib. According to al-Wâḳidi, it is said by Sufyân ath-Thauri, al-Auzâ'i, Mâlik ibn-Anas, ibn-abi-Lailah, ibn-abi-Dhi'b, abu-Ḥanîfah and abu-Yûsuf that from one of the banu-Taghlib is collected double what is collected from a Moslem, on land, cattle and possessions. But if he is a child or idiot, a double *sadaḳah*—according to the school of al-'Irâḳ—is taken on his land, and nothing on his cattle; and according to the school of al-Ḥijâz, a double *ṣadaḳah* is taken on his cattle and his land. They all, however, agree that what is taken from the banu-Taghlib should be spent in the same way as *kharâj*, because it is a substitute for tax.

CHAPTER III

The Fortifications of the Mesopotamian Frontier

Shimshât. When 'Uthmân ibn-'Affân became caliph, he wrote to Mu'âwiyah conferring on him the governorship of Syria, and assigned 'Umair ibn-Sa'd al-Anṣâri as governor of Mesopotamia. Later he dismissed the latter and combined both Syria and Mesopotamia, including their frontier 184
fortifications [*thughûr*] under Mu'âwiyah, in the meantime ordering Mu'âwiyah to invade or send someone to invade Shimshâṭ,[1] *i. e.,* Armenia IV. Accordingly, Mu'âwiyah sent thereto Ḥabîb ibn-Maslamah-l-Fihri and Ṣafwân ibn-Mu'aṭṭal as-Sulami who, after a few days of camping around it, reduced it and made terms similar to those of ar-Ruha. Ṣafwân took up his abode in Armenia until his death towards the end of Mu'âwiyah's caliphate. It is held by others that Mu'âwiyah himself led the invasion with these two in his company, that he then conferred its governorship on Ṣafwân, who lived in it until his death. After stopping in Malaṭyah in the year 133, Constantine the "tyrant" camped around Shimshâṭ with hostile intentions, but effected nothing. After making a raid on the surrounding places, he departed. Shimshâṭ was included in the *kharâj*-land until the time of al-Mutawakkil who changed it into a tithe-land, putting it on the same level with the other frontier fortresses.

Kamkh. After the conquest of Shimshâṭ, Ḥabîb ibn-

[1] Yâkût, vol. iii, p. 319.

Maslamah attacked Ḥiṣn Kamkh [1] but failed to reduce it. Ṣafwân too attacked it and failed. In the year 59—the year in which he died—Ṣafwân made another attempt on it, at which time he was accompanied by 'Umair ibn-al-Ḥubâb [2] as-Sulami, who climbed the wall and kept struggling single-handed until the Greeks gave way and the Moslems climbed up. Thus the reduction of Kamkh was due to 'Umair ibn-al-Ḥubâb and was the thing in which he boasted and others boasted for him. Later, however, the Greeks succeeded in taking it; but it was recaptured by Maslamah ibn-'Abd-al-Malik. Thus the fort passed back and forth from the hands of the Moslems to the hands of the Greeks until the year 149 in which al-Manṣûr left Baghdâdh for Ḥadîthat al-Mauṣil from which he sent al-Ḥasan ibn-Ḳaḥṭabah and after him Muḥammad ibn-al-Ash'ath, both under the leadership of al-'Abbâs ibn-Muhammad. for the invasion of Kamkh. Muhammad ibn-al-Ash'ath died at Âmid.[3] Al-'Abbâs and al-Ḥasan advanced to Malaṭyah [4] from which they took provisions, and then camped around Kamkh. Al-'Abbâs ordered that mangonels be set upon the fort. The holders of the fort covered it with cypress wood to protect it against the mangonel stones. and killed by the stones they hurled two hundred Moslems. The Moslems then set their mantelets [5] and fought severely until they 18
captured it. Among those in the company of al-'Abbâs ibn-Muhammad ibn-'Ali in this campaign was Maṭar al-Warrâḳ. Once more the Greeks took Kamkh fort, and in the year 177 an attack against it was led by Muhammad ibn-

[1] Ḥauḳal, pp. 129, 130.

[2] *Cf.* Maḥâsin, vol. i, p. 204; Duraid, p. 187.

[3] Diyârbakr.

[4] Yâḳût, vol. iv, pp. 633-634.

[5] Ar. *dabbâbah:* Zaidân, vol. i, p. 143.

Abdallâh ibn-'Abd-ar-Raḥmân ibn-abi-'Amrah-l-Anṣâri, the *'âmil* of 'Abd-al-Malik ibn-Ṣâliḥ over Shimshâṭ, which resulted in its reduction. The fort was entered on the 14th of Rabî' II, 177, and was held by the Moslems until the time of the civil war led by Muḥammad ibn-ar-Rashîd, at which time its holders fled away and the Greeks took possession of it. Some hold that the fort was delivered to the Greeks by 'Ubaidallâh ibn-al-Aḳṭa' who, thereby, saved his son who was held by them as prisoner. In the caliphate of al-Ma'mûn, 'Abdallâh ibn-Ṭâhir reduced it; and it was in the hands of the Moslems until certain Christians from Shimshâṭ, Ḳâliḳala together with Biḳrâṭ ibn-Ashûṭ, the patrician of Khilâṭ, succeeded by subtle means in transferring it to the Greeks, and in this wise winning their favor which the Christians desired because they held crown-lands in the province of Shimshâṭ.

Malaṭyah. Ḥabîb ibn-Maslamah-l-Fihri was sent by 'Iyâḍ ibn-Ghanm from Shimshâṭ to Malaṭyah [1] whose conquest he effected. The city was later lost to the Moslems. When Mu'âwiyah became governor of Syria and Mesopotamia, he sent again Ḥabîb ibn-Maslamah who took it by force and stationed in it a Moslem company of horsemen to keep post on the frontier and a *'âmil.* When Mu'âwiyah visited it on his way to the land of the Greeks, he stationed in it a garrison from Syria, Mesopotamia and other places. It became one of the headquarters for the summer expeditions. In the days of 'Abdallâh ibn-az-Zubair, its inhabitants having left it, the Greeks came and devastated it; but they soon after evacuated it, and it was occupied by Armenian and Nabatean [Aramean] Christians.

Ṭurandah. Muḥammad ibn-Sa'd from al-Wâḳidi:—After its invasion by 'Abdallâh ibn-'Abd-al-Malik in the

[1] Yâḳût, vol. iv, pp. 633-634.

year 83, the Moslems settled in Ṭurandah [1] and built their houses in it. This Ṭurandah is three days' journey from Malaṭyah and lies in the interior of the Byzantine Empire. Malaṭyah at this time was in ruins and inhabited by only a few Armenian *dhimmis* and others. In summer, a detachment of troops from Mesopotamia would come and stay in it until the rain and snow began to fall, at which time they would return. When 'Umar ibn-'Abd-al-'Azîz became 18
caliph, he made the inhabitants of Ṭurandah, against their will, evacuate it, because he feared a raid of the enemy upon them. As they left, they carried away everything on their backs, leaving nothing behind and breaking even the jars of oil and vinegar. 'Umar settled them in Malaṭyah and destroyed Ṭurandah, making Ja'wanah ibn-al-Ḥârith of the banu-'Âmir ibn-Ṣa'ṣa'ah the governor of Malaṭyah.

The Greeks descend upon Malaṭyah. In the year 123, some 20,000 Greeks made a descent on Malaṭyah. Its inhabitants closed the gates; and the women appeared on the wall with turbans on their heads and took part in the fight. The people of Malaṭyah then sent a messenger to appeal for help. He rode on a post-mule and came to Hishâm ibn-'Abd-al-Malik who was then at ar-Ruṣâfah. Hishâm summoned the Moslems to the help of Malaṭyah, but hearing that the Greeks had withdrawn from it, he communicated the news to the messenger and sent him with horsemen to remain at the frontier in readiness for the enemy. Hishâm led an expedition in person, after which he alighted in Malaṭyah where he lay encamped until it was built. On his way, he passed through ar-Raḳḳah which he entered with his sword at his side. This was the first time in his rule in which he carried his sword.

It is reported by al-Wâḳidi that in the year 133, Constan-

[1] Yâḳût, vol. iii, p. 534.

tine the "tyrant" directed his march to Malaṭyah. Kamkh
at that time was in Moslem hands; and its governor was
one of the banu-Sulaim. The people of Kamkh having sent
a call to the people of Malaṭyah for succor, 800 horsemen
sallied forth from it to meet the Greeks. The Greek cavalry
defeated them after a battle, and Constantine camped
around Malaṭyah and invested it. At this time, Mesopotamia was the scene of a civil war and its *'âmil* Mûsa ibn-
Ka'b was at Ḥarrân. Therefore, when the people of Malaṭyah sent a messenger soliciting aid, nobody came. Hearing that, Constantine addressed the people of Malaṭyah
saying, "O people of Malaṭyah, I would not have come to
you had I not realized your state and the fact that your
authorities [*sulṭân*] are too busy to help you. Make peace
therefore with me and leave the city that I may destroy it
and go my way." The people did not comply with his demand; so he set the mangonels. The siege was pressed
so hard and the inhabitants were so exhausted that they
asked Constantine for safe-conduct, which request he accepted. As they prepared to leave, they carried every light
thing they could and threw what was too heavy into wells
and hiding places. As they made their way out, all the
Greeks stood in two rows from the city gates to the end
of the line, with their swords unsheathed and the point of
the one sword on the point of the one opposite to it, thus 187
making an arch. The Greeks saw them off until they got
to their place of safety, upon which they turned toward
Mesopotamia where they settled in various places. Malaṭyah was then razed to the ground by the Greeks, who left
nothing but a granary of which only one side was damaged. Ḥiṣn Ḳalûdhiyah was also destroyed by them.

Malaṭyah rebuilt. In the year 139, al-Manṣûr wrote to
Ṣâliḥ ibn-'Ali ordering him to rebuild and fortify Malaṭyah. He then deemed it best to send 'Abd-al-Wahhâb ibn-

Ibrâhîm al-Imâm as governor over Mesopotamia and its frontier fortresses. Accordingly, 'Abd-al-Wahhâb started in the year 140 at the head of troops from Khurâsân and was accompanied by al-Hasan ibn-Kaḥṭabah. He ordered the people of Syria and Mesopotamia to furnish contingents of troops, which they did to the number of 70,000. With these, he marched to the site of Malaṭyah, gathered workmen from various places and started the construction. Al-Ḥasan ibn-Ḳaḥṭabah himself would sometimes carry a stone and hand it over to the mason. He would also provide the workers with dinners and suppers at his own expense, opening his kitchens to the public. 'Abd-al-Wahhâb was displeased at this and wrote to abu-Ja'far stating that he ['Abd-al-Wahhâb] gave food to the people, but al-Ḥasan distributed many times more, his aim being to contend with him for superiority in beneficence, to spoil what he did, and to disparage him by means of extravagance and hypocrisy; and that al-Ḥasan had special heralds to go round calling people to his meals. To this, abu-Ja'far replied, "Boy, al-Ḥasan feeds people on his own account; and thou feedest them on mine. What thou hast written was due to thy ignominy, deficient energy and base-mindedness." In the meantime, he wrote to al-Ḥasan: "Feed the people, but do not use a herald." Al-Ḥasan used to announce to the workmen that he who, in building a wall, got first to the crown of a cornice would receive so much." This made them put forth special effort to finish the work; and thus was Malaṭyah with its mosque rebuilt in 6 months. For every group of ten to fifteen troops in the army, he built a house of two rooms below and two rooms above and a stable. At a distance of thirty miles from the city, he built a frontier castle and another on a rivulet called Ḳubâḳib that empties its water into the Euphrates. Al-Manṣûr settled in Malaṭyah 4,000 fighters from Mesopotamia, Malaṭyah being one of

the Mesopotamian frontier towns, adding to each man's stipend ten *dînârs,* and giving to each a bounty of one hundred *dînârs,* in addition to the pay allotted to the different tribes. 188
He stationed in the town the necessary garrison, assigned farms to the troops as fief and built the Ḳalûdhiyah fort.

Constantine desists from Jaiḥân. Constantine the "tyrant", at the head of an army of more than 100,000 men, came to Jaiḥân; but hearing of the great number of the Arabs, he desisted from it.

Naṣr ibn-Mâlik and Naṣr ibn-Sa'd accompany 'Abd-al-Wahhâb. I heard it said that 'Abd-al-Wahhâb was accompanied in the expedition mentioned above by Naṣr ibn-Mâlik al-Khuzâ'i and Naṣr ibn-Sa'd al-Kâtib, a freedman of al-Anṣâr. Hence the poet's words:

"Thou hadst on thy sides two Nasrs: Naṣr ibn-Mâlik and Naṣr ibn-Sa'd,
may thy victory [Ar. *naṣr*] be unparallelled!"

Muḥammad ibn-Ibrâhîm goes against Malaṭyah. In the year 141, Muḥammad ibn-Ibrâhîm was sent to invade Malaṭyah at the head of an army from the people of Khurâsân, with al-Musaiyab ibn-Zuhair leading the choice men of the army. He posted a body of horsemen in Malaṭyah so that the enemy should not covet its possession. Those of its old inhabitants who survived returned to it.

Ar-Rashîd humiliates the Greeks. In the days of ar-Rashîd, the Greeks attempted the conquest of Malaṭyah but to no avail. Ar-Rashîd led an invasion, overcame and humiliated them.

Mar'ash. When abu-'Ubaidah ibn-al-Jarrâḥ was in Manbij, he sent Khâlid ibn-al-Walîd to the region of Mar-'ash[1] whose fort Khâlid seized on the condition that its

[1] Germanicia. Mas'ûdi, vol. viii, p. 295; Ḥauḳal, p. 62.

holders be allowed to emigrate to another place, after which he destroyed it. When Sufyân ibn-'Auf al-Ghâmidi made an expedition against the Greeks in the year 30, he started from Mar'ash and made a tour in the land of the Greeks. Mar'ash was built by Mu'âwiyah and populated by him with troops. After the death of Yazîd ibn-Mu'âwiyah, the Greeks reiterated their attacks on the city and so the inhabitants had to desert it. 'Abd-al-Malik ibn-Marwân, after the death of his father, Marwân ibn-al-Ḥakam, and after asserting his claim upon the caliphate, made terms with the Greeks, agreeing to pay them a certain sum. But in the year 74, Muḥammad ibn-Marwân attacked the Greeks, and thus the peace was broken.

In the year 75, Muḥammad ibn-Marwân once more led the summer campaign, and the Greeks went forth in Jumâda I from Mar'ash to al-A'mâḳ [valleys]. The Moslems marched against them under Abân ibn-al-Walîd ibn-'Uḳbah ibn-abi-Mu'aiṭ accompanied by Dînâr ibn-Dînâr, a freedman of 'Abd-al-Malik ibn-Marwân and a governor of Ḳinnasrîn and its districts. The two armies met in 'Amḳ [valley] Mar'ash where a fierce battle was fought, resulting in the defeat of the Greeks. The Moslems chased them, massacring and capturing. In this same year, Dînâr came across a band of Greeks at Jisr [bridge] Yaghra about 189
ten miles from Shimshâṭ, and routed them. Later al-'Abbâs ibn-al-Walîd ibn-'Abd-al-Malik came to Mar'ash, built it, fortified it, moved people into it and erected in it a cathedral mosque. He imposed upon the people of Ḳinnasrîn a contingent of troops to be sent to Mar'ash.

When Marwân ibn-Muḥammad during his caliphate was busy fighting against Ḥimṣ, the Greeks came against Mar'ash and invested it until its inhabitants made terms to evacuate it. Accordingly, they together with their families left for Mesopotamia and the district of Ḳinnasrîn, upon which the Greeks destroyed the city. The *'âmil* of Marwân over the city was at that time al-Kauthar ibn-Zufar ibn-al-Ḥârith al-Kilâbi and the "tyrant" was Constantine son of Leon.[1] When Marwân was through with Ḥimṣ and had destroyed its wall, he sent an army to rebuild Mar'ash. It was rebuilt and made into a city; but the Greeks led an insurrection and destroyed it.

In the caliphate of abu-Ja'far al-Manṣûr, Ṣâliḥ ibn-'Ali rebuilt Mar'ash and fortified it. He invited men to settle in it, promising to increase their stipends. He was succeeded by al-Mahdi who increased its garrison and armed the people.

Muḥammad ibn-Sa'd from al-Wâḳidi:—Mîkhâ'îl [Michael] set out from Darb al-Ḥadath at the head of 80,000 men and came to 'Amḳ Mar'ash, killing, burning and carrying away the Moslems as captives. Thence he advanced to the gate of the city of Mar'ash in which there was 'Îsa ibn-'Ali who in that year was on an expedition. The freedmen of 'Îsa together with the inhabitants of the city and their troops sallied out against Michael and showered on him their lancets and arrows. Michael gave way before them and they followed him until they were outside the city range; at which he turned upon them, killing eight of 'Îsa's freedmen and chasing the rest back to the city. Having gone in, they closed its gates and Michael, after investing the city, departed and stopped at Jaiḥân. When Thumâmah ibn-al-Walid al-'Absi, who was then in Dâbiḳ and who in the year 161 led the summer expedition, heard of that, he despatched against Michael a strong detachment of cavalry most of whom lost their lives. This aroused the anger of al-Mahdi who began preparations for sending al-Ḥasan ibn-Ḳaḥṭabah on an expedition in the following year, *i. e.*, 162.

[1] Ar. Ḳusṭanṭin ibn-Alyûn. He was the successor of Heraclius; Maḥâsin, vol. i, p. 84; Athir, vol. ii, p. 444.

Ḥiṣn al-Ḥadath and Darb al-Ḥadath. Hisn al-Ḥadath was one of the places reduced in the days of 'Umar by Ḥabîb ibn-Maslamah who was sent by 'Iyâd ibn-Ghanm. After that, Mu'âwiyah used to pay frequent attention to it. Darb al-Ḥadath was ominously called by the banu-Umaiyah 190
"as-Salâmah" [safety] because they suffered a great calamity in it, the calamity being, according to some, the occurrence implied in the term Ḥadath [which means occurrence]. Others assert that the Moslems met on the way a youth who fought against them with his companions, hence the name Darb al-Ḥadath.[1]

At the time of the insurrection of Marwân ibn-Muhammad, the Greeks went and destroyed the city of al-Hadath and drove its people out as they had done in the case of Malaṭyah.

In the year 161, Michael went out to 'Amḳ Mar'ash, and al-Mahdi directed al-Ḥasan ibn-Kahtabah to make a tour in the Byzantine Empire. Al-Ḥasan's hand lay so heavily upon the people that they put his picture in their churches. His entrance to the land of the Greeks [Asia Minor] was through Darb al-Ḥadath where he examined the site of its city [al-Ḥadath] which he was told was evacuated by Michael. Al-Ḥasan chose that site for his city, and when he departed he spoke to al-Mahdi regarding the reconstruction of this city as well as that of Ṭarsûs. Al-Mahdi gave orders that al-Ḥadath be built first. Among the companions of al-Ḥasan in this campaign were Mandal al-'Anazi[2]—the Kufite traditionist, and Mu'tamir ibn-Sulaimân al-Baṣri. Al-Ḥadath was rebuilt by 'Ali ibn-Sulaimân ibn-'Ali, the governor of Mesopotamia and Ḳinnasrîn, and was called al-Muḥammadîyah. The death of al-Mahdi

[1] "The pass of the youth."

[2] *Cf.* Dhahabi, *Mushtabih*, p. 377.

coincided with the completion of its building, so it is really al-Mahdîyah as well as al-Muḥammadîyah. Brick was the material used in its construction. The death of al-Mahdi fell in the year 169.

Al-Mahdi was succeeded by his son Mûsa-l-Hâdi who dismissed 'Ali ibn-Sulaimân and conferred the governorship of Mesopotamia and Ḳinnasrîn upon Muḥammad ibn-Ibrâhîm ibn-Muḥammad ibn-'Ali. Since 'Ali ibn-Sulaimân had by this time completed the building of the city of al-Ḥadath, Muḥammad assigned to it troops from Syria, Mesopotamia and Khurâsân, fixing forty *dînârs* as the stipend of each soldier. To these he assigned the houses as fiefs, and bestowed three hundred *dirhams* on every one of them. The city was completed in 169.

According to abu-l-Khaṭṭâb, 'Ali ibn-Sulaimân assigned 4,000 paid troops to al-Ḥadath and settled them in it, transferring 2,000 men into it from Malaṭyah, Shimshâṭ, Sumaisâṭ, Kaisûm, Dulûk and Ra'bân.

It was stated by al-Wâḳidi that when the building of al-Ḥadath was completed, winter set in and rain and snow fell in great quantities. The houses of the city, not being 191
strongly built or provided with the necessary precautions, had their walls soon covered with cracks and fell to pieces. The Greeks then occupied it and the troops together with the people that were in it were scattered. Hearing that, Mûsa conscripted a contingent of troops headed by al-Musaiyab [not al-Musaiyib] ibn-Zuhair, another by Rauḥ ibn-Ḥâtim and still another by Hamzah ibn-Mâlik. Mûsa, however, died before they were sent out.

After that, ar-Rashîd became caliph, and he gave orders to rebuild the city, fortify it, station a garrison in it and assign to its fighters dwellings and lands as fiefs.

It was stated by others than al-Wâḳidi that when al-Ḥadath was built, one of the great patricians of the Greeks made a descent upon it with a strong host. The city was built with bricks, one placed on top of the other, without mortar intervening and which were damaged by the snow. The *'âmil* with all those in the city took to flight, and the enemy entered it, putting its mosque to flames, destroying the city and carrying away the movable possessions of the people. When ar-Rashîd became caliph, he rebuilt it.

I was informed by one from Manbij that ar-Rashîd wrote to Muḥammad ibn-Ibrâhîm confirming him in the work he was doing. Thus the erection of the city of al-Ḥadath and its peopling were carried out by him on behalf of ar-Rashîd. Later, Muḥammad was dismissed by ar-Rashîd.

Rahwat Mâlik. In the year 46, Mâlik ibn-'Abdallâh al-Khath'ami, nicknamed Mâlik aṣ-Ṣawâ'if [summer expeditions] and who was a Palestinian, made an expedition to the Byzantine territory and returned with great booty. On his way back he stopped at a place called ar-Rahwat, fifteen miles from Darb al-Ḥadath. There he spent three days during which he sold the booty and divided its shares. Therefore the place was called Rahwat Mâlik.

Marj 'Abd-al-Wâḥid. Marj 'Abd-al-Wâḥid was a pasture-land devoted to the exclusive use of the Moslem cavalry, which after the erection of al-Ḥadath and Zibaṭrah was of no more use and therefore was changed into a sown land.

Zibaṭrah. Zibaṭrah was an old Greek fort that was reduced together with the old Ḥadath[1] fort by Ḥabîb ibn-Maslamah-l-Fihri. The fort stood until it was destroyed by the Greeks in the days of al-Walîd ibn-Yazîd. It was then rebuilt, but not so strongly, therefore the Greeks made another attack on it at the time of the insurrection of Mar-

[1] Caetani, vol. iv, p. 60, note 1.

wân ibn-Muḥammad and destroyed it. Al-Manṣur built it again and it was once more torn into pieces by the Greeks. It was then rebuilt by ar-Rashîd under the supervision of Muḥammad ibn-Ibrâhîm who stationed a garrison in it.
When al-Ma'mûn became caliph, the Greeks made another 192
descent on it and tore it into pieces, after which they made a raid on the pasturing cattle of its holders and carried away some cattle. Al-Ma'mûn gave orders for repairing and fortifying it. In the year 210, the deputies of the Greek "tyrant" came asking for peace, which al-Ma'mûn refused. In pursuance of his orders, his *'âmils* [lieutenants] in the frontier fortresses made tours in Asia Minor where they wrought heavy slaughter, subdued the land and won many brilliant victories. One misfortune was the loss of the life of Yaḳẓân ibn-'Abd-al-A'la ibn-Aḥmad ibn-Yazîd ibn-Asîd as-Sulami.

In the days of al-Mu'taṣim-Billâh abu-Isḥâḳ ibn-ar-Rashîd, the Greeks made a sally against Zibaṭrah[1] in the course of which they killed the men, captured the women and destroyed the city. This greatly aroused the anger of al-Mu'taṣim who chased them as far as 'Ammûriyah, destroying many forts on the way. He camped against 'Ammûriyah until he reduced it, putting its fighters to death and carrying off the women and children as prisoners. He then destroyed 'Ammûriyah, and ordered that Zibaṭrah be rebuilt. He also fortified and garrisoned it. The Greeks after that tried to reduce it but failed.

Ḥiṣn Manṣûr. According to abu-'Amr al-Bâhili and others the Manṣûr fort was named after Manṣûr ibn-Ja'wanah ibn-al-Ḥârith al-'Âmiri of Ḳais who had charge of building and repairing it, and who occupied it in the days of Marwân with a large host of the troops of Syria and Mesopotamia in order to repulse the enemy.

[1] Yâḳût, vol. ii, p. 914.

This same Manṣûr was governor of ar-Ruha when its inhabitants rebelled in the early part of the [Abbasid] dynasty and were besieged by al-Manṣûr, the *'âmil* of abu-l-'Abbâs over Mesopotamia and Armenia. When al-Manṣûr captured the city, Manṣûr took to flight; but when he was later given safe-conduct, he appeared on the scene. When 'Abdallâh ibn-'Ali dismissed abu-Ja'far al-Manṣûr, 'Abdallâh made Manṣûr the chief of the guard in his district. When 'Abdallâh fled to al-Basrah, Manṣûr disappeared but was discovered in the year 141 and brought before al-Manṣûr, who, on his way from Jerusalem, put him to death at ar-Raḳḳah. According to others, Manṣûr was given safe-conduct and appeared after the flight of [Abdallâh] ibn-'Ali. After this there were found letters on him directed to the Greeks and betraying Islâm. When al-Manṣûr, in the year 141, arrived at ar-Raḳḳah from Jerusalem, he sent someone who brought him; and he was beheaded at ar-Raḳḳah. Al-Mansûr then departed for al-Hâshimîyah [1] at al-Kûfah.

In the caliphate of al-Mahdi, ar-Rashîd built the Manṣûr fort and stationed a garrison in it.

[1] Yâḳût, vol. iv. p. 946: *Baghdâd under the Abbasid Caliphate*, p. 5.

CHAPTER IV

Arabic made the Language of the State Registers 193

Greek remained the language of the state registers [1] until the reign of 'Abd-al-Malik ibn-Marwân, who in the year 81 ordered it changed. The reason was that a Greek clerk desiring to write something and finding no ink urined in the inkstand. Hearing this, 'Abd-al-Malik punished the man and gave orders to Sulaimân ibn-Sa'd to change the language of the registers. Sulaimân requested 'Abd-al-Malik to give him as subsidy the *kharâj* of the Jordan province for one year. 'Abd-al-Malik granted his request and assigned him to the governorship of the Jordan. No sooner had the year ended, than the change of the language was finished and Sulaimân brought the registers to 'Abd-al-Malik. The latter called Sarjûn [Sergius] and presented to him the new plan. Sarjûn was greatly chagrined and left 'Abd-al-Malik sorrowful. Meeting certain Greek clerks, he said to them, "Seek your livelihood in any other profession than this, for God has cut it off from you."

The total tax of the Jordan which was thus assigned as subsidy [2] was 180,000 *dînârs,* that of Palestine was 350,000; that of Damascus 400,000; that of Ḥimṣ with Ḳinnasrîn and the regions called to-day al-'Awâṣim, 800,000, and according to others 700,000.

[1] Ar. *dîwân* which may also be used in the sense of office or bureau.

[2] Ar. *ma'ûnah*; see Mubarrad, *Kâmil*, p. 76, last line.

PART IV

ARMENIA

CHAPTER I

The Conquest of Armenia

Traditions have been communicated to me by Muḥammad ibn-Ismâ'îl of Bardha'ah and others on the authority of abu-Barâ' 'Anbasah ibn-Baḥr al-Armani; by Muḥammad ibn-Bishr al-Ḳâli on the authority of his *sheikhs*; by Barmak ibn-'Abdallâh ad-Dabîli, Muḥammad ibn-al-Mukhaiyis al-Khilâṭi and others on the authority of some well versed in the affairs of Armenia. These traditions I herewith transmit, having pieced them up together into one whole, to wit:—

The four provinces. Shimshâṭ, Ḳâlîḳala, Khilâṭ Arjîsh and Bajunais constituted Armenia IV; the district of al- 194
Busfurrajân [Waspurakan], Dabîl [Dwîn], Sirâj Ṭair and Baghrawand constituted Armenia III; Jurzân [Georgia] constituted Armenia II; as-Sîsajân and Arrân constituted Armenia I.[1] According to others, Shimshâṭ alone constituted Armenia IV; Ḳâlîḳala, Khilâṭ, Arjîsh and Bâjunais, Armenia III; Sirâj Ṭair, Baghrawand, Dabîl, and al-Busfurrajân, Armenia II; and as-Sîsajân, Arrân [Albania], and Taflîs, Armenia I.[2] Jurzân and Arrân were held by the Khazar, while the rest of Armenia was held by the Greeks under the governorship of "the Lord of Armaniyâḳus".

Ḳubâdh ibn-Fairûz builds many cities. Al-Khazar used from time to time to make raids and reach as far as ad-Dînawar. Because of it, Ḳubâdh ibn-Fairûz *al-Malik*[3]

[1] *The Encyclopaedia of Islâm*, vol. i, p. 444.

[2] Khurdâdhbih, pp. 122-123.

[3] *i. e.*, the king. He belonged to the Sassanian Dynasty.

despatched one of his great generals at the head of 12,000 men, who ravaged the land of Arrân and conquered the region lying between ar-Rass river and Sharwân. Ḳubâdh then followed him and built in Arrân the city of al-Bailaḳân, the city of Bardha'ah—which is the capital of the whole frontier region, and the city of Ḳabalah, *i. e.*, al-Khazar. After that he erected Sudd al-Libn [brick dam] lying between the land of Sharwân and al-Lan gate. Along this Sudd, he established 360 cities which fell into ruins after the erection of the city of al-Bâb wa-l-Abwâb.

Anûshirwân builds other cities. Ḳubâdh was succeeded by his son Anûshirwân Kisra who built the cities of ash-Shâbirân and Maskaṭ, and later al-Bâb wa-l-Abwâb [1] which was called Abwâb because it was built on a road in the mountain. He settled in the places he built a people whom he called as-Siyâsijûn.[2] In the land of Arrân, he established Abwâb Shakkan,[3] al-Ḳamîbarân, and Abwâb ad-Dûdânîyah. Ad-Dûdânîyah are a tribe who claim to be descended from the banu-Dûdân ibn-Asad ibn-Khuzaimah. 195
He also built ad-Durdhûkîyah [4] which consisted of twelve gates,[5] each one of which was a castle of stone. In the land of Jurzân he established a city, Sughdabîl, which he populated with a body of as-Sughd [Sogdians] and Persians, making it a fortified town. Next to the Greek lands in the region of Jurzân, he built a castle and called it Bâb Fairûzi-ḳubâdh; another called Bâb Lâdhiḳah; still another Bâb

[1] Derbend. See Meynard, *Dictionnaire de la Perse*, p. 68; Hamadhâni, pp. 286-288; Ḥauḳal, pp. 241-242.

[2] *Cf.* St. Martin, *Mémoires sur l'Arménie*, vol. i, pp. 207-214.

[3] Hamadhâni, p. 288, "Shakka"; Yâḳût, "Shaḳa"; Ḥauḳal, p. 254, "Shakka".

[4] Hamadhâni, p. 288, "ad-Durzûḳîyah"; St. Martin, vol. ii, p. 189.

[5] *Cf.* Hamadhâni, p. 288.

Bârikah which lies on the Ṭarabazundah sea [Black Sea]. He also erected Bâb al-Lân, Bâb Samsakhi,[1] al-Jardamân fort, and Samshulda fort. Moreover, Anûshirwân conquered all the forts of Armenia held by the Greeks, built and fortified the city of Dabîl, built an-Nashawa—the capital of the al-Busfurrajân district, the fort of Waiṣ and other castles in the land of as-Sîsajân including al-Kilâb and Sâhyûnis castles. In the forts and castles, he stationed Siyâsijîyah men noted for valor and efficiency in warfare.

Anûshirwân builds a wall between his domain and that of the Turks. Anûshirwân then wrote to the king of the Turks asking for reconciliation and peace and for action in unison. In order to assure him of his friendliness, Anûshirwân sought his daughter's hand and expressed a desire to be his son-in-law. Meanwhile, he sent him a maid of his, who was adopted by one of his wives, and said she was his daughter. Consequently, the Turk presented his daughter to Anûshirwân and came to see him. The two met at al-Barshaliyah where they caroused together for some days, and each felt the other was friendly to him and expressed his loyalty. Anûshirwân ordered some of his friends in whom he confided to wait for nightfall and set fire to a part of the Turkish camp, which they did. In the morning, the Turkish king complained to Anûshirwân; but the latter denied having ordered it or known that his men had done it. After a few nights, Anûshirwân gave his orders to repeat the act, and his men did. The Turk grumbled so much at the act that Anûshirwân had to show sympathy for him 196
and apologized to him, upon which he was appeased. By order of Anûshirwân, fire was set in a corner of his own camp where nothing but cottages of straw and twigs stood. In the morning, Anûshirwân grumbled to the Turk, saying,

[1] Brosset, *Histoire de la Georgie*, vol. i, p. 238.

"Thy men were on the point of destroying my camp; and thou rewardest me by throwing suspicion upon me!" The Turk swore that he knew no reason for the act, upon which Anûshirwân addressed him, saying, "Brother, thy troops and mine look with disfavor on the peace we made, because they have thereby lost the booty depending on razzias and wars that might be carried out between us. I fear they undertake things to corrupt our hearts after our mutual agreement of sincerity, so that we may once more have recourse to enmity after our new blood relationship and our friendship. I deem it wise, therefore, that thou allowest me to build a wall between thee and me with one gate through which none from us will go to you and from you to us, except the ones thou wishest and we wish." The Turk accepted the proposal and left for his own land.

Anûshirwân commenced building the wall. He built the side of it that faced the sea with rock and lead. Its width he made 300 *dhirâ'ṣ,* and its height reached the mountain heights. He ordered that stones be carried in boats and dropped into the sea, so that when they appeared above the surface, he could build on them. The wall extended over a distance of three miles in the sea. When the construction was completed, he fixed on its entrance iron gates and entrusted it to one hundred horsemen to guard it. Before this, it took 50,000 troops to guard the place. On this wall he also set a mantelet. The Khaḳân [1] was later told, "Anûshirwân has deceived thee and given thee for wife one who is not his daughter and fortified himself against thee"; but Khaḳân was no match for such wiles.

Anûshirwân assigns kings. Anûshirwân assigned kings, stationed them in different districts, and conferred on each one of them the governorship [made him Shâh] of one dis-

[1] The Turkish king.

trict. One of these was "Khakân al-Jabal" [lord of the mountain] who bore the title "Ṣâḥib as-Sarîr"[1] [holder of the throne] and was named Wahrârzân-shâh. Another was the king of Fîlân surnamed Fîlân-shâh. Others were Ṭabarsarân-shâh, the king of al-Lakz—surnamed Jarshân-shâh—the king of Maskaṭ (whose kingship has been abolished), the king of Lîrân—surnamed Lîrân-shâh—and the king of Sharwân called Sharwân-shâh. He also made 197
the chief of Bukh[2] its king, and the chief of Zirîkirân its king. The kings of Jabal al-Ḳabaḳ[3] he left over their kingdoms and made terms with them, stipulating that they pay an annual tribute.

Thus Armenia was in the hands of the Persians until the appearance of Islâm, at which time many Siyâsîjûn abandoned their forts and cities which fell into ruins. The Khazar and Greeks thus got possession of what was once in their hands.

Ḳâlîḳala. At a certain period, the Greek princes were scattered about and some of them became like Mulûk aṭ-Ṭawâ'if,[4] and one ruled over Armaniyâḳus. After the death of the latter, his wife succeeded him and her name was Ḳâli.[5] She built the city of Ḳâlîḳala[6] which she named Ḳâliḳâlah. The meaning of the word is "the benevolence of Ḳâli." She set her picture on one of the city gates. The Arabs arabicized Ḳâliḳâlah into Ḳâlîḳala.

Ḳâlîḳala reduced. When 'Uthmân ibn-'Affân became caliph, he wrote to Mu'âwiyah, his *'âmil* over Syria and

[1] Iṣṭakhri, p. 191, note f; Mas'ûdi, vol. ii, pp. 41-42.

[2] St. Martin, vol. i, p. 76.

[3] *Cf.* Meynard, p. 437, "Qabq (Caucase)".

[4] Petty kings among whom the Persian kingdom was divided after Alexander. Ṭabari, vol. i, pp. 704-713.

[5] Hamadhâni, p. 292.

[6] Armen. *Karin*, modern Erzerum.

Mesopotamia together with their frontier cities, ordering him to send Ḥabib ibn-Maslamah-l-Fihri into Armenia.[1] Ḥabib had left a good impression in connection with the conquest of Syria and the invasion of the Greeks. This fact was fully realized by 'Umar, by 'Uthmân and by 'Uthmân's successor. Others say that 'Uthmân wrote [directly] to Ḥabîb ordering him to make an expedition against Armenia. The former view is more authentic. Accordingly, Ḥabîb went against it at the head of 6,000, but according to another estimate, 8,000, of the people of Syria and Mesopotamia. Arriving in Ḳâliḳala, he camped around it; and when its people came out against him, he fought them and drove them to the city. They then asked for peace, agreeing to evacuate the place and pay the tax. Many of them left the city and went as far as Asia Minor. Ḥabîb remained in the city with his men for a few months. He then learned that the patrician of Armaniyâkus had massed a large army against the Moslems and was reinforced by troops from al-Lân, Afkhâz and from Samandar in al-Khazar. Therefore, he wrote to 'Uthmân asking for reinforcement. 'Uthmân wrote to Mu'âwiyah asking him to send to Ḥabîb a body of men from Syria and Mesopotamia interested in the "holy war" and booty. Accordingly, Mu'âwiyah sent 2,000 men who were settled in Ḳâlîḳala, given fiefs and stationed as horsemen guard to keep post in it. 19
At the receipt of Ḥabîb's request, 'Uthmân also wrote to Sa'îd ibn-al-'Âṣi ibn-Sa'îd ibn-al-'Âṣi ibn-Umaiyah, his *'âmil* over al-Kûfah, ordering him to reinforce Ḥabîb with an army headed by Salmân ibn-Rabî'ah-l-Bâhili who bore the title "Salmân al-Khail" [the Salmân of horsemen] and who was generous, benevolent and of a warlike nature. Salmân set out at the head of 6,000 Kufites. The Greeks

[1] Müller, *Der Islam in Morgen- und Abendland*, pp. 259-260.

and their followers had already arrived and encamped on the Euphrates, before Ḥabîb received the reinforcement. Taking advantage of the night, the Moslems swept over them and killed their chief. That evening Ḥabîb's wife, umm-'Abdallâh, daughter of Yazîd of the Kalb tribe, asked Ḥabîb, "Where shall I meet thee?" To this, Ḥabîb replied, "Either at the tents of the 'tyrant',[1] or in Paradise!" When he got to those tents he found her there.

When the Moslems were done with their enemy, Salmân returned. The Kufite troops wanted to have a share in the booty but were refused, which led into a verbal dispute between Ḥabîb and Salmân. Some Moslems threatened Salmân with death, regarding which the poet said:

> "If ye kill Salmân, we kill your Ḥabîb;
> and if ye depart towards ibn-'Affân, we would also depart."[2]

'Uthmân was communicated with, and he wrote back, "The spoils belong wholly to the Syrians by right." Meanwhile, he wrote to Salmân ordering him to invade Arrân.

It is reported by others that in the caliphate of 'Uthmân, Salmân ibn-Rabî'ah went to Armenia, made captives and plundered, returning in the year 25 to al-Walîd ibn-'Uḳbah at Ḥadîthat al-Mauṣil. Al-Walîd received a letter from 'Uthmân informing him that Mu'âwiyah had written him to the effect that the Greeks were gathered against the Moslems in great numbers, and that the Moslems wanted reinforcements, and ordering him to send 8,000 men.[3] Accordingly, al-Walîd sent 8,000 men under Salmân ibn-Rabî'ah-l-Bâhili. Mu'âwiyah sent an equal number under Ḥabîb ibn-Maslamah-l-Fihri. The two leaders reduced many

[1] Referring to the Greek general.

[2] Ṭabari, vol. i, pp. 2893-2894.

[3] *Ibid.*, vol. i, pp. 2807-2808.

forts, carried away many prisoners and fell to dispute regarding the general leadership. The Syrians wanted to kill Salmân, hence the verse quoted above. The former report, however, is more authentic and was orally communicated to me by many from Ḳâliḳala and in writing by al-'Attâf ibn-Sufyân abu-l-Aṣbagh, the *ḳâḍi* of Ḳâliḳala.

Ḥabîb kills al-Mauriyân. Muḥammad ibn-Sa'd from 'Abd-al-Ḥamîd ibn-Ja'far's father:—Ḥabîb ibn-Maslamah besieged the inhabitants of Dabîl and camped around the city. Al-Mauriyân ar-Rûmi [1] came against him; but under the cover of the night, Ḥabîb killed him and plundered what was in his camp. Salmân then joined Ḥabîb. The authorities of this tradition believe that Ḥabîb fell upon the Greek at Ḳâliḳala. 199

Kûsân subdues Ḳâliḳala. Muḥammad ibn-Bishr al-Ḳâli and ibn-Warz al-Ḳâli from the *sheikhs* of Ḳâliḳala:—Ever since its conquest, the city of Ḳâliḳala held out against attacks until the year 133 in which "the tyrant" set out, besieged Malaṭyah, destroyed its wall and expelled the Moslems that were in it to Mesopotamia, after which he encamped at Marj al-Ḥaṣa whence he directed Kûsân al-Armani against Ḳâliḳala. Kûsân came and invested the city, whose inhabitants at that time were few and whose *'âmil* was abu-Karîmah. In the course of the siege, two Armenian brothers who lived in the city made a breach through a rampart in its wall, went out to Kûsân and brought him in to the city. Thus Kûsân subdued the city, killed [many], took captives and razed it to the ground, carrying off what he plundered to "the tyrant". The captives he distributed among his companions.

Al-Manṣûr rebuilds and al-Mu'taṣim fortifies Ḳâliḳala.

[1] Patrician of Armaniyâḳus which province is listed in De Goeje's edition of Balâdhuri as a name of person.

According to al-Wâkidi, in the year 139 al-Manṣûr gave ransom [1] for those of the captives of Ḳâliḳala who survived; and he rebuilt Ḳâliḳala, populated it, and returned them into it. He also invited to it troops from Mesopotamia and other places to live in it. In the caliphate of al-Mu'taṣim-Billâh, the Greek "tyrant" came to Ḳâliḳala and threw projectiles on its wall until it was on the point of falling. Thereupon al-Mu'taṣim had to spend 500,000 *dirhams* to make the city strong again.

The patricians of Khilâṭ and Muks. After having captured Ḳâliḳala, Ḥabîb marched to Mirbâla where the patrician of Khilâṭ brought him a statement written by 'Iyâḍ ibn-Ghanm, who had guaranteed to the patrician the security of his life, possessions and country and had concluded a treaty with him stipulating that the patrician should pay tax. Ḥabîb sanctioned the terms of the statement. He then occupied a house between al-Harak [2] and Dasht al-Warak. The patrician of Khilâṭ brought him the money he owed and offered a present which Ḥabîb refused to accept. Ḥabîb then visited Khilâṭ and passed to aṣ-Ṣabâbah [?] [3] where he was met by the chief of Muks,[4] one of the districts of al-Busfurrajân. Ḥabîb made peace with him in exchange for an annual tax to be paid for his land, sent a 200
man with him and wrote him a statement of peace and safety.

Arjîsh, Bâjunais and aṭ-Ṭirrîkh. To the villages of Arjîsh and Bâjunais, Ḥabîb sent a body of men who subdued them and laid poll-tax on them. The leading men of these villages came to Ḥabîb and made a treaty agreeing to

[1] Ar. *fâda bihim*; see Mawardi, pp. 82 and 232.

[2] St. Martin, vol. i, p. 101.

[3] Original not clear.

[4] St. Martin, vol. i, p. 175.

pay the *kharâj* on their lands. As for aṭ-Ṭirrîkh lake, he did not interfere with it, and it was used by the public until Muḥammad ibn-Marwân ibn-al-Ḥakam became governor of Mesopotamia and Armenia, upon which he took possession of its fish and sold them, making an income out of it. The lake after that became the property of Marwân ibn-Muḥammad and was thus lost to Muḥammad.

Dabîl and other towns sue for peace. Ḥabîb now came to Azdisâṭ,[1] the chief village of al-Hurmuz,[2] crossed Nahr al-Akrâd and encamped at Marj Dabîl. Thence he sent the cavalry against Dabîl and marched until he reached its gate. The people took to the fortifications and threw projectiles on him. Ḥabîb set a mangonel against the city and used it until they sued for peace and capitulation. This he granted them. His cavalry wandered around, occupied Jurna,[3] reached as far as Ashûsh, dhât-al-Lujum, al-Jabal Kûntah[4] and Wâdi-l-Aḥrâr and subdued all the villages of Dabîl. He also despatched a force against Sirâj Ṭair and against Baghrawand whose patrician came and made terms, agreeing to pay an annual tribute, to be loyal to the Moslems, to entertain them, and to aid them against the enemy. The text of the treaty with Dabîl ran as follows:

"In the name of Allah, the compassionate, the merciful. This is a treaty of Ḥabîb ibn-Maslamah with the Christians, Magians and Jews of Dabîl, including those present and absent. I have granted you safety for your lives, possessions, churches, places of worship, and city wall. Thus ye are safe and we are bound to fulfil our covenant, so long as ye fulfil yours and pay poll-tax and *kharâj*. Thereunto

[1] "Aschdischad," St. Martin, vol. i, p. 101; Yâḳût, vol. i, p. 199, "Ardashât".

[2] Balâdhuri reads "Ḳirmiz," which is a clerical error.

[3] *Marâṣid,* vol. i, p. 25.

[4] Original not clear.

Allah is witness; and it suffices to have him for witness. Signed by Ḥabîb ibn-Maslamah."

An-Nashawa and al-Busfurrajân. Ḥabîb after this proceeded to an-Nashawa and took possession of it on terms similar to those of Dabîl. The patrician of al-Busfurrajân came and made terms regarding all of his country together with the land of Haṣâtiltah[1] [?] and Afâristah [?], agreeing to pay a certain tax every year.

As-Sîsajân. Ḥabîb then moved to as-Sîsajân[2] whose people resisted him but were defeated. He also conquered Waiṣ; and made terms with the holders of the forts at as- 201
Sîsajân to the effect that they pay tax. He then proceeded to Jurzân.

Dhât-al-Lujum. I was informed by certain *sheikhs* from Dabîl, among whom was Barmak ibn-'Abdallâh, that Ḥabîb ibn-Maslamah marched with his men bent on Jurzân. When they got to dhât-al-Lujum, they left some of their horses and mules to graze, leaving their bridles together in one place. Suddenly, a band of the "uncircumcised" fell upon them before they could bridle their animals. In the fight that ensued, the "uncircumcised" drove the Moslems away and seized the bridles together with as many horses and mules as they could. Later, the Moslems returned to them, massacred them and took back what has been carried away from them. That is why this spot was called "dhât-al-Lujum" [the place of the bridles].

As Ḥabîb was advancing against the patrician of Jurzân, he was met by a messenger of the patrician and the inhabitants of the town, who presented a written message and asked for a treaty of peace and security. Accordingly, Ḥabîb wrote to them:—

[1] Certain diacritical points missing.

[2] Meynard, p. 335.

"Your messenger, Nuḳla,[1] came to me and my companions 'the Believers' saying on your behalf that we are a nation whom Allah has honored and given superiority, which Allah did, great praise be to Allah, and prayer and peace be on Muḥammad his Prophet and noblest creature! Ye also stated that ye would like to make peace with us. As for your present, I have estimated its value and considered it a part of your tax. I have made a treaty of peace with you and inserted one condition in it. If ye accept the condition and live up to it, well and good. Otherwise 'announce ye a war waged by Allah and his Prophet[2]'. Peace be to those who follow the proper guidance."

The treaty with the people of Taflîs. Ḥabîb thence proceeded to Taflîs [Tiflis] and made the following statement of peace to its people:—

"In the name of Allah, the compassionate, the merciful. This is a statement from Ḥabîb ibn-Maslamah to the inhabitants of Taflîs which lies in Manjalîs[3] at Jurzân al-Hurmuz,[4] securing them safety for their lives, churches, convents, religious services and faith, provided they acknowledge their humiliation and pay tax to the amount of one *dînâr* on every household. Ye are not to combine more than one household into one in order to reduce the tax, nor are we to divide the same household into more than one in order to increase it. Ye owe us counsel and support against the enemies of Allah and his Prophet to the utmost of your ability, and are bound to entertain the needy Moslem for one night and provide him with that food used by 'the people of the Book' and which it is legal for us to partake of.

[1] *Cf.* Ṭabari, vol. i, p. 2674.

[2] Kor., 2:279.

[3] Brosset, vol. i, pp. 245, 248.

[4] and not "Ḳirmiz" as Balâdhuri has it. See Ṭabari, vol. i, p. 2674.

If a Moslem is cut off from his companions and falls into your hands, ye are bound to deliver him to the nearest body of the 'Believers', unless something stands in the way. 202
If ye return to the obedience [1] of Allah and observe prayer, ye are our brethren in faith, otherwise poll-tax is incumbent on you. In case an enemy of yours attacks and subjugates you while the Moslems are too busy to come to your aid, the Moslems are not held responsible, nor is it a violation of the covenant with you. The above are your rights and obligations to which Allah and his angels are witness and it is sufficient to have Allah for witness."

The following is a copy of the treaty made by al-Jarrâḥ ibn-'Abdallâh-l-Ḥakami with the people of Taflîs:

"In the name of Allah, the compassionate, the merciful. This is a treaty made by al-Jarrâḥ ibn-'Abdallâh with the inhabitants of Taflîs in the district of Manjalîs and the province of Jurzân. They have shown me the treaty made with them by Ḥabîb ibn-Maslamah to the effect that they accept the humiliation of the tax, and that he made terms with them regarding lands belonging to them, vineyards, and mills, called Awâra and Sabîna in the district of Manjalîs, and regarding Ṭa'âm and Dîdûna in the district of Ḳuḥuwîṭ in the province of Jurzân, stipulating that they pay on these mills and vineyards a tax of 100 *dirhams* per annum without repeating it. These terms of peace and security I put into effect and ordered that the sum be never increased on them. Let no one, therefore, to whom this my treaty is read increase the tax on them; so Allah wills. Written by—."

Various places conquered by Ḥabîb. Ḥabîb conquered Ḥawâriḥ, Kasfaryabs [?],[2] Kisâl, Khunân, Samsakhi, al-

[1] Ṭabari, vol. i, p. 2675: "become Moslem".

[2] Lacking in diacritical points.

Jardamân, Kastasji,[1] Shaushit,[2] and Bâzalît,[3] which capitulated on the terms that the lives of the inhabitants be spared, that places of worship and their walls be not molested and that they pay annual tribute on their lands and persons. The people of Ḳalarjît, Tharyâlît,[4] Khâkhît,[5] Khûkhîṭ,[6] 203
Arṭahâl,[7] and Bâb al-Lâl [8] also made terms with Ḥabîb. Aṣ-Ṣanârîyah and ad-Dûdânîyah made terms, agreeing to pay an annual tax.

Al-Bailaḳân. By order of 'Uthmân, Salmân ibn-Rabî'ah-l-Bâhili proceeded to Arrân. Here he conquered the city of al-Bailaḳân which capitulated on terms stipulating that he guarantee the safety of their lives, possessions and city walls, and that they pay poll-tax and *kharâj.*

Bardha'ah and other places. Thence Salmân advanced to Bardha'ah and camped on ath-Thurthûr [9] river which flows at a distance of less than one parasang from the city. The inhabitants closed their city gates against him; and he made an attempt on it for many days, making raids on its villages. It was the time for reaping the harvest. At last, its people made terms similar to those of al-Bailaḳân and opened their gates. Thus he made his entrance and occupied the city. Salmân then sent his cavalry which conquered Shifshîn, al-Misfawân, Ûdh, al-Misryân,[10] al-Hur-

[1] Brosset, vol. i, p. 512.

[2] St. Martin: "Schauscheth"; *cf.* Ḳazwîni, vol. ii, p. 413, line 20.

[3] Brosset, vol. i, pp. 45, 86.

[4] "Thrialeth," Brosset, vol. i, pp. 248, 285.

[5] "Kakheth" in Brosset, *l. l.*

[6] "Kukhet," Brosset, vol. i, pp. 315, 349; St. Martin, vol. ii, p. 198.

[7] Brosset, vol. i, p. 39.

[8] St. Martin, vol. ii, p. 227.

[9] St. Martin, vol. i, p. 87.

[10] Text not clear.

ḥilyân and Tabâr, all of which are districts. Other places in Arrân were reduced. The Kurds of al-Balâsajân [1] he summoned to Islâm; but they fought against him and were subjugated. Some were made to pay tax and others *ṣadaḳah*; but the latter were few.

Shamkûr. I was informed by some people from Bardha'ah that Shamkûr was an ancient city to which Salmân ibn-Rabî'ah sent someone who reduced it. It was well populated and flourishing until it was destroyed by as-Sâwardîyah, who after the departure of Yazîd ibn-Usaid from Armenia came together and became a source of trouble and misfortune. In the year 240, the city was rebuilt by Bugha, the freedman of al-Mu'taṣim and the governor of Armenia, Adharbaijân and Shimshâṭ. He settled in it people from al-Khazar who, because of their interest in Islâm came, and sought security. He also transplanted merchants to it from Bardha'ah and called it al-Mutawakkilîyah.

Ḳabalah and other places. Salmân thence advanced to the junction of ar-Rass and al-Kurr behind Bardîj. Crossing al-Kurr he reduced Ḳabalah; and the chief of Shakkan and al-Ḳamîbarân capitulated, agreeing to pay annual tax. In like manner did the people of Khaizân,[2] the king of 204
Sharwân and the other kings of al-Jibâl, the people of Masḳaṭ, ash-Shâbirân and the city of al-Bâb capitulate. The city of al-Bâb was closed after him. Khâḳân with his cavalry met Salmân beyond al-Balanjar river. The latter was killed with 4,000 Moslems who in that critical position were heard shouting "Allah is great!" [3]

[1] Yâḳût, vol. i, p. 173, and vol. ii, p. 780.

[2] St. Martin, vol. i, pp. 175 *seq.*; Yâḳût, vol. ii, p. 507: "Khaizâr"; Mas'ûdi, vol. ii, pp. 39-40; Meynard, p. 350.

[3] Ya'ḳûbi, vol. ii, p. 194.

Salmân the first ḳâḍi of al-Kûfah. This Salmân ibn-Rabî'ah was the first to hold the position of *ḳâḍi* in al-Kûfah,[1] where he spent forty days without hearing a case. He transmitted traditions on 'Umar ibn-al-Khaṭṭâb's authority. Says ibn-Jumânah-l-Bâhili referring to Salmân and Ḳutaibah ibn-Muslim:

" We have two tombs one at Balanjar
 and another at Ṣîn-Istân [China] and what a tomb that is!
The one who lies in China has brought about conquests in all places;
 and the merits of the other cause abundant rain to fall."[2]

Among the companions of Salmân at Balanjar was Ḳarẓah ibn-Ka'b al-Anṣâri. It was he who carried the news of Salmân's death to 'Uthmân.

Ḥabîb put by 'Uthmân in charge of the frontier fortresses. Having made these conquests in Armenia, Ḥabîb reported his success to 'Uthmân ibn-'Affân who received his letter immediately after the news of Salmân's death. 'Uthmân was on the point of assigning Ḥabîb over all Armenia; but he then deemed it best to put him in charge of the campaigns on the frontiers of Syria and Mesopotamia, because of his efficiency in doing what he intended to do. 'Uthmân conferred on Ḥudhaifah ibn-al-Yamân al-'Absi the governorship of the frontier fortresses of Armenia; and the latter left for Bardha'ah and sent his *'âmils* to the places that lay between it and Ḳâlîkala and up to Khaizân. He then received 'Uthmân's message instructing him to depart and leave in his place Ṣilah ibn-Zufar al-'Absi who was in his company. Ḥudhaifah assigned Ṣilah as his successor.

Ḥabîb returned to Syria and began his campaigns against the Greeks. He settled in Ḥimṣ, but Mu'âwiyah moved him to Damascus, where he died in the year 42, aged 35. Once

[1] Gottheil, *Egyptian Cadis*, page VI.

[2] For an explanation see ibn-Ḳutaibah, *Kitâb al-Ma'ârif*, p. 221.

when 'Uthmân was besieged, Mu'âwiyah sent this Ḥabîb at the head of an army to his relief. Having arrived in Wâdi-l-Ḳura, Ḥabîb heard of the death of 'Uthmân and 205
took his way back.[1]

Various governors of Adharbaijân and Armenia. 'Uthmân appointed al-Mughîrah ibn-Shu'bah governor of Adharbaijân[2] and Armenia, but dismissed him later, and appointed al-Ḳâsim ibn-Rabî'ah ibn-Umaiyah ibn-abi-aṣ-Ṣalt ath-Thaḳafi governor of Armenia. Others say he appointed 'Amr ibn-Mu'âwiyah ibn-al-Muntafiḳ al-'Uḳaili governor of Armenia; and still others say that for 15 years after al-Mughîrah, one of the banu-Kilâb ruled over Armenia, and that he was succeeded by al-'Uḳaili. Under 'Ali ibn-abi-Ṭâlib, al-Ash'ath ibn Ḳais ruled over Armenia and Adharbaijân. He was followed by 'Abdallâh ibn-Ḥâtim ibn-an-Nu'mân ibn-'Amr al-Bâhili who ruled over it in the name of Mu'âwiyah. 'Abdallâh died in it and was succeeded by his brother 'Abd-al-'Azîz ibn-Ḥâtim ibn-an-Nu'mân, who built the city of Dabîl, fortified it and enlarged its mosque. He also built the city of an-Nashawa and repaired the city of Bardha'ah. Others say he rebuilt Bardha'ah and deepened the trenches around it. He also rebuilt the city of al-Bailaḳân. These cities were dilapidated and ready to fall into ruins. According to others, it was Muhammad ibn-Marwân who in the days of 'Abd-al-Malik ibn-Marwân rebuilt Bardha'ah. Al-Wâḳidi states that 'Abd-al-Malik built Bardha'ah under the supervision of Ḥâtim ibn-an-Nu'mân al-Bâhili or his son. This 'Abd-al-Malik appointed 'Uthmân ibn-al-Walid ibn-'Uḳbah ibn-abi-Mu'aiṭ to the governorship of Armenia.

[1] Ghazarian, "Armenien unter der Arab Herrschaft," *Zeitschrift für Armen. Philol.*, vol. ii, pp. 177-182 (Marburg, 1904).

[2] Meynard, pp. 14-17.

Armenia rebels. During the insurrection of ibn-az-Zubair, Armenia rose and its nobles [1] with their followers threw off their allegiance. When Muḥammad ibn-Marwân held under his brother 'Abd-al-Malik the governorship of Armenia, he led the fight against them and won the victory, slaughtering and taking captives. Thus, he subdued the land. He promised those who survived higher stipends than the ordinary soldiers' pay. For that purpose they assembled in churches in the province of Khilâṭ where he locked them in and put guards on the door, and then he frightened them. In this campaign umm-Yazîd ibn-Usaid was taken captive from as-Sîsajân, she being the daughter of as-Sîsajân's patrician.

'Adi governor of Armenia. Sulaimân ibn-'Abd-al-Malik made 'Adi ibn-'Adi ibn-'Amîrah [2]-l-Kindi governor of Armenia. 'Adi ibn-'Amîrah was one of those who had left 'Ali ibn-abi-Ṭâlib and settled in ar-Raḳḳah. He was later made the governor of Armenia by 'Umar ibn-'Abd-al-'Azîz. This 'Adi was the one after whom the Nahr 'Adi at al-Bailaḳân was named. According to others, the *'âmil* of 'Umar was Ḥâtim ibn-an-Nu'mân, but that is not confirmed. 206

Mi'laḳ and al-Ḥârith as governors. Yazîd ibn-'Abd-al-Malik conferred the governorship on Mi'laḳ ibn-Ṣaffâr al-Bahrâni, but he later dismissed him and assigned al-Ḥârith ibn-'Amr aṭ-Ṭâ'i, who made an incursion against the inhabitants of al-Lakz [3] conquering the district of Ḥasmadân.[4]

Al-Jarrâḥ as governor. When al-Jarrâḥ ibn-'Abdallâh

[1] Ar. *aḥrâr,* the class that constituted the aristocracy of Armenia before the Persian rule; see Yâḳût, vol. i, pp. 222, 438.

[2] Ṭabari, vol. ii, p. 887: "'Umairah".

[3] Yâḳût, vol. iv, p. 364.

[4] "Jashmadân," Iṣṭakhri, p. 187.

al-Ḥakami of Madhḥij became governor of Armenia, he stopped at Bardha'ah where his attention was called to the different measures and weights used by the people and which he fixed according to the standards of justice and honesty introducing a new measure, called al-Jarrâḥi, with which they deal until to-day. After crossing al-Kurr,[1] he marched until he went over the river known by the name of as-Samûr and came to al-Khazar, among whom he wrought a great slaughter. He also fought against the inhabitants of the land of Ḥamzîn[2] and made terms with them stipulating that they be transplanted to the district of Khaizân where he gave them two villages. He then attacked the people of Ghûmîk[3] and captured some of them. Turning back, he came to Shakka, and his army spent the winter at Bardha'ah and al-Bailaḳân. Al-Khazar assembled their troops and crossed ar-Rass.[4] He fought against them in Saḥrâ' [desert] Warthân, and when they withdrew to the region of Ardabîl[5] he engaged them in battle at a distance of four parasangs from Armenia. After a three days' battle, he suffered martyrdom together with his men, and therefore was the river called Nahr al-Jarrâḥ. A bridge spanning it also bore the same name.

Maslamah as governor. Hishâm ibn-'Abd-al-Malik after that appointed Maslamah ibn-'Abd-al-Malik to the governorship of Armenia, put at the head of the van of his [Maslamah's] army Sa'îd ibn-'Amr ibn-Aswad al-Jurashi, and accompanied him by Isḥâḳ ibn-Muslim al-'Uḳaili with his brothers, Ja'wanah ibn-al-Ḥârith ibn-Khâlid of the banu-

[1] Iṣṭakhri, p. 187.

[2] "Ḥamrîn," Maḥâsin, vol. i, p. 318.

[3] "Ghumîk," Iṣṭakhri, p. 185; *cf.* Mas'ûdi, vol. ii, p. 40; "'Amîk" in Yâḳût, vol. i, p. 438.

[4] Iṣṭakhri, p. 187; Yâḳût, vol. ii, p. 779.

[5] Meynard, pp. 21-22.

Rabî'ah ibn-'Âmir ibn-Ṣa'ṣa'ah, Dhufâfah and Khâlid—the two sons of 'Umair ibn-al-Ḥubâb as-Sulami—al-Furât ibn-Salmân al-Bâhili, and al-Walîd ibn-al-Ḳa'ḳâ' al-'Absi. Sa'îd engaged in conflict with al-Khazar who were at this time besieging Warthân, and forced them to withdraw, putting them to flight. Al-Khazar came to Maimadh in Adharbaijân; and as Sa'îd was preparing for the conflict with them, he received a message from Maslamah ibn-'Abd-al-Malik blaming him for attacking al-Khazar before his [Maslamah's] arrival, and informing him that he had assigned in his place over the army 'Abd-al-Malik ibn-Muslim al-'Uḳaili. As soon as Sa'îd turned over the army to his successor, he was arrested by Maslamah's messenger who fettered him and carried him to Bardha'ah where he was thrown into its prison. Al-Khazar left and 207
Maslamah followed them. When Maslamah communicated the news to Hishâm, Hishâm wrote back:

> "Dost thou leave them at Maimadh where thou canst see them,
> and then seek them beyond the limit of soil [where sand begins]?"

Thereupon Hishâm ordered that al-Jurashi be released from prison.

Maslamah made peace with the people of Khaizân, and by his order, its fort was dismantled. He appropriated in it estates for himself. It is known to-day by the name of Ḥauz Khaizân. The kings of al-Jibâl also made peace with him. The Shâhs of Sharwân, Lîrân, Ṭabarsarân, Fîlân and Jarshân presented themselves before him; and so did the chief of Masḳaṭ. Maslamah, thereupon, betook himself to the city of al-Bâb, which he reduced. In its castle were a thousand families of al-Khazar whom he besieged and against whom he hurled stones and then pieces of iron shaped like stones. All that, however, was of no avail. He, therefore, resorted to the spring, the water of which Anûshirwân had conducted into their cistern, and slew on it cows and sheep throwing the contents of their stomachs and some assafœtida into the water. It did not take the water more than one night before it bred worms, became vitiated and corrupted. Therefore, the holders of the castle fled under the cover of the night and vacated the castle. In the city of al-Bâb wa-l-Abwâb, 24,000 Syrians were settled by Maslamah ibn-'Abd-al-Malik and assigned stipends. Accordingly, the inhabitants of al-Bâb to-day do not allow any *'âmil* to enter their city unless he has money to distribute among them. He, moreover, built a granary for food, another for barley, and an armory. He ordered that the cistern be filled with earth, repaired the city, and provided it with embattlements. In the company of Maslamah was Marwân ibn-Muḥammad who took part in the attack against al-Khazar and distinguished himself in fighting. After Maslamah, Hishâm appointed Sa'îd al-Jurashi who spent two years in the frontier region.

Marwân as governor. Marwân ibn-Muḥammad [1] then became the ruler of the frontier and took up his abode at Kisâl. Marwân was the one who built the city of Kisâl. This city lies 40 parasangs from Bardha'ah and 20 from Taflîs. Marwân then entered the country of al-Khazar next to Bâb al-Lân and made Asîd [2] ibn-Zâfir as-Sulami abu-Yazîd, accompanied by the kings of al-Jibâl, enter it from the side of al-Bâb wa-l-Abwâb. Then Marwân made an incursion on the Slavs who were in the land of al-Kha- 208
zar and captured 20,000 families whom he settled in Khâkhîṭ. When they later put their commander to death and took to flight, Marwân pursued and slaughtered them.

When the chief of al-Khazar learned of the great num-

[1] Brosset, vol. i, pp. 238 *seq.*

[2] "Usaid" in Duraid, p. 187, line before last.

ber of men with whom Marwân had swept over his land and of their equipment and strength, his heart was filled with cowardice and fear. When Marwân came close to him, he sent him a messenger inviting him to "Islâm or war", to which he replied, "I have accepted Islâm. Send therefore someone to present it to me." Marwân did so. The chief professed Islâm and made a treaty with Marwân according to which Marwân confirmed him as ruler of his kingdom. Marwân with a host of al-Khazar accompanied the chief; and al-Khazar were made to settle in the plain of the province of al-Lakz between as-Samûr and ash-Shâbirân.

The land of as-Sarîr. After that, Marwân made his entrance to the land of as-Sarîr, slaughtered its inhabitants, and reduced certain forts in it. Its king offered him submission and allegiance and made terms, agreeing to give every year 1,000 youths—500 lads and 500 maids—with black hair and eyebrows and with long eyelashes, together with 100,000 modii [1] to be poured in the granaries of al-Bâb. Marwân took from him a pledge.

The people of Tûmân made terms with Marwân, agreeing to give every year 100 youths—50 maids and 50 lads—each 5 spans in height, with black hair and eyebrows and with long eyelashes, together with 20,000 modii for the granaries.

The land of Zirîkirân. He then entered the land of Zirîkirân,[2] whose king made terms, agreeing to offer fifty youths, and 10,000 modii for the granaries every year. Thence he proceeded to the land of Ḥamzîn which refused to make terms and whose fort, after an investment of one month, he reduced. He then set fire to the fort and de-

[1] Wheat measure.

[2] Original not clear.

stroyed it. The terms agreed upon were that they give 500 youths only once and not to be responsible for such a gift any more, and that they carry 30,000 modii every year to the granaries of al-Bâb. Then he advanced to Sindân,[1] which capitulated on condition that it offer 100 youths to be given by its chief only once and not to be responsible for such a gift in the future, together with 5,000 modii to be carried every year to the granaries of al-Bâb. On the followers of the Shâh of Ṭabarsarân, Marwân assessed 10,000 modii to be carried per annum to the granaries of al-Bâb;
but on the Shâh of Fîlân he did not assess anything, because 209
of his distinction in warfare, ability in conflict and the praiseworthiness of his cause.

Al-Lakz, Khirsh and other places. Marwân thence made a descent on al-Lakz castle [whose chief] had refused to pay anything of what was assessed, had set out to meet the chief of al-Khazar and was killed by a shepherd who shot an arrow at him without knowing him. The people of al-Lakz then made terms, agreeing to give 20,000 modii to be carried to the granaries. Having appointed Khashram as-Sulami as their ruler, Marwân came to the castle of the chief of Sharwân which was called Khirsh and which lay on the sea shore. The chief rendered submission and agreed to leave the height.[2] Marwân imposed 10,000 modii on the people of Sharwân per annum, and made it a condition on their chief to be in the van of the army when the Moslems start the attack against al-Khazar, and in the rear when they return; and on the Shâh of Fîlân that he should only take part in the attack; on the Shâh of Ṭabarsarân that he be in the rear when the Moslems start, and in the van when they return.

1 Lacking in diacritical points, d'Ohsson, p. 68; "Misdâr" in Maḥâsin, vol. i, p. 318.

2 Surrender the castle.

Thâbit rebels. Marwân then advanced to ad-Dûdânîyah and slaughtered its people. The news of the death of al-Walîd ibn-Yazîd then came to him, and Thâbit ibn-Nu'aim al-Judhâmi rose against him.[1] Musâfir al-Kaṣṣâb, who was one of those established in al-Bâb by aḍ-Ḍaḥḥâk al-Khâriji [the rebel], now came to Thâbit, espoused his cause and was made by him governor over Armenia and Adharbaijân. Musâfir then came to Ardabîl in disguise, where he was joined by a group of the ash-Shurat, and they all came to Bâjarwân[2] in which they found people with similar views and were joined by them. Thence they came to Warthân from whose inhabitants a large body of men, who held similar views, joined them; and they all crossed over to al-Bailaḳân where they were joined by a large crowd holding similar views. Marwân then came to Yûnân.[3] Isḥâḳ ibn-Muslim was made governor of Armenia by Marwân ibn-Muḥammad and never ceased to fight against Musâfir who was at al-Kilâb castle in as-Sîsajân.

When the "blessed dynasty" appeared and abu-Ja'far al-Manṣûr was made ruler of Mesopotamia and Armenia in the caliphate of as-Saffâḥ abu-l-'Abbâs, he sent against Musâfir and his followers a general from Khurâsân, who fought them until he overpowered them and slew Musâfir. The inhabitants of al-Bailaḳân, who had fortified themselves in al-Kilâb castle under the leadership of Ḳadad ibn-Aṣfar al-Bailaḳâni, surrendered.

The governorship of Yazîd. When al-Manṣûr became caliph, he made Yazîd ibn-Usaid as-Sulami governor of
Armenia. The latter reduced Bâb al-Lân and stationed in 210

[1] Ṭabari, vol. ii, pp. 1892 *seq.*

[2] Meynard, p. 74.

[3] First syllable mutilated in the original; *cf.* Iṣṭakhri, p. 192; Ḥauḳal, p. 251.

it a cavalry guard with stipends. He also subdued aṣ-Ṣanârîyah, whose inhabitants paid *kharâj*. In compliance with al-Manṣûr's orders, he married the daughter of the king of al-Khazar. She gave birth to a child which did not live; she herself died in child-birth. Yazîd sent someone to the naphtha and salt mines of the land of Sharwân and levied tax on them. He put someone in charge of them. He also built the city of Arjîl aṣ-Ṣughra [the Less] and Arjîl al-Kubra [the Great], and settled people from Palestine in them.

Ash-Shamâkhîyah. Muḥammad ibn-Ismâ'îl from certain *sheikhs* from Bardha'ah:—Ash-Shamâkhîyah [1] which lay in the province of Sharwân was thus called after ash-Shamâkh ibn-Shujâ', who was the king of Sharwân during the rule of Sa'îd ibn-Sâlim [2] al-Bâhili over Armenia.

Al-Hasan suppresses the revolt. Muḥammad ibn-Ismâ'îl from certain *sheikhs*:—After the dismissal of ibn-Usaid and Bakkâr ibn-Muslim al-'Uḳaili, and during the governorship of al-Ḥasan ibn-Ḳaḥṭabah aṭ-Ṭâ'i, the Armenians broke off their allegiance under their chief Mûshâ'il [3] al-Armani. Al-Manṣûr sent reinforcements under 'Âmir ibn-Ismâ'îl. Al-Ḥasan engaged himself in fight with Mûshâ'il and killed him, dispersing his troops. Things went on well with al-Ḥasan. The Nahr al-Ḥasan in al-Bailaḳân is named after this al-Ḥasan; and so are the Bâgh [4] at Bardha'ah named Bâgh al-Ḥasan, and the crown-lands known as al-Ḥasanîyah.

Different governors of Armenia. 'Uthmân ibn-'Umârah ibn-Khuraim succeeded al-Ḥasan ibn-Ḳaḥṭabah, and then

[1] Muḳaddasi, p. 276; Iṣṭakhri, p. 192; Meynard, p. 353: "Shamâkhi."

[2] "Salm," Ṭabari, vol. iii, p. 305.

[3] St. Martin, vol. i, p. 342; Brosset, vol. i, p. 159.

[4] Persian—garden, vineyard.

came Rauḥ ibn-Ḥâtim al-Muhallabi, Khuzaimah ibn-Khâzim, Yazîd ibn-Mazyad ash-Shaibâni, 'Ubaidallâh ibn-al-Mahdi, al-Faḍl ibn-Yaḥya, Sa'îd ibn-Sâlim, and Muḥammad ibn-Yazîd ibn-Mazyad. Of these rulers, Khuzaimah was the severest. It was he who introduced the system by which Dabîl and an-Nashawa paid land tax according to the area, not the produce. The Armenian patricians did not cease to hold their lands as usual, each trying to protect his own region; and whenever a *'âmil* came to the frontier they would coax him; and if they found in him purity and severity, as well as force and equipment, they would give the *kharâj* and render submission, otherwise they would 211
deem him weak and look down upon him.

The governorship of Khâlid ibn-Yazîd. In the caliphate of al-Ma'mûn, the Armenian patricians were under the rule of Khâlid ibn-Yazîd ibn-Mazyad, who accepted their presents and associated personally with them. This corrupted them and encouraged them against the *'âmils* of al-Ma-mûn who came after him.

Al-Ḥasan ibn-'Ali over the frontier region. Al-Mu'taṣim-Billâh appointed to the governorship of the frontier region al-Ḥasan ibn-'Ali-l-Bâdhaghîsi, better known as al-Ma'-mûni, who let its patricians and nobles go their way, and dealt so leniently with them that they became more disloyal to the Sultan and more severe on the people who came under their rule. Jurzân was subdued by Isḥâḳ ibn-Ismâ'îl ibn-Shu'aib, a freedman of the banu-Umaiyah. Sahl ibn-Sanbâṭ, the patrician, rose against the *'âmil* of Ḥaidar ibn-Kâwus al-Afshîn over Armenia and killed his secretary and had a narrow escape by flight. Armenia after this was ruled by *'âmils* who would remit to its people what was due from them, and accept whatever *kharâj* could be offered.

The governorship of Yûsuf ibn-Muḥammad. Two years

after al-Mutawakkil became caliph, he conferred the governorship of Armenia upon Yûsuf ibn-Muḥammad ibn-Yûsuf al-Marwazi. As he passed through Khilâṭ, Yûsuf seized its patrician Buḳrâṭ ibn-Ashûṭ and carried him off to Surra-man-ra'a, which act greatly offended the patricians, nobles and feudal lords [Ar. *mutaghallibah*]. Later a *'âmil* of his, named al-'Alâ' ibn-Aḥmad, went to a convent at as-Sîsajân, called Dair al-Aḳdâḥ, which was highly respected and richly endowed with gifts by the Armenian Christians, and carried away all what was in it and oppressed its occupants. This act was too much for the patricians, who held communication with each other and urged each other to throw off their allegiance and rise in revolt. They instigated al-Khuwaithiyah,[1] who were "uncircumcised" and were known by the name of al-Arṭân, to fall upon Yûsuf, and urged them against him in revenge for the carrying-away of their patrician Buḳrâṭ. Meanwhile, every one of the patricians and feudal lords sent them horses and men to help them bring that about. Accordingly, they fell upon Yûsuf at Ṭarûn, after he had distributed his followers in the villages, and slew him, carrying away all that his camp contained.

The governorship of Bugha the Elder. Al-Mutawakkil assigned to the governorship of Armenia Bugha-l-Kabîr [the Elder] who, arriving in Badlîs, seized Mûsa ibn-Zurârah who, in revenge for Buḳrâṭ, had favored and taken part 212
in killing Yûsuf. Bugha warred against al-Khuwaithiyah, slaughtering a great number, and carrying many away as captives. He then invested Ashûṭ ibn-Ḥamzah ibn-Jâjik, the patrician of al-Busfurrajân, at al-Bâḳ,[2] compelled him to surrender his castle and carried him as captive to Surra-

[1] St. Martin, vol. i, p. 100.

[2] Khurdâdhbih, p. 123, line 11; Ṭabari, vol. iii, p. 1410, line 3.

man-ra'a. He then advanced to Jurzân and succeeded in laying hold on Isḥâḳ ibn-Ismâ'îl, whom he kept in confinement until his death. Bugha reduced Jurzân, and carried away those Christians and non-Christians of Arrân, of the elevated region of Armenia,[1] and of as-Sîsajân, who belonged to the revolutionary party. Thus the political state of affairs in that frontier region became so quiet as never before. In the year 241, he came to Surra-man-ra'a.

[1] Text corrupt.

PART V

NORTHERN AFRICA

CHAPTER I

The Conquest of Egypt and al-Maghrib [Mauritania]

'Amr moves against Egypt. After the battle of al-Yarmûk, 'Amr ibn-al-'Âṣi laid siege to Caesarea [Ḳaisârîyah]. When Yazîd ibn-abi-Sufyân assumed power, 'Amr left his son in his place at Caesarea and led, all of his own accord, an army of 3,500 to Egypt. 'Umar was angry because of it and wrote to him, rebuking and reprimanding him for following his own opinion, without consulting 'Umar, and ordering him to return home in case the message was received before his arrival in Egypt. 'Amr, however, received the message in al-'Arîsh.[1] It is asserted by others that 'Umar wrote to 'Amr ibn-al-'Âṣi, ordering him to proceed to Egypt. 'Amr received the message as he was besieging Caesarea. The one who delivered the message was Sharîk ibn-'Abdah, to whom 'Amr gave 1,000 *dînârs,* which Sharîk refused to accept. 'Amr asked him to conceal the matter and not disclose it to 'Umar.

Al-Fusṭâṭ. The advance of 'Amr against Egypt took place in the year 19. He first stopped at al-'Arîsh and then proceeded to al-Faramâ',[2] in which were troops ready for the fight. 'Amr fought and defeated them, taking possession of their camp. Thence he advanced straight on to al-

[1] Al-Makrizi, *al-Khiṭaṭ*, vol. ii, p. 63 (Cairo, 1325): "Rafj"; Zaidân, *Ta'rikh Miṣr al-Ḥadith*, vol. i, p. 77; "Rafḥ . . . modern Raf', ten hours' journey from al-'Arish."

[2] Pelusium. Maḥâsin, vol. i, p. 8.

Fusṭâṭ and camped at the myrtle gardens, as the people of al-Fusṭâṭ had dug moats. The name of the city was Alyûnah,[1] but the Moslems called it Fusṭâṭ because they said, "This is the meeting place [Ar. *fusṭâṭ*] of the people, and the place where they assemble." Others say that 'Amr pitched a tent [also *fusṭâṭ*] in it, and it bore its name from it.[2] 213

As 'Amr ibn-al-Âṣi was besieging al-Fusṭâṭ, he was joined by az-Zubair ibn-al-'Auwâm ibn-Khuwailid at the head of 10,000—others say 12,000 men—among whom were Khârijah ibn-Ḥudhâfah-l-'Adawi and 'Umair ibn-Wahb al-Jumaḥi. Az-Zubair was on the point of leading an incursion and wanted to go to Antioch; but 'Umar said to him, "Abu-'Abdallâh, wouldst thou like to take the governorship of Egypt?" To this az-Zubair replied, "I do not care for it, but would like to go there on a holy war and co-operate with the Moslems. If I find that 'Amr has already reduced it, I would not interfere with his affairs, but would go to some sea-coast and keep post at it; but if I find him in the struggle, I shall fight on his side." With this understanding, he left.

Az-Zubair led the attack on one side, and 'Amr ibn-al-'Âṣi on the other. Finally az-Zubair brought a ladder and climbed on it until, with his sword unsheathed, he looked down upon the fort and exclaimed, "Allah is great!" and so did the Moslems exclaim and follow him up. Thus he took the fort by assault, and the Moslems considered it legal to take all that was in it. 'Amr made its holders *dhimmis*, imposed a poll-tax on their person and *kharâj* on their land, and communicated that to 'Umar ibn-al-Khaṭṭâb who endorsed it. Az-Zubair marked certain lots in Miṣr [Old

[1] Yâkût, vol. i, pp. 355, 450.

[2] Makrîzi, vol. ii, pp. 75-76.

Cairo] for himself [*ikhtaṭṭa*] and built a well-known mansion in which 'Abdallâh ibn-az-Zubair resided when he invaded Ifrîḳiyah[1] in the company of ibn-abi-Sarḥ. The ladder which az-Zubair used is still in Miṣr.

'Affân ibn-Muslim from Hishâm ibn-'Urwah:—Az-Zubair was sent to Miṣr; and when he was told there were in it warfare and pest, he replied, "We have come here only for warfare and pest." The Moslems put ladders up and climbed on them.

'Amr an-Nâḳid from Yazîd ibn-abi-Ḥabîb:—'Amr ibn-al-'Âṣi entered Egypt with 3,500 men. When 'Umar ibn-al-Khaṭṭâb heard about the situation in Egypt, he was affected with solicitude and fear and despatched az-Zubair ibn-al-'Auwâm at the head of 12,000 men. Az-Zubair 214
took part in the conquest of Miṣr and marked out in it certain lots.[2]

The division of the land. 'Amr an-Nâḳid from Sufyân ibn-Wahb al-Khaulâni:—When we conquered Miṣr without making a covenant with it, az-Zubair rose and said to 'Amr, "Divide it"; but 'Amr refused. Then az-Zubair said, "By Allah, thou shouldst divide it as the Prophet divided Khaibar." 'Amr wrote that to 'Umar who wrote back, saying, "Leave it as it is, so that the descendants of the descendants[3] may profit by it."

A tradition to the same effect was communicated to me by 'Abdallâh ibn-Wahb on the authority of Sufyân ibn-Wahb.

'Amr and az-Zubair conquer Egypt. Al-Ḳâsim ibn-Sallâm from Yazîd ibn-abi-Ḥabîb:—'Amr ibn-al-'Âṣi entered

[1] Africa = Tunis. Ibn-'Adhâri, *al-Bayân al-Mughrib*, vol. i, pp. 3 *seq.*

[2] Ar. *khiṭaṭ*. See Maḳrîzi, vol. ii, pp. 76 *seq.*

[3] Ar. *ḥabal al-ḥabalah*. See Muṭarrizi, p. 105; Caetani, vol. iv, p. 247; Maḳrîzi, vol. ii, p. 72, line 23; p. 73, line 25; *an-Nihâyah*, vol. i, p. 198.

Egypt at the head of 3,500 men. Just before that, 'Umar was affected with solicitude and fear and sent az-Zubair ibn-al-'Auwâm at the head of 12,000 men. Az-Zubair took part with 'Amr in the conquest of Egypt and marked out for himself two lots in Miṣr and Alexandria.

Ibrâhîm ibn-Muslim al-Khawârizmi from 'Abdallâh ibn-'Amr ibn-al-'Âṣi:—The latter said, "There is a disagreement regarding the conquest of Miṣr: some say it was conquered by force, and others by capitulation. The fact is that my father ['Amr ibn-al-'Âṣi] arrived in it and was resisted by the people of Alyûnah. He finally took possession of it by force and led the Moslems in. Az-Zubair was the first to climb its fort. The chief of Miṣr said to my father, 'We have heard of what ye did in Syria and how ye assessed poll-tax on the Christians and Jews, leaving the land in the hands of its owners to utilize it and pay its *kharâj*. If ye treat us the same way, it would do you more good than to kill, capture and expel us.' My father consulted with the Moslems and they all advised him to accept the terms, with the exception of a few men who asked him to divide the land among them. Accordingly, he assessed on every adult, excepting the poor, two *dînârs* as poll-tax, and on every land-owner, in addition to the two *dînârs*, 215
three *irdabbs* of wheat, two *ḳisṭs* of oil, two *ḳisṭs* of honey and two *ḳisṭs* of vinegar, to be given as a subsistence allowance to the Moslems, and gathered in the public house of provision [*dâr-ar-rizḳ*], where it is divided among them. A census was taken of the Moslems, and the inhabitants of Miṣr were required to provide every one of the Moslems with a woolen upper gown, an upper cloak or turban, breeches and a pair of shoes [1] per annum. Instead of the woolen gown, a Coptic robe would do. To this end, a state-

[1] Dozy, *Noms des Vêtements, s. v. jubbah, burnus, 'amâmah, sirwâl* and *khuff*.

ment was written, in which it was stipulated that so long as they lived up to these terms, their women and children would neither be sold nor taken captives, and their possessions and treasures would be kept in their hands.[1] The statement was submitted to 'Umar, the 'Commander of the Believers,' who endorsed it. Thus, the whole land became *kharâj*-land. Because, however, 'Amr signed the contract and the statement, some people thought that Miṣr was taken by capitulation." [2]

After the king of Alyûnah had made arrangements for himself and for the people in his city, he made terms on behalf of all the Egyptians similar to the terms of Alyûnah. The Egyptians consented, saying, "If those of us who are protected by fortifications have accepted such terms, and were content with them, how much more should we be content who are weak and have no power of resistance." *Kharâj* was assessed on the land of Egypt to the amount of one *dînâr* and three *irdabbs* of wheat on every *jarîb*, and two *dînârs* on every adult. The statement was submitted to 'Umar ibn-al-Khaṭṭâb.

The terms made with 'Amr. 'Amr an-Nâkid from Yazîd ibn-abi-Ḥabîb:—Al-Muḳauḳis [3] made terms with 'Amr ibn-al-'Âṣi, stipulating that 'Amr should let those of the Greeks go who wanted to leave, and keep those who wanted to stay, on certain conditions, which he specified, and that he would assess on the Copts, two *dînârs* per head. Hearing this, the king of the Greeks was enraged and sent his

[1] Gottheil, "Dhimmis and Moslems in Egypt", *O. T. and Semitic Studies*, vol. ii, p. 363.

[2] Maḳrîzi, vol. ii, pp. 72-74.

[3] Ibn-Ḳurḳub al-Yûnâni—perhaps Cyrus, the viceroy and archbishop of Alexandria under Heraclius. See Butler, *The Arab Conquest of Egypt*, pp. 508, 521; *Byzant. Zeitschrift*, year 1903, p. 1606; Casanova, *Moḥammed et la Fin du Monde*, p. 26.

troops, who, closing the gates of Alexandria, announced to 'Umar their readiness for war. Al-Mukaukis presented himself before 'Amr and said, "I have three requests to make: do not offer to the Greeks the same terms thou hast offered me, because they have distrusted me; do not violate the terms made with the Copts, for the violation was not started by them; and when I die, give orders that I be buried in a church at Alexandria (which he named)." 'Amr answered, "The last is the easiest [1] for me."

Bilhît, al-Khais, Sulṭais and Alexandria. Certain villages in Egypt resisted the advance of the Moslems, and 'Amr carried away some of their inhabitants as prisoners. These were the following: Bilhît,[2] al-Khais,[3] and Sulṭais.[4] Their captives were carried away to al-Madînah. 'Umar ibn-al- 216
Khaṭṭâb sent them back and made them, together with the Coptic community, *dhimmis*. The covenant they had, they did not violate. The following is the report of the conquest of Alexandria made by 'Amr to 'Umar: "Allah has given to us the possession of Alexandria by force and against its will, without covenant or contract". According to Yazîd ibn-abi-Ḥabîb, however, the city was taken by capitulation.

The tax of Egypt. Abu-Aiyûb ar-Raḳḳi from Yazîd ibn-abi-Ḥabib:—The *kharâj* and poll-tax which 'Amr raised from Egypt amounted to 2,000,000 *dînârs*; but that raised by 'Abdallâh ibn-Sa'd ibn-Abi-Sarḥ, 4,000,000. When 'Uthmân remarked to 'Amr, saying, "After thee the milch camels have yielded more milk", 'Amr replied, "This is because ye have emaciated their young".[5]

In the year 21, 'Umar ibn-al-Khattâb wrote to 'Amr ibn-

[1] Maḳrîzi, vol. i, p. 263.

[2] *Cf.* "Balhîb" in Yâḳût, vol. i, p. 733.

[3] Butler, p. 289, and note; ibn-Duḳmâḳ, *Kitâb al-Intisâr li-Wâsiṭat 'Iḳd al-Amṣâr*, vol. v, p. 118 (Bûlâḳ, 1893).

[4] *Cf.* Duḳmâḳ, vol. v, pp. 118-119.

[5] Maḳrîzi, vol. i, p. 159.

al-'Âṣi informing him of the straits in which the inhabitants of al-Madinah were, and ordering him to transport by sea to al-Madinah all the food he had collected as *kharâj*. Accordingly, the food with the oil was carried there; and when it reached al-Jâr,[1] it was received by Sa'd al-Jâr.[2] Later it was kept in a special house at al-Madînah and distributed among the Moslems by measure. At the time of the first insurrection, the supply was cut off. In the days of Mu'âwiyah and Yazîd, it was again carried to al-Madînah. Then it was cut off until the time of 'Abd-al-Malik ibn-Marwân, after which it was carried until the caliphate of abu-Ja'far, or a little previous to that.

Bakr ibn-al-Haitham from Yazîd ibn-abi-Ḥabîb:—After the first peace was made, the tax-payers in Egypt made new terms in the caliphate of 'Umar, stipulating that instead of the wheat, oil, honey and vinegar they offered, they would pay two *dînârs* in addition to the other two *dînârs*. Each one thus was bound to pay four *dînârs*; and they consented to that and preferred it.

'Ain Shams, al-Faiyûm and other places reduced. Abu-Aiyûb ar-Raḳḳi from al-Jaishâni:—The latter said, "I heard it stated by a number of those who witnessed the conquest of Egypt that when 'Amr ibn-al-'Âṣi reduced al-Fusṭâṭ, he despatched to 'Ain Shams[3] 'Abdallâh ibn-Ḥudhâfah as-Sahmi, who took possession of its land and made 217
terms with the inhabitants of its villages similar to those of al-Fustât. Likewise 'Amr despatched Khârijah ibn-Ḥudhâfah al-'Adawi to al-Faiyûm,[4] al-Ushmûnain, Ikh-

[1] Hamdâni, *Ṣifat Jazîrat al-'Arab*, p. 47, line 17 (ed. Müller).

[2] Sa'd al-Jâri mentioned in Dhahabi, *al-Mushtabih*, p. 81; *cf.* ibn-Sa'd, vol. iii[1], p. 240; Yâḳût, vol. ii. p. 6.

[3] Heliopolis; confused by some historians with Bâb Alyûnah (Babylon); Butler, p. 212, note.

[4] Maḳrîzi, vol. i, pp. 402-403.

mim, al-Basharûdât [1] and the villages of upper Egypt, which he reduced on the same terms. 'Amr also sent 'Umair ibn-Wahb al-Jumaḥi to Tinnîs, Dimyâṭ, Tûnah, Damirah, Shaṭa, Diḳahlah,[2] Bana and Bûṣîr, which he reduced on the same terms. 'Amr also sent 'Uḳbah ibn-'Âmir al-Juhani (others say 'Amr's freedman, Wardân after whom Sûḳ [market] Wardân in Egypt is named) to the rest of the villages in the lower part of the country; and he did the same. Thus did 'Amr ibn-al-'Âṣi effect the conquest of all Egypt and make its land *kharâj*-land."

The Copts have no covenant. Al-Ḳâsim ibn-Sallâm from Aiyûb ibn-abi-l-'Âliyah's father:—The latter said, "I heard 'Amr ibn-al-'Âṣi say from the pulpit, 'I have occupied this position and am bound to none of the Egyptian Copts by covenant or contract. If I want, I can kill; if I want, I can take one-fifth of the possessions; if I want, I can sell captives. The people of Anṭâbulus are excluded because they have a covenant which must be kept'."

Al-Maghrib and Egypt taken by force. Al-Ḳâsim ibn-Sallâm from Mûsa ibn-'Ali ibn-Rabâḥ al-Lakhmi's father:—All al-Maghrib was taken by force.

Abu-'Ubaid from aṣ-Ṣalt ibn-abi-'Âṣim, the secretary of Ḥaiyân ibn-Shuraiḥ:—The latter said that he read the letter of 'Umar ibn-'Abd-al-'Aziz to Ḥaiyân, his *'âmil* over Egypt, stating that Egypt was taken by force, with no covenant or contract.

Poll-tax of the Copts not to be increased. Abu-'Ubaid from 'Ubaidallâh ibn-abi-Ja'far:—Mu'âwiyah wrote to Wardân, a freedman of 'Amr, ordering him to increase the poll-tax of every Copt by one *ḳîrâṭ*, but Wardân wrote back, "How can I increase it while it is stated in their covenant that their tax should not be increased?"

[1] *Cf.* Bakri, vol. i, p. 166.

[2] Yâḳût, vol. ii, p. 581.

Egyptians overtaxed. Muḥammad ibn-Sa'd from 'Abd-al-Ḥamîd ibn-Ja'far's father:—The latter heard 'Urwah ibn-az-Zubair say, "I spent seven years in Egypt and was married in it. I found its people exhausted, being burdened with more than they could bear. The country was conquered by 'Amr through capitulation, covenant and some- 218
thing assessed on the inhabitants."

The statement of 'Amr. Bakr ibn-al-Haitham from 'Uḳbah ibn-'Âmir al-Juhani:—The Egyptians had a covenant and a contract. 'Amr gave them a statement to the effect that they were secure with respect to their possessions, lives and children, and that none of them would be sold as slaves. He imposed on them a *kharâj* not to be increased, and promised to expel all fear of attack by an enemy. 'Uḳbah added, "And I was a witness thereunto".

The division of the land. Al-Ḥusain ibn-al-Aswad from Sufyân ibn-Wahb al-Khaulâni:—The latter said, "At the conquest of Miṣr by us, which was effected without covenant, az-Zubair ibn-al-'Auwâm rose and said, ''Amr, divide it between us!' 'Amr replied, 'By Allah, I will not divide it before I consult 'Umar.' He wrote to 'Umar, and the latter wrote back, 'Leave it as it is, so that the descendants of the descendants may profit by it.'"

Its kharâj. Muḥammad ibn-Sa'd from Usâmah ibn-Zaid ibn-Aslam's grandfather:—In the year 20, 'Amr ibn-al-'Âṣi, accompanied by az-Zubair, subdued Egypt. When Egypt was conquered, the people made terms, agreeing to pay something he imposed on them, which was two *dînârs* on every man, excluding women and boys. The *kharâj* of Egypt during his governorship amounted to 2,000,000 *dînârs*; but later it reached 4,000,000.

Two dînârs on each Copt. Abu-'Ubaid from Yazîd ibn-abi-Ḥabîb:—Al-Muḳauḳis, the chief of Egypt, made terms with 'Amr ibn-al-'Âṣi, stipulating that each Copt pays two *dînârs.* Hearing this, Heraclius, the chief of the Greeks, was enraged with anger and sent the troops to Alexandria and closed its gates; but 'Amr reduced the city by force.

The poll-tax of the native village of umm-Ibrâhîm annulled. Ibn-al-Kattât, *i. e.*, abu-Mas'ûd, from ash-Sha'bi:—'Ali ibn-al-Ḥusain, or al-Ḥusain himself, interceded with Mu'âwiyah regarding the poll-tax of the fellow-villagers in 219
Egypt of the mother of Ibrâhîm,[1] the Prophet's son; and it was cancelled. The Prophet himself used to recommend that the Copts be favorably treated.

The Prophet recommends the Copts. 'Amr from Mâliḳ, and al-Laith from a son of Ka'b ibn-Mâlik:—The Prophet said, "If ye conquer Egypt, treat the Copts favorably, because they have *dhimmah* and blood-relationship." It is stated by al-Laith that umm-Ismâ'îl[2] was a Copt.

'Umar confiscates 'Amr's possessions. Abu-l-Ḥasan al-Madâ'ini from 'Abdallâh ibn-al-Mubârak:—'Umar ibn-al-Khattâb used to record the possessions of his *'âmils* at the time of their appointment; and whatsoever was later added was partly or wholly confiscated by him. He once wrote to 'Amr ibn-al-'Âṣi, "It has become revealed that thou ownest commodities, slaves, vases and animals which thou didst not possess when thou wert made governor of Egypt." 'Amr wrote back, "Our land is a land of agriculture and trade; we, therefore, get as income more than what is necessary for our expenses." To this, 'Umar replied, "I have had enough experience with the wicked *'âmils.* Thy letter is the letter of one disturbed because justice has been meted out to him. Therefore, my suspicion has been aroused against thee, and I have sent to thee Muḥammad ibn-Maslamah with a view to dividing with thee what thou hast. Reveal to him thy secret,

[1] Mâriyah, the Copt; Nawâwi, p. 853.

[2] The reference is to Hagar.

and give out whatever he demands of thee; thereby thou wouldst be spared his severity. What is concealed has been revealed.[1]" Thus were 'Amr's possessions confiscated by 'Umar.

Al-Madâ'ini from 'Îsa ibn-Yazîd:—When Muḥammad ibn-Maslamah divided with 'Amr ibn-al-'Âṣi his possessions, 'Amr made this remark, "An age in which the son of Hantamah[2] treats us in this manner is certainly an evil age. Al-'Âṣi used to put on silk garments with brocade borders!" "Hush," said Muḥammad, "had it not been for this age of ibn-Ḥantamah which thou hatest, thou wouldst be found bending in the court-yard of thy house, at the feet of a goat, whose abundance of milk would please thee and scarcity would displease thee."[3] "I beg thee by Allah," exclaimed 'Amr, "report not what I have just uttered to 'Umar. A conversation is always confidential." Muḥammad replied, "So long as 'Umar lives, I shall not mention anything that took place between us."

Egypt taken by force. 'Amr an-Nâḳid from 'Abdallâh ibn-Hubairah:—Egypt was taken by force.

'Amr from ibn-An'am's grandfather (who witnessed the conquest of Egypt):—Egypt was taken by force without covenant or contract. 220

[1] Freytag, *Prov.*, vol. i, p. 160, number 33.

[2] 'Umar ibn-al-Khaṭṭâb's mother; Nawâwi, p. 447.

[3] Caetani, vol. iv, pp. 618-619.

CHAPTER II

THE CONQUEST OF ALEXANDRIA

The battle of al-Kiryaun. When 'Amr ibn-al-'Âṣi conquered Miṣr, he settled in it and wrote to 'Umar ibn-al-Khaṭṭâb soliciting his orders to march against Alexandria [al-Iskandarîyah].[1] 'Umar wrote and ordered him to do so; so 'Amr marched against it in the year 21, leaving as his substitute [lieutenant] over Miṣr Khârijah ibn-Ḥudhâfah ibn-Ghânim ibn-'Âmir ibn-'Abdallâh ibn-'Ubaid ibn-'Awîj ibn-'Adi ibn-Ka'b ibn-Lu'ai ibn-Ghâlib. In the meantime, those Greeks and Copts who lived below Alexandria had gathered and said, "Let us attack him in al-Fusṭâṭ before he reaches here and makes an attempt on Alexandria." 'Amr met them at al-Kiryaun[2] and defeated them with a great slaughter. In their ranks were men from Sakha, Bilhît, al-Khais and Sulṭais, and others who came to their assistance and support.

Alexandria reduced. 'Amr kept his way until he arrived in Alexandria, whose inhabitants he found ready to resist him, but the Copts in it preferred peace. Al-Muḳauḳis communicated with 'Amr and asked him for peace and a truce for a time; but 'Amr refused. Al-Muḳauḳis then ordered that the women stand on the wall with their faces turned towards the city, and that the men stand armed, with their faces towards the Moslems, thus hoping to scare them

[1] Duḳmâḳ, vol. v, p. 121.

[2] Chaereum, Butler, pp. 288-289; al-Idrîsi, *Ṣifat al-Maghrib, as-Sûdân, Miṣr w-al-Andalus,* p. 160.

[Moslems]. 'Amr sent word, saying, "We see what thou hast done. It was not by mere numbers that we conquered those we have conquered. We have met your king Heraclius, and there befell him what has befallen him." Hearing this, al-Muḳauḳis said to his followers, "These people are telling the truth. They have chased our king from his kingdom as far as Constantinople. It is much more preferable, therefore, that we submit." His followers, however, spoke harshly to him and insisted on fighting. The Moslems fought fiercely against them and invested them for three months. At last, 'Amr reduced the city[1] by the sword
and plundered all that was in it, sparing its inhabitants of 221
whom none was killed or taken captive. He reduced them to the position of *dhimmis* like the people of Alyûnah. He communicated the news of the victory to 'Umar through Mu'âwiyah ibn-Ḥudaij al-Kindi (later as-Sakûni) and sent with him the [usual] fifth.

Some state that al-Muḳauḳis made terms with 'Amr to the effect that he should pay 13,000 *dînârs*, that those who prefer to leave Alexandria should leave, and those who prefer to stay should stay, and that two *dînârs* be assessed on every adult Copt. To this end, 'Amr wrote a statement. He then left in his place over Alexandria 'Abdallâh ibn-Ḥudhâfah ibn-Ḳais ibn-'Adi ibn-Sa'd ibn-Sahm ibn-'Amr ibn-Huṣaiṣ ibn-Ka'b ibn-Lu'ai at the head of a cavalry guard of the Moslems, and departed for al-Fusṭâṭ.[2]

Manuwîl captures Alexandria. The Greeks wrote to Constantine, son of Heraclius, who was their king at that time, telling him how few the Moslems in Alexandria were, and how humiliating the Greeks' condition was, and how they had to pay poll-tax. Constantine sent one of his men, called

[1] *Cf.* ibn-Iyâs, *Ta'rîkh Miṣr*, vol. I, p. 22.

[2] Maḳrîzi, vol. i, pp. 263 *seq.*

Manuwîl[1] [Manuel], with three hundred ships full of fighters. Manuwîl entered Alexandria and killed all the guard that was in it, with the exception of a few who by the use of subtle means took to flight and escaped. This took place in the year 25. Hearing the news, 'Amr set out at the head of 15,000 men and found the Greek fighters doing mischief in the Egyptian villages next to Alexandria. The Moslems met them and for one hour were subjected to a shower of arrows, during which they were covered by their shields. They then advanced boldly and the battle raged with great ferocity until the "polytheists" were routed; and nothing could divert or stop them before they reached Alexandria. Here they fortified themselves and set mangonels. 'Amr made a heavy assault, set the ballistae and destroyed the walls of the city. He pressed the fight so hard until he entered the city by assault, killed the fighters and carried away the children as captives. Some of its Greek inhabitants left to join the Greeks somewhere else; and Allah's enemy, Manuwîl, was killed. 'Amr and the Moslems destroyed the wall of Alexandria in pursuance of a vow that 'Amr had made to that effect, in case he reduced the city.

According to certain reports, this invasion took place in the year 23; and according to others, the insurrection took place in the years 23 and 25; but Allah knows best. 'Amr 222
assessed on the land of Alexandria *kharâj*; and on its people, poll-tax.

Al-Mukaukis. Some report that al-Mukaukis forsook the people of Alexandria when they violated the covenant, but 'Amr reinstated him with his people on the terms of their first capitulation. Others assert that he died before this invasion.

Alexandria taken by capitulation. Muhammad ibn-Sa'd

[1] Butler, pp. 468-475.

from 'Umar ibn-'Abd-al-'Azîz:—The latter said, "Not a town in al-Maghrib did we take by capitulation except three: Alexandria, Kafarṭîs and Sulṭais. 'Umar used to say, 'Whosoever of the inhabitants of these places accepts Islâm will be set free together with his possessions'."

How the dwellings were divided. 'Amr an-Nâkid from Yazîd ibn-abi-Ḥabîb:—'Amr ibn-al-'Âṣi conquered Alexandria, and some Moslems took up their abode in it as a cavalry guard. Later, they withdrew, after which they made an assault and hastened to secure dwellings. Some of them would come to the houses they once occupied and find them already held by a fellow Moslem. Regarding this, 'Amr remarked, "I am afraid the dwellings would fall into ruins if different ones of you should occupy them in turn." Consequently, when the invasion was made and the Moslems arrived in al-Kiryaun, he said, "Go with Allah's blessing. Whosoever of you sticks his lancet into a house, that house is his and his father's sons'." Thus, the Moslem would enter a house and stick his lancet into some apartment of it; then another would come and stand his lancet in the same house. The same house would thereby be in the possession of two or three persons,[1] which they would occupy until their withdrawal, at which the Greeks would come and occupy it.

Yazîd ibn-abi-Ḥabîb used to say, "No money from the rent of these houses is legal.[2] They can neither be sold nor bequeathed, but they are dwelling-places for the Moslems during the time they hold their post as guard."

The second conflict. During the second conflict with Alexandria, when Manuwîl, the Greek eunuch, came, the people closed the gates; but 'Amr reduced it and destroyed its wall.

[1] Makrizi, vol. i, p. 269: "tribes".

[2] Dukmâk, vol. v, p. 118.

'Abdallâh ibn-Sa'd replaces 'Amr. No sooner had 'Amr returned to al-Fusṭâṭ after assigning his freedman, Wardân, as governor of Alexandria, than he was dismissed. In the place of 'Amr, 'Uthmân appointed 'Abdallâh ibn-Sa'd ibn-abi-Sarḥ ibn-al-Ḥârith of the banu-'Amr ibn-Lu'ai,[1] 'Uthmân's foster-brother. That took place in the year 25.

According to others, 'Abdallâh ibn-Sa'd was in charge of the *kharâj* of Egypt in behalf of 'Uthmân. Between 'Abdallâh and 'Amr, a verbal dispute arose and 'Abdallâh wrote and accused 'Amr. 'Amr was dismissed by 'Uthmân, who assigned 'Abdallâh to both functions, and wrote him saying that Alexandria was taken once by force and revolted two times, and ordering him to station in it a cavalry guard that would never depart from it, and to assign abundant subsistence allowances to the guard, and change its personnel once in every six months.[2] 223

Ibn-Hurmuz. Muḥammad ibn-Sa'd from al-Wâḳidi:—ibn-Hurmuz al-A'raj al-Ḳâri [the lame "reader"] used to say, "Your best coast, from the standpoint of guard, is Alexandria." At last he left al-Madînah and joined the guard stationed in Alexandria, where he died in the year 117.

The capitation tax. Bakr ibn-al-Haitham from Mûsa ibn-'Ali's father:—The capitation tax from Alexandria was 18,000 *dînârs*; but when Hishâm ibn-'Abd-al-Malik became caliph, it amounted to 36,000.[3]

'Abdallâh ibn-Sa'd made governor. 'Amr from Yazîd ibn-abi-Ḥabîb:—'Uthmân dismissed 'Amr ibn-al-'Âṣi from Egypt and assigned in his place 'Abdallâh ibn-Sa'd. But when the Greeks occupied Alexandria, the Egyptians asked

[1] Nawâwi, pp. 345-347.

[2] Maḳrîzi, vol. i, p. 270.

[3] Maḳrîzi, vol. i, p. 269.

'Uthmân to keep 'Amr until he was through with the fight against the Greeks, because he had special knowledge of warfare and inspired awe in the enemy. 'Uthmân did so; and 'Amr defeated the Greeks. 'Uthmân then wanted 'Amr to be in charge of the army, and 'Abdallâh in charge of the *kharâj*; but 'Amr refused, saying, "My case is that of one who holds the horns of the cow while the chief milks it." 'Uthmân then appointed ibn-Sa'd to the governorship of Egypt.

The Abyssinians of al-Bîma. For seven years after the conquest of Egypt, the Abyssinians of al-Bîma[1] kept up their resistance, and could not be subjugated because of the water with which they flooded their thickets.

The second conquest of Alexandria. 'Abdallâh ibn-Wahb from Mûsa ibn-'Ali's father:—'Amr conquered Alexandria for the second time by capitulation, which conquest took place in the caliphate of 'Uthmân after the death of 'Umar.

[1] Ṭabari, vol. iii, p. 1106.

CHAPTER III

THE CONQUEST OF BARKAH AND ZAWÎLAH 224

Barkah makes terms. Muḥammad ibn-Sa'd from 'Abdallâh ibn-Hubairah:—After reducing Alexandria, 'Amr ibn-al-'Âṣi led his army intent upon the conquest of al-Maghrib [Mauritania] until he arrived in Barḳah, the chief city of Anṭâbulus,[1] whose inhabitants made terms on a poll-tax of 13,000 *dînârs* to be raised as the price of those of their children whom they desired to sell.[2]

Bakr ibn-al-Haitham from 'Abdallâh ibn-Hubairah:—After investing and fighting the people of Anṭâbulus and its city, Barḳah,[3] which lay between Egypt and Ifrîḳiyah [Africa = Tunis], 'Amr ibn-al-'Âṣi made terms with them, stipulating that they pay a poll-tax which might include the price of those of their children whom they desired to sell. 'Amr wrote a statement to that effect.

Muḥammad ibn-Sa'd from Isḥâḳ ibn-'Abdallâh ibn-abi-Farwah:—The inhabitants of Barḳah used to send their *kharâj* to the governor of Egypt without having anyone come to urge them for it.[4] Their land was the most fertile land of al-Maghrib, and it never saw an insurrection.

Al-Wâḳidi states that 'Abdallâh ibn-'Amr ibn-al-'Âṣi used to say, "Had it not been for my possessions in al-

[1] Pentapolis. Khurdâdhbih, p. 91. *Cf. Caetani,* vol. iv, p. 534.

[2] Caetani in vol. iv, p. 533, nota, thinks it must have meant the right to offer to the Moslems their children as slaves according to a fixed price.

[3] Barca. Butler, p. 429.

[4] As-Suyûṭi, *Ḥusn al-Muḥâḍarah,* vol. i, p. 86.

Ḥijâz, I would live in Barḳah, because I know of no place that is more safe or isolated than it."

'Amr's report to 'Umar. Bakr ibn-al-Haitham from Mu'âwiyah ibn-Ṣâliḥ:—'Amr ibn-al-'Âsi wrote to 'Umar ibn-al-Khaṭṭâb informing him that he had appointed 'Uḳbah ibn-Nâfi' al-Fihri governor of al-Maghrib and that the latter had reached as far as Zawîlah. He also informed him that peace prevailed among all between Zawîlah [1] and Barḳah, that their allegiance was strong and that the Moslems among them had paid *ṣadaḳah* and the "people of the covenant" acknowledged the poll-tax imposed. 'Amr also wrote that he had assessed on the inhabitants of Zawîlah and on those living in the region between his town and Zawîlah, what he saw would be tolerated by them, and ordered all his *'âmils* to collect *ṣadaḳah* from the rich to be 225
distributed among the poor, and poll-tax from the *dhimmis* to be carried to 'Amr in Egypt, and to raise from Moslem lands the tithe and half the tithe, and from those who capitulated, what had been agreed upon.

The origin of the Berbers. Bakr ibn-al-Haitham once told me, "I asked 'Abdallâh ibn-Ṣâliḥ regarding the Berbers,[2] and he said, 'They claim to be the descendants of Barr ibn-Ḳais; but Ḳais had no son with the name, Barr. In fact they are descended from the race of the giants [Philistines] against whom David fought. In ancient times, their home was Palestine; and they were tent-dwellers. Later on, they came to al-Maghrib, where they multiplied'."

The Berbers of Luwâtah. Abu-'Ubaid al-Ḳâsim ibn-Sallâm from Yazîd ibn-abi-Ḥabîb:—'Amr ibn-al-'Âṣi made this a condition on the Berber inhabitants of Luwâtah [3] at

[1] Ṭabari, vol. i, p. 2646.

[2] See article on Berbers in the *Encyclopædia of Islâm*.

[3] Butler, p. 430.

Barḳah. "Ye have to sell your children and wives in order to pay the poll-tax on you." Commenting on this, al-Laith said, "If they were slaves, that would not be a legal thing for them to do."

Bakr ibn-al-Haitham from Yazîd ibn-abi-Ḥabîb:—'Umar ibn-'Abd-al-'Azîz wrote regarding the Luwâtah women, "Whoever has a Luwâtah woman, let him either be engaged to her through her father, or return her to her people." Luwâtah [1] is a village inhabited by Berbers who had a covenant.

[1] *Cf.* Khurdâdhbih, pp. 90 and 91; ibn-Khaldûn, *Kitâb al-'Ibar fi-Aîyâm al-'Arab w-al-'Ajam w-al-Barbar,* vol. ii², p. 128 (Bûlâḳ, 1284).

CHAPTER IV

THE CONQUEST OF TRIPOLI

Bakr ibn-al-Haitham from 'Ali ibn-abi-Ṭalḥah:—In the year 22,[1] 'Amr ibn-al-'Âṣi advanced to Tripoli.[2] He met resistance but reduced the place by force, carrying away many loads of fine silk brocade from its merchants. This booty he sold and divided its price among the Moslems. He wrote to 'Umar ibn-al-Khaṭṭâb, "We have arrived in Tripoli which lies nine days from Ifrîḳiyah. If the 'Commander of the Believers' thinks it best to allow us to invade the latter, it will be well." 'Umar wrote back, 226
ordering him not to go, saying, "This should not be called Ifrîḳiyah, but Mufarriḳah,[3] which is treacherous to others, and to which others are treacherous." 'Umar wrote that because its inhabitants used to pay something to the king of the Greeks and often treated him treacherously, while the king of al-Andalus, who had made terms with them, treated them treacherously. These facts were known to 'Umar.

According to a tradition communicated to me by 'Amr an-Nâḳid on the authority of certain *sheikhs*, Tripoli was taken by 'Amr ibn-al-'Âsi through a covenant made by him.

[1] Weil, *Geschichte der Chalifen*, vol. i, p. 124 note: "year 23".

[2] Tripolis; Ar. Aṭrâbulus. Yâḳût, vol. i, p. 309; Ya'ḳûbi, *Buldân*, p. 346.

[3] Pun on words. Mufarriḳah means causing deviation from the right course.

CHAPTER V

The Conquest of Ifrîḳiyah

'Uthmân reinforces ibn-Sa'd. When 'Abdallâh ibn-Sa'd ibn-abi-Sarḥ, was appointed governor over Egypt and al-Maghrib, he sent out the Moslems in cavalry detachments, and they plundered as far as the extremities of Ifrîḳiyah [modern Tunis]. 'Uthmân ibn-'Affân first hesitated to attack Ifrîḳiyah; but after consultation, he made up his mind to do so, and wrote to 'Abdallâh in the year 27 (others say 28, still others 29), ordering him to lead the attack, and reinforced him with a large army in which were Ma'bad ibn-al-'Abbâs ibn-'Abd-al-Muṭṭalib, Marwân ibn-al-Ḥakam ibn-abi-l-'Âṣi ibn-Umaiyah and his brother al-Ḥârith ibn-al-Ḥakam, 'Abdallâh ibn-az-Zubair ibn-al-'Auwâm, al-Miswar ibn-Makhramah ibn-Naufal ibn-Uhaib ibn-'Abd-Manâf ibn-Zuhrah ibn-Kilâb, 'Abd-ar-Raḥmân ibn-Zaid ibn-al-Khaṭṭâb, 'Abdallâh ibn-'Umar ibn-al-Khaṭṭâb, 'Âṣim ibn-'Umar, 'Ubaidallâh ibn-'Umar, 'Abd-ar-Raḥmân ibn-abi-Bakr, 'Abdallâh ibn-'Amr ibn-al-'Âṣi, Busr ibn-Abi-Arṭâh ibn-'Uwaimir al-'Âmiri, and abu-Dhu'aib Khuwailid ibn-Khâlid al-Hudhali, the poet. Abu-Dhu'aib died in this campaign and ibn-az-Zubair had charge of the burial. In this campaign, a great host of the Arabs from the environs of al-Madînah took part.

The magnates of Ifrîḳiyah make terms with 'Abdallâh. Muḥammad ibn-Sa'd from 'Abdallâh ibn-az-Zubair:—The
latter said:—" 'Uthmân ibn-'Affân sent us on an expedition 22
against Ifrîḳiyah, whose patrician exercised authority from

Tripoli to Ṭanjah [Tangiers]. 'Abdallâh ibn-Sa'd ibn-abi-Sarḥ marched against him and occupied 'Aḳûbah. After a few days' fight, I was enabled to kill, by Allah's help, the patrician. His army took to flight and was torn to pieces. Ibn-abi-Sarḥ sent detachments and scattered them all over the country; and they carried away a large booty and drove before them all the cattle they could. Seeing that, the great men of Ifrîḳiyah met together and offered 'Abdallâh ibn-Sa'd 300 quintals [1] of gold provided he would let them alone and leave their land. Their request was granted."

Muḥammad ibn-Sa'd from ibn-Ka'b:—'Abdallâh ibn-Sa'd ibn-abi-Sarḥ made terms with the patrician of Ifrîḳiyah, stipulating that the latter should pay 2,500,000 *dînârs.*

'Uḳbah ibn-Nâfi'. Muḥammad ibn-Sa'd from Mûsa ibn-Ḍamrah-l-Mâzini's father:—When 'Abdallâh ibn-Sa'd made terms with the patrician of Ifrîḳiyah, he returned to Egypt without appointing anyone to the governorship of Ifrîḳiyah, which at that time had no meeting-place [2] or central town. When 'Uthmân was murdered and Muḥammad ibn-abi-Ḥudhaifah ibn-'Utbah ibn-Rabî'ah ruled over Egypt, he sent nobody to Ifrîḳiyah; but when Mu'âwiyah ibn-abi-Sufyân came to power, he assigned over Egypt Mu-'âwiyah ibn-Ḥudaij as-Sakûni who, in the year 20, sent 'Uḳbah ibn-Nâfi' ibn-'Abd-Ḳais ibn-Laḳît al-Fihri to Ifrîḳiyah. 'Uḳbah invaded it and parceled it out into lots among the Moslems.

'Ukbah sent Busr ibn-abi-Arṭâh [3] to a castle in al-Ḳairawân, which he reduced, killing and capturing many. It is now known as Ḳal'at Busr and lies near a city called Majjânah, near the silver mine.

[1] Ar. *ḳinṭâr* = "1,200 *dînârs,* and in the language of Barbar = 1,000 *mithḳâls* of gold or silver"; *T.'A.*

[2] Ar. *ḳairawân.* See De Goeje's edition of Balâdhuri, gloss., pp. 92-93.

[3] Maḳrizi, vol. i, p. 272, does not have "abi" in the name.

I heard it said that Mûsa ibn-Nuṣair sent Busr, who was then 82 years old, to this castle; and the latter reduced it.
This Busr was born two years before the Prophet's death. 228
Others than al-Wâkidi claim that Busr was one of those who transmitted traditions from the Prophet; but Allah knows better.

Various governors. It was stated by al-Wâḳidi that 'Abdallâh ibn-Sa'd held the governorship until Muḥammad ibn-abi-Ḥudhaifah assumed authority over Egypt, which he had made to rise in rebellion against 'Uthmân. Later on, 'Ali assigned Ḳais ibn-Sa'd ibn-'Ubâdah-l-Anṣâri as governor of Egypt, after which he dismissed him and chose Muḥammad ibn-abi-Bakr aṣ-Ṣiddîḳ. The latter he also dismissed and assigned Mâlik al-Ashtar, who was taken sick [1] at al-Ḳulzum [Suez]. 'Ali once more assigned Muḥammad ibn-abi-Bakr, who was later killed by Mu'âwiyah ibn-Ḥudaij and burned in a donkey's belly.[2]

'Amr ibn-al-'Âṣi ruled in the name of Mu'âwiyah ibn-abi-Sufyân. He died in Egypt on the feast of the breaking of the fast of Ramaḍân [*al-fiṭr*] in the year 42 (others say 43), and was succeeded by his son 'Abdallâh whom Mu'âwiyah dismissed. Mu'âwiyah assigned ibn-Ḥudaij, who spent four years in Egypt; at the close of which he made a razzia and plundered. After that he returned to Egypt and sent there 'Uḳbah ibn-Nâfi' al-Fihri. Others say that 'Uḳbah was appointed by Mu'âwiyah over al-Maghrib; and so he invaded Ifrîḳiyah at the head of 10,000 Moslems and reduced it. He parceled out its Ḳairawân [3] in lots among the Moslems, the site being a thicket covered with tamarisk and other trees and which nobody could attempt because of

[1] Maḥâsin, vol. i, pp. 116-117.

[2] *Ibid.*, vol. i, p. 125; Khaldûn, vol. ii^{2}, p. 182.

[3] 'Adhâri, vol. i, p. 12.

the beasts, snakes and deadly scorpions. This ibn-Nâfi' was a righteous man whose prayer was answered. He prayed to his Lord, who made the scorpions disappear; even the beasts had to carry their young and run away.

Al-Wâḳidi says, " I once said to Mûsa ibn-'Ali, ' Thou hast seen the buildings in Ifrîḳiyah that are connected together and that we still see to-day. Who was it that built them? ' And Mûsa replied, ' The first one was 'Uḳbah ibn-Nâfi' al-Fihri who marked out the plans for the buildings, himself built a home, and the Moslems at the same time built houses and dwelling-places. He also built the cathedral mosque that is in Ifrîḳiyah.' "

It was in Ifrîḳiyah that Ma'bad ibn-al-'Abbâs fell a martyr in the campaign of ibn-abi-Sarḥ during the caliphate of 'Uthmân. Others say he met natural death during the war; but that he fell a martyr is the more authentic report.

According to al-Wâḳidi and others, Mu'âwiyah ibn-abi-Sufyân dismissed Mu'âwiyah ibn-Ḥudaij [1] and conferred the governorship of Egypt and al-Maghrib on Maslamah ibn-Mukhallad al-Anṣâri,[2] who appointed his freedman, abu-l-Muhâjir, governor of al-Maghrib. When Yazîd ibn-Mu'âwiyah, however, came to power, he reinstated 'Uḳbah ibn-Nâfi' in his position, and the latter invaded as-Sûs al- 229
Adna,[3] which lay behind Ṭanjah. There he went about without being molested or fought by anybody. At last he departed.

Yazîd ibn-Mu'âwiyah died and his son Mu'âwiyah ibn-Yazîd, surnamed abu-Laila, was proclaimed caliph. Mu-'âwiyah called a general public prayer meeting, and resigned the caliphate. He retired to his home where he died after

[1] 'Adhâri, vol. i, p. 14.

[2] Suyûṭi, *Ḥusn*, vol. ii, 7.

[3] *i. e.*, the nearer (= Dar'ah) in distinction from al-Aḳṣa—the farther; Ya'ḳûbi, *Buldân*, pp. 359-360.

two months. Later came the rule of Marwân ibn-al-Ḥakam and the insurrection of ibn-az-Zubair.

Then came 'Abd-al-Malik ibn-Marwân to power; and everything went smoothly with him. He assigned as *'âmil* over Egypt his brother 'Abd-al-'Azîz who put over Ifrîḳiyah Zuhair ibn-Ḳais al-Balawi.[1] Zuhair conquered Tûnis and left for Barḳah. Hearing that a band of Greeks had landed from their ships and were doing mischief, he went against them with a cavalry detachment. On meeting them, he fell a martyr with his companions. His tomb is still there. His and his companions' tombs are called *Kubûr ash-Shuhadâ'* [the martyrs' tombs].

Then Ḥassân ibn-an-Nu'mân al-Ghassâni [2] became ruler. He made an incursion against al-Kâhinah,[3] the queen of the Berbers. He was defeated by her and came and occupied certain castles within the territory of Barḳah. These castles were included within one whose roof was an arched structure upon which one could cross over. Since then, these castles were called Ḳuṣûr Ḥassân.[4]

Ḥassân made another incursion, killed the queen and carried into captivity many Berbers whom he sent to 'Abd-al-'Azîz. Regarding these captives, the poet, abu-Miḥjan Nuṣaib, used to say, " I have seen in 'Abd-al-'Azîz's home Berber captives who have faces more beautiful than which I never saw."

According to ibn-al-Kalbi, Hishâm assigned Kulthûm ibn-'Iyâḍ ibn-Waḥwaḥ al-Ḳushairi to the governorship of Ifrîḳiyah, whose people rebelled and put him to death. Ibn-al-Kalbi also states that Ifrîkiyah was subdued in pre-

[1] 'Adhâri, vol. i, p. 16.

[2] *Ibid.*, vol. i, pp. 18 *seq.*

[3] Fem. of *kâhin* = soothsayer.

[4] 'Adhâri, vol. i, p. 21.

Islamic times by Ifrikis ibn-Ḳais ibn-Ṣaifi-l-Ḥimyari and was named after him. He killed Jurjir [1] [Gregory] its king and said regarding the Berbers, "How barbarous they are!" Hence the name, Berbers.

Al-Ḳairawân. According to a tradition communicated to me by certain inhabitants of Ifrikiyah on the authority of their *sheikhs,* when 'Uḳbah ibn-Nâfi' al-Fihri wanted to build al-Ḳairawân,[2] he began to think regarding the site of the mosque, and he saw in a dream as if a man called to prayer at a certain spot where he later erected the minaret. When he awoke, he started to erect the boundary marks where he had seen the man stand, after which he built the mosque.

Muḥammad ibn-Sa'd from al-Wâḳidi:—Muḥammad ibn-al-Ash'ath al-Khuzâ'fi ruled over Ifrikiyah in the name of abu-l-'Abbâs "the Commander of the Believers", and repaired the city of al-Ḳairawân with its mosque. He was later dismissed by al-Manṣûr, who assigned 'Umar ibn-Ḥafṣ Hizârmard [3] in his place.

[1] *Cf.* 'Adhâri, vol. i, pp. 5-6.
[2] Iṣṭakhri, pp. 39-40.
[3] 'Adhâri, vol. i, p. 64. "'Amr ibn-Ḥafṣ ibn-Ḳabiṣah."

CHAPTER VI

The Conquest of Ṭanjah [Tangiers]

According to al-Wâḳidi, 'Abd-al-'Azîz ibn-Marwân made Mûsa ibn-Nuṣair,[1] a freedman of the banu-Umaiyah and who came originally from 'Ain at-Tamr (some say he belonged to the clan of Arâshah, a branch of the Bali; others say, to the clan of Lakhm) governor over Ifrîḳiyah. According to others, Mûsa ruled over it in the time of al-Walîd ibn-'Abd-al-Malik, in the year 89. He reduced Ṭanjah and occupied it, he being the first to occupy and mark it in lots for the Moslems. His horsemen went as far as as-Sûs al-Adna,[2] which was over twenty days' journey from as-Sûs al-Aḳṣa [the farther as-Sûs = modern Morocco]. Thus he subjugated as-Sûs al-Aḳṣa, carrying many captives from the inhabitants and receiving homage. His *'âmil* collected from them *ṣadaḳah*. Later he assigned Ṭâriḳ ibn-Ziyâd, his freedman, over it [Ṭanjah and environs] and departed to Ḳairawân Ifrîḳiyah.

[1] 'Adhâri, vol. i, pp. 24 *seq.*

[2] *Ibid.*, vol. i, p. 27.

PART VI

ANDALUSIA

CHAPTER I

The Conquest of Andalusia

Ṭârik crosses the Straits. According to al-Wâkidi, the first to invade Andalusia [1] was Ṭârik ibn-Ziyâd,[2] the *'âmil* of Mûsa ibn-Nuṣair, and that was in the year 92. Ṭârik was met by Ulyân, the commander of the Majâz [3] al-Andalus, whom he promised safety provided he would transport him with his companions to Andalusia in his ships. When he arrived there, Ṭârik was resisted by the people, but he effected the conquest of the land in the year 92.[4] The king of Andalusia, it is claimed, belonged to the Ashbân [Spanish] people whose origin was from Iṣbahân.[5] Mûsa
ibn-Nuṣair wrote Ṭârik a severe letter for risking the lives 231
of the Moslems and following his own opinion without consulting Mûsa as regards the campaign. In the meantime, he ordered him not to go beyond Cordova [Ar. Ḳurṭubah].[6] Mûsa himself proceeded to Cordova in Andalusia; and Ṭârik sought and was reinstated in his favor. Ṭârik then reduced the city of Ṭulaiṭulah,[7] the capital of the kingdom

1 Al-Andalus, Spain. Ya'ḳûbi, *Buldân*, pp. 353-355.

2 'Adhâri, vol. ii, pp. 11 *seq.*

3 "The straits separating Morocco from Andalusia," al-Marâkishi, *al-Mu'jib fi-Talkhîṣ Akhbâr al-Maghrib*, p. 6.

4 'Adhâri, vol. ii, pp. 5 *seq.*

5 Ispahan of Persia. The Arabs were misled to this conclusion by the accidental similarity between the two names. See Mas'ûdi, vol. ii, pp. 326-327.

6 Idrisi, *Ṣifat al-Maghrib*, pp. 208-214.

7 Toledo. Muḳaddasi, p. 235; Khurdâdhbih, p. 89.

of Andalusia and which lies next to France [Ar. Faranjah]. Here he carried off a wonderful table[1] which Mûṣa ibn-Nuṣair, on his return in the year 96, offered as a present to al-Walîd ibn-'Abd-al-Malik in Damascus, who was sick at that time. When Sulaimân ibn-'Abd-al-Malik came to power, he demanded 100,000 *dînârs* from Mûsa ibn-Nuṣair; but when Yazîd ibn-al-Muhallab interceded in Mûsa's behalf, he was spared.

Ismâ'îl governor of al-Maghrib. When 'Umar ibn-'Abd-al-'Azîz became caliph, he appointed over al-Maghrib Ismâ'îl ibn-'Abdallâh ibn-abi-l-Muhâjir, a freedman of the banu-Makhzûm, who behaved according to the best standards and invited the Berbers to Islâm. 'Umar ibn-'Abd-al-'Azîz also wrote them letters to that effect, which were read to them in the different districts by Ismâ'îl. Thus did Islâm prevail over al-Maghrib.

Yazîd as governor. When Yazîd ibn-'Abd-al-Malik assumed power, he appointed Yazîd ibn-abi-Muslim, a freedman of al-Ḥajjâj ibn-Yûsuf, over Ifrîḳiyah and al-Maghrib. The latter arrived in Ifrîḳiyah in the year 102, and had his guard of Berbers. On the hand of every guard, he inscribed the word " Guard ",[2] which act displeased them and made them impatient with him. Some of them entered into a conspiracy and agreed to kill him. One evening, he went out for the sunset prayer, and they killed him in his place of worship. Yazîd then appointed Bishr ibn-Ṣafwân al-Kalbi. Bishr beheaded 'Abdallâh ibn-Mûsa ibn-Nuṣair in revenge for Yazîd [ibn-abi-Muslim] on the ground that he was suspected of killing him and arousing people against him.

Bishr and other governors. Hishâm ibn-'Abd-al-Malik

[1] " Once owned by king Solomon ". Marâkishi, p. 8.

[2] Ar. *ḥarasi.* 'Adhâri, vol. i, p. 34.

again appointed Bishr ibn-Ṣafwân.[1] The latter died in al-Ḳairawân in the year 109. Hishâm appointed in his place 'Ubaidah ibn-'Abd-ar-Raḥmân al-Ḳaisi,[2] after whom Hishâm appointed 'Abdallâh[3] ibn-al-Ḥabḥâb, a freedman of the banu-Salûl. 'Abdallâh sent 'Abd-ar-Raḥmân ibn-Ḥabîb ibn-abi-'Ubaidah ibn-'Uḳbah ibn-Nâfi' al-Fihri to the invasion of as-Sûs[4] and the land of as-Sûdân. The
victories won by 'Abd-ar-Raḥmân were unparalleled, and 232
among the booty he carried away were two of the women slaves of that region, each with one bosom. These people are known by the name of Tarâjân.

After ibn-al-Ḥabḥâb, Hishâm appointed Kulthûm ibn-'Iyâḍ al-Ḳushairi who arrived in Ifrîḳiyah in the year 23[5] and was killed in it. Hishâm appointed after Kulthûm, Ḥanẓalah ibn-Ṣafwân al-Kalbi,[6] a brother of Bishr, who fought against the Kharijites[7] and died there while he held the governorship.

When al-Walîd ibn-Yazîd ibn-'Abd-al-Malik assumed power, 'Abd-ar-Raḥmân ibn-Ḥabîb al-Fihri rose against him. 'Abd-ar-Raḥmân was in good favor with the inhabitants of this frontier region [northern Africa and al-Maghrib], because of the good deeds done in it by his grandfather 'Uḳbah ibn-Nâfi'. Consequently, 'Abd-ar-Raḥmân subdued this region; and Ḥanẓalah departed, leaving 'Abd-ar-Raḥmân over it.

[1] 'Adhâri, vol. i, p. 35.

[2] *Ibid.*, vol. i, p. 36: "as-Sulami".

[3] *Ibid.*, vol. i, p. 38: "'Ubaidallâh"; *cf.* Maḥâsin, vol. i, p. 319.

[4] Idrîsi, *Ṣifat al-Maghrib*, p. 165.

[5] 'Adhâri, vol. i, p. 41.

[6] Al-Kindi, *Kitâb al-Wulât w-al-Ḳuḍât*, pp. 71-72, 80-82 (ed. Guest).

[7] *Al-Khawârij.* Rebels led by the heretic 'Ukkâshah aṣ-Ṣufri; see 'Adhâri, vol. i, pp. 45-47.

When Yazid ibn-al-Walîd assumed the caliphate, he did not send to al-Maghrib any *'âmil.*

Then came Marwân ibn-Muḥammad to power. 'Abd-ar-Raḥmân ibn-Ḥabîb communicated with him and professed homage and sent him presents. Marwân had a secretary, Khâlid ibn-Rabî'ah-l-Ifrîḳi, who was a special friend of 'Abd-al-Ḥamîd ibn-Yaḥya and kept up a correspondence with him. Marwân confirmed 'Abd-ar-Raḥmân as governor of the region, and appointed after him Ilyâs ibn-Ḥabîb, and after that, Ḥabîb ibn-'Abd-ar-Raḥmân. After this, the Ibâḍites [1] and the Berbers of the Khârijites had the upper hand.

Towards the end of abu-l-'Abbâs' caliphate, Muḥammad ibn-al-Ash'ath al-Khuzâ'i came to Ifrîḳiyah as its ruler at the head of 70,000 men, according to others, 40,000. His rule lasted for four years, during which he repaired the city of al-Ḳairawân. At last, the troops of the city rose against him together with others. I heard it reported that the inhabitants of the town and the troops that were in it rose against him and he held out against them in his castle for 40 days, during which his followers from Khurâsân, and others who owed him allegiance, came to his help. Consequently, he succeeded in laying hold on those who fought against him. He then went over the names and put to death every one whose name was Mu'âwiyah, Sufyân, Marwân or any other name that is borne by anyone of the banu-Umaiyah, sparing only those who had different names. He was thereupon dismissed by al-Manṣûr.

'Umar ibn-Ḥafṣ ibn-'Uthmân ibn-Ḳabîṣah ibn-abi-Ṣufrah-l-'Ataki, known as Hizârmard, was then made governor by al-Manṣûr, who had great admiration for him. 'Umar entered Ifrîḳiyah and launched in it a campaign that carried

[1] Ash-Shahrastâni, *Kitâb al-Milal w-an-Niḥal,* p. 100 (ed. Cureton).

him to the extremity of the land of the Berbers, where he built a city which he called al-'Abbâsîyah. Abu-Ḥâ- 233
tim as-Saddarâti-l-Ibâḍi (one of the inhabitants of Saddarâtah and a freedman of the Kindah) fought against Hizârmard; and the latter suffered martyrdom together with some members of his family. The frontier region broke out in revolt, and the city he had established was destroyed.

Hizârmard was succeeded by Yazîd ibn-Ḥâtim ibn-Ḳabîṣah ibn-al-Muhallab,[1] who rebelled at the head of 50,000 men and was accompanied to Jerusalem by abu-Ja'far al-Manṣûr who spent large sums of money on him. Yazîd advanced until he met abu-Ḥâtim in Tripoli [Ar. Aṭrâbulus]. He killed him and made his entrance to Ifrîḳiyah, where everything went smoothly with him.

Yazîd ibn-Ḥâtim was succeeded by Rauḥ ibn-Ḥâtim, and the latter by al-Faḍl ibn-Rauḥ, who was slain by the troops that rose up against him.

I was informed by Aḥmad ibn-Nâḳid, a freedman of the banu-l-Aghlab, that al-Aghlab ibn-Sâlim at-Tamîmi,[2] of Maru ar-Rûdh,[3] was among those who came from Khurâsân with al-Musauwidah.[4] Al-Aghlab was appointed by Mûsa-l-Hâdi governor of al-Maghrib. When al-Aghlab came to Ḳairawân Ifrîḳiyah, Ḥarîsh, who was once in the army of the frontier region of Tûnis, gathered a body of men, with whom he marched against him and besieged him. Al-Aghlab later made a sortie, and in the battle which followed was hit by an arrow and fell dead. Neither his followers nor those of Ḥarîsh knew of it. At last Ḥarîsh

[1] Kindi, pp. 111-117.

[2] *Ibid.*, p. 110.

[3] Hamadhâni, *Buldân*, pp. 319-322.

[4] The partisans of the Abbasid dynasty, so called because they wore black clothes.

was defeated with his army and were pursued by the men of al-Aghlab for three days, during which many were killed, including Ḥarîsh himself, who fell in a place called Sûḳ al-Aḥad. Al-Aghlab after this was called "the martyr" [*ash-Shahîd*].

Ibrâhîm ibn-al-Aghlab, one of the leading men of the Egyptian army, arose one day with twelve men and carried away from the treasury the exact value of their subsistence allowances and no more. They ran away to a place called az-Zâb which lay at a distance of more than ten days from al-Ḳairawân. The *'âmil* of this frontier region, at that time under ar-Rashîd Hârûn, was Harthamah ibn-A'yan.[1] Ibrâhîm ibn-al-Aghlab assumed the commandership of the troops that were in that region and offered presents to Harthamah, showing him kindness and telling him in writing that he did not rebel or disobey, but was rather forced 234
to what he did by urgency and necessity. Harthamah assigned him to be governor of the region and intrusted to him its affairs.

When Harthamah's resignation from the governorship of this region [Ifrîḳiyah] was accepted, he was succeeded by ibn-al-'Akki,[2] whose rule was so bad that the people rose up against him. Ar-Rashîd consulted Harthamah regarding a man whom he could assign to that post and intrust to him its management, and Harthamah advised him that Ibrâhîm be reconciled, won over and appointed over the region. Accordingly, ar-Rashîd wrote to Ibrâhîm, stating that he had forgiven him his crime, excused his fault and thought it wise to assign him to the governorship of al-Maghrib as an act of favor, expecting to receive from him loyalty and good counsel. Ibrâhîm became ruler of the region and managed its affairs thoroughly.

[1] Kindi, p. 136.

[2] 'Adhâri, vol. i, p. 80.

One of the city troops named 'Imran ibn-Mujâlid rose in a revolt and was joined by the army of the region who demanded that their subsistence allowances be given them, and laid siege to Ibrâhîm in al-Ḳairawân. Soon after that, those who pay allowances and stipends came bringing money from the *kharâj* of Egypt; and when the dues were given, they [the rebels] dispersed themselves. Ibrâhîm built al-Ḳaṣr al-Abyaḍ [the white citadel] two miles to the *ḳiblah* of al-Ḳairawân, and parceled out the land around it among the Moslems, who established themselves and their residences there. Thus did that section become populated. Ibrâhîm also built a cathedral mosque with gypsum and brick and marble columns, and covered it with cedar wood, making it 200 *dhirâ's* in length and almost 200 *dhirâ's* in width. He bought slaves to the number of 5,000, emancipated them and made them settle around it. This city he called al-'Abbâsîyah, which is still flourishing to-day.

Al-'Abbâsîyah. Muḥammad ibn-al-Aghlab ibn-Ibrâhîm ibn-al-Aghlab [1] built in the year 239 a city near Tâhart [2] and named it al-'Abbâsîyah, too. This city was destroyed by Aflaḥ ibn-'Abd-al-Wahhâb al-Ibâḍi, who wrote to the Umaiyad chief of Andalusia, informing him of his act in order to win his favor. The Umaiyad chief sent him 100,000 *dirhams.*

Bârah. There lies in al-Maghrib a land known as al-Arḍ al-Kabîrah [3] [the big land], situated at a distance of 15 days, more or less, from Barḳah. In it lies a city on the coast, called Bârah, whose inhabitants were Christians, but not Greeks. This city was invaded by Ḥablah,[4] the freed-

[1] 'Adhâri, vol. i, p. 107.

[2] Ṭabari, vol. iii, p. 562.

[3] Idrîsi, *Ṣifat al-Maghrib*, p. 56.

[4] "Ḥayah" in Athîr, vol. vi, p. 370.

man of al-Aghlab, who failed to reduce it. It was later invaded by Khalfûn al-Barbari (supposed to have been a freedman of the Rabî'ah) who reduced it in the early part 235
of al-Mutawakkil's caliphate.

Al-Mufarraj ibn-Sallâm. After Khalfûn there arose one called al-Mufarraj ibn-Sallâm who conquered and brought under his control 24 forts. He then forwarded the news of the situation to the Master of the post [1] in Egypt, and told him that he and his followers could conduct no [public] prayer unless the *imâm* confirms him over his district and makes him its ruler, so that he may not be included in the category of usurpers. Al-Mufarraj erected a cathedral mosque. Finally his men rose up against him and killed him.

Sûrân. He was followed by Sûran who sent his messenger to al-Mutawakkil, the "Commander of the Believers," asking for a confirmation and a letter of appointment to a governorship. Al-Mutawakkil, however, died before his messenger departed with the message to Sûrân.

Al-Muntaṣir-Billâh died after holding the caliphate for six months. Then came al-Musta'în-Billâh Aḥmad ibn-Muḥammad ibn-al-Mu'taṣim who ordered his *'âmil* over al-Maghrib, Ûtâmish, a freedman of the "Commander of the Believers", to confirm Sûrân; but no sooner had the messenger started from Surra-man-ra'a, than Ûtâmish was slain.[2] That region was after that governed by Waṣîf, a freedman of the caliph, who confirmed Sûrân in his position.

[1] *Ṣâḥib al-barîd.* Ibn-aṭ-Ṭiḳṭaḳa, *al-Fakhri,* p. 129.

[2] Ṭabari, vol. iii, pp. 1512, 1513.

PART VII

ISLANDS IN THE SEA

CHAPTER I

The Conquest of Certain Islands in the Sea

Sicily. The first to invade Sicily [1] was Mu'âwiyah ibn-Ḥudaij al-Kindi [2] in the days of Mu'âwiyah ibn-abi-Sufyân. It was continually invaded after that. The descendants of al-Aghlab ibn-Sâlim al-Ifriḳi conquered more than 20 cities in it, which are still in the hands of the Moslems. In the caliphate of al-Mutawakkil, Aḥmad ibn-Muḥammad ibn-al-Aghlab reduced in it the Yânah castle and Ghalyânah [3] fortress.

It is stated by al-Wâḳidi that 'Abdallâh ibn-Ḳais ibn-Makhlad ad-Dizaḳi plundered Sicily and carried off idols of gold and silver studded with pearls, which he sent to Mu'â-wiyah. Mu'âwiyah sent them to al-Baṣrah to be carried into India and sold there with a view to getting a higher price for them.

Rhodes. Mu'âwiyah ibn-abi-Sufyân sent expeditions by
sea and by land. He sent to Rhodes [4] Junâdah ibn-abi- 236
Umaiyah-l-Azdi. Junâdah was one of those on whose authority traditions were reported. He had chance to meet abu-Bakr, 'Umar and Mu'adh ibn-Jabal, and died in the year 80. Junâdah took Rhodes by force. Rhodes was a thicket in the sea. In pursuance of Mu'âwiyah's order, Junâdah caused Moslems to settle in it. This took place in the year 52.

[1] Ar. Siḳilliyah. Idrîsi, "Italy", in *Nuzhat al-Mushtâḳ fi-Ikhtirâḳ al-Âfâk*, pp. 57-58 (Rome, 1878).

[2] Kindi, pp. 17-19, 27-30.

[3] *Cf.* Idrîsi, "Italy", p. 49; Amari, *Bibliotheca Arabo-Sicula*, p. 60.

[4] Rûdis. See Kindi, p. 38.

Rhodes is one of the most fertile of all islands, and is about sixty miles in size. It is rich in olive trees, vineyards, fruits and fresh water.

Muḥammad ibn-Sa'd from al-Wâkidi and others:—The Moslems occupied Rhodes for seven years, living in a fort made for them. At the death of Mu'âwiyah, Yazîd wrote to Junâdah ordering him to destroy the fort and return. Mu'âwiyah used to alternate its occupants, making them live there in turns. Mujâhid ibn-Jabr [1] lived in it and taught the Koran.

Arwâd. In the year 54, Junâdah ibn-abi-Umaiyah reduced Arwâd,[2] and Mu'âwiyah made the Moslems settle in it. Among those who took part in conquering it was Mujâhid and Tubai',[3] a son of Ka'b al-Aḥbâr's [4] wife. It was here that Mujâhid taught Tubai' the Koran. Others say that he did it in Rhodes. This Arwâd is an island lying near Constantinople [al-Ḳusṭanṭînîyah].

Crete. Junâdah led a razzia against Crete [Iḳrîṭish],[5] a part of which he conquered at the time of al-Walîd. Later, the island was lost to the Moslems. In the caliphate of ar-Rashîd it was invaded again by Ḥumaid ibn-Ma'yûḳ al-Ḥamdâni, who reduced a part of it. In the caliphate of al-Ma'mûn, it was invaded by abu-Ḥafṣ 'Umar ibn-'Îsa-l-Andalusi, known by the name of al-Ikrîṭishi, who first reduced one fort and occupied it. Then he kept on reducing one part after another until none of the Greeks were left. He also dismantled their forts.

[1] Kindi, p. 39.

[2] Ṭabari, vol. ii, p. 163.

[3] Ṭabari, vol. ii, p. 163; Dhahabi, p. 69.

[4] A Jewish rabbi of Ḥimyar converted to Islâm in the time of 'Umar. Muir, *Annals*, p. 236, note 1.

[5] Idrîsi, "Italy", p. 19; Rustah, p. 85; "Iḳrîṭiyah".

PART VIII

NUBIA

CHAPTER I

Terms made with Nubia

'Ukbah leads the attack. Muḥammad ibn-Saʻd from abu--Khair:—When the Moslems subdued Egypt, ʻAmr ibn-al-ʻĀṣi sent to the surrounding villages, in order to overrun and pillage them, a detachment of cavalry under ʻUḳbah ibn-Nâfiʻ al-Fihri (Nâfiʻ being a brother of al-Âṣi on his mother's side). The cavalry entered the land of Nubia [1] as the summer expeditions of the Greeks do. The Moslems met in Nubia determined resistance. They were subjected to such severe showers of arrows until most of them were wounded and had to return with many wounds and blinded eyes. Therefore were the Nubians called the " archers of the eyes ".

The terms made. This state of affairs continued until ʻAbdallâh ibn-Saʻd ibn-abi-Sarḥ ruled over Egypt. The Nubians asked for peace and conciliation from ʻAbdallâh, who granted their request, the terms being that they pay no tax but offer as a present three hundred slaves per annum; and that the Moslems offer them as a present food equivalent to the value of the slaves.

The Nubians as archers. Muḥammad ibn-Saʻd from a *sheikh* of the tribe of Ḥimyar:—The latter said, " I have been to Nubia twice during the caliphate of ʻUmar ibn-al-Khaṭṭâb, and I never saw a people who are sharper in warfare than they. I heard one of them say to the Moslem, ʻ Where do you want me to hit you with my arrow?' and

---

[1] An-Nûbah. See Idrîsi, *Sifat al-Maghrib*, p. 19.

in case the Moslem would disdainfully say, 'In such a spot', the Nubian would never miss it. They were fond of fighting with arrows; but their arrows would scarcely ever hit on the ground.[1] One day, they arrayed themselves against us and we were desirous to carry the conflict with the sword; but they were too quick for us and shot their arrows, putting out our eyes. The eyes that were put out numbered 150. We at last thought that the best thing to do with such a people was to make peace. We could carry very little booty away from them; and their ability to inflict injury was great. 'Amr, however, refused to make peace with them and went on contending against them until he was dismissed and was succeeded by 'Abdallâh ibn-Sa'd ibn-abi-Sarḥ, who concluded peace with them."

According to al-Wâḳidi, Mu'âwiyah ibn-Ḥudaij al-Kindi lost his eye in Nubia and thus became one-eyed.

The legality of selling their children as slaves. Abu-'Ubaid al-Ḳâsim ibn-Sallâm from Yazîd ibn-abi-Ḥabîb:—The latter said, "Between us and the black tribes [Ar. *asâwid*], no treaty or covenant exists. Only a truce was arranged between us, according to which we agreed to give them some wheat and lentils, and they to give us slaves. It is all right to buy their slaves from them or from others."

Abu-'Ubaid from al-Laith ibn-Sa'd:—The latter said, "The terms we made with the Nubians stipulated only that we neither fight against them nor they against us, that they give slaves and we give them their value in terms of food. 238
If they desire, therefore, to sell their wives or children, there is no reason why they should not be bought."

In a report of abu-l-Bukhturi and others, it is stated that 'Abdallâh ibn-Sa'd ibn-abi-Sarḥ made terms with the Nubians to the effect that they give four hundred slaves per

[1] *i. e.* they scarcely ever missed their aim.

year, whom they shall bring forth and for whom they shall receive food in exchange.

The caliph al-Mahdi ordered that Nubia be held responsible every year for 360 slaves and one giraffe, and that they be given wheat, vinegar, wine, clothes and mattresses or the value thereof.

The Nubians recently claimed that the tribute [1] is not due on them every year, and that it was demanded from them in the caliphate of al-Mahdi, at which time they told the caliph that the tribute was a part of what they took as slaves from their enemies and therefore they had, if they could not get enough slaves, to use their own children and offer them. Al-Mahdi ordered that they be tolerated, and that the tribute of one year be considered as if for three. No confirmation, however, could be found in the registers of al-Ḥaḍrah; [2] but it was found in the register in Egypt.

Al-Ḳummi in al-Bujah. Al-Mutawakkil ordered one, Muhammad ibn-'Abdallâh, known as al-Ḳummi, to be sent and put in charge of al-Ma'din [3] in Egypt. He also put him in charge of al-Ḳulzum [Suez], the road of al-Ḥijâz, and the furnishing of guides to the Egyptians when on holy pilgrimage. Arriving in al-Ma'din, he conveyed provisions in ships from al-Ḳulzum to the land of al-Bujah. He then proceeded to a sea-coast, called 'Aidhâb,[4] where the ships met him. With these provisions, he and his followers were strengthened and fed until they came to the castle of the king of al-Bujah. Al-Ḳummi attacked him in

[1] Ar. *baḳt*, Quatremère, *Mémoires Géographiques et Historiques sur l'Égypte*, vol. ii, pp. 42, 53.

[2] Perhaps al-Khaḍrâ'. See Idrîsi, *Ṣifat al-Maghrib*, p. 84; Hamadhani, *Buldân*, pp. 79-80.

[3] The mine land. Maḳrîzi, vol. i, pp. 313, 318; Mas'ûdi, *Tanbîh*, p. 330.

[4] Idrîsi, *Ṣifat al-Maghrib*, p. 27.

small force, and the king of al-Bujah made a sally with his numerous men on camels fastened with girths. Al-Ḳummi brought bells and put them on his horses. As soon as the camels heard the bell sounds, they ran away with the al-Bujah men over hills and valleys. The chief of al-Bujah was killed and was succeeded by his sister's son,[1] whose father was one of the kings of al-Bujah. He sued for a
truce, which al-Mutawakkil granted only on condition that 239
he [the chief] should tread on his [al-Mutawakkil's] carpet. Accordingly, he came to Surra-man-ra'a and made terms in the year 241, agreeing to pay tribute in money and slaves. He was then sent back with al-Ḳummi. Thus, the people
of al-Bujah are in a state of truce in which they pay tax 240
and do not prevent the Moslems from working in the gold mine, which terms are mentioned in the conditions imposed upon their chief.

[1] Maḳrîzi, vol. i, p. 317: "his brother's son"; *cf.* Quatremère, *op. cit.*, vol. ii, p. 136.

CHAPTER II

THE KARAṬIS [1]

THE Greeks used to get the *karâṭis* from Egypt,[2] and the Arabs used to get the *dînârs* from the Greeks. 'Abd-al-Malik ibn-Marwân was the first to inscribe on the upper part of these fabrics such phrases as "Declare: Allah is one!" and others with the name of Allah. One day, he received from the Byzantine king a message, saying, "You have recently introduced upon your *karâṭîs* some inscription that we hate. If you leave that out, well and good; otherwise, you shall see on the *dînârs* the name of your Prophet associated with things you hate." This was too much for 'Abd-al-Malik, who hated to abolish a worthy law that he had established. He thereupon sent for Khâlid ibn-Yazîd ibn-Mu'âwiyah and said to him, "O abu-Hâshim! It is a calamity!" Khâlid replied, "Be free from your fright, 'Commander of the Believers'; declare the use of their *dînârs* illegal; strike new coinage in place of them, and let not these infidels be free from what they hate to see on the fabrics." "Thou hast eased my mind," said 'Abd-al-Malik, "may Allah give thee ease!" He then struck the *dînârs*.

According to 'Awânah ibn-al-Ḥakam, the Copts used to

[1] Rolls of papyrus for writing; also, cloth of Egyptian fabric used for carrying vases or clothes. Zaidân, *Ta'rîkh at-Tamaddun*, vol. i, p. 103; *Zeitschrift für Assyrologie*, pp 187-190, yr. 1908.

[2] Al-Kindi, *Faḍâ'il Miṣr*, p. 209, lines 9-10 (ed. Oestrup).

[3] Ar. *ṭawâmîr*. Fraenkel, *op cit.*, p. 251.

inscribe the word " Christ " at the top part of the *ḳarâṭîs,* and to ascribe divinity to him (may Allah be highly exalted above that!); and they used to put the sign of the cross in place of " In the name of Allah, the compassionate, the merciful ". That is why the Byzantine king was disgusted and his anger was aroused with the change that 'Abd-al-Malik introduced.

According to al-Madâ'ini, it was stated by Maslamah ibn-Muḥârib that Khâlid ibn-Yazîd advised 'Abd-al-Malik to declare the use of the Greek *dînârs* illegal, to prohibit their circulation and to stop the sending of the *ḳarâṭîs* to the Byzantine empire. Accordingly, no *ḳarâṭîs* were carried there for some time.

PART IX

AL-'IRÂK AND PERSIA

CHAPTER I

THE CONQUEST OF AS-SAWÂD 241

THE CALIPHATE OF ABU-BAKR AṢ-ṢIDDÎḲ

Al-Muthanna invades as-Sawâd. Al-Muthanna ibn-Ḥârithah ibn-Salamah ibn-Ḍamḍam ash-Shaibâni used to lead incursions with some of his men against as-Sawâd.[1] Having heard of it, abu-Bakr made inquiries regarding him and learned from Ḳais ibn-'Âṣim ibn-Sinân al-Minḳari that that was not a man with no reputation, or of unknown origin, or of no support; but it was al-Muthanna ibn-Ḥârithah ash-Shaibâni. Later, al-Muthanna presented himself before abu-Bakr and said to him, "Caliph of the Prophet of Allah, make me your lieutenant over those of my people who have accepted Islâm, that I may fight against those foreigners, the Persians." Abu-Bakr wrote him a covenant to that effect. Al-Muthanna proceeded till he came to Khaffân; and inviting his people to Islam, they accepted it.

Khâlid in al-Ubullah. Abu-Bakr then wrote to Khâlid ibn-al-Walîd al-Makhzûmi, ordering him to go against al-'Irâḳ. Others say that he sent him from al-Madînah. In the meantime, abu-Bakr wrote to al-Muthanna ibn-Ḥârithah ordering him to receive Khâlid and obey his word.

Previous to this, Madh'ûr ibn-'Adi-l-'Ijli had written to abu-Bakr presenting his case and the case of his people, and asking to be put in charge of the campaign against the Persians. Now, abu-Bakr wrote and ordered him to join Khâlid, stop with him when he stopped and move with him

[1] 'Irâḳ, the region west of the Tigris. Rustah, p. 104.

when he moved. On the arrival of Khâlid in an-Nibâj,[1] he was met by al-Muthanna ibn-Ḥârithah. Thence Khâlid proceeded to al-Baṣrah in which there was at this time Suwaid ibn-Ḳuṭbah adh-Dhuhli (others than abu-Mikhnaf say that there was in it Ḳuṭbah ibn-Ḳatâdah adh-Dhuhli) of the tribe of Bakr ibn-Wâ'il, accompanied by a band of followers. Suwaid had designs regarding al-Baṣrah similar to those of al-Muthanna regarding al-Ḳûfah, which at that time was not called al-Kûfah but al-Ḥîrah. Suwaid said to Khâlid, "The inhabitants of al-Ubullah had assembled against me but failed to make the attack simply because of thy presence, as I believe." "If that is so," answered Khâlid "the advisable thing for me would be to leave al-Baṣrah in the day time and return in the night, at which time my companions would enter thy camp and we will fight together." Accordingly, Khâlid left in the direction 242
of al-Ḥîrah and when darkness fell, he turned back until he got to the camp of Suwaid, which he entered with his men. In the morning, the inhabitants of al-Ubullah, hearing that Khâlid had left al-Baṣrah, advanced towards Suwaid. Seeing the great number of men in his army, they were confounded and turned back. Thereupon, Khâlid shouted, "On them! I see in them the looks of a people whose hearts Allah has filled with terror!" Then the Moslems charged them, put them to flight, and by Allah's help, killed a great number and caused others to drown in Dijlat al-Baṣrah.[2] Thence Khâlid passed through al-Khuraibah,[3] reduced it and carried its inhabitants away into captivity. He left over it in his place—as it is reported by al-Kalbi—Shuraiḥ ibn-

[1] Khurdâdhbih, pp. 146, 147.

[2] or Dijlat al-'Aura = the united course of the Tigris and the Euphrates before they empty into the Persian Gulf. Yâḳût, vol. iii, p. 745.

[3] Hamadhâni, *Buldân*, p. 189.

'Âmir ibn-Ḳain [1] of the banu-Sa'd ibn-Bakr ibn-Hawâzin. The city was a fortified frontier town for the Persians.

Nahr al-Mar'ah. It is also reported that Khâlid came to the river known as al-Mar'ah [2] river, with whose people he made terms. He then fought against a body of men assembled at al-Madhâr.[3]

Khâlid proceeds to al-Ḥîrah. Khâlid then proceeded to al-Ḥîrah,[4] and left Suwaid ibn-Ḳuṭbah to rule over his district, saying, "We have crushed the Persians in thy district in a way that will humiliate them before thee."

Others report that when Khâlid was in the district of al-Yamâmah, he wrote to abu-Bakr for reinforcements; and abu-Bakr sent him Jarîr ibn-'Abdallâh al-Bajali. Jarîr met Khâlid as the latter was on his way out of al-Yamâmah, joined him and attacked the al-Madhâr's chief by Khâlid's orders. Allah knows if that is so.

Al-Wâḳidi states, "Our friends in al-Ḥijâz maintain that Khâlid left for al-'Irâḳ, passing by Faid [5] and ath-Tha'labîyah,[6] after which he came to al-Ḥîrah.

Zandaward, Durna and other places reduced by Khâlid. Khâlid ibn-al-Walîd passed through Zandaward in Kaskar and reduced it; he also reduced Durna and its territory, which capitulated after one hour's shooting by the people of Zandaward on the Moslems.

He then proceeded to Hurmuzjarad, to the inhabitants of which he made a promise of security. The city itself was taken. Khâlid then came to Ullais. Jâbân,[7] the chief

[1] Ṭabari, vol. i, p. 2382.

[2] *i. e.*, the woman's river; Ṭabari, vol. i, p. 2026.

[3] Yâḳût, vol. iv, p. 468; Hamadhâni, p. 211.

[4] Ḥauḳal, p. 163.

[5] A town in central Najd. Muḳaddasi, p. 254.

[6] On the west bank of the Euphrates. Kuhrdâdhbih, p. 127.

[7] Ṭabari, vol. i, p. 2018.

of the Persians, set out against him and Khâlid sent ahead al-Muthanna ibn-Ḥârithah ash-Shaibâni who met Jabân at Nahr ad-Damm [sanguine canal]. Khâlid made terms with the inhabitants of Ullais, stipulating that they act as spies, guides and helpers to the Moslems against the Persians.

Khâlid in al-Ḥîrah. Khâlid then proceeded to Mujtama' al-Anhâr[1] [confluence of canals], where he was met by Azâdhbih, the holder of the frontier fortifications of Kisra that lay between the Persian and the Arab territories. The 243
Moslems fought against him and defeated him. Then Khâlid came and stopped at Khaffân. Others say he proceeded directly to al-Ḥîrah, where he was met by 'Abd-al-Masîḥ ibn-'Amr ibn-Ḳais ibn-Ḥaiyân ibn-Buḳailah[2] (Buḳailah's proper name being al-Ḥârith) of the Azd, Hâni' ibn-Ḳabîṣah ibn-Mas'ûd ash-Shaibâni and Iyâs ibn-Ḳabîṣah aṭ-Ṭâ'i (others say Farwah ibn-Iyâs), Iyâs being the *'âmil* of Kisra Abarwîz over al-Ḥîrah after an-Nu'mân ibn-al-Mundhir. These men made terms with Khâlid, stipulating that they pay 100,000 *dirhams* per year, others say 80,000 per year, that they act as spies for the Moslems against the Persians, and that Khâlid would not destroy any of their churches or citadels.

It was reported by abu-Mikhnaf, on the authority of abu-l-Muthannah-l-Walîd ibn-al-Ḳaṭâmi, who is the same as ash-Sharki ibn-al-Ḳaṭâmi-l-Kalbi, that 'Abd-al-Masiḥ, who was an aged man, appeared before Khâlid who asked him, "Where dost thou come from, old man?" And he replied, "From my father's back."—"What didst thou come out from?"—"From my mother's womb."—"Woe unto thee! Where art thou now?"—"In my clothes."—"Woe

[1] Wellhausen, *Skizzen*, vol. vi, p. 42; Caetani, vol. ii, p. 937.

[2] Duraid, p. 285; Ṭabari, vol. i, p. 2019; Mas'ûdi, vol. i, p. 217.

to thee! Where dost thou stand now?"—"On the ground."—"Dost thou have reason [Ar. *ta'ḳul*]?"—"Yes, I can bind [*a'ḳul*] and tie up [a camel]." [1]—"Woe to thee! I am speaking to thee like a man!"—"And I am answering thee like a man."—"Art thou for peace or for war?"—"For peace."—"What are these forts then?"—"We built them for the rogue until the meek comes." [2] The two then discussed the question of peace and it was agreed that 100-000 [*dirhams*] be offered the Moslems every year. The money taken from these people was the first sum carried to al-Madînah from al-'Irâk. It was also stipulated that they seek no evil for the Moslems and that they act as spies against the Persians. All that took place in the year 12.

Al-Ḥusain ibn-al-Aswad from Yaḥya ibn-Âdam:—The latter said. "I heard it said that the people of al-Ḥîrah were 6,000 men, on each one of whom 14 *dirhams,* each having the weight of 5 *ḳîrâṭs,* were assessed, making 84,000 *dirhams* in all, of 5 *ḳîrâṭs* each, or 60,000 of 7 each. To that end, he [Khâlid] wrote them a statement which I myself have read." 244

It is reported that Yazîd ibn-Nubaishah-l-'Âmiri said, "We came to al-'Irâḳ with Khâlid and went as far as the frontier fort of al-'Udhaib. We then came to al-Ḥîrah whose people had fortified themselves in al-Ḳaṣr al-Abyaḍ [white citadel], Ḳaṣr ibn-Buḳailah and Ḳaṣr al-'Adasîyin. We went around on horseback in the open spaces among their buildings, after which they made terms with us." (According to ibn-al-Kalbi al-'Adasîyin were a branch of the Kalb, and were named after their mother who was also of the Kalb tribe.)

[1] Pun on words. Caetani, vol. iv, p. 657 takes it to mean, "I am rich enough to pay the blood-wit [*'aḳl*] and to retaliate by killing [*ḳawad*]".

[2] *Cf.* Mas'ûdi, vol. i, p. 218; Ṭabari, vol. i, p. 2019; Caetani, vol. iv. p. 657.

Abu-Mas'ud al-Kûfi from ash-Sha'bi:—Khuraim[1] ibn-Aus ibn-Ḥârithah ibn-Lâm aṭ-Ṭâ'i said to the Prophet, "If Allah enables thee to reduce al-Ḥirah, I shall ask thee to give me Buḳailah's daughter." When Khâlid wanted to make terms with the inhabitants of al-Ḥirah, Khuraim said to him, "The Prophet has given me Buḳailah's daughter. She should not therefore be included in thy terms." This was testified to by Bashîr ibn-Sa'd and Muḥammad ibn-Maslamah of the *Anṣâr*; and therefore, Khâlid did not include her in the terms, but turned her over to Khuraim. She was then bought from Khuraim for 1,000 *dirhams,* she being too old for Khuraim to marry her. Some one remarked to Khuraim, "She was sold very cheap. Her people would have paid thee many times the price thou hast charged." And he replied, "I never thought there was a number above ten hundred."

Another tradition has it that the one who asked the Prophet to give him Buḳailah's daughter was one of the Rabî'ah. The former view, however, is more authentic.

Bâniḳiya taken. Khâlid ibn-al-Walîd despatched Bashîr ibn-Sa'd abu-an-Nu'mân ibn-Bashîr of the *Anṣâr* to Bâniḳiya.[2] Bashîr was met by the Persian horsemen headed by Farrukhbundâdh. Bashîr's men were shot with arrows; but he led the charge and put the enemy to flight, killing Farrukhbundâdh. He then returned with a wound which became recrudescent, when he came to 'Ain at-Tamr, and caused his death. Others say that Khâlid himself, accompanied by Bashîr, met Farrukhbundâdh.

Khâlid then sent Jarîr ibn-'Abdallâh al-Bajali to the people of Bâniḳiya. Jarîr was met by Buṣbuhra ibn-Ṣalûba, who refused to fight and proposed to make peace. Jarîr

[1] Mawardi, p. 333; Ṭabari, vol. i, pp. 2047-2048.

[2] Hamadhâni, p. 165.

made terms with him on 100,000 *dirhams* and one mantle.[1] Others say that ibn-Ṣalûba came to Khâlid and, refusing to fight, made those terms. After the battle of an-Nukhailah 245
and the death of Mihrân, Jarîr came and received from ibn-Ṣalûba's people and from the people of al-Ḥîrah the sum agreed upon, and wrote them a receipt. Others deny that Jarîr ibn-'Abdallâh ever came to al-'Irâḳ except in the caliphate of 'Umar ibn-al-Khaṭṭâb. Abu-Mikhnaf and al-Wâḳidi, however, repeat that he went there twice.

Khâlid wrote a statement to Buṣbuhra ibn-Ṣalûba and sent the mantle to abu-Bakr together with the money from al-Ḥîrah and the thousand *dirhams*. Abu-Bakr offered the mantle as a present to al-Ḥusain ibn-'Ali.

Abu-Naṣr at-Tammâr from 'Abdallâh ibn-Mughaffal [2] al-Muzani:—No part of al-'Irâḳ made covenant [with the Moslems] except al-Ḥîrah, Ullais and Bâniḳiya.

Al-Ḥusain ibn-al-Aswad from ibn-Mughaffal:—No land below al-Jabal [3] is fit for sale except the land of the banu-Ṣalûba and the land of al-Ḥîrah.

Al-Ḥusain ibn-al-Aswad from al-Aswad ibn-Ḳais's father:—The latter said, "We arrived in al-Ḥîrah and made terms on so much money and a camel's saddle." In answer to my question, "What did ye do with the saddle?" he replied, "One of us had no saddle and we gave it to him."

Abu-'Ubaid from Ḥumaid ibn-Hilâl:—When Khâlid arrived in al-Ḥîrah, its inhabitants made terms without offering any resistance. The following verse was written by Ḍirâr ibn-al-Azwar al-Asadi:

1 Ar. *ṭailasân* = Persian apparel of dark wool. Dozy, *Vêtements*, pp 278-280.

2 Mughaffal and not Mughaffil as Balâdhuri has it. See Dhahabi, p. 477.

3 Al-Jabal or al-Jibâl = Media. Hamadhâni, pp. 209 *seq.*

"I had insomnia in Bânikiya and whosoever receives
what I received there—a wound, would certainly have insomnia."

Al-Wâkidi states, "Our companions agree that this Dirâr was slain in al-Yamâmah."

Al-Falâlîj and Tustar. From Bânikiya, Khâlid came to al-Falâlîj,[1] in which was massed a host of Greeks. They were soon dispersed, and Khâlid, meeting no resistance, re- 246
turned to al-Hîrah. Hearing that Jâbân was at the head of a great army in Tustar,[2] Khâlid sent against him al-Muthanna ibn-Hârithah ash-Shaibâni and Hanzalah ibn-ar Rabî'[3] ibn-Rabâh al-Usaidi of the banu-Tamim (he is the one called Hanzalah-l-Kâtib [the scribe]). No sooner had these two come to the place where Jâbân was, than he fled.

Sûk Baghdâd and al Anbar. Khâlid proceeded to al-Anbâr[4] whose people betook themselves to their fortifications. Here some one came to Khâlid and pointed out to him Sûk [market] Baghdâdh[5] which later [after Baghdâdh was founded] was called as Sûk al-'Atîk [the old market] and which lay near Karn as-Sarât.[6] Khâlid sent al-Muthanna who made a raid on this market, and the Moslems filled their hands with gold and silver and commodities light to carry. They spent the night at as-Sailahîn, and then came to al-Anbâr where Khâlid was. The Moslems then invested the inhabitants of al-Anbâr and set fire to places in its district. Al-Anbâr was thus called because the Persian granaries were in it and the friends and protégés of an-Nu'

[1] Pl. of Fallûjah. Yâkût, vol. iii, p. 908.

[2] Haukal, p. 172.

[3] "Rabî'ah" in Duraid, p. 127; and "Rabî'ah ibn-Saifi" in Kutaibah, *Ma'ârif*, p. 153.

[4] Iştakhri, p. 77

[5] Le Strange, *Baghdâd during the Abbasid Caliphate*, p. 12.

[6] As-Sarât Point where aş-Sarât canal disembogued to the Tigris. See Ya'kûbi, *Buldân*, p. 235.

mân used to get their subsistence allowances from it. Seeing what had befallen them, the inhabitants of al-Anbâr made terms which satisfied Khâlid, and so he left them in their homes.

Others assert that Khâlid sent al-Muthanna before him to Baghdâdh and then followed him and directed the raid against it, after which he returned to al-Anbâr. This, however, is not authentic.

Al-Ḥusain ibn-al-Aswad from ash-Sha'bi:—The people of al-Anbâr have a covenant [with the Moslems].

A tradition communicated to me by certain *sheikhs* from al-Anbâr states that terms were concluded with the people of al-Anbâr in the caliphate of 'Umar in which it was stipulated that they pay for their canton [*ṭassûj*] 400,000 *dirhams* and 1,000 cloaks fabricated in Ḳaṭawân, per year. The terms were made by Jarîr ibn-'Abdallâh al-Bajali. Others say that the sum was 80,000; but Allah knows best.

Jarîr reduced Bawâzîj al-Anbâr in which are to-day many of his freedmen.

According to a report there came to Khâlid ibn-al-Walîd someone who pointed out to him a market above al-Anbâr in which the Kalb, Bakr ibn-Wâ'il and others from the tribe of Ḳuḍâ'ah used to meet. Khâlid despatched against this place al-Muthanna ibn-Ḥârithah who made a raid against it, carried as booty what there was in it, slaughtered and took captives.

'Ain at-Tamr. Thence Khâlid advanced to 'Ain at-Tamr [1] and invested its fort in which a great frontier guard of Persians was stationed. The holders of the fort made a sally and fought, but after that, they confined themselves to their fort, where Khâlid and the Moslems besieged them 247
until they sued for peace. Khâlid refused to give them

[1] Yaḳut, vol. iii, p. 759.

promise of security and reduced the fort by force, slaughtering and carrying away captives. Here he found certain persons in a church whom he took captives. Among these captives was (1) Ḥumrân ibn-Abân ibn-Khâlid at-Tamri. Others say his father's name was Abba. This Ḥumrân was the freedman of 'Uthmân. He first belonged to al-Musaiyab ibn-Najabah-l-Fazâri from whom 'Uthmân bought him, and then released him. 'Uthmân later sent him to al-Kûfah to make inquiry regarding the conduct of his *'âmil* there, on which occasion Ḥumrân did not tell the truth. So 'Uthmân denied him the rights of protection [Ar. *jiwâr*] and Ḥumrân went and settled in al-Baṣrah. Among other captives were (2) Sirîn, father of Muḥammad ibn-Sîrîn,[1] whose brothers were Yaḥya ibn-Sîrîn, Anas ibn-Sirîn, and Ma'bad ibn-Sîrîn, Muḥammad being the eldest brother, and all being the freedmen of Anas ibn-Mâlik al-Anṣâri; (3) abu-'Amrah, a grandfather of 'Abdallâh ibn-'Abd-al-A'la, the poet; (4) Yasâr, a grandfather of Muḥammad ibn-Isḥâḳ—the author of *as-Sîrah*[2]—and a freedman of Ḳais ibn-Makhramah ibn-al-Muṭṭalib ibn-'Abd-Manâf; (5) Murrah abu-'Ubaid, a grandfather of Muḥammad ibn-Zaid ibn-'Ubaid ibn-Murrah (Nafis ibn-Muḥammad ibn-Zaid ibn-'Ubaid ibn-Murrah, the owner of the citadel [*ḳaṣr*] near al-Ḥarrah [volcanic tract of al-Madînah] was a son of this Muḥammad. His descendants give the name of their ancestor as 'Ubaid ibn-Murrah ibn-al-Mu'alla-l-Anṣâri and later az-Zuraḳi); (6) Nuṣair, the father of Mûsa ibn-Nuṣair, the governor of al-Maghrib. This Nuṣair was a freedman of the banu-Umaiyah, as it is asserted by freedmen in the frontier towns descended from slaves whom he

[1] Bakri, p. 199.

[2] The biography of the Prophet from which ibn-Hishâm's was abridged.

had released. Ibn-al-Kalbi says that abu-Farwah 'Abd ar-Raḥmân ibn-al-Aswad and Nuṣair abu-Mûsa ibn-Nuṣair were both Arabs of [the clan of] Arâshah of [the tribe of] Bali and that they were taken captives from Jabal al-Jalîl [Mt. Galilee] in Syria during the caliphate of abu-Bakr. Nuṣair's name was originally Naṣr which was later used in the diminutive form—Nuṣair. Some one of the banu-Umaiyah gave him his liberty; and he returned to Syria where in a village called Kafarmara[1] his son Mûsa was born. Mûsa was lame. Al-Kalbi adds that some one said that the two [Nuṣair and abu-Farwah] were brothers taken captives from 'Ain at-Tamr, and that they owed their liberty to the banu-Ḍabbah.

According to 'Ali ibn-Muḥammad al-Madâ'ini, it is stated by someone that abu-Farwah and Nuṣair were of the captives of 'Ain at-Tamr. Abu-Farwah was bought by Nâ'im al-Asadi who sold him later to 'Uthmân who used him for digging graves. When the people rose up against 'Uthmân, 248
abu-Farwah joined them and said to 'Uthmân, "Restore what thou hast wrongfully taken from others!" To this 'Uthmân replied, "Thou representest the first thing. I bought thee out of the *ṣadaḳah* funds that thou mayest dig the tombs; but thou hast left that." His son 'Abdallâh ibn-abi-Farwah was one of the illustrious freedmen. One of his descendants[2] was ar-Rabî' ibn-Yûnus ibn-Muḥammad ibn-abi-Farwah, a companion of al-Manṣûr. Abu-Farwah was thus called because of a furred garment [Ar. *farwah*] which he had on when he was taken captive.[3]

According to certain reports, Khâlid made terms with the

[1] "Kafarmathra" in *Marâṣid*, vol. ii, p. 504.

[2] Caetani, vol. ii, p. 945.

[3] *Aghâni*, vol. iii, p. 127, adds Kaisân, one of the ancestors of abu-l-'Atâhiyah, to the list of captives.

holders of 'Ain at-Tamr fort and these captives [mentioned above] were found in a church in a certain canton.[1] Some say that Sîrîn was one of the inhabitants of Jarjarâya and that he came there on a visit to a relative of his and was taken captive together with those in the church.

Al-Ḥusain ibn-al-Aswad from Yaḥya ibn-Âdam from ash-Sha'bi:—Khâlid ibn-al-Walîd made terms with the people of al-Ḥîrah and 'Ain at-Tamr, and stated them in a letter to abu-Bakr, which the latter endorsed. Yaḥya adds, "I asked al-Ḥasan ibn-Ṣâliḥ,[2] 'Have the people of 'Ain at-Tamr, like those of al-Ḥîrah, to pay something for their lands, but nothing for their persons?' To this al-Ḥasan replied, 'Yes.'"

It is stated by someone that there was at 'Ain at-Tamr at the head of the an-Namir ibn-Ḳâsiṭ tribe, Hilâl ibn-'Akkah ibn-Ḳais ibn-al-Bishr an-Namiri,[3] who gathered an army and fought against Khâlid. He was defeated, killed and crucified. According to ibn-al-Kalbi, there was at the head of the an-Namir at that time 'Akkah ibn-Ḳais ibn-al-Bishr himself.

The wound of Bashîr ibn-Sa'd al-Anṣâri became recrudescent and caused his death. He was buried at 'Ain at-Tamr. By his side was buried 'Umair ibn-Ri'âb ibn-Muhashshim ibn-Sa'îd ibn-Sahm ibn-'Amr, who was hit by an arrow at 'Ain at-Tamr and fell a martyr.

The razzias of an-Nusair ibn-Daisam. When Khâlid ibn-al-Walîd was at 'Ain at-Tamr he sent an-Nusair ibn-Daisam ibn-Thaur to a spring of water by which were settled the banu-Taghlib, whom he surprised by night, killing and carrying away many captives. One of the prisoners

[1] *ṭassûj*. Noldeke *ZDMG*, 1874, vol. xxviii, p. 94, note.

[2] One of the intermediate authorities of this tradition.

[3] Ṭabari, vol. i, p. 2122: "an-Namari".

asked Khâlid to release him, promising to point out to him a quarter inhabited by the banu-Rabî'ah. Khâlid did so and an-Nusair came to the Rabî'ah quarter, where he fell upon them in the night-time and carried away booty and captives. He then proceeded inland towards Takrît. Thus did the Moslems enrich themselves with booty. 249

According to a tradition communicated to me by abu-Mas'ûd al-Kûfi, on the authority of Muḥammad ibn-Marwân, an-Nusair came to 'Ukbarâ' and gave promise of security to its inhabitants, who brought forth food for his men and their animals. He then passed through al-Baradân, whose people hurried to present themselves before the Moslems. An-Nusair said, "Never mind!", which was enough to guarantee their safety.

Thence an-Nusair advanced to al-Mukharrim which according to abu-Mas'ûd was not called then Mukharrim,[1] but was so called after being occupied by a certain descendant of Mukharrim ibn-Ḥazn ibn-Ziyâd ibn-Anas ibn-ad-Daiyân al-Ḥârithi, as it is mentioned by Hishâm ibn-Muḥammad al-Kalbi.

The Moslems then crossed a bridge lying near Ḳaṣr [castle] Sâbûr, known to-day by the name of Ḳaṣr 'Îsa ibn-'Ali. The bridge was in charge of Khurzâd ibn-Mâhibundâdh who went out against the Moslems, but was fought and defeated by them. The Moslems then retreated to 'Ain at-Tamr.

An-Nusair and Ḥudhaifah. It is stated by al-Wâkidi that after the battle of al-Jisr [bridge] and after making the Moslems withdraw to Khaffân, al-Muthanna ibn-Ḥârithah sent in the caliphate of 'Umar ibn-al-Khaṭṭâb an-Nusair and Ḥudhaifah ibn-Miḥṣan at the head of a body of horsemen, who destroyed a band of the banu-Taghlib

[1] Ya'ḳubi, *Buldân*, p. 253.

and crossed over to Takrît from which they carried away camels and goats.

"One of the things told me by abu-Mas'ûd," said 'Attâb ibn-Ibrâhîm, "was that an-Nusair and Ḥudhaifah promised security to the people of Takrît and wrote a statement which was carried out by 'Utbah ibn-Farḳad as-Sulami when he reduced aṭ-Ṭîrhân [or Ṭîrahân] and al-Mauṣil. He also mentioned the fact that an-Nusair, directed by Khâlid ibn-al-Walîd, made a raid against villages in Maskin and Ḳaṭrabbul [or Ḳuṭrubbul] from which he carried off large booty."

From 'Ain at-Tamr, Khâlid advanced to Syria and said to al-Muthanna ibn-Ḥârithah, "Return [to al-Ḥîrah?]—may Allah have mercy on thee—to thy Sultan, untired and unfailing." [1]

The departure of Khâlid for Syria took place in Rabî' II, 250
according to others, Rabî' I, year 13. It is claimed by some that Khâlid came from 'Ain at-Tamr to Dûmah,[2] which he reduced, and after that he proceeded to al-Ḥîrah and thence to Syria. That he departed for Syria from 'Ain at-Tamr, is, however, more reliable.

[1] Certain verses describing the battles referred to above are here omitted from the translation. This was done in a few other cases.

[2] *Skizzen*, vol. iv, p. 47, n. 3. De Goeje, *Mémoire*, p. 15, takes this to be Dûmah al-Ḥîrah and not al-Jandal. *Cf.* Müller, *Der Islâm*, vol. i, p. 229, note.

CHAPTER II

The Caliphate of 'Umar ibn-al-Khaṭṭâb

Abu-'Ubaid chief commander. When 'Umar ibn-al-Khaṭṭâb was proclaimed caliph, he directed abu-'Ubaid ibn-Mas'ûd ibn-'Amr ibn-'Umair ibn-'Auf ibn-'Uḳdah ibn-Ghiyarah ibn-'Auf ibn-Thaḳîf (who is identical with abu-l-Mukhtâr ibn-abi-'Ubaid) to al-'Irâḳ with 1,000 men. Meanwhile, he wrote to al-Muthanna ibn-Ḥârithah, ordering him to receive abu-'Ubaid and obey his word. In the company of abu-'Ubaid, he sent Salîṭ ibn-Ḳais ibn-'Amr al-al-Anṣâri, saying to him, "Had it not been for the fact that thou art too hasty, I would have put thee in chief command. But warfare is a stubborn thing, and only the cautious man is fit for it."

Abu-'Ubaid defeats Jâbân, al-Jâlînûs and other Persian chiefs. Abu-'Ubaid marched forward and left no Arab tribe by which he passed without arousing its interest in the "holy war" and plunder. Thus, he was joined by a large host. On arriving in al-'Udhaib, he heard that Jâbân,
the Persian, was at Tustar with a large body of men. Abu- 251
'Ubaid met Jâbân and put his troops to flight, taking some of them captive.

Thence abu-'Ubaid proceeded to Durna [1] in which there was assembled a body of Persians. These abu-'Ubaid chased to Kaskar. He then advanced to meet al-Jâlînûs,[2]

[1] Ṭabari, vol. i, p. 2169: "Durtha"; *cf.* Yâḳût, vol. ii, pp. 565, 569; Bakri, p. 345.

[2] "Jâlînûs", in Ṭabari, vol. i, p. 2170.

who was at Bârûsma [or Mârûsma]; but ibn-al-Andarz-'azz [1] made terms with him, agreeing to pay four *dirhams* on every person, provided abu-'Ubaid should keep his way.

Abu-'Ubaid sent al-Muthanna to Zandaward,[2] and finding that its inhabitants had violated their covenant, al-Muthanna fought against them, won the victory and carried away [many] captives. Abu-'Ubaid also sent 'Urwah ibn-Zaid-al-Khail aṭ-Ṭâ'i to az-Zawâbi, with whose chief [*dihḳân*] me made terms similar to those made with Bârûsma.

[1] Ṭabari, vol. i, pp. 2029 *seq.*

[2] Yâḳût, vol. ii, pp. 951-952.

CHAPTER III

THE BATTLE OF ḲUSS AN-NÂṬIF, OR THE BATTLE OF AL-JISR

Dhu-l-Ḥâjib. Hearing that the Arabs were massing their forces, the Persians sent dhu-l-Ḥâjib [the eye-browed] Mardânshâh who was nicknamed by Anûshirwân "Bahman" [potent, endowed with great means] because he augured good from him.[1] He was called dhu-l-Ḥâjib because, in his pride, he tied up his brows, to lift them above his eyes. His name, it is said, was Rustam.[2]

The elephant. Abu-'Ubaid ordered that the bridge [on the Euphrates] be erected; and it was, the people of Bâniḳiya helping in the construction. It is said that this bridge once belonged to the people of al-Ḥîrah on which they crossed over to their farms. Being in ruins, abu-'Ubaid ordered it repaired. Over this bridge, abu-'Ubaid and the Moslems crossed from al-Marwaḥah[3] and met dhu-l-Ḥâjib who was accompanied by 4,000 men armed from head to foot, and one elephant—others say many elephants. A fierce fight ensued, in the course of which many wounds were inflicted on the Moslems. At this, Salîṭ ibn-Ḳais said to abu-'Ubaid, "I have warned thee against crossing this bridge and advised thee to withdraw to some quarter and write for reinforcements to the 'Commander of the Believers'; but thou hast refused." Salîṭ fought until he was killed. Abu-'Ubaid asked, "Which is the vulnerable point in this creature?" and he was told that it was its trunk, 252
upon which he made a rush and struck the trunk of the ele-

[1] *Cf.* Caetani, vol. iii, p. 148.

[2] Ya'ḳûbi, vol. ii, p. 161.

[3] Yâḳût, vol. iv, p. 505.

phant. Abu-Miḥjan ibn-Ḥabîb ath-Thaḳafi also charged the elephant and struck and broke its leg. The "polytheists", thereupon, made an attack which resulted in the death of abu-'Ubaid. Others say that the elephant threw its weight upon him and crushed him.[1]

The Moslems who fell. After abu-'Ubaid, the flag was carried by his brother, al-Ḥakam, who was then killed, and the flag passed to the hands of his son, Jabr, who also fell. Al-Muthanna[2] ibn-Ḥârithah carried it for one hour, after which he withdrew his men as some of them defended the others. On this occasion, 'Urwah ibn-Zaid al-Khail fought so fiercely that his action was estimated to be equivalent to that of a whole group of men.

Among those who took part in the defense of the Moslems on the west bank of the river, was the poet abu-Zubaid aṭ-Ṭâ'i, who happened to be at al-Ḥîrah on some personal business. Abu-Zubaid was a Christian.

Al-Muthanna came and occupied Ullais and communicated the news in a letter to 'Umar ibn-al-Khaṭṭâb sent with 'Urwah ibn-Zaid.

Among those killed in the battle of al-Jisr [the bridge], according to abu-Mikhnaf, was abu-Zaid al-Anṣâri, one of those who compiled the Koran in the days of the Prophet.

The battle of al-Jisr was fought on Saturday at the end of Ramaḍân, year 13.

Abu-'Ubaid al-Ḳâsim ibn-Sallâm from Ḳais ibn-abi-Ḥâzim:—As abu-'Ubaid was crossing Bâniḳiya with a band of followers, the "polytheists" cut the bridge and many of his men lost their lives. Ismâ'îl ibn-abi-Khâlid adds that abu-'Amr ash-Shaibâni stated that the battle of Mihrân was fought at the beginning of the year, and al-Ḳâdisîyah at the end of it.

[1] Ṭabari, vol. i, pp. 2178-2179; Athir, vol. ii, pp. 332-333.

[2] Dinawari, p. 119.

CHAPTER IV

The Battle of Mihrân or an-Nukhailah 253

Jarîr ibn-'Abdallâh's campaign in al-'Irâḳ. According to abu-Mikhnaf and others, for one year after the calamity that befell abu-'Ubaid and Salîṭ, 'Umar ibn-al-Khaṭṭâb refrained from the mention of the name of al-'Irâḳ. In the meantime, al-Muthanna ibn-Ḥârithah was staying in the region of Ullais summoning the Arabs to the " holy war ". At last 'Umar invited the Moslems to an expedition to al-'Irâḳ, but they kept aloof and hesitated to go there, so much so that he was on the point of carrying the expedition in person. Now, a body of al-Azd came to 'Umar intent on the invasion of Syria; but he asked them to go to al-'Irâḳ and aroused their interest in the spoils to be taken from the Kisra family. They left it for him to choose for them, and he ordered them to start [for al-'Irâḳ].

Jarîr ibn-'Abdallâh came from as-Sarâh at the head of the Bajîlah [1] tribe, and offered to go to al-'Irâḳ, provided one-quarter of what they took possession of be allotted to him and his men. 'Umar accepted the offer and Jarîr started towards al-'Irâḳ. Some claim that he went via al-Baṣrah and had a conflict with the satrap [Marzubân] of al-Madhâr, whom he defeated. Others claim that the conflict with the Marzubân took place when Jarîr was in the company of Khâlid ibn-al-Walîd. Still others assert that Jarîr took the road to al-'Udhaib, passing through Faid and ath-Tha'labîyah.

[1] Ṭabari, vol. i, p. 2186; Caetani, vol. iii, p. 155.

'Affân ibn-Muslim from ash-Sha'bi:—After the death of abu-'Ubaid, who was the first to be directed by 'Umar to al-Kûfah, 'Umar directed Jarîr ibn-'Abdallâh there, saying, "Wouldst thou go to al-'Irâḳ if I allow thee one-third of the spoils after the [usual] fifth has been taken?" and Jarîr said, "I will."

Dair Hind. The Moslems assembled in Dair Hind[1] in the year 14 immediately after the death of Shîrawaih, and the succession of Bûrân, daughter of Kisra, who was to rule until Yazdajird ibn-Shahriyâr came of age. Yazdajird[2] sent against them Mihrân ibn-Mihribundâdh al-Hamadhâni at the head of 12,000 men. The Moslems offered no resistance until he crossed the bridge on the Euphrates and arrived next to Dair al-A'war.[3]

The battle of al-Buwaib. It is reported by Saif that Mihrân, after crossing al-Jisr [the bridge], came to a place called al-Buwaib.[4] It was in this place that he was killed.

Someone has said that the irregularities in the land of al-Buwaib were filled up with bones in the time of the civil 254
war,[5] made level with the surface and covered with powdered soil [and that whenever the soil was removed the bones were seen].[6] The spot lay between as-Sakûn [canal] and the banu-Sulaim [canal].[7] This was the place in which the water of the Euphrates sank in the time of the Kisras and from which it poured into al-Jauf.[8]

[1] A convent near al-Ḥirah. Hamadhâni, *Buldân*, p. 183; Bakri, pp. 362-364; Yâḳût, vol. ii, pp. 707-709.

[2] *Cf.* Dinawari, p. 125; Ṭabari, vol. i, p. 2163.

[3] Yâḳût, vol. ii, p. 644.

[4] *Ibid.*, vol. i, p. 764.

[5] The reference is, perhaps, to the insurrection of Muṣ'ab ibn-az-Zubair.

[6] The text is corrupt.

[7] Ṭabari, vol. i, p. 2191.

[8] *Ibid.*, vol. i, p. 2187, lines 12-13; *cf.* Caetani, vol. iii, pp. 256-257.

The Moslems camped at an-Nukhailah [1] and were led, according to the Bajîlah, by Jarîr ibn-'Abdallâh, and, according to the Rabî'ah, by al-Muthanna ibn-Ḥârithah. Others affirm that the Moslems were commanded in turn by the heads of the various tribes. The Moslems met their enemy, and Shuraḥbîl ibn-as-Simṭ al-Kindi distinguished himself in the fight that ensued. Mas'ûd ibn-Hârithah was slain. So al-Muthanna said, " Fear not, Moslems, because my brother is killed. Such is the fate of the best among you." Upon this, the Moslems charged, as if they were one body, with confidence and patience which resulted, by Allah's help, in the death of Mihrân and the defeat of the " infidels ".[2] The Moslems pursued them with slaughter; and few were those who escaped. On this day, Kurṭ ibn-Jammâḥ al-'Abdi applied his sword until its edge was bent. When the night fell, they returned to their camp. This took place in the year 14.

The death of Mihrân was effected by Jarîr ibn-'Abdallâh and al-Mundhir ibn-Ḥassân ibn-Dirâr ad-Dabbi, each one of whom claimed that he had killed him, which led to a fierce dispute.[3] At last, al-Mundhir carried away Mihrân's belt; and Jarîr, the rest of the spoils from him. Some assert that among those who killed him was al-Ḥiṣn ibn-Ma'bad ibn-Zurârah ibn-'Udas at-Tamîmi.

Moslem raids. After this victory, the Moslems did not cease to make raids in the regions between al-Ḥîrah and Kaskar, Sûra, Barbîsma [?] and Sarât [4] Jâmâsib and between al-Fallûjatain, an-Nahrain and 'Ain-at-Tamr.[5]

[1] Yâḳût, vol. iv, pp. 771-772.

[2] *Cf.* Mas'ûdi, vol. iv, pp. 205-206.

[3] Yûsuf, p. 16, lines 16-17.

[4] *Cf.* Dînawari, p. 121.

[5] See Le Strange, *The Lands of the Eastern Caliphate*, p. 25, map.

The Moslems also attacked Ḥiṣn Malîḳiya, which was a watching post, and reduced it. They drove the Persians from other watching posts at aṭ-Ṭaff, the Persians by this time having become emaciated and having become weak and feeble in power. Certain Moslems crossed Nahr [canal] Sûra and came to Kûtha, Nahr al-Malik and Bâdûraiya; some reaching as far as Kalwâdha. The Arabs in these raz- 255
zias lived on what they plundered.

There are those who say that between the battles of Mihrân and al-Ḳâdisîyah, 18 months elapsed.

CHAPTER V

The Battle of al-Ḳâdisîyah

'Umar sends Sa'd ibn-abi-Waḳḳâṣ. The Moslems wrote to 'Umar ibn-al-Khaṭṭâb telling him of the great number of the Persians massing against them, and asked for reinforcements. 'Umar desired to lead the razzia in person and collected an army for that purpose; but he was advised by al-'Abbâs ibn-'Abd-al-Muṭṭalib and other *sheikhs* from among the Companions of the Prophet to stay at home and send out the forces and troops; and 'Umar did that. 'Ali ibn-abi-Ṭâlib advised him to go himself; but 'Umar replied, "I have made up my mind to stay." 'Umar proposed to 'Ali the idea of going; but the latter refused, upon which 'Umar wanted Sa'îd ibn-Zaid ibn-'Amr ibn-Nufail al-'Adawi to go. Finally, it occurred to him to send Sa'd ibn-abi-Waḳḳâṣ, which he did. The name of abu-Waḳḳâṣ was Mâlik ibn-Uhaib ibn-'Abd-Manâf ibn-Zuhrah ibn-Kilâb. Sa'd was a man of valor and a good shot. Others say that at this time Sa'îd ibn-Zaid ibn-'Amr was on an expedition in Syria.

Sa'd proceeded to al-'Irâk and stayed at ath-Tha'labîyah for three months, in the course of which all the troops overtook him. Thence he came, in the year 15, to al-'Udhaib. Al-Muthanna ibn-Ḥârithah happened to be ill at that time, and he advised Sa'd to meet the enemy between al-Ḳâdisîyah and al-'Udhaib. His case soon became serious and he was carried to his clan among whom he died. Sa'd married his wife.

Rustam. According to al-Wâḳidi, al-Muthanna died before Rustam came to al-Ḳâdisîyah. This Rustam, who was from ar-Rai—or from Hamadhân as others say—came and occupied Burs from which he left for a place between al-Ḥîrah and as-Sailaḥîn, where he stayed for four months without trying measures or fighting with the Moslems. The Moslems, in the meantime, lay camped between al-'Udhaib and al-Ḳâdisîyah. Rustam sent ahead of him dhu-l-Ḥâjib, who camped at Ṭîzanâbâdh. The "polytheists" numbered about 120,000, and were accompanied by thirty elephants, and had a great banner called Dirafsh Kâbiyân;[1]
while the Moslems, taken together, numbered between 9,000 256
and 10,000. When the Moslems were in need of fodder or food, they sent horsemen into the interior of the land who would make raids along the lower course of the Euphrates. From al-Madînah, 'Umar used to send them sheep and camels for slaughter.

Al-Mughîrah reinforces Sa'd. Al-Baṣrah was built sometime between the battle of an-Nukhailah and al-Ḳâdisîyah by 'Utbah ibn-Ghazwân. When 'Utbah asked leave for a pilgrimage, he assigned as successor al-Mughîrah ibn-Shu'bah, who was confirmed in his position by a letter from 'Umar. Before long, the charge[2] that was brought against al-Mughîrah was brought against him, and 'Umar appointed abu-Mûsa governor of al-Basrah and recalled al-Mughîrah to al-Madînah. Later, 'Umar sent al-Mughîrah back to al-Baṣrah together with those who gave witness against him. Now, on the day of the battle of al-Ḳâdisîyah, 'Umar wrote to abu-Mûsa, ordering him to reinforce

[1] or Dirafshikâbiyân. In Persian: dirafsh-i-Kâwiyân = the royal standard of the Sassanians; see Vullers' *Persian Dictionary;* Ṭabari, vol. i, p. 2175.

[2] Of having immoral relations with umm-Jamîl, which is discussed later by al-Balâdhuri. See abu-l-Fida, vol. i, p. 163.

Sa'd; upon which abu-Mûsa sent al-Mughîrah with 800 (others say 400) men. Having taken part in the battle, al-Mughîrah returned to al-Madînah.

Ḳais reinforces Sa'd. In the meantime, 'Umar wrote to abu-'Ubaidah ibn-al-Jarrâḥ, and he sent to the reinforcement of Sa'd Ḳais ibn-Hubairah ibn-al-Makshûḥ al-Murâdi, who according to some, took part in the battle of al-Ḳâdisîyah, and according to others, did not arrive until the battle was over. Ḳais commanded 700 men.

The battle of al-Kâdisîyah took place at the end of the year 16. Some say that it was 'Utbah ibn-Ghazwân who sent al-Mughîrah to the reinforcement of Sa'd, that al-Mughîrah was assigned governor of al-Baṣrah only after he returned from al-Ḳâdisîyah and that 'Umar, after calling al-Mughîrah back to al-Madînah because of the charge brought against him, never sent him out of al-Madînah except when he assigned him governor of al-Kûfah.

Al-'Abbâs ibn-al-Walîd an-Narsi from ash-Sha'bi:—'Umar wrote to abu-'Ubaidah, "Send to al-Ḳâdisîyah Ḳais ibn-Makshûḥ at the head of the men he invites to join him." Ḳais summoned a body of men and arrived, at the head of 700 of them, to find the victory already won by Sa'd. Ḳais's men asked for a share in the booty. Sa'd wrote to 'Umar, who wrote back, "If Ḳais arrived before the burial of those that were killed, then thou shouldst give him his share."

Al-Mughîrah's interview with Rustam. Rustam asked Sa'd to send some companions of his to consult with him. Sa'd delegated al-Mughîrah ibn-Shu'bah. Al-Mughîrah betook himself towards Rustam's throne, in order to sit by him, but was not allowed to do so by the Persian cavalry guard [*asâwirah*]. Rustam said many things, among which was the following, "I have learned that ye were forced to what ye are doing by nothing but the narrow 257 means of livelihood and by poverty. We are ready to give you what will satisfy you, and to see you leave with certain things that ye choose."[1] Al-Mughîrah answered, "Allah has sent us his Prophet by following and obeying whom we were made prosperous, and he has ordered us to fight those who differ from our faith 'Until they pay tribute out of hand and in a humbled state'.[2] We, therefore, call thee to the worship of Allah alone and the belief in his Prophet, which if thou shouldst do, well and good; otherwise, the sword will decide between us." Rustam, snorting with anger, said, "By the sun and by the moon, the day will not break to-morrow before we kill you all." "No strength and no force but in Allah," answered al-Mughîrah, and departed riding a lean horse with a sword broken at its edge and wrapped up in rags.[3]

'Amr and al-Ash'ath interview Rustam. 'Umar wrote to Sa'd instructing him to send to the magnate of the Persians a delegation to invite him to Islâm. Accordingly, Sa'd sent 'Amr ibn-Ma'dikarib az-Zubaidi and al-Ash'ath ibn-Ḳais al-Kindi at the head of a delegation. They passed by Rustam, and on being brought before him, he asked them, "To whom are ye going?" to which they replied, "To your chief." A long conversation followed in which they said, "Our Prophet has promised us the conquest of your land," upon which Rustam called for a palm-leaf basket full of soil and said, "This is for you from our land!" 'Amr ibn-Ma'dikarib immediately arose, spread his cloak and departed, carrying in it some of the soil. When he was asked later, "Why didst thou do that?". 'Amr replied, "Because I considered it a good omen, indicating that

[1] Dînawari, p. 127; Ṭabari, vol. i, p. 2271.

[2] Koran, 9:29.

[3] Ṭabari, vol. i, p. 2270.

their land will one day be ours, and we will take possession of it." Finally, they presented themselves before the king and invited him to Islâm. The king became angry and ordered them to leave, saying, "Had ye not been envoys, I would have put you to death!" He also wrote and rebuked Rustam for sending them to him.

A Moslem forage expedition. Later, a forage expedition [1] of the Moslems, headed by Zuhrah ibn-Ḥawîyah ibn-'Abdallâh ibn-Ḳatâdah at-Tamîmi—later as-Sa'di—(others say it was headed by Ḳatâdah ibn-Ḥawîyah[2]), came across some Persian cavalry, which was the occasion for the final conflict. The Persians rallied to the succor of their cavalry, 258
and the Moslems to those on their expedition; and a fierce battle raged between the two. The time was an afternoon. 'Amr ibn-Ma'dikarib az-Zubaidi rushed forward and, seizing a Persian chief by the neck, lifted him to the saddle in front of him, saying [to his men], "I am abu-Thaur! Do ye as I do!" He then stabbed the nose of one of the elephants, saying, "Apply your swords to their trunks; the vulnerable point in the elephant is his trunk."

Sa'd slaps his wife. Sa'd ibn-abi-Waḳḳâṣ had, for a special reason, appointed Khâlid ibn-'Urfuṭah-l-'Udhri, an ally of the banu-Zuhrah, to be commander of the army and director of the affairs of the Moslems. Sa'd lived in Ḳaṣr [tower] al-'Udhaib. His wife, Salma, daughter of Ḥafṣah of the tribe of the banu-Taimallâh ibn-Tha'labah, and formerly the wife of al-Muthanna ibn-Ḥârithah, often repeated, "O, Muthanna! But there is no more Muthanna to aid the cavalry!" Hearing that, Sa'd slapped her on the face; upon which she said, "Is it jealousy or cowardice, Sa'd?"

[1] Ar. *'allâfah.*

[2] Ḥajar, vol. ii, p. 23.

Abu-Mihjan in prison. Abu-Mihjan ath-Thakafi [1] was alienated to Bâḍi' [2] by 'Umar ibn-al-Khaṭṭâb in punishment for his being addicted to wine. He somehow managed to run away and followed Sa'd; he, according to al-Wâkidi, not being one of those who had started with Sa'd. In the army of Sa'd, abu-Mihjan again drank wine on account of which Sa'd flogged and imprisoned him in al-'Udhaib tower. Here he asked Zabrâ', a concubine of Sa'd, to release him that he might take part in the fight, promising to return to his fetters.[3] She made him swear by Allah that he would do so if released. Riding on Sa'd's mare, he rushed on the Persians, pierced through their line and thrust his sword into the nose of the white elephant. Sa'd who was watching him, said, "The mare is mine; but the charge is that of abu-Mihjan." Abu-Mihjan then returned to his fetters. Others say that it was Salma, daughter of Ḥafṣah, who gave him the mare; but the former report is more authentic. When the question of Rustam was settled, Sa'd said to abu-Mihjan, "By Allah, I shall never punish thee for wine after seeing what I saw of thee." "As for me," answered abu-Mihjan, "by Allah, I shall never drink it again." [4]

The slayer of Rustam. On that day, Ṭulaiḥah ibn-Khuwailid al-Asadi distinguished himself in fighting, and with a blow, cut the under-helmet of al-Jâlînûs, but did not injure his head. On the same occasion, Kais ibn-Makshûh turned to the people and said, "To be killed is the fate of the noble. Let not those 'uncircumcised' have more pa-

[1] Yûsuf, pp. 17-18; Mas'ûdi, vol. iv, pp. 213-219; *al-'Iḳd al-Farîd*, vol. iii, p. 407.

[2] Hamdâni, p. 133, l. 22; p. 41, l. 7: "Nâṣi'"; Yâḳût, vol. i, p. 471; Ṭabari, vol. i, p. 2480.

[3] Dinawari, p. 129.

[4] Mas'ûdi, vol. iv, p. 219; Athîr, vol. ii, p. 369.

tience or be more anxious to die than yourselves." Saying this, he rushed and fought fiercely. By Allah's help, Rus- 259
tam was slain and his body was found covered with so many blows and stabs that the one who gave the fatal blow could not be determined. 'Amr ibn-Ma'dikarib, Ṭulaihah ibn-Khuwailid al-Asadi, Ḳurṭ ibn-Jammâḥ al-'Abdi and Ḍirâr ibn-al-Azwar al-Asadi had all rushed at him. This Ḍirâr, according to al-Wâḳidi, was killed in the battle of al-Yamâmah. Some say that Rustam was killed by Zuhair ibn-'Abd-Shams al-Bajali; others, by 'Auwâm ibn-'Abd-Shams; and still others by Hilâl ibn-'Ullafah at-Taimi.[1]

This battle of al-Ḳâdisîyah was fought on Thursday, Friday and the night of Saturday, which last was since called "Lailat al-Harîr".[2] The night of the battle of Ṣiffîn was also thus called.

Some say that Ḳais ibn-Makshûḥ took no part in the fight at al-Kâdisîyah, having arrived there after the Moslems had been through with the fighting.

Salmân ibn-Rabî'ah's part. Ahmad ibn-Salmân al-Bâhili from certain *sheikhs*:—Salmân ibn-Rabî'ah invaded Syria in the company of abu-Umâmah aṣ-Ṣudai ibn-'Ajlân al-Bâhili, and took part in the battles fought by the Moslems there. He then went forth to al-'Irâk together with those who, under great urgency, hastened to al-Ḳâdisîyah as a reinforcement, and took part in the decisive conflict. He settled at al-Kûfah and was killed in Balanjar.

According to al-Wâḳidi, a group of Persians, planting their banner firmly in the ground, said, "We shall not leave our position until we die;" upon which Salmân ibn-Rabî'ah-l-Bâhili made an attack and killed them, carrying their banner away.

[1] Ya'ḳûbi, vol. ii, p. 165.

[2] The night of yells of pain. Caetani, vol. iii, pp. 643, 675; *Skizzen*, vol. vi, p. 75; Ṭabari, vol. i, p. 2327.

Khâlid ibn-'Urfuṭah's part. Sa'd sent Khâlid ibn-'Urfuṭah at the head of the cavalry charged with pursuing the enemy. Khâlid and his men killed every one they overtook until they arrived in Burs. Here Khâlid was the guest of one, Bisṭâm, who treated him with kindness and loyalty. A canal that ran there was called Nahr Bisṭâm. Khâlid then passed through aṣ-Ṣarâh [canal] and caught up with Jâlinûs. Kathîr ibn-Shihâb al-Ḥârithi charged Jâlinûs and stabbed him, and according to others, killed him. Ibn-al-Kalbi says that it was Zuhrah ibn-Ḥawîyah aṣ-Sa'di who killed him. The former report is more authentic.

The Persians fled to al-Madâ'in, following Yazdajird [their king]. Sa'd immediately communicated with 'Umar, announcing the victory and giving the names of those who had fallen.

The Persian arrows. Abu-Rajâ' al-Fârisi from his grandfather:—The latter said: "I took part in the battle of al-Ḳâdisîyah when I was still a Magian. When the Arabs sent their arrows against us, we began to shout, 260
'dûk! dûk!'[1] by which we meant, spindles. These spindles, however, continued to shower upon us, until we were overwhelmed. Our archer would send the arrow from his Nâwakîyah bow, but it would not do more than attach itself to the garment of an Arab; whereas their arrow would tear the coat of mail and the double cuirass that we had on."

According to Hishâm ibn-al-Kalbi, the first to kill a Persian in the battle of al-Ḳâdisîyah was Rabî'ah ibn-'Uthmân ibn-Rabî'ah of the banu-Naṣr ibn-Mu'âwiyah ibn-Bakr ibn-Hawâzin ibn-Manṣûr.

In this battle, Sa'd ibn-'Ubaid al-Anṣâri fell a martyr. 262
His death afflicted 'Umar so much that he said, "His death almost marred the joy of the victory for me."

[1] Yûsuf, p. 16: "dûs!" *Cf.* Ṭabari, vol. i, p. 2236.

CHAPTER VI

THE CONQUEST OF AL-MADÂ'IN

An-Nakhîrkhân slain by Zuhair. After the battle of al-Ḳâdisîyah, the Moslems started off, and after passing Dair [monastery] Ka'b [?],[1] they were met by an-Nakhîrkhân,[2] who appeared at the head of a large body of men from al-Madâ'in.[3] In the conflict that ensued, Zuhair ibn-Sulaim al-Azdi seized an-Nakhîrkhân by the neck; and they both fell to the ground. Zuhair took a dagger that was in the other man's belt and cut open his abdomen, thereby putting him to death.

Bahurasîr. Sa'd and the Moslems went and occupied Sâbâṭ. They then assembled in the city of Bahurasîr,[4] which lay in the Shikk al-Kûfah [western bank of the Tigris], where they spent nine months (others say 18),[5] during which they ate fresh dates for two seasons. The inhabitants of that city fought against them until they could offer no more resistance, at which the Moslems entered the city. When the city was thus reduced, Yazdajird ibn-Shahriyâr, the Persian king, resolved to flee and was suspended in a basket from the wall of al-Abyaḍ fort in al-Madâ'in
and was therefore called by the Nabateans Barzabîl [the 263

[1] Yûsuf, p. 17, l. 8: "Dair al-Masâlih" (?).

[2] Tabari, in Nöldeke, *Geschichte der Perser*, pp. 152-153.

[3] Seleucia-Ctesiphon. Meynard, *Dictionnaire de la Perse*, p. 518.

[4] Nöldeke, *Perser*, p. 16, n. 4.

[5] Dînawari, p. 133.

son of the basket]. Yazdajird thence left for Ḥulwân [1] with the principal dignitaries of his kingdom, and carried with him the treasury of the kingdom, his precious but light [2] pieces of furniture, private treasury, wives and children. In the year in which he fled, plague and famine ravaged all Persia. The Moslems then crossed [the Tigris] through a ford, and took possession of the city on the eastern bank of the river.

The Arabs cross the Tigris. 'Affân ibn-Muslim from abu-Wâ'il:—The latter said, "When the Persians were put to flight at al-Ḳâdisîyah, we pursued them. They reunited at Kûtha [3] and we pursued them until we reached the Tigris, at which the Moslems said, 'Why do you gaze at this small body of water? Let us wade through.' [4] Accordingly, we waded through, and once more put the enemy to flight."

Muḥammad ibn-Sa'd from Abân ibn-Ṣâliḥ:—When they were defeated at al-Ḳâdisîyah, the fugitive Persians came to al-Madâ'in. The Moslems having arrived at the Tigris, whose water was flowing higher than ever, found that the Persians had removed the ships and ferry-boats to the eastern bank and burned the bridge. Sa'd and the Moslems finding no way to cross over were greatly afflicted. At last, Sa'd chose one of the Moslems who swam across on horseback. Likewise, the other Moslems crossed on horseback and, on landing, made the owners of the ships transport the baggage. Seeing that, the Persians said, "By Allah, those we are fighting are nothing less than demons [*jinn*]!" and they took to flight.

[1] Yâḳût, vol. ii, p. 312.

[2] Ar. *khiff;* Caetani, vol. iii, p. 724, takes it to be *khaffa* and stretches the meaning into "ma abbandonando in gran parte le sue masserizie". *Cf.* Dînawari, p. 133.

[3] Yâḳût, vol. iv, p. 318.

[4] Text not clear. Caetani, vol. iii, p. 723.

Sâbâṭ and ar-Rûmîyah. 'Abbâs ibn-Hishâm from 'Awânah ibn-al-Ḥakam, and abu-'Ubaidah Ma'mar ibn-al-Muthanna from abu-'Amr ibn-al-'Alâ' :—Sa'd ibn-abi-Waḳḳâṣ sent at the head of the van of his army Khâlid ibn-'Urfuṭah, who succeeded in reducing Sâbâṭ [1] before Sa'd's arrival. Khâlid proceeded and camped at ar-Rûmîyah [2] until its people made terms, agreeing to have those of them who wanted to leave, do so, and those who wanted to stay, stay, on condition that they offer homage and give counsel, pay *kharâj,* and act as guides for the Moslems, without entertaining any treachery against them. Sa'd [in crossing the river] found no ferry-boats, but was shown a ferry near aṣ-Ṣaiyâdîn village. The horses waded through while the Persians shot them with their arrows. All the Moslems, however, escaped, and only one of them from the tribe of 264
Ṭaiyi', whose full name was Salîl ibn-Yazîd ibn-Mâlik as-Sinbisi, was killed.

Kisra's concubines. 'Abdallâh ibn-Ṣâliḥ from ash-Sha'bi :—The latter said, "In the battle of al-Madâ'in, the Moslems carried away many of Kisra's maids [concubines] who had been brought from all quarters of the world and lavishly adorned for him. My mother was one of them. On that day, too, the Moslems found camphor and, taking it for salt, put it in their cooking-pans." [3]

According to al-Wâḳidi, Sa'd was all done with the conquest of al-Madâ'in and Jalûlâ' in the year 16.

[1] Sometimes called Sâbât Kisra. Yâḳût, vol. i, p. 3; Caetani, vol. iii, p 724, l. 4.

[2] Perhaps a suburb of Madâ'in. Yâḳût, vol. ii, p. 867.

[3] Dînawari, p. 134; Yûsuf, p. 17.

CHAPTER VII

THE BATTLE OF JALÛLÂ'

A description of the battle. After spending several days in al-Madâ'in, the Moslems received word that Yazdajird had massed a great host, which was then at Jalûlâ', and had directed it against them. Sa'd ibn-abi-Waḳḳâṣ thereupon dispatched Hâshim ibn-'Utbah ibn-abi-Waḳḳâṣ at the head of 12,000 men to meet them. The Moslems found that the Persians, having left their families and heavy baggage at Khâniḳîn,[1] had dug trenches and fortified themselves, binding themselves with a pledge never to flee. Reinforcements were coming to them all the time from Ḥulwân and al-Jibâl [the mountains, *i. e.*, Media]. The Moslems, thinking it best to hasten the attack before the reinforcements became too strong, met them with Ḥujr ibn-'Adi-l-Kindi commanding the right wing, 'Amr ibn-Ma'dikarib commanding the cavalry and Tulaiḥah ibn-Khuwailid commanding the infantry. The Persians were on this occasion led by Khurrazâd, a brother of Rustam. The fight that ensued was the fiercest they ever had, in which arrows and lances were used until broken to pieces, and swords were applied until they were bent. Finally the Moslems altogether made one onslaught and drove the Persians from their position, putting them to flight. The Persians fled away and the Moslems kept pursuing them at their very heels with fearful slaughter until darkness intervened and they had to return to their camp.

[1] Yâḳût, vol. ii, p. 393.

Hâshim ibn-'Utbah left Jarîr ibn-'Abdallâh in Jalûlâ' with a heavy force of cavalry to act as a check between the Moslems and their enemy. Yazdajird thereupon left Hul- 265
wân.

Mahrûdh. The Moslems carried on many raids in the regions of as-Sawâd on the east bank of the Tigris. Coming to Mahrûdh,[1] Hâshim made terms with its *dihḳân,* stipulating that the latter should pay a *jarîb* of *dirhams* [?] and the former should not kill any of the men.

Ad-Daskarah. On a charge of treachery, against the Moslems, Hâshim put the *dihḳân* of ad-Daskarah [2] to death.

Al-Bandanijain. Hâshim then proceeded to al-Bandanijain,[3] whose inhabitants sued for peace, agreeing to pay tax and *kharâj*. Consequently, Hâshim promised them security.

Khâniḳîn. At Khâniḳîn there was a small remnant of the Persians against whom Jarîr ibn-'Abdallâh now marched and whom he put to death. Thus was no region of the Sawâd Dijlah left unconquered by the Moslems or unpossessed by them.

According to Hishâm ibn-al-Kalbi, the leader of the army in the battle of Jalûlâ' in behalf of Sa'd was 'Amr ibn-'Utbah ibn-Naufal ibn-Uhaib ibn-'Abd-Manâf ibn-Zuhrah whose mother was 'Âtikah, daughter of abu-Wakkâṣ.

After the battle of Jalûlâ', Sa'd left for al-Madâ'in where he gathered a host of men, and then kept on his way to the region of al-Ḥirah.

The battle of Jalûlâ' took place at the close of the year 16.

The converts. Those who embraced Islâm were among others, Buṣbuhra—the *dihḳân* of al-Falâlîj and an-Nahrain,

[1] Yâḳût, vol. iv, p. 700.

[2] *Ibid.*, vol. ii, p. 575; Nöldeke, *Perser*, p. 295, n. 1.

[3] Persian: Bandanîkân; Yâḳût, vol. i, p. 745.

Bisṭâm ibn-Narsi—the *dihḳân* of Bâbil and Khuṭarniyah,[1] ar-Rufail—the *dihḳân* of al-'Âl,[2] and Fairuz—the *dihḳân* of Nahr al-Malik[3] and Kûtha. 'Umar ibn-al-Khaṭṭâb did not interfere with them but left their lands in their own hands and annulled the poll-tax they paid.

Hâshim's campaign. Abu-Mas'ûd al-Kûfi from 'Awânah's father:—Sa'd ibn-abi-Waḳḳâṣ dispatched Hâshim ibn-'Utbah ibn-abi-Waḳḳâṣ accompanied by al-Ash'ath ibn-Ḳais al-Kindi. Hâṣhim passed through ar-Râdhânât[4] and visited Daḳûḳa and Khânîjâr, conquering all that region together with all the district of Bâjarma. Hâshim penetrated towards Sinn Bârimma[5] and Bawâzîj al-Mulk as far as the border of Shahrazûr.

'Umar's message to Sa'd. Al-Ḥusain ibn-al-Aswad from Yazîd ibn-abi-Ḥabîb:—When Sa'd ibn-abi-Waḳḳâṣ completed the conquest of as-Sawâd, he received the following letter from 'Umar ibn-al-Khaṭṭâb:

"I have received thy letter in which thou statest that thy men have asked thee to divide among them whatever spoils 266
Allah has assigned them. At the receipt of my letter, find out what possessions and horses the troops on 'horses and camels'[6] have acquired and divide that among them, after taking away one-fifth. As for the land and camels, leave them in the hands of those men who work them, so that they may be included in the stipends [pensions] of the Moslems. If thou dividest them among those present, nothing will be left for those who come after them."

[1] Yâḳût, vol. ii, p. 453.
[2] Yâḳût, vol. iii, p. 592.
[3] *Ibid.*, vol. iv, p. 846.
[4] *Ibid.*, vol. ii, p. 729.
[5] *Ibid.*, vol. iii, p. 169.
[6] Kor., 59:6.

How the land and the inhabitants of as-Sawâd should be considered. Al-Ḥusain from 'Abdallâh ibn-Ḥâzim:—The latter said, "I once asked Mujâhid regarding the land of as-Sawâd and he answered, 'It can neither be bought nor sold.' This is because it was taken by force and was not divided. It belongs to all the Moslems."

Al-Walîd ibn-Ṣâliḥ from Sulaimân ibn-Yasâr:—'Umar ibn-al-Khaṭṭâb left as-Sawâd for those who were still in men's loins and mothers' wombs [*i. e.*, posterity], considering the inhabitants *dhimmis* from whom tax should be taken on their person, and *kharâj* on their land. They are therefore *dhimmis* and cannot be sold as slaves.

The following statement was made by Sulaimân: "Al-Walîd ibn-'Abd-al-Malik wanted to consider the inhabitants of as-Sawâd as having been acquired without fighting [Ar. *fai'*]; but when I told him of the position 'Umar took regarding them, Allah prevented him from doing so."

Al-Ḥûsain ibn-al-Aswad from Ḥârithah ibn-Muḍarrib:—'Umar ibn-al-Khaṭṭâb, desiring to divide as-Sawâd among the Moslems, ordered that they be counted. Each Moslem had three peasants for his share. 'Umar took the advice of the Prophet's Companions, and 'Ali said, "Leave them that they may become a source of revenue and aid [1] for the Moslems." Accordingly, 'Umar sent 'Uthmân ibn-Ḥunaif al-Anṣâri who assessed on each man 48, 24, or 12 [*dirhams*].

Abu-Naṣr at-Tammâr from 'Ali:—The latter said, "If ye were not to strike one another on the face [have civil war] I would divide as-Sawâd among you."

Al-Ḥusain ibn-al-Aswad from 'Âmir:—The people of as-Sawâd have no covenant, rather they came under our control by surrender.

[1] Ar. *mâddah*; see *an-Nihâyah*, vol. iv, p. 84.

Al-Husain from ash-Sha'bi:—The latter was asked 267
whether the people of as-Sawâd had a covenant, to which he replied, "At first, they had none; but when the Moslems consented to take *kharâj* from them, then they came to have one."

Al-Ḥusain from 'Âmir:—The latter said, "The people of as-Sawâd have no covenant."

The Magians. 'Amr an-Nâkid from Ja'far ibn-Muḥammad's father:—The Emigrants had a sitting place in the mosque in which 'Umar used to discuss with them the news he received from the different regions. One day he said, "I know not how to treat the Magians;" upon which 'Abd-ar-Raḥmân ibn-'Auf rose and said, "I bear witness that the Prophet said, 'Treat them according to the same law with which ye treat the People of the Book'."

The Bajîlah's share in as-Sawâd. Muhammad ibn-aṣ-Sabbâh al-Bazzâz from Ḳais ibn-abi-Hâzim:—The Bajîlah tribe constituted one-fourth of the Moslems in the battle of al-Ḳâdisîyah, and 'Umar had allotted them one-fourth of as-Sawâd. Once when Jarîr [ibn-'Abdallâh] called on 'Umar, the latter said, "Had I not been responsible for what I divide, I would leave to you the share already given; but I see that the Moslems have multiplied, so ye have to restore what ye have taken." Jarîr and the others did as 'Umar said; and 'Umar offered Jarîr a present of 80 *dînârs*.[1]

A woman of the tribe of Bajîlah, called umm-Kurz, came to 'Umar and said, "My father died and his share in as-Sawâd holds good. I shall never deliver it!" 'Umar turned to her and said, "But, umm-Kurz, thy people have all consented to do so." "I shall never consent," said she, "unless thou carry me on a submissive she-camel covered with

[1] Yûsuf, p. 18.

a red nappy mantle [Ar. *ḳaṭîfah*] and fill both of my hands with gold," which 'Umar did.

Al-Ḥusain from Jarîr:—'Umar gave to the Bajîlah one-quarter of as-Sawâd which they held for three years.

Ḳais said:—" Jarîr ibn-'Abdallâh accompanied by 'Ammâr ibn-Yâsir called on 'Umar who said, 'Had I not been 268
held responsible for what I divide, I would leave to you the shares already given; but I see now that ye ought to restore what ye have taken.' And they did, upon which 'Umar offered a present of 80 *dînârs* to Jarîr."[1]

According to a tradition communicated by al-Ḥasan[2] ibn-'Uthmân az-Ziyâdi on the authority of Kais, 'Umar gave Jarîr ibn-'Abdallâh 400 *dînârs*.

Ḥumaid ibn-ar-Rabî' from al-Hasan ibn-Sâlih:—'Umar gave the Bajîlah, in exchange for the fourth of as-Sawâd they held, a stipend of 2,000 *dirhams*.

Al-Walîd ibn-Ṣâliḥ from Jarîr ibn-Yazîd ibn-Jarîr ibn-'Abdallâh's grandfather:—'Umar allotted to Jarîr and his men one-quarter of what they had conquered in as-Sawâd. When the spoils of Jalûlâ' were brought together, Jarîr demanded his quarter. Sa'd communicated the demand to 'Umar who wrote back as follows: "If Jarîr wants himself considered as having with his men, fought for a pay similar to the pay of *al-Mu'allafah Kulûbuhum*,[3] then ye may give them their pay. If, however, they have fought in Allah's cause and will accept his remuneration, then they are part of the Moslems, having their rights and their obligations." Hearing that, Jarîr said, "Truly and honestly has the 'Commander of the Believers' spoken. We do not want our quarter."

[1] Yaḥya ibn-Âdam, pp. 29 *seq.*

[2] Dhahabi, p. 244.

[3] Those whose hearts are won to Islâm by special gifts. See De Goeje, *Mémoire*, p. 51; Ṭabari, vol. i, p. 1679; Kor., 9:60.

Al-Ḥusain from Ibrâhîm an-Nakha'i:—Someone came to 'Umar ibn-al-Khaṭṭâb, saying, "I have accepted Islâm and ask thee to exempt my piece from the land-*kharâj,*" to which 'Umar replied, "Thy land has been taken by force."

Khalaf ibn-Hishâm al-Bazzâr from Ibrâhîm at-Taimi:—When 'Umar conquered as-Sawâd, the troops said to him, "Divide it among us because we have reduced it by force through our swords." But 'Umar refused, saying, "What will then be left for those Moslems who come after you? Moreover, I am afraid that if I divide it, ye may come to be at variance with one another on account of its water." 'Umar, therefore, left the people of as-Sawâd in possession of their lands, assessing a tax on their person and a fixed tax [1] on their lands which he did not divide.

A survey of as-Sawâd. Al-Ḳâsim ibn-Sallâm from ash- 269
Sha'bi:—'Umar ibn-al-Khaṭṭâb sent 'Uthmân ibn-Ḥunaif al-Anṣâri to make a survey [*yamsaḥ*] of as-Sawâd, which he found to be 36,000,000 *jarîbs,* on every *jarîb* of which he assessed one *dirham* and one *ḳafîz.* Al-Ḳâsim adds, "I heard that the *ḳafîz* was a measure of theirs also called *ash-shâburḳân.*" [2] According to Yaḥya ibn-Âdam, it is equivalent to *al-makhtûm al-Ḥajjâji.*[3]

The tax assessed. 'Amr an-Nâḳid from Muḥammad ibn-'Abdallâh ath-Thaḳafi:—'Umar assessed on every *jarîb* in as-Sawâd, whether cultivated or uncultivated, provided it was accessible to water, one *dirham* and one *ḳafîz,* on every *jarîb* of *raṭbah* [trefoil or clover] five *dirhams* and five *ḳafîzes,* and on every *jarîb* of trees ten *dirhams* and ten *ḳa-*

[1] Ar. *ṭasḳ* or *ṭisḳ.* J. Wellhausen, *Das Arabische Reich,* pp. 172-173, Nöldeke, *Perser,* p. 241, n. 1; Caetani, vol. ii, p. 930, n. 6.

[2] Mâwardi, pp. 272, 304.

[3] Introduced through al-Ḥajjâj ibn-Yûsuf who died in the year 90 A. H.

fîzes (palm trees not mentioned). On every man, he assessed 48, 24, or 12 *dirhams* as poll-tax.

Al-Ḳâsim ibn-Sallâm from abu-Mijlaz Lâḥiḳ ibn-Ḥumaid:—'Umar ibn-al-Khaṭṭâb assigned 'Ammâr ibn-Yâsir to act as religious head [1] for the people of al-Kûfah and to command their militia, 'Abdallâh ibn-Mas'ûd to be their *ḳâḍi* and treasurer, and 'Uthmân ibn-Ḥunaif to measure the land. To these three, he assigned each day one goat, one-half of which, together with the appendages [2] to be taken by 'Ammâr and the other half to be divided between the other two. 'Uthmân ibn-Ḥunaif measured the land and assessed on each *jarîb* of palm trees, 10 *dirhams*; of vine trees, 10 *dirhams*; of sugar-cane, 6 *dirhams*; of wheat, 4 *dirhams*; and of barley, 2 *dirhams*. To this end, he wrote to 'Umar, who endorsed the assessments.

Al-Ḥusain ibn-al-Aswad from 'Amr ibn-Maimûn:—'Umar ibn-al-Khaṭṭâb sent Ḥudhaifah ibn-al-Yamân beyond the Tigris, and 'Uthmân ibn-Ḥunaif below the Tigris; and they assessed on every *jarîb* one *ḳafîz* and one *dirham*.

Al-Ḥusain from Muḥammad ibn-'Abdallâh ath-Tha- 270
ḳafi:—When al-Mughîrab ibn-Shu'bah was governor of as-Sawâd, he wrote, "We find here other products than wheat and barley," and mentioned Indian peas, grapes, clover [3] and sesame, upon each of which he assessed 8 *dirhams* and excluded palm-trees.[4]

Khalaf al-Bazzâr from al-'Aizâr ibn-Ḥuraith:—'Umar ibn-al-Khaṭṭâb assessed on one *jarîb* of wheat two *dirhams* and two *jarîbs*; on one *jarîb* of barley, one *dirham*, and

[1] Ar. *âla aṣ-ṣalâh*; Caetani, vol. iii, p. 756, translates: "l'autorità civile."

[2] Ar. *sawâḳit*. Yûsuf, p. 20: "*baṭn*" = belly.

[3] Ar. *raṭbah* or *ruṭbah* may also be applied to cucumber, melon and the like; see Caetani, vol. v, pp. 370 and 371; Yûsuf, pp. 20-22.

[4] *Cf.* Adam, p. 98.

one *jarîb*; and on every two *jarîbs* in the uncultivated land that can be sown, one *dirham*.

Khalaf al-Bazzâr from al-'Aizâr ibn-Huraith:—'Umar assessed on one *jarîb* of vine-trees 10 *dirhams*, on one *jarîb* of clover, 10; of cotton, 5; on one Fârisi palm-tree, one *dirham* and if of inferior quality, one *dirham* on two trees.

'Amr an-Nâkid from abu-Mijlaz:—'Umar assessed on a *jarîb* of palm-trees 8 *dirhams*.

Al-Husain ibn-al-Aswad from ash-Sha'bi:—'Umar ibn-al-Khattâb sent 'Uthmân ibn-Hunaif [1] who assessed on the people of as-Sawâd 5 *dirhams* on one *jarîb* of clover, and 10 *dirhams* on one *jarîb* of vine-trees; but he assessed no tax on what was grown among the vines.

Al-Walîd ibn-Ṣâliḥ from al-Miswar ibn-Rifâ'ah:—'Umar ibn-'Abd-al-'Azîz said that the *kharâj* of as-Sawâd in the time of 'Umar ibn-al-Khaṭṭâb was 100,000,000 *dirḥams;* but in the time of al-Hajjâj, it amounted to 40,-000,000.

Al-Walîd from Aiyûb ibn-abi-Umâmah ibn-Sahl ibn-Ḥunaif's father.—'Uthmân ibn-Hunaif put seals around 271
the necks [2] of 550,000 of the "uncircumcised", and the *kharâj* during his governorship amounted to 100,000,000.

Al-Walîd ibn-Sâlih from Mus'ab ibn-Yazîd abu-Zaid al-Ansâri's father:—The latter said, "'Ali-ibn-abi-Tâlib sent me to the land irrigated by the Euphrates, mentioning different cantons and villages, and naming Nahr al-Malik [3] Kûtha, Bahurasîr, ar-Rûmakân, Nahr Jaubar, Nahr Durkît and al-Bihkubâdhât. He ordered me to assess on every *jarîb* of wheat, if thickly sown, one *dirham* and a half and one *ṣâ'*; if thinly sown, two-thirds of a *dirham* and if not so

[1] Ya'ḳûbi, vol. ii, pp. 173-175.

[2] Yûsuf, p. 73, l. 12-16; Caetani, vol. v, pp. 371-372.

[3] Yâḳût, vol. iv, p. 846.

thickly or thinly sown one *dirham*; and on barley, one-half of that. He also ordered me to assess on the gardens that include palm-trees and other kinds, 10 *dirhams* per *jarîb*; on one *jarîb* of vine-trees, if its trees had been planted for three full years and a part of the fourth, and if it bears fruit, ten *dirhams*, with nothing on palm-trees that are outside the villages and the fruits of which are eaten by the passers-by. On vegetables, including cucumbers, grains, sesame and cotton, he ordered me not to assess anything. On those landlords [*dihkâns*] who ride mules and wear rings of gold around their feet, he ordered me to assess 48 *dirhams* each; and on those of them who are merchants of medium means, 24 *dirhams* per annum each; but on the farmers and the rest of them, 12 *dirhams* each."

Humaid ibn-ar-Rabî' from al-Hasan ibn-Sâlih:—The latter said, "I asked al-Ḥasan, 'What are those different rates of assessed land-tax [*ṭasḳ*]?' And he replied, 'They, one after the other, have been assessed according to the nearness and distance of the land from the markets[1] and the drinking places in the river [*furaḍ*].' Yaḥya ibn- 272
Âdam says, 'The Moslems of as-Sawâd asked al-Manṣûr towards the end of his caliphate to introduce the system by which they turn over to the authorities as tax a part of the produce of the land;[2] but he died before the system was introduced. Later, by al-Mahdi's orders, the system was introduced in all places with the exception of 'Akabat Hulwân.'"

[1]Mâwardi, p. 306, l. 12.

[2] Ar. *muḳâsamah*, as contrasted with *misâḥah*, is the system of land tenure by which the *kharâj* is levied on the produce and not the area and is from one-tenth to one-half of the produce of the lands. *Cf.* Mâwardi, p. 260; De Goeje's Balâdhuri "Glossarium", pp. 86-87; ibn-Ṭiḳṭaḳa, p. 215, l. 16, p. 260, l. 5; Berchem, *La Propriété Territoriale*, p. 45.

The survey of Ḥudhaifah. 'Abdallâh ibn-Ṣâliḥ al-'Ijli from certain authorities:—Ḥudhaifah who measured the surface of the land irrigated by the Tigris, died at al-Madâ'in. The Ḳanâṭir Ḥudhaifah [arches of Ḥudhaifah] are named after him, because he camped near them; but others say because he renewed them. His cubit [Ar. *dhirâ'*], like that of ibn-Ḥunaif, is the length of a man's arm, hand and thumb, stretched out. When the inhabitants of as-Sawâd had the system of *kharâj* proportioned to the produce of the land, after they had that based on the area [*misâḥah*], one of the officials said: "The tithe levied on the fiefs was a tenth which was not equivalent [?] to one-fifth of the half levied on the *istâns* [administrative districts]. Therefore, it is necessary that there should be levied on the *jarîb* of the fiefs subject to the area [*misâḥah*] system of *kharâj* also one-fifth of what is levied on the *jarîb* of the *istâns* [?]."[1] Such was the case.

Abu-'Ubaid from Maimûn ibn-Mihrân:—'Umar sent Ḥudhaifah and ibn-Ḥunaif to Khânikîn, which was one of the first places they conquered; and after they attached seals to the necks of the *dhimmis*, they collected its *kharâj*.

Lands confiscated by 'Umar. Al-Ḥusain ibn-al-Aswad from 'Abd-al-Malik ibn-abi-Ḥurrah's father:—The latter said, "'Umar ibn-al-Khaṭṭâb confiscated for himself ten pieces of land in as-Sawâd of which I remember seven, the remaining three having slipped me. The lands he confiscated were (1) a piece covered with woods; (2) one covered with marshes; (3) one belonging to king Kisra; (4) all of Dair Yazîd;[2] (5) the land of those who were killed during the war; (6) the land of those who fled the country.

[1] Caetani, vol. v, p. 374; Muḳaddasi, p. 133.

[2] Caetani, vol. v, p. 373, gives it "dayr mubad (? nel testo: barîd)". *Cf.* Yûsuf, p. 32, l. 20.

This state of affairs lasted until the register was burned in
the days of al-Ḥajjâj ibn-Yûsuf, upon which the people 273
seized the [domanial] land bordering on their property."[1]

Abu-'Abd-ar-Raḥmân al-Ju'fi from 'Abd-al-Malik ibn-abi-Ḥurrah's father:—'Umar ibn-al-Khaṭṭâb confiscated in as-Sawâd the land of those who were killed during the war, the land of those who fled the country, all the land of king Kisra, all the land belonging to Kisra's family, every swampy place, all Dair Yazîd and all the land that was appropriated by Kisra for himself. Thus, the value of what 'Umar took amounted to 7,000,000 *dirhams*. In the battle of [Dair] al-Jamâjim, the people burnt the register and every one of them seized what bordered on his land.

Fiefs assigned by 'Uthmân. Al-Ḥusain and 'Amr an-Nâḳid from Mûsa ibn-Ṭalḥah:—'Uthmân assigned as fief to 'Abdallâh ibn-Mas'ûd a piece of land in an-Nahrain; to 'Ammâr ibn-Yâsir, Asbîna;[2] to Khabbâb ibn-al-Aratt, Sa'naba; and to Sa'd [ibn-abi-Waḳḳâṣ] the village of Hurmuz.

'Abdallâh ibn-Ṣâliḥ al-'Ijli from ash-Sha'bi:—'Uthmân ibn-'Affân assigned as fief to Ṭalḥah ibn-'Ubaidallâh an-Nashâstaj;[3] and to Usâmah ibn-Zaid, a piece of land which he later sold.

Shaibân ibn-Farrûkh from Mûsa ibn-Ṭalḥah:—'Uthmân ibn-'Affân gave fiefs to five of the Companions of the Prophet: 'Abdallâh ibn-Mas'ûd, Sa'd ibn-Mâlik az-Zuhri, az-Zubair ibn-al-'Auwâm,[4] Khabbâb ibn-al-Aratt and Usâmah ibn-Zaid.[5] Mûsa ibn-Ṭalḥah adds, "I noticed that ibn-

[1] Athîr, vol. ii, p. 407; Âdam, pp. 45-46.

[2] Yûsuf, p. 25, l. 9: "Istîniya."

[3] Yâḳût, vol. iv, p. 783.

[4] Ibn-Sa'd, vol. iii[1], pp. 75-77.

[5] *Cf.* Ya'ḳûbi, vol. ii, p. 202, l. 4.

Mas'ûd and Sa'd, who were my neighbors, used to cultivate their lands for one-third and one-fourth [of the produce]."

Al-Walîd ibn-Ṣâliḥ from Mûsa ibn-Talḥah:—The first one to give out al-'Irâk in fiefs was 'Uthmân ibn-'Affân who gave out pieces of land appropriated by Kisra, and others evacuated by their owners. Thus, he assigned to Ṭalḥah as fief an-Nashâstaj; to Wâ'il ibn-Hujr al-Had 274
rami, the land bordering on Zurârah's; to Khabbâb ibn-al Aratt, Asbîna; to 'Adi ibn-Hâtim at-Ṭâ'i, ar-Rauhâ', to Khâlid ibn-'Urfuṭah, a piece of land near Ḥammâm [bath] A'yan; to al-Ash'ath ibn-Kais al-Kindi, Tîzanâbâdh; and to Jarîr ibn-'Abdallâh al-Bajali, his land on the bank of the Euphrates.

Ajamat Burs. Al-Husain ibn-al-Aswad from al-Ḥasan ibn-Sâlih:—The latter said, "I was informed that 'Ali assessed on the owners of Ajamat [forest] Burs 4,000 *dirhams*; and to that end, he wrote them a statement on a piece of parchment.[1]

I was told by Aḥmad ibn-Ḥammâd al-Kûfi that Ajamat Burs lies in the vicinity of the Namrûdh [Nimrod] palace in Bâbil [Babylon]. In this forest, there is a precipice of great depth, which, according to some, is a well from the soil of which the bricks of the palace were made, and which, according to others, is a landslide.

Nahr Sa'd. I learnt from abu-Mas'ûd and others that the landlords [*dihkâns*] of al-Anbâr asked Sa'd ibn-abi-Waḳḳâṣ to dig for them a canal which they had previously asked the Persian magnate [king] to dig[2] for them. Sa'd wrote to Sa'd ibn-'Amr ibn-Harâm, ordering him to dig the canal for them. Accordingly, they dug until they reached a mountain which they could not cut through, upon

[1] Âdam, p. 18.

[2] *Cf.* Mas'ûdi, vol. i, p. 225.

which they gave it up. But when al-Ḥajjâj became governor of al-'Irâḳ, he gathered workmen from all regions, and said to his superintendents, "Take note of what one of the diggers eats per day. If it is the weight of what he digs out, then continue the work." Thus, they spent money[1] on it until it was completed. The mountain excavated was therefore named after al-Ḥajjâj; but the canal, after Sa'd ibn-'Amr ibn-Ḥarâm.[2]

Nahr Maḥdûd. Al-Khaizurân, the mother of the caliphs, [*umm-al-khulafâ'*] ordered that the canal known by the name of Maḥdûd be dug; and she gave it the name of ar-Raiyân.[3] Her superintendent over the work had divided it into sections, put limits for every section, and put it in charge of a group of men to dig; hence the name Maḥdûd [*i. e.*, limited].

Nahr Shaila. As for the canal known by the name of Shaila, it is claimed by the banu-Shaila ibn-Farrukhzâdân al-Marwazi that Sâbûr [Persian king] had dug it out for their grandfather when he sent him to guard the frontier of the dominion at Nighya in the canton of al-Anbâr. According to others, however, the canal was so called after 275
one, Shaila, who made a contract for digging the canal in the days of the caliph al-Manṣûr; the canal being old but buried, al-Manṣûr ordered that it be excavated. Before the work was brought to an end, al-Manṣûr died and the work was completed in the caliphate of al-Mahdi. According to others, al-Manṣûr ordered that a mouth [only] be dug for the canal above its old mouth; but he did not complete the work. Al-Mahdi completed it.

[1] *Cf.* Caetani, vol. iii, p. 864.

[2] *Cf. Marâṣid*, vol. iii, p. 248.

[3] *Marâṣid*, vol. iii, p. 48: "al-Marbân."

CHAPTER VIII

THE FOUNDING OF AL-KÛFAH

Al-Kûfah chosen. Muḥammad ibn-Sa'd from 'Abd-al-Ḥamîd ibn-Ja'far and others:—'Umar ibn-al-Khaṭṭâb wrote to Sa'd ibn-abi-Waḳḳâṣ ordering him to adopt for the Moslems a place to which they could emigrate, and which they could use as a meeting place [*ḳairawân*], provided that between him ['Umar] and the Moslems, no sea should intervene. Accordingly, Sa'd came to al-Anbâr [1] with the idea of occupying it. Here, however, flies were so numerous, that Sa'd had to move to another place, which proved to be unsatisfactory, and therefore he moved to al-Kûfah which he divided into lots, giving the houses as fiefs and settling the different tribes in their quarters. He also erected its mosque. All this took place in the year 17.

Sûḳ Ḥakamah. The following was communicated to me by 'Ali ibn-al-Mughîrah-l-Athram, on the authority of *sheikhs* from al-Kûfah:—When Sa'd ibn-abi-Waḳḳâṣ was through with the battle of al-Ḳâdisîyah, he went to al-Madâ'in, made terms with the inhabitants of ar-Rûmiyah and Bahurasîr, reduced al-Madâ'in,[2] Asbânbur [2] and Kurdbandâdh [3] and settled his troops in them. The troops occupied these places. Subsequently, Sa'd was ordered [by 'Umar] to remove them; and so he removed them to Sûḳ Ḥakamah, others say to Kuwaifah on this side of al-Kûfah. Ac-

[1] Dînawari, p. 131.

[2] The Arabic and Persian names of Ctesiphon; Yâḳût, vol. i, p. 237.

[3] Perhaps a quarter in Ctesiphon; Caetani, vol. iii, p. 848.

cording to al-Athram, the word *takauwuf* [1] means "the reunion of people". Others say that circular places when sandy are called *kûfah*; and still others call the land rich in pebbles, mud and sand, *kûfah*.

Mosquitoes in al-Madâ'in. It is stated that when the Moslems in al-Madâ'in were attacked by the mosquitoes, Sa'd wrote to 'Umar telling him that they were badly affected by them; in answer to which 'Umar wrote back, 276
"Arabs are like camels; whatever is good for the camels is good for them. Choose for them, therefore, a habitable place; and let no sea intervene between them and me." The determining of the dwelling-place was entrusted to abu-l-Haiyâj al-Asadi 'Amr ibn-Mâlik ibn-Junâdah.

Al-Kûfah founded. Then 'Abd al-Masîḥ ibn-Buḳailah presented himself before Sa'd and said to him, "I can point out to thee a site which is outside the waterless desert, and higher than the muddy places where mosquitoes abound." [2] Saying this, he pointed out the site of al-Kûfah which was then called Sûristân. When Sa'd arrived on the spot destined to be the site of the mosque, a man shot, by his orders. an arrow towards the *ḳiblah*, another towards the north, another to the south, a fourth to the east, and marked the spots where the arrows fell. Sa'd then established the mosque and the governor's residence on the spot where the man who shot the arrows had stood, fencing in all the space around that spot. He then drew lots with two arrows between the tribe of Nizâr and the tribes of al-Yaman, promising the left side, which was the better of the two, to the one whose arrow was drawn first. The people of al-Yaman had theirs first; and they were, therefore, allotted the pieces on the east side. The pieces allotted to the Nizâr fell on

[1] From which noun Kûfah comes.

[2] *Cf.* Ṭabari, vol. i, p. 2389.

the west side beyond the boundaries fixed for the mosque, leaving what was fenced in within the marks for the mosque and the governor's residence. Later, al-Mughîrah ibn-Shu'bah enlarged the mosque; and Ziyâd [1] [ibn-Abîhi] rebuilt it strongly and rebuilt the governor's residence. Ziyâd often repeated, "On every one of the pillars of the mosque at al-Kûfah, I spent 1,800 [*dirhams*]." Another building was established by 'Amr ibn-Ḥuraith al-Makhzûmi, whom Ziyâd used to leave in his place over al-Kûfah whenever he absented himself in al-Baṣrah. Ziyâd's agents erected many buildings which made the place crowded and thickly set.[2]

The lane called Kuḳâḳ 'Amr in al-Kûfah takes its name from the banu-'Amr ibn-Ḥuraith ibn-'Amr ibn-'Uthmân ibn-'Abdallâh ibn-'Umar ibn-Makhzûm ibn-Yaḳaẓah.

The Yamanites. Wahb ibn-Baḳîyah-l-Wâsiṭi from ash-Sha'bi:—The latter said, "We (the Yamanites) were 12,000 men; the Nizâr were 8,000; from which you can easily see that we constituted the majority of the settlers 277
of al-Kûfah. Our arrow went to the east side of the mosque. That is why we hold the pieces we now hold."

The mosque. 'Ali ibn-Muḥammad al-Madâ'ini from Maslamah ibn-Muḥârib and others:—Al-Mughîrah enlarged the mosque [3] of al-Kûfah and rebuilt it. Ziyâd later enlarged it still more. Pebbles were spread in this mosque and in that of al-Baṣrah, because when people prayed their hands were covered with dust, which they used to remove by clapping their hands. This made Ziyâd say, "I am afraid that in course of time, the clapping of hands will be taken for a part of the religious ceremony." When he, therefore, en-

[1] Yâḳût, vol. iv, pp. 323-324.

[2] Athir, vol. ii, pp. 410 *seq.*

[3] Hamadhâni, pp. 173-174.

larged the mosque and added to it, he ordered that pebbles be strewn in the courtyard of the mosque. The overseers of the work used to oppress those who gathered the pebbles, saying, "Bring us only this kind which we show you", choosing special samples, and asking for similar ones. By such means, they enriched themselves. Hence, the saying, "It is good to be in authority even over stones." [1] This saying, however, is, according to al-Athram, explained by abu-'Ubaidah by the fact that al-Ḥajjâj ibn-'Atîk ath-Thaḳafi, or his son, had charge of cutting the pillars for the al-Baṣrah mosque from Jabal al-Ahwâz where he discovered a mine. This gave rise to the expression: "It is good to be in authority even over stones."

Abu-'Ubaidah states that the colonization of al-Kûfah took place in the year 18.

Ziyâd took for himself in the al-Kûfah mosque a *maḳṣûrah* which afterwards was renewed by Khâlid ibn-'Abdallâh al-Ḳasri.

The version of al-Haitham. Ḥafṣ ibn-'Umar al-'Umari from al-Haitham ibn-'Adi aṭ-Ṭâ'i:—After having settled in al-Madâ'in, planned it out and established a mosque, the Moslems found the place too dirty and productive of pestilence. Sa'd ibn-abi-Waḳḳâṣ communicated the fact to 'Umar who wrote back that they should move westward. Sa'd came to Kuwaifah ibn-'Umar, but finding the water all around it, the Moslems left it and came to the site on which al-Kûfah now stands. They hit on the ridge called Khadd al-'Adhrâ' [the virgin's cheek] on which lavender, daisies, broom-plants [*shîḥ* and *ḳaiṣûm*] and poppies grew. On this site, they established themselves.

I was told by a Kufite *sheikh* that the region between al-Kûfah and al-Ḥirah was known by the name of al- 278
Milṭâṭ.

[1] Freytag, vol. ii, p. 917, n. 47.

The house of 'Abd-al-Malik ibn-'Umair was used for entertaining guests, 'Umar having ordered that some house be put to that use for those who came from the different provinces.

Charges against Sa'd. Al-'Abbâs ibn-Hishâm al-Kalbi from Muḥammad ibn-Isḥâḳ:—Sa'd ibn-abi-Waḳḳâṣ made a wooden door for his mansion which he surrounded with a fence of reeds. 'Umar ibn-al-Khaṭṭâb sent Muḥammad ibn-Maslamah-l-Anṣâri who set fire to the door and fence, and made Sa'd leader in the mosques of al-Kûfah where nothing but good was spoken of him.

Al-'Abbâs ibn-al-Walîd an-Narsi and Ibrâhîm al-'Allâf al-Baṣri from Jâbir ibn-Samurah:—The people of al-Kûfah reported Sa'd ibn-abi-Waḳḳâṣ to 'Umar on the ground that he did not lead properly in prayers. In answer to the charge, Sa'd said, "As for me, I have always followed the prayer of the Prophet and never deviated from it. In the first two [prostrations] I repeat prayer slowly, in the last two, quickly."[1] "That was what was thought of thee, abu-Isḥâḳ," said 'Umar. 'Umar then sent certain men to inquire in al-Kûfah regarding Sa'd, about whom nothing but good was told in the different mosques, until they came to the mosque of the banu-'Abs. Here someone called abu-Sa'dah said, "As for Sa'd, he does not divide shares equally, nor judge cases justly." Hearing this, Sa'd exclaimed, "O God, if he is telling a lie, make his age long, perpetuate his poverty, take away his eyesight and expose him to troubles!" 'Abd-al-Malik said, "I later saw abu-Sa'dah intercepting the way of the maids in the streets; and when somebody asked him, 'How are you, abu-Sa'dah?' he always replied, 'I am old and crazed, being afflicted with the curse of Sa'd'."

[1] Bukhâri, vol. i, p. 195; Zamakhshari, *Fâ'iḳ*, vol. i, p. 212.

In another tradition transmitted by al-'Abbâs an-Narsi, Sa'd made the following petition, regarding the people of al-Kûfah: "O God, let no ruler be satisfied with them, and let them be never satisfied with a ruler!"

I was informed by al-'Abbâs an-Narsi that al-Mukhtâr ibn-abi-'Ubaid, or someone else, said, "To love the people of al-Kûfah is honor; and to hate them is destruction."

Al-Ḥasan ibn-'Uthmân az-Ziyâdi from ash-Sha'bi:—
After the victory of al-Ḳâdisîyah, 'Amr ibn-Ma'dikarib 279
visited 'Umar ibn-al-Khaṭṭâb and was asked by him about Sa'd and whether the people were satisfied with him. 'Amr gave the following answer, "I left him laying up for them as an ant lays up, having as much sympathy with them as a kind mother. In his love of dates, he is an Arab; in the collection of taxes, he is Nabatean. He divides shares equitably, judges cases justly and leads the bands successfully." "It looks," said 'Umar, "as if ye both have agreed to compensate each other with praise (Sa'd having before written to 'Umar in commendation of 'Amr)." "No, 'Commander of the Believers'," answered 'Amr, "I rather said what I knew." "Well, 'Amr," said 'Umar, "describe war." "It is bitter in taste when waged. He, who perseveres in it, becomes known, but he who grows weak, perishes."—"Describe the arms."—"Ask me about whichever thou wantest."—"The lancet?"—"It is a brother which may betray thee."—"The arrows?"—"Arrows are messengers of death which either err or hit."—"The shield?"—"That is the defense which has most to suffer."—"The coat of mail?"—"Something that keeps the horseman busy; a nuisance for the footman; but in all cases, a strong protection."—"The sword?"—"May it be the cause of thy death!"—"*Thy* death!"—"The fever has abased me to thee."[1]

[1] A proverb applied to the case of abasement on the occasion of need. Lane's "Dictionary" *s. v. aḍra'a.*

'Umar appoints 'Ammâr and then al-Mughîrah. At last, 'Umar dismissed Sa'd and appointed 'Ammâr ibn-Yâsir. A complaint was made against 'Ammâr to the effect that he was weak and knew nothing about politics. He was therefore dismissed after holding the office of governor over al-Kûfah for one year and nine months. In this connection, 'Umar remarked, "What am I to do with the people of al-Kûfah? If I appoint a strong man over them, they attribute transgression to him; and if a weak man, they despise him."[1] Calling al-Mughîrah ibn-Shu'bah, he asked him, "Wouldst thou commit again what thou didst once commit, if I should assign thee over al-Kûfah?" And al-Mughîrah answered, "No." Al-Mughîrah went to al-Madînah, after the conquest of al-Kâdisîyah, and was appointed by 'Umar over al-Kûfah, which position he held until 'Umar's death.

Sa'd, then al-Walîd, then Sa'îd as governors. Then came 'Uthmân ibn-'Affân and appointed over al-Kûfah Sa'd; but later dismissed him and appointed al-Walîd ibn-'Ukbah ibn-abi-Mu'aiṭ ibn-abi-'Amr ibn-Umaiyah. When al-Walîd visited Sa'd, the latter said, "Either thou hast become intelligent after me, or I have become foolish after thee." Al-Walîd was later dismissed and Sa'îd ibn-al-Âṣi ibn-Sa'îd 280
ibn-al-Âṣi ibn-Umaiyah was nominated to his place.

Persians unite with the Arabs. Abu-Mas'ûd al-Kûfi from Mis'ar ibn-Kidâm:—In the battle of al-Ḳâdisîyah, Rustam led 4,000 men called Jund [army] Shahânshâh, who asked for peace provided they be allowed to settle wherever they wanted, be confederates with whomever they wanted and receive soldiers' stipends. Their request having been granted, they united in a confederacy with Zuhrah

[1] *'Iḳd*, vol. iii, p. 360; Ḥamadhâni, p. 184; Ḳazwîni, *Âthâr al-Bilâd*, p. 167.

ibn-Ḥawîyah as-Sa'di of the banu-Tamîm. Sa'd [ibn-abi-Waḳḳâṣ] allowed them to settle where they chose, and assigned 1,000,000 *dirhams* for stipends. Their chief [*naḳîb*] was one of them called Dailam;[1] hence the name of the place Ḥamrâ' Dailam. Later Ziyâd [ibn-Abîhi], following the orders of Mu'âwiyah, sent some of them to Syria where they are called al-Furs [Persians], others to al-Baṣrah where they were combined with the Asâwirah [Persian cavalry].

According to abu-Mas'ûd, the Arabs call the non-Arabs Ḥamrâ' [the red], and would say, "I came from Ḥamrâ' Dailam," as they would say, "I came from Juhainah" or some other place. Abu-Mas'ûd adds, "I heard someone say that these Asâwirah lived near ad-Dailam and when they were attacked by the Moslems in Ḳazwîn, they accepted Islâm on the same terms as the Asâwirah of al-Baṣrah. Then they came to al-Kûfah and settled in it."

According to al-Madâ'ini, Abarwîz brought from ad-Dailam 4,000 men who acted as his servants and escort, which position they held until the Arab invasion. They then took part in the battle of al-Ḳâdisîyah under Rustam. When Rustam was killed and the Magians were defeated, they withdrew, saying, "We are different from those others [*i. e.*, Arabs]; we have no refuge, and have already left a bad impression on the Moslems. Let us then adopt their faith, and we will be strengthened by them." Having deserted to the Moslem camp, Sa'd wanted to know the cause; and al-Mughîrah ibn-Shu'bah asked them about it. Thus, they presented their case, saying, "We will adopt your faith." Al-Mughîrah came back to Sa'd and told him about it. Sa'd promised them security; and they accepted Islâm. They witnessed the conquest of al-Ma-

[1] "Dîlam" in Persian.

dâ'in under Sa'd and the conquest of Jalûlâ'; after which they returned to al-Kûfah where they settled with the Moslems.

Places of interest and the persons after whom they are named.[1] The Jabbânat [cemetery] as-Sabî', after a son of as-Sabî' ibn-Sabu' ibn-Ṣa'b al-Hamdâni.

The Ṣaḥrâ [desert] Uthair,[2] after Uthair of the banu-Asad. 281

The Dukkân [shop] 'Abd-al-Ḥamîd, after 'Abd-al-Ḥamîd ibn-'Abd-ar-Raḥmân ibn-Zaid ibn-al-Khaṭṭâb, the *'âmil* of 'Umar ibn-'Abd-al-'Azîz over al-Kûfah.

The Saḥrâ bani-Ḳirâr after the banu-Ḳirâr ibn-Tha'-labah. . . . ibn-Nizâr.

Dâr ar-Rûmîyin was a dunghill where the inhabitants of al-Kûfah cast their rubbish and which was taken as fief from Yazîd ibn-'Abd-al-Malik by 'Anbasah ibn-Sa'îd ibn-al-Âṣi, who removed the soil in it for 150,000 *dirhams.*

The Sûḳ [market] Yûsuf in al-Ḥîrah, after Yûsuf ibn-'Umar . . . ath-Thaḳafi.

Ḥammâm [bath] A'yan, after A'yan, a freedman of Sa'd ibn-abi-Waḳḳâṣ.

Bî'at [church] bani-Mâzin in al-Ḥîrah, after some of al-Azd of Ghassân.

Ḥammâm 'Umar, after 'Umar ibn-Sa'd ibn-abi-Waḳḳâṣ.

Shahârsûj Bajîlah in al-Kûfah, after the banu-Bajlah.[3]

Jabbânat 'Arzam, after a certain 'Arzam, who used to shake in it milk in a skin [so that its butter might come forth]. 282

Jabbânat Bishr, after Bishr ibn-Rabî'ah . . . ibn-Ḳumair al-Khuth'ami.

Zurârah, after Zurârah ibn-Yazîd . . . ibn-Ṣa'ṣa'ah.

[1] The following list is a shortened form of the original.

[2] Dhahabi, pp. 5-6.

[3] Yâḳût, vol. iii, p. 338; Hamadhâni, p. 182; *Marâṣid*, vol. ii, p. 135.

Dâr [house] Ḥukaim in al-Kûfah, after Ḥukaim ibn-Sa'd ibn-Thaur al-Bukâ'i.

Ḳaṣr [castle] Mukâtil, after Mukâtil ibn-Ḥassân[1] . . . of the banu-Amru'i-l-Ḳais.

As-Sawâdiyah[2] in al-Kûfah, after Sawâd ibn-Zaid ibn- 283
'Adi. . . .

Ḳaryat [village] abi-Ṣalâbah on the Euphrates, after Ṣalâbah ibn-Mâlik ibn-Ṭârik. . . .

Aksâs Mâlik, after Mâlik ibn-Ḳais . . . ibn-Nizâr.

Dair [monastery] al-A'war, after one of the Iyâd of the banu-Umaiyah.

Dair Ḳurrah after Ḳurrah of the banu-Umaiyah ibn-Hudhâfah.

Dair as-Sawa, after the same banu-Umaiyah.

Dair al-Jamâjim, after the Iyâd tribe who in a battle with the banu-Bahrâ' and the banu-l-Ḳain lost many who were buried there and whose skulls [*jamâjim*] were later excavated as one was digging in the ground.

Dair Ka'b, after the Iyâd.

Dair Hind, after the mother of 'Amr ibn-Hind.

Dâr Ḳumâm, after the daughter of al-Ḥârith ibn-Hâ- 284
ni' al-Kindi.

Bi'at bani-'Adi, after the banu-'Adi ibn-adh-Dhumail of the Lakhm.

Ṭizanâbâdh, after aḍ-Ḍaizan ibn-Mu'âwiyah ibn-al-'Abîd as-Saliḥi.

Masjid [mosque] Simâk in al-Kûfah, after Simâk ibn-Makhramah ibn-Ḥumain al-Asadi. . . .

Mahallat [quarter] bani-Shaiṭân, after Shaiṭân ibn-Zuhair[3] . . . ibn-Tamîm.

[1] *Ḳâmûs*, vol. iv, p. 36, l. 22: "Ḥaiyân."

[2] "Sauwârîyah" in Hamadhâni, p. 182; *cf. Tâj al-'Arûs*, vol. ii, p. 390; Yâḳût, vol. iii, p. 180.

[3] "Zubair" in Yâḳût, vol. iii, p. 356, l. 12; *cf.* Ḥajar, vol. i, p. 585.

The site of Dâr 'Îsa ibn-Mûsa belonged to al-'Alâ' ibn-'Abd-ar-Raḥmân . . . ibn-'Abd-Manâf. 285

There is a path in al-Kûfah named after 'Amîrah ibn-Shihâb. . . .

Ṣaḥrâ' Shabath, after Shabath ibn-Rib'i ar-Riyâḥi of the banu-Tamîm.

Dâr Ḥujair in al-Kûfah, after Ḥujair ibn-al-Ja'd al-Jumaḥi.

Bi'r [well] al-Mubârik [Mubarak ?], after al-Mubârik [Mubarak ?] ibn-'Ikrimah ibn-Ḥumairi [Ḥimyari ?]-l-Ju'fi.

Raḥa [hand-mill] 'Umârah, after 'Umârah ibn-'Uḳbah . . . ibn-Umaiyah.

Jabbânat Sâlim, after Sâlim ibn-'Ammâr . . . ibn-Hawâzin.

Ṣaḥrâ' Albardakht, after the poet Albardakht aḍ-Ḍabbi.

Masjid bani-'Anz, after the banu-'Anz ibn-Wâ'il ibn-Ḳâsiṭ.

Masjid bani-Jadhîmah, after the banu-Jadhîmah ibn-Mâlik ibn-Naṣr . . . ibn-Asad.

There is a mosque in al-Kûfah named after the banu-l-Maḳâṣif.

Masjid bani-Bahdalah, after the banu-Bahdalah ibn-al-Mithl ibn-Mu'âwiyah of the Kindah.

Bi'r al-Ja'd in al-Kûfah, after al-Ja'd, a freedman of Hamdân. 286

Dâr abi-Arṭât, after Arṭât ibn-Mâlik al-Bajali.

Dâr al-Muḳaṭṭa', after al-Muḳaṭṭa' ibn-Sunain al-Kalbi.

Ḳaṣr al-'Adasîyîn at the extremity of al-Ḥîrah, after the banu-'Ammâr ibn-'Abd-al-Masîḥ. . . .

The cathedral mosque in al-Kûfah was built with material taken from the ruins of the castles in al-Ḥîrah that belonged to the al-Mundhir clan, the price of that material constituting a part of the tax paid by the people of al-Ḥîrah.

Sikkat al-Barîd [post-office] in al-Kûfah was once a

church built by Khâlid ibn-'Abdallâh . . . of the Bajîlah for his mother, who was a Christian.

Khâlid built shops, dug the canal called al-Jâmi', and erected the Ḳaṣr Khâlid.

Sûḳ Asad, after Asad ibn-'Abdallâh, Khâlid's brother.

Ḳanṭarat [arch] al-Kûfah was built by 'Umar ibn-Hubairah, and later repaired by Khâlid and others.

Al-Hâshimîyah. The following tradition was transmitted to me by abu-Mas'ûd and others:—Yazîd ibn-'Umar ibn-Hubairah laid out a city in al-Kûfah on the Euphrates and occupied it before it was fully completed. He then received a letter from Marwân, ordering him to avoid the neighborhood of the people of al-Kûfah; and he, therefore, left it and built the castle known by the name of Ḳaṣr ibn-Hubairah near the Sûra bridge.

When caliph abu-l-'Abbâs came to power, he occupied this city, completed the erection of certain mansions [*maḳṣûrahs*] defended by walls in it, established new buildings and called it al-Hâshimîyah. People in general called it by its old name after ibn-Hubairah; and abu-l-'Abbâs making the remark, "I see that the name of ibn-Hubairah will always cling to it", gave it up and established on a site opposite to it another city by the name of al-Hâshimîyah. After residing there for some time, he decided to settle in al-Anbâr, where he built his well-known city [1] in which he was buried.

Madînat as-Salâm. When abu-Ja'far al-Manṣûr became caliph, he occupied the city of al-Hâshimîyah in al-Kûfah after completing its erection, enlarging it and preparing it according to his own idea. Later, he abandoned it in favor of Baghdâdh, where he built his city. He founded Baghdâdh and called it Madînat as-Salâm,[2] and repaired its old

[1] Le Strange, *Baghdâd*, pp. 5-6.

[2] "The city of peace." Le Strange, p. 10.

wall which begins at the Tigris and ends at aṣ-Ṣarât [canal].

It was in this al-Hâshimîyah that al-Manṣûr imprisoned 'Abdallâh ibn-Ḥasan ibn-Ḥasan ibn-'Ali ibn-abi-Ṭâlib because of his two sons Muḥammad and Ibrâhim; and it was here that he was buried.

Ar-Ruṣâfah. Al-Manṣûr built in al-Kûfah ar-Ruṣâfah [causeway] and by his orders, his freedman abu-l-Khaṣib Marzûḳ built for him on an old foundation the castle that bears his name: abu-l-Khaṣib. Others say that abu-l-Khaṣîb built the castle for himself; and al-Manṣûr used to visit him in it.

Al-Khawarnaḳ. As for al-Khawarnaḳ, it was an old Persian castle built by an-Nu'mân ibn-Amru'i-l-Ḳais (whose mother was ash-Shaḳiḳah, daughter of abu-Rabî'ah ibn-Dhuhl ibn-Shaibân) for Bahrâm Jûr ibn-Yazdajird ibn-Bahrâm ibn-Sâbûr dhu-l-Aktâf, who was brought up in the home of an-Nu'mân.[1] It was this same an-Nu'mân who left his kingdom and traveled around, as mentioned by 'Adi ibn-Zaid al-'Ibâdi in his poem. When the "blessed dynasty" appeared, al-Khawarnaḳ was given as fief to Ibrâhîm ibn-Salamah, one of their propagandists in Khurâsân
and a grandfather of 'Abd-ar-Raḥmân ibn-Isḥâḳ al- 288
Ḳâḍi. During the caliphate of al-Ma'mûn and al-Mu'taṣim, Ibrâhîm lived in Madînat as-Salâm and was a freedman of ar-Ribâb. In the caliphate of abu-l-'Abbâs, he erected the dome of al-Khawarnaḳ which did not exist before.

Bâb al-Fîl. Abu-Mas'ûd al-Kûfi from certain *sheikhs* of al-Kûfah:—When the Moslems conquered al-Madâ'in, they captured an elephant; all the other elephants they came across before having been killed by them. They wrote to

[1] Tha'âlibi, *Mulûk al-Furs*, pp. 530-540 (ed. Zotenberg); Hamadhâni, pp. 178-179.

'Umar about it and he told them to sell it if possible. The elephant was bought by a man from al-Ḥîrah who used to cover its back with a cloak and go round the villages exhibiting it. Sometime after that, umm-Aiyûb, daughter of 'Umârah ibn-'Uḳbah ibn-abi-Mu'aiṭ (who was the wife of al-Mughîrah ibn-Shu'bah and later of Ziyâd) wanted to see the elephant as she was in her father's home. The elephant was brought before her and stood at the door of the mosque which is now termed Bâb al-Fîl. After looking at it, she gave its owner something and dismissed him. But no sooner had the elephant taken a few strides, than it fell dead. That is why the door was called Bâb al-Fîl.[1] Some say that the one who looked at it was the wife of al-Walîd ibn-'Uḳbah ibn-abi-Mu'aiṭ; others that it was a sorcerer who made the people see an elephant appearing from the door riding on a donkey; still others that the trough of the mosque was brought on an elephant and passed through this door, which was for that reason called Bâb al-Fîl. These explanations are false. There are those who claim that the trough of the mosque was carried on an elephant and brought in through this door. Others think that an elephant owned by one of the governors once rushed against this door which was later called after it. The first explanation, however, is the most authentic.

Jabbânat Maimûn. According to abu-Mas'ûd, the Maimûn cemetery at al-Kûfah was named after Maimûn, a freedman of Muḥammad ibn-'Ali ibn-'Abdallâh, surnamed abu-Bishr, who built aṭ-Ṭâḳât[2] in Baghdâdh near Bâb ash-Shâm.[3]

[1] "The elephant door"; *cf.* Ṭabari, vol. ii, p. 27.

[2] Archways or arcades. *Cf.* Le Strange, *Baghdâd*, p. 130.

[3] "The Syrian gate", Le Strange, pp. 17-18; Hamadhâni, p. 184; Ya'ḳûbi, pp. 240-242.

Sahrâ' umm-Salamah. The umm-Salamah desert was so called after umm-Salamah, daughter of Ya'kûb ibn-Salamah . . . ibn-Makhzûm and the wife of abu-l-'Abbâs. 289

Al-Kûfah moat. I was told by abu-Mas'ûd that al-Manṣûr held the people of al-Kûfah responsible for its moat and that he imposed on every one of them forty *dirhams* to meet its expenses, he being displeased with them on account of their tendencies toward the Ṭâlibite party and their spreading false news regarding the *sulṭân* [the chief authority].

The inhabitants of al-Kûfah commended. Al-Ḥusain ibn-al-Aswad from 'Âmir:—'Umar writing to the people of al-Kûfah called them "the head of the Arabs."

Al-Ḥusain from Nâfi' ibn-Jubair ibn-Muṭ'im:—'Umar said, "In al-Kûfah are the most distinguished men."

Al-Ḥusain and Ibrâhîm ibn-Muslim al-Khawârizmi from ash-Sha'bi:—'Umar in addressing the people of al-Kûfah wrote, "To the head of Islâm."

Al-Ḥusain ibn-al-Aswad from Shamir ibn-'Aṭîyah:—'Umar said regarding the people of al-Kûfah, "They are the lance of Allah, the treasure of the faith, the cranium of the Arabs, who protect their own frontier forts and reinforce other Arabs."

Abu-Naṣr at-Tammâr from Salmân:—The latter said:—"Al-Kûfah is the dome of Islâm. There will be a time in which every believer will either be in it or will have his heart set upon it."

CHAPTER IX

WÂSIṬ AL-'IRÂḲ

The first cathedral mosques. 'Abd-al-Ḥamîd ibn-Wâsi' al-Khatli-l-Ḥâsib from al-Ḥasan ibn-Ṣâliḥ:—The first cathedral mosque[1] built in as-Sawâd was that of al-Madâ'in built by Sa'd and his companions. It was later made larger and stronger under the supervision of Ḥudhaifah ibn-al-Yamân who died at al-Madâ'in in the year 36. After that, Sa'd established the mosque of al-Kûfah and 290
that of al-Anbâr.

Wâsiṭ built by al-Ḥajjâj. The city of Wâsiṭ was built in the year 83 or 84 by al-Ḥajjâj who also built its mosque, castle and Ḳubbat al-Khaḍrâ'.[2] The site of Wâsiṭ having been covered with reeds [*ḳaṣab*], the city acquired the name of Wâsiṭ al-Ḳaṣab. This city is equidistant from al-Ahwâz, al-Baṣrah and al-Kûfah. Ibn-al-Ḳirrîyah remarks, "He [al-Ḥajjâj] has built it but not in his town, and shall leave it but not for his son."

One of the *sheikhs* of Wâsiṭ from other *sheikhs*:—When al-Ḥajjâj completed the erection of Wâsiṭ, he wrote to 'Abd-al-Malik ibn-Marwân, "I have built a city in a hollow of the ground [*kirsh*] between al-Jabal and al-Miṣrain, and called it Wâsiṭ [lying halfway between]." That is why the people of Wâsiṭ were called the Kirshîyûn.[3] Before he

[1] *Masjid jâmi'* = the chief mosque of the city in which people assemble on Friday for prayer and the *khuṭbah*.

[2] *i. e.*, "the green dome." It was later occupied by al-Manṣûr and called Bâb adh-Dhahab. Le Strange, 31 *seq.*; Yâḳût, vol. i, p. 683; Ya'ḳûbi, *Buldân*, p. 240, and *Ta'rîkh*, vol. ii, p. 450; Ṭabari, vol. iii, p. 326.

[3] *Tâj al-'Arûs*, *s. v. kirsh.*

erected Wâsiṭ, al-Ḥajjâj had the idea of taking up his abode in aṣ-Ṣin of Kaskar. He, therefore, dug Nahr [canal] aṣ-Ṣin and ordered that the workmen be chained together so that none of them might run away as a deserter. After that it occurred to him to establish Wâsiṭ [1] which he later occupied, then he dug out an-Nîl [2] and az-Zâbi canals. The latter was so called because it branched off from the old Zâbi. He thus reclaimed the land around these two canals and erected the city called an-Nîl [3] and populated it. He then turned his attention to certain crown-domains which 'Abdallâh ibn-Darrâj, a freedman of Mu'âwiyah ibn-abi-Sufyân, had reclaimed (when with al-Mughîrah ibn-Shu'bah he had charge of the *kharâj* of al-Kûfah) for Mu'âwiyah. These domains included waste lands, swamps, ditches and thickets. Al-Ḥajjâj built dams [4] in these domains; uprooted the reeds in them and added them to the domains of 'Abd-al-Malik ibn-Marwân after populating them.

To his castle and the cathedral mosque in Wâsiṭ, al-Ḥajjâj brought doors from Zandaward,[5] ad-Daukarah, Dârûsâṭ, Dair Mâsirjasân [6] and Sharabîṭ, whose people protested, saying, "We have been guaranteed the security of our cities and possessions;" but he did not mind what they said.

Al-Mubarak. Al-Mubarak [7] canal was dug by Khâlid ibn-'Abdallâh-l-Ḳasri al-Mubarak and commemorated by al-Farazdaḳ in certain verses.

[1] Ḳazwîni, pp. 320-321; Ḥauḳal, pp. 162-163.

[2] Ya'ḳûbi, *Buldân*, p. 322.

[3] *Tanbîh*, p. 52.

[4] *musannayât; Tâj al-'Arûs, s. v. saniya*; Mâwardi, p. 311.

[5] Ṭabari, vol. iii, p. 321.

[6] Marâṣid, vol. i, p. 439.

[7] Ṭabari, vol. iii, pp. 1981, 1985.

Khâlid's bridge. Muḥammad ibn-Khâlid ibn-'Abdallâh 291
aṭ-Ṭaḥḥân from his *sheikhs*:—Khâlid ibn-'Abdallâh al-Ḳasri wrote to Hishâm ibn-'Abd-al-Malik asking for permission to make an arch over the Tigris. Hishâm wrote back, "If this were possible, the Persians would have done it." Khâlid wrote again; and Hishâm answered: "If thou art sure that it is feasible, thou mayst do it." Khâlid built the arch at a great expense; but it was soon destroyed by the water. Hishâm made Khâlid pay the expenses out of his own pocket.

Al-Bazzâḳ. The canal known by the name of al-Bazzâḳ was an old one of which the Nabatean form is al-Bassâḳ, which means that which cuts the water off from what comes after it and takes it over to itself. In this canal the superfluous water from as-Sîb jungles and some water of the Euphrates gather. This name was corrupted into al-Bazzâḳ.

Al-Maimûn. As for al-Maimûn [1] it was first dug out by Sa'îd ibn-Zaid, an agent of umm-Ja'far Zubaidah, daughter of Ja'far ibn-al-Manṣûr. The mouth of al-Maimûn was near a village called Maimûn. In the time of al-Wâthiḳ-Billâh, the position of the mouth was shifted by 'Umar ibn-Faraj ar-Rukhkhaji, but the river kept its old name al-Maimûn [the auspicious], lest the idea of auspiciousness be dissociated from it.

I was informed by Muḥammad ibn-Khâlid that by the order of caliph al-Mahdi, Nahr aṣ-Ṣilah was dug out and the lands around it were entrusted to farmers. The income thereof was used as stipends to the inhabitants of the sacred territories of Makkah and al-Madînah [*ahl al-Haramain*] and for other expenses there. It was stipulated on the tenants who came to those lands that they should yield two-

[1] Tabari, vol. iii, p. 1760: "Nahr Maimûn."

fifths [?] of the produce, with the understanding that after holding their share for fifty years, they should yield as tax one-half of its produce. This stipulation is still in force.[1]

Al-Amîr. As regards Nahr al-Amîr, it was ascribed to 292
'Îsa ibn-'Ali and lay in his fief.

Mashra'at al-Fîl. We were informed by Muḥammad ibn-Khâlid that Muḥammad ibn-al-Ḳâsim presented to al-Ḥajjâj an elephant from as-Sind[2] which was transported through al-Baṭâ'iḥ [the great swamp] on a ship and was landed at a watering place, which has since been called Mashra'at al-Fîl or Furḍat[3] al-Fîl.

[1] *Cf.* Ḳudâmah, pp. 241-242.

[2] A country bordering upon India, Karmân and Sijistân; Meynard, p. 324.

[3] *mashra'at* = wharf; *furḍat* = harbor.

CHAPTER X

Al-Baṭâ'iḥ

Al-'Aurâ'. I was informed by certain learned men that the Persians often discussed the future fall of their kingdom and thought that earthquakes and floods would be the sign thereof. Now, the Tigris emptied its water into Dijlat al-Baṣrah, also called al-'Aurâ',[1] by means of branching streams which drew their water from the main stream which carried the rest of the water and looked like one of those streams.

The formation of al-Baṭâ'iḥ. In the days of Ḳubâdh ibn-Fairûz,[2] the water at the lower part of Kaskar broke through a great breach which was neglected until its waters drowned large, flourishing tracts of land. Ḳubâdh was a feeble man and cared little for the breach. But when his son Anûshirwân came to rule, he ordered that dams be made and thus the water was stopped and some of the lands flourished again.

When the year came in which the Prophet sent 'Abdallâh ibn-Ḥudhâfah as-Sahmi to Kisra Abarwîz, which was the year 7 A. H. (others say 6), the waters of the Tigris and the Euphrates rose to a height never reached before or since, causing many great breaches. Abarwîz made special effort to stop the breaches; but the water had the better of him,

[1] The united course of the Tigris and Euphrates before they empty into the Persian Gulf. Yâḳût, vol. ii, p. 745.

[2] Tha'âlibi, pp. 586-603.

turned towards al-Baṭâ'iḥ [1] and overflowed the buildings and plants, drowning many cantons that were there. Kisra [2] rode out in person to block the breaches; he scattered money right and left, put many workmen to death and, according to a report, crucified on certain breaches forty dam builders in one day; but all that was of no avail against the force of water.[3]

With the advent of the Arabs into al-'Irâḳ, the Persians 293
were kept too busy fighting to mind the breaches which would burst and no one would mind them; and the feudal lords [*dihḳâns*] failed to block them. Consequently, al-Baṭîḥah was made wider and more extensive.[4]

'Abdallâh ibn-Darrâj. When Mu'âwiyah ibn-abi-Sufyân became ruler, he appointed 'Abdallâh ibn-Darrâj, his freedman, over the *kharâj* of al-'Irâḳ. 'Abdallâh, by cutting down the reeds and stopping the water by dams, reclaimed for his master lands in al-Baṭâ'iḥ, the income of which amounted to 5,000,000 [*dirhams*].

Hassân an-Nabaṭi. Then came Ḥassân an-Nabaṭi, the freedman of the banu-Ḍabbah, the builder of Ḥauḍ [reservoir] Ḥassân in al-Baṣrah and the one after whom Manârat [light-house] Ḥassân in al-Batâ'iḥ is named. Ḥassân reclaimed certain lands in al-Baṭâ'iḥ for al-Ḥajjâj in the days of al-Walîd and for Hishâm ibn-'Abd-al-Malik.[5]

Al-Janb canal. Before al-Baṭâ'iḥ was formed, there was at Kaskar a canal called al-Janb, along the south bank of which ran the post-road to Maisân, Dastumaisân and al-Ahwâz. When al-Baṭâ'iḥ was formed, that part of the

[1] The great swamp in which water overflowing from the Tigris and Euphrates disappeared. Rustah, p. 94.

[2] Anûshirwân; Tha'âlibi, p. 603.

[3] Mas'ûdi, vol. i, p. 225.

[4] Ḳudâmah, p. 240.

[5] *Cf.* Ḳudâmah, p. 240.

post-road which became a thicket was called Âjâm al-Barid; and the other part was called Âjâm Aghmarbathi [1] in which the great thickets lie. The canal is now seen in the *al-Jâmidah* [solid] lands that have recently been reclaimed and rendered fit for use.

The version of abu-Mas'ûd. Abu-Mas'ûd al-Kûfi from his *sheikhs*:—Al-Baṭâ'iḥ was formed after the "flight" of the Prophet and during the reign of Abarwîz over the Persians. Many great fissures were formed which Kisra was unable to block, thus making the rivers overflow and producing al-Baṭâ'iḥ. At the time of the Moslem wars with the Persians, the water overflowed and no one took the trouble to block the fissures. This enlarged the Baṭîḥah and made it wider. The banu-Umaiyah had reclaimed a part of the Baṭîḥah, which part was again sunk in the time of al-Ḥajjâj when new breaches appeared which al-Ḥajjâj did not care to block, trying thereby to injure the Persian feudal lords whom he suspected to be on the side of ibn-al-Ash'ath who had broken off his allegiance to al-Ḥajjâj. Ḥassân an-Nabaṭi reclaimed for Hishâm certain tracts of the Baṭîḥah land.

Abu-l-Asad. Abu-l-Asad, from whom Nahr abu-l-Asad takes its name, was one of the generals of the caliph al-Manṣûr, and one of those sent to al-Baṣrah when 'Adballâh 294
ibn-'Ali resided in it. It was this abu-l-Asad who made 'Abdallâh ibn-'Ali enter al-Kûfah.

I was told by 'Umar ibn-Bukair that al-Manṣûr dispatched his freedman abu-l-Asad, who pitched his camp between al-Manṣûr and the army of 'Îsa ibn-Mûsa as al-Manṣûr was fighting against Ibrâhîm ibn-'Abdallâh ibn-al-Ḥasan ibn-al-Ḥasan ibn-'Ali ibn-abi-Ṭâlib. The same abu-l-Asad dug the canal near al-Baṭîḥah which bears his name.

[1] "A Nabatean word which means the great thickets;" Ḳudâmah, p. 241.

Others say that abu-l-Asad, reaching the mouth of the canal and finding it too narrow for the ships, widened it; and, therefore, it was named after him.

It is stated by abu-Mas'ûd that in the time of the "blessed dynasty" certain breaches were formed which made al-Baṭâ'iḥ larger. Because of the water of the Euphrates, many thickets grew, of which some were reclaimed and made tillable land.

Maslamah reclaims new lands. Abu-Mas'ûd from 'Awânah:—In the days of al-Ḥajjâj, new breaches were made. Al-Ḥajjâj wrote to al-Walîd ibn-'Abd-al-Malik stating that he estimated that 3,000,000 *dirhams* would be required for blocking them. Al-Walîd thought that too much. Maslamah ibn-'Abd-al-Malik said to al-Walîd, "I offer to pay the expenses provided thou givest me as fief the depressed tracts in which the water remains, after spending 3,000,000 *dirhams,* which sum shall be spent under the direct supervision of thy counsellor and trusted man, al-Ḥajjâj." Al-Walîd accepted the offer. Maslamah gained possession of lands that had many cantons close together. He dug as-Sîbain [1] and induced the farmers and tenants to come and hold land. Thus the land flourished; and in order to secure his protection, many landowners voluntarily turned their farms over to him, and then held them from him as fief. When the "blessed dynasty" came and the possessions of the banu-Umaiyah were confiscated, all as-Sîbain was assigned as fief to Dâ'ûd ibn-'Ali ibn-'Abdallâh ibn-al-'Abbâs, from whose heirs it was bought with its rights and boundaries and was included in the crown-domains [*ḍiyâ' al-khilâfah*].

[1] The dual form of as-Sîb.

CHAPTER XI

Madînat as-Salâm

Built by al-Manṣûr. Baghdâdh [1] was an ancient city, but al-Manṣûr colonized it, and added a city to it [2] which 295
he began in the year 145. Hearing that Muḥammad and Ibrâhîm, the sons of 'Abdallâh ibn-Ḥasan ibn-Ḥasan, had thrown off their allegiance to him, al-Manṣûr returned to al-Kûfah. In the year 146, he transferred the public treasures [*buyût al-mâl*], repositories, and registers from al-Kûfah to Baghdâdh, and called it Madînat as-Salâm [the city of peace]. In the year 147, the wall of this city, with everything else connected with it, and the wall of ancient Baghdâdh were completed. Al-Manṣûr died in Makkah in the year 158 and was buried near the well of Maimûn ibn-al-Ḥadrami, an ally of the banu-Umaiyah.

Ar-Ruṣâfah. Ar-Ruṣâfah [3] was built for al-Mahdi by al-Manṣûr on the east side of Baghdâdh. This side was called 'Askar [camp] al-Mahdi [4] because al-Mahdi camped in it on his way to ar-Rai. When he returned from ar-Rai, he settled in ar-Ruṣâfah, although it had occurred to al-Manṣûr to direct him to settle in Khurâsân. This took place in the year 151. Before al-Mahdi had occupied the

[1] A Persian word meaning the city "founded by God," see Le Strange, *Baghdâd*, pp. 10-11.

[2] Ḥaukal, p. 164.

[3] *i. e.*, causeway, the eastern suburb of Baghdâd. Iṣṭakhri, pp. 83, 84; *Tanbîh*, p. 360.

[4] Ya'ḳûbi, *Buldân*, p. 251.

east side, a palace was built for him by al-Manṣûr's order; the one variously known as Ḳaṣr al-Waḍḍâḥ, Ḳaṣr al-Mahdi and ash-Sharḳîyah.[1] It lay on the other side of Bâb al-Karkh. Al-Waḍḍâḥ, after whom it is sometimes called, was a man from al-Anbâr who had charge of the expenses.

Al-Manṣûr as a builder. Al-Manṣûr built the two mosques of Madînat as-Salâm and the new bridge over aṣ-Ṣarât [canal]. The site of the city he bought from the owners of the villages of Bâdûraiya, Ḳaṭrabbul [or Ḳuṭrubbul], Nahr Bûḳ and Nahr Bîn. He gave the city as fief to members of his household, his generals, soldiers, companions and secretaries. He made the meeting place of the streets at al-Karkh, and ordered the merchants to build their shops and held them responsible for the rent.[2]

Places of interest in Baghdâd.[3] The al-Mukharrim quarter[4] in Baghdâdh takes its name from Mukharrim ibn-Shuraiḥ[5] ibn-Ḥazn al-Ḥârithi.

The Ḳanṭarat al-Baradân quarter, from as-Sari ibn-al-Ḥuṭaim,[6] the builder of al-Ḥuṭamîyah.

Aṣ-Ṣâliḥîyah, from Ṣâliḥ ibn-al-Manṣûr.

Al-Ḥarbîyah, from Ḥarb ibn-'Abdallâh al-Balkhi,[7] the
commander of the guard in al-Mauṣil under Ja'far ibn-abi- 296
Ja'far.

Az-Zuhairîyah or Bâb at-Tibn, from Zuhair ibn-Muḥammad of the inhabitants of Abîward.

[1] *i. e.*, "the oriental palace". Ya'ḳûbi, p. 245.

[2] Ar. *ghallah* = rent paid for buildings standing on the property of the state.

[3] The following list is an abridged form of the original.

[4] Le Strange, pp. 217-230.

[5] Duraid, p. 238, omits "ibn-Shuraiḥ".

[6] *Marâṣid*, vol. ii, p. 453: "as-Surai ibn-al-Ḥuṭam".

[7] *Cf.* Maḥâsin, vol. i, p. 397.

'Îsâbâdh, from 'Îsa ibn-al-Mahdi.[1]

Ḳaṣr 'Abdawaih standing opposite Barâtha, from 'Abdawaih, a notable of the Azd.

Al-Manṣûr assigned as fief to Sulaimân ibn-Mujâlid the site of his home; to Muhalhil ibn-Ṣafwân, after whom Darb Muhalhil is named, a special fief; to 'Umârah ibn-Ḥamzah, the quarter that bears his name; to Maimûn abu-Bishr after whom Ṭâḳât Bishr are named, a special fief near Bustân al-Ḳass;[2] to Shubail, his freedman, a fief near Dâr Yaḳṭîn; to umm-'Ubaidah, a freedmaid of Muḥammad ibn-'Ali, a fief; to Munîrah, a freedmaid of Muḥammad ibn-'Ali and after whom Darb Munîrah and Khân [inn] Munîrah are named, a special fief; and to Raisânah[3] a spot known by the name of Masjid bani-Raghbân.[4]

Darb [path] Mihrawaih takes its name from Mihra- 297
waih ar-Râzi who was one of the captives of Sinfâdh and was set free by al-Mahdi.

The city a residence for the caliphs. Al-Manṣûr lived in Madînat as-Salâm to the last days of his caliphate. He made a pilgrimage from it and died in Makkah. The city was then occupied by the caliph al-Mahdi. Later, al-Mahdi left for Mâsabadhân, where he died. Most of the time he spent in Madînat as-Salâm was passed in palaces he built at 'Îsâbâdh.

Madînat as-Salâm was then occupied by al-Hâdi Mûsa ibn-al-Mahdi, who died in it. Ar-Rashîd Hârûn also resided in it, and later left it for ar-Râfiḳah where he stayed for a while and then departed for Khurâsân, and died at Ṭûs. The city became after that the residence of Muḥammad ibn-ar-Rashîd, who was slain in it.

[1] *Tanbîh*, pp. 343-344.

[2] Ya'ḳûbi, p. 247.

[3] *Marâṣid*, vol. ii, p. 433.

[4] Dhahabi, p. 227; Ya'ḳûbi, pp. 244-245.

Al-Ma'mûn 'Abdallâh ibn-ar-Rashîd came to the city from Khurâsân and took up his abode in it. He then left on an expedition during which he died at al-Fadhandûn and was buried at Ṭarsûs.

Surra-man-ra'a, a residence for the caliphs. Caliph al-Mu'taṣim-Billâh made his residence in it and then left it for al-Ḳâṭûl [1] where he occupied the Ḳaṣr ar-Rashîd which was built when ar-Rashîd dug out Ḳâṭûlah [canal] and called it abu-l-Jund [the father of the army] because the land watered by it produced enough provisions for the army. Al-Mu'taṣim erected in al-Ḳâṭûl a building which he occupied, and offered the Ḳaṣr to Ashnâs at-Turki [the Turk], his freedman. He started to colonize that region and after beginning a new city, he gave it up and built the city of Surra-man-ra'a.[2] He transplanted people to it and made it his residence. At the meeting point of the streets, he built a cathedral mosque, and called the city Surra-man-ra'a. Al-Mu'taṣim made his freedman, Ashnâs, together with the other generals who had joined him [Ashnâs], settle at Karkh Fairûz. Other generals were given the houses called al-'Arabâya.[3] Al-Mu'taṣim died in Surra-man-ra'a in the year 227.

Hârûn al-Wâthiḳ-Billâh lived to the last day of his life in a house which he built at Surra-man-ra'a and called al-Hârûni.

When in dhu-l-Ḥijjah, year 232, the caliph Ja'far al-Mutawakkil-'Alallâh was installed, he made al-Hârûni his residence. He erected many buildings and assigned to different men fiefs in a place back of Surra-man-ra'a called al- 298

[1] *Tanbîh*, pp. 356-357.

[2] Ya'ḳûbi, pp. 256-257; Yâḳût, vol. iii, p. 14; Ṭabari, vol. iii, pp. 1179-1180.

[3] *Marâṣid*, vol. v, p. 501, n.; *Mushtarik*, p. 183.

Ḥâ'ir [1] in which al-Mu'taṣim had put him in confinement, thus giving more space for the inhabitants. Al-Mutawakkil also built a great cathedral mosque and lavished enormous sums of money on it, making the minaret so high that the voices of the muezzins could be easily heard, and the minaret could be seen at a distance of many parasangs. The Moslems gave up the first mosque and held Friday prayers in it.

Al-Mutawakkilîyah. Al-Mutawakkil founded a city which he called al-Mutawakkilîyah. He built it between al-Karkh, known by the name of Fairûz, and al-Ḳâṭûl, known by the name of Kisra, chose it for his abode and gave fiefs in it. The houses and the villages known as al-Mâḥûzah [2] were included in it. Al-Mutawakkil built in this city a cathedral mosque. From the time he started the city to the time he occupied it, only a few months elapsed, the occupation having taken place at the beginning of the year 246. Here he died in Shauwâl, [2] 47.

In the same night on which he died, al-Muntaṣir-Billâh was proclaimed caliph; and on Tuesday the 10th of Shauwâl, he left al-Mutawakkilîyah for Surra-man-ra'a, where he died.

'Uyûn aṭ-Ṭaff. 'Uyûn [springs] aṭ-Ṭaff [3] which include 'Ain aṣ-Ṣaid, al-Ḳuṭḳuṭânah, ar-Ruhaimah, 'Ain Jamal and the lands that belonged to them, were held by the garrisons that guarded the frontier forts beyond as-Ṣawâd. These springs lay near Khandaḳ [trench] Sâbûr, which Sâbûr had dug between him and the Arabs who guarded the frontier and the other Arabs who lived there. Sâbûr allowed them the use of the land as fief without collecting *kharâj* from them.

[1] Ṭabari, vol. iii, p. 752, and Ya'ḳûbi, p. 258: "al-Ḥair". *Cf.* Yâḳût, vol. ii, p. 189.

[2] Athîr, vol. vii, pp. 56, 68: "al-Mâkhûrah".

[3] Yâḳût, vol. iii, p. 539; Hamadhâni, p. 187.

In the battle of dhu-Ḳâr in which Allah through his Prophet gave the Arabs the victory, the Arabs gained possession of some of these springs, the rest remaining in the hands of the Persians. When the Arabs advanced to al-Ḥîrah, the Persians took to flight after covering over with earth all the springs in their lands. The Arabs who held the remaining springs embraced Islâm; and the land which they cultivated became tithe-land.

After the battles of al-Ḳâdisîyah and al Madâ'in, the lands whose owners had evacuated them, were turned over to the Moslems and given out as fiefs, thus becoming tithe-lands. Such was the case with 'Uyûn aṭ-Ṭaff whose lands
are treated like the villages in the valley of al-Madînah and 299
the villages of Najd, all the *ṣadaḳah* thereof being given to the *'âmils* of al-Madînah.

When Isḥâḳ ibn-Ibrâhîm ibn-Muṣ'ab ruled over as-Sawâd in the name of al-Mutawakkil, he added these 'Uyûn and their lands to what he already controlled; and he collected their tithe, treating them as any other land in as-Sawâd, which status they still retain. The Moslems later dug out many other springs which irrigate lands that are treated in a similar way.

'Ain al-Jamal. I was told by a *sheikh* that 'Ain al-Jamal[1] was so called because a camel [Ar. *jamal*] died near it. Others say that the one who dug it out was called Jamal.

'Ain aṣ-Ṣaid. 'Ain aṣ-Ṣaid[2] [fishing spring] was so called because fish gathered in it. I was told by certain Kuraiẓîyûn [?] that this spring was one of those covered with earth. As one of the Moslems was passing there, the legs of his horse sank in the mud. He dismounted and dug in the ground; and the water appeared. With the help of

[1] Rustah, p. 180: "'Ain Jamal".

[2] *Ibid.*, p. 180: "'Ain Ṣaid"; *cf.* Khurdâdhbih, p. 146.

certain men he called, the earth and soil were removed, the course was opened and the water issued as before. The spring then passed to the hands of 'Îsâ ibn-'Ali, who bought it from a son of Ḥasan ibn-Ḥasan ibn-'Ali ibn-abi-Ṭâlib. One of 'Îsa's wives was umm-Kalthûm, daughter of Ḥasan ibn-Ḥasan. Mu'âwiyah in exchange for the caliphate, assigned, together with other things, 'Ain aṣ-Ṣaid as fief to al-Ḥasan ibn-'Ali.

'Ain ar-Raḥbah. 'Ain ar-Raḥbah was also one of the springs buried of old. A pilgrim from Karmân once saw it leaking; and when he returned from his pilgrimage, he advised 'Îsa ibn-Mûsa regarding it and pointed it out to him. This Karmân man took it as fief with its land and dug it out. He cultivated the lands around it and planted the palm-trees which stand on al-'Udhaib road.

'Uyûn al-'Irḳ. A few parasangs from Hît lie certain springs called al-'Irḳ which are similar to 'Uyûn aṭ-Ṭaff, and whose tithes are taken by the chief of Hît.

The meaning of Sawâd. Al-Athram from abu-'Amr ibn-al-'Alâ':—When the Arabs saw the great number of villages, palm and other trees, they exclaimed, "Never did we see a greater number of *sawâd*!" *i. e.*, objects. Hence the name of the country as-Sawâd.

The market compared to the place of worship. Al-Ḳâsim ibn-Sallâm from Muḥammad ibn-abi-Mûsa:—One day 'Ali went out to the market and saw that his relatives 300
had secured special places, upon which he remarked, "That can not be. For the Moslems, the market is similar to the place of worship: he who arrives first can hold his seat all day until he leaves it."

Abu-'Ubaid from 'Abd-ar-Raḥmân ibn-'Ubaid's father:—The latter said, "In the time of al-Mughîrah ibn-Shu'bah, we used to go early into the market; and when one sat in a place, he had claim on it until the nightfall. But when

Ziyâd came, he ordered that he who sat in a place, could claim it so long as he occupied it."

According to Marwân, al-Mughîrah held the governorship of al-Kûfah twice: once for 'Umar and another time for Mu'âwiyah.

CHAPTER XII

Arabic Made the Language of the Register

Al-Madâ'ini 'Ali ibn-Muḥammad ibn-abi-Saif from his *sheikhs*:—Persian was the language of the register of the *kharâj* of as-Sawâd and the rest of al-'Irâḳ. When al-Ḥajjâj became ruler of al-'Irâḳ he chose Zâdân Farrûkh ibn-Yabra for secretary, and the latter was assisted by Ṣâliḥ ibn-'Abd-ar-Raḥmân, a freedman of the banu-Tamim, who knew both Arabic and Persian. Ṣâliḥ's father was one of the captives of Sijistân. Through Zâdân Farrûkh, Ṣâliḥ was acquainted with al-Ḥajjâj, who found him acceptable. One day Ṣâliḥ said to Zâdân, "Thou art the means by which I became acquainted with the governor; and I see that he has found me acceptable. I, therefore, do not wonder if he should promote me over thee, in which case thou wouldst fall." "Never believe that," answered Zâdân; "he has more use for me than I for him, because none but myself can be found to keep his books." "By Allah," retorted Ṣâliḥ, "if thou so desire, I could change the accounts into Arabic." "Try a part of it," said Zâdân, "and I will see." Ṣâliḥ having done that, Zâdân asked him to feign illness, which he did. Al-Ḥajjâj sent his own physician, but found nothing wrong with Ṣâliḥ. Hearing that, Zâdân ordered him to appear.

In the days of 'Abd-ar-Raḥmân ibn-Muḥammad ibn-al-Ash'ath al-Kindi, Zâdân Farrûkh was killed on his way from some house to his own home, or some other man's home. Thereupon, al-Ḥajjâj made Ṣâliḥ secretary in the

place of Zâdân. Ṣâliḥ reported to al-Ḥajjâj the conversation that took place between him and Zâdân relative to the change of the language of the register. Al-Ḥajjâj 301
immediately made up his mind to adopt Arabic as the language of the register and charged Ṣâliḥ with the task. Mardânshâh ibn-Zâdân Farrûkh asked Ṣâliḥ, "What wouldst thou do with *dahwiyah* and *shashwiyah*?" To this, Ṣâliḥ replied, "I shall use instead *'ushr* [tenth] and *nuṣf'ushr*[1] [half-tenth]."—"And what about *wîd*?"—"I shall use *aiḍan*" (*wîd* means excess).[2] Hearing that, Mardânshâh said, "May God efface thy trace from the world as thou hast effaced the trace of the Persian!" Ṣâliḥ was later offered 100,000 *dirhams* in order to show that it was impossible to change the language of the register and to refrain from doing it; but he refused and carried out the plan. 'Abd-al-Ḥamîd ibn-Yaḥya, the secretary of Marwân ibn-Muḥammad used to say, "Great is Ṣâliḥ, and great is the favor he has bestowed upon the secretaries!"

'Umar ibn-Shabbah from Sahl ibn-abi-aṣ-Ṣalt:—Al-Ḥajjâj assigned for Ṣâliḥ ibn-'Abd-ar-Raḥmân a certain period in which to change the language of the register.[3]

[1] These are the Arabic equivalent of the Persian terms *dahwiyah* and *shashwiyah; shash* means six.

[2] *wîd* or *waid* is used to-day in Persian in the sense of "little". Ar. *aiḍan* corresponds to *ditto.*

[3] *Cf.* Mâwardi, p. 350.

PART X

MEDIA [AL-JIBÂL]

CHAPTER I

Ḥulwân

Ḥulwân capitulates. After the decisive battle of Jalûlâ' had been won by the Moslems, Hâshim ibn-'Utbah ibn-abi-Waḳḳâṣ added to the forces of Jarîr ibn-'Abdallâh al-Bajali a heavy detachment of cavalry and stationed him at Jalûlâ' between the Moslems and their enemy [the Persians].

Later on, Sa'd sent Jarîr about 3,000 Moslems and ordered him to advance with them and his forces to Ḥulwân.[1] No sooner had Jarîr approached Ḥulwân than Yazdajird fled away in the direction of Iṣbahân. Ḥulwân capitulated; and Jarîr promised to spare the people and guarantee their lives and possessions without interfering with those who preferred to flee the land.

Ḳarmâsîn. Leaving in Ḥulwân a part of his forces [?] with 'Azrah ibn-Ḳais ibn-Ghazîyah-l-Bajali, Jarîr pushed towards ad-Dînawar, which he failed to reduce. He, however, reduced Ḳarmâsîn[2] on the same terms as Ḥulwân. He then returned to Ḥulwân and held its governorship until the arrival of 'Ammâr ibn-Yâsir in al-Kûfah. 'Ammâr wrote to Jarîr that 'Umar ibn-al-Khaṭṭâb wanted him to reinforce abu-Mûsa-l-Ash'ari [in Tustar]. Accordingly, Jarîr left 'Azrah ibn-Ḳais over Ḥulwân, and in the year 19 made 302
his way to join abu-Mûsa.

Muḥammad ibn-Sa'd from 'Â'ishah, daughter of Sa'd ibn-

[1] Rustah, pp. 164-165.

[2] Yâḳût, vol. iv, p. 68.

abi-Waḳḳâṣ:—The latter said, "When Mu'âwiyah put Ḥujr ibn-'Adi-l-Kindi [1] to death, my father made the following remark, 'If Mu'âwiyah had seen the part Ḥujr had taken [2] in the reduction of Ḥulwân, he would have realized of what great value he was to Islâm'."

According to al-Wâḳidi, certain sons of Jarîr ibn-Abdallâh settled in Ḥulwân, where their descendants are still living.

[1] *Aghâni*, vol. xvi, pp. 3-4; Athîr, vol. iii, pp. 392 *seq.*; Mas'ûdi, vol. v, pp. 15 *seq.*

[2] Text not clear. *Cf.* Ḥajar, vol. i, p. 645.

CHAPTER II

The Conquest of Nihâwand

An-Nu'mân in chief command. In the year 19, when Yazdajird fled away from Ḥulwân, the Persians and the people of ar-Rai, Ḳûmis,[1] Iṣbahân, Hamadhân and al-Mâhain communicated with one another and, in the year 20, joined Yazdajird. The latter put at their head Mardânshâh dhu-l-Ḥâjib and they unfurled their flag ad-Dirafshikâbiyân. These "polytheists" numbered 60,000, and according to other estimates, 100,000. When 'Ammâr ibn-Yâsir communicated this news to 'Umar ibn-al-Khaṭṭâb, the latter was on the point of leading an expedition in person against them, but desisted lest the Arabs should then prevail over Najd and other places. The advice to let the Syrians lead the attack from Syria and the Yamanites from al-Yaman was also discarded, lest the Greeks should return to their home, and the Abyssinians should subjugate what was next to them. Consequently, he wrote to the people of al-Kûfah ordering that two-thirds of them should set out and one-third should stay for the defense of their homes and country. From the people of al-Baṣrah, he also sent a group of men. He then said, "I shall use over the army someone who shall be the first to expose himself to the spears."[2] Accordingly, 'Umar wrote to an-Nu'mân ibn-'Amr ibn-Muḳarrin al-Muzani, who was at that time with as-Sâ'ib ibn-al-

[1] In Ṭabaristân. Yâḳût, vol. iv, p. 203; Meynard, pp. 464-465.

[2] The original is obscure. *Cf.* Dînawari, p. 142; Caetani, vol. iv, p. 215, n. 1.

Akra' ath-Thakafi, assigning him to the leadership of the army, saying, "In case thou art killed, Hudhaifah ibn-al-Yamân shall be the leader; if he should be killed, then Jarîr 303
ibn-'Abdallâh al-Bajali; if he should be killed, then al-Mughîrah ibn-Shu'bah; and if he should be killed, al-Ash'ath ibn-Kais." This an-Nu'mân was at that time the *'âmil* over Kaskar and its territory. Others say he was in al-Madînah, and when he received his appointment over this army from 'Umar by word of mouth, he started from it.

Shaibân from Ma'kil ibn-Yasâr:—When 'Umar ibn-al-Khattâb sought the advice of al-Hurmuzân, saying, "Shall we begin with Isbahân or Adharbaijân [Atrapatakan]?" al-Hurmuzân replied, "Isbahân is the head, and Adharbaijân the wings. Cut off the head, and the wings will fall off together with it."[1]

Al-Mughîrah as envoy. When 'Umar entered the mosque [in al-Madînah], his eyes fell on an-Nu'mân ibn-Mukarrin; so he took a seat by his side. When he was through with his prayer, 'Umar said, "I want thee to be my *'âmil* [lieutenant]". An-Nu'mân replied, "If a collecting-*'âmil*, no; but if an invading-*'âmil*, yes." "An invading one," said 'Umar. Thus 'Umar sent an-Nu'mân and wrote to the people of al-Kûfah to reinforce him, which they did, sending among others al-Mughîrah ibn-Shu'bah. An-Nu'mân sent al-Mughîrah to dhu-l-Hâjibain,[2] the Persian chief at Nihâwand.[3] Al-Mughîrah [reaching the Persian camp] drew his sword and began cutting the rugs to pieces until he presented himself before the chief, upon which he took his seat on the throne. By dhu-l-Hâjib's

[1] *Cf.* Tabari, vol. i, pp. 2600-2601; Mas'ûdi, vol. iv, p. 230.

[2] He is also called dhu-l-Hâjib Mardânshâh.

[3] or Nahâwand. Müller, vol. i, p. 245; Meynard, pp. 573-576; Yâkût, vol. iv, pp. 406, 827.

order, al-Mughirah was dragged out. So he exclaimed: "[Remember that] I am an envoy!"

The battle fought. When the Moslems met the "polytheists", they found them fastened in chains, in tens and fives, so that they might not flee. Before the fight started they shot their arrows and wounded some of the Moslems. Then an-Nu'mân said, "I noticed that when the Prophet did not carry on the fight in the morning, he would wait until the sun set and the wind blew; then the victory would be assured."[1] An-Nu'mân added, "I shall now shake the standard I carry three times. After the first shake, let each perform the ablutions and satisfy his natural wants. After the second shake, let each turn to his sword (he may have said sandal-thong) and get ready, putting everything in order. When the third shake is, by Allah's will, made, then rush and let none of you heed the other." Saying this, an-Nu'mân shook the standard and they did as he had ordered them. His coat of mail was too 304
heavy for him; but he fought and his men fought; and he was the first Moslem to be killed.

The Persian [dhu-l-Ḥâjib] fell from his mule and his belly was cut open.

Ma'ḳil ibn-Yasâr [the narrator of this tradition] adds, "Coming to an-Nu'mân and finding that life had not yet fully departed from him, I washed his face with some water I carried in a vessel; upon which he asked, 'Who art thou?'—'Ma'ḳil.'—'How did the Moslems fare?'—'I have glad tidings; Allah has given us conquest and victory!'—'Praise be to Allah! Write and tell 'Umar about it.'"

The news carried to 'Umar. Shaibân from abu-'Uthmân an-Nahdi:—The latter said, "I myself carried the glad news to 'Umar who asked, 'And what about an-Nu'-

[1] *Cf.* Ṭabari, vol. i, p. 2603.

mân?' 'He was killed,' said I. 'We are Allah's,' remarked 'Umar, 'and to Allah we return.' Saying this, he began to cry. I then said, 'By Allah, he was killed with others whom I know not.' 'But whom Allah knows,' said he."

Aḥmad ibn-Ibrâhîm from abu-'Uthmân an-Nahdi:—The latter said, "When 'Umar ibn-al-Khaṭṭâb received the news of the death of an-Nu'mân ibn-Muḳarrin, he covered his face with his hands and began to cry."

The version of as-Sâ'ib. Al-Ḳâsim ibn-Sallâm from as-Sâ'ib ibn-al-Aḳra':—The latter said, "An army, the similar to which was never seen before, marched against the Moslems." He then cited the tradition regarding 'Umar's intention to lead the expedition in person, his appointment of an-Nu'mân ibn-Muḳarrin, the forwarding with as-Sâ'ib (whom 'Umar put in charge of the booty) of the appointment in which these words occur: "Bring no false case to my attention, and never hold justice from anyone." [1] The tradition then gives an account of the battle and mentions that an-Nu'mân was the first to be killed in the battle of Nihâwand, upon which Ḥudhaifah carried the standard and Allah gave them [the Arabs] victory. As-Sâ'ib adds, "I gathered the booty and divided it. After that there came to me a spy,[2] saying, 'The treasure of an-Nakhîrkhân [3] is in 305
the castle.' When I climbed up there, I found two chests containing pearls, the similar to which I never saw before. I then made my way to 'Umar who, having not yet received the news, was roaming in the streets [of al-Madînah] and making inquiries. Seeing me, 'Umar exclaimed, 'Oh! what news?' I gave him an account of the battle and the death

[1] *Cf.* Ṭabari, vol. i, p. 2597.

[2] *Cf.* Dînawari, p. 145.

[3] *Ibid.*, p. 145: "Nukhârijân".

of an-Nu'mân and mentioned the case of the two chests. 'Umar said 'Go and sell the chests and divide the price among the Moslems.' Accordingly, I took them to al-Kûfah, where I met a young man of the Ḳuraish, 'Amr ibn-Ḥuraith, by name, who paid their price from the stipends of [his own] family and the warriors of its members. One chest he took to al-Ḥîrah, where he sold it for the same price he had paid me for both; and the other he kept. This was the first part of the fortune 'Amr amassed."

Other versions. A certain biographer reports that the battle of Nihâwand was fought on Wednesday and Thursday and, after a short cessation, fighting was continued on Friday. He reports in describing the battle a similar tradition to that reported by Ḥammâd ibn-Salamah.

Ibn-al-Kalbi from abu-Mikhnaf:—An-Nu'mân camped at al-Isbîdhahâr[1] with al-Ash'ath ibn-Ḳais commanding his right wing and al-Mughîrah ibn-Shu'bah, the left wing. In the fight that ensued, an-Nu'mân was killed. At last the Moslems won the victory; and that conquest was termed "the victory of victories." The conquest of Nihâwand took place on Wednesday, year 19, and according to others, 20.

Ar-Rifâ'i from al-Ḥasan and Muḥammad:—The battle of Nihâwand took place in the year 21. A similar tradition was communicated to me by ar-Rifâ'i on the authority of Muḥammad ibn-Ka'b.[2]

Dînâr makes terms for the city. Others report that after the defeat of the Persian army and the victory of the Moslems, Ḥudhaifah, who was at that time the leader, laid siege to Nihâwand, whose inhabitants made sorties but were de-

[1] Hamadhâni, pp. 211, 259, and Dînawari, p. 143: "al-Isfîdhahân"; Yâḳût, vol. i, p. 239: "Isbîdhahân".

[2] *Cf.* Weil, vol. i, pp. 88-94; Muir, *Annals*, pp. 255-258; Muir, *Caliphate*, pp. 178-180; Wellhausen, *Skizzen*, vol. vi, p. 97.

feated. One day Simâk ibn-'Ubaid al-'Absi chased a Persian who was accompanied by 8 horsemen. Simâk killed all eight, as each of them in turn turned against him. Seeing that he was left alone, the man chased yielded and laid 306
down his arms. Simâk took him as prisoner; but as he spoke Persian, Simâk called someone who understood him and translated what he said, which was, "I shall go to your leader that I may make terms with him on this land, pay him poll-tax, and give thee for taking me as prisoner whatever thou requestest. To thee I owe a great deal because thou didst spare my life." Simâk asked, "What is thy name?" and he replied, "Dînâr". Simâk led him to Ḥudhaifah who made terms with him, stipulating that the *kharâj* and poll-tax be paid, and that the safety of the possessions, walls and dwellings of the inhabitants of his city, Nihâwand, be guaranteed. Nihâwand was thereafter called Mâh Dînâr. Dînâr often came after that to Simâk, offering him presents and showing his loyalty.

Mâh al-Baṣrah and Mâh al-Kûfah. Abu-Mas'ûd al-Kûfi from al-Mubârak ibn-Sa'd's father:—Nihâwand was one of the places conquered by the people of al-Kûfah, whereas ad-Dînawar was one of those conquered by the people of al-Baṣrah. The increase of the Moslems at al-Kûfah made it necessary that the lands the *kharâj* of which was divided among them be increased. Consequently, [the district of] ad-Dînawar was given them, in exchange for which the people of al-Baṣrah were given [the district of] Nihâwand which formed a part of [the province of] Iṣbahân. The excess of the *kharâj* of ad-Dînawar over that of Nihâwand was therefore a gain for the people of al-Kûfah.[1] Nihâwand was thereafter called Mâh al-Baṣrah; and ad-Dînawar, Mâh al-Kûfah. All this took place during the caliphate of Mu'âwiyah.

[1] *Cf.* Caetani, vol. iv, p. 502.

The meaning of "al-Yamân". I have been informed by certain men of learning that Ḥudhaifah ibn-al-Yamân was the son of Ḥusail [Ḥisl] ibn-Jâbir al-'Absi. He was an ally of the banu-'Abd-al-Ashhal of *al-Anṣâr*; and his mother was ar-Rabâb, daughter of Ka'b ibn-'Adi of the 'Abd-al-Ashhal tribe. His father was killed in the battle of Uḥud by 'Abdallâh ibn-Mas'ûd al-Hudhali, who killed him by mistake, taking him for an "unbeliever". In accordance with the Prophet's order, the blood money was paid; but Ḥudhaifah distributed it among the Moslems. According to al-Wâḳidi, Ḥusail was nicknamed al-Yamân because he had commercial interests in al-Yaman; and whenever he arrived in al-Madînah, people would say, "Here comes al-Yamâni [of which al-Yamân is a shortened form]." According to al-Kalbi, however, Ḥudhaifah was the son of Ḥusail ibn-Jâbir ibn-Rabî'ah ibn-'Amr ibn-Jurwah, Jurwah being the one nicknamed al-Yamâni after whom Ḥudhaifah was so called, although between the two many generations intervened. Jurwah, in pre-Islamic times, killed someone 307
and fled to al-Madînah, where he became an ally of the banu-'Abd-al-Ashhal. His people called him al-Yamâni because he made an alliance with the Yamanites.

CHAPTER III

Ad-Dînawar, Mâsabadhân and Mihrijânkadhaf

Ad-Dînawar makes terms. Abu-Mûsa-l-Ash'ari left Nihâwand, to which he had come with the army of al-Baṣrah for the reinforcement of an-Nu'mân ibn-Muḳarrin. On his way, he passed by ad-Dînawar where he camped for five days, in which he was offered resistance for only one day. The people of ad-Dînawar then agreed to pay tax and *kharâj*, and sought safety for their lives, possessions and children. Abu-Mûsa granted their request and left over the city his *'âmil*, together with some horsemen, and proceeded to Mâsabadhân, whose people offered no resistance.[1]

As-Sîrawân makes terms. The people of as-Sîrawân made terms similar to those of ad-Dînawar, agreeing to pay poll-tax and *kharâj;* and abu-Mûsa sent detachments and conquered all the lands of ad-Dînawar. Others assert that abu-Mûsa conquered Mâsabadhân before the battle of Nihâwand.

Aṣ-Ṣaimarah capitulates. Abu-Mûsa 'Abdallâh ibn-Ḳais al-Ash'ari sent as-Sâ'ib ibn-al-Aḳra' ath-Thaḳafi—who was his son-in-law through his daughter umm-Muḥammad ibn-as-Sâ'ib—to aṣ-Ṣaimarah the chief city of Mihrijânḳadhaf. The city capitulated; and it was agreed that the lives of the inhabitants be spared, that no captives be taken, and that no pieces of gold or silver be carried away, pro-

[1] *Cf.* Athir, vol. ii, p. 409; Ṭabari, vol. i, p. 2477; Yâḳût, vol. iv, p. 393.

vided the inhabitants paid poll-tax and *kharâj* on the land. As-Sâ'ib reduced all the districts of Mihrijânkadhaf. The more reliable report is that abu-Mûsa dispatched as-Sâ'ib from al-Ahwâz; and the latter reduced Mihrijânkadhaf.

Sinn Sumairah. Muḥammad ibn-'Uḳbah ibn-Muṣrim [1] aḍ-Ḍabbi from certain *sheikhs* of al-Kûfah:—When the Moslems invaded al-Jibâl, they passed by the eastern summit called Sinn Sumairah, Sumairah being a woman of the Ḍabbah [a branch] of the banu-Mu'âwiyah ibn-Ka'b ibn-Tha'labah ibn-Sa'd ibn-Ḍabbah and one of the Emigrants. Sumairah had a tooth [*sinn* protruding beyond the others];[2] hence the name of the peak Sinn Sumairah.

Ḳanâṭir an-Nu'mân. Ḳanâṭir [arches] an-Nu'mân, according to ibn-Hishâm al-Kalbi, were named after an-Nu'mân ibn-'Amr ibn-Mukarrin al-Muzani, who camped by these Ḳanâṭir, which had been standing from ancient time.

Kathîr ibn-Shihâb. Al-'Abbâs ibn-Hishâm al-Kalbi from 'Awânah:—Kathîr ibn-Shihâb ibn-al-Ḥusain ibn-dhi-l-Ghuṣṣah-l-Ḥârithi belonged to the 'Uthmân party and often spoke evil of 'Ali ibn-abi-Ṭâlib, and dissuaded men from following al-Ḥusain. He died either before or at the beginning of the rebellion of al-Mukhtâr ibn-abi-'Ubaid. Al-Mukhtâr ibn-abi-'Ubaid referred to him when he said: "By the Lord of heavens, the severe in punishment, the revealer of the Book, I shall surely dig the grave of Kathir ibn-Shihâb, the transgressor, the liar." Mu'âwiyah gave him for some time the governorship of ar-Rai and Dastaba, which he held on behalf of Mu'âwiyah and his two *'âmils,* Ziyâd and al-Mughîrah ibn-Shu'bah. After that, he incurred Mu'âwiyah's anger and was flogged and imprisoned by him in

---

[1] *Cf.* Maḥâsin, vol. i, p. 700, and Ṭabari, vol. i, p. 2458: "'Uḳbah ibn-Mukram".

[2] Ṭabari, vol. i, p. 2648.

Damascus. Shuraiḥ ibn-Hâni' al-Muradi interceded in favor of Kathîr; and he was released. Yazîd ibn-Mu'âwiyah, for selfish reasons, approved of following Kathîr and siding with him, and wrote to 'Ubaidallâh ibn-Ziyâd, asking him to appoint Kathîr over Mâsabadhân, Mihrijânḳadhaf, Ḥulwân and al-Mâhain [the two Mâhs], which he did, giving Kathîr many villages of the crown-domains in al-Jabal [1] as fief. Here Kathîr built the castle which bears his name and which lies in ad-Dînawar. Zuhrah ibn-al-Ḥârith ibn-Manṣûr ibn-Ḳais ibn-Kathîr ibn-Shihâb had secured many crown-villages at Mâsabadhân.

Al-Khashârimah. I learned from a descendant of Khashram ibn-Mâlik ibn-Hubairah-l-Asadi that the Khashârimah came first to Mâsabadhân towards the end of the Umaiyad dynasty, their grandfather being an emigrant from al-Kûfah.

Kathîr made governor. Al-'Umari from al-Haitham ibn-'Adi:—Ziyâd was one day on a trip when the belt of his robe became loose. Kathîr ibn-Shihâb immediately drew a needle, that was stuck in his cap, and a thread and mended the belt. Seeing that, Ziyâd said, "Thou art a man of discretion; and such a one should never go without an office." Saying this, he appointed him governor over a part of al-Jabal.

[1] or al-Jibâl = Persian 'Irâḳ or Media. Meynard, p. 151; Ḳazwini, p. 228; Hamadhâni, p. 209; Rustah, p. 106.

CHAPTER IV

THE CONQUEST OF HAMADHÂN 309

Jarîr reduces Hamadhân. In the year 23 A. H., al-Mughîrah ibn-Shu'bah who, after the dismissal of 'Ammâr ibn-Yâsir, was the *'âmil* of 'Umar ibn-al-Khaṭṭâb over al-Kûfah, dispatched Jarîr ibn-'Abdallâh al-Bajali to Hamadhân.[1] The inhabitants of Hamadhân offered resistance and repelled his attacks, in the course of which Jarîr received an arrow in his eye; and he remarked, "I give up my eye, seeking recompense from Allah who decorated with it my face and provided me by means of it with light, so long as he willed, and then deprived me of it as I was in his cause!" After that he reduced Hamadhân, which made terms similar to those of Nihâwand. This took place toward the close of the year 23. Its inhabitants, having later rebelled, drove Jarîr back; but he finally took their land by force.[2]

Other versions. According to al-Wâḳidi, Jarîr reduced Nihâwand in the year 24, six months after the death of 'Umar ibn-al-Khaṭṭâb.

It is reported by others that al-Mughîrah ibn-Shu'bah, with Jarîr leading the vanguard, marched against Hamadhân and, after reducing it, put it in charge of Kathîr ibn-Shihâb al-Ḥârithi.

The terms with al-'Alâ'. 'Abbâs ibn-Hishâm from his grandfather and 'Awânah ibn-al-Ḥakam:—When Sa'd ibn-

[1] Ecbatana. See Meynard, pp. 597-608.

[2] *Cf.* Yâḳût, vol. iv, p. 981; Athîr, vol. iii, p. 16.

abi-Waḳḳâṣ ruled over al-Kûfah in behalf of 'Uthmân ibn-'Affân, he assigned over Mâh and Hamadhân al-'Alâ' ibn-Wahb ibn-'Abd ibn-Wahbân of the banu-'Âmir ibn-Lu'ai. The people of Hamadhân acted treacherously and violated the covenant, on account of which al-'Alâ' fought against them until they surrendered. The terms he made with them stipulated that, on the one hand, they should pay *kharâj* on their land and tax on their person and deliver to him 100,000 *dirhams* for the Moslems; and that, on the other hand, he should not interfere with their possessions, inviolable rights and children.

Mâdharân. According to ibn-al-Kalbi, the castle known by the name of Mâdharân was so called after as-Sari ibn-Nusair [1] ibn-Thaur al-'Ijli, who camped around it until he reduced it.

Sîsar. Ziyâd ibn-'Abd-ar-Raḥmân al-Balkhi from certain *sheikhs* of Sîsar:—Sîsar was so called because it lay in 310
a depression surrounded by thirty hills. Hence its other name "Thalâthûn Ra's" [thirty summits]. It was also called Sîsar Ṣadkhâniyah which means thirty summits and a hundred springs, because it has as many as one hundred springs.

Sîsar and the adjoining region were pasture-lands for the Kurds and others. It also had meadows for the beasts of burden and the cattle of caliph al-Mahdi, and was entrusted to a freedman of his called Sulaimân ibn-Ḳirâṭ—whose name Saḥrâ' Ḳirâṭ in Madînat as-Salâm bears—and to a partner of his, Sallâm aṭ-Ṭaifûri, Ṭaifûr having been a freedman of abu-Ja'far al-Manṣûr and having been given by him as present to al-Mahdi. When in the caliphate of al-Mahdi the destitute [*ṣa'âlîk*] and villain became numerous and spread over al-Jabal, they chose this region for their refuge and

[1] *Cf. Marâṣid*, vol. iii, p. 27.

stronghold, to which they resorted after acting as highwaymen, and from which they could not be called back, because it was a boundary line between Hamadhân, ad-Dînawar and Adharbaijân. Sulaimân and his colleague wrote to al-Mahdi, reporting the case of those who interfered with their beasts and cattle. Thereupon, al-Mahdi directed against them a great army and wrote to Sulaimân and Sallâm, ordering them to build a city and occupy it with their associates and shepherds and use it as a refuge for their beasts and cattle against those who threatened them. Accordingly, they built the city of Sîsar, fortified it, and made people settle in it. The district [*rustâḳ*] of Mâyanharaj[1] in ad-Dînawar, and that of al-Jûdhamah in Adharbaijân which is a part of the province of Barzah, together with Rusṭuf[2] and Khâbanjar were added to Sîsar; and the whole was made into one district that was put under one *'âmil* to whom its *kharâj* was paid.[3]

Later, in the caliphate of ar-Rashîd, this band of destitute multiplied and badly damaged Sîsar. Ar-Rashîd ordered that it be repaired and fortified, stationing in it 1,000 of the men of Khâḳân al-Khâdim as-Sughdi, whose descendants are still in it. Towards the end of his cali- 311
phate, ar-Rashîd appointed Murrah ibn-abi-Murrah ar-Rudaini-l-'Ijli over Sîsar. 'Uthmân al-Audi attempted to wrest it from his hands, but failed, succeeding[4] only in wresting all or most of what Murrah already held at Adharbaijân. Until the time of the insurrection, Murrah ibn-ar-Rudaini did not cease in the days of Muḥammad ibn-ar-Rashîd to pay the fixed *kharâj* of Sîsar which he had

[1] Khurdâdhbih, p. 120. Hamadhâni, p. 240: "Mâyanmaraj".

[2] ? perhaps *rustâḳ*; *cf.* Yâḳût, vol. iii, p. 216.

[3] Hamadhâni, pp. 239-240.

[4] According to Hamadhâni, p. 240, he failed in that, too.

agreed to pay annually.[1] In the caliphate of al-Ma'mûn, Sîsar was taken from the hand of 'Âṣim ibn-Murrah and once more added to the crown-domains [*ḍiyâ' al-khilâfah*].

Al-Mafâzah. I was told by certain *sheikhs* from al-Mafâzah, which is situated near Sîsar, that when al-Jurashi[2] ruled over al-Jabal the inhabitants of al-Mafâzah evacuated their town. Al-Jurashi had a general, Hammâm ibn-Hâni' al-'Abdi, to whom most of the people of al-Mafâzah yielded their villages and held them as tenants in order to enjoy his protection. Hammâm appropriated the villages to himself and used to pay the treasury what was due on them until he died. His sons were too weak to hold them. After the death of Muḥammad ibn-Zubaidah, when al-Ma'mûn was on his way from Khurâsân to Madinat as-Salâm, he was met by certain sons of Hammâm and a man from al-Mafâzah named Muḥammad ibn-al-'Abbâs, who told him the story of the place and informed him of the desire of all the people to give up their lands to him and act as his tenants in it provided they be protected and strengthened against the destitute bands and others. Al-Ma'mûn accepted their offer and ordered that they be reinforced and strengthened in order to cultivate the lands and repair them. Thus these lands were added to the crown-domains.

Laila-l-Akhyalîyah. According to a tradition communicated to me by al-Madâ'ini, Laila-l-Akhyalîyah paid a visit to al-Ḥajjâj. He gave her a present, and she requested him to write and recommend her to his *'âmil* at ar-Rai. On her way back, Laila died at Sâwah, where she was buried.

[1] Ar. *muḳâṭa'ah*; M. V. Berchem, *La Propriété Territoriale et l'Impôt Foncier sous les Premiers Califes*, p. 45.

[2] *Cf.* "al-Ḥarashi" in Ya'ḳûbi, p. 253.

CHAPTER V

Ḳumm, Ḳâshân and Iṣbahân

312

Ḳumm and Kâshân reduced. Leaving Nihâwand, abu-Mûsa 'Abdallâh ibn-Ḳais al-Ash'ari came to al-Ahwâz, and after passing through it, stopped at Ḳumm which he reduced after a few days' fight. He then directed al-Aḥnaf ibn-Ḳais, whose name was aḍ-Ḍaḥḥâk ibn-Ḳais at-Tamîmi to Ḳâshân, which he took by force. Abu-Mûsa then overtook him.[1]

Jai and al-Yahûdîyah capitulate. In the year 23, 'Umar ibn-al-Khaṭṭâb directed 'Abdallâh ibn-Budail ibn-Warḳâ' al-Khuzâ'i to Iṣbahân. Others assert that 'Umar wrote to abu-Mûsa-l-Ash'ari ordering him to direct 'Abdallâh at the head of an army to Iṣbahân, which abu-Mûsa did. 'Abdallâh ibn-Budail conquered Jai,[2] which capitulated after a fight, agreeing to pay *kharâj* and poll-tax, provided the population be guaranteed the safety of their lives and all possessions with the exception of the arms in their hands.

'Abdallâh ibn-Budail then directed al-Aḥnaf ibn-Ḳais, who was in his army, to al-Yahûdîyah,[3] whose inhabitants made terms similar to those of Jai.

Thus ibn-Budail effected the conquest of the territory of Iṣbahân with its districts over which he acted as *'âmil* to

[1] *Cf.* Yâḳût, vol. iv, pp. 15, 175.

[2] A part of Iṣbahân. Iṣṭakhri, p. 198, note *n*; Ḥauḳal, p. 261; Yâḳût, vol. ii, p. 181; Meynard, pp. 188-189.

[3] Another suburb of Iṣbahân. Yâḳût, vol. iv, p. 1045.

the end of the first year of 'Uthmân's caliphate, at which time 'Uthmân appointed as-Sâ'ib ibn-al-Aḳra'.

Bashîr's version. Muḥammad ibn-Sa'd, a freedman of the banu-Hâshim, from Bashîr ibn-abi-Umaiyah:—Al-Ash'ari camped at Iṣbahân and proposed to the people the idea of Islâm, which they refused. He then proposed that they pay tax, upon which they made terms agreeing to pay it. The very next morning they rebelled; and he fought against them and, by Allah's help, defeated them. Muḥammad ibn-Sa'd, however, adds, "In my view this refers to the inhabitants of Ḳumm."

The satrap of Iṣbahân. Muḥammad ibn-Sa'd from Muḥammad ibn-Isḥâḳ:—'Umar sent ibn-Budail al-Khuzâ'i to Iṣbahân, whose satrap [*marzubân*] was an aged man called al-Fâdûsafân.[1] Ibn-Budail besieged the city and wrote to the people inciting them to forsake him. Seeing the luke- 313
warmness of his men, al-Fâdûsafân chose thirty archers, in whose courage and obedience he confided, and fled away from the city towards Karmân with a view to joining Yazdajird. As soon as 'Abdallâh knew of it, he sent after him a heavy detachment of cavalry. As the Persian reached a high place, he looked behind and said to 'Abdallâh, "Take heed for thyself, no arrow of ours misses its mark. If thou charge, we shoot; and if thou fight a duel, we will fight!" A duel followed in the course of which the Persian gave 'Abdallâh[2] a blow [with the sword] which, falling on the pommel of his saddle, broke it and cut the breast-girth [of the horse]. The Persian then said to 'Abdallâh, "I hate to kill thee because I see thou art wise and brave. Wouldst thou let me go back with thee that I may arrange terms with thee and pay tax for my towns-

[1] Ṭabari, vol. i, p. 2639: "al-Fâdhûsafân".

[2] Caetani, vol. v, p. 10, takes 'Abdallâh to be the one who delivered the blow. *Cf.* Ṭabari, vol. i, p. 2639.

men, of whom those who stay will be considered *dhimmis*, and those who flee will not be interfered with? The city I will turn over to thee." Ibn-Budail returned with him and took Jai; and the Persian fulfilled his promise, saying, "I saw that ye, people of Iṣbahân, are mean and disunited. Ye, therefore, deserve what I did with you."

The territory of Iṣbahân pays kharâj. Ibn-Budail then passed through the plains and mountains of the territory of Iṣbahân, all of which he conquered, treating them as regards *kharâj* as he had treated the people of al-Ahwâz.

Some say that the conquest of Iṣbahân and its territory was effected partly in the year 23 and partly in the year 24.

Other versions. It is reported by others that 'Umar ibn-al-Khaṭṭâb sent at the head of an army 'Abdallâh ibn-Budail, who met abu-Mûsa, after the latter had conquered Ḳumm and Ḳâshân. They both now led the attack against Iṣbahân with al-Aḥnaf ibn-Ḳais commanding the van of abu-Mûsa's army. Thus they subjugated all al-Yahûdîyah as described above. Ibn-Budail, after that, reduced Jai; and they both marched through the territory of Iṣbahân and reduced it. The most reliable account, however, is that Ḳumm and Ḳâshân were conquered by abu-Mûsa; whereas Jai and al-Yahûdîyah, by 'Abdallâh ibn-Budail.

Abu-Ḥassân az-Ziyâdi from a Thaḳîf man:—In Iṣbahân stands the sanctuary [1] of 'Uthmân ibn-abi-l-'Âṣi ath-Thaḳafi.

Persian nobility embrace Islâm. Muḥammad ibn-Yaḥya at-Tamîmi from his *sheikhs*:—To the nobility of Iṣbahân belonged various strongholds in Jafrabâd in the district of 314
ath-Thaimarah [2]-l-Kubra, in Bihjâwarsân [3] and in the fort

[1] Ar. *mashhad*—a place where a martyr died or is buried.

[2] Ya'ḳûbi, p. 275: "at-Taimara"; *cf.* Rustah, p. 154, *b*; Yâḳût, vol. i, p. 908.

[3] or Ḳahjâwarsân, Pers. Gah Gâwarsan. Yâḳût, vol. ii, p. 11.

of Mârabîn.[1] When Jai was reduced, these nobles offered homage, agreeing to pay the *kharâj*; and because they disdained to pay poll-tax, they became Moslems.

Al-'Anbari in Iṣbahân. It is stated by al-Kalbi and abu-l-Yakẓân that after al-Hudhail ibn-Ḳais al-'Anbari was appointed governor of Iṣbahân in the time of Marwân, the 'Anbari clan moved there.

Idrîs ibn-Ma'ḳil imprisoned. The grandfather of abu-Dulaf (abu-Dulaf being al-Ḳâsim ibn-'Îsa ibn-Idrîs ibn-Ma'ḳil al-'Ijli), whose occupation consisted in preparing perfumes and trading in sheep, came to al-Jabal with a number of his relatives and occupied a village at Hamadhân called Mass. They became wealthy and came to own many [crown] villages. One day Idrîs ibn-Ma'ḳil attacked a merchant who owed him money and choked him. Others say he choked him and took his money. Therefore, he was carried away to al-Kûfah, where he was imprisoned. This took place when Yûsuf ibn-'Umar ath-Thaḳafi ruled over al-'Irâḳ in the days of Hishâm ibn-Abd-al-Malik.

Al-Karaj rebuilt. After that, 'Îsa ibn-Idrîs came to al-Karaj,[2] which he reduced and whose fort, which was dilapidated, he rebuilt. Abu-Dulaf al-Ḳâsim ibn-'Îsa strengthened his position and rose into eminence in the eyes of the *sulṭân*. He enlarged that fort and built the city of al-Karaj which was for that reason called after him Karaj abi-Dulaf. Al-Karaj to-day forms a district by itself.

Ḳumm's rebellion suppressed. The inhabitants of Ḳumm threw off their allegiance and withheld the *kharâj*. Al-Ma'mûn directed against them 'Ali ibn-Hishâm al-Marwazi, recruiting him with troops[3] and ordering him to wage war

[1] *Cf.* Muḳaddasi, p. 402: "Sârimîn"; Ya'ḳûbi, p. 275: "Mirabin"; Yâḳût, vol. iv, p. 382: "Mârabânân"; Hamadhâni, p. 263.

[2] Meynard, pp. 478-479.

[3] Ṭabari, vol. iii, p. 1093.

against them. 'Ali did so, killed their chief, Yaḥya ibn-'Imrân, razed the city wall to the ground and collected over 7,000,000 *dirhams* as tax, although previous to this they used to complain that 2,000,000 were too much for them to pay.

In the caliphate of abu-'Abdallâh al-Mu'tazz-Billâh ibn-al-Mutawakkil-'Alallâh, they once more threw off their allegiance, upon which al-Mu'tazz directed against them Mûsa ibn-Bugha, his *'âmil* over al-Jabal, who was conducting the war against the Ṭâlibites who appeared in Ṭabaristân. Ḳumm was reduced by force and a large number of its inhabitants was slaughtered. Al-Mu'tazz wrote that a group of its leading men should be deported.

CHAPTER VI

The Death of Yazdajird ibn-Shahriyâr ibn-Kisra Abarwîz ibn-Hurmuz ibn-Anûshirwân 315

The flight of Yazdajird. Yazdajird fled from al-Madâ'in to Ḥulwân and thence to Iṣbahân. When the Moslems were done with Nihâwand, he fled from Iṣbahân to Iṣṭakhr, where he was pursued, after the conquest of Isbahân, by 'Abdallâh ibn-Budail ibn-Warḳâ', but to no avail. Abu-Mûsa-l-Ash'ari came to Iṣṭakhr and attempted its conquest, but did not succeed, and likewise did 'Uthmân ibn-abi-l-'Âṣi ath-Thaḳafi try it and fail.

In the year 29 when all Persia with the exception of Iṣṭakhr and Jûr [1] was already reduced, 'Abdallâh ibn-'Âmir ibn-Kuraiz proceeded to al-Baṣrah. Yazdajird was on the point of leaving for Ṭabaristân, whose satrap had invited him, when Yazdajird was still in Iṣbahân, to come to Ṭabaristân which he told him was well fortified. It then occurred to Yazdajird to flee to Karmân, to which ibn-'Âmir sent after him Mujâshi' ibn-Mas'ûd as-Sulami and Harim ibn-Ḥaiyân al-'Abdi. Mujâshi' came and stopped at Biyamand in Karmân, where his army was caught by a snow storm and nearly annihilated, few only surviving. The castle in which he resided was called after him Ḳaṣr Mujâshi'. Mujâshi' then took his way back to ibn-'Âmir.

As Yazdajird was one day sitting in Karmân, its *marzubân* came in; but Yazdajird felt too haughty to speak to

[1] Ṭabari, vol. i, p. 2863: "which is Ardashîr Khurrah". *Cf* Meynard, p. 23.

him, and the *marzubân* ordered that he be driven out, saying, "Not only art thou unworthy of a kingdom but even of a governorship of a village; and if Allah had seen any good in thee, he would not have put thee in such condition!"

Yazdajird left for Sijistân [1] whose king showed regard for him and exalted him. After a few days Yazdajird asked about the *kharâj* which made the king change his attitude towards him.

Seeing that, Yazdajird left for Khurâsân. When he reached the boundary line of Maru he was met by its satrap [*marzubân*] Mâhawaih [2] with great honor and pomp. Here he was also met by Nîzak Ṭarkhân who offered him something to ride upon, gave him presents and entertained him bountifully. Nîzak spent one month with Yazdajird, after which he left him. He then wrote Yazdajird asking for the hand of his daughter. This aroused the anger of Yazdajird, who said, "Write and tell him 'Thou art nothing but one of my slaves; how darest thou then ask for my daughter's hand?'" Yazdajird also ordered that Mâhawaih, the
satrap of Maru, give an account and be asked about the 316
money he had collected. Mâhawaih wrote to Nîzak, instigating him against Yazdajird and saying, "This is the one who came here as a runaway fugitive. Thou hast helped him in order to have his kingdom restored to him; but see what he wrote to thee!" They both then agreed to put him to death.

Yazdajird slain. Nîzak led the Turks to al-Junâbidh [3] where he met the enemy. At first the Turks retreated, but then the tide turned against Yazdajird, his followers

[1] *Cf.* Michel le Syrien, *Chronique*, vol. ii, p. 424 (ed. Chabot).

[2] Tha'âlibi, p. 743: "Mâhawait".

[3] Yunâbidh, Yunâwid or Kunâbidh. Iṣṭakhri, p. 273; Ḥaukal, p. 324; Muḳaddasi, p. 321.

were killed, his camp was plundered, and he fled to the city of Maru. The city refused to open its gates; so he had to dismount at a miller's house standing on the bank of al-Mirghâb.[1] Some say that having heard of that, Mâhawaih sent his messenger who killed him in the miller's house. Others assert that Mâhawaih incited the miller and, by his orders, the miller killed Yazdajird, after which Mâhawaih said, "No slayer of a king should be kept alive", and he ordered that the miller himself be put to death. Still others claim that the miller offered Yazdajird food, which he ate, and drink, which intoxicated him. In the evening, Yazdajird took out his crown and put it on his head. Seeing that, the miller coveted the possession of the crown, and raising a mill-stone dropped it on Yazdajird. After killing him, he took his crown and clothes and threw the body into the water. When the news came to Mâhawaih, he put the miller and his family to death and took the crown and clothes. According to another story, Yazdajird was warned against the messengers of Mâhawaih and fled away, jumping into the water. When the miller was asked about him, he said, "The man has left my house." They found Yazdajird in the water, and he said, "If ye spare me I will give you my belt, ring and crown." He asked them for some money with which he could buy bread, and one of them gave him 4 *dirhams*. Seeing that, Yazdajird laughingly said, "I was told that I will some day feel the need of 4 *dirhams*!" Later he was attacked by certain men sent after him by Mâhawaih, and he said, "Kill me not; rather carry me to the king of the Arabs, and I will make terms with him on your and my behalf, and thus ye will be safe." They refused and choked him by means of a bow-string.

[1] or Marghâb or Murghâb, also called Nahr Maru. Ṭabari, vol. i, p. 2872; Ḥaukal, p. 315.

His clothes they carried away in a pouch; and his body they threw away into the water.[1]

Fairûz taken away by the Turks. It is claimed that Fairûz ibn-Yazdajird fell into the hands of the Turks, who gave him one of their women in marriage; and he settled among them.

[1] *Cf.* Tha'âlibi, pp. 746-747; Ṭabari, vol. i, pp. 2879-2881.

INDEX

Abân b. Sa'îd, 124, 162, 174
Abân b. 'Uthmân, 82
Abân b. al-Walîd, 294
Abân b. Yaḥya, 184
Abânain, 147
Abarwîz, 160, 277, 390, 441, 453, 455
'Abbâs b. al-Walîd, 263, 294
abu-l-'Abbâs as-Saffâḥ, 104, 233, 256, 282, 300, 328, 361, 368, 445, 446
al-'Abbâs b. 'Abd-al-Muṭṭalib, 20, 49, 63, 69, 86, 124, 409
al-'Abbâs b. Jaz', 226
al-'Abbâs b. Muḥammad, 288
al-'Abbâs b. Zufar, 225
al-'Abbâsîyah, 371
al-'Abbâsîyah (built by Hizâr-mard), 369
'Abd-al-'Azîz b. Ḥaiyân, 258
'Abd-al-'Azîz b. Ḥâtim, 321
'Abd-al-'Azîz b. Marwân, 360, 362
'Abd-al-Ḥamîd b. Yaḥya, 368, 466
'Abd b. al-Julanda, 116, 118
'Abd-al-Ḳais, 120, 130
'Abd-al-Malik b. Marwân, 54, 59, 75, 82, 83, 135, 180, 192, 195, 202, 219, 220, 221, 226, 238, 247, 248, 249, 250, 255, 282, 283, 294, 301, 321, 322, 341, 360, 383-385, 449, 450
'Abd-al-Malik b. Muslim, 324
'Abd-al-Malik b. Ṣâliḥ, 203, 238, 262, 289
'Abd-al-Malik b. Shabîb, 21
'Abd-al-Masîḥ b. 'Amr, 390
'Abd-al-Masîḥ b. Buḳailah, 435
'Abd-al-Muṭṭalib, 60, 77
'Abd-ar-Raḥmân b. 'Auf, 34, 424
'Abd-ar-Raḥmân b. abi-Bakr, 135, 356
'Abd-ar-Raḥmân b. Ghanm, 224
'Abd-ar-Raḥmân b. Ḥabîb, 367, 368
'Abd-ar-Raḥmân b. Isḥâḳ, 446
'Abd-ar-Raḥmân b. Muḥammad, 104, 455, 465
'Abd-ar-Raḥmân b. Zaid, 356
'Abd-aṣ-Ṣamad b. 'Ali, 25
'Abd-al-Wahhâb b. Ibrâhîm, 291-292, 293
'Abd-al-Wâḥid b. al-Ḥârith, 283
banu-'Abd-ad-Dâr, 78, 81
'Abdallâh b. 'Abbâs, 30
'Abdallâh b. 'Abd-al-A'la, 396
'Abdallâh b. 'Abd-al-Malik, 255, 289
'Abdallâh b. 'Abdallâh, 129, 139
'Abdallâh b. 'Ali, 193, 233, 300, 455
'Abdallâh b. 'Âmir, 490
'Abdallâh b. 'Amr, 216, 217, 338, 352, 356, 358
'Abdallâh b. Bishr, 237
'Abdallâh b. Budail, 485-487, 490
'Abdallâh b. Darrâj, 450, 454
'Abdallâh b. abi-Farwah, 397
'Abdallâh b. al-Ḥabḥâb, 367
'Abdallâh b. Ḥadhaf, 127
'Abdallâh b. al-Ḥârith b. Ḳais, 139
'Abdallâh b. al-Ḥârith b. Naufal, 82
'Abdallâh b. Ḥasan, 446
'Abdallâh b. Ḥâtim, 321
'Abdallâh b. Ḥudhâfah, 341, 347, 453
'Abdallâh b. Ḳais, 375

'Abdallâh b. Khâlid, 74
'Abdallâh b. Mas'ûd, 133, 143, 427, 431-432, 477
'Abdallâh b. Mûsa, 366
'Abdallâh b. ar-Rabî', 105
'Abdallâh b. Rawâḥah, 44, 47, 48
'Abdallâh b. Sa'd, 337, 340, 350-351, 356-359, 379-380
'Abdallâh b. Sibâ', 80
'Abdallâh b. Sufyân, 83
'Abdallâh b. Suhail, 129
'Abdallâh b. Ṭâhir, 256, 283, 289
'Abdallâh b. 'Umar, see b. 'Umar
'Abdallâh b. Wahb, 140
'Abdallâh b. Zaid b. 'Abdallâh, 120
'Abdallâh b. Zaid b. 'Âṣim, 135, 140
'Abdallâh b. Zaid b. Tha'labah, 135
'Abdallâh b. az-Zubair b. al-'Auwâm, 74, 75, 76, 82, 219, 220, 247, 289, 322, 337, 356, 360
'Abdallâh b. az-Zubair b. 'Abd-al-Muṭṭalib, 174
umm-'Abdallâh, 311
'Âbidîn, 232
al-Abnâ', 160-162
Abyssinia (al-Ḥabashah), 49, 118
Acre ['Akka], 179, 180, 181, 220
'Adan, 107
Adhanah, 260
Adharbaijân, 319, 321, 324, 328, 472, 483
Adhramah, 281
Adhri'ât, 105, 193, 214-215
Adhruḥ, 92-94, 105
'Adi b. 'Adi, 322
'Adi b. Arṭât, 118
'Adi b. Ḥâtim, 141, 432
'Adi b. Zaid, 446
Aflaḥ b. 'Abd-al-Wahhâb, 371
al-Aghlab b. Sâlim, 369-370, 375
Aḥmad b. Muḥammad, 375
al-Aḥnaf b. Ḳais, 485, 487
al-Ahwâz, 139, 449, 455, 479, 487
al-Aḥwâz, 283, 485
Ailah, 92-94, 105, 166
'Ain al-Jamal, 461, 462
'Ain ar-Raḥbah, 463
'Ain ar-Rûmîyah, 281-282
'Ain aṣ-Ṣaid, 461, 462-463
'Ain as-Sallaur, 228
'Ain Shams, 341
'Ain at-Tamr, 30, 96, 169, 218, 302, 392, 394-400, 407
'Ain al-Wardah, *s. v.* Ra's al-'Ain
'Ain Zarbah, 264
al-'Ain al-Ḥâmiḍah, 275
'Â'ishah, daughter of Hishâm, 282
'Â'ishah ("the Mother of the Believers"), 21, 26, 40, 51, 70, 75, 135, 144
'Â'ishah b. Numair, 30
Aiyûb b. abi-Aiyûb, 184
abu-Aiyûb Khâlid, 19, 237
umm-Aiyûb, 447
Ajamat Burs, 432
Ajnâdîn (Ajnâdain), 174-175, 183, 208, 215, 216
Ajyâd, 81
'Aḳabat Baghrâs, 258
'Aḳabat an-Nisâ', 258-259
al-'Aḳiḳ, 20, 27, 28, 39
'Akk, 31, 32
b. al-'Akki, 370
'Aḳûbah, 357
al-'Alâ' b. 'Abdallâh, 120, 121, 122, 123, 124, 127, 128, 129, 130, 131, 137
al-'Alâ' b. Aḥmad, 331
al-'Alâ' b. Wahb, 481-482
Aleppo [Ḥalab], 207, 224-226, 229
Alexandretta [Iskandarûnah], 249, 253
Alexandria [al-Iskandarîyah], 228, 338, 340, 344, 346-351, 352
'Ali b. Hishâm, 488-489
'Ali b. al-Ḥusain, 344
'Ali b. Sulaimân, 280, 296, 297

'Ali b. abi-Ṭâlib, 29, 52, 54, 62, 67, 94, 101, 103, 286, 321, 322, 358, 409, 423, 428, 432, 463, 479
'Ali b. Yaḥya, 263
'Alḳamah b. 'Ulâthah, 197
Âlûsah, 279
Alyûnah, 336, 338, 339, 347
'Amawâs [Emmaus], 213, 215, 270
Âmid, 275, 278, 288
'Âmir b. Fuhairah, 26
'Âmir b. abi-Waḳḳâṣ, 176, 208
abu-'Âmir al-Ash'ari, 85
abu-'Âmir ar-Râhib, 16, 17
banu-'Âmir b. Ṣa'ṣa'ah, 147
'Amḳ Mar'ash, 294, 295, 296
'Amḳ Tizîn, 249, 250
'Ammâr b. Yâsir, 279, 425, 427, 431, 440, 469, 471, 481
'Ammûrîyah, 225, 254, 258, 299
'Amr b. 'Abdallâh, 118, 119
'Amr b. al-'Âṣi, 116, 117, 118, 140, 147, 165-167, 178, 179, 186, 201, 213, 215, 216, 217, 219, 335-345, 346-351, 352-353, 355, 358, 379, 380
'Amr b. Ḥazm, 107, 108
'Amr b. Ḥuraith, 436, 476
'Amr b. al-Jârûd, 133
'Amr b. Ma'dikarib, 183, 185, 412, 413, 415, 420, 439
'Amr b. Mu'âwiyah, 321
'Amr b. Muḍâḍ, 81
'Amr b. Sa'îd al-Ashdaḳ, 184
'Amr b. Sa'îd b. al-'Âṣi, 58, 174, 247
'Amr b. Sâlim, 60, 61
'Amr b. Umaiyah, 34
'Amr b. 'Utbah, 421
'Amr b. az-Zubair, 29
banu-'Amr b. 'Auf, 16
banu-'Amr b. Lu'ai, 135
banu-'Amr b. Mu'âwiyah, 153, 156-157
abu-'Amrah, 396
Anas b. Mâlik, 48, 396
Anas b. Sîrîn, 396
'Ânât, 279, 284
al-Anbâr, 32, 279, 394-395, 432, 433, 434, 445, 449, 488
'Anbasah b. Sa'îd, 184, 442
al-Andalus [Andalusia], 355, 365-372
b. al-Andarz'azz, 402
'Ans, 159
Anṭâbulus, 342, 352
Anṭarṭûs, 205
Antioch [Anṭâkiyah], 175, 176, 180, 189, 202, 207, 209, 211, 213, 226-231, 246, 248, 249, 250, 253, 254, 255, 256, 257, 258, 259, 263, 336
Anûshirwân, 306-308, 324-325, 403, 453, 454
al-'Arabah, 168
al-'Arabâya, 460
Arabia, 13, 103
'Arafah, 61, 62, 77
'Arâjin, 231
Arakah (Arak), 171
'Arandal, 193
Arâshah, of the Bali, 362, 397
'Arbassûs, 241, 242
Ardabîl, 323, 328
al-Arḥaḍîyah, 28
'Arîb b. 'Abd-Kulâl, 109
al-'Arim, *s. v.* Sudd
al-'Arîsh, 335
Arjîl al-Kubra, 329
Arjîl aṣ-Ṣughra, 329
Arjîsh, 305, 313
Armaniyâḳus, 305, 309, 310
Armenia, 207, 231, 275, 300, 305-332
Arrân, 305, 306, 311, 318, 319, 332
al-'Arṣah, 30
Arṭahâl, 318
Arwa, daughter of 'Abd-al-Muṭṭalib, 174
abu-Arwa ad-Dausi, 166

Arwâd, 376
Arzan, 275
Asad b. 'Abdallâh, 445
abu-l-Asad, 455, 456
banu-Asad b. Khuzaimah, 145, 148, 278
al-Asbadhi, 120
Asbânbur, 434
Asbina, 431, 432
al-Ash'ath b. Ḳais b. Ma'dikarib, 153-158, 208, 211, 321, 412, 422, 432, 472, 475
b. al-Ash'ath, 104
al-Ashbân [Spaniards], 365
Ashnâs, 460
Ashûsh, 314
Ashûṭ b. Ḥamzah, 331
Asia Minor [Bilâd ar-Rûm, Byzantine Empire], 195, 207, 209, 232, 239, 253, 254, 260, 261, 263, 284, 285, 289, 290, 294, 296, 298, 299, 310, 384
Asîd b. Zâfir, 325
'Âṣim b. Murrah, 484
'Âṣim b. 'Umar, 356
'Asḳalân, 219, 221-222
al-Aswad al-'Ansi, 156, 159-162
'Attâb b. Asîd, 66, 87
al-Aus, 33
Auṭâs, 85
'Auwâm b. 'Abd-Shams, 415
al-Auzâ'i, 71, 114, 190, 214, 240, 242, 243, 286
al-'Awâsim, 202-203, 223-234, 253, 301
Azâdbih, 390
al-Azd, 31, 32, 33, 116, 117, 390, 405, 442
Azdisâṭ, 314
Azrah b. Ḳais, 469

Bâb Bâriḳah, 306-307
Bâb al-Fîl, 446-447
Bâb al-Lâl, 318
Bâb al-Lân, 306, 307, 325, 328
Bâb Samsakhi, 307
Bâb ash-Shâm, 282, 447
al-Bâb wa-l-Abwâb, 306, 319, 324, 325, 327, 328
al-Bâb ash-Sharḳi, 186, 187, 189, 190
Bâbil, 422, 432
Bâdhâm, 161
Bâḍi', 414
Badlîs, 275, 331
Badr, 129
Bâdûraiya, 408, 458
Baghdâd (Baghdâdh, or Madînat as-Salâm), 262, 263, 280, 282, 288, 395, 445, 446, 447, 457-464, 482, 484
Baghrâs, 228, 258
Baghrawand, 305
al-Baḥrain, 120-131, 140
Bahrâm Jûr, 446
Bahurasîr, 417, 428, 434
al-Bailaḳân, 306, 318, 321, 322, 323, 328, 329
Baisân, 179
Bait 'Ainûn, 197
Bait Jabrîn, 213
Bait Lihya, 200
Bait Mâma, 245
Bait Râs, 179
Bâjarma, 422
Bâjarwân, 328
Bajîlah, 405, 407, 424-425
Bâjuddah, 272
Bâjunais, 305, 313
al-Bâḳ, 331
Bakkâr b. Muslim, 329
Bakr b. Wâ'il, 120, 388, 395
abu-Bakr b. Muḥammad, 71
abu-Bakr aṣ-Ṣiddîḳ, 20, 26, 28, 34, 38, 39, 46, 49, 51, 52, 53, 54, 61, 73, 84, 96, 101, 107, 112, 117, 124, 127, 128, 129, 130, 134, 136, 137, 141, 143-150, 153-155, 160, 162,

165-167, 169, 175, 213, 218, 375, 387, 389, 393, 397, 398
banu-Bakr, 61
abu-Bakrah b. Masrûḥ, 85
Ba'labakk, 171, 180, 198, 201, 228, 236, 245, 247, 251
al-Balanjar, 319, 320, 415
al-Balâsajân, 319
Baldah, 204
Bâlis, 231-233
al-Balḳâ', 173, 193, 197
Bana, 342
al-Bandanijain, 421
Bâniḳiya, 392-394, 403, 404
Barâ' b. Mâlik, 130, 131
al-Baradân, 399
Bârah, 371
Bardha'ah, 305, 318, 319, 320, 321, 322, 324, 325, 329
Bâriḳ, 184
Barḳah (in Africa), 352-354, 360, 371
Barr b. Ḳais, 353
al-Barrîyah, 281
al-Barshaliyah, 307
Bârûsma, 402
Barzah, 186
abu-Barzah-l-Aslami, 66
al-Basharûdât, 342
Bashîr b. al-Audaḥ, 158
Bashîr b. Sa'd, 392, 398
al-Baṣrah, 82, 114, 116, 117, 118, 124, 139, 151, 180, 228, 264, 300, 375, 388, 396, 405, 410, 411, 436, 437, 441, 449, 455, 471, 476, 490
al-Baṭâ'iḥ, 264, 452, 453-456
al-Bathanîyah, 193
Baṭiḥân, Baṭḥân or Buṭḥân, 22, 25, Wâdi—26
Baṭn Marr, 32
al-Baṭrîḳ b. an-Naka, 220
al-Ba'ûḍah, 149
Bawâzîj al-Anbâr, 395
Bawâzîj al-Mulk, 422
Bâzabda, 275
Bâzalît, 318
al-Bazzâḳ, 451
Beirût, 194
Berbers, 123, 253-254, 360, 361, 366, 368, 369
Bihjâwarsân, 487
al-Bihḳubâdhât, 428
Biḳrâṭ b. Ashûṭ, 289
Bilâl, 26
Bilhît, 340
al-Bîma, 351
Bishr b. Maimûn, 282, 459
Bishr b. Ṣafwân, 366, 367
Bisṭâm, 416
Bisṭâm b. Narsi, 422
Biyamand, 490
Bugha (a freedman of al-Mu'taṣim), 319
Bugha-l-Kabîr, 331-332
al-Bujah, 381, 382
Bûḳa, 229, 246, 250, 259
Buḳailah, 392
Bukh, 309
Buḳrâṭ b. Ashûṭ, 331
Bulunyâs, 205
Bûrân, 406
Burs, 410, 416
Buṣbuhra b. Ṣalûba, 392-393, 421
al-Busfurrajân, 305, 307, 313, 315, 331
Bushair b. Yasâr, 45, 46, 47
Bûṣîr, 342
Busr b. abi-Arṭât, 172, 356, 357, 358
Buṣra, 171, 172, 173, 193, 234
al-Buṭâḥ, 149
Buṭnân Ḥabîb, 229
al-Buwaib, 406
Buwailis, 232
al-Buwairah, 36
Buzâkhah, 144, 145, 147
Byzantine Empire, *s. v.* Asia Minor

Constantine [Ḳusṭantîn b. Alyûn], 287, 290-291, 293, 299
Constantine, son of Heraclius, 347
Constantinople, 179, 207, 209, 347, 376
Copts, 339, 340, 342, 343, 344, 346, 347, 383
Cordova [Ḳurṭubah], 365
Crete [Iḳrîṭish], 376
Cyprus [Ḳubrus], 180, 235-243

Dabba, 117
banu-Ḍabbah, 397
Dâbiḳ, 264, 295
Dabîl, 305, 312, 314-315, 321, 330
Dâdhawaih, 161, 162
aḍ-Ḍaḥḥâk b. Ḳais, *s. v.* al-Aḥnaf
aḍ-Ḍaḥḥâk al-Khâriji, 328
Dailam, 441
ad-Dailam, 441
Dair al-A'war, 406, 443
Dair Hind, 406, 443
Dair al-Jamâjim, 431, 443
Dair Ka'b, 417, 443
Dair Khâlid, 186, 198
Daḳûḳa, 422
Ḍamâlu, 263-264
Damascus [Dimashḳ], 167, 172, 173, 176, 178, 182, 183, 186-199, 200, 201, 202, 216, 217, 219, 301, 320, 366, 480
Damîrah, 342
Dâr al-'Ajalah, 80-81
Dâr al-Ḳawârîr, 78, 80-81
Dâr an-Nadwah, 80-81
Dâra, 275
Daraulîyah, 255
Darb al-Ḥadath, 295, 296, 298
ad-Darb (Darb Baghrâs), 210, 254
abu-ad-Dardâ' 'Uwaimir, 186, 216, 217
Dârîn, 129, 130
Dârûsâṭ, 450
Dasht al-Warak, 313
ad-Daskarah, 421
Dastaba, 479
Dastumaisân, 454
Dâthin, 167
Dâ'ûd b.'Ali, 456
ad-Dauḳarah, 450
abu-Dharr al-Ghifâri, 237
abu-Dhu'aib Khuwailid, 356
Dhufâfah b. 'Umair, 324
Dîdûna, 317
Dijlah (district), 259
Dijlah, see Tigris
Dijlat al-Baṣrah, 388, 453
Diḳahlah, 342
Dimyâṭ, 342
Dînâr, 475-476
Dînâr b. Dînâr, 294
ad-Dînawar, 305, 469, 476, 478-480, 483
Ḍirâr b. al-Azwar, 149, 393, 394, 415
Diyâr Muḍar, 278
Diyâr Rabî'ah, 278, 281
ad-Dubbiyah (ad-Dâbiyah), 168
banu-Dûdân, 306
ad-Dûdânîyah, 306, 318, 328
abu-Dujânah Simâk, 35, 36, 37, 135, 139
abu-Dulaf al-Ḳâsim, 488
Dulûk, 202, 231, 297
Dûmat al-Ḥîrah, 96, 97, 400
Dûmat al-Jandal, 95-97, 171
Duraid b. aṣ-Ṣimmah, 85
ad-Durdhûḳîyah, 306
Durna, 389, 401
ad-Dustân, 244

Egypt (Miṣr), 20, 180, 191, 215, 216, 335-345, 351, 352, 353, 356, 358, 359, 360, 371, 372, 379, 381, 383
Euphrates [al-Furât], 232, 279, 284, 285, 293, 311, 403, 406, 410, 428, 432, 443, 445, 451, 453, 456

Fadak, 37, 50-56, 58
Faḍâlah b. 'Ubaid, 237
al-Fadhandûn, 460
al-Faḍl b. al-'Abbâs, 215
al-Faḍl b. Ḳârin, 206
al-Faḍl b. Rauḥ, 369
al-Faḍl b. Yaḥya, 330
al-Fâdûsafân, 486
Faid, 389, 405
Fairûz (*dihḳân*), 422
Fairûz b. ad-Dailami, 160-162
Fairûz b. Jushaish, 129
Fairûz b. Yazdajird, 493
al-Faiyûm, 341
Fakh, 79
Fâkhitah, daughter of 'Âmir, 129
Fâkhitah, daughter of Ḳaraẓah, 235
al-Falâlij, 394, 421
al-Fallûjatain, 407
Fâmiyah, 201-202
al-Farâfiṣah-l-Kalbîyah, 29
Faraj b. Sulaim, *s. v.* abu-Sulaim
Faranjah [France], 366
al-Farazdaḳ, 450
al-Farmâ', 335
Farrukhbundâdh, 392
Farwah b. Iyâs, 390
Farwah b. Musaik, 160
abu-Farwah 'Abd-ar-Raḥmân, 397
umm-Farwah, 155
al-Fasîlah, 229
Fâṭimah, 52, 53, 54, 55, 61, 99
al-Fauwârah, 175
abu-l-Fawâris, 262
banu-Fazârah, 146
Fiḥl, 176-177, 216
Filân, 309, 324, 327
al-Fujâ'ah, 149, 158
Fuḳair, 29
Furât b. Ḥaiyân, 141
al-Furu', 28, 29
al-Fusṭâṭ, 335, 336, 341, 347, 350
al-Ghâbah, 24
al-Ghâbah (the city of), 130
Ghâbat b. Hubairah, 282
umm-Ghaḍbân, 128
al-Ghamr, 147-148
al-Ghamr b. Yazîd, 282
banu-Ghanm b. 'Auf, 17
Ghassân, 32, 83, 96, 172, 209, 254, 442
Ghaṭafân, 144, 148
Ghazzah, 168, 213
Ghûmîk, 323
Ghurâbah, 141
Ghûrah, 141

Habbâr b. Sufyân, 174
Ḥabîb b. 'Abd-ar-Raḥmân, 368
Ḥabîb b. Maslamah, 208, 227, 229, 231, 241, 246, 273, 275, 287, 289, 296, 298, 309, 311-318, 320-321
Ḥabîb b. Zaid, 135, 140
umm-Ḥabîb aṣ-Ṣahbâ', 169
banu-Ḥabîbah, 93, 94
umm-Ḥabîbah, 208
Ḥabtar, 128
al-Hâdi, *s. v.* Mûsa
al-Ḥadîḳah, 135, 141
Ḥâḍir Ḥalab, 224-225
Ḥâḍir Ḳinnasrîn, 223
Ḥâḍir Ṭaiyi', 224-225
al-Ḥadîthah, 280
Ḥadîthat al-Mauṣil, 288, 311
al-Ḥaḍrah, 381
Ḥaḍramaut, 107, 112, 153, 156, 157
Ḥafṣ b. abi-l-'Âṣi, 125
abu-Ḥafṣ 'Umar b. 'Îsa, 376
Ḥaidar b. Kâwus, 330
al-Ḥâ'ir, 460
abu-l-Haitham Mâlik, 50
abu-l-Haiyâj al-Asadi, 435
Hajar, 110, 120, 121, 122, 123, 124
Ḥajar, 151
al-Ḥajjâj b. 'Atîk, 437
al-Ḥajjâj b. al-Ḥârith, 175

al-Ḥajjâj b. Yûsuf, 75, 76, 104, 110, 112, 250, 259, 366, 428, 431, 433, 449-450, 452, 454, 455, 456, 465, 466, 484
Ḥakam b. Sa'd al-'Ashîrah, 32
al-Ḥakam b. Mas'ûd, 404
umm-Ḥakîm, 182
Ḥalab as-Sâjûr, 231
Hamadhân, 410, 471, 481-484, 488
Ḥamâh, 201-202
Hamdân, 109, 160, 444
Ḥammâd al-Barbari, 78, 81
al-Ḥammârin, 82
Ḥamrâ' Dailam, 441
Ḥamzah b. 'Abd-al-Muṭṭalib, 80, 135
Ḥamzah b. Mâlik, 297
Ḥamzah b. an-Nu'mân, 58
Ḥamzîn, 323, 326
Hâni' b. Ḳabîṣah, 390
al-Hani wa-l-Mari, 280-281
umm-Hâni', 52
banu-Ḥanîfah, 133, 134, 135, 136
Ḥanẓalah, b. ar-Rabî', 394
Ḥanẓalah, b. Ṣafwân, 367
banu-Ḥanẓalah, 149, 150
al-Ḥarajah, 112
al-Harak, 313
al-Ḥaram, 70, 72, 73, 75, 76, 77, 82, 84
umm-Ḥarâm, 235, 237
Harim b. Ḥaiyân, 490
Ḥarîsh, 369-370
al-Ḥârith b. 'Abd-Kulâl, 109
al-Ḥârith b. 'Amr, 322
al-Ḥârith b. al-Ḥakam, 356
al-Ḥârith b. Hâni', 443
al-Ḥârith b. al-Ḥârith, 175
al-Ḥârith b. Hishâm, 175, 215
al-Ḥârith b. Khâlid, 83
al-Ḥârith b. abi-Shimr, 209
Ḥârithah b. Tha'labah, 33
banu-Ḥârithah, 24
al-Ḥarnâniyah, 272
al-Ḥarrah, 21, 22, 27, 30, 396
Ḥarrân, 272-274, 282, 291
Harthamah b. A'yan, 221, 261, 262, 370
Hârûn ar-Rashîd, 78, 81, 83, 105, 117, 202, 221, 224, 233, 238, 244, 252, 257, 260, 261, 263, 264, 280, 282, 283, 293, 297-298, 299, 300, 370, 376, 459, 460, 483
abu-Hârûn as-Sulami, 280
al-Hârûnîyah, 264
Ḥasan b. Ḥasan b. 'Ali, 463
al-Ḥasan b. 'Ali, 49, 99, 155
al-Ḥasan b. 'Ali-l-Bâdhaghîsi, 330
al-Ḥasan b. Ḳaḥṭabah, 261, 288, 292, 295, 296, 329
al-Ḥasan b. 'Umar, 281
Hâshim b. Ṣubâbah, 67
Hâshim b. 'Utbah, 208, 420-422, 469
al-Hâshimîyah, 300, 445-446
Ḥasmadân, 322
Ḥassân b. Mâhawaih, 258
Ḥassân b. Mâlik, 190
Ḥassân an-Nabaṭi, 454, 455
Ḥassân b. an-Nu'mân, 360
Ḥassân b. Thâbit, 36, 188, 218
Ḥâtim b. an-Nu'mân, 321, 322
abu-Ḥâtim as-Saddarâti, 369
Haudhah b. 'Ali, 132, 133
abu-l-Haul, 184
Ḥaurân, 173, 193, 197
Ḥawâriḥ, 317
Hawâzin, 85
Heraclius [Hiraḳl], 174, 175, 176, 177, 179, 182, 189, 200, 207, 210, 211, 253, 254, 344
Ḥibâl b. Khuwailid, 145
Ḥibra, 197
al-Ḥijâz, 31, 50, 57, 59, 112, 114, 157, 165, 168, 261, 286, 353, 381, 389
Hilâl b. 'Aḳḳah, 398
Hilâl b. Ḍaigham, 260

Hilâl b. 'Ullafah, 415
Ḥima an-Naḳî', 23
Ḥima ar-Rabadhah, 23
al-Ḥimâr, 210, 379
Ḥimṣ [Emesa], 174, 175, 180, 198, 200-206, 211, 212, 216, 217, 223, 228, 270, 275, 294, 295, 301, 320
Ḥimyar, 108, 109
Hind, daughter of 'Utbah, 207
Hind, daughter of Yâmîn, 155
al-Ḥîrah, 32, 96, 97, 169, 388, 389, 390, 391, 392, 393, 394, 398, 400, 403, 404, 407, 410, 421, 437, 442, 444, 447, 462, 475
Hishâm b. 'Abd-al-Malik, 83, 181, 238, 256, 258, 280, 282, 290, 323, 324, 325, 350, 360, 366, 367, 451, 454, 488
Hishâm b. al-'Âṣi, 147, 175
Ḥiṣn al-Ḥadath, 260, 282, 296-297
Ḥiṣn Ḳalûdhiyah, 291, 293
Ḥiṣn Kamkh, 287-288, 291
Ḥiṣn Maliḳiya, 408
Ḥiṣn Manṣûr, 299-300
Ḥiṣn Mâridîn, 275
Ḥiṣn Salmân, 230
al-Ḥiṣn b. Ma'bad, 407
Hît, 279, 280, 463
Ḥiyâr bani-l-Ḳa'ḳâ', 225-226
Ḥubâbah, 155
al-Ḥubal, 141
Ḥubâsh b. Ḳais, 210
al-Ḥudaibiyah, 45, 49, 60
Ḥudhaifah b. Miḥṣan, 117, 399-400
Ḥudhaifah b. al-Yamân, 320, 427, 430, 449, 472, 474, 475, 476, 477
abu-Ḥudhaifah b. al-Mughîrah, 74
abu-Ḥudhaifah b. 'Utbah, 138
al-Hudhail b. Ḳais, 488
Ḥujair, 138
Ḥujr b. 'Adi, 420, 470
abu-l-Ḥuḳaiḳ, 43, 47
Ḥukaim b. Sa'd, 443
Ḥulwân, 420, 421, 469-470, 471, 480, 490
Ḥumaid b. Ma'yûf, 238, 376
Ḥumrân b. Abân, 396
Ḥunain, 66, 85, 86
abu-Hurairah (ad-Dausi), 22, 30, 63, 64, 124, 125, 126
Ḥuraith b. 'Abd-al-Malik, 96
Ḥurḳûṣ b. an-Nu'mân, 170
Hurmuz (village), 431
al-Hurmuz, 314
b. Hurmuz al-A'raj, 350
al-Hurmuzân, 472
Hurmuzjarad, 389
al-Ḥuṣaid, 169
Ḥusail [Ḥisl] b. Jâbir, 477
Ḥusain b. Muslim, 263
al-Ḥusain b. 'Ali, 49, 99, 344, 393, 479
al-Ḥusain al-Khâdim, 283
al-Ḥusain b. Muḥammad, 112
al-Ḥusain b. Numair, 74, 75
al-Ḥuṭam, 127, 128
al-Ḥuwairith b. Nuḳaidh, 67
Ḥûwârîn, 171
Ḥuyai b. Akhṭab, 41, 43, 44

Ibrâhîm (son of the Prophet), 35, 344
Ibrâhîm b. 'Abdallâh, 446, 455, 457
Ibrâhîm b. al-Aghlab, 370, 371
Ibrâhîm b. al-Mahdi, 228
Ibrâhîm b. Sa'îd, 228
Ibrâhîm b. Salamah, 446
Idrîs b. Ma'ḳil, 488
Ifrîḳiyah, 337, 352, 355, 356-361, 362, 366, 367, 368, 369, 370
Ikhmîm, 340-341
'Ikrimah b. abi-Jahl, 117, 155, 174
Ilyâs b. Ḥabîb, 368
'Imrân b. Mujâlid, 371
al-'Irâḳ, 29, 79, 96, 102, 104, 129, 146, 155, 158, 167, 230, 231, 247, 261, 286, 387, 389, 391, 393, 401, 405, 406, 409, 415, 432, 433, 454, 465, 488
'Irḳah, 194

'Îsa b. 'Ali, 295, 452, 463
'Îsa b. Idrîs, 488
'Îsa b. Ja'far, 117
Iṣbahân, 365, 469, 471, 472, 485-489, 490
al-Isbîdhahâr, 475
Isḥâḳ b. Ibrâhîm, 462
Isḥâḳ b. Ismâ'îl, 330, 332
Isḥâḳ b. Muslim, 323, 328
Ismâ'îl b. 'Abdallâh, 366
Iṣṭakhr, 490
Iyâd, 169, 254, 443
'Iyâḍ b. Ghanm, 215, 216, 226, 227, 229, 230, 231, 269-278, 289, 296, 313
Iyâs b. Ḳabîṣah, 390

al-Jabal, *s. v.* al-Jibâl
Jabal al-Ahwâz, 437
Jabal al-Ḳabaḳ, 309
Jabalah, 204, 205
Jabalah b. al-Aiham, 207-210, 254
Jâbân, 389-390, 394, 401
al-Jâbiyah, 172, 186, 187, 188, 189, 190, 198, 214, 233
Jabr b. abi-'Ubaid, 404
Jabrîl b. Yaḥya, 257
Jabrîn, 230
Jadhîmah, 150
Ja'far, 38
Ja'far b. Sulaimân, 21, 76, 233
abu-Ja'far, *s. v.* al-Manṣûr
umm-Ja'far Zubaidah, *s. v.* Zubaidah
Jafrabâd, 487
Jai, 485, 487, 488
Jaifar, b. al-Julanda, 116, 118
Jaiḥân, 256, 293, 295
al-Jâlînûs, 401, 414, 416
Jalûlâ', 419, 420-433, 469
Jamîl b. Buṣbuhra, 421
al-Janad, 107
al-Janb, 454
al-Jâr, 341
al-Jarâjimah, 246-252, 258
Jarash, 179
al-Jarbâ', 92-94
al-Jardamân, 307, 318
Jarîr b. 'Abdallâh, 159, 160, 389, 392, 393, 395, 405-407, 421, 424, 425, 432, 469, 470, 472, 481
Jarjarâya, 398
al-Jarrâḥ b. 'Abdallâh, 317, 322-323
Jarshân, 309, 324
Jau Ḳurâḳir, 148
al-Jaulân, 179
Ja'wanah b. al-Ḥârith, 290, 323
al-Jazîrah, *s. v.* Mesopotamia
Jerusalem [Bait al-Muḳaddas, Îliyâ'], 15, 30, 182, 213-214, 217, 227, 300, 369
al-Jibâl or al-Jabal, 319, 324, 325, 393, 420, 449, 480, 482, 484, 488, 489
Jidh', 32
al-Jifshîsh al-Kindi, 154
Jisr Manbij, 232, 275
Jisr al-Walîd, 259-260
al-Jisr, 399, 403-404, 406. *Cf.* Ḳuss an-Nâṭif
Jordan [al-Urdunn], 167, 176, 178-181, 193, 201, 202, 216, 217, 244, 301
Jubail, 194
Judhâm, 92, 207, 218
al-Juḥâf w-al-Jurâf, 82
Juhainah, 184, 441
al-Junâbidh, 491
Junâdah b. abi-Umaiyah, 375-376
Jurash, 91
al-Jurf, 28, 39, 114, 165, 218
Jurhum, 31, 32, 74
al-Jurjûmah, 247, 249, 250
Jurna, 314
Jurwah al-Yamâmi, 477
Jurzân, 305, 306, 315, 316, 317, 330, 332

Juwâtha, 127, 128, 129, 140

Ka'b al-Ḥabr, 237
Ḳabalah, 306, 319
Ḳadas, 179
al-Ḳâdisîyah, 277, 404, 408, 409-416, 417-418, 424, 434, 439, 440, 441, 462
Kafarbaiya, 256, 257
Kafarjadda, 282
Kafarmara, 397
Kafarṭis, 349
Kafartûtha, 281
al-Kâhinah, 360
Ḳainuḳâ', 33
al-Ḳairawân, 357, 358, 361, 362, 367, 368, 369, 370, 371
Ḳais b. Hubairah, 160-162, 411
Ḳais b. Makhramah, 396
Ḳais b. Makshûḥ, 208, 414, 415
Ḳais b. Sa'd, 358
Ḳais b. Sakan, 116
Ḳaisârîyah, 216-220, 335
banu-l-Ḳa'ḳâ', 225-226
Ḳalarjît, 318
Kalb, 170, 391, 395
Ḳâliḳala, 289, 305, 309-310, 312-313, 320
Kalthûm b. Hidm, 15
Kalwâdha, 408
al-Ḳamîbarân, 306, 319
Ḳanâṭir an-Nu'mân, 479
Kanîsat aṣ-Ṣulḥ, 263
al-Kanîsat as-Saudâ', 264
dhu-Ḳâr, 462
al-Karaj, 488
Ḳarda, 275
Karkh Fairûz, 460, 461
Ḳarḳîsiya, 171, 274, 275, 279, 281
Karmân, 463, 486, 490
Ḳarmâsîn, 469
Karrâz an-Nukri, 130, 131
Ḳaryat abi-Ṣalâbah, 443
al-Ḳaryatain, 171
Ḳâshân, 485-489
al-Ḳâsim b. Rabî'ah, 321
Ḳâṣirîn, 231-232
Kaskar, 259, 389, 402, 407, 453, 454, 472
Ḳaṣr al-'Adasîyîn, 391, 444
al-Ḳaṣr al-Abyaḍ, 371, 391
al-Ḳaṣṣah, 144, 145
Kastasji, 318
Ḳaṭarghâsh, 258
Kathîr b. Shihâb, 416, 479, 480, 481
al-Katîbah, 45, 46, 49
al-Ḳaṭîf, 124, 129
Ḳaṭrabbul (or Ḳuṭrubbul), 400, 458
Ḳâṭûl Kisra, 461
al-Ḳâṭûl, 460
Ḳâṭûlah, 460
Ḳazwîn, 441
Khâbanjar, 483
Khabbâb b. al-Aratt, 431, 432
al-Khâbûr, 279
Khaffân, 387, 390, 399
Khaibar, 37, 41, 42-49, 50, 51, 52, 57, 58, 337
al-Khais, 340
Khaizân, 319, 320, 323, 324
al-Khaizurân, 433
Khâḳân, 308, 319
Khâḳân al-Khâdim, 483
Khâkhît, 318, 325
Khalfûn al-Barbari, 372
Khâlid b. 'Abdallâh, 437, 445, 450-451
Khâlid b. Mâlik, 159
Khâlid b. Sa'îd, 106, 107, 156, 160, 165, 166, 182, 183
Khâlid b. Thâbit, 214
Khâlid b. 'Umair, 324
Khâlid b. 'Urfuṭah, 413, 416, 419, 432
Khâlid b. al-Walîd, 63, 64, 65, 95, 96, 97, 118, 128, 129, 134, 136, 137, 145, 147-150, 158, 167-168,

169-172, 173, 174, 176, 178, 179, 186-191, 193, 198, 200, 223, 270, 277-278, 293, 387-400, 405
Khâlid b. Yazîd b. Mazyad, 330
Khâlid b. Yazîd b. Mu'âwiyah, 383
Khalîj Banât Nâ'ilah, 29
Khânîjâr, 422
Khânikîn, 420, 421, 430
Khârijah b. Ḥiṣn, 144, 145, 148
Khârijah b. Ḥudhâfah, 336, 341, 346
al-Khashârimah, 480
Khashram b. Mâlik, 480
Khashram as-Sulami, 327
b. Khaṭal al-Adrami, 66, 67
al-Khaṭṭ, 124, 129
Khaulân, 152, 157
Khauwât b. Jubair, 27
al-Khawarnaḳ, 446
al-Khazar, 305, 306, 309, 310, 319, 323, 324-327, 329
al-Khazraj, 19, 33
al-Khiḍrimah, 141
Khilâṭ, 275, 289, 305, 313, 322, 331
Khufâsh, 112
Khûkhîṭ, 318
Khumm, 77, 78
Khunân, 317
Khunâṣir b. 'Amr, 229
Khunâṣirah, 229
al-Khuraibah, 388
Khuraim b. Aus, 392
Khurâsân, 151, 205, 261, 262, 280, 292, 293, 297, 328, 368, 369, 446, 457, 459, 460, 484, 491
Khurrazâd, 420
Khurzâd b. Mâhibundâdh, 399
al-Khuṣûṣ, 256
Khuṭarniyah, 422
Khuzâ'ah, 33, 60, 61, 62, 63, 64, 240
Khuzaimah b. Khâzim, 330
dhu-l-Kilâ', 263
al-Kilâb, 307, 324
banu-Kilâb, 34
Kinânah, 60, 61
Kindah, 107, 153, 154, 156, 157, 169, 211, 369
Ḳinnasrîn, 202, 211, 213, 214, 217, 223-234, 254, 259, 270, 294, 296, 297, 301
al-Kiryaun, 346, 349
Kisâl, 317, 325
Kisra, 124, 129, 160, 390, 405, 406, 419, 430, 431, 432
Ḳu'aiḳi'ân, 81
Ḳubâ', 15, 16, 17, 18
Ḳubâdh b. Fairûz, 305-306, 453
Ḳubâḳib, 292
Ḳubbash, 197
Ḳudâmah b. Maẓ'ûn, 125
al-Kûfah, 97, 102, 103, 104, 105, 133, 155, 169, 180, 211, 212, 228, 279, 300, 310, 320, 388, 396, 405, 411, 415, 427, 434-448, 449, 450, 455, 457, 464, 469, 471, 472, 475, 476, 479, 480, 481, 482, 488
Ḳuḥuwîṭ, 317
Kulthûm b. 'Iyâḍ, 360, 367
al-Ḳulzum, 358, 381
Ḳûmis, 471
Ḳumm, 485-489
Ḳura 'Arabîyah, 53, 143
Ḳuraish, 60, 61, 62, 63, 64, 65, 68, 74, 75, 77, 80, 86, 105, 112, 133, 475
banu-Ḳuraiẓah, 25, 40-41
Ḳurâḳir, 169, 170
Kurdbandâdh, 434
Kurds, 319, 482
al-Kurr, 319, 323
Ḳurrah b. Hubairah, 147
Ḳurṭ b. Jammâḥ, 407, 415
Ḳurṭubah, see Cordova
Ḳûrus, 202, 230
Kurz b. 'Alḳamah, 84
umm-Kurz, 424
Ḳuṣai b. Kilâb, 77, 80
Ḳuṣam, 171

Kûsân al-Armani, 312
al-Kûshân, 244
Ḳuss an-Nâṭif, 403-404
Kûtha, 408, 418, 422, 428
Ḳutham b. Ja'far, 54
al-Ḳuṭḳuṭânah, 461
Kuwaifah, 434, 437

Labbah, 16
al-Lâdhiḳîyah, 203-205
Laila (daughter of al-Jûdi), 96-97
Laila-l-Akhyalîyah, 484
b. abi-Laila, 71, 73, 89, 90, 113, 114, 286
al-Laith b. Sa'd, 238
Lakhm, 92, 207, 362, 443
Laḳîṭ b. Mâlik, 117
al-Lakz, 309, 322, 326, 327
Lîrân, 309, 324
Ludd [Lydda], 213, 220
dhât-al-Lujum, 314-315
Luwâtah, 353-354

Ma'âb, 173
Ma'arrat Miṣrîn, 229
Ma'arrat an-Nu'mân, 202
Ma'bad b. al-'Abbâs, 356, 359
al-Madâ'in, 262, 416, 417-419, 420, 421, 430, 434, 435, 437, 441-442, 446, 449, 462, 490
al-Madhâr, 389, 405
Mâdharân, 482
Madhḥij, 160, 183, 323
Madh'ûr b. 'Adi, 387
al-Ma'din, 381
al-Madînah, 15, 27, 30, 33, 54, 57, 61, 80, 81, 84, 117, 124, 127, 129, 136, 144, 146, 155, 158, 162, 165, 184, 208, 214, 270, 341, 350, 356, 387, 391, 410, 411, 440, 451, 462, 472, 477
Madînat as-Salâm, *s. v.* Baghdâd
al-Mafâzah, 484
al-Maghrib, 256, 335-345, 349, 352-353, 356, 358, 359, 366, 367, 368, 369, 370, 371, 372, 396
Magians, 110, 118, 120, 121, 123, 130, 314, 424, 441
Mâh al-Baṣrah [Nihâwand], 476, 482
Mâh Dinâr, 476
Mâh al-Kûfah [ad-Dînawar], 476
al-Mâhain, 471, 480
Mâhawaih, 491, 492
al-Mahdi, 21, 76, 184, 223, 252, 257, 260, 261, 263, 264, 280, 295, 296, 297, 300, 381, 429, 433, 451, 457, 459, 482, 483
al-Mahdîyah, 297
Mahrûbah, 226
Mahrûdh, 421
al-Mâḥûzah, 461
Maimadh, 324
Maimûn (village), 451
Maimûn b. Ḥamzah, 282
Maimûn al-Jurjumâni, 248
al-Maimûn (canal), 451
Maisarah b. Masrûḳ, 254, 270
Maiyâfâriḳîn, 275
Majâz al-Andalus, 365
Ma'ḳil b. Yasâr, 472, 473
Makkah, 15, 16, 19, 21, 27, 32, 33, 47, 60-76, 77-81, 82-83, 86, 87, 88, 129, 146, 165, 184, 240, 451, 457, 459
Maḳna, 92-94
al-Maḳsalâṭ, 188, 190
Malaṭyah, 287, 288, 289-293, 297, 312
Mâlik b. 'Abdallâh, 298
Mâlik b. Anas, 238
Mâlik al-Ashtar, 254, 358
Mâlik b. 'Auf, 85, 101
Mâlik b. Murârah, 107, 108
Mâlik b. Nuwairah, 149-150
al-Ma'mûn, 54, 56, 83, 141, 229, 233, 256, 257, 281, 289, 299, 330, 376, 446, 460, 484, 488

Manbij, 202, 203, 231, 293, 298
Mandal al-'Anazi, 261, 296
Manjalis, 316, 317
Manṣûr b. Ja'wanah, 299-300
Manṣûr b. al-Mahdi, 228
al-Manṣûr, 76, 78, 238, 251, 256, 257, 259, 260, 280, 288, 291, 292, 295, 299, 300, 312-313, 328, 329, 341, 360, 368, 369, 397, 429, 433, 445, 446, 448, 455, 457-459, 482
Manuwîl, 347-348
Manẓûr b. Zabbân, 144
Mârabîn, 488
Maraḳîyah, 205
Mar'ash, 231, 293-295
Mardânshâh, 403, 410, 471, 472, 473
Mardânshâh b. Zâdân, 466
Ma'rib, 111
Marj 'Abd-al-Wâḥid, 282-283, 298
Marj Dabîl, 314
Marj al-Ḥaṣa, 312
Marj Ḥusain, 263
Marj Râhiṭ, 172
Marj aṣ-Ṣuffar, 174, 182-185, 186, 216
Marj Ṭarsûs, 261
Martaḥwân, 229
Maru, 491, 492
Maru ar-Rûdh, 369
al-Marwah, 71
dhu-l-Marwah, 29, 166
al-Marwaḥah, 403
Marwân b. al-Ḥakam, 20, 54, 79, 84, 184, 294, 356, 360
Marwân b. Muḥammad, 193, 205, 231, 256, 259, 294-295, 296, 299, 314, 325-328, 368, 445, 466, 488
al-Marzubânah, Bâdhâm's wife, 160
Mâsabadhân, 459, 478-480
banu-Mashja'ah, 171
Mashra'at (or Furḍat) al-Fîl, 452
Masḳaṭ, 306, 309, 319, 324
Maskin, 400
Maslamah b. 'Abd-al-Malik, 228-229, 232, 233, 248, 249, 258, 288, 323-325, 456
Maslamah b. Mukhallad, 359
Mass, 488
al-Maṣṣîṣah, 254, 255-259, 260, 264
al-Mauriyân ar-Rûmi, 312
al-Mauṣil, 261, 277, 400, 458
Mâyanharaj, 483
Mâyazdiyâr b. Ḳârin, 206
al-Mâziḥîn, 278
Mesopotamia [al-Jazîrah], 176, 191, 202, 207, 251, 254, 269-283, 287, 289, 290, 291, 292, 294, 296, 297, 299, 300, 309, 312, 313, 314, 320, 328
Mid'am, 57
Midlâj b. 'Amr, 279-280
abu-Miḥjan b. Ḥabîb, 404, 414
Mihrân, 393, 405-408
Mihrijânḳadhaf, 478-480
Mîkhâ'îl, 295, 296
Miḳyas b. Ṣubâbah, 67
Mi'laḳ b. Ṣaffâr, 322
Milḥân b. Zaiyâr, 200
Mirbâla, 313
al-Miṣrain, 83, 449
Mt. Lebanon, 248, 250-251
Mt. al-Lukâm [Amanus], 246, 247
Mu'âdh b. Jabal, 107, 108, 109, 110, 111, 215, 233-234, 242, 375
Mu'âwiyah b. Ḥudaij, 347, 357, 358, 359, 375, 380
Mu'âwiyah b. abi-Sufyân, 54, 59, 64, 79, 84, 86, 103, 135, 151, 155, 179, 180, 183, 184, 191, 194-197, 204, 205, 213, 216-219, 227, 228, 235-238, 250, 255, 269, 271, 278-279, 287, 289, 293, 309, 310, 311, 320, 321, 341, 342, 344, 357, 358, 359, 375, 376, 441, 450, 454, 463, 464, 470, 476, 479
Mu'âwiyah b. Yazîd, 359
al-Mubarak aṭ-Ṭabari, 55, 56

Mudhainib, 25, 26
al-Muffarraj b. Sallâm, 372
al-Mughîrah b. abi-l-'Âṣi, 125
al-Mughîrah b. Shu'bah, 101, 321, 410-412, 427, 436, 440, 441, 447, 450, 463, 464, 472, 473, 475, 479, 481
Muḥaiyiṣah b. Mas'ûd, 50, 51
abu-l-Muhâjir, 359
al-Muhâjir b. abi-Umaiyah, 106, 107, 154-157, 160, 162
Muḥakkim [Muḥakkam] al-Yamâmah, 134-136
Muḥammad b. al-'Abbâs, 484
Muḥammad b. 'Abdallâh b. 'Abd-ar-Raḥmân, 288-289
Muḥammad b. 'Abdallâh b. Ḥasan, 446, 457
Muḥammad b. 'Abdallâh b. al-Ḥasan b. 'Ali, 55, 56
Muḥammad b. 'Abdallâh al-Ḳummi, 381-382
Muḥammad b. 'Abdallâh b. Sa'îd, 184
Muḥammad b. al-Aghlab, 371
Muḥammad b. al-Ash'ath, 155, 288, 361, 368
Muḥammad b. abi-Bakr, 358
Muḥammad b. abi-Ḥudhaifah, 357, 358
Muḥammad b. Ibrâhîm, 293, 297, 298, 299
Muḥammad b. Isḥâḳ, 396
Muḥammad b. al-Ḳâsim, 250, 259, 452
Muḥammad b. Marwân, 202, 294, 314, 321, 322, 399
Muḥammad b. Maslamah, 51, 344-345, 392, 438
Muḥammad b. al-Murtafi', 30
Muḥammad b. Sa'îd, 184
Muḥammad b. Yaḥya, 55
Muḥammad b. Yazîd, 330
Muḥammad b. Yûsuf ath-Thaḳafi, 112
al-Muḥammadîyah, 296
Mujâhid b. Jabr, 376
Mujâshi' b. Mas'ûd, 490
Mujjâ'ah b. Murârah, 132, 134, 136-137, 141
al-Muka'bar al-Fârisi, 129, 130, 131
al-Muḳauḳis, 339, 340, 343, 346-348
al-Mukhabbil, 83
Mukhairîḳ, 35
Mukharrim b. Ḥazn, 399
al-Mukhtâr b. abi-'Ubaid, 439, 479
Muks, 313
Mulûk aṭ-Ṭawâ'if, 309
al-Mundhir b. Ḥassân, 407
al-Mundhir b. Mâ' as-Samâ', 225
al-Mundhir b. an-Nu'mân, 127, 128
al-Mundhir b. Sâwa, 120, 123, 127
al-Muntaṣir, 372
Mûrah, 258
Murrah b. abi-Murrah, 483
Mûsa b. Bugha, 206, 489
Mûsa-l-Hâdi, 184, 185, 297, 369, 459
Mûsa b. Nuṣair, 358, 362, 365-366, 396, 397
abu-Mûsa-l-Ash'ari, 79, 85, 107, 267, 410, 411, 469, 478, 479, 485, 487, 490
al-Muṣ'ab b. az-Zubair, 247
al-Muṣafir al-Ḳaṣṣâb, 328
Musailimah al-Kadhdhâb, 128, 132-140, 151, 159
al-Musaiyab b. Zuhair, 293, 297
Mûshâ'îl al-Armani, 329
Muslim b. 'Abdallâh, 180, 228
al-Musta'în, 372
Mu'tah, 138, 195
Mu'tamir b. Sulaimân, 261, 296
Mutammam b. Nuwairah, 149-150
al-Mu'taṣim, 206, 221, 225, 256, 257, 258, 259, 264, 299, 312-313, 446, 460, 461

al-Mutawakkil, 21, 56, 76, 81, 225, 229, 245, 249-250, 252, 263, 265, 287, 331, 372, 375, 381-382, 460, 461
al-Mutawakkiliyah, 319, 461
al-Mu'tazz, 489
al-Muthanna b. Ḥârithah, 169, 387-388, 390, 394, 395, 399, 400, 401-402, 404, 409-410, 413
Muzaiḳiya, 31

Nabateans, 247, 248, 250, 289, 417
Nâbulus, 213, 245
banu-an-Naḍîr, 33, 34-39, 43, 51
Nafîs b. Muḥammad, 30, 396
Nahr al-Amîr, 452
Nahr ad-Damm, 390
Nahr Durḳiṭ, 428
Nahr Maḥdûd, 433
Nahr al-Malik, 408, 422, 428
Nahr al-Mar'ah, 389
Nahr Maslamah, 232
Nahr Sa'd, 432
Nahr Sa'îd, 280
Nahr Shaila, 433
Nahr aṣ-Ṣilah, 451
Nahr aṣ-Ṣîn, 450
an-Nahrain, 407, 421, 431
umm-Nahshal, 82
Najd, 134, 165, 462
Najrân, 29, 32, 76, 98-105, 107, 157, 240
an-Najrâniyah, 102, 103
an-Nakhîrkhân, 417, 474
an-Namir b. Ḳâsiṭ, 398
an-Nashâstaj, 431, 432
an-Nashawa, 307, 315, 321, 330
Naṣîbîn, 274-275, 278-279
Naṣr b. Mâlik, 293
Naṣr b. Sa'd, 293
an-Naṭât, 45, 46
Nihâwand, 146, 471-477, 478, 481, 485, 490
Niḳâbulus, 230
an-Nîl, 450
Nîzak Ṭarkhân, 491
Nizâr, 435, 436
Nu'aim b. 'Abd-Kulâl, 109
Nu'aim b. Aus, 197
Nubia, 379-382
an-Nujair, 154, 155, 157, 158
an-Nukhailah, 393, 405-408, 410
an-Nu'mân Ḳail dhi-Ru'ain, 109
an-Nu'mân b. al-Mundhir, 127, 390, 394-395
an-Nu'mân b. Zur'ah, 284
Nuṣair abu-Mûsa, 396, 397
an-Nusair b. Daisam, 398-400

Orontes [al-Urunṭ or al-Urund], 200, 227

Palestine [Filasṭîn], 167, 168, 178, 193, 201, 202, 207, 213-222, 227, 232, 244, 301, 329, 353
Persians (Furs), 45, 63, 120, 123, 180, 306, 387, 389, 390, 391, 396, 401, 403, 407, 408, 409, 413, 414, 415, 416, 418, 419, 420, 421, 440, 441, 451, 453, 454, 455, 462, 471

Rabaḍ Ḥarrân, 282
Ra'bân, 202, 231, 297
Rabî'ah, 127, 128, 229, 372, 392, 399, 407
Rabî'ah b. Bujair, 169, 170
Rafaḥ, 213
ar-Râfiḳah, 280, 459
ar-Raḥbah, 281
Rahwat Mâlik, 298
ar-Rai, 410, 457, 471, 479, 484
ar-Raiya, 141, 142
ar-Rajjâl [Raḥḥâl] b. 'Unfuwah, 132, 133, 134
ar-Raḳḳah, 270-272, 274, 275, 278, 280, 281, 282, 290, 300, 322
ar-Ramlah, 220-221
Rammân, 147

Ra's al-'Ain, 275-277, 279
Râskifa, 274, 282
ar-Rass, 306, 319, 323
Rauḥ b. Ḥâtim, 297, 330, 369
"ar-Rawâdîf," 247, 250
Rhodes [Rûdis], 375-376
ar-Ribâb, 151, 446
ar-Ruha, 269, 272-275, 278, 282, 287, 300
ar-Rûmîyah, 419, 434
ar-Ruṣâfah, 446, 457
Ruṣâfat Hishâm, 280, 290
Rustam, 410-415, 420, 440, 441

Sabasṭiyah, 213
Sâbâṭ, 417, 419
as-Sâbûn, 129
Sâbûr, 433, 461
Sa'd b. 'Amr, 169, 279, 280, 432-433
Sa'd b. Khaithamah, 15, 16
Sa'd b. Mâlik, 431, 432
Sa'd b. Mu'âdh, 40, 41
Sa'd b. abi-Waḳḳâṣ, 23, 24, 176, 230, 409-414, 416, 417, 418, 419, 420, 421, 422, 425, 431, 432, 434, 435, 437-442, 449, 469, 481-482
aṣ-Ṣadif, 107, 156
aṣ-Ṣafa, 65, 71
Ṣafîyah, 43-44
aṣ-Ṣa'fûḳah, 142
Ṣafwân b. al-Mu'aṭṭal, 270, 273, 287, 288
Sahl b. Ḥunaif, 36, 37
Sahl b. Sanbâṭ, 330
as-Sâ'ib b. al-Aḳra', 471-472, 474, 478, 479, 486
as-Sâ'ib b. al-'Auwâm, 136, 138
Sa'îd b. 'Âmir, 270, 275, 278
Sa'îd b. 'Amr b. Aswad, 323-325, 484
Sa'îd b. 'Amr b. Sa'îd, 184
Sa'îd b. al-'Âṣi, 184, 310, 440
Sa'îd al-Khair b. 'Abd-al-Malik, 280
Sa'îd b. Sa'd, 81
Sa'îd b. Sâlim, 329, 330
as-Sailaḥîn, 394, 410
aṣ-Ṣaimarah, 478
Sajâḥ, 151
as-Sakûn, 153, 406
Salamyah, 205
Sala'ûs, 282
Ṣâliḥ b. 'Abd-ar-Raḥmân, 465, 466
Ṣâliḥ b. 'Ali, 205, 221, 251, 257, 260, 291, 295
Salîṭ b. Ḳais, 132, 401, 403, 405
Sallâm aṭ-Ṭaifûri, 482, 483
Salma, 413, 414
Salmân b. Rabî'ah, 230-231, 310-312, 318-320, 415
Samaritans, 217, 244-245
aṣ-Ṣamṣâmah sword, 183-185
as-Samûr, 323, 326
Ṣan'â', 106-107, 112, 156, 160, 162
aṣ-Ṣanârîyah, 318, 329
aṣ-Ṣarâh (canal), 396, 416, 446, 458
as-Sarât, 32, 405
as-Sarîr, 326
Sarjûn [Sergius], 301
Sarûj, 274, 282
as-Sawâd, 114, 387-400, 421, 422-431, 449, 461, 462, 463, 465
as-Sâwardîyah, 319, 443
as-Sayâbijah, 250
Sa'yah b. 'Amr, 43
Seleucia [Salûḳîyah], 228
Shabath b. Rib'i, 151, 444
ash-Shâbirân, 306, 319, 326
Shaila, 433
Shaizar, 201
abu-Shajarah 'Amr, 148
Shakkan, 319
abu-Shâkir, 83
ash-Shamâkhîyah, 329
Shamkûr, 319
ash-Sharât, 193-194
Sharwân, 306, 309, 319, 324, 327, 329

ash-Shiḳḳ, 45, 46
Shimshâṭ, 287, 289, 294, 297, 305, 319
Shîrawaih, 406
Shuraḥbîl b. Ḥasanah, 165-167, 177, 178, 179, 186, 190, 201, 215
Shuraḥbîl b. as-Simṭ, 211-212, 406
Shuraiḥ b. 'Âmir, 388-389
Shurât, 118, 328
Sicily [Siḳilliyah], 375
Sidon [Ṣaidâ'], 194
Siffîn, 232, 415
Sijistân, 465, 491
Simâk b. Kharashah, *s. v.* abu-Dujânah
Simâk b. 'Ubaid, 476
as-Simṭ b. al-Aswad, 200-201, 211, 212, 224
Sinân, 255
as-Sind, 250, 252
Sinjâr, 274, 276
Sinn Sumairah, 479
Sirâj Ṭair, 305, 314
as-Sîrawân, 478
Sîrîn abu-Muḥammad, 396, 398
as-Sîsajân, 305, 307, 315, 322, 328, 331, 332
Sîsar, 482-484
Sîsiyah (Sîs), 262
as-Siyâsîjûn, 306, 307, 309
Slavs [Ṣaḳâlibah], 231, 325
St. John's Cathedral, 191-192
as-Sudd al-'Arim, 30, 31
Sufyân b. 'Abdallâh, 89
Sufyân b. 'Auf, 294
Sufyân b. Mujîb, 194, 195
Sufyân b. 'Uyainah, 238, 240
abu-Sufyân b. Ḥarb, 61, 62, 63, 66, 87, 91, 101, 107, 157, 197, 208
Sughdabîl, 306
Suhail b. 'Amr, 129, 215
Suḥaim b. al-Muhâjir, 248
abu-Sulaim Faraj al-Khâdim, 260, 262
banu-Sulaim, 148, 291
Sulaimân b. 'Abd-al-Malik, 54, 198, 220, 222, 366
Sulaimân b. Ḳirâṭ, 482, 483
Sulaimân b. Sa'd, 301
Sulâlim, 45, 46
Sulṭais, 340, 349
Sumaisâṭ, 273-274, 297
Sûrân, 372
Surra-man-ra'a, 330, 332, 372, 382, 460-461
as-Sûs al-Adna, 359, 362
as-Sûs al-Aḳṣa, 362
Suwa, 169-170
Suwaid b. Ḳuṭbah, 388, 389
Syria (ash-Shâm), 16, 17, 20, 32, 46, 50, 61, 75, 92, 96, 102, 103, 111, 146, 155, 158, 162, 165-168, 169, 173, 175, 176, 177, 180, 190, 191, 194, 198, 208, 209, 210, 211, 212, 214, 215, 216, 217, 219, 220, 223, 230, 231, 232, 234, 238, 241, 246, 247, 249, 250, 251, 254, 261, 269, 278, 279, 283, 287, 289, 292, 297, 299, 309, 310, 320, 338, 397, 400, 405, 409, 415, 471

Tabâlah, 91
Ṭabaristân, 489, 490
Ṭabarsarân, 309, 324, 327
Tabûk, 92-94, 105, 167
Tadmur, 171
Taflîs, 241, 305, 316-317, 325
banu-Taghlib, 114, 115, 151, 169, 170, 284-286, 398, 399
aṭ-Ṭâ'if, 28, 61, 62, 85-90, 165, 208
Taimâ', 31, 57-59
Ṭaiyi', 224, 419
Ṭâḳât Bishr, 282, 447, 459
Takrît, 225, 399, 400
Ṭalḥah b. 'Ubaidallâh, 144, 431, 432
Tall 'Afrâ', 282
Tall A'zâz [or 'Azâz], 230
Tall Jubair, 263

Tall Madhâba, 282
Tall Mauzin, 275
Tamîm b. Aus, 197
banu-Tamîm, 120, 129, 149, 151, 278, 394
Ṭanjah [Tangiers], 357, 359, 362
Tanûkh, 223, 224, 254
Ṭarîḳ b. Ziyâd, 362, 365
Ṭarsûs, 253, 254, 260-262, 263, 296, 460
Thâbit b. Ḳais, 139, 145
Thâbit b. Nu'aim, 328
ath-Thabjâ' al-Ḥaḍramiyah, 155
Thaḳîf, 85, 86, 87, 248, 487
Tha'labah b. 'Amr, 32, 33
ath-Tha'labîyah, 389, 405, 409
Thanîyat al-'Uḳâb, 172, 200
Thât b. dhi-l-Ḥirrah, 161
ath-Thughûr al-Jazarîyah [Mesopotamian Frontier Fortifications], 287-300
ath-Thughûr ash-Shâmîyah [Frontier Fortresses of Syria], 253-265
Thumâmah b. al-Walîd, 295
Tiberias [Ṭabaraiyah], 178-179
Tigris, 417, 418, 421, 427, 430, 446, 451, 453
aṭ-Ṭirrîkh, 313-314
Ṭizanâbâdh, 410, 432, 443
Tîzîn, 202, 229
Tripoli [Aṭrâbulus], 194-196
Tripoli (Aṭrâbulus) in Africa, 355, 357, 369
Ṭulaiḥah b. Khuwailid, 145, 146, 147, 414, 415, 420
Ṭulaiṭulah [Toledo], 365
Tûmân, 326
Tûnis, 360, 369
Ṭuraifah b. Ḥâjizah, 149
Ṭurandah, 289-290
Turks, 307, 491, 493
Tustar, 394, 401
Tyre [Ṣûr], 179, 180, 181, 220
'Ubâdah b. al-Ḥârith, 133
'Ubâdah b. aṣ-Ṣâmit, 201, 203-205, 209, 216, 217, 235, 237
Ubai b. Ka'b, 18, 69, 135
'Ubaid b. Murrah, 30, 396
abu-'Ubaid b. Mas'ûd, 401-402, 403-404, 405, 406
'Ubaidah b. 'Abd-ar-Raḥmân, 367
abu-'Ubaidah b. al-Jarrâḥ, 65, 165-166, 172, 173, 176, 177, 178, 179, 186-190, 193, 198, 200, 203, 205, 208, 211, 213-216, 223-224, 226-232, 234, 244, 246, 254, 269, 270, 293, 411
'Ubaidallâh b. al-Mahdî, 330
'Ubaidallâh b. Ziyâd, 151, 480
al-Ubullah, 388
al-'Udhaib, 391, 401, 405, 409, 410, 413, 414, 463
Uḥud, 22, 28, 30, 35, 80, 140, 477
Ukaidir b. 'Abd-al-Malik, 95-97
'Uḳbah b. 'Âmir, 342, 343
'Uḳbah b. Nâfi', 353, 357, 358, 359, 361, 367, 379
'Ukbarâ', 399
'Ukkâshah b. Miḥṣan, 145, 146
Ullais, 389-390, 393, 404, 405
'Umair b. al-Ḥubâb, 288
'Umair b. Sa'd, 209-210, 237, 241, 254, 272, 276-277, 279, 284-285, 287
'Umair b. Wahb, 336, 342
banu-Umaiyah, 52, 53, 135, 193, 221, 233, 251, 258, 296, 330, 368, 396, 397, 443, 455, 456
abu-Umâmah As'ad, 19, 218
abu-Umâmah aṣ-Ṣudai, 168, 230, 415
'Umân, 32, 116-119, 124, 140, 147, 155
'Umar b. 'Abd-al-'Azîz, 20, 21, 28, 49, 52, 53, 54, 58, 70, 88, 92, 103, 104, 105, 112, 118, 190, 192, 204,

220, 238, 255, 258, 280, 290, 322, 342, 349, 354, 366, 428, 442
'Umar b. Ḥafṣ Hizârmard, 361, 368-369
'Umar b. Hubairah, 282, 445
'Umar b. al-Khaṭṭâb, 20, 22, 23, 24, 27, 29, 34, 37, 42, 45, 46, 48, 49, 50, 51, 53, 54, 57, 58, 61, 62, 69, 70, 73, 74, 76, 81, 82, 87, 88, 89, 102, 103, 111, 123, 124, 125, 126, 130, 131, 138, 139, 141, 146, 147, 148, 150, 151, 152, 158, 162, 166, 173, 176, 179, 188, 190, 191, 194, 196, 197, 198, 208, 209, 210, 212, 214-219, 222, 227, 233-234, 235, 240, 241, 242, 253, 269, 270, 272, 273, 275, 276, 277-278, 279, 284-286, 296, 310, 320, 335, 336, 337, 338, 339, 340, 341, 343, 344, 345, 346, 347, 351, 353, 355, 375, 379, 393, 395, 399, 401-402, 404, 405, 406, 409-412, 414, 416, 422-428, 430, 431, 434, 435, 438, 439, 440, 446, 448, 464, 469, 471-475, 481, 485, 487
b. 'Umar, 18, 23, 36, 43, 47, 49, 70, 73, 88, 356
al-Urdunn, *s. v.* Jordan
'Urwah b. Zaid, 402-404
'Urwah b. az-Zubair, 29, 51, 107, 122, 343
'Utbah b. Ghazwân, 125, 410-411
'Utbah b. Rabî'ah, 81
'Uthmân b. 'Affân, 20, 25, 29, 51, 54, 67, 74, 76, 102, 104, 123, 141, 184, 194, 196, 222, 227, 232, 235, 253, 278, 279, 286, 287, 309, 310, 311, 318, 320, 321, 340, 350, 351, 356, 357, 358, 359, 396, 397, 431, 432, 440, 482, 486
'Uthmân b. abi-l-'Âṣi, 90, 124, 125, 487, 490
'Uthmân al-Audi, 483
'Uthmân b. Ḥunaif, 102, 423, 426, 427, 428, 430
'Uyainah b. Ḥiṣn, 145, 146
'Uyûn al-'Irḳ, 463
'Uyûn aṭ-Ṭaff, 461-463

Wâdi-l-Ḳura, 29, 31, 37-39, 321
Wâdi Mahzûr, 24, 25, 26
Waḥshi b. Ḥarb, 80, 135
Waiṣ, 307, 315
banu-Walî'ah, 153-158
al-Walîd b. 'Abd-al-Malik, 20, 54, 76, 192, 193, 195, 220, 249, 250, 259, 260, 280, 362, 366, 376, 423, 454, 456
al-Walîd b. 'Uḳbah, 102, 282, 311, 440, 447
al-Walîd b. Yazîd, 104, 238, 241, 298, 328, 367
Wardân, 342, 350
Warthân, 323, 324, 328
Wâsiṭ, 264, 449-452
Wâsiṭ ar-Raḳḳah, 281
al-Wâthiḳ, 185, 249, 451, 460
al-Waṭîḥ, 45, 46

Yâfa [Jaffa], 213
al-Yahûdîyah, 485, 487
Yaḥya b. 'Imrân, 489
Yaḥya b. Sa'îd, 50, 184
al-Yâḳûṣah, 175
Ya'la b. Munyah, 152, 157
al-Yamâmah, 21, 76, 129, 132-142, 389, 394, 415
al-Yaman, 31, 61, 86, 98, 99, 102, 103, 106-115, 152, 156, 159-162, 165, 183, 226, 261, 435, 471, 477
al-Yarmûk, 175, 188, 207-211, 216, 223, 335
Yathrib (al-Madînah), 31, 33, 34, 44, 86
Yazdajird b. Shahriyâr, 406, 416, 417, 418, 420, 421, 469, 471, 486, 490-493

Yazîd b. 'Abd-al-Malik, 112, 190, 204, 322, 366, 442
Yazîd b. Ḥâtim, 369
Yazîd b. al-Ḥurr, 254
Yazîd b. Makhlad, 262
Yazîd b. Mu'âwiyah, 59, 75, 76, 96, 103, 202, 236, 244, 245, 294, 359, 376, 480
Yazîd b. al-Muhallab, 259, 366
Yazîd b. abi-Muslim, 366
Yazîd b. abi-Sufyân, 58, 166-168, 173, 178, 179, 186, 189, 190, 193, 194, 196, 201, 208, 215-217, 219, 269, 335, 341
Yazîd b. 'Umar, 445
Yazîd b. Usaid, 319, 328-329
Yazîd b. al-Walîd, 238, 241, 368
Yuḥanna b. Ru'bah, 92
Yûsha' b. Nûn al-Yahûdi, 50
Yûsuf b. Muḥammad, 330-331
Yûsuf b. 'Umar, 104, 105, 442, 488

az-Zâb, 370
Zabîd, 107
Zâdân Farrûkh, 465-466
Zaid b. al-Khaṭṭâb, 138, 139, 150
abu-Zaid al-Anṣâri, 116, 117, 118, 404
Zamzam, 77
Zandaward, 389, 402, 450
az-Zârah, 129, 130, 131
az-Zawazân, 275
Zawîlah, 352-354
b. az-Ziba'ra as-Sahmi, 68
Zibaṭrah, 282, 298-299
Zirîkirân, 309, 326
Ziyâd b. Abîhi, 436, 437, 441, 447, 464, 479
Ziyâd b. Labîd, 107, 153-157, 160
abu-Zubaid aṭ-Ṭâ'i, 282, 404
Zubaidah, daughter of abu-l-Faḍl, 81, 281, 451
az-Zubair b. al-'Auwâm, 27, 28, 38, 39, 43, 49, 63, 65, 138, 336-338, 343, 431
Zuhair b. Ḳais, 360
Zuhair b. Sulaim, 417
Zuhrah b. Ḥawîyah, 413, 416, 440-441
banu-Zuhrah, 80, 413
Zur'ah b. dhi-Yazan, 107
Zuraib, 24
Żurârah, 432, 442
az-Zuṭṭ, 250, 251, 259, 264

ERRATA

Page	line	for	read
Page 17,	line 4,	*for* " is ",	*read* " it ".
25,	21,	" Ju'dubah ",	" ibn-Ju'dubah ".
25,	28,	" 'Umri ",	" 'Umari ".
29,	7,	" Warwah ",	" Marwah ".
31,	3,	" Taima' ",	" Taimâ' ".
33,	11,	" al-Arḳam ",	" al-Arḳam ibn-'Amr ".
36,	14 and 26,	" Buwairah ",	" al-Buwairah ".
45,	11,	" Ḥudaibiyah ",	" al-Ḥudaibiyah ".
49,	6,	" al-Ḥassân ",	" al-Ḥasan ".
55,	17,	" al-Mubarik ",	" al-Mubarak ".
56,	2,	" al-Mubarik ",	" al-Mubarak ".
71,	2,	" Sa'id ",	" Sa'îd ".
78,	1,	" Ḥaḍram ",	" Ḥaḍrami ".
78,	9.	" Khadîjah ",	" Khadîjah daughter of Khuwailid ".
78,	11,	" Shufiyah ",	" Shufaiyah ".
80,	8,	" Mus'ab ",	" Muṣ'ab ".
83,	29,	" Ma'mûm ",	" Ma'mûn ".
113,	17,	" al-'Abbâs ".	" 'Abbâs ".
115,	4,	" Zinad ",	" Zinâd ".
117,	11,	" al-Makhzûmi ",	" and 'Ikrimah ibn-abi-Jahl al-Makhzûmi ".
142,	7,	" Sa'fûḳ ",	" Ṣa'fûḳ ".
150,	15,	" Muttamam ",	" Mutammam ".
151,	23,	" 'Abdallâh ",	" 'Ubaidallâh ".
153,	4,	" Bayaḍi ",	" Bayâḍi ".
153,	11, 12, 22, 24,	" Labîd ",	" ibn-Labîd ".
155,	32,	" Yamîn ",	" Yâmîn ".
160,	8,	" Bayaḍi ",	" Bayâḍi ".
166,	13,	" Arwa ",	" abu-Arwa ".
175,	24,	" Yâḳûṣah ",	" al-Yâḳûṣah ".
186	18,	" Abu-ad-Dardâ' appointed ",	" Yazîd appointed abu-ad-Dardâ' ".
194,	4,	" Bierût ",	" Beirût ".
197,	12,	" Ḥuṭai'ah ",	" Ḥuṭai'ah ".
204,	5,	" 'Abd-al-'Azîz ",	" 'Umar ibn-'Abd-al-'Azîz ".
206,	8,	" Mayazdiyâr ",	" Mâyazdiyâr ".

Page 220,	line 29,	*for*	" Baṭriḳ ",	*read* " Baṭrîḳ ".
221	8,		" Abbâs ",	" 'Abbâs ".
227,	28,		"abu- ",	" ibn- ".
250,	20,		" Ḥafs ",	" Ḥafṣ ".
260,	32,		" Hadath ",	" Ḥadath ".
276,	15,		" Amr ",	" 'Amr ".
277,	26,		" 'Umar ibn- ",	" 'Umair ibn- ".
282,	22,		" 'Afra' ",	" 'Afrâ' ".
282,	33,		" Mawardi ",	" Mâwardi ".
287,	13,		" Armenia ",	" Armenia IV ".
305,	11,		" Bajunais ",	" Bâjunais ".
306,	20,		" Durdhûkîyah ",	" Durdhûḳiyah ".
328,	9,		" ash-Shurat ",	" ash-Shurâṭ ".
361,	15,		" Khuzâ'fi ",	" Khuzâ'i ".
375,	19,		" Mu'adh ",	" Mu'âdh ".
376,	21,		" Ma'yûḳ ",	" Ma'yûf ".
392,	32,		" Mawardi ",	" Mâwardi ".
401,	1,		" Khattâb ",	" Khaṭṭâb ".
421,	30,		" Buṣbuhra ",	" Jamîl ibn-Buṣbuhra ".
428,	23,		" Mus'ab ",	" Muṣ'ab ".
432,	8,		" Zurârah's ",	" Zurârah ".